BOOKS BY CHARLOTTE VALE ALLEN

Leftover Dreams
Painted Lives
Night Magic
Dream Train
Illusions
Time/Steps
Matters of the Heart
Pieces of Dreams
Intimate Friends
The Marmalade Man (Destinies)
Daddy's Girl
Promises
Love Life

Leftover Dreams

Leftover

Dreams

CHARLOTTE VALE ALLEN

DOUBLEDAY

NEW YORK LONDON TORONTO SYDNEY AUCKLAND

PUBLISHED BY DOUBLEDAY
a division of Bantam Doubleday Dell Publishing Group, Inc.
666 Fifth Avenue, New York, New York 10103

DOUBLEDAY and the portrayal of an anchor with a dolphin
are registered trademarks of Doubleday,
a division of Bantam Doubleday Dell Publishing Group, Inc.

All of the characters in this book are fictitious,
and any resemblance to actual persons, living or
dead, is purely coincidental.

Library of Congress Cataloging-in-Publication Data

Allen, Charlotte Vale, 1941–
Leftover dreams / Charlotte Vale Allen. — 1st ed.
p.   cm.
I. Title.
PS3551.L392L44   1992
813'.54—dc20   91-20116
CIP

ISBN 0-385-41944-9

Title/Part Title Photograph by Comstock, Inc./Russ Kinne

BOOK DESIGN AND ORNAMENTATION BY CAROL MALCOLM-RUSSO

FOR ARCHIE MACDONALD

$\mathcal{A}$CKNOWLEDGMENTS

I AM GREATLY INDEBTED TO SMITH CORONA—TO THE STAFF at Cortland, New York, at Toronto, and at New Canaan, Connecticut—for their extraordinary assistance in keeping me "up and running." Also, my thanks to Mark Danton for his help with Italian dialogue and to Dr. Michael Weinstock for his medical expertise.

I'm indebted to Linda Cobon, administrator of the Archives of Exhibition Place, for her help in reconstructing the Ex of days gone by.

A big thank-you to Dina Watson for her diligent reading and excellent suggestions during the writing of this manuscript, and to Archie MacDonald, as always, for his hours of research.

Finally, I am grateful to Claire Smith for her insights, her patience, and her willingness to "brainstorm"; to my longtime editor, Judy Kern, for her enthusiasm and her input, and to Steve Rubin for his belief in this project.

Leftover Dreams

Part 1

TORONTO,
1940–59

CHAPTER
ONE

NOLAN GAVE HER THE HIGH SIGN, AND LIKE ONE OF those Russian dogs she'd read about once in some magazine, her insides twisted almost painfully in anticipation. But her face gave nothing away. She worked a few more minutes, then glanced up at the clock.

"One of these days I'm gonna have my goddamned bladder removed," she told her neighbor Flo as she got up from her machine.

Without taking her eyes from the slippery fabric she was feeding under the presser foot, Flo grinned and said, "A woman's gotta do what she's gotta do, eh?"

"Some of us just gotta do it more often than others," Maggie quipped, moving away through the din of the various machines, headed for the side staircase by the washrooms.

The business offices were on the floor below the factory. The receptionist, two secretaries, and the bookkeeper sat at desks at the front of the building. In back of this was the owner's office, with its mahogany paneling and thick carpet. She'd never actually been inside—there was no reason for her to go there, as Nolan was responsible for the employees—but she had glimpsed details through the open door. Nolan's office was situated in a low-traffic area halfway between the storage bays and the shipping department at the rear of the building.

She glanced around. No one in sight. Her palm damp, she turned the knob of Nolan's door and ducked inside, throwing the latch on the lock as she did. Heart racing, already wet, she remained by the door of the darkened office. For years she'd been responding to Nolan's signal. She didn't know if it was the terrible risk involved—he had a wife, and she could be fired if they were ever found out—or her hatred of men that kept bringing her back. But once or twice a week, ever since her second month on the job more than twelve years before, he'd appear on the floor to give her the high sign, and she'd come downstairs. There'd been a few close calls, occasions when they'd almost been caught, but they'd managed to keep what went on between them a secret. No one in the factory, not even Flo, who was a good friend, knew about Maggie and Mr. Nolan.

He was waiting for her. One hand reached up under her skirt as the other closed over the back of her neck, directing her mouth to his. They'd never bothered with preliminaries. For one thing, there wasn't time. And for another, the risk and the secrecy kept her permanently stimulated. Five mornings a week, she inserted her diaphragm as a matter of course, just in case Nolan should decide to summon her. At the beginning, there had been weeks when she'd crept into his office sometimes twice in one day. Of course he'd been younger then. Now he was forty, and slowing down. She didn't care. Twice a week or twice a day, it was all the same to her. Their encounters were like a bitter medicine that briefly relieved her generalized pain.

He undid the top of her dress and opened her brassiere while she got her pants off. Then she stood half naked, with her legs apart, knees locked, while his fingers stroked and rubbed, and his mouth drew at her breasts. She despised both herself and him, and bit down hard on her lower lip as he easily teased her closer and closer to the brink. He knew every part of her body, perhaps better than she did; knew how to excite her and what she did or didn't like.

A minute or so and they were both ready. He positioned her on the edge of the desk, his hands lifting and holding her open while he fed himself smoothly into her. Almost sick with desire and contempt, she locked her legs around his hips, her mouth fastened to his. She kept one hand braced behind her on the desktop while the other signaled in the small of his back as they silently struggled toward their separate pleasures. Three minutes, four, then he buried his face in her neck as he shuddered, flooding inside her. She imagined the tide of his flow crashing against the seawall of her diaphragm, and felt grimly triumphant. Her muscles involuntarily dilating and contracting, she waited. Thirty seconds, sixty. Then, recovered, still joined to her, he eased her back on the desk, delved again with his fingers, and at the same time began the slow driving thrust he knew she needed.

The combined motions inside and out took her into that dark place where there was no thought, only vicious sensation—a spiraling, tightening coil of violent pleasure that culminated in convulsion, an exquisite seizure that sent the framed photographs on his desk toppling as her treacherous body leaped beneath his touch.

He liked to watch her at these moments. She couldn't stand that, and always closed her eyes so she could remain detached from him in her frenzy. He could watch if he wanted, but she was damned if she'd let him *see*. With her eyes tightly shut he didn't exist; she didn't need him, didn't rely on him for these ten or twelve minutes of frantic nakedness. He was nothing, no one, just something she used to ease some of the tremendous tension.

After, while he quickly dressed, she dried herself with a tissue before stepping shakily into her underpants. She felt emptied, hollow, enraged. Her hands shook as she fastened her brassiere then fitted her breasts into the cups. Already, so quickly, the loathing was sweeping through her. And inside, the spiral gradually uncoiled with ever smaller aftershocks as she smoothed her skirt, took a deep breath, then, with uncertain limbs, left the office.

They hadn't spoken. If he'd said a single word she might have picked up the letter opener and stabbed him.

There were times when Maggie Parker's memories were like a fast-burning fuse attached to the highly volatile anger that detonated inside her. She then found herself a servant to its force, unable either to conceal or control it. When this happened at the factory she could relieve herself with Nolan, if his summons happened to coincide with her resurgent anger, or redirect her furious energy to the work at hand—feeding triangles of fabric, in a blurred multicolored frenzy, between the presser foot and feed dog of the industrial sewing machine.

If it occurred while she was waiting tables at the coffee shop, she'd snap at the short-order cook, at the other waitresses, even at the customers, most of whom were regulars who'd long since grown accustomed to Maggie's occasional irascibility. Her coworkers at both the umbrella factory and the restaurant simply shrugged and kept their distance until her mood improved, as it usually did in an hour or two. They accepted her periodic displays of bad temper philosophically, because she commanded their respect.

Everyone knew Maggie had been left to raise her daughters alone, and they could see for themselves she'd done a good job of it. Her girls were clean, well mannered, and obedient—a credit to their hardworking mother, which was precisely how she wanted the world to see them. More than anything else, she wanted it known that she could stand on her own two feet, and that no one, particularly that son of a bitch John Parker, was going to drive her to her knees.

But sometimes, without warning, the recollection of what Parker had done to her set her insides on fire, and then the flames of her outrage scorched everyone indiscriminately. In the aftermath, while her victims sought to nurse their charred sensibilities, it would never have occurred to Maggie to apologize for any damage she'd done, because it was a given that she, more than most people, had cause to give vent to her molten indignation.

Her daughters, Faye and Louise, were her public burden, the upright and transverse pieces of the cross she bore, and whenever the anger overcame her, all she saw when she looked at them were the features they'd inherited from their rotten father. Faye had John Parker's depthless, deep-set gray eyes, his square jaw, and elegant patrician nose. Louise had his high, rounded forehead, his arching, well-defined eyebrows, and his wide, full mouth. The sight of those two faces so clearly bearing John Parker's imprint could send Maggie into such a blind rage that she felt capable of murder.

In more temperate moments she was able to see her own self in the tawny hues of Faye's hair, in her dimpled chin and fair complexion; she recognized herself in Louise's deep blue eyes, the length of her neck, and the tidy conformation of her ears. It was these inherited characteristics of hers that enabled her to live year in and year out with the too-visible, walking, talking reminders of her teenage folly.

She carried around a mental portrait of herself in 1938, the year she was sixteen and met John Parker on a blind date set up by her girlfriend May Greeley. It was the year her life had been ruined. The portrait was always perfectly clear in her mind: Her hair was ear length and done in smart marcel waves; she wore a royal blue drop-waisted dress that set off the color of her eyes; high heels that showed off her slim ankles and shapely calves and made her exactly five feet six; and her mother's pearls. She weighed an even hundred and ten pounds, her breasts were full and firm, and her waist was precisely twenty-four inches. Her eyelashes were subtly darkened with a bit of mascara, her cheeks bore a hint of powdered rouge, and deep pink lipstick accentuated the shape of her mouth. She was virginal, pristine, perfect; filled with a simmering excitement for her own limitless potential. She had a head full of ideas for her future, for the wonderful life she was going to have when she met the man of her dreams.

And then John Parker came along to dazzle her with his snazzy clothes, his glib tongue, and his large persuasive hands. After being introduced, he leaned uncomfortably close to her and said, "You don't know it yet, sister, but you're just wild about me."

He was so much older than the boys she'd dated, and so good-looking, so smooth and confident that she couldn't think of a thing to say. She'd just stared into his deep gray eyes, with her heart hammering and her body all at once overheated, and waited to see what would happen next. She felt imperiled, cut loose from everything familiar, and hoped the sudden rush of moisture between her legs wasn't the start of her period. She hated anyone, even her parents, touching her when she was having the curse.

"No comeback, eh?" he said after a moment. "Good. Tell the boys no if they ask. John Parker's taking you out from now on."

He was a salesman, and he had a car, which impressed her. Hardly anyone had cars in those days. He held the door for her while she climbed in, then he took her for a drive. They wound up parked in the pitch dark somewhere in High Park. He turned on the radio, tossed his cigarette out the window, then reached for her.

That first night he got her so crazy she didn't know what she was doing. She kept saying no, don't, but before she knew it he had the blue dress down around her waist and her step-ins were on the floor somewhere. He wouldn't quit, his hands were all over her. She was scared to death someone would come along and catch them there, but she couldn't stop him. He kept stroking her between her legs and kissing her, and after a while she couldn't even think. He made her come. She didn't even know what was happening. He had to tell her. Then he got her to use her hand on him until he stopped her abruptly, pushing her hand away while he held his hankie over himself.

By the end of the second week he'd convinced her to go all the way. "Don't worry about a thing," he told her, rolling on a safe. "You're gonna love this, Maggie. Now come on over here," he said, pulling her down under him on the back seat of the car. "John Parker's gonna send you to heaven."

Eighteen months later they were married, and the following year, after a nightmarish labor that went on for almost three days, during which time

John Parker was nowhere to be found, she was the mother of a seven pound fifteen ounce baby girl. And sixteen months after that, with John Parker once again conspicuously absent, two days of hellish labor culminated in the forceps delivery of another daughter weighing seven pounds nine ounces. Just when she was beginning to recover from the rigors of this second birth and the exhaustion of coping with two babies under the age of two, he telephoned to say he wouldn't be coming home ever again.

"Let's just chalk it up to experience, kiddo," he said. "It's not working out. These things happen."

The ruthless, conniving bastard didn't even have the guts to tell her in person. Nor did he bother to collect his possessions. He left with only the clothes on his back and vanished for good and always.

She was a twenty-year-old mother of two, with almost no money, a thickened waistline, nipples permanently distended from prolonged nursing, and a vaginal prolapse as a result of her extended labors. She sold for cash every last item that had belonged to John Parker, borrowed money from her father to pay for the necessary internal reconstruction that left her with a tightened vagina the surgeon said was "good as new, Marg," made a deal with her friend Blanche upstairs to look after the babies while she went out to find some work, and, in her final act of creation, gave birth to a deep and abiding mistrust of all men. She liked the fact that they were attracted to her; she enjoyed the sense of power it gave her to know that they were forever wanting to touch her; but her contempt for them was so limitless that her greatest satisfaction came in verbally slapping them into place when they took even the smallest step out of line. She satisfied the lust John Parker had instilled in her with Jerry Nolan in the darkened office at the factory.

She took pride in looking good, and paid top dollar for the few clothes she had so that her appearance stated in no uncertain terms how well she was able to provide for herself and her girls. Since Faye and Louise grew very quickly out of their clothes, it was only sensible to acquire their garments at the lowest possible price. But every last item they put on was meticulously laundered, with not so much as a single button missing. These same rigid standards were applied to the girls themselves. Their hair got washed every three days without fail, and they were bathed—or later, bathed themselves—every other night. Their fingernails and toenails were clipped every two weeks, their ears, faces, and necks were washed nightly, and their teeth were brushed morning and night. These girls represented her in public, and by God, they were going to be at their best!

She gave them the benefit of her hard-earned knowledge about men and about the world, determined no fast-talking smoothie would ever come along and put Faye and Louise down on their backs the way John Parker had put her down on hers. No man was ever going to take advantage of her girls.

When Faye got her first period and mutely presented her mother with her blood-soaked underpants, Maggie underwent a moment of such complete and utter revulsion that her initial instinct was to strike the girl with all the force she could muster. She restrained herself because this was a woman's curse, after all, and Faye could hardly be blamed for having had the misfortune of being born female. Maggie went for the new sanitary belt she'd bought for herself a week earlier, briskly gave it and a box of pads to Faye, then went to the kitchen to make a cup of tea. She sat by the window, alternately staring at the smoke from her cigarette and at the thawing ground of the small back yard, experiencing an interior spasm of combined jealousy and renewed anger.

Faye was no longer a child. She'd soon be fourteen. And now that she'd started menstruating she'd shortly develop breasts and hips. Louise was twelve. She'd be next to come waving the soiled evidence of her maturity in Maggie's face. Before she knew it, she'd be living with two other women. It wasn't enough she'd had to live with them as children. The thought of having to put up with them as grown women was almost more than she could tolerate. There'd be boys at the door, boys on the phone, boys every time she turned around. And they'd all be after only one thing: getting their filthy hands on her daughters' bodies. On top of working five days and three nights a week, she'd have a full-time job just keeping the sons of bitches away from her girls. And there were no guarantees she'd succeed, nor was it likely Faye and Louise would thank her for it. Look how easily that rotten prick had gotten her out of her step-ins! It *was* a curse to be a woman. And it was damned hard to say who was worse: men for thinking with their cocks, or women for letting themselves be used. Goddamned stupid women! Bad enough she had to listen to their pathetic whining at work. Now she'd have to listen to it at home too! She wished to Christ she'd never laid eyes on John Fucking Parker.

CHAPTER

T W O

WITH GREAT BITTERNESS, THEIR MOTHER WAS FOREVER telling them that if John Parker hadn't run off when Faye was sixteen months old and Louise was only a newborn; if the son of a bitch had never come along in the first place to ruin all her chances, she might have been living a decent life now instead of having to work two jobs and worry about making enough to support herself and two children.

Their mother had no time for men, wouldn't give you a nickel for one, and rarely let a day go by without warning the girls: "Never trust a word any man says, and you'll be fine. Get what you want from them, but don't ever be fool enough to give yourself to them heart and soul. The minute you do, the game's over, believe you me. Remember what I tell you, and you'll never look back."

The girls learned very early on to pay close attention to whatever Ma said, because they never knew what would set her off. It might be that she didn't think they'd been listening properly, or that they'd said or done something she didn't like; maybe they'd lost a hair ribbon or got holes in their socks; they'd been snippy; Louise had told a fib, or Faye had had a smart-alecky look on her face. So many things made her mad. It was hard to keep track of them all. And when she did get mad, all hell broke loose. The girls would flee to their room and hope that Ma would forget they were there.

They never talked about what went on at home because they were sure something awful would happen if they did. And when one of the neighborhood kids said, "Boy, I'm late. Am I ever gonna get a licking!" Faye and Louise would exchange a look.

They were scared of their ma. She always told them it was nobody's business what went on inside their house; she said that if anything ever happened to her they'd be sent to an orphanage. "If you think you've got it bad now, think again! And don't imagine you could go running to your grandmother, because she wouldn't want a thing to do with you! I'm the only one who'd ever put up with you two prize packages.''

So they paid attention when Ma told them what a miserable life she had, how rotten men were, what a lousy job it was working in that goddamned factory. "I'm not too crazy about that crummy coffee shop, either, believe you me." They listened when Ma said their father was the biggest bastard who ever lived, and if it hadn't been for him she could've been living in a decent house in a decent neighborhood and having a halfway decent life. They listened, but they didn't believe most of the things she said, because they could see for themselves that lots of men—like Mr. Perlman, the druggist, and Mr. DiStasio upstairs, and Mr. Nolan at the factory—weren't bastards at all. They were nice, kind people.

Faye vowed she'd never be as mean and suspicious as Ma. She wouldn't be at all like her, so no man would talk her into getting married and then walk out on her. Louise was of the opinion that Ma's rotten temper was probably what had driven John Parker away. In bed at night when they talked about the future, the girls assured each other they'd never wind up like their mother. Faye said, "When I get married, I'll be nicer to my children than Ma is to us, and I'll always be there waiting when they get home from school."

Louise said, "I'm not so sure I even want to get married."

Faye was shocked. "Girls *always* get married. You shouldn't *say* things like that. What would you *do* if you didn't get married?"

"I didn't say I never would," Louise defended herself. "I just said I'm not so sure I'd want to. Maybe I'll be rich and live all by myself. Or I might adopt some poor orphan child and give her a lovely home."

"How're you going to get rich?"

"I don't know. I'll think of something," Louise said confidently.

Faye was regularly amazed by some of the things her kid sister said, and by the way Lou could tell lies with a completely straight face. She never lied about anything important. It was more make-believe than actual lying. But even so, Lou's imagination was remarkable, and she could spin out stories that were so convincing Faye would find herself halfway believing them even when she knew they weren't true.

This one time when she was about eight, Lou told a bunch of kids in the schoolyard that she'd met Frankie Laine and Theresa Brewer. The kids all blew mouth farts and said, "Oh yeah, sure," but Lou got very serious and said, "I don't care if you don't believe me. *I* know what's true." She spoke with such conviction that Faye actually tried to think when Lou could have met them. Later on, when Faye called her on it, asking, "How come you said that?" Lou replied, "Well, it could've happened. How's anyone to know?" Faye had to admit Louise had a point, even though when she stopped to think about it the idea of Frankie Laine and Theresa Brewer meeting a little kid like Lou was ridiculous.

╈

The three of them lived on the ground floor of a small house on Manning Avenue just north of Queen Street. The Parkers had been renting the two-bedroom lower half of the house since before Faye was born, while a series of tenants had come and gone from the second floor.

The DiStasios lived upstairs with their two boys until Faye was almost seven and Lou was five and a half, and Blanche DiStasio took care of them both until they were old enough to go to school. Maggie talked the principal into letting Louise start kindergarten a year early since she could already read and print her letters. And with both kids in school, Maggie no longer had to pay Blanche for baby-sitting, which meant she could quit working overtime and take life a little easier.

Blanche and Maggie were best friends, and sometimes went out together for an evening at the movies or to a bingo game, while Blanche's husband, Frankie, sat home with the kids. Blanche was tall and thin, a very pretty woman with thick black hair, pale skin, and large brown eyes. The girls adored her, and secretly wished she was their mother. Even Maggie had to admit Blanche had a sweet nature. But she said it as if having a sweet nature wasn't something that would ever do Blanche any good.

Blanche always spoke softly, never raised her voice. She was a generous woman who remembered the girls' birthdays every year and gave them mitts or scarves she'd knitted. She offered Faye and Louise something to eat whenever they came upstairs to play with her two boys, Renaldo and Rafael. Aldo and Raffie were almost the same ages as the girls, and the four of them had grown up together. They'd walked to school together, made snow angels in the back yard in the winter, and played elaborate games of house in the cool cellar in the summer. Both boys were tall and pale-skinned, with thick black hair like their mother's. They had her same soft manner of speaking but their father's liveliness and exuberant sense of humor.

Frankie DiStasio was dark and energetic, on the short side but muscular. He liked to laugh, and was always on the go. Maggie said he was, "a good provider, a decent man," which was the greatest praise she could offer about any man.

Upon arriving in Canada from Palermo at the age of sixteen, Frankie had gone to work in his cousin's grocery store on Dundas Street. He was exempted from military service because a childhood bout of rheumatic fever had left him with a heart murmur. When the economy picked up during the war he saved every cent he could, and finally bought a store of his own in November of 1947. After a tearful round of goodbyes in the house on Manning Avenue, he moved Blanche and the boys into the apartment over the store.

The girls were devastated by the departure of the DiStasios. Blanche and Maggie stayed good friends, but with Blanche working twelve hours a day in the store they didn't get to spend much time together. The first few months after the DiStasios moved, Maggie would take a walk with the girls up to College Street on a Saturday to buy a few things—Frankie always knocked a couple of cents off the price—and she and Blanche would talk for a while if the store wasn't too busy, while the girls played with Aldo and Raffie in their big new bedroom. But gradually, Maggie and Blanche saw less and less of each other.

Louise and Faye kept up their friendship with the boys. They'd meet to go swimming in the huge pool at Sunnyside, or to catch a Saturday matinee at the Bloor, or the Midtown, or the Orpheum, or to go roller-skating at the Strathcona Roller Rink, which they preferred to the Mutual Arena, where the crowd was bigger, older, and rougher. At the Strathcona they'd put on their rented skates and join the crowd circling the rink under the colored lights, while the music played. For a time Louise dreamed of becoming a professional skater, imagining herself in a short-skirted spangled outfit, spinning in the spotlight. But when she asked her mother if she could take the Saturday morning classes at the rink, Maggie snorted and said, "That'll be the day, sister," and that was the end of that dream.

The girls thought of Aldo and Raffie as their brothers. They'd known them all their lives, and liked the same things. It wasn't much of a walk from Manning Avenue up to College and Markham, and they much preferred the DiStasios' place to their own. The DiStasios were their ideal of the perfect family, people who weren't afraid to show they loved each other.

After the DiStasios moved out, the second floor was rented by a couple who spent every weekend drinking beer until they were falling-down drunk; then they'd get into a fight. These fights were so alarmingly tumultuous that Faye and Louise were convinced someone up there would be killed. They'd hear the woman crying and screaming, and the menacing shouts of her husband, followed by crashes and banging and thuds that shook the walls. An irate Maggie would get up at two or three in the morning to call the police, while the girls crept out into the hall to eavesdrop on the proceedings in anxious, almost giddy silence. The couple upstairs would go very quiet when the police arrived, trying to act innocent even though their slurred speech and the wife's bruises proved Maggie's complaints were legitimate. They'd stay quiet for a week or two after one of these incidents, then on a Friday night it would start all over again.

"I'm never going to drink beer," Faye declared. "The stuff makes people crazy."

"Me, neither," Louise agreed. "And it smells horrible too."

Mr. DiStasio made big bottles of red wine and sometimes when the girls went to visit and stayed for supper, he'd give each of the kids a jigger of his homemade wine to have with their spaghetti. "Don't tella you mama Frankie gives you wine, huh?" he'd tell the girls with a grin. "She maybe no lika me givin' it to you. Okay?"

The girls chorused "okay" each time, and happily sipped the rather sour brew. Mr. DiStasio never got drunk or hit Blanche, so Faye and Louise concluded that wine was obviously safer than beer.

Finally, after seven months of the neighbors' brawling, Maggie declared, "I've had enough of this crap!" and called the landlord. "I've been a good tenant, Mr. Silverman. Nine years and you've never had a minute's trouble from us. You don't get rid of those bums upstairs, I'm moving out—and I hope you get another pair like those two who wreck the place altogether."

A week later the battling couple were gone and a new family moved in —a pale, timid couple with strange blue numbers tattooed on the inside of their forearms, who smiled uncertainly at Louise and Faye as their possessions were unloaded from a truck, and who asked in awkward English if they'd look after their daughter while the furniture was put into place. Flattered at being considered sufficiently mature to baby-sit, the girls eagerly took charge of the fair-haired docile four-year-old. They

played with her on the scrubby patch of grass to one side of the front walk
for the hour it took to remove everything from the truck.

Faye fell in love with Sophie. She loved the little girl's blond ringlets
and tiny fingers; she loved the way Sophie grew flushed and sleepy when
Faye held her on her lap and read her fairy tales from books she'd
borrowed specially from the library. Nobody except Louise had ever
seemed to belong to her the way Sophie did during the almost five years
the Wisznowskis lived upstairs. She got paid fifteen cents an hour to baby-
sit, when she'd happily have done it for free. They invited both girls to
come up for meals when Maggie was at work, and introduced Faye and
Louise to their cheerful friends and relatives, and to *pirogies* and cabbage
rolls and chewy dark bread. In their hesitant, heavily-accented English,
they made it a point to include Maggie in their invitations when she was
home. But she declined every time, making a face as she'd tell the girls,
"It makes me nervous, trying to talk to them. I can't make out a word
they're saying. And all that heavy food gives me indigestion." She never,
however, discouraged the girls from going upstairs to visit. "Don't over-
stay your welcome," she'd say. "And be sure to mind your manners."

It was Faye who spent the most time upstairs. And it was Faye who
stood on the front porch with the Wisznowskis and cried brokenheartedly
the day the truck came to move them into the house they'd bought up
north of St. Clair. "You'll come see us," Mrs. Wisznowski said consolingly. "You'll come see Sophie."

Faye promised she would, and a couple of weeks after the new people,
the Healeys—a stiffly polite pair in their fifties—moved in, she got her
mother's permission, and made the long trip—three transfers on the
streetcar—to their impressive new detached brick two-story house on
Hillcrest Avenue. She stayed over, her first night ever away from home,
but couldn't sleep in the strange bed in the strange house, even though
these were her old friends and Sophie was wild with excitement at having
Faye come to visit. She lay awake in the dark guest room, startled by
every sound, yawning with tiredness but unable to fall asleep without the
familiar warmth of her sister's body at her side. In the morning, she
thanked them, hugged and kissed Sophie goodbye, and walked tearfully
down the tree-lined street toward the streetcar stop. She returned home
to the shabby stucco house on Manning Avenue, with its narrow back yard
and lopsided front porch, with its peeling wallpaper and drafty old-fashioned bathroom with the big high-sided tub that sat on four lion's paws.

She missed Sophie terribly, but was embarrassed to visit the Wisznowskis in their nice new place. It made her miserably aware of her own cheap clothes and ugly shoes.

Ma bought the girls' clothes from the sale tables in Eaton's or Simpson's basements, without ever consulting them. She'd turn up with things "marked down to practically nothing" and gloat, expecting them to be thrilled with outfits that didn't match, in dreadful colors. Both Faye and Louise were bothered by the things their mother expected them to wear, especially when she herself always had nice dresses and fancy high-heeled shoes. If they dared to express any displeasure, she'd say, "You'll wear what I pick out and you'll damned well like it!" and they'd let the matter drop until the next time she came home with mismatched outfits for them. But they couldn't help wondering if Ma dressed them so badly on purpose, as her way of letting them know how she felt about them. After all, she never got anything for herself that wasn't really smart, even if the dresses had all been marked down.

Faye had been able to demonstrate her love for Sophie with hugs and kisses, something she and Lou got from Mr. and Mrs. DiStasio and from their Gramma Perry, but never from their own mother. Maggie Parker didn't believe in making a show of her feelings. "A person who cares about you puts a roof over your head and food on the table. More than that you don't need." So when the Wisznowskis moved away, Sophie's absence left Faye with a hollow feeling in her chest, as if a part of her had been taken away. She wished she and Lou had the kind of mother who gave hugs, or who stroked her children's hair with a gentle hand the way Blanche DiStasio did.

Faye couldn't make sense of her mother, could never figure out what would or wouldn't please her. She was very pretty and wore her blond hair in a pageboy. She had big blue eyes; she wore bright red nail polish, and she never left the house with her hair in curlers the way some of the neighborhood women did. She didn't look like someone who worked in an umbrella factory and waited tables three nights a week. She looked more like somebody who didn't have to work at all, or who had an important office job. If they were out together, Faye would notice the admiring way people looked at her mother, and she'd wonder what they'd think if they knew Ma was only someone who worked in a factory. Maybe they wouldn't admire her if they knew what she was really like. There were moments when Faye wanted to start screaming right in the middle of the street, telling the whole world the truth about Ma. And there were times when Maggie would go running across Queen Street without waiting for the lights to change, and Faye would hang back on the sidewalk, both hoping and afraid that her mother would get hit by a car. She felt as if she wanted her mother dead, but the idea also made her queasy with fear. When the light changed, she'd go running to catch up, looping her arm through her mother's, hoping Maggie wouldn't shake her off as she so often did. Being allowed to walk arm in arm with her mother was such a rare privilege that when it happened Faye was always tricked into believing things were actually going to be all right from then on. Until an hour, or a day, or a week later, when she accidentally spilled the milk or she forgot to scrub the bathtub, and Maggie went crazy again.

Sometimes the girls would meet their mother at the factory after school, and everybody would make a fuss over them, asking how was school, and saying, my oh my, but weren't they getting so grown up. Maggie would drape her arms around the girls' shoulders, saying, "Some kids, eh?" It was all for show, of course, but the girls played along. In an undertone Ma would tell them to say hello to Flo, or Mick, or one of the others, and obediently the girls would go over and reply politely to the questions about school or about what they were going to be when they grew up. They disliked going to the factory and could hardly wait to get away from the noise of the machinery and the smell of glue and of sweating bodies. They did have a good time every year at the factory Christmas party, and the plant manager, Mr. Nolan, would make a point of telling the girls how pretty they were, and how highly he thought of their mother. And every year he asked what kind of careers they were planning. Faye never had an answer, and for some reason his yearly Christmas interest in her future distressed her. She felt as if she was letting this very nice man down by being unable to declare she intended to become a nurse, or a schoolteacher, or a librarian.

Louise, on the other hand, would tell him a whopper, all the while wearing a great big smile. Over the years she'd told Mr. Nolan she wanted to be a dress designer, a streetcar conductor, a roller-skating champion, a singer, a movie star, and a hairdresser. Louise had an answer for every question, no matter who asked. In school, if the teacher asked her something and she didn't know the answer, she'd just make one up. Half the time she was actually right. The teachers were crazy about Louise, while Faye got sent to the principal's office twice in grade five for being what her teacher called "defiant." All she'd done was stand up for herself, once when Mr. Fisher yelled at her for forgetting to bring her homework and once when he said, in front of the whole class, that she was sloppy because the ink in her notebook always got smudged. "It's because I'm left-handed," she'd explained, and he threw a fit at her for answering back and said, "Get out of my classroom! You're to go to the principal's office!" Mr. Stevenson, the gray-haired, mean-mouthed principal, gave her the strap each time, two sizzling whacks across the palm of her right hand—she refused to hold out her left one—then told her he didn't ever want to see her back in his office again. She hated the man, and wouldn't let him see her cry, even though the strap hurt like anything. School was awful, the teachers were old and mean, or what they called "shell-shocked"—like Mr. Fisher, who'd been blown up or something in the First World War and screamed at the kids all the time—and she wished she didn't have to go.

After Lou skipped grade five—she was very smart, everybody said so —and the two of them wound up in grade six together, school wasn't quite so bad. Except for when kids would ask about their father. Then Faye would quickly change the subject, or give vague answers intended to discourage their questions. She found it hard to make friends and usually spent recesses and lunch hours alone, while Louise was always part of a group and was forever having kids over to the house to play. It didn't worry her that Ma would get mad if they made a mess. It also didn't bother her that she and Faye had to carry house keys and let themselves in at lunchtime and after school because there was nobody home. Louise didn't mind making her own lunch or having to run down to the corner with a grocery list in one hand and a two-dollar bill in the other because Maggie hadn't had time to do the shopping. Faye worried sometimes that Lou would one day have so many friends she wouldn't have time for her own sister. She was deeply proud of Louise—of her brightness and her ease with people, of her ability to make up fantastic stories and convince people they were true—but always in the back of her mind was the fear that one day Lou would go off and leave her, and then she'd have no one to love.

CHAPTER

THREE

A T THE END OF JUNE 1953, A DAY AFTER SCHOOL LET OUT
for the summer, a new family moved into the second floor of the house
across the street. Faye and Louise happened to spot an overloaded station
wagon and a pickup truck pull up out front, and sat down on the splintery
front porch steps in the breezeless morning heat to watch.

A thin little boy with stick-doll limbs and a head that seemed too large
for his spindly frame, and a somewhat older, equally thin girl helped
several adults unload the pickup and the car. Faye and Louise speculated
on the ages of the children and whether or not they were just helping out
or if they were actually going to be moving in across the street.

"He looks about five," Faye said, thinking they were two of the
skinniest kids she'd ever seen. "She's maybe seven or eight."

"I was hoping she was older," Louise said disappointedly.

"Maybe she is, Lou," Faye said testily, the heat making her ill-tem-
pered. "Why don't you go ask her, if you're so anxious to have another
friend."

Louise stared at her for a long moment. "You sounded just like Ma,
the way you said that."

Horrified by the thought, Faye said, "I did not."

"You did too. Why're you being so mean?"

"I'm not being mean. I just don't know why you'd be so interested in
some scrawny new kid on the block. It's not as if you don't have tons of
friends already."

"People're supposed to have lots of friends," Louise said, her eyes on
the two kids across the road.

"Well, you'd better go on over and introduce yourself, then."

"Okay, I will," Lou declared, getting up. "What're you so mad about
anyway, Faye?"

"I'm not mad," Faye said, relenting. "It's just too hot. I know you're dying of curiosity." She gave her sister a smile. "Go on. You can tell me all about them when you get back."

Louise sauntered over to the other side of the street. Up close, she could see that the girl was definitely older than eight. Although she was tiny, her features were surprisingly adult: wide-set, tired-looking blue eyes, a dainty nose, sharp, slanting cheekbones, a full mouth, and a pointed chin. Stopping a few feet away, Louise said, "Hi. My name's Louise. Are you going to be living here?"

Without looking up, the girl lifted a battered end table and said, "Uh-huh. That's my brother, Chuckie." She nodded at the wiry little boy who was carrying an orange crate, empty except for half a dozen comic books, through the front door. "I'm Shirley. That your sister over there?" she asked, indicating Faye.

"Yup. Want me to help you with that?" Louise offered. "How old're you?"

"Nah, that's okay," Shirley said. "Twelve. What about you?"

"Me, too," Louise said happily, looking into the rear of the nearly empty station wagon. "I could bring this lamp, if you like."

"Okay," Shirley said, struggling up the walk with the table.

It seemed very dark inside after the daylight glare, and Louise climbed the stairs carefully, curious to see the place. Arriving at the landing, she paused, not sure where to put the lamp, and looked around. Shirley and her brother were in a tiny bedroom at the end of a short hall to her right, at the front of the house. Next to it was a boxy, crowded living room no bigger than the bedroom she shared with Faye at home. In the middle was another bedroom, roughly the same size as the living room, and to her left was a kitchen and a closed door she imagined led to the bathroom. The apartment didn't seem big enough for four people. It was, in fact, about the smallest place she'd ever seen. What little furniture there was looked old and shabby. From where she stood, all she could see in the kids' bedroom were a pair of iron cots and some orange crates. With a jolt, she realized that these people were really poor. And suddenly she understood that despite her mother's endless complaints about never having enough money, compared to this family they were very well off. They had real bedsteads with springs and mattresses, and a nice sofa with matching armchairs. The only orange crates in their house were down in the cellar and filled with old copies of *Liberty, Life, Coronet,* and *Screen Gems* magazines.

A woman came out of the kitchen just as Shirley emerged from the bedroom, and on seeing Louise the woman smiled, saying, ''Hi! Who's this, eh?'' as she lifted the lamp out of Louise's hands. She was an older, more solid version of Shirley, with the same long dark hair, blue eyes, and delicate prettiness.

''I live across the street. I'm Louise.''

''Is that right? How old're you, then, eh?''

''Twelve, the same as Shirley,'' Louise answered, fascinated by the woman's shiny gums. She seemed too young not to have teeth. Louise had always thought only old people lost their teeth. This woman wasn't old at all. Louise wondered if she'd eaten too much candy as a kid. Ma was always telling them their teeth would fall out if they didn't go easy on the chocolate bars.

''That's great, eh Shirl?'' the woman said. ''Someone for you to play with.''

Shirley nodded expressionlessly, coming to stand next to Louise at the top of the stairs.

''Where are you from?'' Louise asked, taken with the woman's husky voice and singsong manner of speaking, which made everything she said sound like a question.

''Me, I come from Montreal, eh?'' The woman gave her another gummy grin. ''But I ben here a long time. Shirley and Chuck, they're born here, like their dad, eh? Why don't you kids go get some ice cream? Me 'n' dad, we'll finish with the rest of the stuff. Hey, Darryl?'' she called over her shoulder. ''Come give the kids money for ice cream.''

From out of the larger bedroom came a tall, dark-haired, narrow-faced man in trousers, with suspenders over the shoulders of a sweat-soaked T-shirt. Squinting against the smoke from the cigarette in the corner of his mouth, he pulled a handful of change out of his pocket and dropped it in his wife's hand. Then, without a word, he turned and went back into the bedroom.

Her mother handed Shirley two quarters, saying, ''Get a carton of Neapolitan, eh Shirl?''

Shirley pocketed the money, said ''Okay'' to her mother, and ''C'mon'' to Louise before starting down the stairs.

As they stepped out into the sunshine Chuckie shouted, ''Where you going?'' as he came clambering down the stairs after the girls.

''To the drugstore for ice cream,'' Shirley said over her shoulder.

"C'n I come, too?"

In answer, Shirley merely shrugged and continued walking.

Louise looked back to see the skinny little boy standing, hands on his hips and a scowl on his face, next to the station wagon.

"I don't mind if he comes," Louise said.

"He'll come if he wants to," Shirley said offhandedly.

Still looking back, Louise saw that Faye was sitting on the porch steps where Louise had left her, elbows on her knees, chin propped on her hands. With a guilty pang, Louise called to her. "Wanna come?"

"No, that's okay. I'm gonna walk up to the DiStasios'," Faye called back, feeling left out and lonely, and wishing yet again that she had her sister's ease with people.

"Okay. See ya later!" Louise waved, then turned to look at her somber-faced new friend. Shirley hadn't smiled once, and both she and her brother were so thin and white they looked as if they'd never been out in the sun. "What grade'll you be going into?" Louise asked.

"Five," Shirley replied, hitching up her yellow-and-white-striped shorts, then tucking in the tails of a fairly grimy blouse.

"How come, if you're twelve already?"

Shirley gave another shrug, then pushed her long limp hair behind her ears. "I get sick a lot. What grade're you going into?"

"Eight. What d'you get sick with?" Louise asked interestedly.

"Just sick," Shirley answered.

"No kidding," Louise said, stealing another look at her.

This girl and her family—at least what Louise had so far seen of them —were very unusual. Shirley seemed to go along with things as they happened, as if she didn't have the energy to disagree or argue. Louise had a strong hunch her mother wouldn't like them. For one thing, Shirley and Chuckie's clothes weren't very clean. And for another thing, she didn't think Ma would be too crazy about the fact that Shirley's mother didn't have any teeth.

At the drugstore, while she waited for Mr. Perlman to take Shirley's money, Louise thought it was too bad Shirley had been told to buy Neapolitan. Louise really hated strawberry ice cream, and when you sliced the block, you got a neat square with chocolate on one end, vanilla on the other, and strawberry in the middle. Whenever they had Neapolitan at home, Louise cut out the strawberry strip and gave it to her sister.

Faye always traded back her vanilla, but Louise didn't think she could ask people she didn't even know to trade their vanilla for her strawberry.

Faye walked along the sidewalk, fingering the dime in her skirt pocket, feeling the sun scorching the top of her head as she looked down at her dusty toes poking out the ends of her sandals. It had to be in the nineties. There wasn't even the hint of a breeze. The air seemed thick with all kinds of different smells. There was the somewhat sour odor of sunflowers, the sweetness of lilacs, the clean, green fragrance of newly mown grass, the richness of a roasting chicken, the cinnamon-spicy sweetness of a fresh-baked apple pie cooling on a windowsill, and the hot chewy smell of melting tar from the road. The sky was absolutely blue, without a single cloud, and the sun was so bright it hurt her eyes to look at it.

She felt very down. Lou had a new friend and would probably spend every single day with her from now on, which meant Faye would have no one to go swimming or roller-skating with, no one to go to the Ex with at the end of August, no one to do anything with. She'd be all by herself the whole summer. She wished she had a job so she could at least earn some pocket money, but she'd asked at all the stores and nobody needed her.

As soon as she got into high school she'd learn how to type. Then she'd be able to get summer jobs and have her own money to buy nice clothes and pay for a show if she felt like going. She and Lou both hated asking Ma for money because she always made such a big production of it. She'd list all the things they hadn't done: Lou hadn't washed the dishes or polished the furniture; Faye had forgotten to buy a paper on the way back from the grocery store; Lou didn't pick up the laundry from the Chinaman's when she should have; they hadn't done this, that, or the other thing. The girls would have to spend two hours with the lemon oil, polishing the furniture, or wash the kitchen floor, then Ma would complain what a lousy job they'd done and dole out a quarter to each of them.

Two little kids were turning somersaults on the pipe fencing outside their house, laughing and throwing themselves over faster and faster. Their sweaty hands made little squeaking sounds as they revolved on the gray pipe. Faye remembered how she and Lou used to do that when they were little, and how much fun it was, how dizzy they'd get. Now that she was going on fourteen and had started getting periods—what their mother called "the curse"—she was very self-conscious about anyone being able to see up her skirt. Whenever she sat out on the porch steps she was careful to make sure her skirt was pulled down over her knees and that she kept her ankles together.

She'd already had three periods and wasn't sure how she felt about having them. She was proud to be so grown up, and thought all the time about how she could actually make a baby, but she was uncomfortable with the way her body was changing. She felt heavier somehow, even though she could still wear last summer's clothes. She hated the downward drag of the sanitary belt on her hips and the bulkiness of the Kotex pads. And her chest hurt. She was astonished and mortified by the hair starting to grow between her legs and under her arms, and really didn't know what to make of it all. Her mother was no help. The only thing she'd said was, "Jeez. You kids are growing up too goddamned fast," which just made Faye feel guilty. She knew her mother made remarks like that because she and Lou were going to need new clothes. Clothes cost money, and both girls knew only too well how their mother hated having to spend any money. When one time last winter Gramma Perry asked, "What're you planning to do with all your money, anyway, Marg?" their mother had snapped, "All *what* money, if you please?"

"Oh come on, Marg," Gramma had said with a coaxing smile, one nylon-clad leg swinging playfully, crossed over the other. "You've probably got the first nickel you ever made squirreled away somewhere." "Your mother," Gramma had said to the girls right in front of Ma, "would sell her very soul if the price was right."

"Jesus!" Maggie had exclaimed. "That's a hell of a thing to say to my kids about your own child!"

"It's the truth, though," Gramma had insisted. "I swear I don't know how you come by it, Marg. You sure didn't get it from me or your father."

"You weren't abandoned and left with two kids to support, were you?" Maggie snapped bitterly. "If I didn't know how to manage money, where would I be? Answer me that!"

"It was just a joke, Marg," Gramma had said, quickly dropping the matter. She put out her cigarette, ran a hand over the back of her upsweep and tucked in a stray wisp of hair before going to the kitchen to lower the heat under the stew she'd fixed for their Sunday supper.

Faye decided that the next time they went to Gramma's she'd try to have a private chat with her. Gramma was a lot easier to talk to, and things didn't bother her the way they did Ma. It was funny, but in many ways Gramma was far more modern than her own daughter. Faye and Louise could always discuss with her things they'd never dare mention to their mother. Gramma never got angry or embarrassed. Sometimes it was hard to believe Ma was actually her child. They looked alike, and they both liked to wear high heels and smart clothes, but it seemed at times as if Ma was the mother and Gramma was her child, instead of the other way around.

Fingering the dime, Faye went along College Street, walking under the awnings where it was cooler, and looking in the store windows. She hoped one of the boys, preferably Raffie, would be home. She was getting too old to hang around with Aldo. She'd be fourteen in January, and Aldo wouldn't be twelve until February. But Raffie would be turning fourteen in November and looked more like sixteen. If Raffie was there, they could go for a walk, or maybe share a lime Coke at the Mars restaurant.

Arriving at the store, she looked at the fruit and vegetables displayed out front, and at the black-crayoned price signs. The cherries were such a deep red they were nearly black; Faye could almost taste their sweet juice. There were enormous watermelons, mounds of fat peaches, blue-black plums, McIntosh apples, Florida oranges, green and red peppers, squat ripe beefsteak tomatoes, and clusters of grapes. Everything looked wonderful.

Mr. DiStasio appeared in the doorway, an apron tied around his waist as usual. Seeing Faye, he broke into a big smile that made his teeth look very white against his dark skin.

"*Ciao, cara!*" he exclaimed. "How you, Faye?"

"I'm fine, thanks, Mr. DiStasio." She smiled back at him, lifted by the warmth of his greeting. "Are the boys home?"

"Aldo, he's gone over to the island, but Raffie, he's helpin' in the store today." Ducking his head back inside, he shouted, "Hey, Raffie! Come on out here." Smiling again at Faye, he reached over to the display and picked up a peach. He wiped it across the front of his apron and held it out to her. "Have a nice peach, Faye." After she thanked him he said, "How'sa you mama? She's good, huh?"

"She's fine, thank you. How's Mrs. DiStasio?"

He shook his head. "She got another headache."

"Oh, that's too bad."

"Yeah, she gettin' them alla the time now. The doctor he don't do nothin'."

Raffie appeared in the doorway and Mr. DiStasio reached up to loop an arm around his older son's neck and gave him a crushing hug as he beamed at Faye, saying, "Look who's here, beautiful girl come to see you!"

Patches of color appeared on Raffie's cheeks as he grinned and said, "Hi, Faye. Pop," he pulled at his father's arm, "you're choking me." Mr. DiStasio released him to go wait on two customers, and Raffie stepped outside, wiping his hands on the apron he wore, like his father, tied around his waist. "Hot, eh?" he said, eyes on the street, trying to look and sound casual even though he was really glad to see her. Faye was his favorite of the sisters, although he liked Lou a lot too. There was just something about Faye that made him feel good when he was with her. She was different from Lou. He liked the way she smiled with her lips closed to try to hide her crooked front tooth. Her laugh was quieter than her sister's, and she didn't talk as much. Most girls didn't listen the way Faye did.

He knew it was wrong, but whenever he locked himself into the bathroom to do *it,* he closed his eyes and imagined he was touching Faye's long dark blond hair, and the breasts she'd started growing. He'd stopped going to confession since he'd started locking himself into the bathroom over four months ago. He didn't want to tell the priest how hardly a day went by that he didn't have to lock himself in at least once, and sometimes two or three times, to jack off. And he definitely didn't want to have to kneel in the confessional and admit that while he was in the bathroom doing *it,* he thought about a girl who wasn't even Catholic.

Lately he thought about Faye all the time. But whenever he saw her, he felt big and hairy next to her, like a gorilla or something. It surprised him that she kept on wanting to hang around with him.

"Yeah, it sure is hot," Faye agreed, rubbing her thumb back and forth over the fuzzy peach. "You have to work all day?"

"Nah. You wanna do something?"

"Sure, but I've only got a dime."

"That's okay. Pop'll give me some money. What d'you wanna do?"

"I don't know. What d'you wanna do?"

"I don't know." Raffie gazed at her, then said, "We could go swimming."

"I'd have to go home to get my suit and stuff," she said doubtfully. She really didn't feel up to walking all the way back home in this heat.

Even with her hair in a ponytail her neck felt itchy and wet, and sweat was running down her sides. She hoped to God she didn't smell. She was dreading it, but she was going to have to ask Ma to buy her some deodorant. Some days she could actually smell herself and she hated that. It angered her that her mother didn't realize she wasn't a kid anymore and needed things like deodorant and, pretty soon, brassieres. Faye was certain other mothers didn't make their kids beg for every last little thing.

"I know!" Raffie said brightly. "We'll go down to the lakeshore. It'll be cooler, and you can wade. Okay?"

"Okay."

"Come on in while I ask Pop if I can go, then we'll make some sandwiches."

Faye stepped inside the store and looked at the long boxes of spaghetti lined up on the floor under the counters. There was every kind, from the thin angel hair to the wide, flat sort Mrs. DiStasio used to make lasagna. Rigatoni, fettuccine, fusilli, linguine, penne—Faye knew all the names and the price per pound of each. She wouldn't have minded working here. She liked the idea of waiting on the customers, putting the fruit and vegetables into the different-sized brown paper bags and writing the prices on the bags with one of the thick black crayons. But she knew Mr. DiStasio didn't need anyone. He had his wife and Aldo and Raffie as well as nieces and nephews, who turned up every so often when things got really busy.

Raffie came back removing his apron, saying, "Come on up, Faye. You can say hi to Mama while I make us some lunch."

Blanche DiStasio was stretched out on the sofa in the living room with the venetian blinds closed, holding a cloth wrapped around a chunk of ice to her head.

"I'm sorry you're not feeling well," Faye said quietly from the threshold of the darkened room.

"Faye, sweetheart," the woman whispered, giving Faye a small smile that seemed to cause her pain. "Come let me give you a kiss."

Faye went to kiss the woman's smooth, cool cheek, then knelt on the floor by the sofa holding Blanche's long elegant hand.

"You get prettier every time I see you," Blanche said. "How's your mama and Louise?"

"They're fine, thank you," Faye answered, automatically stroking the back of the soft hand entrusted into hers.

"You come to see Raffie, sweetheart?"

"We're going to the beach." Faye kept her voice low. "I'd better be going now, and let you rest. I hope you feel better soon." Faye gave her another kiss before getting to her feet.

"Thank you, sweetheart. You and Raffie go and have a nice time." She gave Faye another pained smile and closed her eyes.

Faye went to the kitchen where Raffie was wrapping several sandwiches in waxed paper. She watched him work, intrigued by how grown-up he seemed because of his height and his build and his deep voice. He was already taller than his father by several inches, and looked just as strong.

"We'll grab some fruit on our way out," he said, depositing the sandwiches in a brown paper bag from the store. "I just gotta get my suit and a couple of towels and we're all set." He handed Faye the bag and brushed past her saying, "You go on. I'll be right down."

Carrying the bag of sandwiches and the peach, Faye descended the stairs to the shop, where Mr. DiStasio was weighing onions on the scale and chatting in Italian to a tiny wizened woman dressed entirely in heavy, shapeless black garments. Faye went to wait by the door, wondering what Lou was doing with her new girlfriend. Maybe it wouldn't be such a bad summer after all, she thought, turning to watch Raffie come loping down the stairs. It was funny, but when she was with him, that heavy feeling she had seemed to go away.

CHAPTER

FOUR

LOUISE WAS HELPLESSLY FASCINATED BY THE BEAUVAIS FAMily. As the summer progressed she saw less and less of her other friends and more and more of Shirley. She couldn't seem to stay away from the girl, although Shirley continued to be as offhand—about everything, including Louise—as on the day they had met. When she was with these people Louise was gripped by the same edgy sense of combined fear and pleasure she got whenever she began telling one of her made-up stories. She'd find herself caught up in the drama of her own unfolding creation, and would be forced to play it through to the end in order to see how it would be received. This unusual family seemed to her to be an intriguing ongoing story that somebody else had made up, and even though she'd come into it well after the beginning—as if she had groped her way to a seat in a darkened movie house when the picture was already up on the screen—she was so immediately caught up in what was going on that she had no desire to leave.

Chuckie, who was actually nine but looked six at the most, hung around the girls.

"Wanna see my new comic?" he'd ask Louise whenever she went over to number 17. "I've got a new *Little Lulu*." His eyes would be so hope-filled she wouldn't have the heart to say no.

"Sure," she'd say, and settle with him on the top stair to go through the comic page by page, reading aloud the word balloons and captions while Chuckie, his particular dirty-little-boy scent emanating from him, sat close by her side, his eyes following her pointing finger as it traveled from frame to frame.

Getting to the end of a comic, he'd smile at her and exclaim fervently, "That was *good,* eh?"

"Yup," she'd agree, touched by his gratitude and ignoring Shirley's tap-tapping foot as she leaned on the banister, waiting.

"Wanna read another?" he'd ask.

Shirley would shake her head emphatically, *no.*

"Maybe later," Louise would tell him.

Let down, lonely, the small boy would shrug his thin shoulders and say, "Yeah. Okay. Where you guys goin' anyhow?"

"Just out!" Shirley would state, pushing past him and starting down the stairs, confident Louise would follow.

"Out where?" Chuckie would ask as Louise returned the comic book to him.

"I don't know," Louise would say, tousling the boy's rather greasy hair. "See ya later. Okay?"

"Yeah," he'd sigh, already retreating to the tiny room at the front of the house.

"Bye, Chuckie," Louise would call.

"Bye, Louise." He always waved without bothering to turn. It made her sad, and she wished Shirley were nicer to him.

Louise read a comic book to Chuckie almost every day until he found a playmate, Jimmy Novotny, up the block. Then he went racing off early every morning to knock on his new friend's door.

Ma had raised Louise and Faye to believe it was impolite just to show up at someone's door, so most mornings after breakfast (even though she'd promised herself she'd call one of her other friends) Louise sat down at the telephone and found herself calling Shirley to ask what she was doing that day. Sounding almost bored, Shirley would usually say, "I'm not doing anything. I'll come over to your place." Louise was rarely invited to Shirley's but that was just as well. Her friend's tiny room with its pair of metal cots and its orange-crate tables distressed her. Part of a torn sheet was thumbtacked to the window frame. Dirty clothes littered the floor, and there were cobwebs in the corners of the ceiling.

Mr. Beauvais didn't seem to have a job, or possibly he worked at night, but whenever Louise went over to number 17, he and Mrs. Beauvais would be sitting on the dusty sofa in the living room, both of them holding drinks in one hand and cigarettes in the other. The man never spoke, but Shirley's mother was unfailingly friendly, giving Louise a bright smile. Several times Louise saw the woman with her teeth in, and was startled by the difference they made. She was tempted to tell Mrs. Beauvais she should wear her teeth all the time because they made her look so good, but decided not to say anything. There was always the possibility that, like Ma, Mrs. Beauvais would take it the wrong way and go crazy.

Although the Beauvais apartment always smelled of cooking, Louise never actually saw any of them eating. When asked, Shirley would say they'd just finished, or were just about to have lunch or supper. Louise suspected that these kids didn't eat at home at all. She knew Chuckie had breakfast and lunch and sometimes even supper at Jimmy's house, and Shirley never turned down an offer of food when she came to play.

Another odd thing was that neither of the kids ever bothered to let their parents know where they were going or when they'd be home. If Shirley was over and Louise announced she had permission to go to the pool at Christie Pits or the one at Sunnyside, Shirley would say, "Okay, let's go," and simply borrow Louise's old bathing suit that didn't fit her anymore. She never phoned home to tell her mother where she was going. Chuckie was out from early morning often until as late as ten at night. Faye mentioned several times having seen him playing Manhunt with some of the older neighborhood kids when she was on her way home from the DiStasios'.

Louise was shocked by this. Manhunt was a scary nighttime variation on hide and seek. Whoever was "it" had to search every possible hiding place, including laneways, back yards, front porches, and cellars, in the entire block between Robinson and Queen. The first one to get found became "it," and the game continued. The problem was, the older kids knew all the best places to hide, so you had to be both fearless and clever to find new places. Faye and Louise had played a couple of times when they were younger, but got so scared hiding alone in the dark that they'd agreed never to play again. In view of all this, the idea of scrawny little Chuckie out late at night playing Manhunt really was upsetting.

Louise fussed aloud over it till Faye said, "It's up to his parents to look out for him, Lou. You can't go telling them what to do with their kids."

"I know that," Louise said, "but it's not right, Faye. I mean, he's only little and he could get hurt. Or somebody could come along and kidnap him, and his parents wouldn't even know until they got the ransom note."

Faye laughed, saying, "How do you come up with these things? And anyway, who'd want to kidnap Chuckie, of all people?"

Louise had to laugh, too. "Nobody. But little children do get kidnapped."

"I'll say one thing for those Beauvais," Faye said, dropping her voice to a whisper. "They make Ma look like a real saint."

They looked guiltily at each other and started to laugh. After a while they got into trying new hairstyles and forgot all about Shirley and Chuckie. But Louise continued to be intrigued by the family, curious to see what was going to happen.

🜚

Faye awakened each morning hoping to see Raffie. When he couldn't get away, she'd tie on an apron and work in the store just to be near him. Since Mrs. DiStasio's headaches seemed to be getting worse, Frankie was grateful for Faye's help, and rewarded her with a bag of fruit to take home and occasionally fifty cents or a dollar.

Maggie was mollified by the offerings of fruit and didn't object to the increasing amount of time Faye spent at the store. But she couldn't help wondering if it wasn't Raffie that interested Faye and not the prospect of earning some extra pocket money. Maggie kept a close watch, prepared to whale the daylights out of her if she spotted the slightest sign that Faye was fooling around with the boy.

Faye took great care to be casual whenever she mentioned the DiStasios or Raffie. She was so afraid Ma would forbid her to see him if she suspected there was anything going on that she didn't even dare confide in Louise, which was a strain because they'd always told each other everything. But Raffie was becoming so important to her that even though she longed to share this secret with her sister she couldn't risk it. Every night when they read in bed before going to sleep she could feel the words collecting in her mouth, almost dancing on her tongue, eager to be spoken. But it wasn't safe. Louise might inadvertently let something slip, and Faye could too readily picture Ma going berserk for her having broken the cardinal rule: Faye trusted a man, and she was in the process of giving herself heart and soul.

Everything had started changing between them that day in June when the Beauvais moved into number 17 and Faye ended up going down to the lakeshore with Raffie. He had this special private place at the bottom of Jameson Avenue. To get there they had to cross Lakeshore Boulevard, then climb through thirty yards or so of thick underbrush. But once past that there was a small rock-free area right at the water's edge, with a wide tree stump to sit on.

"I clear away a little more every time I come here," Raffie explained, leading her along the smooth path he'd made on the lake bottom. "You can walk out right up to your waist. When I'm hot, I work underwater, making the path wider."

They were shielded from view by the bushes and trees on either side and behind them, and the secluded spot was inaccessible except by boat or by Raffie's route through the underbrush.

"This is great," she told him, looking at a tanker far out on the lake.

Raffie swam while she waded close to shore, watching him. Then they sat on his towel with the sun quickly drying them, and ate the thick sausage and sweet roasted pepper sandwiches he'd made. She kept stealing glances at him, awed by the way he seemed to have galloped ahead of her in becoming an adult. He'd grown very tall, and the bones of his face had somehow come closer to the surface. His bare chest was broad and very tan, and his long arms and legs were lean and strong. She was captivated by the way the muscles flexed beneath his skin whenever he moved.

She was startled when his newly deep voice said, "You're gonna get burned, Faye," and he draped his shirt around her shoulders. She thanked him as he sat back down, then surprised herself by saying, "You're getting really handsome, Raffie."

He wound his arms around his knees and turned to smile at her. "I'm a gorilla," he said, profoundly aware of how big he was compared to her. He towered over everyone now; his voice came rumbling up from deep in his chest; and he could easily lift an armchair single-handedly.

"No, you're not," she said seriously. "Why would you say that?"

"It's how I feel."

"Well, you shouldn't feel that way. You're *not* a gorilla. What a thing to say!"

"You're getting beautiful," he said, thinking she'd opened this door and fair was fair. He did find her beautiful, especially her eyes. They were so big, and an amazing, luminous gray-blue. Every time he looked at her eyes he had a powerful feeling of wanting to protect her, to take care of her, to touch her.

"I am not. You're only saying that because I said you were handsome."

"No, you are, Faye," he argued. "You know I'd never lie to you."

"You feel like a gorilla," she said, studying his deep brown eyes, "and I feel—heavy. We're a fine pair."

"What? You mean like fat? You're thin as a rail, for Pete's sake."

"Not fat, but *heavy* sort of, as if my bones weigh more all of a sudden or something. It's strange."

"Mama says it's adolescence," he said, squinting at the sun. "She says everybody feels all wrong at our age."

"You talk to your *mother* about things like that?"

"Sure. Don't you?"

"Raffie," she chided. "You know my mother. She'd *never* talk to Lou or me about sex or anything. She looked like she wanted to kill me when I told her—" She broke off abruptly and averted her eyes, chewing on her lower lip.

"Told her what?"

"That I started having periods," she whispered, then covered her face with her hands and laughed with embarrassment. She felt suddenly naked.

"I told Mama the first time I had a wet dream," he admitted.

Faye uncovered her face. "What's that?"

"It's like . . . when you jack off in your sleep without even knowing it."

Chagrined by her ignorance, she ventured to meet his eyes—after all, this was *Raffie,* whom she'd known her entire life. "I've heard the boys talking in the schoolyard, but I'm not sure what you mean."

He blew air out over his lips and tried to think of the best way to explain. "I guess for boys it's the same as starting to have periods. It's when we become able to get girls pregnant. Stuff . . . seeds . . . come out, you know. The thing is, it feels great."

"Oh!" She nodded, and sat back against the tree stump. She was finding out more from Raffie than she'd learned in her entire lifetime from her mother.

"Pop says guys my age jack off all the time."

"God! You're so lucky. You can actually talk to your parents. I've been thinking about having a chat with my gramma." She looked at him anxiously, her eyes wide. "But I'm scared she'll turn around and repeat what I say to my mother."

"Talk to *my* mother," he suggested. "She loves you and Lou, and she's easygoing."

"I think I'd rather just talk to you. I'm used to you, and I know you'd never tell on me."

"I never would," he said soberly.

"I know." She smiled at him.

He smiled back at her, and they were silent for a minute or two. Then he leaned forward and kissed her lightly on the mouth. He shifted away to see if she was mad. She felt a sudden fluttering in her chest as they stared at each other, both of them breathing faster all at once.

Then they kissed again and again, until Raffie suddenly groaned and held her arms very tightly, his eyes shut. Then he jumped up and ran into the lake. When he came back, water sparkling on his dark skin, he said, "We better start heading back. It's getting late."

"What's the matter, Raffie?"

"Nothing," he hedged.

"No, tell me. What happened?"

Avoiding her eyes, he said, "The same thing as a wet dream, only awake. The kissing got me excited, that's all."

"Is that bad?"

"Maybe," he answered, pulling his trousers on over his wet bathing suit. "I don't ever want to do anything that gets either one of us in trouble."

"Me, neither."

"Yeah, but see, my getting excited could mean trouble." He dropped down on his haunches in front of her and scooped up a handful of sand. As it trickled through his fingers he said, "I think a lot about touching you, Faye. And that's a sin."

"Oh! I never knew that."

"Well," he said matter-of-factly, "now you do."

"You're not mad at me, are you?"

"At you? Heck, no. I'm mad at myself because I couldn't stop it from happening, and Pop says guys have to learn self-control." Accepting the shirt she held out to him, he pulled it on saying, "I'd never be mad at you, Faye. You're my best friend and I love you. I just have to learn self-control, like Pop says."

She was able to smile again, deeply pleased. "You're *my* best friend," she said, and started putting on her sandals. "And I love you, too. So that's okay."

↳

Maggie was actually glad when Nolan gave her the high sign late one Friday afternoon in mid August. She hadn't been down to his office in more than a week and she'd started feeling jittery, like some kind of goddamned addict. Every morning when she inserted the diaphragm she felt angry and repelled and bewildered too, wondering what the hell was going on. Was Nolan playing games with her suddenly after all these years? She'd make him sorry he'd ever been born, if he was. *Nobody* played games with her! She called the shots, she decided what she would or wouldn't do, and with whom. But as each day ended and he hadn't appeared on the floor to glance in her direction, giving her the high sign no one else would ever notice, her agitation grew.

Their arrangement suited her down to the ground, and the thought of having to find some other man who'd be satisfied merely to make love without expecting to go out places—never mind talking—made her nervous. The situation with Nolan was perfect. So why, out of the blue, was he staying away from her? She was so nerved up that by the time he did signal her on Friday afternoon she had to remind herself not to bolt out of her chair and go flying downstairs to his office.

"What the hell's going on?" she demanded in a whisper, once inside his office with the door locked.

In the near darkness he frowned and stopped halfway over to her. "Nothing's going on, Mag. What d'you mean?"

"How come it's been ten days?"

The fact that they were talking was so extraordinary he had to smile. "Missed me, eh?"

When she didn't reply, he came closer, automatically reaching to unzip her as he murmured, "Had a bit of a cold and didn't want you to catch it. That's all. You think I'd pass up time with you if I didn't have to?"

Satisfied, she discouraged further conversation, reaching up under her dress to remove her pants.

While they were right in the middle, with Nolan clutching her hips from behind, she had a vision of Faye with Raffie DiStasio and silently vowed that she'd break every bone in the little bitch's body if she ever found out Faye was being stupid enough to throw everything away on some boy.

CHAPTER

FIVE

THE OPENING IN LATE AUGUST OF THE CANADIAN NA-
tional Exhibition, commonly called the Ex, was, and had been since 1879 for most kids in Toronto, both the highlight of the summer and the signal of its end. Once the Ex arrived it was usually only a matter of a week, give or take a day or two, before school started.

Billed as the world's largest annual exhibition, it usually ran for four-teen days, excluding Sundays of course (very little was ever open in the city on Sundays; there were no newspapers on that day and the sale of alcoholic beverages was prohibited), and an average of one hundred and seventy thousand people attended daily. For the price of admission—fifty

cents for adults and ten cents for children under fifty-four inches tall—
you had free access to all the buildings, to the band concerts, to dozens of
displays, and to competitions in everything from fencing or swimming to
voice and piano.

Some kids, like Louise, started saving their money weeks and even
months ahead so they'd have enough to go on all the rides—especially the
new roller coaster, the Flyer, which would be in operation for the first
time that summer of 1953—to play a few of the games, see some of the
sideshows along the midway, possibly go to the live evening shows at the
grandstand or the Coliseum, and still have enough left to stop at a Honeydew stand and buy a big Ritz Carlton hot dog and a waxy-coated cup of
Honeydew, a drink that tasted like melon-flavored orange juice.

No matter how hot it might be, it was always cooler down at the vast
CNE grounds on the lakeshore. And there was so much to see that it was
the rare child who went only once. Aside from the many permanent
structures—the Automotive Building, the Horse Palace, the Horticultural
and Music buildings, among others—there was also an air show, recitals,
fashion shows, a musical comedy production under the Big Top, high
diving on the waterfront, sailing regattas, horseshoe pitching contests,
local celebrities demonstrating how to prepare their favorite recipes,
concerts at the band shell, and fabulous nightly fireworks displays. Most
kids went early in the morning and stayed as late as their parents would
permit, or until their money ran out and all they had left was a streetcar
ticket for the ride home.

In previous years, Louise and Faye had attended once with their mother
and at least two more times on their own, usually on children's days,
when admission and most everything else was half price. Faye was invariably cautious with her money, making it last, while Louise became obsessed with trying to win prizes and played at one game booth after
another until, suddenly, she had nothing left, and they'd only been on the
grounds for an hour or so. Faye inevitably took pity on her and judiciously
doled out nickels and dimes for rides and games and food during the
remainder of the day and evening. They never had enough left to cover
the fifty-cent price of admission to the Grandstand show, but Maggie had
twice taken them to sit way up in the bleachers, where they'd watched
the performers spot-lighted on the stage far below. Louise had been
mightily impressed by the Canadettes, who were advertised as the longest
precision dance line in the world, and talked for weeks afterward about

becoming one. Maggie put an end to her lopsided pirouettes and bent-knee high kicks in the kitchen, saying, "Forget it, sister! I'm not shelling out my hard-earned money for any dance lessons." Louise wasn't all that upset. She knew she'd never have made it, because no matter how hard she tried she just couldn't do the splits. It hurt like anything, and if you had to suffer to be a dancer it wasn't worth it. She'd just have to think of some other way to get rich and famous.

The Ex was an orgy of sights and sounds, smells and tastes. All the newest foreign and domestic cars were on display in the Automotive Building; you could get bite-size samples of everything from cakes to hot dogs in the Food Products Building, as well as special Ex prices on such things as aluminum cookware, cake mixes, and peanut butter; and four cooking shows were held daily at the Kitchen Theatre in the Coliseum Annex. If you were interested (and Faye and Louise never were), there were cat and dog shows in the Horse Palace annex, and livestock was judged in the Coliseum arena. You could see the latest in gadgetry and appliances in the Electrical or Manufacturers' buildings, or admire the nine-room ranch-type bungalow dream home, or go see Elsie the Borden Cow. In the Women's Building craftsmen showed how to make ceramics or jewelry or leather tooling; there was a spelling bee, a square dancing competition, and telescopes at the Province of Ontario Building, so you could have a look at the stars.

Also on the grounds were a baby crèche, a hospital, a parcel check room, a ballpark, a bus station, police and fire departments, a bank, and a post office. There were numerous sit-down restaurants, as well as booths selling hamburgers and rubbery ears of buttered corn, or ice cream sandwiches, which consisted of a slab of vanilla ice cream between two waffles. You could buy a paper cornet of chips, douse them with salt and malt vinegar, and eat them as you strolled along. The air reeked of burned sugar from the cotton candy machines, of hot popcorn and peanuts, of mustard and onions, frying meat, oil, and the tang of vinegar. By midday the grounds were thickly littered with sticky elongated paper cones discarded after the last weightless fragment of cotton candy had dissolved on the tongue; the greasy oblong paper trays from countless ears of corn; crumpled paper napkins; multicolored ticket stubs; paper drink cups that had been stomped flat by teenaged boys who liked to make them sound like guns being fired; gum; peanut shells that crunched underfoot; cigarette butts; leaflets and brochures; and sundry other items contributing to the general debris.

The cacophony of sound was overwhelming: the screams of passengers riding the more alarming rides, shrill mechanical laughter emanating from the speaker over the fun house, vendors selling souvenirs, small children wailing from fatigue, and the hoarse, cajoling voices of the barkers. There were always a few young couples carrying enormous teddy bears or large, amorphous stuffed toys of an improbable pink or neon-green it was generally understood the men had somehow managed to win. Louise eyed these fellows with envy, wishing she could win something wonderful, say, at the steeplechase, or from those monstrously frustrating machines where you tried to direct a claw to pick up a wristwatch or one of the other good prizes resting on a bed of colored gravel. All she ever got were a few stupid stones, or a cheap tin whistle at the fishpond, and since nobody ever lost at the fishpond it wasn't really like winning.

"When I was your age," Gramma Perry told the girls during their regular weekly supper at her house the Sunday before the Ex was due to open, "I'd be worked up for weeks over the Ex. I especially remember the Grandstand show in 1917. Quite the spectacle that was, let me tell you. There were vaudeville skits, ten minutes or so of movies—silents in those days, of course—and then"—she paused dramatically—"the Jubilee Spectacle. Over a thousand performers in front of a huge painting, reenacting Queen Victoria's proclamation of confederation, making us the Dominion of Canada. It was positively thrilling." She gave a little shiver as if seeing it all again, then continued with gusto. "The first thing my parents always did when we got there was to tell me that if for some reason we became separated, Father should meet Mother at the Gooderham Fountain, and I should go to the lost children department. It was a big old tent chock-full of kids who seemed to me to be having a whale of a time. I never did manage to get myself lost," she chuckled. "But not for want of trying. I thought it'd be the height of drama to get lost at the Ex. Your Dad and I always took you when you were a tot, Marg. Remember?"

"Of course I remember," Maggie snapped impatiently. "We went every year, for God's sake. I'd hardly be likely to forget."

"Well, girls," Gramma Perry went on, choosing to ignore her daughter's mood, "I was there two years later in 1919 when the Prince of Wales came for the opening ceremony. I can still see him clear as day, looking *so* handsome in his uniform. He wore high, polished boots with spurs, and he had the loveliest smile. Everyone cheered, and he actually came to the edge of the platform and shook hands with people at the front. It was wonderful."

"Let's see, 1919," Louise said, counting backward as she studied her grandmother, who, as usual, was wearing a dress and high heels and had her hair in a French twist. Gramma was a secretary to some lawyers on Bay Street, and Louise often wondered why somebody so old still went to work every day. Grandmothers were supposed to have white hair and stay at home, but Gramma not only had blond hair like their ma, she hardly ever stayed home. She actually went out on dates to places like the Palace Pier or the Imperial Room at the Royal York. She had a big jar of swizzle sticks from all the places she'd been. It was amazing, Louise thought, that a *grandmother* had dates and got dressed up to go dancing. Whenever Louise asked her about it, Gramma would say, "I may be a widow, honey, but I'm not dead yet."

"That's a long time ago," Louise said, having finished her mental arithmetic.

Gramma laughed. "Not *that* long ago. I know you girls think I'm older than God, but I'll have you know I'm not even fifty yet. I was fifteen years old in 1919, just a little older than you, Faye, and simply crazy about Prince Edward. I kept hoping he'd spot me in the crowd and fall madly in love. But of course no such thing happened."

"There's going to be a whole *bunch* of new rides this year," Louise bubbled. "I can't wait, can you, Faye?"

Faye smiled in her new quiet way and said, "Ma said I could go with Raffie and Aldo the first night, but I'll go again with you, too."

"You planning to go with the girls, Marg?" Gramma asked.

"We'll see," Maggie said. "I wouldn't mind seeing Victor Borge, but as far as I'm concerned the Ex is nothing but a big waste of money."

"Everything all right, dear?" Gramma asked, knowing full well Marg was in one of her moods. There was nothing subtle about her daughter's signals, but it wasn't always easy to be sympathetic to a woman who was bothered by so much. The things other people would pass off were enough to trigger a full-scale spasm of outrage in Marg. And yet the things you were certain would infuriate her quite often went unremarked. She'd always been impossible to read, even as a child. Of course her father had spoiled her, forever fussing over her and making her think she was better than other people. Ellen had tried to warn him, but poor Ronald just couldn't see how giving in to her every whim the way he did might not be good for Marg. So she'd grown up full of herself. But John Parker had put a stop to that in no uncertain terms.

Faye and Louise turned to look at their mother, who was busy lighting a fresh cigarette while the one she'd just put out was still smoldering in the ashtray. Her long fingernails were painted the same shade of red as her lipstick, and when she got her cigarette lit, she drummed her brightly enameled nails on the hand-embroidered white tablecloth.

Louise thought her mother looked very glamorous with her blond hair side-parted like Veronica Lake's and her dark eyelashes casting shadows on her cheek, and wondered, as she did most days, how someone so pretty could be so mean.

Faye saw the telltale signs of an impending blowup—the chain-smoking and fingernail tapping, the crossed leg swinging back and forth metronomically—and was afraid her mother had somehow found out about her and Raffie. She was so nervous she had to keep taking little sips of water to ease the dryness in her throat. She dreaded her mother's outbursts, and wished she and Lou could live a peaceful, quiet life instead of having to worry constantly about inadvertently saying or doing something that would send their mother over the edge.

Maggie was waiting. She wanted to be sure she had proof before confronting the girls about the small sums of money that had been disappearing regularly from the jar of change she kept in the cabinet beside the stove. She doubted it was Faye. Faye was too much of a straight arrow to steal, although she was probably going to be one of those stupid females who were pushovers for good-looking men. Louise, on the other hand, was capable of just about anything. She could lie like a trouper, and you didn't dare believe even half of what she said.

"Everything's just peachy," Maggie told her mother, flashing a quick, too-bright smile that failed to reassure any of them. "I'm tired, that's all."

"What you want is an early night," Ellen Perry said, feigning sympathy. It was completely beyond her why Marg was so hard on Faye and Louise. They were good girls, the kind any mother would be proud to have. But not Marg. She'd been making those children pay for John Parker since the day the man had left her, punishing two innocents for something that wasn't their fault. "You work too hard," Ellen said, knowing a show of understanding would calm Marg right down. "Your mother works too hard," she told Faye and Louise, also aware that they'd long since learned it was often necessary for the sake of peace to pander to their mother's ill humor. The girls nodded sagely, and she marveled again at her daughter's good fortune in having two such bright children. You never had to tell them anything twice. "You take the girls and run along home, dear, get a good night's sleep. Then you'll feel right as rain."

Before they left, Ellen slipped five dollars to each of the girls, whispering, "For the Ex."

Louise hugged her fiercely and whispered, "*Thanks,* Gramma."

Faye gave her grandmother a kiss and a grateful smile, and stood for a moment holding her hand before kissing her again.

"Be sure to come tell me all about it," Gramma said as Maggie and the girls set off.

"I'll tell you *everything* when we come next Sunday," Louise promised.

"Don't wind up in the lost children department," Ellen warned with a laugh.

"Not me," Louise declared. "Bye, Gramma," she sang, hurrying to catch up with her mother and sister.

It had been planned for weeks that Louise and Shirley would go to the Ex together on opening day. Louise had managed to save close to four dollars of the ten Gramma had given her months ago on her birthday, and with the additional five she had almost nine whole dollars to spend—the most she'd ever had at one time in her whole life. She was giddy with anticipation and determined to make her money last for the entire day, the way Faye always did.

Chuckie wanted to go with them but Mrs. Beauvais persuaded him to go instead to Kew Beach with her and Mr. Beauvais, promising they'd take him to the Ex the following day when it might be somewhat less crowded. Chuckie wasn't at all happy about the arrangements, and when the girls set off from Louise's house, he was sitting on the top step of the porch at number 17, elbows on his knees, palms cupping his chin, the very picture of dejection.

Louise called over, "See ya later, Chuckie," and waved to him. The undersized boy merely frowned. "You'll be going tomorrow," she called. "And I'll bring you back a surprise."

At this he perked up and yelled, "What?"

"It'll be a surprise. Okay?"

"Don't forget!" he shouted, waving goodbye.

"I won't," she promised, wondering why Shirley was so mean to her kid brother. Chuckie was okay. He wasn't one of those stupid kids who always wanted to play dumb boy games, but was happy to be the child if she and Shirley wanted to play house, or to be the customer if they played storekeepers. She wanted to ask Shirley about it, but didn't want to get into a fight and spoil the day, so she didn't say anything.

At the corner of Bathurst and Queen they climbed into a southbound streetcar crammed with kids on their way to the Ex.

"I can't wait!" Louise said excitedly, hanging on to the pole near the back doors, feet firmly planted so she wouldn't lose her balance as the car swayed along the tracks. "This is the first time I've been allowed to go by myself."

"You're not by yourself," Shirley said expressionlessly.

"You know what I mean. Without an adult," Louise clarified, wondering why Shirley was forever so glum. She hadn't smiled half a dozen times all summer. Why am I friends with you? Louise asked herself, looking at the shorter girl's oddly grown-up face. I don't even like you, she thought, jolted. It was true. She *didn't* like Shirley. The girl was no fun; all she ever wanted to do was come over and flop on the living room floor with comics, or coloring books, or cutouts. She hardly ever wanted to go swimming, or over to Bellwoods Park, or even to roller-skate in the schoolyard. It was no wonder she was white as flour-and-water paste and had shadows under her eyes. After today, Louise decided, she'd stop hanging around with her. It was time she started seeing some of her other friends again.

Having made this decision, she felt better, eased by the knowledge that she wouldn't have to keep on working so hard to be friends with this secretive, somber girl. Maybe she'd never find out what the end of the Beauvais family story was, but she no longer cared. Shirley was just a big pain and not worth the effort.

There was a huge crowd outside the Princes' Gate, waiting to push in through the turnstiles. Louise could smell the popcorn from the cart just inside the gate that sold candy apples and little white bags of popcorn. The girls paid their ten cents and entered the grounds. Louise was overcome by a sense of occasion and by pride in her ability to take care of herself. Being given permission to go to the Ex with a friend meant she was now considered a responsible person. She felt wonderful as she and Shirley went past the Automotive Building on the left and the Electrical Building on the right, heading for the midway. As they walked along the broad boulevard she could see the new roller coaster and hear the screams of people riding it, and shivered with excitement. "What d'you want to do first?" she asked.

Shirley shrugged, her thin elbows poking outward with the gesture. "I don't care," she said, hands in the pockets of her shorts.

"Well," Louise said patiently, "you want to look around the buildings first, or start on the midway and go on the rides?"

"I don't care," Shirley said again.

Brother! Louise thought, itching to give the girl a punch between her jutting shoulder blades to get her going.

"Let's go to the midway," Shirley said suddenly, and headed off without even waiting for Louise.

Louise stood for a few seconds watching Shirley move away, thinking maybe it hadn't been such a great idea after all to come to the Ex with this girl. She had an awful feeling it wasn't going to be as much fun as she'd imagined.

CHAPTER

SIX

THAT FRIDAY MORNING AFTER MA HAD GONE TO WORK and Lou had left for the Ex, Faye cleaned the apartment—just to be sure Ma would have no excuse for getting mad at her—then got ready to go over to the DiStasios'.

As she came out the front door she spotted Chuckie and his parents heading down to Queen Street, on their way, Faye knew, to Kew Beach. Chuckie was skipping along behind his mother and father, carrying a tin bucket-and-spade set, his bare arms and legs very thin and white. There was something wrong with that family, something Faye couldn't quite pinpoint. With a sudden fierce feeling of protectiveness, she hoped that once school started Lou would stop seeing so much of Shirley. She really didn't like Lou hanging around with that girl.

The streets were quieter than usual with most of the kids down at the Ex. She wondered what Lou was doing at that moment, and if she'd already blown all her money on the games. If she had, poor Lou was probably miserable. And it was highly doubtful that Shirley would offer to treat.

Arriving at the corner of Dundas, Faye looked both ways before crossing. It was too hot to run, even if a streetcar was lumbering along the tracks toward her. And she didn't want to arrive at the store all sweaty. She liked to turn up looking her best, to see the way Raffie's face brightened when he saw her.

Whenever Faye thought of the future—something she and Raffie talked about regularly now when they went to their special private beach, or down to the cellar under the store to sit on the bench behind the furnace, or over to the Mars to sit in one of the two-seater booths and share a lime Coke—she pictured herself and Raffie and their children as a family like the DiStasios. When they were old enough, she and Raffie would get married and have a wonderful life together. They'd already decided they'd have two children, once they'd saved enough to buy a nice house. Raffie would be an engineer and leave for his office every morning wearing a suit and tie and carrying a briefcase. And Faye would stay home to look after the house and the children, raising a happy boy and girl who got lots of hugs and kisses. The mental images of these domestic scenes filled her with satisfaction.

Because it was a Friday, her mother had said she could stay over for an early supper with the family, then go to the Ex afterward with Raffie. Any time the two of them went out in the evening, Faye told her mother she was going with both boys. She and Raffie had agreed that he'd never phone her when Ma was home, because Faye had the idea that if her mother heard Raffie's new deep voice over the line she'd somehow be able to figure out that the two of them were in love. And then Ma would make trouble with Raffie's folks, and Faye couldn't bear the idea of that.

Ma would scream at her, call her an idiot, and tell her she was too young to know what she wanted, that she was throwing her life away. But Faye knew she was going to feel the way she did about Raffie for the rest of her life. When they kissed and touched each other down in the cellar she felt as if she'd die if she lost him. There wasn't anything she wouldn't do for Raffie, and nothing, she knew, that he wouldn't do for her. She could tell just by the look on his face when she let him touch her under her clothes how much he cared about her. She loved being able to show her love for him, using her hand and his handkerchief. It made her so happy to please him. And just the night before last she'd let him put his hand between her legs because he was so anxious to make her feel good, too. She was excited now remembering how good it had felt, and eager to be alone with him again. They loved each other, and one day they were going to get married.

Y

Friday morning just before the coffee break, Nolan gave her the high sign for the second day in a row. Her body reacted as if an electric current had passed through it.

Taking her time, she finished the sections she was sewing, then pushed her chair back from the machine. "The damned coffee's going to kill me one of these days," she told Flo.

"It plays hell with my Ern's guts, that's for sure," Flo commiserated. "You probably wanna think about switching to tea or something."

"Might be a good idea," Maggie said, setting off in the direction of the washrooms.

Nolan was all over her the instant she'd closed and locked the door. "Take everything off," he whispered urgently.

"Are you nuts? There's no time," she whispered back, not in the least averse to the idea but simply bothered by the logistics.

"You'll go back up during the coffee break. No one'll notice," he said, tugging at her zipper.

"All right, all right," she said. "But not my stockings."

"Sure, okay," he said, helping her off with the dress.

When she stood naked except for her garter belt, nylons, and high heels, he gazed at her appreciatively, murmuring, "Christ, you're gorgeous, Mag!"

"Do me a favor and shut the hell up," she said. "Okay?"

"I'll never understand you," he said, looking somewhat wounded.

"Don't even try."

"All these years," he said, "I thought we were friends."

"Well, we're not," she said. "So forget it."

They did it on the leather sofa, with her kneeling astride his lap. And when he'd finished first, as he always did, he surprised her by going down on her—something he hadn't done in years, primarily because there was never enough time.

She could barely get her clothes fastened afterward, she was so wrung out. She wished she could lie down and take a nap instead of having to go back upstairs to her stinking machine.

As she moved to go, Nolan put a hand on her arm, saying, "What about coming out with me one evening?"

She laughed automatically. "Where's your wife gonna be while the two of us are out on the town?"

"We're splitting up, Nora and me."

"Oh? Did you get a special dispensation from the pope or something?"

"Jesus, you're a hard woman, Mag. But yes, as a matter of fact it's something like that. So, what's your answer?"

Her hand on the doorknob, she said, "I wouldn't be caught dead in public with you, Nolan."

"Yes, you would, and you know it. Think about it! We could have a couple of hours in bed instead of ten minutes."

"That's screwing, not dating. I've gotta get back upstairs."

"I meant we'd have dinner too. We'd have a chance to talk for a change. Will you think about it?" he persisted.

"Probably not," she said, and left.

Climbing the stairs back up to the factory, she couldn't help wondering what it'd be like to go out for drinks or a bite to eat with Nolan. He wasn't the worst looking guy she'd ever seen, and he certainly made good money, plus he made love like a champion. Shit! What the hell was she doing? He'd almost tricked her into becoming interested in him. Well, she wasn't about to set one foot outside this factory in Nolan's company. There wasn't a man alive worth the powder to blow him away. The nerve of Nolan, thinking she'd even consider going out with him! And why did he have to go changing things now, after all these years? She felt like marching back down the stairs and smacking him right across the mouth. God, but she hated men!

Louise was hanging on to her money and feeling good about it as she watched Shirley try over and over to win at one game after another. She was stuck waiting, becoming bored, while Shirley played at the steeple-chase, her finger on the trigger of a gun that fired a stream of water at a target. If the water hit the target, her horse moved forward, but Shirley kept missing, so her horse never won. She went on losing, but just pulled one more dime from her pocket, then another and another, oblivious of Lou.

Finally, when the bell went off and for the seventh time in a row someone else instead of Shirley had won, Lou tapped her on the arm and said, "Let's go on some rides now."

"I want to play one more time."

"No!" Louise said firmly. "I'm tired of standing around waiting. We came here to have a good time, not for you to blow all your money on stupid games while I'm stuck doing nothing. Let's *go* on the *rides*."

"Oh, all right," Shirley said peevishly, as if she was humoring a spoiled child. "Come *on!*"

Louise was beginning to hate her. It had been two whole hours since the gates had opened at nine o'clock, and they hadn't done a single worthwhile thing. It probably wouldn't have been so bad if she'd been playing the games, too. But watching Shirley trying so hard to win made Lou see that the games really were dumb, the way Faye had always said, and a complete waste of time. It sickened her now to think of all the money she'd thrown away on them in previous years.

"Let's go on the Giant Rotor!" Louise exclaimed, seeing the line of people waiting to buy tickets. "It's brand new. It goes spinning around and then supposedly the floor drops away and you get stuck to the wall."

"I don't want to," Shirley said. "Let's go on the Ferris wheel instead."

Louise wanted badly to try out the Giant Rotor but she gave in and agreed to go on the Ferris wheel. And that's the way it went for the next couple of hours, with her giving in every single time to what Shirley wanted to do. If Louise said she'd like to go on the roller coaster, Shirley wanted to go see the Man with Two Faces in the sideshow. If Louise said could they please go on the Giant Rotor now, Shirley said she wanted to ride one of the little boats through the Tunnel of Love.

At a quarter to one Louise declared, "I'm hungry. I'm going to get something to eat."

Shirley gave one of her shrugs and trailed Louise over to the booth.

"Aren't you going to eat anything?" Louise asked, handing over a quarter to pay for her Ritz Carlton red hot and a Honeydew.

"I'm not hungry," Shirley said. "You eat while I go play the ring toss."

"Brother," Louise muttered. While she ate, she tried to add up how much Shirley had already spent on the dumb games. It had to be at least four or five dollars. What a waste of good money!

It was so long before Shirley came back that Louise had started getting worried, wondering how she was going to explain to Mrs. Beauvais that Shirley had gone off to play the games and Louise hadn't been able to find her. When she did return, Louise got mad. "Where the *heck* have you been?" she demanded. "I've been waiting *hours,* for Pete's sake! I was beginning to get scared you were lost. Can we go on the Flyer now *finally?*"

"I spent all my money," Shirley said, hands jammed into her shorts' pockets.

"Oh, great!" Louise moaned, wanting to hit her.

"Don't get into a sweat," Shirley said. "I know where I can get some more."

"What? Where? How?"

"Come on. You can keep a lookout for me."

What was she going to do? Louise wondered, going with Shirley back to the part of the midway where most of the rides were located.

Stopping outside the low fence enclosing the Rocket—a lozenge-shaped contraption that turned upside down and spun around—Shirley glanced from side to side, then said, "Okay. Keep a lookout."

Mystified, Louise watched as Shirley climbed quickly over the fence then got down on her hands and knees and started crawling around on the ground under the rotating Rocket. Louise anxiously eyed the two men running the ride, trying to figure out what Shirley was doing, and wishing that whatever it was she'd hurry up. She didn't even know what she was keeping a lookout *for.*

No more than five minutes later Shirley was back, scooting over the fence. Grabbing Louise by the arm, she led her farther along the midway, then stopped. Opening her fist, she counted a handful of coins and then, with a look of extreme satisfaction, said, "Eighty-seven cents. Come on. There's two more good ones."

"What're you *doing?*" Louise asked as Shirley pocketed the change.

"Don't you know *anything?*" Shirley said with a rare show of energy. "I'm getting the money that falls out of peoples' pockets when they're upside down."

Dumbfounded, Louise could only wonder if Shirley had figured that out all by herself, or if somebody had shown her.

Just over half an hour later Shirley had amassed three dollars and eighteen cents. "Okay," she said. "Let's go see King Kong, the Killer."

"I'm sick of the sideshows. That guy didn't have two faces. He just had big lumps on his face. It was revolting," Louise said. "I want to see some of the buildings, get a few free samples, and enter some of the draws. Last year my girlfriend Lily's mother won a Mixmaster."

"What're you gonna do with a *Mixmaster?*"

"They have draws for all kinds of things," Louise said, astonished at how literally Shirley took things. "And I'd kind of like a candy apple, or maybe some cotton candy."

"Oh, all right," Shirley conceded, again with an air of conciliating a difficult child. "Let's go, if we're going."

Both girls collected shopping bags at one stand and quickly filled them with advertising pamphlets and samples of cheese and cookies, tiny bottles of perfume, small boxes of cereal, miniature Coca-Cola bottles, rolls of Lifesavers, and tiny cellophane bags of Planters Peanuts. They stopped to watch a man who was the fastest-talking human being Louise had ever heard demonstrate the fantastic kitchen tool that sliced and diced and shredded potatoes or carrots, even lettuce. Then they went to have a free sugar doughnut and a sample-size cup of Orange Crush.

Louise had almost recovered from her irritation with Shirley when, to her astonishment, she saw the girl reach out and snatch a necklace with a gold-plated heart pendant from a jewelry display. Shirley slipped the necklace into her pocket and kept on walking. Scandalized, Louise whispered, "I saw you do that!"

"So what?" Shirley shrugged.

"That's *stealing!*"

"So what?" Shirley repeated.

"It's not right to steal. You should go give that necklace back."

At this, Shirley turned with a disbelieving expression and said, "Are you kidding? I will not! It's mine!"

Louise stared at Shirley's pallid and stubborn, oddly grown-up features not knowing what to say or do. Reviewing all her possible options, she knew she couldn't do a thing. She prayed someone didn't catch Shirley and accuse Louise of stealing, too, just because she happened to be with her, because now that she was aware of what was going on, she saw

Shirley helping herself to one small thing after another. Growing more and more disgusted, Louise looked around guiltily every time, but no one seemed to notice. By the time they left the General Exhibits Building and started back toward the midway, Louise was actually anxious to go home. It had been the worst and longest day of her life, and to top things off, there was a great big piece of bubble gum stuck to the bottom of her sandal.

"Hold up," she said to Shirley, leaning against a souvenir booth with her shopping bag looped over one arm while she tried to pry the gum off the sole of her shoe with a Popsicle stick she found on the ground. The gum didn't want to come off. She really had to work at it, bent over her upraised right foot, so she wasn't paying any attention to Shirley. She'd just managed to scrape off the last of the gooey stuff when Shirley came strolling around the side of the booth wearing a big black cowboy hat. Louise was about to ask where she'd got it when a man suddenly appeared behind Shirley, dropped a hand on her shoulder and said, "Just a minute there, girlie! Where d'you think you're going with that hat, eh?"

For once Shirley seemed at a loss. Mutely she removed the hat and tried to return it, but the man said, "Oh no you don't! You don't get off that easily. I'm going to have to turn you over to the police."

Frozen to the spot, Louise watched as the man kept one hand firmly fastened to Shirley's shoulder while signaling to another man to come over.

"Caught this one trying to make off with a hat," he told the second man. "You want to book her?"

Louise didn't think the second man was a police officer, but maybe they had officers dress in ordinary clothes at the Ex so they could catch people like Shirley.

"Let's get her name and address, call her folks," the second man said.

"Good idea," replied the first one. "Come on around here," he said, directing Shirley to the front of the booth.

Louise followed, swallowing nervously as the man got a piece of paper and a pencil, then said, "Okay, missy. What's your name?"

"Shirley."

He printed that on the paper. "Shirley what?"

"Shirley Evans," Louise said, causing all of them to turn and look at her.

"Who're you?" the man asked.

"She's my cousin from Winnipeg. She wasn't going to steal your hat, mister. She was just coming to show it to me, to ask if I thought she should buy it. See, I had gum stuck to the bottom of my shoe and I was back there"—she pointed—"trying to get it off. I can show it to you, if you want, and the Popsicle stick I was using. Anyway, you see, she was having a look at your hats while she waited. That's all. She'd never take anything that didn't belong to her. My ma always says Shirley's as honest as the day is long."

"Yeah," he said doubtfully. "Well, I'm still gonna have to give her folks a call. If she's visiting you, you better give me your address and phone number," he said, his eyes returning to Shirley who at once said, "Seventeen . . ."

"Markham Street," Louise said quickly, causing the man to look back at her.

"Okay. What's the phone number?"

"Empire three five six nine seven," Louise rattled off whatever numbers popped into her head.

He finished writing this down and at last released his grip on Shirley's shoulder. "I'm gonna have to tell your folks about this, little girl," he told her. "And the police will warn the other concessionaires about you, give them your description, so don't you go trying to steal anything else here. Got that?"

Shirley's head bobbed up and down.

Louise said, "She honestly wasn't trying to steal that hat, but I'll make sure she doesn't try anything else on. I'm very sorry, sir." With that, she grabbed hold of Shirley's hand and towed her away at a brisk pace.

When they were at a good distance from the scene of Shirley's attempted crime, Louise stopped and whirled around to face the smaller girl. "You nearly got yourself arrested!" she cried, trembling with upset and residual fear. "Are you *crazy?* They could've put you in *jail!* Why do you *do* things like that?" She wanted to take Shirley by the shoulders and shake her as hard as she could, until she lost that po-faced expression.

Shirley just stared blankly at her and shrugged.

"I promised my mother I'd be home by nine. We have to go right now if we don't want to be late!" Louise's voice wobbled up and down, out of control.

"I don't *want* to go yet." Shirley stood with her hands in her pockets, her feet planted slightly apart as if prepared physically to withstand any attempt Louise might make to move her.

"We *have* to!" Louise insisted. "I'm not getting in trouble with my mother because of you. Bad enough I had to get you out of that jam back there. We're going *right now!*"

"Not me. I'm staying."

Louise stopped a passing couple to say, "Could you please tell me the time?"

The woman looked at her watch. "Eight thirty-five, dear. Are you little girls lost?"

"No, we're not," Louise said politely. "Thank you." The couple went on, and she turned back to Shirley. "I'm going to be late because of you," she said furiously. "I'm leaving right this minute. Are you coming or not?"

"No," Shirley said, her pointed chin jutting.

Louise was afraid to leave Shirley there and afraid of what her mother would do to her when she got home late. "Okay, fine," she said nervously. "Then I'm going without you!" She took a few steps thinking Shirley would come along after her but when she turned back Shirley was already out of sight. "Oh, shit!" she whispered, scared now as well as angry. What if something bad happened to that dumb girl? She'd get blamed for it, even if it wasn't her fault. Shirley was a sneak and a thief and a rotten friend, but everybody would blame her for sure if anything happened to the crummy little creep.

Hurrying as fast as she could through the crowd, Louise raced toward the Princes' Gates at the far end of the grounds. It was going to take her at least fifteen minutes just to get to the gates. Damn! Shit! Damn! Here she'd spent a whole day at the Ex and she still had almost five dollars left. Well, she reasoned, trying to look on the bright side, when she came again with Faye she'd at least have some money to spend.

Spotting a pay phone, she decided to call home. If she let her mother know she was going to be late, maybe Ma wouldn't be mad. Sweating, she dropped a nickel into the slot, dialed her number, then waited. When her mother answered, Louise said, "It's me, Ma. I wanted to let you know I'll be a little late, but I'm on my way to the streetcar stop right now."

"You get the hell home now!" her mother yelled.

"I'm coming, I told you," Louise said, so scared she felt as if she were going to wet her pants.

"You just get back here on the double!" Her mother slammed the phone down so hard it hurt Louise's ear.

Hanging up the receiver, she felt as if all her bones had melted, and she was suddenly so tired she could hardly stand up. She hadn't done a single thing wrong but she was in really bad trouble.

"Shit shit shit!" she muttered under her breath. She hated and despised Shirley Beauvais, and they weren't going to be friends anymore. As she was approaching the gates, she saw a souvenir stand and remembered she'd promised Chuckie a surprise. She took a minute to buy a paper bird that was attached to a stick by a long string. When you waved it around, the bird whistled. Chuckie would like it. At least she hadn't broken her promise, she thought grimly, close to tears.

CHAPTER

SEVEN

MAGGIE HADN'T BEEN HOME FROM WORK MORE THAN A few minutes when the telephone rang. Snatching up the receiver she barked a hello, then heard Nolan say, "That's some hell of a way to answer the phone, Mag."

"Jesus, Nolan," she said tiredly, "what d'you want?"

"I want to know if you're going to think about coming out with me."

"I told you, no."

"Yeah, but you didn't mean that."

"Nolan, I meant it. Leave me the hell alone."

"So you won't come out with me and you won't even think about it?"

"Finally he gets it." She gave an exasperated sigh. "Can I go now? I'm tired. I'd like to relax a little after a hard day's work, if that's okay with you."

"We could relax together." It sounded as if he were smiling.

He was being so persistent it was almost funny. "What got you going

on this kick anyway?'' she asked. ''When did you decide to mess everything up and start hounding me?''

''Nothing's messed up. I'm not hounding you. I always had it in the
back of my mind that if my situation ever changed maybe the two of us
could get something going away from work.''

''Where're you calling from?'' she asked suspiciously.

''My office. Where'd you think I was calling from?''

''Never mind. I could care less.''

''Okay, Mag. I can tell you're in no mood to talk.''

''Talking has never been of any interest to me where you're concerned, Nolan. I would've thought you'd've figured that out by now.''

''If you want me to get off the line, just say so,'' he said quietly,
sounding hurt.

''I want you to get off the line,'' she said flatly.

''Okay, Mag, I'm sorry you feel that way. See you Monday.''

The rain started as Louise was leaving the CNE grounds. In the down-
pour, the noise of the Ex diminishing behind her, she trudged along Fleet
Street, following the families and couples headed for the streetcar loop.
Shirley might have been the world's worst companion that day but Louise
couldn't help feeling guilty about leaving her. She hoped nothing bad
happened to the sneaky little jerk, and several times looked back on the
off chance Shirley might be there, but she never was.

Maybe Shirley would get herself electrocuted crawling around looking
for money under the rides. She'd wind up getting herself killed, and
everyone would say it was Louise's fault for going off without her.

While she waited unhappily, impatiently, for the streetcar, willing it to
hurry up and get there, she looked back, seeing the lights from the
midway and the rides shining through the rain. People were pouring out
through the exits now, holding newspapers or jackets over their heads and
laughing as they came running. There wouldn't be any fireworks tonight,
because of the rain. Everything would close up early instead of staying
open until ten-thirty. Louise frowned, trying to remember what she'd
learned in science about electricity and water. Maybe Shirley really would
get electrocuted. Holy cow! she thought, panicky, trying to see if she
could spot Shirley among the people leaving the grounds. No sign of her.
Maybe she'd be the one to get kidnapped instead of Chuckie, and everybody would say it was Louise's fault.

On the streetcar she held the heavy damp shopping bag on her lap and looked out the window, nervously rolling her transfer into a tube. The car was jammed with wet people, and the air smelled like laundry. Her hair was dripping, her blouse and shorts were stuck to her skin, and her feet kept sliding around in her sandals. The car rocked as it climbed up Bathurst Street, the passengers all swaying. She wanted to go to sleep and forget today had ever happened.

While she was waiting for the Queen streetcar with the rain pounding down on her, the shopping bag handles gave way, so she had to fold the top over and carry the bulky bag in her arms. It was probably way after nine now, the latest she'd ever been out after dark by herself, and she didn't even care. She hoped some lunatic murdered her. When they found her dead body lying in some alley next to the garbage cans Ma would be sorry.

It was hard to walk very fast with her sandals slip-sliding every which way. The leather straps cut into the sides of her feet and her ankles as she went up Manning. She was so miserable she almost hoped some murderer did come after her. She wouldn't even try to get away. She'd just tell him to go ahead and kill her.

Maybe Faye was home, she thought, her spirits suddenly lifting a little. She really hoped so, because Faye would stand up for her. She always did. But even if Faye had started for home from the Ex when the rain began she'd never have made it back by now. Her spirits falling again, she struggled along the street knowing no one was going to be there to help her explain to Ma what had happened.

Hearing footsteps on the porch, Maggie paused a moment, listening, then marched down the hall and threw open the front door. Grabbing a fistful of Louise's hair, she yanked the girl into the house, slammed the door shut, and said in a low, deadly voice, *"Where the goddamned hell've you been?"*

Her head dragged painfully to one side, arms wrapped around the sodden shopping bag, Louise said, "I phoned you. I *told* you I was late." Tears sprang to her eyes as her mother pulled her by the hair into the living room.

"I'll teach you to steal!" Maggie hissed. Letting go of Louise's hair, she started slapping her with both hands as hard as she could, hitting whatever part of her was handy—arms, shoulders, the back and side of her head.

Bent over the shopping bag, Louise tried to duck out of range of the blows, bobbing this way and that as her mother chased after her. In a frenzy, her face red and her hands moving too fast to keep track of, Maggie Parker pursued her.

"Why're you *hitting* me?" Louise cried, finding herself trapped in the corner of the room. "I didn't *do* anything." Crouching, she shielded herself with the bag, trying to make herself small enough to hide behind it. She hated her mother and wished she were big enough to hit back. Ma wouldn't stop now until she got tired out, and sometimes that took hours.

Maddened at being unable to get at Louise, Maggie bent down and grabbed for the shopping bag with both hands. The wet paper gave way and the bag's contents spilled out over the hardwood floor.

"What's all this, more stuff you've stolen?"

Deeply wounded by the accusation, Louise began trying to gather up the pamphlets and soggy samples, the fragile whistling paper bird she'd bought for Chuckie. "I didn't steal anything," she sobbed as her mother started kicking at the pile of goods. "Don't *do* that!" Louise cried, her voice rising despite her efforts to keep it down. "You're *breaking* it all!"

"I'll give you *breaking*," Maggie panted, her fury undiminished. It was all she could do not to kick Louise, to pound her senseless. She wanted to, but knew she didn't dare. People could understand punishing an unruly child, but no one would understand what she really longed to do to this monster. She had to push away the images; they were too dangerous. But they stayed right at the edge of her mind like a crowd of onlookers, urging her on as she started whacking Louise on the head with both hands.

Folding her arms protectively over her head, Louise drew her knees up tight to her chest and sobbed. She hadn't done a single thing wrong—even lying to those men for stupid Shirley, and leaving her hadn't really been wrong; she just hadn't liked having to do it. Yes, she'd fibbed to the men. But they'd scared Shirley, and they got their hat back. So everything worked out all right really. It wasn't a bad lie, not anything wicked that would get innocent people in trouble. Why did Ma go crazy this way? Why did she hate her and Faye so much? Why was she always ready to believe the worst about them when they hadn't done anything? The outrageous unfairness of it was like a stone stuck in her throat. She couldn't swallow it and she couldn't spit it out. Her mother kept hitting and hitting, trying again to grab hold of Louise's hair.

"What'd you do with the money, you goddamned thief? Eh? *Eh?* What'd you do with it? *Where is it?*"

"What money?" Louise cried helplessly, head aching and face stinging from the repeated blows.

"The money you stole from the jar in the kitchen. *Where is it? What did you do with it?*"

"I didn't take any of that money!" Louise shouted, wiping her eyes and nose with the back of her hand. "I would never."

"Keep your voice down!" Maggie warned.

"I won't!" Louise screamed. "I won't! I don't steal! I'd never steal! Go ahead and kill me! I don't care!"

"Don't you dare raise your voice to me!" Maggie got out, all but strangling on her rage. Her hand swung out and she struck Louise hard across the face. The blow was so forceful that Louise was thrown into the wall, and Maggie felt a pain shoot through her hand. "You better not have spent it!" she warned, using her left hand on the top of Louise's head, then pounding on the girl's upper arms with her fists. "I'll teach you to take what doesn't belong to you!" she said through her teeth, her voice even lower now as it rode the tidal wave of her rage. She experienced a dark, deepening satisfaction with each blow that connected. Every word she spoke echoed inside her skull and was punctuated by the power pulsing through her bloodstream.

"What're you *doing,* Ma?" Faye asked from the doorway.

"You stay the hell out of this if you know what's good for you!" Maggie warned in a deadly, low voice.

"Why're you hitting her?" Faye came into the room, taking in the sight of her sister cowering in the corner, the scattered contents of the torn shopping bag. "What did she do?"

"Who are you to question me?" Maggie demanded.

"I want to know," Faye insisted implacably.

Taken aback, Maggie hesitated a moment, then said, "She's been stealing from my change jar."

"I HAVE NOT!" Louise shouted, her sister's presence fueling her courage. "I DIDN'T DO ANYTHING! I HATE YOU!"

"You don't *ever* talk that way to me!" Maggie delivered another whack across the side of Louise's face.

"Stop *hitting* her!" Faye exclaimed, clutching her mother's arm. "You're not even listening. *Listen!* Lou didn't take the money. Shirley did." She hadn't realized she knew this, but had no doubt that it was the truth.

Shaking off Faye's hand, Maggie snatched up Louise's plastic change purse from the floor. As she pulled out a folded pair of two dollar bills her face was distorted by a twisted triumphant smile. "Oh, yeah?" she shrilled. "What d'you call this, then?" She felt positively exultant. She had even more proof right in her hand. Let the little scum talk her way out of this!

The girls spoke simultaneously.

"That's *my* money."

"It's *her* money."

"What d'you mean it's *her* money?" Maggie asked, eyes slitted.

The girls looked at each other. If they explained, they'd get Gramma in trouble. But if they didn't explain, their mother would keep on accusing Lou of being a thief, keep on beating her. With a sigh, Faye said, "Gramma gave us each five dollars for the Ex."

"When?" Maggie challenged, convinced it was a lie.

"On Sunday," Faye said. "Ask her if you don't believe us."

"Yeah!" Louise sniffed, still crouched in the corner. "Ask her!"

"Oh I'll ask her all right. You can count on it." Turning, she pointed a finger at Louise, saying, "Don't you bring that Shirley here again. I don't want that girl in my house. Understand?"

"You don't have to worry about that," Louise said sullenly. "We're not friends anymore."

Maggie gave her another smack. "Don't use that tone of voice with me, young lady!"

Louise held a hand to her stinging cheek and sobbed, her chest heaving. A voice in her head whispered, *I hate you hate you hate you. I hope you die.*

"You shouldn't go hitting people without bothering to find out the truth," Faye told her mother, positioning herself in front of Louise. "You're always doing that to us, deciding we've done things when we haven't, beating us up for no good reason. You've got to stop it, Ma. If you hit her again," Faye threatened, a fearful fluttering in her chest, "I'll hit you."

Maggie slapped her across the face. There was silence for a second or two as Faye looked into her mother's eyes, and Louise, unblinking, looked first at her sister and then at her mother. Faye took a breath, then slapped her mother. In the ensuing stunned silence, Faye felt fear darting about inside her like some trapped thing searching madly for a way out. But she also had a new and profound sense of her own power.

Eyes round, mouth agape, Louise shrank into herself, certain Ma would kill them both now. But it'd be worth it. She felt fiercely proud of her older sister.

Maggie instinctively put her hand to her face, so stunned she was temporarily unable to react.

"You made me do that. I warned you," Faye said shakily, starting to cry. It was wrong to hit your own mother. But it was also wrong for a mother to treat her children the way Maggie Parker treated them. All at once the words began pouring out of her. "You're always hitting us and screaming at us when we haven't even done anything, and we're good girls." The words came out in gulps as the tears flowed down her cheeks. Something was ending, and although she wasn't sure quite what it was, it made her terribly sad. "Me and Lou, we always do what we're told. We don't act up, or stay out late, or smoke cigarettes, or do any of the bad things other kids do. We all know Lou likes to tell fibs and make up stories, but it doesn't hurt anybody. And maybe I am sloppy and leave my hair in the sink, but no matter how hard we try, nothing we do is ever right for you. You act like you hate us, always telling us to get the hell away from you, you can't stand the sight of us. I'll tell you what *I* think," she cried, her voice rising. "I think you don't deserve to have us. Lou comes home with the best report cards of anyone in the class and you're not even proud of her. We clean up around here and take out the garbage and you don't even say thank you. Other people's mothers are nicer to us than you are. Mrs. DiStasio and Mrs. Wisznowski, even old Mrs. Healey upstairs acts like she cares more about us than you do. You're an awful mother, and we're too good for you." At the end of this declaration, she stood breathing hard, tears streaming down her face, understanding that it was her childhood that was ending. She could never have it back. It was gone forever, and she already missed it the same way she missed Sophie, with an aching in her chest and a place in her brain that felt bruised whenever she thought about how wonderful it felt to hug Sophie and have the little girl's arms go tight around her neck. It was a terrible, lonely feeling and for a few moments she wished they could go backward and wipe out the last few minutes. She didn't want to give up her childhood yet, she wasn't ready. But it was too late. And if she had to, she'd strike back again. Nobody was going to hurt her or her sister ever again.

When Maggie didn't say anything but just kept standing there with her eyes round and her hand on her cheek, frozen in place like a statue, Faye turned away. She dropped down and began pushing everything back into the torn shopping bag, while an awe-struck Louise looked on.

Maggie couldn't move. She stood with a hand on her smarting cheek, her eyes moving back and forth between the two girls. She wanted to wrap her hands around Faye's throat and choke the life out of her for daring to strike her. But she was so stung by her daughter's words and so thrown by the passionate intensity of her declaration that she was temporarily paralyzed. It had never occurred to her that either of the girls was capable of harboring so many grievances, or that they thought she was such a bad mother. She was a damned *good* mother, had kept them fed and clothed, and had paid for the roof over their heads from the day that bastard John Parker abandoned them. Their ingratitude was galling. At last, knowing she had to say something and determined to preserve her authority, she said, "Go to your room, the two of you!" Her voice sounded wispy, robbed of its force by shock.

"Don't worry," Faye said without looking around. "We're going. We're fed up with the sight of *you*." Hefting the wet bag, she said, "Come on, Lou," and gave her younger sister a hand up.

Maggie backed up a step or two as Faye, chin lifted, an arm around Louise's shoulders, directed her hiccuping sister down the hall to their bedroom.

After they'd gone, Maggie went straight to the kitchen to light a cigarette with shaking hands. Then she picked up the telephone to call her mother.

Louise sat on the side of the bed with her legs dangling, whispering, "I *hate* her! I wish she'd *die!*"

"Don't say that," Faye said automatically.

"I *do* wish it!" Louise repeated stubbornly. "I mean it with all my heart."

"We better get you into the bath," Faye said, wiping her face with both hands.

Louise stared at her, then said, "You sounded just like a mother, the way you said that." She laughed. Then her face folded in on itself and she started crying again. "She hit me so hard, all over. My head hurts."

"I know." She *felt* like the mother now, and wondered if Lou could actually tell.

"It's a good thing you came home or she would've killed me this time. I thought she was going to. She kept on hitting and hitting and wouldn't stop."

"I'll see if the coast's clear, then keep you company while you have your bath." Faye opened the door an inch, listened, then whispered, "She's on the phone, probably calling Gramma to yell at her for giving us the money. Bring your pajamas and come on."

In the tub, Louise sat inspecting the tops of her arms before reaching for the soap and her washcloth.

"You're gonna have bruises," Faye said, upset by the reddened areas all over Lou's back and shoulders and face. Maybe their mother really was crazy and would actually have killed Lou if she hadn't come home in time. The thought was very scary. She'd hit them both many times before, but never like this. Lou's face looked swollen and sore. Her lips were puffy and her eyes were bloodshot from crying. She's just a little kid, Faye thought, studying her sister's flat chest, so pale compared to her tanned arms. "Are you hungry, Lou? You want me to get you something?"

Louise shook her head. "I wish we could go live somewhere else," Louise whispered. *"She* wouldn't care."

Faye said, "As soon's I'm old enough, I'm getting my own place, and you're coming with me."

"What'll we live on?" Louise asked.

"I'll take typing when we get to high school. Then I'll be able to get a good job in an office."

"But what about school?"

Faye shrugged. "The only thing I care about is learning to type. And as soon as I've learned how, I'll quit and go to work."

"You promise you'll take me with you?" Louise asked.

"Cross my heart and hope to die." Faye's left hand crisscrossed her chest. "I'd never go off and leave you, Lou. You're my sister, and I'm going to look out for you from now on. She's never going to hit either one of us ever again. I'll *kill* her if she does."

For the second time that night, Louise gazed with awe at Faye. "I'm *glad* you hit her," she said. "Really, really glad."

Faye looked down at her lap and quietly, almost to herself, said, "I'm not." Then she cleared her throat and looked over at Louise, saying, "Hurry up and get washed or you'll catch a chill."

CHAPTER

EIGHT

ALF HEALEY WAS DISTRESSED WHEN HE MET LOUISE THE next morning as he was returning home with a quart of milk and the Saturday paper and she was on her way out the door.

"You all right, little miss?" he asked quietly, taking in her battered face.

"I'm fine, thank you," she answered soberly. "How are you, Mr. Healey?"

"Oh, me," he said dismissively, always impressed by the fancy manners of the two Parker girls. "I'm right as rain, thanks for asking." Then, his voice dropping to a more confiding tone, he said, "You can always come up to me and the missus, you've got trouble, you know. You and your sister both."

His words reinforced everything Faye had said the night before, and seemed further proof of how much more other people cared about her and Faye than their own mother did. She was touched by his concern, but a lifetime of her mother's warnings not to talk about what went on inside their home held her back. "Thank you very much," she said sincerely, "but I'm okay. I have something important I have to do now, so I better be going. Bye, Mr. Healey." She gave him a smile that made her face hurt, and continued on her way.

Upstairs, as he put the bottle of milk in the fridge, Alf said, "I run into Louise just now. The tyke's black-and-blue, Biddy. I've a good mind to report that mother of theirs to the authorities."

Turning from the stove, her mouth downturned, Biddy Healey said, "I knew something was going on down there last night, the way that child was carrying on. But you go bringing the police in on people, Alf, and next thing you know, we've got nothing but ructions.''

"A'course you're right, Biddy,'' he said sadly, sitting down at the table and folding open the paper. "But somebody oughta do something about a woman beats a child that way.''

"That's the truth all right,'' she agreed, turning back to the sausages spitting in the pan. "It's a disgrace is what it is.''

"Oh my, my,'' Alf exclaimed, gazing at the newspaper. "Come take a look, Bid! Isn't this that child from across the street?''

"Goodness me,'' she said softly. "I do believe you're right, Alf. How dreadful! Those poor people.''

⤙

All night long Louise had dreamed about confronting Shirley. In one dream she got back every last penny Shirley had stolen from the jar, then she went home and threw the money at her mother's feet. Her mother broke down and said she was sorry for falsely accusing her and for hitting her, and could Louise possibly find it in her heart to forgive her. But Louise said, "I'm sorry, but it's too late for that,'' and walked away.

In another dream someone was pounding at the front door. Louise sat up in bed, listening to the rumble of male voices. Then heavy footsteps approached, the bedroom door opened, and her mother said, "There she is,'' pointing at Louise. Two police officers came into the room. One said, "You'll have to come with us,'' and the other had a pair of handcuffs. "You shouldn't have left her all by herself,'' the second officer said. "But she wouldn't come with me!'' Louise cried. "It wasn't my fault!'' No one would listen. Something horrible had happened to Shirley, and Louise was going to be taken to jail in the Black Maria.

What with the awful, angry dreams and Ma's beating, she'd had a very bad night. She woke up determined to make sure Shirley was all right, and then to tell her off but good. Without bothering to wash or brush her teeth, she got dressed. As she marched across to number 17, she rehearsed what she was going to say. She wanted the whole world to know Shirley was a sneak thief and a rotten troublemaker, and hoped Mr. and Mrs. Beauvais gave the rotten skunk the worst licking of her life. She pounded on the door with her fist and waited. The inside of her mouth felt stuffed, as if all the things she wanted to say were pebbles crammed into her cheeks. When she started to speak they'd come flying out and hit Shirley like bullets.

It was Mrs. Beauvais who came to the door. And that was strange. Usually Shirley or Chuckie would come running down the stairs. On top of that the woman looked a bit peculiar, but at first glance Louise couldn't determine why.

Uncertainly, Louise said, "Hi, Mrs. Beauvais. Is Shirley home?"

The woman looked as if she was trying to smile, and Louise wondered if Mrs. Beauvais' face hurt, too, as she said, "Shirley, she can't play wit' you today," and Louise was relieved to know the stupid jerk hadn't got herself killed at the Ex. At least nobody would come blaming Louise for leaving her.

"Is something the matter?" Louise asked, thinking Mrs. Beauvais seemed very tired and her face was kind of gray. She had her teeth in for a change, but today they looked too big for her mouth. Her clothes were rumpled and wrinkled, like she'd been sleeping in them. But that was silly, she chided herself. Grown-ups didn't sleep in their clothes.

"You didn't hear, eh?"

Louise shook her head.

"My Chuckie, he drowned yesterday," Mrs. Beauvais said, her eyes all at once wet underneath.

"I beg your pardon?" Louise was sure she hadn't heard correctly. The woman's accent often made it seem she'd said one thing when she'd actually said something else.

"Chuckie," Mrs. Beauvais repeated, "he drowned."

Louise felt as if she'd been shoved in the chest, and it was suddenly hard for her to breathe.

"At Kew Beach," the woman added, as if these extra few words explained everything. She held a crumpled Kleenex to her nose, saying, "You'll see Shirley another time, eh? You go on home now, okay?" After a moment she carefully closed the door.

Louise stood staring at the cracked brown paint on the door, hearing Mrs. Beauvais inside slowly returning up the stairs. She couldn't make sense of what the woman had told her. It was incomprehensible. Chuckie had been sitting right here on the top step of this very porch yesterday morning, when she and Shirley left for the Ex. She'd bought him a surprise, a whistling bird, just like she'd promised. And as soon as it was dried out she was going to give it to him.

Her eyes kept blinking, there was a funny taste in her mouth, and her chest ached. After a time she turned and went down the steps to stand on the sidewalk looking up and down the early morning street. There was no one around. The air was warm but not hot. The leaves of the horse chestnut tree in front of the house lifted slowly, then fell as if they were tired. A cream-and-red-painted streetcar went rattling past down on Queen Street. Louise put a hand in her pocket and fingered the metal rim of her change purse as she again looked up the tree-lined street, at the cars parked here and there, at the front porch of Mrs. McGarry's house across the street with the lattice-work underneath and the three green-painted steps, the snowball bush that took up most of her front garden. A black and white dog came trotting along the sidewalk, stopped to sniff around the base of the lamppost, trotted another few feet, then lifted his leg on the fire hydrant. Ma had kept the four dollars, but Louise still had eighty-two cents. The dog crossed the road and began sniffing his way down the other side of the street. Somewhere up the block a screen door slammed. An idea beginning to take form, Louise started walking toward Queen, her eyes on the sidewalk.

She'd been sent out a zillion times to buy Ma a paper, but she'd never bought one just for herself. Feeling grown up, but in an unpleasant way, she handed over the pennies and tucked the warm folded newspaper under her arm. Then she walked slowly back up the street, her eyes again on the sidewalk. All at once she remembered—and she made a face at the memory—how she used to pick up wads of gum off the sidewalk when she was little, and chew them. It was positively disgusting. How could she have *done* that? She shook her head hard to get past the memory. When she'd settled on the front step, she opened the paper with a sense of momentousness so powerful she felt a bit sick to her stomach. And there it was, right on the bottom corner of the front page: BOY DROWNS AT KEW BEACH.

The story said Chuckie had fallen from the foot of a pier into the water. Louise gazed at the tidy block of print, trying to believe any of this was real. She read the story again. It said that Mary and Darryl Beauvais, the parents, had gone to sit on a bench while their son, Charles, was playing on the pier. When they went to look for him a short time later he was gone. "Divers," the last lines of the piece said, "had to call off their search for the boy's body as darkness fell last night."

Louise went back over this last part several times, picturing men swimming around in the deep, very cold water of Lake Ontario, looking for Chuckie, who kept hiding from them. If he hadn't been found, it had to mean Chuckie could still be alive. She got up and went inside to tell her sister, who was sitting in bed, chewing on her finger as she read a library book.

"Read this," Louise said, pointing out the story.

Faye read the article while Louise watched her face. "Maybe he's not really dead," she said when Faye had finished reading.

"Maybe," Faye said doubtfully, "but it sure sounds as if he is." Setting the paper aside, she wound her arms around her drawn-up knees, saying, "It'd be so horrible to drown. Poor Chuckie. He was kind of a cute kid. I liked him. I certainly liked him a whole lot more than his sister, that's for sure."

"You honestly, truly think he's dead?" Louise asked, her eyes drawn to the newspaper. If it said so in the paper, it had to be true. But she couldn't seem to make her mind fit around the idea that someone she knew and had seen only the day before could be gone forever. How could that be? She imagined her brain to be like a stretchy bathing cap that fit over most things but just wouldn't fit over the fact of Chuckie being dead. What *was* dead, anyway? And why did it strike her as so completely impossible?

"I'm afraid so," Faye answered. "What happened when you went over there?"

"Mrs. Beauvais came to the door looking kind of funny and said Chuckie drowned at Kew Beach, so Shirley couldn't play today, I could see her another time."

"Funny how?"

"Her face was a strange color, sort of gray, and her eyes were wet underneath. I don't believe it!" Louise declared, wondering what they'd done with Chuckie. Maybe he'd run away or something.

"I do," Faye said softly.

"How come? I mean, it says right there"—she tapped the newspaper with her finger—"that somebody named *Charles* is supposed to have drowned, but they didn't find his body. That's not *Chuckie*."

"Come on, Lou. You know Chuckie's just a nickname for Charles. And they wouldn't print what they did if they hadn't looked everywhere and couldn't find him. He's dead, Lou."

"I promised to bring him a surprise from the Ex. And I did too," Louise said, convinced that when the whistling bird was dry she'd go over to number 17 and give it to him. She could even see the way he'd suddenly grin and go running around to make the bird sing. She retrieved the paper from the bed as Faye swung her legs over the side and went off to the bathroom. She was about to get the scissors to cut out the story when the doorbell rang. For a moment she wondered if the police had come to arrest her for not taking Chuckie along to the Ex. But no, that was crazy. It was Shirley's fault, not hers. She wouldn't have minded if Chuckie had come with them. He *should've* come with them. She'd have had a better time, and people wouldn't be going around now saying he was dead.

Leaving the paper on the desk, she ran to open the door, amazed to see her grandmother standing on the front porch. "Hi, Gramma," she said, and hugged her. "I didn't know you were coming over."

Her grandmother gave her a long hug back then stepped away and tilted Louise's chin up, saying, "It's a surprise visit. Let me look at you." She looked for a long time, becoming visibly angry. Taking Louise firmly by the hand she led her inside, asking, "Where's your sister, Lulu?"

"In the bathroom."

"Is she all right?"

"She's fine, Gramma."

"I'm asking if your mother hit her, too."

"Just once," Louise whispered. "Then Faye *hit her back!*"

"Christ Almighty!" Ellen Perry shook her head, then said, "I want you to tell me the truth now, okay?"

"Okay."

"Has this happened before?"

"All the time," Louise confessed, feeling guilty for telling on Ma, but justified and deeply relieved too. She was tired of keeping this a secret. "But this time was the worst."

"Hell! Why didn't you or Faye ever *tell* me?" Ellen asked sadly, appalled that something so horrendous could have been going on for so long without her knowledge.

"Ma said if we ever told and she got in trouble, you wouldn't want anything to do with us, so we'd get sent to an orphanage. I'm sorry if we got you in trouble, Gramma, but we had to tell her about the money you gave us. She kept saying I *stole* it. And I *never* steal things!" Shirley stole things. Did that have something to do with why Chuckie died? She wished she understood. "I know I don't always tell the truth, but honest to God I'd never ever steal!"

"Never mind about the money. You did what you had to do." With a sigh Ellen looked at her daughter's closed bedroom door, saying, "Now I'm going to do what I have to do. I want you to put some ice on your face, Lulu. You go to the kitchen and do that right now. Okay?"

"Okay, Gramma."

Louise went toward the kitchen as her grandmother opened the bedroom door without knocking. "Get out of that bed!" she heard Gramma say, then the door closed, so Louise was unable to hear any more.

"Is Gramma here?" Faye asked, coming into the kitchen still in her pajamas, her hair not brushed.

Louise nodded, wishing she could hear what was going on in the bedroom. "Gramma looked at my face and got mad. I'm supposed to put ice on it."

Faye got up and went over to the fridge, saying, "You do look awful, Lou." The sight of her sister's face kept making her stomach knot. She felt like taking the bread knife and stabbing her mother. For a second time that morning she was overwhelmed by hatred. She had to take a deep breath to calm herself, then she pulled open the door to the freezer compartment to get the tray of ice cubes.

"I do?" Louise ran down the hall to look at herself in the bathroom mirror. She hadn't connected the soreness in her head, face, chest, and arms to injuries that might actually show. Seeing her reflection, she realized her mother had really hurt her this time, and in places where it showed. Her cheek was all swollen and blue, and her eyes looked smaller. She stared at herself, unable to make sense of what she was seeing. The way she looked was somehow the same as the newspaper saying Chuckie was dead: None of it seemed real. The face in the glass wasn't one she recognized. It was lumpy and discolored. Her lips were big and puffy, and her nose looked wrong, wider than it was supposed to be. Undoing her blouse, she shrugged it off—a pain stabbing her between the shoulder blades as she did—and gaped at the huge purple-red bruises on her arms and chest. The more she saw of her injuries, the more aware she became of the aching tenderness everywhere above her hips.

Buttoning the blouse back on over her undershirt, she returned to the kitchen. Faye was sitting at the table in her short-sleeved pink cotton pajamas, her ankles crossed and her bare feet tucked back under the chair.

"Mr. Healey looked at me funny this morning," Louise told her. "He asked if I was all right. I couldn't figure out why he was asking."

"I guess now you know. You feel okay?"

"My head hurts mostly, but I'm okay," Louise said staunchly. "You want to see the bruises?" she asked, fingers going to her buttons.

"No, thanks. I can imagine. You should have some breakfast, Lou."

"I'm not hungry."

"Neither am I. You better put this on your face." Faye indicated the dish towel she'd wrapped around the ice cubes.

Louise sat at the table and looked over her shoulder down the hall. "I've never seen Gramma so mad. Maybe she'll take us away to live with her."

"I don't think so," Faye said.

"Why not?" Louise turned back to face her sister.

"Ma would never let us go. You know that."

"No, I don't know that. Why?"

"Put the ice on your face. Because she'd have nobody to show off at the factory, and because if she let us go it'd make her look bad, sort of. I mean, she's always making such a big deal out of how she's had to raise us alone, and how she's done this really terrific job of it. If we weren't around, she could hardly go telling people that. Could she?"

Louise ran her finger back and forth over the flowers on the oilcloth covering the table. "I guess not," she said.

"I told you, Lou. Don't worry about it. I'm looking out for you now."

Picking up the towel, Louise held it to her face, asking, "Did you ask Gramma to come over?"

Faye shook her head. "I think she came to see if we were okay. That must've been *some* phone call Ma made last night."

Lou closed her eyes, feeling her face going numb from the cold. She thought of Chuckie and again wondered if he really could be dead.

"If you *ever* raise a hand to those girls again," Ellen Perry said, so upset she could scarcely breathe, "I'll make you one very sorry woman. I've always known you were bitter, but I never *dreamed* . . ." She had to stop and swallow in order to dislodge the lump in her throat. She blinked back tears and gazed accusingly at her daughter.

Cowed by this unique display of her mother's anger, Maggie nodded dumbly, hating the way this was happening: being roused from a sound sleep to listen to threats and accusations. No warning, no chance to recite

the long list of reasons she had for being forced to deal with the girls in
the way she did.

"Those girls are the salt of the earth," Ellen said, having regained her
self-control. "And you've done nothing but heap abuse on their heads.
You've blamed them for every blessed thing that's ever gone wrong in
your life. And now, now I find out you've been *beating* them! If I'd had
any *idea* this was going on, I'd have taken Lulu and Faye away from you
years ago. They are *not* to blame for *your* mistakes. It is *not* their fault that
you let your head be turned by a cheap smoothie most women
wouldn't've given a second look. I'm sick to death of hearing about it.
I'm sick to death of your moods. And you're going to quit taking your
frustrations out on the girls. I'm *warning* you, Marg. You may be my
daughter, and I love you, but as God is my witness, I'll take them away
from you. And how *dare* you tell them I wouldn't want them? What is
wrong with you?" Ellen asked mournfully, then paused to battle back her
tears a second time. If she knew one thing about her daughter, it was that
you could never ever show any weakness when dealing with her. The
moment you did, Marg would find some way to capitalize on it.

"You beat her black and blue," Ellen continued, determined to make
her position unequivocally clear. "A child who wouldn't dream of taking
anything that didn't belong to her. The worst anyone can say about Louise
is that she tends to embroider the truth, lets her imagination get the
better of her now and then. You don't beat a child because she acts up or
tells a few lies. You don't beat children, period. And you're never going
to raise a hand to them again, or you'll live to regret it. You have my
word I'll see to it personally. Now," she said with finality, "I'm taking
them out for the day, and I don't want to hear one word out of you.
You've always got reasons for everything you do, always have had since
you were old enough to talk. But no one in her right mind does what you
did to Lulu last night." With that, Ellen went out, slamming the door
behind her.

Maggie sank back against the headboard, hearing the slamming of the
door echo in her eardrums. First her ungrateful children, and now her
mother had turned against her. Tears burned at the back of her eyes but
she refused to cry. No one understood the weight of the burden she
carried, not even her own mother. She wanted to scream at the unfairness
of it. Nolan hounding her, Faye daring to strike her, her mother threaten-

ing to take her children away. She could feel a headache starting at the base of her skull, and to top it all off she was getting the curse.

⁂

Coming into the kitchen, Ellen said, "Faye, you get dressed. I'm taking you both out to breakfast. Then, if you feel like it, I thought maybe we'd go to the Ex."

"Oh, Gramma, I'd *love* that!" Louise cried.

"What about you, Faye?"

"I'd love it, too, Gramma." Faye smiled and said, "I'll get dressed and be right back."

"Ma kept my four dollars," Louise said, her face falling at the realization that she hadn't any money to spend.

"Never mind," Ellen said, pulling out a chair and sliding into it. "I'll get it back for you. Would you be interested in seeing *Holiday on Ice* at the Coliseum?"

"Oh, could we? I *love* figure skating. It's even better than roller-skating."

"We certainly could," Ellen said, feeling so shaken she had the arbitrary notion that her spine had in some way become unlocked. Her body wanted to crumple in on itself. "While we're waiting for Faye, let's keep that ice on your poor face. It'll take down some of the swelling."

For the fifteen minutes it took Faye to get ready, Louise sat at the table holding the ice to her face, while her grandmother smoked one of her Sweet Caporals and stared at the hallway as if daring her daughter to show her face. But Maggie stayed in her bedroom. Louise kept peeking from behind the ice pack, positively stricken at the sight of her gramma blotting her eyes with one of her lace-edged monogrammed handkerchiefs. She'd never in her entire life seen her grandmother cry and it made her feel terrible.

When Faye returned, Ellen took the ice from Louise and put it in the sink saying, "I thought for a treat we girls would go to Diana Sweets."

"Oh," Louise said, looking down at herself. "I love Diana Sweets, but I should wear a skirt if we're going there. And I have to wash and brush my teeth."

"Go ahead and get ready, Lulu. We'll wait, won't we, Faye?"

"Sure we will," Faye said.

On the streetcar, the three of them sat on one of the long seats behind the conductor. Faye turned to her grandmother and hesitantly said,

"Would it be all right if I make a phone call when we get to the restaurant, Gramma? I'd like to call a friend to say where I'm going."

"Who?" Louise asked at once.

"Would that be all right?" Faye asked, ignoring Louise's question.

"Of course it would," Ellen said.

"You're gonna call Raffie, aren't you?" Louise guessed.

Blushing, Faye said, "What makes you think that?"

"Are you dating Raffie, Faye?" Ellen asked with a smile.

"You wouldn't tell on me, would you, Gramma?" Faye asked imploringly.

"Who on earth would I tell?" Ellen winked at her.

"Don't you dare say a word to Ma!" Faye warned Louise.

"I'd never!" Louise said, looking offended that Faye wouldn't trust her.

"Promise?"

"Cross my heart and hope to die."

"Okay," Faye said, hugely relieved. "Raffie and I are going steady, only nobody knows. And you know how Ma is about men."

Louise nodded, then studied her sister as Faye and Gramma talked, trying to see if there was anything different about her. Except for the new way she had of smiling lately, she seemed the same as ever. But having a boyfriend and going steady was serious, almost like getting engaged. "Are you two getting married?" she asked as the thought occurred to her.

Ellen laughed, and Faye said, "I don't know. Someday, maybe. Jeez, Lou. I won't be fourteen for another five months. Don't rush me."

"You go ahead and enjoy yourself, Faye," Ellen said. "And never mind about your mother. Just because she hates men doesn't mean you have to. Raffie's a darling boy. Now, I want to tell you both something. You girls are to come to me if there's ever a problem. What your mother's been telling you all these years about me is a complete lie. You're the only grandchildren I'm ever going to have. You mean the world to me, and don't ever forget that. Okay?" Both girls nodded, and she said, "I'm sickened by her saying such a thing about me. Sickened."

Faye took hold of her grandmother's hand, wondering why Ma had lied to them. All this time there'd been someone she could've talked to, someone who'd always been on their side, and who didn't think she was throwing everything away just because she and Raffie loved each other.

Louise let her head rest against Gramma's arm and breathed deeply, wondering if things were really going to be okay now.

The following Monday's *Telegram* had a big story about the divers finding Chuckie's body at Kew Beach. There was a photograph with an X marking the spot where the body was found. Louise read every word, then went back and read it all again. Chuckie really was dead. Someone she knew had actually *died*. It was almost too much for her to comprehend. But when she saw the misshapen whistling paper bird she'd bought as Chuckie's surprise from the Ex, her chest began to hurt. She could see him so clearly, sitting on the top step of the porch across the road, with his elbows propped on his knobby knees, all by himself as she and Shirley went off down the street.

People were supposed to cry when someone died, but she couldn't. She felt as if she wanted to, but no tears would come. Maybe there was something wrong with her. Chuckie was dead, and she couldn't cry. It was terrible. She felt very, very sorry about him. Charles Beauvais. She'd known him, they'd played together; and now he was gone for good and always. She was afraid to tell Faye or Gramma about how she was unable to cry for Chuckie, imagining the two of them would be shocked.

Even once school started after Labor Day, she couldn't stop thinking about Chuckie. He'd come into her mind and she'd see his small pointed face and mischievous eyes. She'd recall the way his brown hair stood up in a cowlick at the top of his head, and his grimy hands, his eagerness to play any game at all, and his willingness to run errands. She remembered how he'd go racing up the street first thing in the morning to Jimmy Novotny's house. She was so gripped by the compelling fact of his absence and by her inability to grieve properly for him that she wasn't even mad at Shirley anymore. She kept a lookout, expecting to see her at school or in the playground during recess, but Shirley never did come. In the middle of September the Beauvais family moved away, and Louise never saw her again. Although she hadn't expected to, sometimes she actually missed the undersized, humorless girl. Most of all, though, she missed Chuckie.

CHAPTER

NINE

MAGGIE WAS DREAMING. SHE WAS IN AN APARTMENT, A wonderful place. She liked everything about it: the view from the windows, the furniture, even the kitchen. Best of all, she liked the man who lived there. She had the impression he was good-looking, although it was hard to be sure because his features seemed to keep changing. He was big, though, and had an aura of importance, authority. He was also witty and very clever. She followed him from room to room, anxious to have him slow down and make love to her. But he never paused for more than a few moments, just long enough to embrace her, causing her excitement to mount. Each time he came close, she pressed tender loving kisses on his cheeks and neck and hands. He responded exactly as she wanted him to, with an awareness of how much she cared for him, and with answers to her silent questions.

Yes, he did love her. Yes, he did have children. Ten of them.

Ten? Was that possible?

He laughed and confessed he was only teasing. He hadn't any children at all.

She told him she hadn't any either. It didn't feel like a lie. When she turned to look back over her own history, which spread out behind her like a vast, gently sloping hillside, there were no children playing on the grass.

He unfastened the towel that was wrapped around her, and she readied herself to receive him. But after caressing her ardently for a time, he suddenly said, don't you have to get to the hospital? And unhappily she realized there was an appointment she couldn't miss. It was her final one. If she failed to appear she'd simply have to go again, another time.

You'd better go take your shower, he told her as he headed for the kitchen. I've got to get the food ready.

Reluctantly, her limbs wobbly from overstimulation, she went to the black-tiled bathroom. She showered with the curtain partway open in order to see and hear him as he moved around in the kitchen. As she bathed she wondered why, when it felt as if she loved him, as if he was the perfect man for her, she couldn't bring herself to trust him completely. He kept holding back, kept her constantly on edge, with the result that she feared committing herself, fretted that the moment she did he'd announce he'd merely been teasing, the way he had about having ten children.

Why couldn't she have him? He was so perfect, so absolutely right for her. She liked the size of him, the look and feel and sound of him, and his aura of stature and success. She'd been waiting so long to be with him. All her years of patience worked in her favor now, enabling her to recognize his rightness and to demonstrate her feelings in a way he couldn't possibly misinterpret. Yet every time they were at the brink of joining, something happened to take him away, out of her embrace, and she was growing exhausted from the effort of caring so much for someone who couldn't manage to find enough time to take the step that would cement them together forever.

She wanted him desperately, and finished her shower determined they'd make love before it was time to leave for the hospital. When she approached him in the kitchen he turned to her with a smile that convinced her she'd been foolish not to trust him. They lay down together on the floor and she ran her hands over the broad expanse of his chest, giving him more and more of those tender love-filled kisses, her body gentle with his as it opened expectantly, his weight bearing pleasurably down upon her.

But right at the point when the next logical step would be their joining, he started to talk. And at once her trust in him began dissolving. He was soft, nowhere near ready to enter her; and the people from the hospital had arrived. They were at the door, waiting to take her. He loved her. She knew that. And she knew she could easily arouse him. So why wouldn't he commit himself to her?

She told him she had to go. He smiled and said there was nothing to worry about. Yet even as he was saying this, he was retrieving his knife from the counter and going back to preparing the food. Disappointment was like an aspirin tablet lodged in her throat. It hurt. She kept swallowing, and it started to dissolve, sending its sour taste back up into her mouth. Hopeless. She pulled on her clothes, leaving the towel on the bathroom floor in a small pointless gesture of defiance.

Before going off with the hospital people she looked back. He was standing in his wine-colored heavy silk dressing gown, the knife poised above the chopping board, gazing out the window at the remarkable view. She knew she'd never come back to this place, and wished she understood why he'd played such a cruel game with her, speaking of love and allowing her to hope.

When she awakened, the dream was still very fresh in her mind. She couldn't shake it, and as a result started the day angry. What the hell kind of bullshit dream was that, anyway?

※

The girls continued to be wary, no less careful than they'd always been around their mother. She'd hardly spoken to them following the weekend the Ex opened, but since she'd never really talked to them in the first place, the only thing different was the accusing way she looked at them now. And she stopped doing that after a while too.

After so many years of dreading her unpredictable mood swings and suffering the consequences of setting off her hair-trigger temper, it was difficult for Faye and Louise to believe they no longer had anything to fear. They still flinched if Maggie so much as lifted a hand to smooth her hair. But time passed and she failed to give in to her violent instincts. They could actually *see* her resisting the impulse to strike them; she'd get a killing look on her face and her fists would clench. Then, as if responding to some inner voice, she'd allow her hands to unfold, and the rage would leave her eyes. The girls began to relax a bit now when Maggie was home.

Her new method of punishment began so subtly that at first they hardly noticed. When they did something that displeased her, she'd act wounded, as if slightly sickened by disappointment. They accepted her reproachful looks and tired sighs as being part of a phase, something that would eventually pass.

But it didn't. And she reached the peak of her ability to seem deeply wounded by the things the girls said and did one afternoon in early December, when Faye went to visit the DiStasios after school. Blanche was in the throes of another headache, and after talking softly with her for a few minutes, Faye agreed to go to the drugstore to refill her prescription for painkillers. It took quite some time because the pharmacist had to call the doctor to ask if it was okay to renew it. But it wasn't that simple. The nurse had to get Mrs. DiStasio's file, then have a word with the doctor between patients, before at last calling the drugstore back. While she waited, Faye tried to get some of her homework done, glancing every few minutes at the clock on the wall behind the counter. People kept coming in and the man had to stop work every time to serve them. When he finally called Faye over to pick up the tablets, it was almost five-thirty. She raced back to the store to give Blanche the medicine and her change, exchanged a few whispered words with Raffie, then ran most of the way home.

"I ask you to do a few simple things, but you don't have time," Maggie said in her new wounded tone. "Here I work my fingers to the bone to put clothes on your backs and a roof over your heads, but do I get any help? No. Did you pick up the laundry like I asked? No. You had to stop at the DiStasios, and the Chinaman's was closed by the time you got there. Thank you very much. I really appreciate your help."

Faye apologized and tried to explain, but Maggie said, "Never mind. Other people are more important to you than your own mother, I know. Forget it. I'll pick the stuff up tomorrow on my lunch hour."

Faye went off to do her homework feeling horribly guilty, as though she'd failed at something monumentally important, and also because what Ma had said was true: She *did* care more about Blanche DiStasio than she did about Ma. What distressed her most was that Ma knew it.

A few weeks later, Lou fell in the schoolyard and badly scraped both knees. When Maggie got home, all she seemed to care about was Louise's torn coat. "You know how many hours I had to work to pay for this?" she asked, looking and sounding stricken. "How much time I had to put in at that stinking machine to buy you this? And now look at it! The sleeve's practically ripped out. Couldn't you try to be more careful? Neither one of you has any respect for me."

"I *fell*, Ma," Louise said. "I didn't do it on purpose. I slipped on some ice and fell so hard both my knees are practically *broken!*"

"It wouldn't hurt you not to run for a change," Maggie said, shaking her head as she inspected the coat. "God knows how I'm going to fix this," she said, gazing at the exposed quilted lining. "Every time I turn around, it's something else." She sighed heavily and went for her sewing box.

"Well it wasn't my *fault*," Louise told Faye. "Does she think I *wanted* to break my stupid knees?"

"Come on," Faye said, holding out a hand. "We'll get you cleaned up."

In the bathroom with the door locked, Louise sat on the toilet while Faye opened the medicine cabinet. "Why's she all of a sudden acting like everything we do is on purpose to make her miserable? You see the way she makes out like we're killing her?"

"At least it's better than getting hit all the time," Faye said, knowing exactly what her sister meant.

"I'm not so sure about that," Louise whispered, her eyes on the door. "If she keeps on with this suffering routine it's gonna drive me nuts. She's acting just like that woman with the big eyebrows in that movie. You know the one."

"What one?"

"You *know*, that stupid movie Ma dragged us to a long time ago, about this woman who's got this fabulous house and has a fit if anyone touches a thing."

"I don't remember that." Faye frowned as she poured peroxide on some cotton batting and dropped to her haunches in front of her sister, saying, "This'll sting."

"Come *on!*" Louise insisted. "You do so remember. She's that actress Ma thinks is so gorgeous, with the big black eyebrows and the mean mouth."

"You mean Joan Crawford?"

"Yeah! Her!"

Faye started to laugh.

"Don't you remember we were mad 'cause there weren't any cartoons, and we had to sit through the whole stupid story about how nobody could *stand* living with her because every time somebody moved an ashtray she went nuts."

"Oh, now I remember," Faye said, watching the peroxide bubble up on Lou's knees. "She was awful, but Ma thought she was great."

"You wait and see. Ma's pretending she's that lady."

"How the heck did you do this, anyway?" Faye asked, looking at her sister's scraped and swollen knees.

"It was stupid Aldo's fault. He said he was going to kiss me in front of everybody in the schoolyard. I said like heck he was and gave him a punch, then ran like anything. Next thing I know I'm skidding on the ice and boom!'' She looked down at herself. "That jerk!"

"Aldo was trying to *kiss* you?"

"He's not nice anymore," Louise said seriously, "not like he used to be. Ever since he started hanging around with those Tomasino brothers."

"Why'd you hit him?"

"Are you kidding? You think I was going to let him *kiss* me?"

"I guess not." Faye started laughing again.

"What's so funny, eh?"

"That stuff about Joan Crawford," Faye giggled. "How d'you suppose she ever got to be a movie star? She's not one bit pretty, not like Piper Laurie. I just love *her*. Or Suzy Parker. She's so beautiful. Imagine being a famous model and getting to wear all those terrific clothes!"

"I like Yvonne De Carlo."

"She's not beautiful."

"Yeah, but she's *Canadian!* Suzy Parker isn't even an actress, for Pete's sake! Ow! What're you *doing?*"

"I've got to make sure there's no dirt in these scrapes. Stop being such a baby."

Louise swatted the top of Faye's head. "I am *not* a baby. You wait and see," she said. "I'll bet you anything Ma's going to get worse and worse."

The day before Christmas, Faye dusted and waxed the furniture, rubbing the lemon oil into the wood until it gleamed. And Louise washed the breakfast dishes before rushing to clean the bathroom. Satisfied they'd done a heck of a good job on everything Ma had asked them to do, they changed into their second-best outfits—Faye's was a dark red dress with long sleeves and a circle skirt that was a little too small on her, and Louise's was a royal blue pinafore and a long-sleeved white blouse with a Peter Pan collar—and walked through the snow down to the factory on King Street for the annual staff party that started at noon.

Most of the kids were the same ones they saw every year: Flo's son, Ernie junior, and her daughter, Cass; Mick's three boys; the Morelli twins; Mrs. Theodopolus's daughter Christine; and a dozen or so others. Since they were all roughly the same age, between eleven and sixteen, and had been meeting at these parties for as long as they could remember, most of them made out that they were too old for the annual family bash and complained about the corny Christmas music and the presents they received from Santa who was, everybody knew, Freddie Hauser, the foreman, who dressed up in the costume every year.

While they were eating the sandwiches (salmon, egg salad, ham) and salads (potato and coleslaw), which were also the same every year, Mr. Nolan came over to say hello.

"You girls get prettier every time I see you," he said with a wide smile. "You've got two beautiful girls here, Maggie."

Maggie gave him a tight little smile, then took another puff on her cigarette, wondering if he was trying to butter her up. He kept asking her to go out, wouldn't take no for an answer, and brought it up now whenever she went down to his office. She didn't even bother answering anymore, just got on with what she'd gone there to do.

"You say that every year, Mr. Nolan," Louise laughed. "We look the exact same as always."

"No. You're both getting prettier by the minute. So," he said, "what did Santa bring you?"

"I got a doll," Louise said. "And Faye got a teddy bear. They're really cute."

"Oh dear me!" Nolan said, looking embarrassed. "I guess it's time Santa realized you're not little girls anymore. We'll have to drop him a note, remind him for next year's party."

"I like my doll," Louise declared. "I've been thinking about starting to play with dolls again."

Following her sister's lead, Faye said, "It's a sweet teddy bear, Mr. Nolan."

Nolan looked at Faye with her expressive, luminous gray eyes and shy smile, and at Louise with her deep blue eyes and impish grin, and wondered how a woman as difficult and unreadable as Maggie had managed to produce two such kind, good-natured children. Most of the other kids had complained audibly about their presents, but not these two. And they weren't just being polite, either. He could tell. Remarkable, he thought. There was a strong physical resemblance but otherwise little similarity between Maggie and them. "You're good girls," he said, meaning it, and wishing yet again that he could've had kids of his own. But Nora had never conceived and he'd only learned this past summer that, without his knowledge, she'd been using birth control all along. He'd been hurt and saddened when she told him, forever putting an end to his dream. He'd have given a lot to be father to a pair of girls as lovely as these, and often wondered whether that was part of Maggie's appeal. He'd even day-dreamed a time or two about marrying Mag and becoming their stepfather. He imagined himself taking them out to supper, or the three of them going on a family trip. He saw snapshots accumulating in a big family album. He knew his longtime fondness for these girls could easily turn into love. But Mag wouldn't even go out for a drink with him.

Maggie watched him making a fuss over Faye and Louise, and couldn't figure out why he was sucking up to them. She didn't like it. If he thought he'd get to her through her kids, he had another think coming! And what the hell were the two of them up to, playing up to Nolan and making out that they liked him? If he ever laid so much as a finger on Faye or Louise, she'd fix him but good. He wasn't fooling her, and neither were those two little bitches.

Before they left the party, Maggie cornered Nolan. "Don't get any funny ideas about my girls," she warned.

Looking first shocked and then hurt, he said, "What's the matter with you, Mag? I'm fond of them. And it's Christmas, for God's sake. Can't you ever let up for a minute?"

"Never you mind," she insisted. "You just watch your p's and q's, if you know what's good for you."

He stared at her, offended by the implication that he was a man who'd molest young girls. What kind of woman was she? Could she conceivably be jealous of her own children? Unable to come up with an answer, he gave her a smile, saying, "Take it easy, Mag. They're just kids, and I've always had a soft spot for them. What're you getting so worked up about?"

Somewhat deflated, she nevertheless had to have the last word. "You worry about yourself," she said, "and I'll worry about Faye and Louise." Dissatisfied with the way the exchange had gone, she headed back across the factory to where the girls were sitting on the side of one of the big cutting tables, talking to Flo's daughter, Cass, who was two years older than Faye and in grade ten at Central Commerce, taking a secretarial course.

"Shorthand's hard," Cass was telling an interested Faye. "And so's bookkeeping. I always hated arithmetic. But typing's a snap. You'll see."

"We're going now," Maggie interrupted.

"Okay, Ma, in just one second," Faye said. "Do you have to have your own typewriter?" she asked Cass.

"Uh-uh. You use the ones at school. But"—Cass looked around and dropped her voice—"I think Mum's getting me a portable for Christmas."

"Wow! Are you ever lucky!" Faye exclaimed.

"Yeah," Cass grinned.

"I'd love to have a typewriter," Louise said. "I could write stories and books."

"Time to go," Maggie said impatiently.

Louise hopped down off the table and stood waiting with her Baby Wetums doll tucked under her arm. Seeing her mother's expression, she tugged on Faye's sleeve, saying, "Come on."

"Maybe I'll call you," Faye told Cass, slipping down off the table. "I'd really like to hear more about it."

"Sure. We could even go to the show sometime, if you want."

While they were putting on their coats and boots in the cloakroom, Maggie put on her wounded look and said, "How dare you keep me waiting, like I'm nobody?"

"Sorry, Ma," Faye apologized. "It's just that Commerce sounds like a really good school, and I was—"

"I'm not a servant, you know, that you keep me waiting," Maggie said.

"She said she was sorry," Louise interjected.

"Sorry's not good enough," Maggie said. "You don't treat your mother like she's a salesgirl or something. Why do you treat me that way?"

Both girls went quiet and attended to getting their boots on.

"All I've done for you and this is the thanks I get," Maggie went on. "I hope to God someday you have children who treat you this way. Then you'll know!"

When they arrived home Maggie took a look around and said, "Did you have to use so *much* oil? Now the dust will stick like glue to every last thing in the house. And there's hair all over the bathroom floor. Can't you two ever do anything right?" Instead of blowing up as they expected, she sighed and put on an apron, then got a clean rag to go over the furniture again, ignoring the girls' offer to do the work a second time.

"We'll do it, Ma," Faye said. "You have a cup of tea, and me and Lou'll clean up. We know you worked all morning."

Louise gave her sister a look that said no, we won't, but Faye ignored her, anxious to keep peace over Christmas.

Maggie said, "What's the use? I might as well have done it myself in the first place."

Feeling guilty and offended, Louise dragged her sister off to the bedroom.

"Didn't I *tell* you she was gonna keep doing this? She turns everything around now, so that no matter what happens she's always the one who gets hurt. She only asks us to do things so she can complain about what a lousy job we do. Then she acts all put-upon and makes a big show of doing the whole thing over herself."

"I think it makes her feel good," Faye answered astutely. "I think from now on, whatever we do, it's never going to be good enough."

"Maybe we should just *let* her do everything herself."

"We can't do that," Faye said. "It wouldn't be right."

"And I suppose what she's doing is right?"

"No, but . . . I don't know."

"It's gonna be a rotten Christmas. I just know it."

"No, it won't, Lou. You'll see. We always have a good time at Gramma's."

"It's gonna be rotten, I'm telling you. She's gonna spend the rest of her life trying to make us miserable. You'll see."

Gramma loved the teacup and saucer the girls gave her. "This is beautiful," she said, giving them each a kiss. "Isn't this beautiful, Marg?"

Maggie gave one of her suffering smiles.

Ellen paid no attention. "I'll have my tea in it with dessert," she said. "It'll be the prize of my collection."

"Open your presents, Ma," Faye said, stroking the wonderful yellow angora sweater Gramma had given her.

"Yeah, come on!" Louise urged, carefully returning her new blue sweater to its box. "Let's see what you got!"

With a small sigh, Maggie put out her cigarette and turned to accept the package Louise handed her.

"Open this first. It's from Gramma," Louise said.

The girls were sitting on the floor beside the tree, watching their mother on the sofa. Ellen, in the armchair, was also watching her, more than a little annoyed by the way Marg seemed determined to spoil Christmas for the girls. So far, she'd commented several times on how tired she was and had made a point of telling Faye and Louise to be sure to help in the kitchen—as if they didn't always volunteer.

Maggie unwrapped the gift from her mother and couldn't conceal her delight at the sight of the familiar blue Birk's Jewelers box she knew held her mother's pearls. "You can't give me these!" she protested, having wanted the pearls all her life.

"Of course I can," Ellen said. "I know you've always loved them, and I always planned to give them to you."

"No, I can't," Maggie insisted, with a sad smile and a shake of her head returning the box. "I really can't take them."

For a few seconds, Ellen couldn't speak. Marg was playing some kind of game, pretending to a nobility they all knew wasn't natural to her. But then, thinking it through, Ellen decided to play along. Suddenly inspired, she said, "If that's the way you feel, Marg, then I guess you won't mind if I give them to Faye." The look of outraged disbelief on Maggie's face was all the proof Ellen needed of her daughter's insincerity in refusing the pearls. That'll teach you, she thought with satisfaction, fed up to the teeth with Marg's games.

"Oh, Gramma!" Faye exclaimed, awed. "You mean it?"

"I certainly do," Ellen said, presenting her with the box. "Have them and wear them in good health, dear."

Maggie looked at her daughter's flushed, beaming face, despising her, and wondering why the hell she'd told her mother she couldn't take the goddamned pearls.

"Wow!" Louise was saying, her head close to her sister's as the two of them examined the gleaming pearl necklace with its gold clasp. "Are you ever *lucky,* Faye!"

"I'll take very good care of them, Gramma," Faye promised, going over to embrace her grandmother. "Thank you."

"You're welcome," Ellen said. "Well, let's see what else you got, Marg."

Maggie was so enraged she wanted to attack all three of them—her mother for taking her so literally, Faye for accepting the pearls without hesitation, and Louise just for being there. But she swallowed it down with a mouthful of smoke, put out her cigarette, and turned to take the package Louise was holding out to her.

"This one's from me'n Faye," Louise said proudly, sitting on her knees and watching expectantly as Maggie went to work on the wrapping paper. She and Faye had saved for ages and spent weeks deciding on just the right present. Then the two of them had gone after school to Morgan's on Bloor Street, a department store they both thought was truly elegant, to make their purchase.

"Oh, Marg," Ellen said, "isn't it gorgeous!"

The girls nodded, pleased, waiting to hear what their mother would say about the Liberty silk scarf the very nice saleslady at Morgan's had said was something any woman would be thrilled to receive.

Maggie folded open the scarf and said stiffly, "Thank you. It's very nice."

Faye and Louise were crushed.

"Don't you like it, Ma?" Louise asked, regretting the question the moment the words came out of her mouth.

"It's very pretty," Maggie said politely, carefully folding it back into the box.

—¥—

"Didn't I tell you she'd wreck Christmas?" Louise muttered to Faye later while they were washing the dishes. "Didn't I *tell* you! We should've just got her some dumb old stockings or something instead of spending all our money on that scarf. She'll never wear it."

"Sure she will," Faye said, although she doubted it.

"She never will," Louise insisted. "Bet you a million bucks."

"Never mind, Lou. It doesn't matter."

"It does so. We went to all that trouble and she's never even going to wear it. We should've given it to Gramma. She thought it was beautiful. We *wasted* our money."

"No, we didn't," Faye said softly. "We had a good time buying it. Didn't we? Just remember that and forget the rest of it."

"Maybe *you* can," Louise said, "but I'll never forget it as long as I live. Never! She only wanted to get back at us because Gramma gave you the pearls."

"D'you think I should give them back?" Faye asked, anxious to keep the peace.

"Don't you dare! Gramma *gave* them to you."

"I know, but if Ma really wants them . . . ."

"The *hell* with her!" Louise swore fiercely. "They're *yours* and she can't *have* them! I *hate* her!"

"Don't say that, Lou."

"I will so say it! I hate her, and so do you."

"No, I don't," Faye said softly, looking over her sister's shoulder at the doorway. "I feel sorry for her."

"What the heck for?"

"I don't know. I guess because she's made such a mess of her life and the only thing she can do is take it out on us."

"Why did you do that?" Ellen asked in a furious whisper. "They gave you a beautiful present and you acted like it was garbage."

"I *said* it was very pretty," Maggie defended herself.

"You made it perfectly clear you didn't like it," Ellen argued. "They went to a lot of trouble, spent all their money to buy you something special, and you didn't even have the decency to make a fuss."

"I said I liked it and I thanked them. What d'you *want* from my life?" Maggie said peevishly.

Ellen looked at the woman sitting on the sofa, with her long red fingernails and side-parted hairdo, with her sullen expression and long-suffering manner, and wondered who she was. Once upon a time she'd been a beautiful infant, a laughing toddler who showed signs of willfulness, a little girl basking in her father's overindulgence. It seemed only minutes later she was a sixteen-year-old with a swollen mouth and glazed eyes announcing she was going to get married. And minutes after that, she was the abandoned wife and mother of two babies; a woman so bloated with bitterness it seemed to ooze from her every pore. Looking at her now, Ellen felt deeply ashamed at having produced a child so hateful.

"They'll never forgive you, Marg," she said. "Do you realize you'll never be able to make up for the dreadful things you've done to them? Do you care?"

"Don't be ridiculous!" Maggie said, thrusting her chin out. "I've been a damned good mother. They're lucky to have me. Somebody else would've put them up for adoption."

Laughter erupted out of Ellen's mouth. "It's hopeless," she said, "trying to talk sense to you. You don't live in the same world as the rest of us."

"Of course I do," Maggie declared indignantly.

"I give up," Ellen said, slumping back in her chair. "I just give up. You'll never change."

"Why should I change?" Maggie asked, looking genuinely bewildered. "What's so terrible about me that I should change?"

"Forget I said anything," Ellen said, massaging her temple with her fingertips. "You're a wonderful mother, the world's best."

Maggie took her literally and gave her a satisfied smile. For the first time, Ellen had to wonder if Marg wasn't possibly a little crazy. How else could you explain her behavior?

CHAPTER
TEN

"I DON'T UNDERSTAND HER," FAYE SAID SOFTLY, LOOKING at the sooty black surface of the furnace. "Last night she called Lou a slut because she left her clothes in the bathroom. She came barging in without even knocking and woke us up, telling Lou to get the hell into the bathroom and pick up her goddamned clothes. A slut, she called her. What a thing to call your own child. It's as if she hates us."

"How could she hate you?" Raffie asked, finding the idea inconceivable. "She's your mother. Mothers don't hate their kids."

"You can't imagine it, can you, Raffie?" she said with a sad smile. Having grown up with Ma made her feel older than him, and more knowledgeable, too. There were things she knew, experiences she'd had that created a distance between them. She kept trying to close that distance by telling him, little by little, how it had been for her and Lou growing up with Ma, without a father. She was convinced that if she could make Raffie understand—even though she was barely able to make sense of it all herself—they'd know each other so completely that nothing could ever part them. They'd always be two separate people, but they'd have one complete set of memories and thoughts. "You think of her as being nice," she went on, "because she pretends for other people. But I'll bet if your mom knew what Ma was really like she probably wouldn't be friends with her. When I was little, you know, I used to think I'd give *anything* to have a mother like yours. She was so kind, and she let you know how much she loved you. I thought you and Aldo were the luckiest kids in the world, to have the mother you did. Now all I want is to get away, and take Lou with me.''

''Where would you go?'' he asked, a little afraid she might say she'd go off and leave him. Every time she raised the subject of getting away from her mother he went tense, fearing she'd made up her mind to go so far away he'd never see her again. His heart seemed to stop while he waited to hear what she'd say. Then it would start up again once she began elaborating on her plans, which always, to his relief, included him. It amazed and reassured him to hear her talk about the way things were going to be, because he was so much a part of those plans that he could actually see himself doing the things she talked about. He could see himself putting their kids to bed, telling them stories while their eyes grew heavy and they slipped into sleep. He could see himself putting on a suit and tie, picking up his briefcase and going off to work. And, best of all, he could see the two of them naked in bed together, making love whenever they felt like it, without any sneaking around, without having to steal a few minutes to be alone together behind the furnace in the cellar, hearing people walking around in the store right over their heads.

''A place of our own,'' she said, ''a place Lou and I could have together. I'll be taking typing when we go back to school next month. Once I know how to type I'll be able to get a good office job.''

''I still think you should've enrolled at Commerce. Then you could've taken a real secretarial course. Harbord's a tough school.''

''I know. But Commerce is so far away, and the only person I'd've known there is Cass Malenkowski. This way I'll be with Lou, and Central Tech's just a few blocks away, remember. So we'll be able to meet for lunch every day.''

''It'll be great,'' he said, momentarily sidetracked by all the prospects. He was finally going to fit in. The past year in grade eight had been rotten. Most of the kids looked half his age, even though a lot of them were older, and he'd been painfully self-conscious of his size, his deep voice, every last thing that set him apart. He was anxious to lose himself in a crowd of guys who looked as if they belonged where they were, guys who'd already started shaving, who had girlfriends, too, and who didn't have to put up with a lot of guff from apple-cheeked little kids chanting in the schoolyard, ''Raffie's got a girlfriend, Raffie's got a girlfriend,'' dancing around him like he was a performing bear. "I can hardly wait," he said with feeling.

She squeezed his hand. It wouldn't be long now before she and Lou were free, living in their own apartment. She'd get dressed in smart-looking clothes she'd picked out for herself, then go to work every day in a nice office while Lou finished school, maybe even went to university. They'd have a quiet, happy life, going to visit Gramma, even having her and the DiStasios over to supper; they wouldn't have to dread going home every day, knowing Ma would get back at five-thirty and start right in on them. Ma's controlled, bitter voice even whispered in her dreams. She wondered often if Lou dreamed of it, too. She kept meaning to ask Lou if she heard Ma's voice suddenly start up in her head when she was out with her friends, or right in the middle of having a good time. Faye heard it all the time. She'd be out with Raffie, or helping Mr. DiStasio in the store and suddenly she'd hear Ma saying, "You're nothing special. Don't ever think for one minute you're any better than anyone else, 'cause you're not. You're dumb as a goddamned post, can't remember a thing anyone tells you." Ma's voice inside her head would remind her she was slow and stupid and ugly, and she'd look nervously at the customers in the store, convinced they were angry with her for taking so long to weigh their onions or add up how much they owed. Every time it happened she wondered if it was true, if people only smiled at her to be kind because they felt sorry for her.

"What?" Raffie asked, seeing her frown.

She put her arms around him, her face in the smooth warmth of his neck, and felt safe in his approval. For him, everything about her was right. She wasn't dumb, or ugly, or useless. "I love you so much," she whispered, breathing in his clean soap-and-water fragrance. He'd be a wonderful father, a man who loved his children as well as his wife. He thought she was beautiful and clever, and told her so every chance he got.

"I love you, Faye," he whispered back, his lips moving against her thick silky hair. Sometimes, when she told him about the things her mother had said and done to her, he wanted to go marching up to the woman and hit her as hard as he could. He'd never do it. You didn't go hitting anybody, especially women. But it wasn't right, her saying and doing those things to Faye, making her feel so bad about herself. He wished he could show her how he felt about her now, using his hands to do it, but there wasn't time. They hardly ever had time lately. Pop was great about letting him take off for a few hours, but he didn't like to push it. Pop was too good-natured, and Aldo always took advantage, saying he couldn't work because he promised the guys he'd go to the island with them, or he had to go bowling, or he just remembered he'd told the Tomasino twins he'd go skating with them. So Raffie worked the extra hours, then went upstairs to make the supper so his mother wouldn't have to. The headaches made her so sick she couldn't even eat, but Raffie knew she'd stand over the stove for hours if it meant everybody else got a good supper. "We better get going," he said, his hand on her cheek. "I gotta cook supper. And I don't want you getting in trouble for being late."

"She used to hit us, you know, Raffie," she said, her pulse suddenly beating dangerously hard in her throat. She was crossing over into perilous territory, doing the other thing Ma had warned her and Lou never to do: to tell people what went on inside their house. But she had to tell. If she didn't, Raffie would never be able to understand why she had to get away, and they'd never be as close as she needed them to be. "She'd hit us and warn us not to cry out loud. If we cried and anyone heard us, she said, she'd kill us." She closed her eyes, seeing her mother's twisted face, hearing her hiss, *Shut up! Shut up!*

"You mean she beat you up?" he asked, his dark eyes very round.

"Yeah," she nodded.

"How come you never *told* me, Faye?"

"I couldn't. No one was ever supposed to know."

He had a picture all at once of Faye and Louise, the way they used to be when they were little, and his sudden outrage was like red paint poured over that picture. He put his arms around her and held her tightly, thinking he'd kill anyone who ever hurt her again. He'd *kill* them.

"That's all over now," he declared, determined to protect her, with his life if he had to. "Nobody's ever gonna hit you again. Not as long as I'm around." He kissed her eyes, then her mouth. When she opened her eyes, he smiled at her and got up, tugging at her hand. "Come on. We gotta get going."

"I know," she said, feeling very shaky and wishing she never had to go home. "I'll just come up and say goodbye to your mother." So what if she was late? Ma would yell at her anyway. And if she ever dared start hitting them again, Raffie would make her good and sorry.

Blanche was in the kitchen, the ingredients for supper spread out in front of her. She was standing by the counter looking at the food, the fingertips of both hands pressed to her temples.

"Mom," Raffie said at once, going over to her, "I'll do it. You sit down and take it easy." An arm around her shoulders, he directed her to a chair.

She caught hold of his hand and held it as she smiled at Faye. "How're you, sweetheart?" she asked, pressing Raffie's hand to her cheek before releasing him.

"I'm fine, Mrs. DiStasio," Faye answered, returning the smile. Blanche was pale and very thin; her eyes looked enormous. Her long black hair was pulled back in a clip at the nape of her long neck. On impulse, Faye crossed the room to give her a careful hug, feeling the woman's bones through her clothing. "How're you?" she asked with concern, sitting down in the chair beside her and looking at Blanche's beautiful hands. Her skin was so translucent Faye could see the deep blue veins beneath the surface, traveling upward into her bare fleshless arms. Despite her age and height, Faye thought she looked like a kid. No makeup, and you could see everything in her eyes, the way you could with Sophie when she first came to live upstairs. Faye wanted to say, I love you, but thought that might seem strange, so she just put her hand over Blanche's and held it. She was scared, suddenly, because Blanche had been sick for such a long time and it was possible she'd die. But she was too young to die, Faye told herself. What a horrible thing to think! Maybe everything Ma had done to her had harmed her mind, causing her to think such awful things. Maybe Blanche would die and it'd be all her fault because she'd thought of it.

"Oh, I'm okay." Blanche continued to smile. "You're getting so grown up, starting high school. You excited, sweetheart?"

"Uh-huh." Faye stroked the cool delicate hand beneath her own. She felt like a monster for sitting there thinking about someone she loved dying. Only sick people had thoughts like that.

"And how's your mama?" Blanche asked, turning her hand palm up and closing her fingers around Faye's. "I hardly see her these days."

"She's fine. She keeps saying she means to call you."

"She's very busy," Blanche said understandingly. "She works so hard, your poor mama."

Not *that* busy, Faye thought angrily. She could've found the time to visit someone who was supposed to be her best friend. "I'll tell her to call you," she said, getting up reluctantly. "I better go. I promised to pick up some meat from the butcher on my way home."

Raffie was chopping green peppers. He put down the knife, saying, "I'll walk Faye out, Mom." He placed a hand on his mother's shoulder. "Don't touch anything. Okay? I'll do it."

"You shouldn't be doing my work, Raffie."

"I don't mind. I'll be right back."

"Maybe I'll lie down for a while," Blanche said, looking at the table-top, her eyes going vague, her smile vanishing. It seemed to Faye that she was looking at something inside her own mind, something that troubled her.

"Sure. You lie down," Raffie said.

"Bye, Mrs. DiStasio," Faye said from the doorway. "I hope you feel better soon. I'll tell Ma to call you."

Blanche looked over blankly, then blinked and smiled as if suddenly remembering she was supposed to, and said, "You're so pretty, Faye, got the face of an angel."

Faye automatically shook her head, and said goodbye again.

Raffie took her hand saying, "She sure does. Be back in a couple of minutes."

"I love your mother," Faye said quietly as they went down the stairs, her throat aching. "I wish they could do something about her headaches."

"Yeah. We all do."

Frankie was busy with customers. Faye called goodbye to him and he blew her a kiss before returning his attention to the penciled figures he was totaling on a brown bag.

At the corner, Raffie released her hand, saying, "Pa said I could have tomorrow afternoon off. If the weather's good we can go to the beach."

"Okay. I'll bring my stuff."

He glanced up and down the street, then gave her a quick kiss, whispering, "I love you."

"I love you, too," she told him, thinking how unfair it was that she had to leave him, to go home to a mother who hated her.

They parted, each turning back to wave. Then Faye darted across College and ran to get to the butcher's before the store closed.

Louise had to wait ages for a streetcar, which made her even more furious than she already was. Instead of having a swell day at the beach with her girlfriends she'd had the worst time of her life. And all because of that stinking Aldo and those creeps, the Tomasino twins.

Aldo began pestering her the minute she came out of the changing area and pushed through the turnstile, with Lucy Kovacs right behind her.

"Hey, Louise!" he shouted. And when she turned to look, he started wriggling, doing a hootchy-kootchy dance, with his tongue hanging out and his eyes rolling.

She groaned and looked away, and Lucy started laughing, saying, "Boy, is he ever ridiculous!"

"Don't laugh, for Pete's sake," Louise told her. "You'll just encourage him."

"But it's hilarious, Lou."

"I'm telling you, don't encourage him."

Right then and there she wanted to go home. But of course she could hardly do that when she'd only just got there. So she put her towel on the sand next to Lucy's—all four of the girls were in a row—and pretended she didn't see or hear him. Which was impossible since he put his towel down right next to hers, with the twins next to him.

When he wasn't trying every trick in the book to get her attention, he sat making remarks about every single girl he saw. "Look at the bazongas on that one, eh?" or "Jeez! If she knew how ugly she was she'd never come outa the house," or he'd bark and moan, trying to sound like a coyote or something to show he thought some girl was sexy.

Fed up, she moved all the way over beside Carolyn. And no sooner was she settled than Aldo and the two goons came trotting over and plonked themselves down next to her.

"Leave me alone, Aldo!" she warned him. "Go away and bother somebody else."

"Aw, you know you're nuts about me," he said, grinning.

"I loathe and despise you," she declared. "You and your idiotic friends too." Turning to Carolyn, she said, "Let's go in the water."

Carolyn said, "Okay," and turned to Lucy and Irene saying, "We're going in. Come on."

So all four of them got up, and Aldo and the twins started whistling and making more disgusting remarks.

"Ooooh baaaby! Shake it, shake it!"

"Lookit those legs, eh?"

Aldo barking, then howling, then yelling, "Wiggling and jiggling, yeah, yeah!"

"Jiggle jiggle jiggle!"

"Hey, you're meltin' my ice cream!"

Louise was so angry and embarrassed she couldn't even pretend not to hear them. She waded into the water, which was so icy cold it made the breath catch in her throat. She tried to understand how someone who used to be so nice could've turned into such a complete jerk.

When she was in up to her knees, she took a deep breath and dived under the next wave washing in. The shock made her lungs seize up and sent her heart crazy. But it felt good too, and she stayed under until she was used to it. Then she came up for air, knuckling the water out of her eyes, and looked back to see the other three giggling and splashing each other, shrieking when a spray of cold water caught them. "Come on, you guys!" she called. "Don't be such cowards!"

"It's *freezing!*" Lucy cried, her arms windmilling as she tried to get back out of the way as Carolyn splashed at the water with the side of her hand.

"It's okay once you get used to it," Louise laughed, watching her friends from maybe thirty feet away. She watched for another minute or two, then floated on her back, squinting up at the sun. It felt great, the sun warming the top of her while she drifted on the cold swells. She closed her eyes, thinking it'd be easy to fall asleep and get carried by the tide right out into the middle of the lake. She could hear Lucy and Carolyn and Irene laughing and yelling at each other, and kept her eyes closed, bobbing up and down on the water.

Suddenly, terrifyingly, something had hold of her ankles and was dragging her under. She fought, struggling against whatever it was, certain she'd drown because she'd swallowed a mouthful of water and couldn't breathe. She wanted to scream, her heart pounding frantically as she strove to get back up to the surface. Her lungs hurt, wanting air, and her mouth wanted to open but she kept it closed, trying to kick free but not strong enough. Panicked, she thought she was going to die. There was a pain inside her head, her lungs were bursting. She tried desperately, using her arms, to get away, but she was held down, the weight on her ankles tremendous, the grip around each one like iron. Then all at once she was light again, the weight gone. She kicked hard and shot to the surface, her mouth opening to gulp air into her aching lungs. She sobbed with fear as she began frantically swimming for shore. Finally her feet touched bottom and she stood with her arms wrapped around her chest, gasping and crying, shivering, chilled right through.

Aldo popped up in front of her, laughing, pointing at her. "Scared ya, eh?" he laughed. "Boy, that was great!"

She screamed so hard she could feel and taste and see blood, and lunged at him, wanting to kill him. He laughed and dived underwater, and she whirled around in a circle, trying to see where he went. She started walking through the heavy water, making her way back to the shore, swearing she'd get hold of him and pull his hair out, scratch that laugh right off his ugly face.

She hadn't gone far when there was a rush in the water behind her, a sudden pulling, and her bathing suit was down around her waist. Utterly humiliated, enraged, she glanced around, praying nobody had seen as she pulled her suit back up and tried to run, hearing Aldo laughing behind her. Gaining speed as she got to the shallower water, she ran right past Lucy and Carolyn and Irene, who called, "What's the matter? What's wrong?"

"I'm going home!" she cried, racing across the sand, one hand keeping a firm grip on the top of her suit. She hated Aldo DiStasio, despised him, hoped he'd die, hoped he'd get hit by a streetcar, or be electrocuted, or run over by a car. Scarcely pausing to snatch up her things, she raced to the changing rooms, the sand burning hot under her feet. She stepped down on something hard and sharp that made her gasp, but she didn't stop to look, just kept on going.

Shaking, teeth chattering, hair dripping in her eyes, she got her wet suit off but couldn't dry herself because there was too much sand in her towel. So she struggled into her clothes—they felt wonderfully warm—stuffed the bathing suit and towel into her bag, and strapped on her sandals. Then she slammed out of the cubicle and marched to the exit. That rotten bastard! She wanted him to die, prayed for it. Come on, God! Make him die! She ground her teeth while she waited for the stupid streetcar to come. He doesn't deserve to live, so kill him!

When she finally got home, she shook out the towel and hung it and her bathing suit on the line in the back yard. Then she started the water running in the tub while she went to get a glass of milk. She put the milk bottle back in the fridge, went to pick up the glass, and dropped it. Don't break don't break! she prayed as the milk went everywhere and the glass hit the side of the table and smashed into a million pieces on the floor.

"Shit, shit!" she muttered, grabbing the dishrag to clean up the mess. It took ages. She had to use a wet newspaper to make sure she got every last bit of glass. Finally finished, she carried the package of glass out to the garbage can, then came back in, realizing with a start that she'd left the water running in the tub. She flew to the bathroom but the water was already spreading over the floor. Crying, "Oh, no!" and breaking into tears, she got the water turned off, pulled the plug, then ran to get the mop.

She cried, hiccuping, the whole time she mopped up the water. She cried when she couldn't wring all the water out of the bath mat and had to hang it, heavy and dripping, over the line outside. She cried even harder when she realized she'd used up all the hot water so that now she couldn't have a bath.

When she was finally able to stop crying, she went to the bedroom to get her piggy bank and, using a knife in the slot, shook out some quarters and dimes, returning the pennies. Then she trudged down to the hardware store on Queen street to buy another glass, keeping her fingers crossed all the way there, hoping they'd have one like the one she'd broken or Ma would go crazy.

Mr. Winters wrapped the glass in newspaper, then put it in a bag before taking her dollar and thirty cents. "What's wrong, Louise?" he asked as he handed her the penny change.

She shook her head. "Nothing. Thanks, Mr. Winters."

"Any time," he said. "How's your mother and your sister?"

"Everybody's fine," she answered morosely. "Bye."

She walked over the uneven wooden floor to the door, opened it, looked up at the bell overhead as it tinkled, made a face, and went out, hearing the bell tinkling behind her. Hope you die die die, she thought, keeping her eyes on the sidewalk as she headed leadenly home. I hope you rot in hell, you stupid shithead. She'd almost drowned because of him, and he thought that was funny. Then he'd pulled her top down right in front of a whole beachfull of people. He'd ruined her entire day, and she hated him more than anyone else in the world. She hoped he stayed in the water too long, got a cramp, and drowned. She'd put on her best dress and go to the funeral and be secretly glad while everybody else cried.

CHAPTER
ELEVEN

LOUISE'S FOOT STARTED HURTING ON THE WALK HOME from the hardware store. After washing the new glass and putting it away, she sat down, undid her sandal, and hiked her foot into her lap.

"What's the matter?" Faye asked, coming into the kitchen with a package of pork chops.

"I stepped on something at the beach," Louise answered, cautiously prodding the area around the bloodied, sand-encrusted cut on the ball of her toe. "It hurts."

"It's full of sand," Faye said, bending to look.

"I think it's still in there," Louise said fearfully. "I can feel it."

"Go wash off the sand and I'll have a look," Faye told her, getting out some potatoes and opening the drawer for the peeler.

Louise lifted her foot into the bathroom sink and held it under the cold-water faucet, wincing as the flow of water washed away most of the dried blood and sand and whitened the edges of what she now saw was quite a deep gash.

Hobbling back to the kitchen, careful to keep her weight off the throbbing foot, she said, "There's definitely something in it."

Faye got down on her knees, gently touching the area with a fingertip. "Something *is* in there," she confirmed. "What'd you step on?"

"I don't know," Louise said, trying not to start crying again. "I didn't stop to look."

"You should go to the doctor."

"No. You get it out."

"Lou, I can't! It's way in there. And if it isn't taken out you'll get infected."

"If I have to go to the doctor, Ma will have a fit."

"That's just too bad, isn't it?" Faye said defiantly. "Keep off it for now, and we'll wait till Ma looks at it."

"I'm not letting her touch it! Remember the last time when I got that big splinter under my fingernail and she tried to use her tweezers to get it out? She nearly killed me before she'd finally let me go to the doctor. And he had to freeze it and cut off half my nail before he could get the stupid thing out."

"Well, what d'you want me to do, Lou?" Faye asked irritably.

"Why're you getting mad at me?" Louise asked, vowing the next time she saw Aldo DiStasio she'd kick him as hard as she could right between the legs.

"I'm not getting mad at you," Faye said. "I'm just imagining what Ma's going to say."

"She'll say I'm stupid and clumsy and it's my own damn fault," Louise said hotly. "Except it's Aldo's fault, that *idiot!*"

"Did he try to kiss you again?" Faye couldn't help smiling.

"It's not *funny!* First he nearly *drowned* me. Then he pulled down my bathing suit in front of the entire world." Louise crossed her arms tightly over her chest.

"What d'you mean he tried to drown you?"

"Exactly what I said. I was swimming out a ways, and he got hold of my ankles and dragged me under. I've never *been* so scared. He wouldn't let go." She suddenly remembered Chuckie and wondered if he'd been terrified too, being underwater.

"What a crummy thing to do," Faye commiserated.

"And then, *then* he pulled down my bathing suit!" Despite her efforts, tears came to her eyes.

Knowing how embarrassing it had to have been, Faye went over to put an arm around her shoulders. Louise at once pressed her wet face into Faye's belly. "He didn't have to do that!" she wailed, convinced everyone on that beach had seen her half naked.

"No, he didn't," Faye agreed, wondering why Aldo would do such a rotten thing. "You want me to say something to the DiStasios tomorrow?"

Louise shook her head as she pulled away, wiping her eyes on her forearm. "He'd only lie and say he didn't do it, the stinking creep. I hate him so much!"

"I'll bet," Faye sympathized. "Anybody ever did that to me, I'd kill him. Poor Lou."

"Yeah," Louise nodded. "Poor me."

Maggie looked, made a face, and said, "It's one damned thing after another with you. Faye, after supper you'll take your sister over to Sick Children's. I've got to go out tonight. Now let's eat before it gets cold."

"Where are you going?" Louise asked.

"Out," Maggie said flatly. After months of his nagging, she'd finally given in and agreed to meet Nolan for a drink. It was the only way she could think of to shut him up. She was in no mood to go anywhere, especially not to the Silver Rail. The tank of live lobsters in the front window was enough to make her stomach turn. But that's where he wanted to go, so she'd go—for the first and last time.

"Mrs. DiStasio was asking for you," Faye said quietly. "I told her you'd phone."

Instead of getting angry, as Faye expected, Maggie seemed suddenly thoughtful, saying, "God, that's right. I must remember to call her."

"She'd really like that," Faye said with an encouraging smile. "You two hardly see each other anymore."

"Maybe I'll drop by on Saturday," Maggie said. "How're her headaches?"

"Bad. She gets them all the time now."

"Frankie should take her to another doctor. The one she's got isn't doing a damned thing for her."

"I think they did," Faye said.

"Doctors," Maggie said disdainfully. "What do they know?"

Louise was atypically quiet during the streetcar ride to the hospital, and she remained quiet throughout the two and a half hours they had to wait in the emergency room before they were finally taken into a curtained cubicle where they waited another half hour before a very young, curly-haired doctor came whistling in.

He broke into a big smile at the sight of them, then said, "Which one's Louise?"

Louise held up her hand, as if she were in a classroom.

"Okay, Louise. Why don't you hop up here"—he patted the examining table—"and we'll see what we can do for you."

He examined her foot, asking, "What'd you step on?"

"She doesn't know," Faye answered.

"I think maybe it was glass," Louise said nervously, convinced whatever he did to her was going to hurt.

"I'll have to open this up," he said, spreading the cut so that Louise grabbed the sides of the examining table and bit her lip, thinking, I knew it; this is going to be murder. "Just relax now," he said, giving her a pat on the knee. "I know that hurt, but that's about as bad as it's going to get. I'll be back in a couple of minutes and we'll get you fixed up. Okay?"

Louise sniffed and said, "Okay."

"Hey," he said, lifting her chin with the side of his hand. "It'll be okay. Cross my heart."

That got a little smile from her.

"Sit tight, and I'll be right back. Okay?"

"Okay."

Faye held her hand, watching Lou's face as the doctor injected a local anesthetic into her foot. Louise bore down on her hand, her face contorting as tears leaked from the corners of her tightly closed eyes. But she didn't make a sound.

"It'll take a minute for that to start working," the doctor told them, setting aside the syringe. He picked up a small box of tissues and handed it to Louise, saying, "Good girl. I thought maybe we'd have to get six nurses in here to hold you down, but you're a real trouper."

Louise gave him a watery smile and blotted her face. "That hurt like the dickens."

"I know. But that really is the worst of it. The rest'll be a breeze. You'll see. So," he said, leaning against the side of the table, "you're sisters, eh?"

"That's right," Faye answered.

"Yeah. You look a lot alike."

"You think so?" Louise asked, propping herself up on her elbows.

"Sure. People must tell you that all the time."

He was so young and so pleasant that Faye smiled, thinking how nice he was. Not like Dr. Steele, their family physician, who always seemed impatient with them, acting the way Ma did, as if they were stupid to have hurt themselves or to have picked up some virus.

Louise said, "I don't think we look alike."

"Well, you do," he grinned. "A couple of really pretty girls. Your mother must be some doll."

Faye and Louise exchanged a look but didn't say anything.

"Okay," he said after another moment or two, "let's see what's in here now." He moved back around to the foot of the table.

Louise continued to grip Faye's hand, expecting it to start hurting at any moment, but all she felt was a kind of tugging. She kept her eyes closed until she heard the doctor say, "Well now, what've we got here?"

"What?" she asked, opening her eyes and propping herself up again on her elbows.

"A nice hunk of glass," he said, holding it up with a pair of long shiny tongs.

The three of them gazed at the bloodied fragment that was about half an inch long by about a quarter of an inch wide.

"What's it from?" Faye asked, feeling queasy.

"Beats me," he said, studying the glass a moment longer before dropping it into a metal basin. "Okay, Lulu," he said, automatically calling her by her nickname. "We'll just make sure there's nothing else in here."

"My gramma calls me Lulu," she said, liking him.

"Maybe I know your gramma, eh?" He looked up and winked, then said, "Lie back down and we'll get this cleaned up, then we'll close it."

"Do I have to have stitches?" she asked worriedly.

"Nope. I'll tape it up nice and tight. A week or so and you'll be good as new, back dancing with the National Ballet."

Louise laughed, and Faye smiled, shaking her head.

"I used to think I wanted to be a Canadette," Louise told him.

"That right? What changed your mind?"

"I couldn't do the splits, and you have to be able to if you're a Canadette."

He laughed out loud. "You're a real pistol," he said.

"Yeah," Louise agreed with satisfaction. "I am."

Watching her, Faye felt a sudden rush of love for her sister. She was such a good kid, so funny and bright. Everybody was always crazy about her.

When he'd finished, he helped Lou to sit on the side of the table, saying, "Now, I want you to keep it dry. Okay?"

"What'll I do when I have to take a bath?"

"Just keep that foot out of the water. Prop it on the side of the tub." He got some gauze pads and a roll of adhesive tape and gave them to Faye. "Change your sister's dressing in three or four days. Okay?"

"Okay."

He patted Louise on the knee again and said, "You were great, Lulu. A real champ. Watch where you're walking next time. Okay?"

"Okay. Thanks a lot."

"My pleasure. So long, Faye. And don't forget to keep that foot dry."

He left, and Faye started to strap Lou's sandal back on, saying, "He was nice."

"He sure was," Louise agreed.

Relieved that it hadn't been worse, Louise perked up considerably on the way home. "I don't think we look alike," she said while they were waiting to transfer to the Bathurst streetcar. "Do you?"

Faye was looking down College Street, knowing it was too late for Raffie to be out, but hoping she might see him anyway. "I don't know," she answered distractedly. "I guess so."

"It must be really late," Louise said. "There's hardly anybody out."

"It was twenty past nine when we left the hospital," Faye said, finally turning around. "Does your foot hurt?"

"It's okay. I should've asked if I could keep the glass."

"What for?"

"To show everybody, of course. They'll never believe me when I say how big it was."

Maggie sipped at her Tom Collins then took a puff of her cigarette, thinking this was nothing but a waste of time. Going to the trouble to take a bath and put on a decent dress just to sit in a bar with Jerry Nolan. As if she didn't see enough of him five days a week at work.

"You look terrific," Nolan said, admiring the way the black dress set off her fair skin and blond hair.

"Thank you." She tapped her fingernails on the tabletop, looking around the room. Christ, this was boring!

"How's your drink?" he asked.

"Fine."

"Are you hungry? We could get something to eat."

"I've already eaten," she said, not bothering to look at him.

"If you don't like it here, we could go somewhere else."

She turned slowly. "I didn't even want to come here," she said. "And I sure as hell don't want to go anyplace else. Let me have my drink in peace, all right?"

He audibly drew in his breath. Then, in a cool voice she'd never heard him use before, he said, "You know, Maggie, all these months I thought you kept turning me down because you didn't believe I was serious, that I was making fun of you or something. But I was wrong, wasn't I? You turned me down because you meant it when you said you wouldn't be caught dead in public with me. You really meant that, didn't you?"

"I don't say things because I'm so crazy about the sound of my own voice," she said, her hand wrapped around the tall, sweating glass.

"No, I realize that now." He was looking at her in a way that set her on edge. "I'm nobody's fool, Maggie, least of all yours." Reaching into his pocket, he brought out his wallet. "Come on. I'll run you home." He pulled out some bills and laid them on the table.

"Wait a minute," she said uncertainly. He was her boss; he could fire her if he wanted to. What the hell would she do if that happened? The only thing she knew how to do was run that damned sewing machine. "At least let me finish my drink," she said, trying to buy time while she reconsidered.

"I don't feel like sitting here with someone who can't stand the sight of me," he said, returning the wallet to his pocket and pushing his chair back from the table.

"I didn't say that," she said, completely thrown. "I just don't like to waste time talking. I mean, we don't ever *have* that much time."

"We do now. All the time in the world." He made an expansive gesture with his hands. "But you're still acting like it's a waste of your energy trying to talk to me. Christ! You think I *enjoy* being treated this way?" He kept his voice down, but she had the feeling people were turning to look at them. *"Do* you?"

"Well, no, I guess not," she said, entirely at a loss as to how to deal with the situation. She wanted to go home, but she didn't want him walking out on her, leaving her a laughingstock in a public bar. She also didn't want to get fired. It suddenly occurred to her she didn't know a thing about this man, except how he made love. Oh, she'd seen how he dealt with the employees, but that didn't mean she had any idea of what he might be capable of saying or doing. "I uhm . . ." She picked up her cigarette, took a hard drag, then made herself look at him through the smoke. Like a respectable business man, he was dressed as always in a suit and shirt and tie, his good-looking silver cuff links catching the light. He could be anyone. She knew nothing about him.

"What?" he said, appearing ready to get up and leave at any moment. "What were you going to say?" When she didn't respond he leaned toward her across the table and said, "You think all these years, what we've been doing all this time, I don't have any feelings about it? You think I'm the kind of man who goes after a woman just because she's handy?" He stared at her. "That's exactly what you think, isn't it? Because it's the way *you* think." His eyes narrowing briefly, his mouth curved into a slight smile. "I'm beginning to figure you out," he said. "And you know what? I made a big mistake. I thought you behaved the way you do because you got burned once, so you're being careful. But I was wrong, wasn't I? You behave the way you do because you don't give a damn. All you're interested in is a quickie once or twice a week. Right?" Without waiting for an answer, he got up. "Come on. I'll run you home."

Left with no alternative but to comply, she picked up her cigarettes and matches and followed him out.

As they walked in silence to his car, which was parked a couple of blocks away, she tried to think what to do. If she didn't say or do something, she was going to find herself out on the street without a job. She *knew* she should've kept saying no to him. But he wouldn't quit; he'd finally worn down her resistance. And now look what was happening.

"What did you expect?" she asked at last, seeing his anger in the set of his jaw and in the way he was striding purposefully toward his car, unconcerned with whether or not she could keep up with him in her high heels.

"Expect?" he repeated, stopping abruptly on the sidewalk and turning to face her. "How about common decency, good manners? You've said things to me I wouldn't take from anyone. But I've taken them from you. Implying I'm the kind of man who'd molest young girls, hinting I've got ulterior motives because I happen to be fond of Faye and Louise. Not even bothering to turn me down nicely, but laughing in my face and telling me you wouldn't be seen dead with me. You're some piece of work. You know that?"

"I see. You wanted me to pretend," she said, standing with one hand on her hip.

"No. I wanted you to be *civilized.*"

"I *told* you I didn't want to go out but you wouldn't accept that. So now I'm uncivilized, because I told the truth."

"You are, but not because you told the truth. Because you don't give a damn about anyone but yourself. And that not only makes you uncivilized, it makes you goddamned well inhuman!" He glared at her for several seconds, then turned and walked on.

"How would you know?" she challenged, hurrying to catch up with him. "You don't know anything about me."

"That's absolutely correct. I don't. I thought I did, but I was wrong." He fished the keys out of his pocket and opened the passenger door, then stood waiting for her to get into the car.

"What're you going to do?" she asked, anxious to know where she stood. "Are you going to fire me now?"

He slapped his hand on the roof of the car and laughed. Then folding his arms, he leaned against the side of the car, his expression once more serious. "Nobody's firing anyone," he said, sounding tired now. "Not everybody thinks the way you do, Maggie."

"What's that supposed to mean?"

"It means, we're not all scum. We don't all *use* people. What goes on between you and me in private has nothing to do with the factory."

"Oh!" Not sure now what to do, she waited for him to say something.

"Twelve, thirteen years—I even forget now how long it's been, but it's a hell of a long time—we've been making love. I guess I'm naive, when you get right down to it. I figured your feelings were involved. Goes to show you how far off the mark you can be."

She looked around, saying, "Maybe I'll get a cab."

"Get the hell in the car and I'll drive you home," he said, straightening. "I've had enough of this crap for one night."

She got in. He shut the door and walked around to the driver's side, rolling down the window before he put the key in the ignition. The radio came on when the engine started. He turned it off, released the hand brake, put on the headlights, then sat staring out the windshield. "I feel tired and stupid," he said. "Forty-one years old and here I'm day-dreaming like some teenager about the two of us getting together, having a nice place with plenty of room for the girls; we'd be a family. Isn't that a hot one?" He put the car in gear, checked the oncoming traffic, then pulled out.

Nervously lighting a cigarette, she rolled her window down halfway, stunned. He'd been thinking about getting *married?* It was the last thing she'd expected. And now, when he'd made it clear he was no longer thinking in those terms, she wished she'd made an effort to be a little nicer. It wouldn't have killed her. He was good-looking; he had some money; he even liked the girls.

"Look," she said, fairly desperate to salvage what she could of the situation. "I'm sorry. All right? How was I supposed to know what you were thinking?"

"Most people," he said, "they leave some room for possibilities."

"You were married, for God's sake!"

"Nora and I split up almost a year ago."

The ensuing silence lasted until they were nearing Manning Avenue. "Could we drive around for a while?" she asked.

"Why?"

"I don't think we should leave things the way they are."

He didn't speak but kept driving west on Queen. Relieved, she lit another cigarette. "I said I was sorry."

"I heard you," he said curtly, speeding up to pass a streetcar in the inside lane, then slowing once he was past it. "Saying you're sorry doesn't make everything right again."

"Well, what will? What do you want?"

"It's too late," he sighed tiredly.

"We could go somewhere," she said meaningfully.

He turned right at the next corner, then began cutting back along side streets. She thought perhaps he was taking her to his place. But then she saw he was heading back to Manning Avenue. What did he want from her? she wondered, becoming depressed. She'd apologized, for God's sake. She'd said she was sorry; she'd even offered to make love. Maybe she'd been too subtle.

"If you want," she said, "we can go to your place."

"I got it the first time, Maggie. I'm not in the mood tonight," he said quietly, heading along Robinson now. "You're just north of Queen, aren't you?"

"That's right," she said, sinking rapidly now.

He pulled up in front of the house, put the shift in neutral, set the hand brake, then got out and walked around the front of the car to open her door. She stepped out onto the sidewalk and looked at the house. The lights were off. The girls weren't back from the hospital.

"Do you want to come in?" she asked, frightened. Bringing him into the house was a dangerous move; it might set a precedent.

He looked at the house. "What about the girls?"

"They're out for a couple of hours."

"Some other time," he said, and took her arm to see her to the door. He waited until she got the door unlocked, then moved to go. Panicked, she put a hand on his arm to stop him.

"Come in," she said thickly, thinking that if he left now after making her beg she'd never forgive him.

He stood staring at her for several seconds then went off down the steps. She felt positively suicidal. Tears suddenly filled her eyes. She pushed the door open and stepped inside, then heard the car engine stop. She exhaled shakily. He was coming in. Relief made her knees weak. She pulled herself erect, sucking in her stomach. "We'll have to make it quick," she said, leading him to her bedroom. "I don't know how long the girls are going to be."

He began removing his jacket and she smiled. It was all right. She could feel her power surging back. In future, she'd be more careful how she dealt with him.

Louise lowered her book and looked at Faye, who was sitting with her own book propped on her drawn-up knees, winding a strand of hair around her finger.

"Maybe it's never going to happen," she said.

"What?" Faye asked, not taking her eyes from the page.

"You know."

"What?"

"You got it when you were thirteen."

Faye finally turned. "Not everybody's the same, you know."

"Everybody else already has it."

Faye closed her book. "It's no big deal, Lou."

"It is too. Everyone I know wears a bra, except me. I haven't grown a single inch in almost an entire year. People think I'm ten years old, for heaven's sake. I'm the shortest of the girls and the only one with no chest."

"Don't worry about it. It'll happen."

"Yeah. When?"

"I promise, it'll *happen*."

"Yeah, but what if it doesn't?"

Faye laughed and ran a hand over her sister's hair. "Believe me, it happens to everyone. Why're you so worried about it?"

"I'm going into high school, for Pete's sake! I'll probably be the only girl in the entire school who doesn't have her period yet. It's *embarrassing.*"

"You don't have to tell people."

"They can tell just by looking at me."

"They can not. Don't be silly!"

"It isn't silly. People can tell because I don't have a chest. And now the entire city probably knows I don't, because of stinking Aldo." She crossed her arms angrily. "I hope he *sits* on broken glass!"

"I'll bet nobody even noticed," Faye said kindly.

Lou sulked, staring at her bandaged foot. "What's it like?" she asked after a moment.

"What's what like?"

"Having a boyfriend, necking and stuff."

Faye's face turned red. "I'm not telling you *that*. Are you *crazy?*"

"Well, do you like it?"

"Of course I like it. I wouldn't do it if I didn't."

"But what d'you *do?*" Louise asked. "There's kissing, I know. What else do you do? Do you touch under your clothes?"

"Louise!" Faye exclaimed in a low voice. "I am *not* discussing that with you. Okay?"

"Don't have a fit. I just wanted to know. What're you getting so worked up about?"

Faye thought of the way she and Raffie touched each other, and blushed even harder. "There are some things," she said with dignity, "that people just don't talk about."

"That's right!" Louise pounced. "And if nobody talks about them, how's anybody supposed to know, eh?"

"You're *not* supposed to know."

"Right. But *you* do! So if I'm not supposed to know, and nobody's supposed to talk about it, how come you're doing it?"

"I . . . we . . . God, Lou! Why're you asking me these things? It's *private.*"

"I want to know what it's like, that's all. Is it like the movies? D'you get all mushy? Do you both take your clothes off? What? Tell me!"

"No, we don't take our clothes off! Not really. It's just . . . nice. Okay? It feels good."

"What does?"

"All of it. Now read your book and leave me alone."

"All of it," Louise repeated. "Do you go all the way?"

"Of course not!" Faye was shocked. "What d'you think I am, anyway?"

"I never said you were anything. I'm only asking. I'd like to *know,* that's all. Do you let him touch your chest?"

"I'm not saying another thing." She picked up her book, found her place and pretended to read, feeling Lou watching her every move. "Stop staring at me!" she said. "The discussion's over."

"So you do," Louise said shrewdly. "Where else?"

Faye pretended to ignore her.

"Would you *want* to go all the way?"

"Louise, I'm warning you! I do *not* want to talk about this."

"No, come on. Would you?"

"I might. Okay? Are you happy? Now *leave me alone!*"

"Wow!" Louise sat back against her pillow, mightily impressed. "You must really love him."

"I'm not saying another word."

"You really must love him, if you'd be willing to go all the way."

"Not one more word."

"Are you ever lucky," Louise said, awed. "I've never even had a date. Probably never will." She hooked a finger into her pajama top and gazed down the inside at her completely flat chest. "Boys only like girls with chests. You've got a really good chest, I've noticed. D'you think you're still growing? I'd hate to have a great big chest, like Lucy. Hers are *enormous.* You should've seen those jerky Tomasino twins staring at her. It was disgusting. And pukey Aldo making shapes in the air with his dumb hands. He's the biggest pig I've ever seen."

Faye slammed her book shut. "I'm going to sleep," she declared, and reached to turn out the light.

Louise continued to sit, gazing into space, repeating, "You're so lucky."

"Good night!" Faye said, punching her pillow. "Go to sleep."

"I'd better get it soon," Louise said in the dark. "I refuse to be the only girl to go through five whole years of high school never having a date.''

''You'll *get* it!'' Faye groaned. *''Go to sleep!''*

''In a minute,'' Louise said, imagining herself with a boyfriend, going for walks together, holding hands. She wasn't so sure about kissing and the rest of it, though. Every time they got to the smoochy part in a movie, she wanted them to hurry up and get it over with. It looked so gorpy. But maybe once you started getting periods it wasn't gorpy anymore. With her luck, and never mind what Faye said, she'd probably be the first girl in the entire world who never got it.

CHAPTER

T W E L V E

LOUISE LOVED BEING IN HIGH SCHOOL. SHE LOVED HAVING different teachers for each subject who addressed her as Miss Parker, and the noisy rush of kids in the corridors between classes. She loved going down to the cramped room in the basement to eat lunch with her friends. She even loved several of her teachers: the hefty and always jovial young woman who taught health and phys ed; the elegant, willowy older woman who was the head of the French department and her homeroom teacher; and the dapper, darkly handsome English teacher who gave her a funny feeling in the pit of her stomach whenever he looked at her. The history teacher, white-haired, portly, and given to lengthy, incomprehensible digressions, was, everyone agreed, a boring old poop. For Latin she had a tall, narrow-faced middle-aged man who wore the same baggy suit and stained striped tie every day, which aroused considerably more interest than anything he attempted to teach. The math teacher appeared to be a raving maniac. With his hair sticking out in all directions and thick glasses that made his eyes seem huge, he had the habit of wiping his chalky hands on his clothes so that by day's end he looked like a demented, slowly disappearing ghost. But he was a great teacher and surprisingly patient,

willing to explain endlessly if anyone found a problem particularly difficult.

Her favorite subjects were English and French. English, because there
was something exciting and faintly dangerous about the young teacher,
with his well-cut suits, his crisp clean-smelling aftershave, and his unsettling gaze. And French, because she was enchanted by the idea of learning
a second language, especially one that sounded as romantic as French.
While a good half of the kids complained that it was a waste of time—
they were never going to live in Quebec, so why the heck was French
compulsory anyway?—Louise could hardly wait to get to class every day,
first to see what the tall, silver-haired Mademoiselle Castle would be
wearing and second to see the day's vocabulary assignment.

She went around reciting constantly: *la chaise,* the chair; *la table,* the
table; *la fenêtre,* the window; *le fauteuil,* the armchair.

Je m'appelle Louise. Ma soeur s'appelle Faye.

Bonjour. Comment allez-vous?

Avez-vous une pomme? Non? Ah, quel dommage.

Great stuff! She *loved* it. She even translated her thoughts into French,
frustrated when her vocabulary proved too limited. She went around the
house chanting declensions: *je suis, tu es, il/elle est, nous sommes, vous êtes,
ils/elles sont; je vais, tu vas, il/elle va, nous allons, vous allez, ils/elles vont.*

She did it so much that Maggie went nuts. "Shut the hell up with that
crap, for Chrissake! I'm sick of hearing it."

After that, she simply recited silently at home.

Faye was intimidated by the crowds of kids, by their tidal force as they
flowed along the corridors between classes. She was nervous about entering the packed, overly warm lunchroom on those days when she wasn't
meeting Raffie. The many compulsory subjects were bewildering. She fell
behind almost immediately in French, and only managed to maintain a
passing grade because of Lou's endless recitations. Latin was a nonsensical
nightmare, history was dreary, algebra was impossible, science was occasionally interesting, English was okay except for Shakespeare's *Julius Cae-
sar,* the language of which defeated her, but typing was unadulterated
pleasure.

While Louise went everywhere either silently reciting to herself or
translating aloud every last thing she saw into French, Faye typed in her
head. Her fingers skipped over an imagined keyboard, typing her
thoughts, even her feelings. And once past the basic lessons—fsf jkj fsf jkj,

ala fjf ala, repeated dozens of times—she raced ahead, quickly memoriz-
ing the entire keyboard and outstripping the rest of the class (twenty-six
girls and two boys) to the delight of the ever-smiling, barrel-shaped,
ancient Miss Giddings.

"You're my star pupil," Miss Giddings declared, standing with a surprisingly dainty hand on Faye's shoulder as she admired the sample business letter Faye was reproducing perfectly. "Splendid, my dear! Simply
splendid!" Faye adored the woman, with her short, wispy brown hair,
her lurid lipstick, her clunky lace-up shoes, and ugly mannish wool suits.
When Miss Giddings greeted her in the corridors, Faye felt strengthened.
There was one place, at least, in the H-shaped three-story building where
she was completely comfortable. And Miss Giddings made her feel special.

The sisters only occasionally ran into each other at school, but met up
most days to walk home together. Often they stopped at the DiStasios'.
They'd visit briefly with Blanche, taking care to speak softly to her, and
pressing light kisses on her cheeks or forehead before tiptoeing from the
permanently darkened living room. Some afternoons they helped out in
the store. Or if it was quiet, Louise would sit on the stool by the cash
register, doing her homework and keeping an eye on things while Frankie
ran errands or went upstairs to look in on his wife, and Faye and Raffie
slipped down to the cellar for ten or fifteen minutes on their bench behind
the furnace. Louise became their enthusiastic lookout, letting a book fall
heavily to the floor or stamping with her foot if Frankie came in unexpectedly, if there was a sudden rush of customers, or if Aldo came swaggering
in and started pestering her.

After forty minutes or an hour, the girls would continue on their way
home, stopping en route to pick up anything Maggie had told them she
needed. They'd peel the potatoes or carrots, or put the meat loaf in the
oven, do whatever cleaning Maggie had assigned, then sit at the kitchen
table with their homework spread out on the oilcloth until it was time for
supper. On the three nights a week when their mother was working, Faye
would go out to meet Raffie for a couple of hours while Louise puttered
around the house, listening to the radio and trying to translate song lyrics
into French while she put her hair in rollers. Occasionally she'd have
friends in. They'd drape themselves over the living room furniture or flop
on the floor, the radio blaring while they discussed boys, their teachers, or
the clothes in the latest issue of *Seventeen*. Faye tried not to be home on

those occasions, feeling too much of a misfit. When the conversation turned to boys or school, she simply listened, unable to feign any interest. She hated school. She had a boyfriend. And the teachers didn't interest her. All she wanted was to be done with school and to spend every possible moment with Raffie.

The only difficulty she encountered in being with Raffie was Aldo. As Louise had said, Aldo had turned into a real jerk. He never missed an opportunity to rag Louise about being a "brain" because she was already in high school, while he, although seven weeks older than she, was only in grade eight. And doing badly. He played hooky constantly. Notes were sent home to Frankie on a regular basis. Aldo of course never delivered them. There were telephone calls Frankie found incomprehensible, and he didn't like to disturb Blanche to come talk to these people and find out what they were saying about his youngest son.

Aldo had taken to dressing like the Tomasino twins, in shirts with the collars turned up and tight pants, with his hair greased into a DA, and a pack of Export A's prominently displayed in his shirt pocket, a comb in his back pocket, and a wad of chewing gum working between his surprisingly white even teeth.

He wasn't as big or as tall as Raffie, nor as muscular. With his large brown eyes and pale skin, he'd inherited his mother's high-cheekboned good looks, but the acne flourishing on his forehead and cheeks, his heavy-lidded gaze, and perpetual sneer rendered him menacing rather than sexy as he thought. Whenever he approached a group of girls in the schoolyard, they'd clutch each other's hands and giggle nervously, collectively finding the courage to tell him to get lost. When he approached those same girls individually, they'd freeze in place, their eyes darting from side to side as if looking either for help or for an escape, silently suffering while he—sometimes alone, but usually with the twins—made explicit suggestions that terrified them.

Aldo loved the power he felt threatening the kids in the schoolyard, and sometimes after dark, if he and the twins happened to spot some kid hurrying along the street with a bag of groceries, they'd close in and scare the living crap out of the kid. If it was a boy, they'd take pokes at him, making moves as if they were going to grab his crotch, trying to pull the bag of groceries out of his arms. If they happened to spot a girl, they'd start following her along the sidewalk, making just enough noise to let her know they were there. Invariably, she'd look back over her shoulder, spot the trio of black-jacketed, slick-haired boys, and take off at a run. Then they'd give chase, letting her get good and scared. The girl would go pounding along the sidewalk, then race up the front walk and fling herself through the door to her house. The boys would laugh, congratulating each other, then get the hell out of there before the father or the police arrived.

The only girl who wasn't scared of Aldo was Louise. She had nothing but contempt for him, and wouldn't even bother to look at him. If he tried to speak to her, she'd either ignore him altogether or make some crack that made him so mad he wanted to bust her one. After that day at the beach, if he even said hello, trying to be nice, she'd cut him down. "You're a pathetic greaseball," she'd say. "Get out of my sight, Aldo, or you'll be walking funny for the rest of your life."

The one time he got together with the twins to throw a scare into her as she was walking home alone from the store, she wound up scaring the crap out of them. It was the end of October, a cold evening. There were leaves all over the sidewalks and the smell of woodsmoke in the air.

Aldo ran over to get the twins, telling them what he wanted to do as they hid out in a laneway on Manning just south of Dundas. As she came down the street, they sauntered out of the lane to stand abreast, blocking the sidewalk and watching her approach. Aldo was thinking this time he'd fix her but good. Except that she didn't do a thing, didn't cross over to the other side to avoid them the way they expected, didn't slow down or even look around to see if there was anyone around who'd help her. She just kept coming toward them, and they glanced at each other, wondering if she was crazy or stupid. When she was about six feet away, walking with her arms wrapped around her load of schoolbooks, she smiled, then opened her mouth and let out an ungodly scream. It sounded as if she was being murdered. She stood on the sidewalk with her head back and screamed so loud and hard that people came running out of their houses, looking out doors and windows, shouting, "What's going on out there?" Louise kept screaming. And suddenly men were coming at them from all directions. Aldo and the twins looked at each other and took off, the twins heading south and Aldo heading north, the three of them dodging guys who chased after them.

In less than a minute, Louise was surrounded by concerned residents asking if she was all right. She thanked them, saying, "I'll be all right now. Thank you," then looked up the street at Aldo being pursued by half a dozen men in their shirtsleeves. "I hope they catch him," she said seriously. "Those three should be locked up." Then she continued on her way home, wishing with all her heart she'd read in tomorrow's paper that Aldo and the twins had been arrested.

The twins managed to get away, but Aldo got roughed up by half a dozen old guys who closed him into the middle of a tight circle. They slapped him around and warned him that if they ever saw him on their block again he'd be one sorry wop. They shoved him back and forth between them, slapped him some more, then gave him a final shove, saying, "Don't come around here no more, punk!" He went home swearing he'd remember every one of their faces and make them sorry they'd ever fucked with him, and despising that smart-ass bitch Lou Parker. But after that, whenever he ran into her at the store, he kept his distance, grateful only that she hadn't, for some reason, told his parents.

✝

Nolan and Maggie had stopped meeting in his office. There was no longer any need for the clandestine ten or fifteen minute encounters. On average, one night a week Nolan would pick her up from the diner and they'd go to his place. If she knew the girls were going to be out for the evening, despite the anxiety and irritation it caused her, she'd let him come to the house.

In mid November, Flo turned to her one morning during the coffee break and said with a smile, "So, I see you got your bladder problem fixed, eh?"

"What?"

Flo said, "You don't have to go all the time now, like you used to."

"Oh, right." Maggie took a drag on her cigarette.

"So what d'you do now?" Flo asked straight-faced. "You go to his place, or yours?"

"*What?*"

"Come on, Maggie!" Flo grinned. "Don't act like you don't know what I'm talking about."

"Well, I don't," Maggie said, suddenly very aware of her cheekbones and jaw and how they moved in stiff concert when she spoke.

"I always thought if I wasn't hooked up with Ern I wouldn't mind having Jerry Nolan's shoes parked under my bed," Flo said playfully.

"What the *hell* are you *talking* about?" Maggie said, her stomach contracting unpleasantly. Did the whole stinking factory know about her and Nolan? And if they did, how did they find out?

"Come on, girl," Flo said good-naturedly. "All these years, and you thought nobody noticed? Jerry would come upstairs, say this or that to a couple of the girls, or Mike Morelli, then five minutes later off you'd go. I personally happen to think the whole thing was kind of exciting, though I could never figure what the two of you managed to get up to in ten minutes. What *were* the two of you doing, anyway?" Flo asked conspiratorially.

"Nothing!" Maggie snapped, feeling as if the whole building had suddenly tilted. "I never *dreamed* you had such a dirty mind. I certainly hope you haven't been spreading that absurd story all over the factory."

Hurt, Flo's head jerked back as if she'd been struck. "There's no need to get mean," she said quietly. "I was just making conversation."

"I don't happen to consider that kind of cheap talk conversation," Maggie said, stabbing out her cigarette. "And for your information, Nolan and I are just friends."

"So you're just friends. There's no need to take my head off."

"I don't appreciate gossip," Maggie said, and with her chin lifted she made her way back to her machine, feeling as if everyone in the staff room was looking at her.

"Bitch!" Flo said under her breath.

"What was *that* about?" Bets Theodopolus wanted to know.

"I was asking was she dating Nolan these days, instead of whatever it was the two of them got up to in his office," Flo said, her eyes still on Maggie, "and she took my head off."

"Why'd you go bringing that up?" Bets asked her.

"I figured after thirteen years we're friends, you know. My mistake," she said, wounded. "I won't go making that mistake again, I can tell you."

"No," Bets agreed sagely. "You don't want to go doing that. Her being next to Nolan like she is, it could cost you your job."

"Jesus!" Flo said. "I never even thought of that." Turning to look at Bets, she said, "She wouldn't. Would she?"

"You never can tell with her. Take my advice and forget it. Just be like always. You know how she is, blows hot and cold."

"I couldn't afford to lose this job, you know," Flo said. "Maybe I'll go patch things up."

Returning to her machine, Flo stopped beside Maggie. "I didn't mean for you to get upset you know, Maggie. I'm sorry if you took me the wrong way. I didn't mean no harm."

"Let's forget it," Maggie said, aligning triangles of fabric. "You made a mistake, that's all."

"Right. So no hard feelings. Okay?"

"That's fine," Maggie said, her knee trembling against the drive control as she made herself look up at Flo and smile. She wanted to grab Flo's hand, hold it down with the presser foot and run it under the needle.

Relieved, Flo smiled back, sat down, and got to work. Jesus! she thought. She was going to have to be very careful from now on what she said to that bitch.

Business was lousy at the diner that night, so Maggie clocked off early and walked home, still in a foul mood because of Flo and her stinking big mouth.

The girls hadn't come home yet, and after changing out of her uniform she couldn't seem to settle down. There was nothing on the radio she wanted to hear, and she didn't feel like reading the paper. She'd had too much coffee that day and didn't want anything to drink. She paced through the house for a time, then paused outside the girls' bedroom. If they'd left the room in a mess, she'd rip them limb from limb.

Anticipating a good excuse to give them a tongue lashing, she opened the door and reached inside to switch on the light. Neat as a pin. The bed made, not so much as a sock on the floor. Even the top of the desk, usually cluttered with Louise's magazines and papers, was clear. She stood in the middle of the room, annoyed at its atypical order. What were they up to? she wondered, looking around. She opened the closet door, expecting to find a mess, but their clothes were properly hung up, their shoes in a row on the floor. Sweaters and some old magazines on the shelf. She shut the door and went to the chest. The top two drawers were Faye's. Underwear, socks, more sweaters, and the blue Birk's box with the pearls. The sight of it made her jaws clench. The bottom two drawers were Louise's. Underwear, socks, sweaters. And under the sweaters, pushed to the back, a notebook.

It was a diary. Closing the drawer, she took the notebook to the kitchen and sat down at the table with a cigarette to read it. It started on the first day of school and was just a bunch of crap about teachers and girlfriends, notes about what she and her sister had done each day. Initials instead of names, French words. Only one reference to Maggie: "Ma out again tonight." That was on the third of November. Some indecipherable reference to "F and R in c. as usual." On the fourth, "Mrs. D. sleeping, sick again." And the last entry, "No p yet! 13$1/2$ already."

Disappointed, Maggie put the book back where she'd found it and was about to put the kettle on when the phone rang.

"What do you say to a meal Sunday with the girls?" Nolan asked cheerfully.

"You know we go to my mother's on Sunday."

"Okay, how about Saturday?"

"The girls have plans."

"You and me, then, Saturday, eh? We'll take in the show at the Casino. How does that sound?"

"That sounds fine, Jerry," she said, forcing a pleasant tone.

"Good, good. I suppose you're too tired for a visitor now."

Just the way his old high sign used to turn her body instantly receptive, any conversational suggestion pertaining to sex now had the same effect. "I'd better not," she said, looking down the hallway. "I don't know what time they'll be home."

"Fair enough," he said. "I'll see you Saturday then."

They exchanged goodbyes and she put the receiver down feeling trapped. Ever since that night she'd gone out for a drink with him he'd been acting as if he owned her, assuming they'd see each other regularly, expecting her to be available. And worst of all, she was obliged to talk to him. She couldn't simply go to his apartment and get into bed with him, then get dressed and go home again. No. He had to fix her a drink and invite her to sit in the living room while he put on some music, then came to sit beside her, wanting to talk. Or he wanted to take her to the Colonial to listen to that noise he called music, or to George's Spaghetti House to sit in practically pitch darkness listening to jazz and trying to figure out what the hell they'd put on the rigatoni. She wished she'd never agreed to meet him that night at the Silver Rail. She'd liked it a lot better when they were doing it at the factory. Just getting down to it without talking, just *doing* it.

Thinking of the factory reminded her of the run-in with Flo and sent her blood pressure skyrocketing. Was Flo just running off at the mouth, or did everyone in the whole goddamned place know about her and

Nolan? Christ! She hated the idea of having to go to work in the morning, more now than ever before. If only she'd listened to her mother and taken a secretarial course she'd have had some skills and been able to get a job somewhere else. A quarter to ten. Where the hell were those two? And what were they up to?

The phone rang and she thought if it was Nolan again she'd scream.

It was her mother.

"How come you're calling so late?" Maggie asked, reaching for her cigarettes.

"I've got some news, Marg, and I thought you'd be getting home about now," her mother said, sounding a bit breathless.

"What news?"

"I hope you're sitting down," Ellen Perry said.

"What?"

"I'm getting married," she laughed.

"You're getting married?" she said disbelievingly. "Who to?"

"My boss, Robert Wolford."

"Wait a minute," Maggie said. "You're getting married to that lawyer you work for, the one you've been dating for, what, five, six years?"

"That's right," Ellen said happily.

"What brought this on?"

"I don't think you're in a mood to talk about this now, Marg," her mother said less brightly. "I'll tell you all about it on Sunday. I just wanted you to be the first to know."

"What're you getting married for at your age? You'd think at over fifty you'd be glad to be out of that whole mess."

"Congratulations, Mother. I couldn't be happier for you, Mother. Thank you for your good wishes, Margaret. I'll see you and the girls on Sunday," she said coldly, and hung up.

"Jesus H. Christ!" Maggie said, staring at the telephone. "What next?"

CHAPTER

T H I R T E E N

"OH, WOW!" LOUISE YELPED, RUNNING OVER TO GIVE her grandmother a big hug. "That's terrific! Isn't that terrific, Faye?"

Faye also hurried to hug her grandmother. "It's wonderful," she said, suddenly very glad to know Gramma wasn't going to have to spend the rest of her life alone. Until this moment she hadn't known it concerned her, but she knew now that she'd never thought it was right that someone as peppy and attractive and kind as Gramma should live alone with no one to love her or look after her. "I'm so happy for you," she said tearfully, able to see and feel her grandmother's happiness.

The three of them turned to look at Maggie, who, as always, had seated herself on the sofa and was busy lighting a cigarette.

"Isn't it great, Ma?" Louise said somewhat spitefully, knowing precisely what her mother thought. Maggie had been ranting about nothing else for three days, shaking her head and saying she couldn't imagine what her mother thought she was doing, getting married at her age.

"It's great." Maggie flashed a quick, too-bright smile.

"You girls help me get the food on the table, then I'll tell you all about it," Ellen said, directing Faye and Louise out to the kitchen. "Bob and I want to take the two of you out to dinner next Friday night," she said, taking the roast from the oven. "Would you like to do that?"

"We'd love to!" Louise answered for both of them.

"Good. I think you'll like him."

"Do you love him, Gramma?" Faye asked, putting an arm around her grandmother's waist.

"Does he love you?" Louise asked, arranging the roasted potatoes in the serving bowl.

"We love each other," Ellen answered, touched. "You're so good-hearted, you two." Enigmatically, she said, "It must've skipped a generation." Then she shook her head and smiled. "Let's get this food on the table or your mother will think we're plotting some conspiracy against her.''

Once the platters had been passed and they each had a plateful of food, Ellen said, ''Obviously, my getting married means some things are going to change. Bob and I have rented a lovely apartment on Avenue Road, and I'll be selling this house.'' She looked around the dining room, then at Maggie, who appeared ready to object. ''The money from the sale will go into a trust fund for the girls, to pay for university if they want to go, or to get them started when they're out on their own.''

Louise clutched Faye's hand under the table, so excited she felt as if she might wet her pants, but frightened by the expression on their mother's face.

''Now, before you say one word, Marg,'' Ellen warned, holding up a hand to silence her, ''there are a few things I want to say to you. First of all, you're welcome to have any of the furniture you might want. Naturally, I'll be keeping my china and glass and the silver. But anything else you're free to take. Secondly, I can see you're ready to explode at the idea of the girls getting the money and not you.'' She gave her daughter a sad smile. ''I can read you like a book, Marg. I know you inside out. You're sitting there thinking, What about me? It's written all over you. Well, this isn't about you, my dear. This is about me, and about my being in a position now to offer Faye and Louise the same opportunities you had but didn't take.''

''What *opportunities?*'' Maggie asked hotly, appalled that her mother hadn't even offered to let her and the girls live in the house. No. She'd just gone ahead and done everything without even discussing it. And the idea that she'd give the money to Faye and Louise was so insane she could scarcely believe any of this was happening. As usual, she was getting the pointy end of the stick.

''If you hadn't made up your mind to leave school and marry John, you could have gone on to complete your education. But you were bound and determined to get married, so your father and I gave you a nice wedding. We paid for your honeymoon, and we paid the hospital bills when the girls were born, and afterward we also laid out the money for your surgery, you'll remember. That money could've gone toward your education, but instead it went for those things. That was your choice, Marg. Lulu and Faye have the right to make their own choices, and I'm in a position now to help them.''

"Now," she went on quickly, leaving no room for Maggie to voice her objections, "Bob's anxious to have you three at the wedding, which is just going to be a quick ceremony at city hall. He's a generous man, and he's prepared to accept my family as his own. He has two sons, by the way," she told the girls, "nineteen and twenty-one. Darling boys." She smiled. "They'll be here for the wedding and the party after. Anyway," she said, turning back to her daughter, "that's about it for the time being. If there's someone you'd like to bring along to the party, by all means bring him." She smiled at the girls, saying, "That means the two of you, too."

Faye at once thought of Raffie, then realized the only way she could invite him to come would be if she included Aldo. And that was out of the question, not only for Lou's sake but also for her own. Lately he'd been making Faye feel uncomfortable, staring at her breasts or trying to touch her every time he went past. She didn't hate him the way Lou did, but she wished he'd leave her alone.

"And who am I supposed to bring?" Maggie challenged, with the feeling that her mother was somehow mocking her.

"I don't know, Marg," Ellen said mildly. "A boyfriend, if you have one. Or else just a friend."

"You know perfectly well I'm not seeing anyone!"

"If you say so, dear."

"What's that supposed to mean?"

"Don't try to pick a fight," Ellen warned. "It's what you're angling after. It's what you always do when you can't have your own way. Don't spoil this, Marg," she said softly, and gazed steadily at Maggie for several long moments. Then, picking up her knife and fork, she turned to Faye and Louise saying, "One day this week I'd like you girls to meet me downtown after school and we'll go shopping. I want you both to have pretty new outfits for the wedding."

"Oh, fantastic!" Louise cried. "This is so exciting, I could just *die!* What's he like, Gramma? Where's the new apartment? What're you gonna wear? I want to know *everything.*"

Simmering, Maggie began sawing her roast beef into tiny pieces, listening to her mother gush sickeningly, like a teenager.

"Bob's a dream," Ellen said. "I know you'll be crazy about him."

"What does he look like?" Faye asked, her food forgotten. "Is he handsome?"

"He's tall, with brown hair just going gray at the temples."

"That's *sooo* sexy," Louise said.

"Yes, it is," Ellen agreed giddily. "He has lovely blue eyes and a glorious smile, and he's a brilliant lawyer."

"What happened to his wife?" Faye asked.

"She died, dear, years ago. He raised those two darling boys on his own with a housekeeper. Of course they're both grown now, and off at university. The younger one's at Western, in London, and the other's at McGill; very bright boys. We've been seeing one another for years, you know."

"You have?" Louise asked. "How come we've never met him?"

Ellen glanced over at Maggie, then said, "I don't really know why. I suppose I kept expecting him to meet someone else."

"But why would he want to meet someone else?" Faye asked.

"Well," Ellen said, coloring. "It's a little secret just between you and me."

"What?" Louise asked, moving closer.

"Naturally, Bob knows, but no one else does."

"What?" Louise asked, on the edge of her seat.

"I'm five years older than he is," Ellen whispered, knowing she'd just supplied her daughter with the ammunition for a major attack.

"That doesn't matter," Faye said with conviction, "not as long as you love each other."

"I swear to God I'm going to be sick," Maggie muttered, putting down her knife and fork.

"Oh, *shut up,* Margaret!" Ellen said, losing her temper. "Either be quiet or leave right now. I won't allow you to spoil this for me. If you can't keep a civil tongue in your head, go home and let the girls and me enjoy ourselves. And if you can't make an effort even to *pretend* to be happy for me, don't bother to come to my wedding."

Shocked, the girls waited to see what would happen.

"Why do I get the feeling you don't want me there?" Maggie asked suspiciously.

"Because Margaret," Ellen said quietly, "I *don't.* You'll do everything in your power to ruin it, and this time I'm not letting that happen. All your life your first thought in every situation has been for yourself. Your father let you get away with that, and I did, too, for far too long. But not this time. You're not going to make yourself the center of attention, and you're not going to put a damper on the occasion. I have a chance for a new life with someone I care for who happens to care for me, too. I'm very lucky to be getting a chance like this, and I want to treasure every moment of it with people who have the capacity to be happy with me. I don't think you're capable of being happy about *anything*. To tell you the truth, if you weren't my daughter, Margaret, I wouldn't spend ten minutes with you. I love you, but I truly do not like you. And I will never forgive you if you ruin my wedding. I love this man. When I was seventeen I thought I was in love with your father. I grew to care for him, and to respect him. But I didn't know a thing about real love. I've learned a lot about it, being your mother, and living alone all these years since your father died. Robert Wolford *loves* me. He thinks I'm special, and because of him, I *am* special. I won't let you poison the only genuine happiness I've ever known with your bitterness.''

"I don't have to sit here and take this!" Maggie stated, convinced her mother had lost her mind.

"No, you don't," Ellen agreed calmly. "It's your choice entirely."

"Come on!" Maggie barked at the girls, jumping to her feet. "We're going!"

"Don't you two move!" Ellen told Faye and Louise. "They're staying," she told Maggie. "They're the only people in this family who are sincerely happy for me, and I want them here. And don't you dare make their lives a misery once you get them home. Bad enough you haven't learned a *thing* from your mistakes, but I won't let you punish them because I've made decisions that don't include you. You are *not* the center of the universe. The sun does *not* rise and fall according to your whims. And Lulu and Faye are going to get a chance to see for themselves that all men are not bastards and that some of us consider ourselves very damned fortunate to find one who makes us happy."

Maggie slowly sat back down. Walking out now would be pointless.

"Once Bob and I are married, I'm going to be in a position to take a more active interest in the girls' lives," Ellen said, her eyes remaining fixed on her daughter's, "and I intend to do just that."

"Meaning what?" Maggie asked, a caustic edge to her voice.

"Meaning I won't be working, so I'll have more time to spend with Lulu and Faye. I'll be keeping an eye on them," she said, staring Maggie down. "I also intend to see that they get some decent clothes and new winter coats. I'm tired of seeing them look like a pair of refugees. They're beautiful girls and I want them going out in the world dressed to show that someone cares about them.''

"Where on Avenue Road is the new apartment, Gramma?'' Louise asked, hoping to redirect the conversation and avoid a big fight.

"Just below Davenport, in that lovely new building on the east side,'' Ellen answered. "We're on the twelfth floor facing west, with a wonderful view. You can see Casa Loma from the balcony. And we've got three bedrooms, in case you girls or his boys want to stay over.'' Aglow again with excitement, she said, "We've ordered furniture from the Art Shoppe, and gorgeous deep-gray broadloom, with pearl gray drapes. Everything's being painted white, and we've chosen burgundy as an accent color. I can't wait for you to see it. Bob has wonderful taste. We agreed we'd only keep small personal things, and buy everything new together, to start fresh.''

"It sounds so nice,'' Faye said, picturing the apartment.

"When's the wedding?'' Louise asked.

"December fifth, in the afternoon.''

"Wow! That's in two weeks. We'd better hurry up if we're going to get new outfits,'' she said to Faye. "What about tomorrow after school?''

"Tomorrow's okay with me,'' Faye said, looking at her grandmother. "Is it okay with you?''

"Perfect. I'll leave early and meet you at the Yonge and Queen entrance to Simpsons at four.''

"By the Elizabeth Arden counter, right?'' Louise said, knowing how much her grandmother loved Blue Grass cologne.

"Right,'' Ellen confirmed.

"This is so exciting,'' Louise bubbled. "What're you gonna wear to get married, Gramma?''

"I thought the two of you could help me pick something.'' She smiled at the girls.

"Really?'' Faye said.

"Really. And now we'd better eat before this goes stone cold,'' Ellen said, casting a quick glance at Maggie, who looked exactly as she had at the age of eleven when Ellen told her in no uncertain terms that she could not go to the expensive private school she'd made up her mind to attend because she admired the uniforms. She'd sat, sulking and resentful, with her arms crossed, glaring at her mother with hate-filled eyes, just the way she was glaring at her now. "I hope you're going to eat that, Marg," she said lightly. "You're looking a bit on the thin side these days."

Unable to fix on any one of the too-many thoughts colliding like bumper cars inside her head, Maggie looked down at her plate and began eating mechanically. What was that crap about keeping an eye on the girls? And that snide reference to bringing someone to the wedding? Did her mother know about Nolan too? Why was everyone ganging up on her all of a sudden?

Faye got a sheath dress in a blue so dark it was almost black. It had long sleeves and a big white collar and was very flattering to her figure and to her fair hair and complexion. Gramma said, "It's time you got your first pair of high heels and some nylons." And while they were in the lingerie department she bought both girls slips, lacy garter belts, silky underpants, and several pairs of nylons each.

Louise's dress was black with fine white stripes. It had puffy sleeves, a sweetheart neckline, and a full circle skirt with a crinoline. Gramma picked out a pair of black patent leather shoes cut low in front and with little Empire heels. It was the most wonderful outfit Louise had ever owned, and she couldn't wait to wear it.

After due deliberation, they agreed Ellen should buy an off-white shantung silk suit. It had a slim skirt with a kick pleat in the back and a round-necked collarless jacket worn over a matching off-white silk blouse with tiny round pearl buttons down the front. Because it was winter, she decided to buy black suede high-heeled pumps rather than the beige leather pair that were her first choice.

Faye picked out a double-breasted camel-hair coat, and Louise opted for a navy swing coat with full, cuffed sleeves. Having completed their shopping, Ellen dropped them off at Manning Avenue in a taxi. Before the girls climbed out of the car, she said, "No matter what your mother says, smile and ignore it. Don't let her spoil the fun we're having. Bob and I will pick you up Friday at six-thirty. I know you'll like him."

"Thanks for everything, Gramma," Louise said, giving her grandmother a kiss. Then she got out and waited on the sidewalk for her sister.

"It's like a dream," Faye said. "I'm so glad you're going to have someone to be with. Really," she said, getting choked up. "You deserve someone nice to care about you."

Ellen put her arms around her and held her tightly, then released her, saying, "Try not to care quite so much, Faye. Sometimes you've got to hold a little back for yourself."

"I don't understand."

"Come on, Faye," Louise said, bending down to see what was taking her so long.

"Just a minute, Lulu," Ellen said, then turned back to Faye. "There are times when you have to take things on faith, dear heart. No amount of your caring will change anything. I'll be all right, and so will your sister. Even your mother, in her own dismal fashion, will get along. Don't worry so much about the rest of us, Faye. The people who love you know how much you care."

"It's just that I want everyone to be happy," Faye said.

"I know that, and I love you for it. You're a girl after my own heart. You run along now. And remember, pretend you don't hear her when she starts in on the two of you."

"Okay, Gramma. Thank you for everything."

"You're more than welcome. I'll see you Friday."

The girls waved as the taxi drove off up the street. When the car was out of sight, they ran up the porch steps and let themselves in.

The first thing Maggie said was, "It's about bloody time! I hope you've eaten, because I certainly wasn't about to sit around waiting for the two of you to decide to come home." Eyeing their shopping bags she said, "It must be nice . . ." and started for her bedroom. "I'm going out. Make sure you get your homework done. And you'd better not leave a mess in the kitchen for me to clean up."

"Where are you going?" Louise asked politely.

"I'm meeting someone for a drink, if you must know."

"Oh, yeah?" Louise said interestedly. "Who?"

"None of your goddamned business!"

"That's nice," Louise muttered, following Faye into their bedroom. Closing the door, she whispered, "You think she's got a *date?*"

Faye shrugged, carefully placing her new dress on a hanger. "Who knows? She's probably trying to make it sound important so we'll think we're missing out on something."

"What were you and Gramma talking about for so long?" Louise asked, opening the lid to admire her fabulous new shoes. Actual heels instead of flats. "These are *so* sharp. Wait till I show Lucy and Carolyn! They'll *die!*"

"Nothing special," Faye answered, laying her new coat on the bed and standing back to admire it. "I can't wait for Raffie to see this," she said softly. "I wish he could come to the party."

"Gramma said you could bring someone."

Faye shook her head. "We'd have to invite Aldo too."

"*Yarrghhh!*" Louise exclaimed. "I'd rather put my wet finger in a socket than go anywhere with that *moron!*"

"Me, too," Faye agreed, gazing at the coat. "Are you going to invite one of your friends?"

Louise thought for a moment, then said, "Not if you're not."

"No, that's okay, Lou. You should if you want to."

"Uh-uh. Let's just keep it the two of us. Besides, Gramma says Bob's two sons are dee-vine. Maybe the younger one will fall madly in love with me and I'll have to break his heart and tell him he's too old for me."

Faye laughed. "Yeah. Well, I wouldn't get too worked up about that, if I were you. He's nineteen, for Pete's sake. He'll probably think we're both children."

"I happen to be very mature for my age," Louise said. "Especially in these shoes."

"Right. Let's put everything away and get something to eat. I'm starving."

"Hey!" Louise said. "Ma's going out. You got any money? We could go over to Pickup's and get some fish and chips. I'd *die* for fish and chips right now."

"Why was she making such a big deal about us doing our homework?" Faye said, looking over at the door. "Since when does she care?"

"Have you *got* any *money?*" Louise repeated. "I *need* fish and chips."

"I don't know," Faye said, still looking at the door. "I've got about thirty-five cents."

"Great! I've got twenty. Soon as she leaves, let's run down. Okay?"

"Sure, okay. Something's going on," Faye said, her brows drawing together. "I just know it."

"You heard what Gramma said. She's only trying to spoil it for everybody."

"I know, but she's up to something. I can *feel* it."

"Are you going to wear your new coat to school, or save it for good?"

"I haven't decided yet," Faye answered, puzzling over what Ma was up to.

"Well, I'm wearing mine!" Louise declared, holding the coat to herself and whirling around in a circle. "We're going to get new clothes! I could *die!*"

"Sshhh! She's on the phone," Faye said, her ear to the door.

"What?" Louise asked in a whisper, coming to stand next to her, trying to hear what their mother was saying.

"Damn! I didn't hear." Faye crossed the room and sat down on the side of the bed. In a hushed voice, she said, "I think she's been going out with some man. And I think he's been here."

"How come?"

"Last week, you know that night you went over to Irene's and I met Raffie at the skating rink near Dundas? I got home before you, remember?"

"Yeah. So?"

"Ma was in her bathrobe, and it was only nine-thirty."

"So what?"

"When did you ever see her walk around here in her bathrobe at nine-thirty? Never, that's when. And you know what else?"

"What?"

"She was just coming out of her room when I got home. And she tried to shut her door real fast, but I looked in, and her bed was messed up."

"So she took a nap," Louise said.

Faye gave her a look. "When did she ever take naps?"

Louise put a hand over her mouth, her eyes opening very wide.

"Right," Faye said. "She had somebody over, and the two of them were in her bedroom."

"Holy shit!" Louise said.

"You wait and see," Faye said. "Something's gonna happen. I can feel it in my bones."

CHAPTER

F O U R T E E N

MAGGIE WAS WORKING THAT FRIDAY NIGHT. THE GIRLS rushed home from school, taking the streetcar for a change, to save time. They knew they'd have the place to themselves and could get ready for the evening without any interference from their mother.

First they decided what to wear. Faye settled for her plain gray skirt, the yellow angora sweater Gramma had given her the previous Christmas, her new black high heels, and Gramma's pearls. Louise would wear Faye's old best dress, the dark red one with the long sleeves and full skirt, and her new patent leather shoes with the Empire heels.

They made each other up—a little rouge, some powder, and pale pink lipstick—then did each other's hair. Faye wore hers up in a bun, and Louise wore hers down, center parted with her favorite gold barrettes holding the hair back from her face.

After a careful inspection, they agreed they looked good. Then, new coats at the ready, thankful it hadn't snowed again so they didn't have to wear their clunky boots, they sat in the living room to wait.

"You look so grown up," Louise said, admiring her sister sitting in the armchair with her legs crossed. "Honest to God, you really do. The heels are fantastic."

"I'm not used to walking in them yet," Faye said, lifting her crossed leg to look at her foot. "But I love them. Don't you?"

"Yeah." Louise looked down at her own feet planted firmly on the floor, ankles together. "You're sure I don't look ten years old?"

"You look really sweet," Faye said critically. "That dress suits you better than it did me."

"I can't *wait* to see what he looks like." Louise turned and sat on her knees to look out the window. "Gramma's getting married," she said softly, awed. "It's like a fairy tale. D'you think he's rich?"

"That's not important."

"I know, but d'you think he is?"

"I don't know, Lou. How would I know a thing like that?"

"What time is it?"

"Twenty-five past."

Louise continued to gaze out the window, scanning the street. "Do you realize," she said over her shoulder, "that you're going to be *fifteen* next month? Another year and you'll be sixteen. I can't *wait* to be sixteen. Then you're an *adult.*"

"You're not legally an adult until you're eighteen. Or maybe it's twenty-one."

"Bob's a lawyer. He'll know. I'll ask him." Turning back to the window, she saw a car pulling up to the curb. "Oh holy cow!" she cried, jumping off the sofa. "They're here! Quick, get your coat!"

When the bell rang, Louise raced to the door expecting to see her grandmother. But standing on the front porch was an unbelievably attractive man in a black overcoat with a velvet collar who smiled and said, "You must be Louise," and held out his hand. "I'm Bob Wolford." Enclosing her hand in his, he said, "I'm delighted to meet you." His eyes lifting, he said, "And you're Faye." He shook her hand too, then stepped aside extending his arm. "Your grandmother's waiting in the car, if you girls are ready."

The car was a gleaming black Cadillac, and Louise skipped down the front steps, gratified to know that Gramma was marrying a man who was not only handsome, but rich too.

The girls climbed into the back of the car and their grandmother turned to smile at them as Bob slid behind the wheel. "You both look lovely," she said.

"So do you, Gramma," Louise said. It was true. She'd never seen her grandmother look the way she did now—radiating happiness and contentment. With a jolt, she realized that her grandmother was beautiful. She looked like Ma, but without the suspicion that always kept Ma's eyes slightly narrowed, and without the anger that was in the set of Ma's mouth. Gramma looked the way Ma would've looked if she'd ever been happy.

Settling back for the ride, Louise could tell Faye was seeing it, too. The funny thing was that with her hair up, and in the half-light of the back of the luxurious car, Louise could see how strongly Faye resembled Ma. And Gramma and Faye looked somehow like the same person. For a few moments Louise couldn't stop staring at the two of them. Her eyes going back and forth between them as the silent Cadillac slid almost magically along the street, Louise had the oddest feeling that Gramma and Faye *were* the same person. Like in some incredible science fiction movie, the two women seemed to be separate images, one older, one younger, of the same person.

"What're you staring at?" Faye asked in a whisper, touching a hand to the back of her head. "Is my hair coming down?"

Reaching out, not even knowing she was going to say it, she gave Faye's hand a squeeze and said, "I love you, Faye."

Her expression of concern disappearing, Faye grinned—she didn't even keep her lips closed the way she usually did to hide her crooked tooth—and whispered, "I love you, too."

✦

They went to the Royal York. The uniformed doorman came hurrying over, touching two fingers to his hat as he said, "Good evening, Mr. Wolford," and rushed around the car to open the door for Gramma, offering his hand to assist her out. Then he opened the back door, again offering his gloved hand first to Faye and then to Louise.

Bob accepted a ticket from the man, slipped it into his pocket, then took Gramma's arm, and the four of them went inside and up the short flight of stairs and along the thickly carpeted corridor leading to the vast lobby that rose three storys and had two mezzanines. They proceeded through the lobby and up three more steps to a checkroom where they surrendered their coats to a smiling woman who gave Bob another ticket.

"All set?" Bob asked the girls, then turned to look at Ellen, saying, "Three lovely women. I'm a lucky fellow."

Their grandmother was wearing a dress neither of the girls had seen before. It was of black crepe, form-fitting and low-cut, and showed off her small waist and what Louise considered to be a very good chest, rounded and creamy-looking but not too big. She had her hair up in a French twist, and smelled as ever of Blue Grass. As the two girls went with Bob and their grandmother through the doorway into the Imperial Room, Louise felt buoyant with excitement and expectation, and was suffused with pride as the man at the door broke into a wide smile and shook Bob's hand, saying, "Ah, Mr. Wolford, good evening." He smiled at Gramma too, saying, "Good to see you again, madame." Then to Bob, "I have a very good table for you tonight," and led the way down the wide steps into a big room with lots of tables on two levels and an orchestra playing up on the stage, taking them to a table right in the middle at the very front of the dance floor.

Faye couldn't shake the sensation that she was dreaming, even as a waiter handed them each large menus then stood by, waiting to know what everyone would have to drink. Bob put his menu down on the table and rested one hand on top of it as he turned to Ellen to ask what she'd like. Then he asked the girls.

Louise said, "You order for me," and Faye, impressed by her cleverness, at once said, "I'd like that, too."

"Since it's a special occasion," Bob told the waiter, "we'll have a bottle of Piper Heidsick with dinner. And for now, rye and ginger ale for the lady." He smiled at Ellen. "I'll have a very dry martini, and two extra special Shirley Temples for the young ladies."

"Very good, sir," the waiter said, and went off.

Louise was dancing in her seat to the music of the orchestra, looking around at the people at nearby tables. Faye's eyes returned to her grandmother who was, Faye could tell, holding hands under the table with this man who was going to marry her. It was miraculous, thrilling: the two of them gazing at each other with such evident caring, the dim, flattering light, the live music, the people all around dressed in evening clothes, the laughter, the clink and tinkle of glasses and cutlery touching china. Bob and her grandmother said something Faye didn't catch and got up to dance. Faye touched the tips of her fingers to the base of her throat, letting them rest in the little dip between the bones there, touching the place where there was a small ache of appreciation and longing and something else that was nameless but deeply significant. She watched the way her grandmother went into this man's arms, saw how he held her, bending his head so he could hear what she was saying; she noted the fit of their bodies and the way they moved together as if they'd come together in just this way hundreds of times before; she saw them as one entity and suddenly with all her heart wanted precisely that for herself. She wanted it so utterly and was at the same time so overwhelmingly glad that it belonged to her grandmother that she simply couldn't contain the emotion. It filled her and overflowed.

Louise touched her arm, stricken. "Faye, what's the matter? What's wrong?"

Faye could only shake her head and try to smile for her sister, lacking the words and the ability to say what all this meant to her. With a sudden crying laugh, she said, "I'm okay." Her eyes returned to the pair on the dance floor while she blotted her face with her napkin. "I'm just so happy for Gramma, that's all."

"Yeah," Louise agreed soberly. "Me, too. Isn't he *nice?*"

"Yes, he is," Faye said, with another crying laugh, then cried even harder.

Laughing now, Louise stroked her hand up and down her sister's arm. "His nails are *manicured*. Did you see?" Faye nodded, holding the napkin to her cheek. "And he's so *distinguished*. Gramma looks *fabulous*. This is the best time I've ever *had!*"

Louise was so emphatic that Faye had to laugh, the tears ending as abruptly as they'd begun. "You're so funny," she told Louise fondly.

"Well, he *is,* and she *does,*" Louise insisted, looking at the orchestra bathed in pink light, and then at her grandmother and Bob gliding smoothly around the floor. She leaned on her elbow and sighed. "It's *so* romantic. Do you and Raffie dance?"

"We danced at the sock hop, remember?"

"Oh, right." Louise looked at her sister. "That was the *worst* time I've ever had. I don't even know why I went. Not one single person asked me to dance."

"They will, Lou. Give it time."

"And I'm probably the best dancer in the entire school too. None of the girls can jive as well as me. Bob's a really good dancer, isn't he? So's Gramma. Aren't you just *dying* to see their new apartment?"

"Uh-huh."

"I *love* this place!" she declared, looking around. "When I start dating, I'm gonna come here with my boyfriends."

"I think it's probably too expensive."

"So I'll get a rich boyfriend."

Faye laughed.

Nolan showed up at the coffee shop and took a table for two at her station.

"What're you doing here?" Maggie asked, getting the pencil from behind her ear and holding it poised over her order pad as she looked sidelong at the owner, who was busy at the cash register. "You want to get me fired?"

"Take it easy," Nolan said with a smile. "I came in to get a bite to eat."

"This is hardly your neighborhood hangout."

He opened the menu and scanned the handwritten sheet of specials. "Combining business with pleasure," he said. "How's the meat loaf?"

"Like sawdust."

"Fair enough. How's the liver?"

"Like shoe leather."

"Well, then," he looked up at her. "What do you recommend?"

"Another restaurant."

He laughed. "Hamburgers any good?"

"They're real meat at least."

"Fine. I'll have a deluxe burger and coffee." He closed the menu and slid it back into place behind the condiments. "Not too busy," he said, getting out his cigarettes and lighter.

"Not too," she agreed, tearing his order from the pad and walking away.

He lit his cigarette and sat back to have a look at the *Star,* asking himself for at least the thousandth time why he bothered with this woman. It was the challenge, he supposed. Underneath the toughness, he was convinced there was a woman who, if he could ever dig her out, actually liked him despite the evidence to the contrary. How ironic! he thought. Here he'd been married to Nora all those years and he'd known the how and why of her better than he'd ever known her body. Nora was a physically cold woman who found sex about as appetizing as coming upon someone else's bowel movement in a public washroom. And Mag was a sexually torrid woman whose body and preferences he knew as well as his own, but whose mind remained an utter mystery to him.

As she went by with plates of food for a couple at the far end of the restaurant, he watched her hips move under the white uniform and admired her legs. He'd always had a weakness for fair-haired women with shapely bodies and well-turned ankles. Nora was fair but rather on the thin side. They'd met and married in a rush because he'd already enlisted and expected to be sent overseas at any time. They'd made love for the first time on their wedding night, and thereafter she treated their sexual encounters like a messy but necessary indignity she was bound by the laws of church and state to tolerate. They'd been married two months when he was shipped out. Slightly over two years later, having stopped a piece of shrapnel with his knee, he was discharged from active service. Nora was as repelled by lovemaking upon his return as she'd been before. Disillusioned, when he'd recovered sufficient mobility he went back to work, and only a few months into the job he'd taken up with Maggie. She'd come down to his office to discuss a discrepancy in her overtime pay, and not five minutes later they had the door locked and were making love on the floor. Her sexual accessibility not only provided a tremendous release, it also took much of the tension out of his marriage. Ironically, he liked Nora far more than he did Maggie. Nora was fiercely intelligent, independent, and ambitious. When they parted she was head nurse at St. Peter's hospital and a thoroughly lapsed Catholic.

"You can't see small children die," she'd said, "and believe in an all-seeing Father. No truly benevolent god would take those lives so cruelly, leaving behind such devastation. I can't accept that."

It didn't shock or surprise him. He'd been losing his own faith in slow degrees since graduating from St. Michael's College and going out on his own, away from his mother's and the teaching brothers' powerful influence. Nora was so thoughtful and articulate, such a caring person, that he was actually grateful to Maggie for providing an outlet that relieved his wife of all but a minimal percentage of his sexual attention.

He justified their arrangement with the thought that it had preserved his marriage. He guessed, correctly, that a fair number of the staff knew of or suspected their involvement. But there'd never been any rumors or comments, because unlike Maggie, who was generally disliked, he was very well liked. He respected the people in his employ, seeing them as diligent, responsible men and women who believed in an honest day's work for a decent rate of pay. There was an abiding mutual respect between him and the staff.

Now, of course, he no longer felt any guilt regarding his affair with Mag, but the ongoing effort he put into pursuing her was beginning to wear him down. When he stopped to think about it, it seemed to be a feckless notion on his part to be actively wooing a woman he liked less with each passing day. He was daily getting closer to the point where he knew he'd throw in the towel.

Maggie slid a plate down in front of him. Then, to his surprise, she sat down and with a smile helped herself to one of his cigarettes. "I'm taking a break," she explained.

"Well, now, this is pleasant," he smiled back at her.

Holding his lighter to her cigarette, she looked at him. One thing she had to admit, he was a damned good-looking man.

"My mother's getting married," she told him.

"Isn't that great!" he said. "Is she elderly, your mother?"

Maggie emitted a bark of laughter. "My mother's fifty-one."

"That's very young." He picked up his knife and carefully cut the hamburger in half. "The women in your family marry young."

"You can say that again. She was seventeen. So was I."

"You expect your girls to follow that tradition?" he asked innocently, biting into the hamburger.

"Not if they know what's good for them," she said sharply.

"So," he said, "when's the big event?"

"December fifth."

"And you'd like the day off, I take it."

"As a matter of fact I would." She hesitated, and for a moment seemed most unlike her usual tightly guarded self.

"Well, of course," he said, and popped a chip into his mouth. "That's not a problem."

"I was wondering," she said, "if you'd like to go with me."

"To the wedding?" he asked, flabbergasted.

"And the party after," she added.

"You're asking me to come with you to your mother's wedding, and to the festivities following?" He put down the hamburger and wiped his hands on a paper napkin he pulled from the dispenser.

"That's right."

"Why?" he asked, trying to see if this heralded a new direction to their affair.

"Don't give me the third degree here, Jerry!" she snapped. "Do you want to come or not?"

"I'd be honored," he said. "Are you quite sure you want to spring me on your family this way?"

"Quite sure," she said decisively, thinking she'd show her mother a thing or two. Making cracks about bringing a friend. *If* she had a boyfriend. She could hardly wait to see her mother's face when she showed up at the wedding with Nolan.

There was a floor show after dinner. A woman came on and stood in the spotlight and sang for over half an hour. Everyone applauded, and then the orchestra went back to playing dance music.

Faye felt her ears go hot when Bob said, "Would you like to dance, Faye?"

Gramma smiled and said, "Go on, dear. Bob's a wonderful dancer."

"Go on, Faye," Louise urged, giving her a nudge.

Faye obediently got up and went to dance with the man her grandmother was going to marry. His hand was warm and very smooth, and he did dance beautifully. He made her feel graceful.

"Are you having a good time?" he asked.

"It's wonderful," she said, looking up at him. He did, as Gramma had said, have a glorious smile. "I'm very happy for the two of you."

"That's kind of you, Faye," he said, gazing directly into her eyes. "It's taken me a long time to talk her into it. Your grandmother can be very stubborn, you know."

"Can she?"

"Yes, she can. I've been trying to get her to marry me for a good four years now. I was beginning to think she'd never agree."

"But she did," Faye smiled.

"Yes, she did. And I want you to know that once we're settled, you and your sister will always be welcome in our home."

"Thank you," she said shyly. "That's very nice."

"I mean it," he said. "I know you girls haven't had an easy time of it. And if you ever need help of any kind, I want you to feel free to come to me."

His saying this brought the ache back to her throat. She nodded. He gave her hand an encouraging little squeeze, and turned her so that she was facing the table and could see her sister and grandmother watching. Louise rolled her eyes, clasped her hands together and laid her cheek against the back of her right hand, gesturing how romantic she thought this was. Faye laughed. Bob looked over, caught Louise mid-gesture, and laughed, too. "She's a delight, your sister."

"Yes, she is," Faye agreed.

The girls were having dessert and Gramma and Bob were drinking cognac when the orchestra swung into an up-tempo number. Louise was tapping her feet under the table and dancing in her seat as she finished the most fantastic chocolate cake she'd ever tasted. Someone touched her on the shoulder and she looked up to see a boy standing there. "Would you care to dance?" he asked.

Not sure of the protocol, she looked over at her grandmother, who grinned and said, "Go on, Lulu."

"Okay," she said. "Sure. I'd love it." The boy, who looked at least sixteen, actually took her hand as they walked onto the dance floor.

"What's your name?" he asked, taking hold of her other hand and getting into position to jive.

"Louise. What's yours?"

"Philip," he said. "Philip Townsend-Post."

"What's Townsend, your middle name?"

"Double-barreled surname, actually," he said apologetically.

"You're English, aren't you?"

"That's right. We're visiting from London, staying in the hotel."

"That's great!" she laughed as they swung into the dance, and he expertly turned her out, then spun her back. "You're a terrific dancer!" she told him happily. "How long're you staying in Toronto?"

"We leave in the morning for New York."

"That's too bad."

"It is rather, isn't it? You're a super dancer. How old are you? If you don't mind my asking."

"I don't mind. I'm thirteen and a half. What about you?"

"I'll be sixteen February twenty-eighth. Or, if you prefer, I'll be four, given that I only have a birthday every four years."

She laughed, and he gave her a closed-mouth smile just like Faye's. "Do you have a chipped front tooth?" she asked.

In answer, he pulled his lips back to reveal twin rows of braces. "They're hideous," he told her. "And frightfully uncomfortable. But my mother insisted."

"They don't look so bad," she said charitably, as with their hands joined they both twisted in and out, then in again.

"You're very kind."

"I love your accent," she said.

They stopped talking to concentrate on their dancing. He had great moves she'd never done before, and he spun her about six times in a row so that her dress went way out in a big circle. When the number finished, Louise clapped spontaneously, turning to grin at the orchestra before looking back at her new friend.

The next number was a slow one and Philip said, "I'm afraid I'm not terribly good at slow dances," and took her hand again to lead her off the floor. "May I introduce you to my family?" he asked.

"Sure," she replied, and went with him to a table in the middle of the room where his parents and a girl about her own age were sitting.

"Mother, father, Rachel, I'd like you to meet Louise. Oh, sorry," he said. "Afraid I didn't ask your surname."

"Parker," Louise said. "Hi. It's nice to meet you. Philip's a terrific dancer."

"I taught him," Rachel said. "He was hopeless before that. That's ever such a pretty dress."

Louise looked down at herself and said, "Thank you."

"Do you live here, Louise?" Philip's mother asked.

"Yes, I do. It's a shame you're leaving tomorrow."

"We've enjoyed our stay here very much," Philip's father said. "Would you care to join us?"

"I'd better not. But thank you anyway. I really should get back. Nice to meet you," Louise said, and turned to go, realizing she'd been holding Philip's hand the whole time.

"I'll see you back to your table," he said, coming along with her. "And perhaps if they play another fast number, we'll have another dance."

"I'd love it." Inspired by his display of courtesy, she said, "Would you like me to introduce you?"

"If you like."

"Sure," she said. "This is my grandmother, Mrs. Perry. Except she's getting married so she'll have a new name. And this is my sister, Faye. And this is Mr. Wolford, who's going to marry my grandmother."

Bob Wolford rose to shake hands, saying, "Good to meet you. The two of you danced up a storm there."

"Thank you, sir."

"Sit down, Philip," Bob invited, reseating himself.

"I'd best return to my table," he said politely. "Thank you for the dance, Louise." He at last released her hand and headed back across the room.

"Isn't he *nice?*" Louise said. "And don't you *love* his accent? He introduced me to his parents and his sister. They're really nice, too. I'm having the best time of my entire life!"

Ellen laughed and reached over to pinch Louise's cheek. "You're adorable, Lulu."

Louise took hold of her grandmother's hand and planted a kiss on the back of it. *"You're* adorable!" she declared. And they all laughed.

The rest of the numbers were slow dances. Louise looked over to wave at Philip from time to time, then sat back and watched everyone dancing.

As they were getting up to leave, Philip came over to say, "I've brought you my father's card. If you ever come to London, please do ring me and I'll take you dancing."

Louise accepted the card, saying, "Wow! Thank you. It was really great meeting you and I hope you have a terrific time in New York."

"I very much enjoyed meeting all of you," he said. "Perhaps we'll see one another in London sometime," he told Louise. "I'm away at boarding school during term but if you come in the summer I'll be at home."

"You go to boarding school?" Louise asked, impressed.

"Afraid so. Well, goodnight everyone." He shook hands again with Bob, made a little bow to Ellen and Faye, then started back to his table.

"Quite a fellow," Bob said as they climbed the stairs and made their way out to the checkroom.

"I liked him," Louise said quietly, running her fingers over the embossed lettering on the card. "Too bad he's leaving."

Bob helped them on with their coats. And impulsively, as they were walking through the lobby, Louise looped her arm through his, saying, "I'm so glad we're going to have you in the family." Leaning around in front of him to address her grandmother, she said, "Gramma, you should've married him *ages* ago!"

*C*HAPTER

FIFTEEN

B<small>OB'S SONS WERE TO PICK UP MAGGIE AND THE GIRLS AND</small>
take them to city hall, where they'd meet up with Bob and Gramma. Faye
and Louise were looking forward not only to meeting the boys but also to
the ceremony itself, as well as to the party being given by Bob's sister at
her house in Rosedale.

Since the wedding was scheduled for four o'clock, Maggie insisted that
the girls go to school in the morning. Louise grumbled about it all the way
there. "We'll still have hours to get ready," Faye said reasonably. "Bob's
sons aren't picking us up until three-twenty."

"Yeah, but *she* gets the whole day to get ready. It's not fair."

"Forget it, Lou. Don't let her wreck it for you."

"That's what she's trying to do, isn't it?" Louise said as they headed
for their lockers. "You're right," she decided. "The heck with her."

When they got home at twelve-twenty, Maggie was in her bedroom.
Faye went to take her bath first, promising to make it fast. Louise laid out
her new things on the bed, and spent several minutes admiring her dress
before getting into her bathrobe. Then she went to the kitchen to make a
couple of bologna sandwiches. She sat at the table and looked out the back
window while she ate. It was a sunny, quite mild day, but she had a hunch
it was going to snow. She could always smell it when there was snow in
the air, and she was hardly ever wrong. She didn't care, as long as it
didn't start snowing until after they left the house, because by then it
would be too late for Ma to force them to wear boots.

She tried to imagine what her grandmother was doing at that moment,
and pictured her having a cup of tea and one of her Sweet Caps in the
kitchen before she went upstairs to get ready. She was probably excited,
with her stomach doing little jumps, the way Louise's was.

"Your turn," Faye said, coming into the kitchen. "Whose sandwich is
this?"

"Yours. I made it for you." Louise put her glass in the sink.

"Thanks, Lou. Will you help me do my hair after?"

"If you do my makeup."

"Deal."

Louise inspected herself in the mirror while the tub was filling. Nothing yet. She still had the chest of an eight-year-old, no waist, no hips. Pathetic. Pinning up her hair to keep it dry, she posed, pouting, turning this way and that. Truly pathetic. With a groan, she turned away from the mirror. Everybody in the entire world had a chest but her. In five months and seven days she'd be fourteen years old. Maybe she'd become a medical phenomenon, the only girl never to get her period.

When they emerged from their bedroom at five past three, Ma was pacing back and forth in the living room with a cigarette. Both girls stopped dead in the doorway, gaping.

Maggie turned, saw the girls, zeroed in on Faye, and was positively assaulted by the sight of her.

Louise felt a sudden clutching in her chest, watching her mother's face. She looked at her sister, then back at Ma, and could see Ma was startled by how pretty and grown-up Faye looked. And she could tell from the slight shift in Ma's features that she was going to try to make Faye feel bad, because for some reason Louise couldn't begin to guess Ma didn't like it that Faye looked so good. Desperate to stop it from happening, she said, "Wow, Ma! Where'd you get the *dress?*"

No good. Ma didn't even hear her; she was pointing at Faye with the two fingers holding her cigarette, saying, "You're not going anywhere looking like that!"

Faye felt as if someone had pushed her in the chest. Her mouth opened, but nothing came out.

"What's wrong with the way she looks?" Louise asked. "She looks sensational."

Still no good. It was as if Ma had gone deaf.

"You get in the bathroom and clean that crap off your face!" Maggie demanded.

"What crap?" Louise asked, affronted, knowing Ma was only mad because Faye looked so terrific. "She doesn't have any crap on her face."

"You shut up!" Maggie said, still pointing with the cigarette at Faye. "Did you hear what I told you?"

Faye seemed ready to cry. Maggie felt better, but she was nowhere near finished. No one was going out of this house looking better than she did. Faye's appearance was like a physical attack, an assault on her pride. "Go on!" she ordered.

"There's nothing wrong with the way she looks!" Louise insisted, as Faye's shoulders slumped and she turned to go. "Leave her alone!"

"It's okay, Lou," Faye got out, moving toward the bathroom.

"She looks *fine!*" Louise said loudly, ready to start screaming over the unfairness of what was happening.

Then the doorbell rang. "Too late!" Louise crowed, running to open the door. Instead of Bob's sons, there stood Mr. Nolan, from the factory. "Hi, Mr. Nolan," Louise said. "Boy, is this ever a surprise!"

"Hi, Louise. Don't you look splendid!"

"I know," she said, patting her full skirt with both hands. "Isn't it terrific? Did you come to see Ma?"

"Don't be stupid!" Ma said from behind her, pulling on her coat. "Who the hell else would he be coming to see?"

"But what're you doing?" Louise asked, confused. "Where're you going?"

"Jerry's taking me. We'll meet you there."

"How come?" Louise wanted to know as Maggie elbowed her aside, telling Nolan, "I'm ready."

"What about us?" Louise asked, mystified.

"You'll go with the boys when they get here," Maggie said.

Mr. Nolan gave Louise a confused, apologetic half-smile before turning to follow Maggie down the porch steps. Louise slowly closed the door, saying, "What's going on? Since when has she been going out with Mr. Nolan?" Then, clapping her hand over her mouth, she turned to look wide-eyed at her sister. "D'you think he's the *one?*"

"It wouldn't surprise me. Get your coat, Lou," Faye said. "They'll be here any minute."

"But what's going *on?*"

"Gramma was right," Faye said hoarsely, convinced she was ugly and looked terrible in the new dress. Maybe she should've worn her hair down instead of letting Louise put it up in a bun. "She's going to try to spoil it."

"With Mr. Nolan? How would that spoil anything? He's really nice," she said, accepting her coat from Faye. "Do you think he really is the one, Faye? And did you *see* that *dress?*"

"It's not something you wear to a wedding," Faye said quietly, wishing she wasn't going. Maybe she'd tell Louise she felt sick and stay home.

"That's for sure! You could see practically her *entire* chest!"

Louise looked so scandalized that Faye had to smile. And suddenly she knew that nothing would stop her from going to the wedding. "All you ever talk about these days is chests."

"Well, they're important." Louise spun in a circle, making her coat billow. "Without a chest, you're just a little kid." Hearing footsteps on the porch, she darted over to open the door.

Two young men who looked a lot like their father but appeared somewhat unsure of themselves stood one in front of the other on the porch. The older one said, "Hi, we're Mike and Bob junior. I mean, I'm Bob junior, and this is Mike."

Mike, almost hidden behind his older brother, ducked out, smiled and waggled his fingers. Louise bent to one side, smiled and waggled her fingers back at him, saying, "I'm Louise. That's Faye."

Bob junior suddenly smiled just the way his father did and said, "You guys look really good. The car's over there." He turned and pointed.

"We're ready," Louise said, and ran down the steps, turning to Mike. "Are you excited? I'm *so* excited."

"I don't know about excited," Mike said bashfully. "More like nervous, sort of."

"How come?"

"It's kind of a big change, that's all. I mean, we've met your grandmother tons of times. But it's not the same thing as having her for a stepmother."

"You'll like her," Louise said confidently. "She's a very fair person. Gee! That's right. She's gonna be your stepmother. I hadn't thought of that. Gramma's gonna be their stepmother, Faye," she turned back to tell her sister.

"I know that, Lou." Faye was taking short, careful steps because of her high heels and the narrow skirt of her new dress. To Bob junior, Faye explained, "Lou always thinks when she finds something out, it's the first time anyone in the world ever figured it out."

Bob junior shot a smile at Louise, then said to Faye, "I know what you mean. I've got a roommate like that."

"Why didn't you tell the girls I was coming to the wedding?" Nolan asked, suspecting he was being used in some fashion.

"I don't tell them everything I do," Maggie said, fixing her coat across her lap.

"Well, now," he said, "this isn't an everyday occurrence, is it?"

"It certainly isn't," she replied, her chin jutting and a satisfied smile on her mouth. "This is a day for the books."

"Close to your mother, are you?"

"I wouldn't go that far," she said, still stinging from her mother's failure to include her in the dinner at the Royal York. "She's just my mother. Everybody has one." She shrugged and began with the fingers of one hand pushing the fingers of the other more firmly into her tight-fitting black leather gloves.

He glanced over, finding her activity slightly unnerving. It appeared as if she were preparing to commit some potentially lethal act with those leather-clad hands, the way she was flexing them, then turning them over to inspect the palms before flexing them again.

Ellen and Bob were sitting on a bench in the hall outside the room where the ceremony was to be performed. At her first sight of Maggie approaching along the corridor in an extremely low-cut, skin-tight, flaming red dress, her coat thrown over her arm and an attractive man at her side, Ellen reflexively gripped Bob's hand.

"Your daughter, I take it," he said, marveling over the exquisitely bad taste of the dress. It was, he thought, the quintessence of inappropriateness.

Ellen nodded, whispering, "She's determined to spoil it. Didn't I tell you?"

"Don't rise to the bait," he counseled. "She can only succeed if you allow it."

For several seconds Ellen felt like weeping. How had she managed to produce this monster? Had she critical failings as a mother of which she was unaware? What sin had she committed to warrant this punishment?

Very quietly, he said, "Treat her like a difficult guest you've had to invite for political reasons. Kill her with charm, Ellie. You can do it."

Ellen moved forward to let her cheek rest against his for a moment, gripped by the irrational fear that she'd lose this man because of her daughter. And she couldn't bear the idea of not having him in her life. Who was Marg? she wondered yet again. What made her do the things she did? She touched her lips lightly to his cheek, then sat back with a smile. "Good. You're right on time," she said as Margaret reached them.

"Naturally," Maggie said, waiting to be introduced.

There was an awkward silence while each of them wondered who should take the first step. Then Jerry stepped forward, extending his hand to Ellen, saying, "Your daughter very kindly invited me to come today. I'm Jerry Nolan."

Ellen shook his hand, unable to see anything but good intentions in his remarkably bright blue eyes. "I've heard Marg speak of you, Mr. Nolan."

"Jerry, please."

"Jerry. I'm delighted you could come. This is Bob."

The two men shook hands as the young people came hurrying up the corridor. The girls went directly to their grandmother, making a fuss over her and telling her how wonderful she looked, while Bob introduced Nolan to his sons.

Completely ignored by everyone, Maggie stood holding her coat, a brilliant red island between the group of men and the small cluster of females. She was seething.

"Gramma, you look so beautiful," Louise said. Then whispered, "Did you *see* Ma's dress?"

"Hard to miss it," Ellen whispered back. "You both look lovely."

"Are you nervous?" Louise asked.

Ellen laughed. "Petrified. Ridiculous, isn't it?"

"Everything's going to be fine, Gramma," Faye said.

Noticing Maggie standing alone, Ellen beckoned to Bob, saying, "You haven't met my daughter, Margaret."

Bob shook Maggie's gloved hand, having to work to hang on to his smile. He'd never seen eyes like hers. They were hard and flat and somehow dead. There wasn't a trace of her mother in Margaret, not even the faintest hint of Ellen's warmth. His dislike was so immediate and intense he could hardly stand to look at her, decked out as she was like a tart in her obscene dress. If anything, Ellen had understated the case when she'd spoken of her daughter as being difficult. He found it almost impossible to believe that the chilly creature in front of him was the mother of two very lovable girls and the child of the woman he loved. "So glad you could be here today," he said, and turned from Maggie the instant common decency permitted, to ask Nolan, who seemed a likable man, what business he was in.

Nolan explained his position as Maggie's employer, feeling Mag's eyes boring holes in the side of his head as he chatted with her soon-to-be stepfather. He was acutely embarrassed for Maggie, and wondered what had possessed her to wear such a dress to her mother's wedding.

When it came time for the wedding party to proceed into the chamber, Nolan hung back, saying, "I'll wait out here. This is a family matter."

Ellen, whose fondness for him was as immediate and complete as Bob's enmity toward Maggie, said, "I wouldn't dream of having you sit out here alone, Mr. Nolan. Please come in with us."

"Yeah, come on," Louise said, taking him by the hand. "It isn't like we don't know you. Is it, Faye?"

Faye said, "That's right," glancing at her mother's incredible red dress. "We certainly know you, Mr. Nolan."

"It's very good of you," Nolan said. "I don't like to impose."

"Not at all," Bob said cordially. "It's a pleasure to have you."

⤙

During the brief ceremony, Faye studied Bob and her grandmother, thinking how well they suited one another, and what an exceptional occasion this was. When Bob took hold of her grandmother's hand and slid the diamond band on her finger, Faye's lungs heaved as if she were being held under water. Chewing on her lower lip to keep from making a sound, she began to cry.

⤙

Keeping her eyes on her grandmother, Louise took hold of her sister's hand. Faye always got emotional when it came to man-woman stuff, especially lately. Louise guessed it was because of her being in love with Raffie, although Faye had always cried easily if she felt strongly about something. Louise sighed, mouthing "I do" every time Gramma did. This was the most romantic event she'd ever witnessed, and she didn't want to miss one second of it. Even the judge looked as if he thought it was romantic, smiling as he presided. Bob was *sooo* handsome. And Gramma looked gorgeous in her silk suit. She'd had her hair done, and it lifted away from her face in a gleaming sweep that was twisted at the back in an elaborate figure eight. Louise sighed again.

⤙

Nolan, impressed by Ellen's dignified bearing and beauty, wondered what the woman must think of her daughter. He found it hard to believe the two were related. Their resemblance notwithstanding, Maggie was brittle, sarcastic, and self-important, while her mother was gracious, warm, and welcoming. He'd caught the way Bob had looked at Mag during the introductions, and knew Mag had made an enemy there. What he still couldn't understand was what Mag had hoped to accomplish not only by wearing that shocking dress but also by inviting him along. Whatever her motives, he had the distinct impression she hadn't succeeded. Seeing Maggie today outside her usual milieu he found her appeal for him considerably diminished. He was, in point of fact, embarrassed to be seen with her all decked out like a trollop.

Bob junior kept glancing covertly at Faye, very taken with her. He was so busy watching Faye he missed most of the ceremony and was only just in time to see his dad kiss their new stepmother. It was the first time he'd ever seen his father kiss a woman other than their mother. It'd been just the three of them for so long now that for long periods of time he actually forgot he and Mike had once had a mother. She'd been dead for fourteen years—forever. Dad had been alone way too long. And Ellen was okay. She'd never tried to get too chummy with him or Mike, had never done any of the embarrassing stuff some of the other women Dad had dated used to pull. Dad was crazy about her. And Bob could see why.

Mike followed the ceremony, feeling awkward and wishing he could put his hands in his pockets. But it wouldn't look good. So he kept them folded together in front of him, amazed to think these two people were actually getting *married*. It was such a big thing to do. How could you know for sure you wanted to spend the rest of your whole life with someone?

He had only very vague memories of his mother. He remembered her falling down once in the living room. He'd thought it was a game, and he'd laughed. Kids could be so stupid. He remembered the way his father's face looked the day he told them she'd died. At six years old Mike had believed everybody had this little flame inside them, sort of like the pilot light on the stove. And when Dad sat down with the two of them to tell them Mom wouldn't be coming home from the hospital, Mike kept thinking his father looked as if someone had blown his flame out. And

Mike had been scared because he didn't know how to get the light going again, and anyway he'd been warned not to play with matches. So the whole time Dad was telling him and Bobby that Mom had died, Mike had been getting more and more worked up worrying how he'd be able to turn that light back on.

Watching his father now, Mike thought he looked very happy, as if he really did have a flame inside. It made Mike feel good. She was nice, Ellen. When they were little and used to go to the office, she'd always talk to them and let them play office at her desk. Boy! He had to smile, thinking about the crazy things he remembered.

Maggie held her coat tightly in her arms, wishing she hadn't bought the goddamned dress. She'd never felt so out of place in her life. First thing tomorrow, she'd return it and get her money back. She'd just have to be very careful not to get anything on it. Gazing fixedly at her mother, she wondered how she'd managed to keep quiet about Wolford all these years, referring to her dates but never once saying anything more than that she'd had dinner with the man a few times. She'd obviously had a hell of a lot more than dinner with him. Christ! She'd probably been sleeping with him since day one. Not letting on, not even a hint. Keeping secrets from her own daughter! Some mother. The two of them were listening to the judge, and the silence in the room was so intense she could actually hear Nolan breathing beside her. What was the point of this? Going through all this mumbo jumbo, exchanging rings and taking vows, when marriage was nothing. You could walk away from it without a second thought. She shifted her weight from one hip to the other, waiting for it to be over. She was tempted to get Nolan to drive her home so she could change, maybe put on the black dress. Maybe she'd do that. The store would never be able to tell she'd worn the red dress for a couple of hours. That's what she'd do. She'd have Nolan run her back to the house, hurry in, and change. And tomorrow she'd get her money back.

When it was finally over, she watched the way the two of them kissed, saw how her mother smiled up at Wolford, and she suddenly understood that she'd just been cut out of her mother's life. There'd be no more Sunday afternoons at her house with the girls. That was all over now. After today she'd have to wait to be invited over, and when she was she'd have to sit around with her mother's new husband, making chitchat instead of being able to relax and let her hair down. What the hell was she supposed to do from now on?

—✦—

As they were leaving city hall, Maggie held Nolan back for a moment, saying, "Find out the address. There's something I have to do before we go to the party."

"What?" he asked.

"I want to go home and change into another dress."

Pleased, thinking she'd at last come to her senses, he said, "All right," and stopped Bob junior to get the address in Rosedale. "We'll catch up with you there," he told the others, then took Maggie firmly by the arm and hurried her out to the car.

He was prepared to sit in the car while she went inside to change, but she turned and gave him an unmistakable look, saying, "You might as well come in."

"Do you think this is the right time for that, Mag?"

"Why not?" she said, slipping out of the car.

It really didn't feel right. He opened his door saying, "I'll just nip down to the corner for cigarettes, Mag. Do you need any?"

Taken aback, she said, "No," and went inside, slamming the door behind her.

He shrugged and went to get his wedding gift from the trunk of the car. Two crystal flutes and a bottle of Dom Perignon. He hoped the happy couple wouldn't think it presumptuous of him. They were awfully nice people, and he felt rather sad that he had to be going to their wedding party—which was bound to be a first-rate affair—with Mag. He'd actually have been more comfortable going on his own.

CHAPTER
SIXTEEN

NANCY VICKERS, BOB'S SISTER, WAS FORTY-ONE, NEWLY divorced, and not in the least sorry about it. She looked very much like her brother—tall, with rich chestnut hair, blue eyes, and a smile as dazzling as his. She'd met Ellen on numerous occasions over the years and was genuinely delighted that her brother had at long last won her over.

Nancy loved to entertain and, upon hearing of the wedding plans, volunteered at once to give the party. She'd gone all out for the occasion, hiring caterers, waiters, a bartender, and a band. There were immense floral arrangements everywhere, and a buffet had been set up in the dining room. The band was installed in the glassed-in garden room Nancy and her former husband had added to the house soon after moving in sixteen years before. A fair number of friends and associates from the law firm had already arrived by the time Faye and Louise got there with Bob's sons.

While Bob junior and Mike engaged in a low-level, good-natured competition for Faye's attention, Nancy's fourteen-year-old daughter, Katharine, who was in grade nine at Branksome Hall, took an immediate shine to Louise.

Having taken their time driving up from city hall, Bob pulled the car over to the curb a block away from his sister's house. He put on the parking brake, turned off the lights, and turned to Ellen. "Now, tell me the truth. How are you?"

Ellen shifted on the seat, reaching for his hand. "You really want to know?"

"Absolutely," he said, moving closer.

"I feel happy, but very shaky. I'm finding it hard to believe this is real." She looked past him at the snow that had begun to fall. Thick, fat flakes dissolved on contact with the car's warmth, just the way she'd dissolved and been transformed by close contact with this man.

She'd worked so hard not to fall in love with him, very aware of the difference in their ages and conscious of the daunting changes her body had started undergoing once she passed forty. Her flesh seemed like an ill-fitting dress she was obliged to wear, and her features had subtly redefined themselves with an angularity she occasionally found startling when she confronted her bathroom mirror. It was exceedingly difficult to reconcile the reality of an ever-changing face and body with a brain that was as flexible and effective as it had been at sixteen. It didn't make sense to her that her mind could remain permanently youthful and elastic while her physical self succumbed to the passage of time.

Regardless of the fact that she was trim and in excellent health, it wasn't possible for her to ignore the age factor. Men seemed to retain their youth far longer than women. But she couldn't help wondering if she thought that way because she'd married very young, been widowed early, and had lived alone for so many years. Then, too, it seemed perilously risky to allow herself to care, because it came too easily. She could feel everything inside her lift expectantly simply at the sight of Bob's smile. And even though he pursued her more and more actively once they'd started dating, she was convinced some younger woman would come along and displace her. So she cherished his company, grateful for whatever interest he demonstrated, and kept a stranglehold on her emotions. For four years she succeeded, although every time she stepped out on a dance floor with him she found it suddenly difficult to breathe. She wanted to abandon all thought and rationality and attach herself to him like some improbable graft; she wanted his hands on her body and his mouth to breathe into hers; she wanted to touch his bare knees, to kiss him behind his ears, to run her tongue over the translucent flesh between his fingers; she wanted to do things she'd never before even imagined, but that with him in mind became weighted with thrillingly explicit sexual possibilities.

Instead, every time, she smiled and tried to savor the synchronous drift of their perfectly attuned limbs, following where he led but maintaining an iron grip on her unruly, swelling emotions.

They would talk, often for hours, and she'd listen to his words while his resonant voice enveloped her and his smile caused what she felt to be the shabby old garment of flesh she wore to shrink and grow moist in response. Never for a moment did she believe he could possibly see her as anything more than a comfortably familiar partner for a relaxing evening out.

Then one night when he saw her to her door and she turned to give him her usual chaste good-night kiss, he took hold of her saying, "This is ridiculous, Ellen. I think we both want more. I know I do, and I'm convinced you do, too. Am I wrong?"

That tidy package of emotions burst out of its lengthy containment and her many misgivings began waging war on her enormous desires. There was so much she wanted to say that she couldn't utter a word. What was he telling her? And what did he want? Was it possible that he felt a longing, too, every time they went into each other's arms? She couldn't think how to respond. It had been so long since she'd revealed herself, so many years since anyone had touched her that she was fairly paralyzed by apprehension and by her ludicrous need. It would take so little to shatter her. Love was the most dangerous of all the emotions. If you didn't pay close attention it could range out of control, do you in.

She was silent for too long, her heart battering inside her like some trapped creature trying to escape from her body as she looked up at him, weighted down not only by her heavy winter coat but by too many questions, too much fear.

Finally, he said, "You're afraid," and she nodded, glad he understood that much at least.

"So am I," he said. "But we shouldn't let that stop us."

"I'm fifty years old," she said, her voice cracked and lacking volume. Every last bit of her energy was being used to prevent her emotions from consuming her common sense.

"I know that," he said patiently. "So what? Don't you know I'm in love with you?"

She shook her head, and he gave her one of his remarkable smiles, saying, "Ellen, what do you think these four years have been about?"

She said, "I honestly don't know. It's cold out here. I think you'd better come in." And with a numbed, trembling hand she got the key in the lock and opened the door.

When she'd moved to turn on the light he stopped her, saying, "Don't," and took hold of her again, engaging her in a kiss that robbed her of the larger part of her ability to think. Her body was an independent entity that had no reservations but simply asserted its right to act. And her last rational and ungovernable thought was, I'm not *that* old. Then she took him upstairs to her bedroom where, grateful for the darkness, she prepared to give herself, in what felt like a form of suicide.

Making love with Bob that first time was an act that required every last bit of her courage. Offering her flawed self naked into his embrace was the single most frightening thing she'd ever done. Despite his most welcome declaration of caring and her treacherous body's insistence, she couldn't help feeling that for a woman of fifty it was foolish and even possibly vain to risk baring herself body and soul to this man.

But Bob took her down on her bed and led her to a state of explosive enlightenment. He expressed such pleasure in every nuance of her construction that she no longer felt old. It was a gift of vast proportions. He made her feel eminently desirable, and with words and gestures and ardent skill, he introduced her to herself. He made her flesh sing, made her hungry for the taste and feel of him, turned her shameless and bold before joining with her in an utterly perfect dance that culminated in an ecstatic convulsion. She held him in her heaving body, overwhelmed by sensation and love, undone by the realization that she'd gained and lost herself all at the same time. She'd been permitted to know and comprehend the arcane dynamics of desire and of completion, and regardless of what happened in the future, she'd never again be the woman she'd been up until only an hour before. And in the year since that first encounter, she'd left her ravenous lingering kisses and caresses on every part of his anatomy, refining and honing her insatiable appetite as she discovered numerous new routes to that same sweetly piercing conclusion.

The snow falling more thickly now, accumulating on the windows and isolating them inside a dim cocoon, she held his hand with both her own. "I adore you. I thought I had a life, you know. But now I don't know what it was. It's scary to be as happy as I am at this moment."

He drew her closer saying, "Why scary?"

"Because I know what I'd be losing if I lost you."

"You're not going to lose me," he said, his hand on her throat as he looked into her eyes.

"I didn't want you to meet Margaret," she said, looking at his mouth. "I was so afraid she'd ruin everything, the way she tried with that dreadful dress . . . God almighty!" she said, looking away from him. "We're supposed to love our children. But what do you do when you get a child like her?"

"You get on with your own life, Ellen," he said sensibly. "She's a grown woman, no longer your responsibility."

Her eyes returned to him. "I knew you wouldn't like her. And I was right. You don't have to say a word. I know exactly how you felt about her." Ashamedly, she said, "It's how *I* too often feel about her. I had the idea that if you met her you'd lose whatever feeling you had for me. I know it's ridiculous, but it's how I felt. And now you've seen for yourself why I was afraid."

"She's got nothing to do with us," he said, stroking the silken column of her throat, then kissing the side of her neck, gratified by her responsive shiver, the acceleration of her breathing.

"We'd better get going," she said, ready to make love to him there and then. "They'll be wondering where we are."

He lifted his head, saying, "I feel so damned lucky. I've *got* you. Every night from now on I'm going to be coming home, not to an empty house, but to you." He kissed her lightly on the mouth, smiled again and said, "It's going to be rough getting through the next few hours without dragging you off into one of my sister's spare bedrooms."

She laughed softly. "We'll both survive it somehow."

It took Maggie less than ten minutes to change. She came rushing out of the house and Nolan opened the passenger door hoping she'd put on something more appropriate to the occasion than that frightful red dress.

"That didn't take long, did it?" she said, sounding pleased with herself as they set off.

"Not at all," he answered. "It's starting to snow. They're forecasting quite a big fall. It may be tricky getting home."

"Let's worry about that later," she said, opening her bag for a cigarette. "What did you think of my mother's new husband?"

He shot a quick look at her to see what sort of expression she had on her face. She appeared merely curious.

"He seems a very decent man," he said cautiously. "He's obviously mad for your mother."

"And what did you think of my mother?"

"She's a lovely person."

"You say that like you're surprised."

"I suppose I was, a bit."

"Why?" she asked.

"I don't know, Mag. We form mental pictures of people. They're usually inaccurate. I expected her to be older, for one thing. She doesn't look her age. Had I not known she was your mother, I'd've thought she was your sister."

"What's that supposed to mean? Are you saying I look old for my age?"

Feeling wearied, he said, "Not at all. Are you warm enough?" He put his hand on the heater control.

"I'm fine," she said curtly, crossing her legs. "She's been seeing him for five years and today's the first time I ever laid eyes on him. What a way to treat your own daughter!"

There was nothing he could think of that was safe to say, so he busied himself with the radio, trying to find a station playing decent music.

"What's that in the back?" she asked, twisting to look at the gift-wrapped box on the back seat.

"A small gift for the bride and groom."

She looked at him in disbelief. "Why'd you do that?"

"It's customary," he said lightly.

"What is it?"

"Just something small," he said, reluctant to discuss the gift with her. Heading north on Jarvis, he said, "When we were first married, Nora and I had a flat on Glen Road in Rosedale."

"That's nice."

"Every now and then I'll come for a walk here, look at the houses. It's my favorite part of the city."

"A lot of rich people with big fancy houses," she said disdainfully.

"A lot of very beautiful houses," he said, "of a kind they don't build anymore."

"With a lot of snooty rich people."

He allowed the conversation to dry up as he bore to the right onto Mt. Pleasant, signaling for a left turn at South Drive to enter the looping, somewhat randomly laid out streets of the area. He liked the eccentricity of Rosedale, as compared with the careful gridwork of most of the rest of the city. Here roads meandered, circled back on themselves. The large houses, each entirely different from its neighbor, each with its own architectural peculiarities: cut-glass fanlights over the front doors, cupolas, balustraded porches, gray stone porticoes, bay windows here, casement windows there, mock Tudor on one corner, stolid red brick on the other.

Huge shade trees, leafless now, supported a steady accumulation of snow. A gate house on one property, a carriage house on the next. It wasn't the aura of wealth he enjoyed so much as the evident striving for individuality each builder had demonstrated. Here and there were comparatively modest houses standing cheek by jowl with a small version of Casa Loma, that wonderful castle on its hill overlooking the city; Sir Henry Pellatt's monument to an immense ego, with its secret passageways, its greenhouses and stables, and commanding position. He loved this city, with its self-conscious citizens who required great amounts of time in which to discard their instinctive mistrust of newcomers but who, once having accepted them, were friends for life. He thought of Toronto with affection, as a very proper, very proud matron of pleasing proportions, who harbored a secret yearning to be just the slightest bit naughty, but who was so scandalized by her darkly kept secret that she exercised an ever more stringent self-control.

Both sides of the street were already lined with cars. Pulling up in front, he said, "I'll let you out here, Mag, then find someplace to park."

"I'm not going in there alone!" she declared.

"But it's cold and I may have to park blocks away."

"I'm not going in there alone," she repeated, as if daring him to defy her.

"Suit yourself," he said, and drove on.

He ended up having to park well along Crescent Road, then had to keep a firm grip on Maggie's arm as they made the walk back to the house on Cluny Drive. The sidewalks were icy, and her high heels weren't made for this kind of weather. By the time they got to the house she was complaining volubly about the long walk, and he clamped his teeth together, determined not to say he'd warned her.

"Here we are," he said, and she looked at the formidable gray stone house feeling suddenly uncertain. The place was a goddamned *mansion*. Bob's sister was probably one of those Rosedale bitches with a mink coat, a membership in the Granite Club, and an attitude of superiority that made Maggie's stomach turn whenever she saw one of them stepping into a taxi outside someplace like Owen's & Elm's or Creed's. She hated those women, with their hundred-dollar handbags and their pompous, rich husbands. And her mother was going to be one of them. Maggie had known it the minute she laid eyes on Robert Wolford, taking in his custom-tailored three-piece suit, his highly polished shoes, his manicured nails, and his gold tiepin and cuff links. Now she was going to have it all shoved down her throat for an entire evening. By the time Nolan was pressing the doorbell she felt like murdering someone.

The door opened and Nolan looked at the tall brightly smiling woman standing there, deluged by instant and multiple reactions. He thought she was the most immediately appealing woman he'd ever seen, and he'd have given almost anything to be on his own, without Mag.

Maggie said, "I'm Ellen's daughter," articulating the words as if laying down a challenge.

The slightest, almost imperceptible reaction registered in Nancy's large, wide-set eyes but only someone watching as closely as Nolan would have seen it. She extended her hand saying, "I'm so glad you could come," then turned to Nolan fully expecting Maggie to introduce her escort.

Seeing Maggie wasn't going to do that, he spoke up. "Jerry Nolan," he said, grasping her large strong hand and feeling a charged current travel between their palms.

"Please come in," Nancy said, her eyes resting an extra moment on Nolan as she stepped back from the door. "I'm Nancy Vickers, Bob's sister."

Maggie was paying no attention, her eyes taking in the house as she handed her coat to a uniformed maid.

"Let me hold that for you," Nancy said, relieving Nolan of the gift while he got out of his coat and gave it to the waiting maid. "The gifts are along here," she said, "if you'd like to come this way."

Nolan looked to Maggie, who, with a little flick of her hand, said, "You go on. I'll get myself a drink."

Relieved to see that Mag had put on an attractive black dress and that she clearly had no objection to being separated from him, he turned to go with Nancy Vickers to a sitting room where a table was piled high with wedding presents.

"It's a lovely house," Jerry said, adding his gift to those already there. "I've admired it many times."

"Have you?" Nancy said interestedly. "Why? When?" She leaned against the doorway with her hand in a pocket of the rust-colored evening dress that was flattering to her auburn hair and slightly tawny skin.

"I like to walk along here, study the houses," he said, reaching for his cigarettes and offering her one. She declined with a smile that made him want suddenly to say or do anything that would keep her smiling. "We lived in Rosedale years ago, my former wife and I."

"You're divorced?"

"In the process."

"Takes forever, doesn't it?" she said, as if the two of them were privy to a knowledge few others shared. "Mine was finalized four months ago. What do you do, Jerry?"

"Nothing terribly exciting," he told her. "I manage a factory. And what do *you* do?" he asked with a bit of wickedness he couldn't manage to repress.

She took him off guard, saying, "I actually do quite a bit. And I work, too." She watched his eyes to see how he'd respond, hoping he was as quick-witted as he seemed.

He laughed, then said, "Wonderful. And you work, to boot."

Pushing away from the doorway, she said, "I do fashion illustrations for Simpson's." She turned her head toward the noise of the party.

"Do you now," he said. "That's impressive."

"Not really. It's something I do instead of serious painting."

The doorbell rang and she said, "Please make yourself at home, Jerry Nolan. I'll catch up with you later."

He watched her walk away, admiring her slim legs and the shift of her hips in the full-skirted dress, so immediately smitten that he felt a pang of guilt at the sight of Maggie, drink in hand, waiting for him. He knew as he crossed the foyer that his involvement with her was at an end, and it heightened his guilt as she asked petulantly, "What the hell took you so long?"

"Sorry, Mag. We got to talking." He surveyed the crowd. "The bride and groom haven't arrived yet."

"I *know* that," she said. "I'm not blind."

"I hope they haven't had a mishap," he said, wondering why she always had to be so unpleasant, so difficult; why she made it impossible for people to like her. Mag engineered her own undoing so skillfully, yet so unknowingly. On one level he felt sorry for her, but on another, self-preserving level, he knew he had to get away from her. If she was determined to have everyone hate her, he really didn't want to be hated by association.

"What the hell do you care?" she asked.

He had to look at her, quietly saying, "I do care. Don't you?"

She didn't answer but simply gazed at him as if he were crazy. Turning away, he spotted Louise waving to him and went toward her with a smile, wondering if it was possible that Maggie wanted everyone else to be as miserable as she was. Whatever it was she wanted no longer concerned him. Just a few minutes' chatting with another woman, and Maggie was already of his past.

✝

Bob maneuvered Ellen into a dark corner of the party room and stood very close to her so that his body blocked her view.

"Having a good time?" he asked, kissing the corner of her mouth.

"Wonderful. Are you?"

He kissed the other corner of her mouth. "Your daughter seems to have undergone a change of heart, not to mention wardrobe."

"I'm astonished," she admitted.

"I'd really like to mess up your hair," he said directly into her ear. "How would you feel about that?"

"I'd be heartbroken if you didn't," she replied. "But you're going to have to wait."

Letting his arm rest on the wall above her head, he studied her for several seconds then said, "You are my wife. We're actually married."

"I know. I feel exactly the same way."

"What took us so long?"

"I did," she said truthfully. "I thought you were just lonely."

"I was."

"So was I," she said.

"So why did it take us five years?"

"Because I was afraid to let myself fall in love with you. I tried very hard not to let it happen."

"Ellie, why?"

She took a deep breath and said, "Because I'm her mother, Bob. That had to mean that somehow, in some way, I made her what she is. And I thought that if I actually was responsible it meant there was something terribly wrong with me. I've tried all her life to give her what I thought she needed, but it was never enough, or right, or something. I just don't know. And aside from that I thought it was inevitable you'd meet someone younger, more right for you."

"That hurts me," he said sadly. "Whatever Margaret is, she came with her components built in. We can't, any of us, do more than our best. You tried, but it didn't work. That happens. That's point number one. Point number two is I've been crazy about you for *years.* No one of *any* age could ever be more right for me than you. I love everything about you. I especially," he said, lowering his gaze, "love the fact that my saying that just did this." And, shifting to conceal his action from view, he touched his fingertips to her stiffened nipple.

She flushed and whispered, "My God! You'll get us arrested."

He laughed, gave her a quick kiss on the mouth, then took her hand and leaned against the wall beside her, his eyes moving over the faces of his friends and associates and family. "I think," he said, "my sister's interested in Nolan."

"Is she?" Ellen said, feeling a quick jab of fear as she focused on Jerry Nolan dancing with Nancy. "I think you're right," she said, able to see in their animated features their attraction to one another. Where was Margaret? she wondered, scanning the room. Her eyes came to rest on the far corner. There, talking to one of the firm's junior partners while her eyes tracked Nolan and Bob's sister, was Ellen's daughter. Poor Maggie, she thought. Something else gone wrong in her life for which she'd blame everyone but herself. And poor Nolan. There'd be hell to pay for this.

"Dance?" Bob asked.

Making an effort, she drew her eyes away from her daughter, and turned to stand very close to Bob in exactly the way he'd stood before her a few minutes before. Tugging at his hand, she signaled. He bent his head and she kissed him, drugged as always by their extraordinary intimacy. "We might be able to slip away in another half hour," she told him.

In response, he kissed her again, then lifted his head and gave a happy laugh. "We're like a pair of teenagers."

"Teenagers," she said with certainty, "have *no idea,* my dear. None. I speak from firsthand experience. We," she said, "are like a pair of adults, thank God."

CHAPTER
SEVENTEEN

MAGGIE KNEW WHAT WAS HAPPENING. NOLAN HAD THE hots for Nancy Vickers. He asked her if she'd mind if he asked their hostess to dance, and Maggie said she didn't care. She could practically read his mind. And she really didn't give a shit one way or another who he had his eye on. But if he thought he was going to make a fool of her in front of a hundred other people, he had another think coming. She stood nursing a gin and tonic, looking around while one of the boring lawyers from Bob's firm droned away in her ear. To her right through the archway, she could see Louise and Nancy's kid on one of the half dozen sofas in the ridiculously large living room, yacking away to Bob's younger son, who was sitting on a big round ottoman in front of them. Opposite her, in the extreme far corner of the so-called party room, her mother was holding hands with Bob while the two of them watched the dancers. Then her mother turned and kissed him. It made Maggie want to vomit. She was willing to bet her mother had never kissed poor Daddy that way. He'd deserved someone better, someone who really appreciated him. Eleven years he'd been dead, and her mother probably never gave a thought to the husband she'd had for twenty-three years. God! She'd never forget her mother's quiet voice on the telephone when she called at the factory to tell her Daddy had fallen over dead at breakfast with a heart attack. The only person who'd ever really loved her was dead, just like that, with no warning. He used to slip her some extra money on Sundays when she brought the babies to the house. And her goddamned mother would start in, saying, "Why would you take money from your father when I just gave you some? You've got to stop taking advantage of us, and trying to pit us against each other. Why do you do it, Marg?" she'd ask, with this faked hurt expression on her face. "We're not wealthy people. Your father and I work hard for what we have, and we give you as much as we can, but nothing ever seems to be enough for you. What more can we *do?* If we knew what would make you happy, don't you think we'd give it to you?'' She'd go on and on until Maggie despised her, wanted to kill her.

The woman had always resented the closeness she and Daddy had; she'd never understood either of them. All he'd wanted was some loving kindness, which he probably didn't get from his wife, although he refused to hear it when Maggie tried to make him see that Ellen was jealous of her and Daddy, jealous of her own daughter, and never mind that big act she put on to show how much she cared for her and the girls. Maggie could spot an act from a mile away, and she'd known all her life that her mother was a phony. Everywhere she turned she was surrounded by them, everybody jealous of her, out to get her. Oh, she knew how they operated, smiling to your face while they were getting ready to stab you in the back. "Don't ever let me hear you say things like that about your mother, Marg," Daddy would say. "Your mother's a kind, caring woman and she doesn't deserve that. After all your mother's done for you, it makes me sick at heart to hear you talk about her that way." She hated it when he took sides and they ganged up on her. And he did it every damned time, making her feel there was no one in the world she could trust. Sooner or later they all turned against her. Her stupid father refused to see that the woman he'd married wasn't good enough for him, that she only pretended to care. Her big hugs and kisses, the fussing over the kids, was just to make herself look good. Now here she was fussing over another man, and paying no attention as usual to her own daughter.

She had to look away. It was making her too angry. Her eyes went again to Nolan, dancing a bit stiffly because of his bum knee, and beaming at that Nancy. What was so hot about her anyway? she wondered, studying her competition. Thick russet hair side-parted and falling precisely to her shoulders; high forehead, sharp pointed nose, full mouth enclosing big white teeth, a squared chin; wide shoulders and no breasts to speak of; long, long legs—the woman was near as tall as Nolan, with big narrow feet in a pair of dyed-to-match rust-colored shoes; diamond earrings and a diamond bracelet, and an emerald pendant that sat precisely between her shallow breasts. The only difference between them, Maggie decided, was money. She was far better-looking, not to mention younger. What was he trying to do, make her jealous? If that was his plan, it wasn't working. He was just getting her mad.

The band finished the number and announced they were taking a short break. Instead of coming back to the person who'd brought him, Nolan was going out through the far archway with that bitch. Abandoning the lawyer, Maggie tracked the pair into the living room. Distractedly, she noticed the kids had gone. An older couple was sitting on the sofa with plates of food. When she looked back, Nolan and Nancy were nowhere to be seen. Returning to the foyer, she sat down to wait on the bench to one side of the stairs. She'd fix his wagon but good. Crossing her legs, she watched people file past the buffet, then carry their plates into the living room. She looked at her watch. Eight-twenty. It felt as if she'd been here for days. Calm down and think! she told herself, knowing she had to prepare a plan of action. It was one thing if she decided to get rid of him, but it was something else entirely if he thought he was going to get rid of her. Nobody was ever going to do that to her again.

"Are you involved with Ellen's daughter?" Nancy asked straight out.

"It's complicated," Nolan answered, knowing he should be downstairs with Maggie. "I'm not sure I can explain it."

"If it requires explaining, it's messy. And I dislike messy situations." She sat on the end of one of the twin beds in the guest room at the rear of the house to which they'd come via the back stairs.

"Yes, so do I." He sat on the corner of the adjoining bed. "But I'm planning to take care of the situation." He paused, then said, "I think you and I are going to be seeing one another." He said this without the slightest trace of egotism.

She leaned back on her hands and studied him, as if measuring the light in his eyes for degrees of truthfulness. "I know," she confirmed. "And I'd like that. But only if I don't find myself embroiled in anything unpleasant. I've had enough of that to last me a lifetime."

"I understand," he said. He was embroiled up to his eyebrows in an epic mess, but hadn't, until meeting Nancy, put it in quite those terms. It was remarkable how meeting her had clarified matters, defined them very specifically for him.

"My former husband was very attractive," she said, convinced by the guilelessness of his gaze that he was being honest with her. "Especially to other women." She gave him a small self-mocking smile. "For a while we played this game of tit for tat. I went at it with a vengeance, hating myself and hating him. It was depressing and pointless, so I put an end to all of it, the marriage and the demoralizing affairs." She looked at him for several moments. "I've never discussed this with anyone. I'm not sure why I'm telling you." She could feel her pulse quickening, as if she'd stepped into an elevator only to have it plunge downward, out of control.

"Marriage never seems to be what we expect," he said thoughtfully. "Ways and means," he said obliquely, again thinking of Maggie. Why had he felt he had no other options? He'd subjected himself to a lot of unpleasantness because he'd grown accustomed to her, and because it hadn't occurred to him that he might meet someone who could feel as right for him as this lovely long-limbed woman with her penetrating gaze. Jesus! He'd actually considered marrying Mag. The idea now was nightmarish; he'd have spent the rest of his life trying to satisfy a woman who was incapable of being satisfied. "We do things with the idea in mind of preserving what we have," he said. "But in the end it turns out nothing we said or did could have changed any of it. We're left feeling empty and foolish, wondering why we tried so hard to keep it intact."

She smiled again. "We make the commitment, then become contortionists trying to honor it. You have a good face," she said critically, her brows drawing together for a moment. "Remarkable coloring. You'd be good to paint."

"I don't know what to say to that," he smiled back at her, unaccustomed to compliments. "We really should get back downstairs."

"You're not required to say anything. It's a statement of fact. I like your face. I'm attracted to you. I'm also hungry, and you're right. We've both got to go back down." Decisively, she got up to pull open one of the desk drawers, quickly jotted down her number, folded the paper, and handed it to him. "Call me," she said, moving to the door. "Perhaps I'll paint you."

He moved to her side. "Wait a minute."

She stopped, curious to see what he'd do. He put a hand to her hair, spreading his fingers so the thick strands slid through them. Her eyes were bold, bright with intelligence and humor. And her mouth was too luscious to resist. He touched her lips with the tip of his forefinger, saying, as if to himself, "The moment I saw you I knew I'd have to rearrange my life. You're larger than life and twice as grand."

Her lips shaped themselves into a smile beneath his finger. She liked him even more now for not having thrown himself at her, as so many of the others had. He understood restraint, and she found that admirable.

"You're so Irish. I love all that bullshit," she said, and ran her tongue across his fingertip.

Her action galvanized him. He slipped his hand under her hair and around over the warm downy skin at the back of her neck and put his mouth to hers. She sighed, placed her hands on either side of his face, inviting the kiss to deepen, lengthen. He kissed sweetly, and she decided he'd be wonderful in bed. Gently she pushed him away. "There's a bathroom through there," she said, pointing. "It has a door to the hallway." Then, running her fingers over the damp hollow beneath her lower lip, she turned, opened the door, and went out.

He came down the stairs and there was Maggie. Atypically she smiled and stood up saying, "There you are."

"Just nipped up to the washroom," he said, thrown by her smile. It occurred to him she rarely smiled. It altered the entire look of her. "I hope I wasn't too long."

Putting her arm through his, she said, "I've been waiting for you so we could eat. I'm starved."

"By all means," he said, feeling the weight of her arm, of her complete presence, like chains pulling him down. Despite her sudden affability, he was anxious now to be done with her demands, her peculiarities, her suspicions, her unaccountable and abrupt changes of mood.

Bob found his sister as she was arriving at the bottom of the stairs. She leaned forward and draped her arms across his shoulders. "Like your party?" she asked, smiling into his face.

"It's sensational. Ellen and I are going to disappear. You won't mind, will you?"

"I don't mind at all. But I am envious." She laughed softly and touched her nose to his. "The two of you deserve each other. I'm very, very happy for you, big brother."

"Your turn will come, Nance," he said fondly.

"Hmmmn," she murmured. "I think maybe it already has." Her eyes shifted away briefly then returned to him.

"A word to the wise," he said. "Be careful. The daughter's not like her mother."

Sobering, she said, "That's all too obvious. Do you suppose Ellen adopted her?"

Bob laughed. "You're rotten."

"That is true. What do you know?"

"Very little, except that he's her boss, and she sprung him on Ellen at the wedding hoping for some effect that hasn't come off. He seems like a decent enough man, but I have a hunch she can be dangerous. And I know how impetuous you can be. This time be careful. Okay?"

"Yes. Go sneak away with your darling new wife," she said, smiling again, closing her arms around him. "I love you to death."

"Love you, too, Nance. Thanks for the party. It was wonderful, as usual."

"You're welcome," she said, and released him, watching him work his way through the guests. With the hum of the party in her ears, sudden laughter, the band starting up again, she relived the kiss in the guest room, feeling a darting thrill shoot down through the center of her body. What was she getting herself into? Her brother was no fool. He seldom had a bad word to say about anyone, so when he advised caution it was worth heeding his advice. Touching the tip of her forefinger to her lips in unconscious duplication of Jerry Nolan's gesture, she decided it was nothing she couldn't handle. And after another moment, seeing Katharine giggling over by the fireplace with that wonderfully gamine little Louise, she smiled and descended the last step. She wanted to hug her daughter, and she also wanted a closer look at Katharine's irrepressibly bright new girlfriend.

Dancing, her body glued to his, Maggie looked up and said, "Take me home, Nolan," and to be sure he got her meaning, she put her leg directly between his as they took the next step.

"What about the girls?" he asked, responding in spite of himself and feeling disloyal to Nancy.

"They'll get a lift. There's all kinds of people here who'll give them a ride home."

"It's early still," he said, turning his wrist to check his watch. "It's just gone nine."

She gave him another of those rare smiles and said, "Good. It'll give us more time."

He couldn't think of any way to get out of it. He'd brought her; he was obliged to take her home. And it would give him an opportunity to talk to her, explain that the affair was over. "All right," he gave in, and led her out of the room. "I'll get the coats, then we'll make our goodbyes." God be wi' ye, he thought, breaking the word down into its components. God be with me. He had an intimation of pending disaster.

Maggie had no interest in saying goodbye or anything else to the woman she had already written off as a high-class whore. "You thank her for me," she said. "I'll just let the girls know we're leaving." Nolan went off to find Nancy, and Maggie searched for the girls. Faye wasn't around, but Louise was dancing with Bob's younger son. Maggie went over to them. "We're going now. You can stay. Just make sure you're home before midnight."

"Midnight?" Louise couldn't believe it. Ma never let her and Faye stay out that late. "You mean it?"

"I mean it. Find someone to give you a ride."

"Bobby and I will bring the girls home, Mrs. . . . ah . . ." Mike stalled, realizing he didn't know her name.

"Parker," Louise helped him out.

"Mrs. Parker," he said. "Don't worry about a thing."

"Believe me, I won't," Maggie said, and walked away, purposely avoiding the sight of Nolan with their hostess over in the same corner where her mother had been busy kissing her new husband. She went to wait by the front door, tapping her toe on the marble floor, with a pretty damned good idea what the two of them were saying to one another.

"I'll call you tomorrow," Nolan said, maneuvering her even farther into the corner. "Will you come out with me sometime soon?"

"Very probably," Nancy said, lacing her fingers through his. "Why are you leaving so early?"

"She wants to go. I've got no choice. Jesus, you're lovely," he said, looking at her full, beautifully shaped mouth.

"Don't call before ten. Now go on. I don't want that woman coming after me with a knife."

He looked startled, even possibly alarmed. "We'll talk tomorrow," he promised, then released her hands, and left.

"Okay?" Maggie asked, smiling away at him unnervingly.

"All set. You wait inside. I'll get the car."

"No, I'll come with you."

"Suit yourself," he said, and opened the door to see that a thick layer of snow blanketed the street and was still falling steadily. "You can't walk in those shoes," he told her. "Wait and I'll get the car."

As he went along the hushed street, blinking snowflakes out of his eyes, he felt a tremendous sense of urgency. Get her home and put an end to this silly business once and for all. It wasn't right to be pursuing another woman while he was still involved with Mag, but that sense of urgency overcame any thoughts of right or wrong. Besides, Mag had made it more than clear, for months now, that she didn't give a tinker's damn for him.

The roads were slick under the snow. The plows hadn't hit the side streets yet, but the main arteries would likely be clear. He drove slowly. Unable to find anywhere safe to turn, he had to drive around the block and come back along Roxborough to Cluny Drive. It took a while and he assumed Maggie would be fuming as he left the car running and went up the front walk to get her. But no. Still all smiles she was, taking his arm and actually laughing as she went slip-sliding down the walk to the car.

When he finally drew up outside her house, she said, "Come in, Nolan," and put both hands on his right arm, pulling at him.

"The weather's bad, Mag. I think it'd be best if I get right on home." He imagined himself returning to the party, and Nancy's surprise to find him back, his own pleasure at the sight of her. Of course he wouldn't go back.

"Come inside," Maggie insisted, her hand delving between his thighs. "We've got hours before the girls get back. Come *on*."

He was rising, like a trained animal getting up on its hind legs. "I don't think so," he said, catching hold of her hands, trying to get her to pay attention. "I think we need to talk, Maggie," he said, determined never again to succumb to her.

She pulled her hands free and sat back, saying, "Go ahead and talk. I'm listening." She opened her bag for a cigarette, got it lit and waited, knowing full well what he was going to say.

"I've decided we shouldn't see each other any more," he said.

"I see. It's that Rosedale bitch, isn't it?"

"I won't listen to that."

He sounded so much like her father saying, Don't ever let me hear you say things like that about your mother, Marg.

"You'll regret this, Nolan," she said menacingly.

"Don't try to threaten me, Mag," he said wearily. "I'm sorry, but we've run our course. It isn't as if we've had anything more going for us than sex. And much as I'll admit I've enjoyed that, it's not enough to build on.''

"You're trying to get rid of me so you can chase after that rich whore.''

"I told you I won't listen to that,'' he said angrily. "I'm *trying* to hold a reasonable conversation with you. If you can't talk without being abusive, perhaps you should go on inside now, and we'll call it a night.''

"You can call it whatever you goddamned want, but you're not dumping me like a sack of garbage.''

"That's not quite the way it is . . .''

She had the door open and was climbing out of the car. "You take your 'reasonable conversation,' Nolan, and shove it straight up your ass! You go when *I* tell you you can go. You don't drop me just because you've got the hots for that horse-faced whore.'' She slammed the door so hard the car rocked. Then she went slipping up the snow-covered walk, tossing away her cigarette.

He considered going after her, but he knew she wouldn't listen to a word he said. She was impossible, a woman who had only one view of any situation and that was her own. He waited until she'd gone into the house, slamming the front door after her, then he put the car in gear and steered his way cautiously down the middle of the snow-covered road. He felt awful about the way things had gone. But then, things always went badly where Mag was concerned. Now that he thought about it, he couldn't recall a single occasion in the past year when he'd parted from her feeling good.

Before he could call Nancy he had to try to speak to Mag, settle things once and for all. It wouldn't be right to go anywhere near Nancy until he'd made it absolutely clear to Maggie that the only contact they'd be having in future would be strictly business.

He dialed her number, dreading having one of the girls answer. But it was Maggie herself who said hello.

"It's Nolan,'' he said. "There's something I have to say to you, and I want you to know I mean it as much this morning as I did last night. We won't be seeing each other any more, Maggie. It's over. I won't argue about it, and I won't discuss it. I want you to be very clear on this.''

"Oh, I'm clear all right,'' she said coldly. "And you're going to be one very sorry son of a bitch when I'm through with you.''

"Stop threatening me," he said. "You're really in no position to do that, and I suggest you think very carefully about what I mean. I'm sorry you feel the only way you can deal with this situation is by making ugly threats. I hope you'll have reconsidered by the time you come to work on Monday morning. Goodbye, Mag," he said, and set the receiver back in its cradle. His hands were shaking as he lit a cigarette. He had to get up and walk the length of his apartment, back and forth, several times, before he was sufficiently calm to sit down again at the telephone.

Her voice when she answered was throaty, low.

"Good morning," he said. "It's Jerry Nolan."

"I knew it was you," she said, sounding nicely amused. "It's ten on the dot."

"I was wondering if you'd care to go out for a meal one evening next week."

"I've got a better idea," she said, smiling first at the housekeeper, who was filling the percolator at the sink, then over at Katharine, who was sitting at the table reading a magazine and holding a box of cornflakes upright over her empty bowl. "Come have breakfast with me. Afterward, we can go for a nice long walk in the snow."

"You don't think that's rushing things a bit?" he asked.

"Yes. But so what? Do you really want to wait a week?"

"Not really. What about your girl?" he asked, anxious to get off on the right foot this time.

"Would you like me to get her permission?" she asked, as Katharine looked over with raised eyebrows and put down the box of cereal.

"Actually, I would," he said.

"That's very sweet. Hold on a minute." She placed one hand over the mouthpiece and said, "Do you remember that tall red-haired man last evening?"

"The one who came with Ellen's daughter?"

"That's right. Do you mind if he comes to have breakfast?"

Katharine smiled widely. "Uh-oh," she said, then sang, *"Yes, it's me and I'm in love again."*

Nancy asked, "Yes or no?"

"Is he nice?"

"Very. He won't come unless you agree."

"Boy, that's different. Sure, tell him I said it's okay. Brother! I better go get dressed." She jumped up and ran barefoot out of the kitchen.

"My daughter says it's okay," Nancy said into the mouthpiece.

"Fine. Half an hour," he said. "I'm looking forward to seeing you."

"Me, too," she said, and hung up to tell the housekeeper there'd be a third for breakfast. She put a hand to her throat and closed her eyes for a moment, then went upstairs to dress.

Maggie sat, livid, waiting for the kettle to boil, her fingernails drumming on the tabletop. That stinking son of a bitch! That rotten bastard! They were all the same. They changed their minds at the drop of a hat and thought all they had to do was say they wanted out, make a fucking phone call and they were off the hook. Not this time! Not this goddamned time! She'd fix his wagon but good.

"I'll bet that was Mr. Nolan," Louise whispered to Faye. "I think he just broke up with Ma. Did you *hear* her?"

"He has to be the one she's been having over when we're out," Faye said.

"Well, he won't be coming over anymore," Louise said, lying on her stomach, chin propped on her hands.

"I'm not going anywhere near her today," Faye said.

"Me, neither." Louise got up and went to look out the window. "Faye," she exclaimed, "you should see all the snow! It looks just like the icing on Gramma's cake."

Faye went to stand beside her at the window. "Wasn't it wonderful?" she said. "The wedding and the party, and that fabulous house, all those nice people."

"It was tremendous," Louise said. "Katharine said she'd go skating with me today. I'm gonna go phone her."

"Don't phone her if Ma's in the kitchen," Faye advised.

"Why not?" Louise asked, her hand on the doorknob.

"Cause Ma didn't like Nancy. Nolan danced with her, and I saw the way Ma was watching them."

"So what's that got to do with me and Katharine?"

"Just don't, okay? She'll take her tea and go back to her bedroom. You can wait fifteen minutes, can't you?"

"Oh, all right," Louise said, returning to the window. "What d'you think Gramma and Bob are doing right now?"

Faye thought for a moment. "They're probably just being happy to-gether," she said at last.

Louise sighed, gazing out at the perfectly smooth snow. "It's *sooo* romantic," she said, and smiled.

*C*HAPTER

E I G H T E E N

"*A*ND WHERE D'YOU THINK YOU'RE GOING?" MAGGIE DE-manded. If anybody so much as looked at her sideways today, she'd commit murder.

"Skating." Louise pulled on her mittens, trying to ignore the danger signs: her mother's thinned lips and narrowed eyes, the combative pos-ture of hands on hips, the forward-thrusting jaw.

"Who with?"

"A girlfriend," Louise said innocently, recalling her sister's warning.

"What girlfriend?"

"Just a girlfriend." Louise was hot, standing there with her heavy clothes on, the ice skates tied by their laces slung around her neck. "Well, I'm going now. I'll see you later, Ma." She started down the hall.

"It's that girl from last night, isn't it?" Maggie guessd.

"Uh-huh." Louise kept aiming for the door.

"You're not going *anywhere* with her."

Faye emerged from the bedroom dressed to go out, and stood watching and listening.

"Yes I am, Ma," Louise said, at the door now.

"No you are *not!"*

Louise turned back. "I'm *going,*" she insisted.

"Did you *hear* me? I said *no!*" Maggie advanced toward her.

"Leave her alone, Ma," Faye said softly.

"And where d'you think *you're* going?" Maggie rounded on her.

"I'm going up to the Distasios', and Lou's going skating. Leave us alone. Okay?'' Faye went to stand beside her sister. "Just because you're in a bad mood, don't take it out on us.''

"Who the hell do you think you're talking to?'' Maggie said in the low deadly voice she used to use before she started hitting them.

"We're talking to you, Ma,'' Faye said, her tone less soft. "We're answering your questions. That's all.''

"You little bitches.'' Maggie's hands curled into fists. She longed to pound them, beat them to a pulp. But she didn't dare. Her goddamned mother would find out and kick up a fuss. "Get out of my sight!'' she barked. "Just get the hell out!''

"That's what we're trying to do,'' Faye said evenly.

Louise got the door open. Faye pushed her out, following right behind.

Maggie hesitated a moment, then tore to the door saying, "You're shoveling these steps and the walk before you go anywhere!''

Lou started to protest, but Faye said, "Okay. We'll do that. Go get the shovel, Lou.''

Maggie slammed back inside. Faye got the broom and started sweeping away the drift that was thick by the railing and just a sprinkling halfway across the porch. Louise came back dragging the shovel, muttering to herself.

"We'll take turns,'' Faye told her. "It won't take long, and then we can go.''

"She can't tell me who my friends are,'' Louise said hotly.

"Don't push her now, Lou. She'll go nuts. Didn't you see the way she looked? It was scary.'' Faye gave herself a little shake, as if physically ridding herself of the image. "Let's finish shoveling, then we'll go.'' Faye began sweeping the steps, anxious to get away. Something had happened and Ma was ready to kill. The best thing she and Lou could do was keep out of her way.

╬

Maggie was determined to make Nolan pay for the way he'd treated her. She could think of nothing else. As she marched into the store to return the red dress ideas tumbled through her mind and she tried to sort through them, to settle on the best course of action.

When the woman who ran the store finally made up her mind to pay attention, Maggie put the bag with the dress on the counter saying, "I'm returning this. I've decided it doesn't really suit me.''

The woman lost her smile and was all business as she removed the dress from the bag and began examining it carefully.

"I took off the tag," Maggie said. "It's there in the bag." What the hell was she looking for?

"This dress has been worn," the woman said. "I'm afraid I can't take it back."

"What're you *talking* about? It has not been worn."

"Oh, but it has, madam," the woman said knowingly, sniffing the fabric. "It smells of perfume. And if you'll look here . . ."

"I was wearing perfume when I tried it on," Maggie cut her off. "What're you trying to pull?"

"We can't take back a dress that's been worn. If you'll look," she tried to show Maggie something about the inside of the dress, but Maggie wasn't interested.

"I'm telling you that dress hasn't been worn!" she insisted, her voice deepening as the anger began throbbing in her temples. "I bought the damned thing yesterday, for Chrissake! When am I supposed to have worn it?"

The woman shook her head apologetically, and Maggie saw her as yet another imbecile trying to make trouble for her. "You give me back my goddamned money," Maggie said, "or I'll make you wish you'd never been born."

Taking a step back, the woman continued to shake her head, saying, "I'm sorry, but it's been worn. There's nothing I can do."

"You give me back my money," Maggie told her, rage coating everything she saw with a film of red, "or I'll break your goddamned windows. I'll wreck everything in the place."

Looking alarmed now but trying not to reveal it, the woman turned to the young salesgirl who'd come to stand beside her, quietly saying, "Call the police, Barb." Then to Maggie: "The dress has been worn and it's store policy. We don't give refunds on garments that have been worn."

Maggie pounded her fist on the glass counter and whirled around, eyes raking the racks of dresses. "Fine! Store policy! You want to argue, I'll just exchange it! I'll take that"—she pointed wildly to a navy dress that caught her eye—"in exchange."

"No refunds," the woman said implacably, "and no exchanges. I'm very sorry but that's our policy."

"Are you calling me a *liar?*" Maggie leaned across the counter, her face red, fists resting on the glass. "Is that what you're saying?"

"I'm saying the dress has been worn and we can't take it back." Holding it up, she pointed at the lining saying, "It has perspiration stains, Madame. A dress doesn't get stains like this just from being tried on."

Maggie grabbed the dress out of her hands. "Where d'you see stains?" she demanded. "Where? There's not a mark on this!"

The other salesgirl came up behind the counter, saying, "May I see it?" and Maggie threw the dress at her. The girl gave Maggie a startled glance, then began to inspect the garment. "I don't see . . ."

"Be quiet, Barb!" the older woman snapped. "It's been worn, and that's all there is to it."

"She can tell it doesn't have a mark on it!" Maggie pounced, pointing an accusing finger. "She knows. What the hell're you trying to pull?"

"It's been worn."

"It damned well hasn't!"

The two women glared at each other as a smiling patrolman opened the door and came inside saying, "Okay, ladies. What seems to be the trouble?"

Both Maggie and the woman tried to speak at the same time. The officer held up a hand and said to the woman behind the counter, "You first."

"She brought back a dress that's been worn and insists we refund her money. She says if we don't, she'll break the windows, wreck everything in here."

The officer turned to Maggie.

"The dress hasn't been worn. Ask her!" Maggie indicated the young salesgirl. "She'll tell you. That one just doesn't want to give me my money back."

"And what's your opinion, miss?" he asked the salesgirl who was still holding the dress in question.

"Well," she said, casting a nervous look at the older woman. "It doesn't look worn to me."

"She doesn't have my years of experience," the woman cut in.

"Let her finish, ma'am, please."

"It doesn't look to me as if it's been worn," said the salesgirl, certain she'd be fired for this, if the expression on the manager's face was anything to go by.

"Let's have a look at that," the policeman said, holding out one large hand. "When did you buy this?" he asked Maggie, turning the dress this way and that.

"Yesterday, for God's sake! She's out of her mind."

"You don't want to go threatening to break windows," he said, handing the dress back to the manager. "It looks brand new to me. Why don't you give her back the money and have done with this?"

Elated at having additional support, Maggie gave the patrolman a wide smile and said, "Thank you. I'll certainly never come in here again. What a way to treat customers!"

Seeing she was on the verge of defeat, the woman played her final card. "Where's your sales slip?" she asked.

Triumphantly, Maggie opened her purse, found the slip and slapped it down on the counter.

Exasperated, knowing full well the dress had been worn and that this raving lunatic had just taken her for a ride, the woman snatched it up and went to the cash register. Pulling bills from the compartmented tray, she got the exact amount of the purchase, slammed the register drawer shut then returned to put the money down on the counter in front of Maggie. "Don't ever come back here," she said.

"I wouldn't dream of it," Maggie said, stuffing the money into her purse. "And you can be sure I'll tell my friends about the way you do business." To the young salesgirl, she said, "Thank you for being truthful," then with the patrolman holding open the door, she swept out. All the way home she gloated over besting that bitch.

Her satisfaction made her restless; her body was filled with an energy that shouted for some decisive act. She went to put on the kettle, then stood by the stove looking at the telephone. On impulse, she snatched up the receiver and dialed Nolan's number, let it ring fifteen times. Getting the phone book, she concentrated, trying to remember the woman's last name. Nancy . . . what? V something. Vickers. No listing. The operator said, "That's an unlisted number. I'm sorry."

"But it's an emergency," Maggie said.

"I'm sorry," the operator repeated.

"Yeah, I'll bet you are!" Maggie threw down the receiver. The kettle was boiling. She turned off the gas, lit a cigarette, and paced. Nolan had dropped her like a hot rock to take up with that cow, and her own kid was suddenly bosom buddies with the daughter.

She went for Louise's diary and sat on the bed to read the latest entries, hoping to get some idea which direction she might take.

Fab. time, *real* champagne, AGAIN! F. sad because R. not there, but good time anyway. B. and M. *so* nice. Had snowball fight on way to car. Stayed up till almost one!

Boring crap. Initials for everything. A complete waste of time. She'd have to keep thinking.

Monday morning during the coffee break, she went downstairs to Nolan's office. He was at his desk. Looking over, he smiled and said, "Is there something you want, Maggie?"

She smiled back even though she wanted to stab him through the heart with his letter opener, and leaned provocatively against the door, saying, "Isn't there something *you* want?"

"No, I'm afraid not. I thought we'd settled all that."

"Oh, I think you do," she said, arching her back, her legs apart. She despised him for forcing her to grovel. But she knew what made him tick, knew how to get him excited. She had a power he couldn't resist.

He put down his pen, and said very quietly, "Please don't do this, Mag. I meant what I said over the weekend. It should have ended a long time ago, but we both let it continue. Let's not embarrass each other by trying to make out it was more than it was. There's no reason why we can't be civilized about it and continue our working relationship. Now," he said, taking a deep breath, "unless you have anything to add to what I've already said, I'd appreciate it if we could both get back to work." He smiled again, picking up his pen.

"Don't think you can treat me this way and get away with it," she said in a husky whisper, rage and humiliation squeezing the air out of her lungs. Who the hell did he think he was kidding with the polite act?

"What way?" he asked, genuinely taken aback. "I'm treating you politely and professionally. What are you *talking* about, Mag?"

"I know what you're up to," she said in that same whisper, her eyes slitting. "You don't fool me for a minute."

"I'm not trying to fool you," he said, bewildered. "I'm sorry you're choosing to interpret the things I've said and done as in any way insulting. The plain truth is I'm no longer comfortable with our . . . arrangement. I was under the impression you weren't particularly comfortable with it either. Given that, it seemed only reasonable to call it quits.''

Groping behind her, her hand found the doorknob and turned it. ''You'll be sorry,'' she whispered, humiliated, and stormed away.

Bemused, he reviewed everything he'd said, trying to see what could have offended her. He didn't think he'd been out of line. Granted, the timing left something to be desired; things had happened so abruptly. But, no. He hadn't said or done anything offensive. Still puzzled, he went back to the bills of lading.

Maggie's hunger for vengeance kept her preoccupied. All day at work, and all night while she slept, her mind was roiling with confrontational vignettes, scenes of carnage featuring her and Nolan, or Nolan and Nancy Vickers, or all three of them. She triumphed each time, demonstrating once and for all that no one made a fool of her and got away with it. She visualized herself bursting into Nancy's bedroom in the dark dead of night, catching the two of them naked, and reducing the pair to a state of abject terror as she menaced them with a variety of weapons ranging from a butcher's knife to a cutthroat razor. She wanted these two cowering, fearfully uttering apologies while she stood with a high-heeled foot placed firmly on the back of Nancy's neck.

And while she went over these scenes again and again, embellishing them with ever more details and snippets of dialogue, clever cutting things she said, life continued on around her without either her active participation or her interest. The girls came and went. Christmas, then Boxing Day, and the new year came and went. She scarcely noticed, and put in the least time possible with her mother and her new husband over the holidays. Their swanky apartment, their lovey-dovey behavior, their gifts, all made her stomach turn. She couldn't stand being around them, couldn't tolerate her mother's phony shows of interest and affection, and was more than willing to leave the girls there and go home.

She completely forgot Faye's birthday in January. When Louise came tiptoeing into the kitchen to ask in a whisper, ''Aren't you going to get Faye a card or anything?'' Maggie barked, ''What the hell for?'' before she realized what Louise was talking about. Her mother was likely fussing over Faye's birthday, just to make her look bad. She said, ''I forgot. All right? I suppose your grandmother's throwing a dinner party at the Royal York or something.''

Louise kept silent and waited.

"Don't hang over me," Maggie said. "I'll go out on my lunch hour tomorrow and get her one of those belated cards and a present. Okay?"

Louise said, "Okay," and went back to her room.

One more goddamned thing to think about, as if she didn't have enough on her plate.

✦

She decided to give it one last try. He was a man after all, and men wanted only one thing. Convinced she could win him over, Maggie left her machine and went downstairs to his office.

She slipped inside and with a smile closed the door then leaned against it. He looked up from his work. She raised her skirt slowly, still smiling.

He said, "Stop that and sit down, please, Mag."

"C'mon, Nolan," she said knowingly, lifting her skirt higher. "We don't have all day."

"Please," he said more strongly. "Stop that now and sit down. Since you're here, we might as well talk."

"You know talking's not what you really have in mind." She arched her back, one hand under her breast.

"Sit down!" he said sharply. "Now!"

She did, hating the fact that he had the upper hand here. Outside the factory, she was the one in charge. She sat back and crossed her legs, making sure he got a good eyeful.

"I want all this to stop."

Affecting a confused expression, she said, "I haven't the faintest idea what you're talking about. I'm only doing what you've always wanted me to do."

"Please, don't play games," he said. "I was hoping we could resolve this situation like grown-ups. Obviously, I was mistaken. I'm sorry it's come to this, but either you stop, or you'll have to go."

Inspired, she said, "I'll go to the union. They'll want to know why you're firing me. What're you going to tell them?"

"Why are you behaving this way?" he asked, knowing he'd never get a straight answer.

"I'm not doing anything," she said with childish stubbornness. *"You're* the one threatening to fire *me."*

Losing all patience, he got up and came out from behind the desk. Placing his hands on either arm of her chair, he put his face close to hers and said, "You're very foolish, Mag. Don't you know the people here dislike you? If you persist with this, you'll leave me no alternative but to let you go. And as for the union, the rep will believe whatever I tell him, and the water will close over your head without so much as a ripple. Stop trying to start things up again, Maggie, or you'll have to go." He pushed himself upright looking unhappy. "It's your choice," he said, sitting on the edge of the desk. "But don't try to set me against the union, because you'll come out the loser. If it comes down to whose word they're going to take, it'll be mine over yours, pure and simple. Please consider very carefully what you're doing. There's really no need for any of this. I know you're angry and you feel I've played unfairly. Perhaps I have. If that's the case, I apologize. Will you accept my apology and stop all this now?" He waited for her answer.

She glared at him, her entire body trembling. "You can't fire me," she said at last.

"I don't want to. I just want you to stop coming down here, throwing yourself at my head. Go back to work, and it will all be forgotten."

"You don't get rid of me that easily," she got out, loathing him, that film of red coating her vision again.

"You have a *choice*," he said, frustrated. "It's up to *you*. All you have to do is stop harassing me, and it'll be over."

"I know what you're up to," she whispered. "And it won't work."

"What won't work? What is it you imagine I'm trying to do?"

"Never you mind." Blindly, she got up and found her way out of the office. She had to stop halfway up the stairs to catch her breath, her nails digging deep into her palms. Everything in her was insisting she should race back to his office, sweep up the letter opener and plunge it into his neck. Saying one thing but meaning something else. Oh, she knew what he was up to, all right.

At noon she left the building and walked without direction, brimming with furious energy. It was only as she was passing a drugstore that she remembered Faye's goddamned birthday, and backtracked to buy a card and a giftbox of Evening in Paris cologne and dusting powder. It wasn't something she'd have given the kid under normal circumstances but she couldn't waste any time. She needed to think. At a coffee shop, she wolfed down a cheeseburger between gulps of scalding tasteless coffee, her appetite enormous. She could have eaten two more burgers but wouldn't spend the money. Leaving a fifteen cent tip on the counter, she headed along the slushy street, back to the factory. She'd fix that prick Nolan's wagon. He thought he held all the cards, but she had a few tricks up her sleeve. Just let him try to fire her! A fat lot he knew, trying to make out everybody in the factory hated her. The truth was they all hated him. One way or another she'd show him!

CHAPTER
NINETEEN

LOUISE'S LAST CLASS EACH DAY WAS ENGLISH, WITH MR. Craven. She liked his teaching; she liked him. He was younger than most of the other teachers, and completely different. He wore terrific clothes and always looked fresh, whether it was first thing in the morning or the end of the day; he had a low, unaccented speaking voice; he even smelled good.

Occasionally when he patrolled the aisles during a test, Louise breathed in the cool citrus fragrance of his cologne and felt the slightest bit dizzy. If he stopped to read over her shoulder, she lost her concentration and had to wait for him to move on before she could continue working. She was most comfortable in his class when he remained at the front of the room, usually perched on the corner of the desk, with one foot on the floor and the other dangling. Then she'd absorb the essence of what he was saying while she studied his dark good looks, his deep brown eyes and the way his mouth moved when he talked. She took note of every detail: the gold signet ring on the little finger of his right hand, the meticulous knot in his tie, the precision of his side-parted haircut, the shapely grace of his hands as they rested on his thigh, the polished leather of his shoes. He fascinated and frightened her. She left his classroom each time gulping down air the way she had the day Aldo nearly drowned her at Sunnyside Beach.

From time to time, with no warning, she'd find herself daydreaming about him and she'd gaze inward, rapt, as he opened the door to the apartment where she imagined he lived, and beckoned her inside. Her dreams never progressed beyond the point where she entered his home.

But over and over she saw herself approaching his door, saw him open it and wordlessly invite her to step across the threshold.

She'd emerge from these abbreviated dreams feeling edgy and excited —and embarrassed. She knew if her girlfriends ever found out they'd tease her relentlessly, accusing her of having a crush on her teacher. Half the girls at school were in love with Mr. Craven. *Daniel.* They'd sigh together, in groups of two and three, whispering his name as if it were a magical incantation. She'd rather die than be one of those gorpy girls rolling their eyes and getting red in the face, swooning and giggling if he happened to pass them in the hall. He just made her nervous, that was all, and she wished she'd stop having that dumb daydream about him.

One Friday early in the new term the bell rang, and Louise, along with the rest of her class, began stacking her books. Mr. Craven said, as he always did, "I haven't dismissed you people yet. Miss Parker, I'd like to see you for a minute. The rest of you"—he gave them a smile, as he always did—"hit the road. And have a good weekend."

He slipped off the edge of his desk as the kids poured out both doors, and Louise went up to the front of the room, books and binder clutched to her chest.

"Don't look so nervous, Miss Parker." He smiled, and her stomach filled with air and started rising inside of her. "I wanted to ask if you'd be interested in contributing to the *Review.*"

"I don't know. You mean a story or something?"

"A story, a poem. You write well. I thought you might want to try. We're a little short on material."

"I don't know," she repeated doubtfully.

"Think about it," he said with a smile. "If you decide you want to contribute something, let me know. There's still plenty of time."

"Okay. I will. Thanks a lot." She started for the door, the palms of her hands damp and her stomach like a balloon she'd swallowed.

As she came out of the room she was amazed to see her grandmother standing by the lockers, waiting for her.

"Gramma, hi!" Louise rushed over, shifting the books to her left arm to give her grandmother a hug. "Am I ever surprised! What're you doing here?"

"I wanted to see you," Ellen said. "I miss seeing you every Sunday."

"You didn't have to come all the way over here. You could've called me and I would've come over after school.'' Taking her grandmother's hand, she said, ''My locker's just around the corner.''

Walking with her, Ellen said, ''I needed some air, so I decided to walk over. I thought if you had no plans, you might like to come home with me, and the three of us could go out for supper later.''

''I'd love it. What about Faye?''

''I spoke to her a few minutes ago. She's going out tonight.''

''With Raffie.''

''That's right.'' Ellen watched Louise flip the dial on her combination lock then pull it open. ''She's going over to the store to wait for him. Apparently he's got an appointment with the dentist. After supper they're going to the movies.''

''They'll hold hands and smooch,'' Louise said, stowing several books, then bending to pull on her boots. She tossed her shoes into the bottom of the locker and reached for her coat. ''Neither one of them'll know a single thing that happened in the movie.''

Ellen laughed and lifted Louise's hair out over her collar. ''There are worse ways to spend a couple of hours, you know, Lulu.''

Louise pulled a face. ''It's gorpy.''

''Next year you might not think so.''

''Oh, I probably will,'' Louise said airily, closing the locker. ''Should I call Ma at work and tell her I won't be home?''

''I've already spoken to her, too.''

''Did she get mad?'' Louise asked somewhat anxiously. The past few weeks Ma had been watching her and Faye like a hawk, waiting to pounce if they said or did anything she didn't like.

''No,'' Ellen told her. ''She said she'd be glad of a little peace and quiet.''

Louise grinned and put her arm through her grandmother's as they set off. ''This is great,'' she said. ''I get to have you and Uncle Bob all to myself.''

They walked up Euclid on their way to Bloor Street, heads down against the stingingly cold wind that whipped up tiny daggerlike flakes from the snowbanks at the edges of the sidewalk.

''It's gonna snow some more,'' Louise huffed, her eyes slitted. ''I can smell it.''

''You're probably right,'' Ellen said, her gloved left hand holding her coat collar tight to her throat.

By the time they climbed into the Bloor streetcar their faces were bright red from the cold. When they sat down, Ellen opened her bag for a handkerchief and blotted her eyes and nose, both streaming in the relative heat of the car. Louise pulled a Kleenex out of her pocket and blew her nose with a loud honk, then looked at her grandmother and laughed.

Ellen laughed, too, gripped by a sudden surge of caring. "You're so adorable," she said, filled with wonder. In spite of Margaret, Louise had somehow managed to grow into a healthy girl, confident and loving and adaptable. Faye, on the other hand, was tentative, hoarding her emotions until she felt sure of a situation, then holding nothing back. She was full to the brim with feelings that bubbled over almost visibly. Everything touched her, yet she seemed unable to believe people could actually reciprocate her feelings. Louise, though, went unselfconsciously into the midst of any group, any set of circumstances. Where did such exceptional self-confidence come from?

"Do you miss the old house, Gramma?" Louise asked. "And what did you do with the furniture and stuff?"

"Your mother said she didn't want any of it, so I sold it," Ellen answered. "You'd think I'd miss the place, wouldn't you? But I don't, not a bit. It's as if I lived there a long, long time ago, as some other person."

"You were different when you lived on St. George," Louise said. "You're way happier now. I mean, you were happy then too. But it was . . . quiet, kind of. Not that you're noisy or anything now." She laughed at her poor choice of words. "To me, it was sort of like you'd decided nothing was ever going to change, and that was okay. Not the greatest, but okay. So you'd just go along and have the best time you could, even if you weren't expecting much. Does that make sense?"

Ellen looked at her in surprise for a moment. "It not only makes sense, it happens to be the truth. How could you know something like that, Lulu? You're still a child."

Louise shook her head. "I think it's only numbers that make you a child, Gramma," she said, feeling her way through her ideas. "Me and Faye, we've had to watch everybody all our lives, deciding who was okay and who might turn out to be like Ma. Maybe when you have to be careful all the time, you don't get to be a little kid for very long. Oh, sometimes we do dumb stuff like other kids, but we're always being careful, in case people suddenly change on us and start saying and doing scary things.''

"I'm sorry," Ellen said quietly. "I know it hasn't been easy for you. If only I'd known . . .''

"It's okay, Gramma. Me and Faye, we're fine. We've always got each other. You know?''

"I know.''

"How come you came to the school, really?''

"I was bored and needed to get out," Ellen admitted. "I've worked most of my adult life you know, Lulu. I always thought I'd like nothing better than to stay home, with time to relax, go shopping, putter about, try new recipes. The first few weeks were fine. I enjoyed getting the apartment fixed up. But lately I've been killing time. Bob hasn't found anyone to replace me. So he's had a temp in from an agency. Just between you and me, I think he's too used to working with me. So we talked it over, and Monday I'm starting back at the office. It suits us both down to the ground. He can stop interviewing, and I can stop twiddling my thumbs.''

"Well, that's great then," Louise said. "As long as you're happy.''

"I am," Ellen assured her. "Very happy. What about you, Lulu? Are you happy?''

Louise looked surprised. "Sure," she said. "So's Faye. We're fine, Gramma. Honestly.''

"You'd tell me if there was a problem, wouldn't you?''

"Course I would. But everything's really okay. Cross my heart.''

The wind at the intersection of Avenue Road and Bloor was fierce, sending newspapers spiraling across the street, and forcing men to dart into the road to retrieve their hats. As they waited in front of the Royal Ontario Museum for the lights to change, vehicles and people moved as if in slow motion. The air seemed a solid icy mass they had to push their way through.

By the time they entered the apartment building the wind had filled with snow and was driving it downward at an oblique angle. The cars and buses had their headlights on and wipers going.

"Maybe," Louise said happily as they waited for the elevator, "we'll get snowed in and I'll have to sleep over.''

"Maybe." Ellen gave her a conspiratorial smile. "I bought a few things, just in case.''

Frankie looked up when Faye came into the store, and said, "Cara! I'ma so glad you come. I been waiting for Aldo but just now he calls up tellin' me he's going somewhere. I gotta go alla the way out to Malton to pick up a package from the customs people at the airport. You'll stay and look after the store for me, eh?"

"Sure," Faye agreed. "I'll be glad to."

He pinched her cheek. "You're a good girl," he grinned. "I just get my coat, then I go."

He hurried off upstairs, and Faye went to the back of the store to hang up her coat and remove her boots. By the time he came down, she'd tied on an apron and was settled on the stool by the cash register with her library copy of *East of Eden*.

"It's gonna take a couple hours," he told her, looking out the window at the falling snow. "I don't go now I gotta wait 'til Monday, eh? I try to get back fast as I can. But Raffie, he oughta get home ina time to close up. Okay?"

"Okay. I'll look after everything. Don't worry."

"*Gràzie, cara!*" He got his ring of keys from the hook beside the cash register, then went out the rear door to the truck parked behind the store.

Faye sat with the book unopened on her lap and watched the snow fall. The wind whined at the front door, pushing in around the frame. People went past on the sidewalk, bent forward as they battled the gusting snow. The streetcars were oddly quiet, as if skating along the tracks. An occasional car with tire chains went rattling by, the chains making a muffled clanking. Inside the store everything seemed very clear, the colors astonishingly vivid in contrast to the swirling gray whiteness outside. She heard the furnace rumbling in the cellar and thought of how warm it would be down in their secret place. She felt a little leap of excitement at the thought of being alone with Raffie, the two of them touching and kissing.

She opened the book and began to read, glancing up every few minutes as another dark, bundled figure pushed homeward through the accumulating snow.

There were few customers. People were anxious to get home before the storm stopped traffic altogether. She was just giving a woman her change when the door opened and Aldo came in with the Tomasino twins.

The twins remained by the door, hands jammed in their pea-jacket pockets, while Aldo swaggered over saying, "How's it going there, Faye?"

"Just fine," she answered, hoping he'd leave quickly. She'd come to dislike Aldo during the past year, and it set her on edge being anywhere near him.

"Where's the old man?" he asked, reaching past her to hit the NO SALE key on the cash register.

"What're you doing, Aldo?"

"Don't get your tits in an uproar. I'm taking a couple of bucks."

"Did you ask permission?"

He slammed shut the drawer and leered at her. "Did you ask permission?" he mimicked. "It's *my* goddamned store, case you forgot." He turned to the hulking twins, who hadn't moved. "I gotta tell the old lady I'm going. Grab an apple or something, you guys."

The twins nodded. Tony turned, picked up two McIntosh apples with one enormous hand, gave one to his brother and put the other into his pocket. Bruno, his eyes on Faye, sank his teeth into the apple. Faye opened her book and stared at the page, her heart beating too fast. Upstairs, Aldo was loudly telling his mother he was going out. Faye winced, imagining his piercing voice cutting through Blanche's head. Aldo was such a pig. He didn't care about anyone, not even his own mother.

After a minute he came clumping down the stairs, the open clasps on his galoshes rattling. "Don't take any wooden nickles, there, Faye, and keep your muff warm. Come on, guys." He pulled open the door, and the twins, like identical robots, turned and followed him out, leaving the door wide open.

Faye got up and went to close it, then stood by the window display watching as the trio headed east toward Bathurst. The traffic on the wide street was barely moving, except for the streetcars sliding soundlessly along the slick-looking silver tracks. The wind had died away and now the snow drifted straight down, accumulating quickly. It felt odd to be inside and warm while inches away the city was being smothered. She breathed in the tart, somewhat winy aroma of the winter apples, a polished pyramid those idiotic Tomasino twins had disturbed. Hearing a sound, she turned to see Blanche coming slowly down the stairs, one tread at a time, her hand very white on the banister.

Faye went across the store to the bottom of the stairs. Looking up, she said softly, "Hi, Mrs. DiStasio. How are you?"

Blanche seemed to be concentrating very hard on getting from one step to the next. When she had both feet on the second step from the bottom, her left hand still gripping the railing, she lifted her head and looked at Faye.

In little more than a whisper, she said, "Faye." Looking dazed, she paused, then said, "Have to sit down," and lowered herself to the step.

Uncertainly, Faye sat down beside her, taking hold of Blanche's hand. It was shockingly cold. At once Faye began trying to warm it. "You're so cold. Why don't I go up and get your sweater?"

The cold hand stopped her. "Stay with me," Blanche whispered, her left hand releasing its grip on the banister. "I don't feel right, Faye," she said, turning to look into Faye's eyes.

"Maybe I should get your pills." Again, Faye moved to go.

"No, stay."

Faye gazed at the woman, returning automatically to trying to warm the icy hand that lay between hers. Blanche was completely without color. Her skin looked like wax that had been melted in a thin, unblemished white layer over the bones of her face, sinking deep into the hollows of her large, very dark eyes.

"I'm scared, Faye," she said. And Faye could see the fear shining in her eyes. "The pain." She wet her lips, her eyes clinging to Faye's as her left hand lifted, wavering, then touched cold against Faye's cheek. Every movement seemed to require tremendous effort, and Faye was all at once very afraid. She glanced over at the door, hoping someone would come in and help. Raffie would be home any minute now. She hoped he'd be there soon. She didn't know what to do.

"I can't see right," Blanche whispered. "Everything's double, one on top of the other. And my hand." Again she wet her lips as she slid her right hand out of Faye's grasp and held it up, looking at it as she flexed her fingers slightly. "It's numb," she said, touching it almost wonderingly with her left hand, eyes shifting back to Faye, both hands falling slowly to her lap. "So tired," she sighed.

Faye put an arm around her. "Rest for a little while," she said. "Then I'll help you back upstairs."

Sighing again, Blanche murmured, "So kind, Faye," and let her head come to rest on Faye's shoulder, her eyes closing.

Faye shifted, turning, so that she held Blanche cradled in both arms, like a child. She didn't weigh much more than a child. Holding her, Faye remembered Sophie and the way the little girl used to go to sleep in her arms, just the way Blanche was going to sleep now. Rocking her gently, Faye stroked her cool forehead, her long thick hair, while with her eyes on the door she willed someone to come. She wanted to get help but didn't dare leave Blanche. She was afraid even to move. There was nothing she could do but hold her, humming under her breath, every so often murmuring, "It's okay, it's okay. You sleep now. Sleep. That's right. You'll feel better when you wake up."

Outside it was dark. The snow fluttered past the window, past the pyramids of winter apples, Florida oranges and grapefruits, green peppers and Prince Edward Island potatoes, golden mounds of cooking onions, imported tomatoes. Not a sound except Blanche's shallow breathing and the creak of the stair tread as Faye held her gently, rocking slowly, slowly. "It's okay. You sleep now, sleep. Everything'll be all right." Blanche looked like a lovely wax doll, sleeping in her arms the way Faye and Lou had slept in this woman's arms as babies. All silence. Minutes ticking away on the big electric clock over the cash register.

Then Blanche breathed deeply in her sleep, once, twice. She exhaled: a long, long sigh that seemed to settle her farther into Faye's arms, her weight somehow greater. Faye looked down, still stroking the thick springy hair. Blanche was perfectly still. Nothing moved, not her eyelashes or her eyes beneath the lids, not her lips. Nothing. No part of her moved. Faye laid a hand on Blanche's chest, but there wasn't a hint of movement beneath her palm. Take another breath! Faye concentrated hard on getting Blanche to breathe, as if by the power of her own determination. But the woman remained motionless. She lay against Faye's breast, those beautiful hands she and Lou had always admired utterly still, terribly cold.

Faye resumed rocking, holding her secure with one hand while with the other she tried to massage some warmth into Blanche's long fingers. Raffie would come home soon and the two of them would get his mother back upstairs to the sofa. They'd cover her with blankets, make sure she was warm. Then they'd go to the kitchen to cook supper together. She'd do the cutting and chopping while Raffie did the actual cooking, knowing just how much spaghetti to put into the pot of boiling water, and just how much oregano, crushed garlic, and red wine to stir into the simmering sauce.

Why didn't anyone come? Didn't people need some of the long Italian tomatoes, or some spaghettini, or maybe a half pound of fusilli for their supper? Didn't anyone want a half dozen fat Florida oranges or some lemons for their tea? Wasn't *anyone* going to come? She looked down. There was tears on Blanche's face. Her headache was so bad she was crying. Poor Blanche. "Don't worry," she crooned. "Raffie will be home soon." Her chest was pumping hard, hurting. "Everything'll be all right now." Please, somebody come!

✦

Raffie hated going to the dentist. He'd already been sitting in the waiting room for forty minutes, looking at old copies of *National Geographic* and tattered issues of *Maclean's* while everybody else went ahead of him. He sat leafing through the magazines, his stomach growling, hoping nobody could hear it, praying he didn't have any cavities. Maybe he was a coward, but he hated the drill. He'd only had four fillings in his life but he remembered vividly the agonizing pain when the drill touched a nerve, and the scorched stink of tooth enamel. He shuddered and looked again at the nurse, who sat with her back to him. There were only four patients, including him, left waiting now. He hoped he was next, so he could get this over and done with. Here he had a four o'clock appointment and it was already getting on for five. He could hear Dr. Winger's voice and the sickening whir of the drill and felt himself break into a sweat. At this rate he wouldn't get home much before six. And Faye was waiting for him. He hoped Aldo had gone out somewhere with his two bonehead buddies instead of hanging around making wiseass cracks and getting Faye nervous. What the hell was wrong with Aldo, anyway?

When he'd first started turning mean, Raffie had blamed Tony and Bruno, convinced they were a bad influence. But after spending some time with the twins he saw he had things backward. It was Aldo who influenced them. The twins were basically two overgrown, not very bright guys who pretty much did what they were told. And Aldo had them doing all kinds of rotten stuff, like throwing a scare into little kids after dark and talking dirty to girls. Raffie covered for him a lot of the time, because if Pop ever found out some of the things Aldo got up to, he'd take a strap to him. And Raffie didn't want that, mostly because he couldn't help believing that somewhere under the greasy DA and the black outfits and the dirty mouth was the decent kid brother Aldo had been up until a couple of years before.

It was getting harder and harder, though, to find any trace of that kid.

Raffie tried repeatedly to talk to him, but it was like talking to a wall. The only thing that got through to Aldo was a direct physical threat, and that only worked because Raffie was so much bigger and because underneath the tough-guy crap, Aldo was a chicken. He could only play tough when he had the twins to back him up. Alone, all it took was one light poke in the arm and Aldo turned to jelly. But that didn't stop him from giving lip to Pop, or from cutting school, or from pretty much ignoring their mother. And it was anybody's guess what other stuff he got up to with Tony and Bruno.

He was forever making cracks at Faye. Raffie caught him at it time and again and threatened to break both his arms if he didn't quit. So Aldo would give it a rest for a few days or a week, then he'd start in again. The only one he couldn't get to was Louise. The moment Aldo opened his mouth she ridiculed him, treating him with contempt and shattering his pride with deadly accurate comments. She laughed at him, and called him a pathetic bully. Aldo would turn red and storm away. Louise sure had his number. He didn't scare her one bit.

If Raffie got home and found out Aldo had been mouthing off to Faye again he'd have to take him out back to the lane and smack him around until he got the message. Because as long as Raffie was around, *no one* was ever again going to upset or hurt the girl he loved.

Tossing aside the magazine he'd been holding, he put the ankle of his right foot up on his left knee and wrapped his hands around his bent leg. It'd probably be too late to go to the show tonight. By the time he got supper on the table it'd be after seven. And when they finished eating and got the dishes done, it'd be way after eight. Faye would be disappointed. She'd been looking forward to seeing *From Here to Eternity*. Well, he'd make it up to her. And if they weren't going to the show, maybe they'd go down to the cellar for a while.

He glanced around the waiting room. Nobody was taking any notice of him. Dr. Winger's voice murmured beyond the closed door, and the drill kept whirring away. Raffie folded his arms across his chest and tucked his fists into his armpits. If the stores were still open he'd stop on the way home and get some vanilla ice cream for his mother. It was one of the few things she could still eat. Brother! What was *taking* so long? He wanted to get *out* of there.

CHAPTER

TWENTY

LOUISE COULD TELL HER GRANDMOTHER WAS ON EDGE. IT was a quarter after six and Bob hadn't come home yet. Every few minutes Ellen got up and went to look out the window. Avenue Road was blocked in both directions with slow-moving traffic, and the snow kept on falling. The outer edge of the balcony was already a good foot deep in it.

"He'll be here soon, Gramma," Louise said, sensing her concern. Going to stand beside her at the window, she put an arm around her waist. "He's just stuck in the traffic."

"Of course he is," Ellen said. "It's silly of me to worry."

Louise moved even closer. "You're not silly. I think it's nice that you worry."

Ellen laughed and kissed the top of her head. "It doesn't look as if we'll be going out. We'd better get started on some supper."

"Okay." Louise took her grandmother's hand. "Let's see what we've got."

Ellen allowed herself to be led into the kitchen. Standing next to Louise, she looked at the contents of the fridge and thought how painful it was to care. Once your feelings were committed you opened yourself to extremes of emotion, so that small things that wouldn't have mattered before were now horribly significant. Someone you loved was late getting home and you imagined all the worst possible scenarios. It was what she'd told Bob the day of the wedding: She knew now what she'd be losing if she lost him. And so almost daily she steeled herself for that possibility. The reverse side of love was loss, and she couldn't ignore the glimpses she had regularly of the dull underside of that currency. The most difficult aspect of loving was the knowledge that arbitrary, irrational incidents could so easily eliminate the object of your love.

She told herself to snap out of it. Her worrying wouldn't change anything. It was a pointless waste of energy. "What should we have, honey?'' she asked her sprite-like granddaughter, unable for the moment to make even a decision so elemental as what to cook. Snap out of it! she told herself.

"Let's see. There's chicken. Oh, and asparagus. I *love* asparagus, don't you?"

Ellen looked at the girl as she peered into the refrigerator, dark blond hair falling forward to conceal the lower half of her face. "I love it, too," she said, her mood mercifully lightened simply by the sight of Lulu moving things around on the shelves. "Take out whatever appeals to you, and I'll get some potatoes."

"I could help cook," Louise offered tentatively.

Ellen opened a drawer and handed her an apron. "You're good for me. Do you know that?"

"Yeah? I'm glad. You're good for me, too. I *love* to cook but Ma only ever lets us put things in the oven or peel potatoes. She never actually lets us make anything."

"Well, this is your golden opportunity. You can cook the entire meal if you want."

"Really, honestly?"

"Honestly."

"Great!" Louise moved to wash her hands at the sink. "You'll help, won't you?" she asked.

"Of course I will." Ellen leaned against the opposite counter.

"Did your mother let you cook when you were my age?"

"Uh-huh." Ellen reached for her pack of Sweet Caporals. "We were very close, my mother and I. She lost her first child, my older brother."

"You had an older brother? I didn't know that."

"He was born in Bergen, before my parents left Norway to come to Canada. I don't remember him at all. I was two when he died."

"That's so sad. What did he die of?"

"Meningitis. He was four and a half. Anyway, my mother and I were always very close after that. She couldn't have any more children, although they kept trying for a long time. So, yes," she said, smiling, "my mother let me cook. She let me do a lot of things my friends weren't allowed to do."

"You're so lucky."

"Yes," Ellen agreed. "I was."

"Did you want to have more children?" Louise asked, unwrapping the package of chicken.

Ellen paused. "No. Not at the time. But, looking back, I think maybe it was a mistake. I should have had at least one more."

"I don't think I'll have any," Louise said. "I don't even know if I want to be married." She looked over to see her grandmother's reaction to this.

Instead of being shocked, the way Faye was whenever Louise said something along these lines, her grandmother said, "For some people marriage isn't the answer. It's a decision you have to make for yourself, Lulu. Only you can know what's right for you."

"It wasn't right for Ma, was it?"

"She made a poor choice. Otherwise, it could have been right. It's hard to say. Maybe if she'd picked a different man, she'd have been happy."

"Was he so awful? Ma makes him sound really horrible."

"He was just a weak man who got more than he bargained for. And your mother got a lot less. We tried to talk her out of it, but she wouldn't listen. She's always been very stubborn."

"Is she *ever*," Louise concurred.

"That doesn't excuse what he did, though. Running off and leaving her that way. She's had a hard time."

"Yeah," Louise said. "But so've a lot of other people."

"Your mother's not like other people."

"Boy! I'll say!" Louise said with energy. "Me and Faye can't wait until we're old enough to have a place of our own."

"I'm always here for the two of you, Lulu. You know that, don't you?"

"I know that, Gramma."

The minute hand crept around the clock face. Faye sat on the steps holding Blanche, her body aching from the strain of remaining in one position for so long. But she wasn't going to move an inch until Raffie or Mr. DiStasio got back. She didn't want to take a chance on disturbing Blanche when she was sleeping so peacefully.

At five-thirty a woman came into the store. Closing the door behind her she looked over at Faye, her eyebrows lifting. Faye held a finger to her lips, then signaled the woman to help herself. The woman smiled, pulled off her mitts, got several bags and began filling them with potatoes, onions, and carrots. She weighed each bag, picked up a crayon to mark down the price, and when she was finished got out her change purse and again looked questioningly over at Faye. Faye nodded. The woman rang up the amount of the sale, put a two dollar bill in the register drawer, took change, and slid the drawer closed. Mitts on, the bag of vegetables in her arm, she smiled again at Faye, and went back out into the storm.

Faye continued to rock Blanche, humming softly.

Raffie was so relieved to learn he had no cavities that he actually laughed several times while his teeth were being cleaned. No drill. No probing with pointed metal instruments that touched a sensitive area and sent a bolt of pain shooting through his head. He wouldn't have to come back here for a whole year. He spat, then rinsed the gritty polish from his mouth, said goodbye and thanks a lot, and hurried to the waiting room for his coat.

When he opened the outside door he stopped in surprise at the sight of the snow. There'd only been a few flakes coming down when he'd arrived. In the space of less than two hours at least eight or ten inches had fallen. Spadina Road was clogged with cars, and arriving at the corner, he saw Bloor was, too. He'd planned to take the streetcar but it was obvious it would be faster to walk. He turned onto Bloor and started west. What a mess! Not a snowplow in sight. The storm probably caught them by surprise. Storms always caught them by surprise. He couldn't remember one time in his entire life when the plows and sanders had been ready to go at the onset of a snowfall. You would've thought they'd have figured out by now that every winter was the same, with a big fall around the end of November, followed by three or four in December, and then one after another right through until maybe the end of March. Toronto got a lot of snow. But the plows and sanders were never ready, and the traffic always backed up and finally stopped, with cars abandoned everywhere so that when the plows did at last come through they had to make detours around the ones left smack in the middle of the road.

It was slow going, hard to see with the stuff blowing right in his eyes. The sidewalks were reduced to single-file paths. He had to keep stepping off into the deep drifts to let people get by. It took him close to twenty minutes just to get over to Bathurst.

Starting south, he thought again of Faye sitting, waiting for him, and tried to put some speed on. The pedestrian traffic on Bathurst wasn't as heavy as it had been on Bloor so there wasn't any kind of a path, just deep random footsteps in the snow. He kicked through from one footstep to the next, leaving a path in his wake. His boots were filling with snow and his ankles were burning from the wet cold.

For a time, as his body moved him closer to home, he thought about Faye, feeling as he always did, a fierce protectiveness combined with longing. His parents accepted her; she was a part of the family, Raffie's girl. They loved her as much as he did. She was so good to his mother, so helpful to his Pop. He was the luckiest guy going. Now if they could just find a doctor who'd be able to figure out why his mother kept getting those rotten headaches, everything would be perfect. It scared him to see her so sick all the time. Her hands trembled, and even though she smiled a lot, he could tell she was feeling lousy. And damned Aldo wouldn't even keep his voice down around the house, or do anything to help. He left his clothes on the floor, left the bathroom a mess every time he used it, never bothered to put things back in the fridge. Pop begged him but Aldo said, "What's the big deal, eh?" and went off, leaving a mess for other people to clean up.

Raffie went into the variety store a few doors down from his place to get a package of Silverwood's vanilla ice cream, knowing his mother would be pleased. The smallest things gave her such a kick. Faye was the same. He'd bought her a box of stationery for her birthday and you'd have thought he'd given her diamonds, or something as important as the portable typewriter her grandmother and Bob had given her for Christmas. It didn't matter what it was, Faye acted every time as if no one had ever given her anything more wonderful. He loved that about her.

When he opened the door and saw Faye on the steps with his mother in her arms, he knew. He knew, but couldn't make himself believe it. Reaching behind him, he flipped the sign on the door from OPEN to CLOSED, then turned the lock. Faye looked up and held a finger to her lips so he'd be quiet. He obeyed, tiptoeing across the store in his galoshes as if he didn't already know. Faye was acting as if Mom was only asleep. Why was she pretending? Or did she actually believe that?

He stood a few feet away, the bag with the ice cream still in his gloved hand, and felt sorrow wedge itself into his chest, pushing painfully between his ribs. Faye slowly rocked his mother back and forth, back and forth, like a baby. Didn't she know? What should he do? In one moment, he went from feeling grown-up and in charge of himself to feeling help-lessly young and uncertain. And just as suddenly he felt old and very weary. The warmth of the store wrapped itself around him. He could smell the fruit ripening in the artificial heat and light, the bananas becom-ing speckled, the skin of the tomatoes shrinking as the pulp inside started to dry. It struck him that every last fruit and vegetable was in the process of dying.

"How long've you been sitting here, Faye?" he asked thickly.

"Ages," she whispered. "I didn't want to disturb her." She pressed her lips to Blanche's forehead, then resumed her rocking.

He put the ice cream down on the floor. "Let me take her."

Faye shook her head no, and hung on, her arms tightening around Blanche.

"It's okay, Faye," he said. But like a little kid Faye shook her head, refusing to let go. He dropped down on his haunches and put one gloved hand under her chin. "Look here at me, Faye." When she raised her head slightly, her eyes large and pearly gray, fearful, he said, "Let me take her upstairs and put her to bed. Okay?"

"She's comfortable where she is, Raffie."

"No, she isn't, Faye. And neither are you. Come on now. Let me take her." He reached to lift his mother out of Faye's arms, and Faye stopped resisting.

He'd carried his mother dozens of times in the past few months, when she'd been too nauseated even to stand up. Her body was rigid now, heavier than before, her arms and legs dangling. Faye slid to one side and he started up the stairs thinking they'd have to call somebody. Who did you call when your mother died? What were you supposed to do?

"Your father had to go to the airport to pick up a package," Faye explained, getting stiffly to her feet. Her legs and hips ached as she followed Raffie up the stairs and down the hall to his parents' room, where he carefully set his mother on the bed. She had a desperate need to make him understand. He had to know it wasn't her fault, she hadn't done anything wrong. But if she hadn't done something wrong, this wouldn't have happened.

"We'd better call someone," he said as Faye's hand crept into his, both of them looking at his mother.

"I didn't know what to do," Faye said, starting to cry, her hand clinging to his. "I'm sorry, Raffie. I didn't know what to *do!*" She wept, huge gulping sobs shaking her body. Blanche was dead, and it was all her fault for keeping her on the stairs where it was drafty. Or maybe it was because Aldo had talked so loudly to her. She was terrified Raffie would blame her, and terrified by how easily, how silently Blanche had stopped living. She couldn't pretend anymore that she didn't know what had happened. And now, for the rest of her life, she'd carry this death around with her, hearing again and again that long slow exhalation, and feeling the increased heaviness of the body in her arms.

Raffie automatically held her, unable to take his eyes off his mother. He felt Faye trembling inside his arms. Snow from his galoshes puddled on the floor. At last, drawing a deep tremulous breath, he said, "We'd better call someone." He pulled the comforter up over his mother's shoulders, then took Faye's hand to lead her out.

In the living room, with Faye still clutching his hand, still sobbing, he was astonished when she cried, "It's all my fault, I know."

"No, it isn't, Faye. Why would you think that?"

"I don't know!" she wailed. "I just don't want you to blame me."

"I'd never blame you," he said. "I'm glad she wasn't all alone, that you were with her. It's not your fault."

He picked up the receiver with his free hand, hooked it between his chin and shoulder, and dialed the operator.

"I need to talk to someone," he said, finding it hard to speak.

"What about?" the operator asked impatiently.

"My mother died. I don't know what I'm supposed to do."

"Oh," the operator said. "I'm sorry. Hold the line, dear. I'll put you through to someone who'll help."

"Thank you," he said, enormously grateful. He was going to cry, and tried to hold it back. He'd have plenty of time to cry later. Right now he needed someone to tell him what to do.

The diner was dead. They hadn't had a customer in forty minutes.

"Might as well close up," Mack said at last.

About time, Maggie thought. She'd spent the last hour refilling the napkin dispensers, topping off the salt and pepper shakers, adding a few drops of water and vinegar to the ketchup bottles then pouring off the watery dregs into other bottles—Mack's cheapskate way of stretching a dollar. The counters and tabletops had been cleaned, so all she and Joyce had to do was drain the coffee urn and get it filled, ready for morning.

Two hours work and she'd made less than two dollars in tips. A complete waste of time. She changed quickly out of her uniform, pulled on her boots, then her coat. Outside the diner she stood and looked up and down the street. She didn't feel like going home. An eastbound streetcar was coming. She waited and got on. Sitting near the back she thought about quitting Mack's place, going after a part-time job at one of the good restaurants downtown where she'd make decent tips and maybe meet some halfway decent people instead of the bums who came staggering in from the Horseshoe or one of the other taverns, looking to sober up on some black coffee before they headed home.

At Yonge Street she got off the streetcar and followed a number of other passengers down into the subway. She'd only been on it a couple of times since it opened a year or so before.

Waiting on the packed northbound platform, she tried not to breathe in the stink of wet wool and somebody's garlicky breath blowing right in her face. She couldn't get away from it and conspicuously fanned the air, hoping whoever it was would get the message and buy some goddamned SenSen or something.

Just north of Bloor the train emerged into the storm at ground level. Everything was blanketed in snow. She moved to the doors, and when the train pulled into the Rosedale station, she got off, again following other passengers as they climbed the stairs. Some of the people split off to catch buses in the adjoining loop. The rest pushed out into the blowing snow. She started up Crescent Road, glancing to her left as she crossed the overpass, seeing the train snaking away down below.

A few people and only a couple of cars passed as she pushed ahead through the snow. Not even seven o'clock, and the city was stopped dead. What a place! A little snow, and everything stopped. Montreal probably didn't die because of a little snow, or New York, say. Only good old Hogtown. Sometimes she hated this city, with its rigid blue laws, its rules and regulations, its cautious citizens. Her father used to say the English-speaking Canadians were practitioners of civil obedience. They believed in law and order. They wanted a safe, clean city where they could raise their families without fear. Without fun, too. Clean, safe, and boring. With her lousy luck she'd be stuck here for the rest of her life, stuck at her crummy machine at Raymar, stuck waiting tables in Mack's roach-infested dump just so she could put decent-looking clothes on her back.

For weeks now she'd been waking up in the middle of the night, unable to go back to sleep, spending hours tossing and turning, agitated and outraged. Nolan had come up on the floor a couple of times to talk to the foreman. And he'd given her these polite nods that made her want to march over and smack him right in the mouth. He thought he was calling the shots, lording it over her.

She went directly to the house as if she'd lived in Rosedale all her life. Lit up like a Christmas tree, and Nolan's car parked in the driveway for all the world to see. She stood on the sidewalk and gazed at the windows, then quickly looked both ways to see if anyone was coming. Not a soul in sight. Everybody snug inside, hiding out from the storm. She peeked in each of the windows in turn, seeing only brightly lit empty rooms. Ducking across the walk, she worked her way along the front of the house until she got to the window of the sitting room, where the wedding gifts had been left the night of the party. Raising her head cautiously she saw, with a jolt, Nolan, the bitch, and her kid sitting together on the sofa, watching television.

Her breathing gone haywire, she took it in: Nolan and that woman on either end, their arms extended along the back of the sofa, fingers laced together, with the kid in the middle. Jesus! The sight was like a blow to her midriff. It hurt. She rested for a moment against the white-painted brick wall of the house, refusing to give in to the hurt, refusing to let herself cry because that bastard threw her over for someone with money. It was so damned unfair! She was better looking, had a better shape too. And she'd put money on it that she was ten times better in bed. Sucking in a mouthful of air so cold it made her teeth ache, her eyelashes clotted with flakes, she moved as quickly as she could, anxious to get away. The last thing she needed was Nolan, or that Nancy, to find her there.

As she retraced the route back toward the subway station she wished she'd pounded on the door, forced a confrontation. But what would that have proved? No, it was a good thing she hadn't done that.

When she looked up to get her bearings she saw that she was already at the station. But she had too much energy churning away inside to stand around on a platform waiting for a train. She marched on, head down, until she was crossing Davenport and saw the Morrissey Tavern up ahead. That was the ticket. She'd stop and have a drink and a cigarette before going home.

⊥

Bob finally arrived at twenty past seven. He bent to kiss Ellen, then, with one of his wonderful smiles, said, "Lulu! This is a real treat," and gave her a big hug.

She returned the hug enthusiastically, imagining other kids got to greet their fathers this way every day. All at once she had a strong sense of what she and Faye had missed out on. "I made the supper," she told him proudly, as Ellen took his coat and briefcase, and he peeled off his rubber overshoes.

"You did, eh?"

"Yup. We've got chicken and asparagus and mashed potatoes. You got stuck in the traffic, didn't you? Gramma was worried."

Straightening, he said, "You shouldn't have worried, Ellen."

She shut the closet door saying, "Excuse us for a minute, Lulu," and the two of them went into the bedroom.

As she checked the dining table again, Louise thought maybe she shouldn't have said anything about Gramma being worried. She hoped her grandmother wasn't going to be mad at her. Sometimes she said whatever came into her head, and that was dumb. While she waited for them to come back she stood by the wall-to-wall window, watching the snow. She had kind of a funny ache, and pressed the heels of her hands into the base of her belly on either side of her hip bones. She was starving and hoped they didn't stay too long in the bedroom. Everything was ready, the first meal she'd ever cooked entirely by herself. Crossing her fingers, she said a silent prayer that her grandmother wouldn't be mad at her, and that the snow would keep falling. She was dying to spend the night.

In the bedroom Ellen sat on the side of the bed watching Bob hang up his suit jacket before removing his tie. He undid the top button of his shirt, and sat down beside her. "You shouldn't have worried, Elly."

"There are dozens of things I shouldn't do, but I do them anyway. That's the way I am." She gave him a somewhat self-deprecating smile. "Did you have to leave the car downtown?"

"Nope. I sat in traffic with the rest of the shmoes, listening to the radio announcer telling me nothing was moving." He chuckled, then kissed her. "I should've left the car, but that would have been too intelligent. If I'd hopped on the subway I'd have been home an hour ago. I'm sorry to be so late, but it's kind of nice to know you were worried."

She stood up saying, "After Monday I won't have to wonder where you are. It'll be a relief to stop behaving like such a ninny."

"You, a ninny?" His eyebrows lifted exaggeratedly. "Never!"

"You wouldn't mind, would you, if Lulu spends the night?"

"Not a bit." He pushed off his shoes and flexed his toes. "I'm crazy about that kid. I wouldn't mind having her around all the time."

Stopping with her hand on the door she turned back. "Really, Bob?"

"You ought to know by now I never say things I don't mean."

She put her arms around him, letting her head rest against his chest, breathing in the sweet starchy fragrance of his shirt and the scent that was uniquely his—of imported soap and wonderfully fresh after-shave. His chest rose and fell evenly; she could feel and hear the steady thrumming of his heart. He never questioned these moments when she simply had to be close to him, to confirm the fact of his reality. He accepted her stillness and her timing, understanding the need. Often he felt the same urge to substantiate, by touch, her presence in his life. For long minutes at a time they came close, silently luxuriating in one another's vital signs. Then, reassured, they stepped apart and went on with whatever they'd been doing.

Upon seeing them walking down the hallway, Louise said, "The two of you have to sit down now, and I'll wait on you. Okay?"

Bob and her grandmother both said okay, and Louise ran into the kitchen, then popped out again. "I forgot about drinks," she said. "You can do the drinks, Uncle Bob. Okay?"

"Okay," Bob said, and, grinning, got up from the table.

"This is so much fun," Louise said, carrying serving dishes to the table. "I hope it snows all night. Maybe I'll stay here forever and never go home."

"After supper," Ellen said, "I'll call your mother, tell her you're spending the night."

"Oh, *great!* Boy oh boy oh boy!"

Ellen crossed her arms on the table and watched Bob take a tray of ice cubes from the refrigerator while Louise got the chicken from the oven. A pleasant, simple domestic scene. She could recall countless occasions when she and Ronald had chatted while they'd cooked a meal together, but Marg had never displayed any interest in joining them or in trying her hand at cooking for them.

Like Raffie and Faye, she and Ron had known each other most of their lives. Friends and family had assumed they'd get married and, eventually, they did. It had been a good marriage, with small kindnesses given and received. They'd always treated each other politely, even when they disagreed, which was usually about Margaret, the sole disruptive element in their household. She'd tried, but had never managed to alter her parents' basic regard for each other. They'd agreed early on never to permit their child to come between them, and they never did. They failed, however, to achieve the family happiness and unity they'd strived to attain, because Marg wouldn't or couldn't cooperate. She seemed unable to abide her parents' peaceful mannerly life, and time and again attempted to break down their communication. It was as if she could be happy only when things went wrong. And whenever she was around things invariably did go wrong. Her mystified parents would be left to make hasty repairs in order to preserve the fabric of their relationship, although as the years passed it lost its shape and its fit. In the end what they had was something frayed at the edges and patched so many times it no longer resembled what it had originally been.

Now, all these years later, here was that living picture of family happiness she'd always longed to see. She drank in every detail, able to recognize the significance of the moment, grateful for her second chance, and to have it confirmed, finally, that the previous failure had not been her doing.

✟

Maggie didn't even have to pay for her drink. She hadn't been in the tavern five minutes when the bartender came over to say, "The drink's compliments of Mr. McCutcheon at the table over there."

Maggie turned, saw an attractive, well-dressed middle-aged businessman sitting alone, a briefcase on the empty seat beside him. He smiled, raised his glass to her, then went back to the newspaper folded open on the table in front of him. Shrugging off her coat, she got a cigarette lit before tasting her Tom Collins, thinking it had been a good idea to stop in here.

It was no time at all before the bartender returned. "Mr. McCutcheon would like to know if you'd care to join him. He's a regular, miss, and a decent type. We don't go for any funny stuff in here. But seeing's how it's such a quiet night with the storm 'n' all. . . . If you're not interested, say the word, and that's the end of it."

For a second time, Maggie turned around to look. The businessman had removed his briefcase from the empty chair and beckoned to her with a manicured hand.

"Go on," the bartender encouraged. "Mr. McCutcheon's right as rain."

"Why not," she said, in a mood for rash acts.

"Go on over. I'll bring your drink."

Maggie approached the table and the bartender actually made the introductions, saying, "This is . . . Oops! Didn't catch your name."

"Margaret," she said, deciding it was more appropriate to the occasion than Maggie.

"Right," said the bartender. "This here's Mr. McCutcheon. Looks like the two of you got stuck in the storm, eh?"

Half an hour's polite chitchat, and Mr. McCutcheon was asking in a whisper if she'd be interested in having a nightcap at his place. She looked over at the bartender, who was washing glasses, paying no attention to them.

"Where do you live?" she asked, thinking if she was smart she'd walk out that instant and go straight home. But she didn't feel like going home.

"Nearby," he said. "Just around the corner."

She checked her watch. Only five past eight. "Why not," she said. "But only for a few minutes, then I've got to get home."

The snow wasn't falling quite as heavily when they came out of the tavern and Mr. McCutcheon held his hand under her elbow as they went along Davenport to Collier Street. "This is my house," he said of an elegant three-story narrow Victorian brick building with wood gingerbread trim. "Please come in."

The place was like a museum, with old-fashioned dark wallpaper and antique furniture, lace curtains, and marble fireplaces. He hung her coat in the hall closet while she gazed at the living room. "What do you do?" she asked, looking at the lit painting over the fireplace. A portrait of a black-haired woman in a red dress.

"Antiques and interior design," he said. "Do you like it?"

"I've never seen anything like it," she replied, not sure whether she liked the place or not.

"Let me show you the rest of the house. My name's Craig, by the way." As he directed her up the stairs, he said, "And what do you do, Margaret?"

"I'm a nurse," she lied without hesitation.

"Which hospital?"

"St. Michael's."

"Hmmn. Are you Catholic?"

"No."

"Just wondering. This is the sitting room." He pointed out a cosy room with chintz-covered furniture and matching curtains, then moved down the hall. "And this is my bedroom." He stood aside to allow her an unimpeded view of the ornate four-poster bed with its carved headboard and footboard.

As luck would have it, the diaphragm was in her purse. She went into his bathroom—more antiques, including a tub with lion's paws, exactly like the one at home, but this one looked brand new—and quickly inserted it. This was dangerous. He could be anyone, a murderer for all she knew. But the danger had the same effect Nolan's high sign used to have on her. The diaphragm slipped easily into place. She washed her hands and went back to the bedroom.

At nine-forty as she was walking up Manning, she reached into her coat pocket for her keys and felt what seemed to be a piece of folded paper. Pulling it out, she saw that it was money. Two twenties and a ten. She was torn between an immediate urge to scratch McCutcheon's eyes out, and delight at having been given a great deal of money for doing something she'd enjoyed. She decided to be flattered. He'd given her for an hour what she worked a forty-hour week to earn at the factory. And he'd asked for her phone number, which she'd refused to tell him. So he'd given her his card, and said to call him if she was in the neighborhood again. Well, maybe she'd do that little thing. Serve Nolan right, thinking he was the only fish in the sea. By the time she'd put on the kettle for tea and lit a cigarette, she was feeling better than she had in quite some time. Craig McCutcheon wasn't some bum. He was a man with something going for him, someone a lot more important than Jerry Nolan.

CHAPTER

TWENTY-ONE

LOUISE INSISTED THAT HER GRANDMOTHER AND BOB RELAX in the living room while she cleaned up. "I want to do it all," she told them, stacking plates and carrying them to the kitchen.

She was enjoying herself. Wearing Gramma's rubber gloves, she stood at the double sinks and transferred each newly washed item from the sink full of suds to the one filled with steaming rinse water. Someday she'd have a wonderful apartment like this, and at the end of the day she'd cook herself a meal, then clean up in her gleaming white kitchen while music played on her hi-fi.

As she neared the end, scrubbing at the baking tin with a Kurly Kate, she felt again that funny dull pain at the base of her belly. Focusing inward, her rubber-gloved hands plunged deep into the soapy water, she considered the peculiar twinging sensation. But as she was trying to analyze the novel inner aching, it stopped, and she continued on with the fantasy that this was her apartment and she was returning it to its customary order.

Finished, the dish towel neatly hung away, she made a trip down the hall to the bathroom and took her time admiring the pretty mint green fingertip towels, the bowl of flower-shaped nuggets of soap, the heavy glass apothecary bottle filled with bath salts, the green-and-white-striped shower curtain, and the thick darker green bath towels folded over the white ceramic towel bar. At last lifting her skirt, she tugged down her underpants, at once noticing an odd stain. It looked like rust. But how could rust get on her underwear? Then, with a marvelous excitement expanding in her chest, she realized what it was. It had finally happened! She wasn't going to stay a chestless child forever.

She was so excited she wanted to rush to the living room to tell her grandmother. But she could hardly do that in front of Bob. She loved him to pieces but she didn't know him well enough for that. She'd have to wait, maybe whisper the great news to Gramma if they had a minute or two alone. After using the toilet, she opened the cabinet under the sink, aware from previous inspections that her grandmother kept Kotex and stuff in there.

For a time she studied a box of Tampax, thinking it'd be much nicer, not to mention tidier, to use one of the tampons. But in the end, having looked over the instructions and found them mildly intimidating, she concluded that virgins probably couldn't use them. So she took a pad, positioned it in her underpants, then straightened her clothing and looked at herself in the mirror while she washed her hands. Not a little kid anymore. No sirree, boy. She was so pleased she laughed softly, made a face at her reflection, then went back to the living room.

Bob and her grandmother were sitting close together on the sofa, with the TV set on. Bob had his long legs propped on the coffee table, an arm around Ellen, who was smoking one of her Sweet Caps. Louise cuddled up beside her grandmother, thinking this was the happiest day of her life.

"I tried to call your mother at the coffee shop," Ellen told her, "but they must have closed up early. Nobody answered at home, either. So I'll try her again in a little while."

"That's fine." Louise impulsively kissed her grandmother's cheek, then settled down to enjoy the program. She was so elated she felt as if she were glowing. Everything was totally, absolutely, completely perfect.

꙳

After the long quiet hours of sitting on the stairs holding Blanche in her arms, Faye was shocked and numbed by the frantic activity that began within half an hour of Raffie's telephone call.

Any number of people started arriving—police and firemen, ambulance attendants, curious neighbors. In the middle of all this, Mr. DiStasio returned home through the back door, carrying a large parcel. He stopped short at the sight of the dozen or so uniformed men milling about in the store and trooping up and down the stairs.

Faye backed away to a corner and watched, her arms wrapped tightly around herself, tears flowing steadily. Periodically she reached into her pocket for some tissues to wipe her eyes and nose, all the while observing the traffic, hearing in the lulls Frankie's disbelieving outbursts of grief and Raffie's deep, quiet voice murmuring, explaining. The front door kept opening and closing. The police officers and firemen left. The ambulance attendants took Blanche away. The crowd in the store went abruptly silent and parted as two men carried a covered stretcher out through the snow to the waiting white vehicle. Then family members began arriving, Frankie's cousins and some of their children, and finally—the crowd again went silent and parted respectfully—Blanche's mother. A tall, darkly handsome woman in a Persian-lamb coat, with the same large liquid eyes as her daughter, she moved regally through the store and climbed the stairs to the apartment above.

Onlookers glanced around the store as if they might never see the place again, then, in twos and threes, they went out the front door. Faye remained invisible, hunched in her corner, her arms still somehow filled with Blanche's unmoving form. She saw that the snow had finally stopped. She looked at the clock over the cash register. Almost ten o'clock. The store was empty. She was alone. Upstairs the tearful voices of the family rose and fell. Phone calls were being made. People went back and forth between the kitchen, where the women were busy preparing food, to the living room, where the telephone was in constant use. At one point Faye heard the word *autopsy,* and understood that Blanche would be opened up, her interior examined in order to determine why she'd died.

Bereft, woozy with exhaustion, Faye left her corner and stood for a time at the foot of the stairs, unable to join the family. She didn't belong, had no comprehension of the rapid-fire Italian being spoken up there. Her neck creaking—the small bones snapped like bursting popcorn kernels— she walked leadenly to the back of the store and began putting on her heavy outerwear. Arms protesting, she wound her scarf around her neck, then bent awkwardly to pull on her boots. Next her coat, so weighty that she felt she might slide to the floor under it as her clumsy fingers fumbled to fasten the buttons. She pulled on her hat, and all sounds were at once diminished by its woolen density. Shoes and schoolbooks in her gloved hands, purse slung over her shoulder, she turned out the lights, made sure the door was on the latch, and let herself out into the shocking cold.

"No, she can *not* spend the night," Maggie declared. "I want her home."

"Marg, be reasonable. What possible difference will it make if she comes home tonight or in the morning?"

"I want her home," Maggie repeated.

"Never mind, Gramma," Louise said. "It's okay. I'll go home."

Keeping a grip on her anger, Ellen said, "All right, Margaret. Bob and

I will bring her home." She put down the receiver and remained silent for a time.

"It's okay, Gramma, really." Louise took her hand and held it. "I'll stay over some other night."

Bob was still sitting on the sofa, both feet now on the floor, his expression grim.

"It's okay, really," Louise told them both. "I'll get the streetcar and be home in no time."

"You are *not* going home alone at night on the streetcar," Ellen said, and looked over at Bob.

"Let's see if we can get a cab." He got up and came across the room to the telephone.

"I'd better get ready." Releasing her grandmother's hand, Louise went to the closet for her coat, listening to Bob on the telephone. She told herself she should've known Ma would never allow her to sleep over. Ma hated the idea of her or Faye having a good time.

"Things are moving again," Bob said. "They'll have a cab here in about ten minutes."

As he said this they could hear the familiar rumble of a snowplow moving ponderously along the street outside.

"I'm sorry, Lulu," Ellen said, standing with Bob, the two of them watching her do up her coat. "We'll come down with you to wait for the taxi."

"You don't have to do that," Louise said. "By the time I get down there it'll probably already be here."

"We'll come down with you," Bob insisted. "I'll just put on my shoes."

The three of them rode down in the elevator in silence, arriving in the lobby as the black-and-orange Diamond Cab pulled up out front. The driver came in and Bob gave him the address and prepaid the fare. Feeling let down but determined not to give in to it, Louise hugged and kissed Bob and her grandmother goodbye, then followed the driver out. All the way home she thought about the look on her grandmother's face, and about how quietly angry Bob had been, and took comfort in the knowledge that they truly hadn't wanted her to go.

Faye was oblivious of the cold and the thick snow on the sidewalks. Lifting one foot ahead of the other, her head down over her armful of books, she headed for home. She wanted only two things: to be close to her sister and to sleep. She'd never felt such bone-deep, blood-weary fatigue. She'd also never felt so alone. Someone she loved had died while she watched, had simply ceased to exist. It was shattering to see that a life could end so easily, so quickly; even more shattering to accept that nothing she could have said or done would have prevented it. It was terrifying in its absolute finality. Alive, and then dead. Where did the essence of the person, the soul, go? Perhaps because they were Catholic it didn't seem quite so final to Raffie and his family; perhaps they were consoled by the belief that the spirit of Blanche, that essence of her, had gone to live on another plane. Maybe they believed that. She couldn't. She didn't have a religion that might have prepared her, with years of Sunday school teachings about where souls went when people you loved died.

Her body kept moving, finding its way home along the streets she'd always known, past the small houses with their snow-filled front yards, some porches still strung with colored Christmas lights although it was well into January. It seemed incredible that she was still alive, could still see and think and feel, even though she'd held Death close in her arms; so close she might inadvertently have been taken along with Blanche. After all, how did Death know where one person left off and another began?

Raffie said he didn't blame her, but she couldn't stop wanting to blame herself. She'd looked at Blanche one day, months before, and it had occurred to her that Blanche was very ill and could die. She'd conceived of the possibility of death, and it had happened. She knew Catholics believed that even the thought of a sin was as bad as actually committing it. She'd thought about Blanche dying. Could she have caused her to die merely by considering it? No. That wasn't right. She didn't have any special powers. She couldn't make people live or die just by thinking about it. If she could, she'd have kept Blanche alive. God! She was so tired.

⤙

Louise let herself into the house and Ma came tearing out of the kitchen, exactly the way she used to, looking ready to kill. Instantly on edge, Louise started toward her room just as Faye's key turned in the lock. Whirling about, Maggie took in Faye's reddened eyes and swollen face, her unsteady movements. Pointing an accusing finger, she said, "You've been drinking!"

Faye gaped at her for a long moment. Then a gulping laugh erupted from her throat. "My God!" she said. "You're so ridiculous." It was the truth. Her mother was a preposterous parody of everything a mother was supposed to be. Seeing this, Faye lost all fear of her. "I wish I *had* been drinking," she said with more energy than she'd known she had left. "What I've been doing, *Mother,* is sitting with a dead woman." Hearing herself say this, the sorrow came flooding back and her eyes filled again. But she continued to stand her ground, eyes locked with her mother's. Go ahead and try something! she thought. Just try!

"What the hell are you talking about?" Maggie asked somewhat nervously, more than a little intimidated by Faye's atypical fearlessness.

"Blanche died," Faye said flatly. "I was looking after the store and she came downstairs saying she felt strange. I sat with her, and she just . . . died. Right in my arms. I was holding her and after about half an hour, maybe more, I don't know, she died."

Hearing this, Louise's mouth dropped open. She went immediately to her sister's side, gazing, astounded at the visible signs of Faye's anguish: the disbelief in her streaming eyes, the quivering of her chin as Faye nodded in answer to Louise's silent question: Was it true?

Maggie made an odd sound and both girls looked at her, flabbergasted. She jammed her fists together under her breasts and her body folded forward as a peculiar squeaking noise came out of her mouth and tears ran from her eyes. They'd never seen their mother cry. Louise was fascinated and appalled by this sudden display of what might be caring. Was she crying because Blanche was dead, or for herself for some reason? Louise no more trusted her tears than she trusted Ma's occasional smiles. It was like having her Baby Wetums doll suddenly stand up and start speaking. It just didn't seem possible that the woman who'd been ranting and raving only moments before was actually human and had real feelings, like everyone else. Louise couldn't stop staring. She simply didn't believe what she was seeing.

Faye felt ashamed and guilty. It had been cruel of her to break the news the way she had. After all, Ma and Blanche had been best friends. Ma had finally gone to visit Blanche just a week or so before. Faye approached her, saying, "I'm sorry, Ma. I didn't mean it to come out that way." She felt so sorry for her mother she instinctively reached to comfort her, putting an arm around her. It was strange. She and Lou had never embraced Ma, never been hugged and kissed by her the way they had by

Blanche and Gramma. Maggie felt lean and hard, unyielding in Faye's attempted embrace. Faye had the idea this might be a breakthrough, that from this point on they might become more like other families. But even as the idea was forming in Faye's mind, Maggie suddenly shoved her away, turned, and went into her room. Faye was left with her arm curved around the empty air where Ma had been. She felt duped, stupid; she'd been tricked by her own feelings. They were never going to be like other families. You had to have real parents, and love, to be a family.

Her fatigue reasserting itself, she let her arm drop heavily and went into the bedroom. Louise followed her, asking, "Did she actually die right in your arms?"

Removing her coat, Faye nodded, then sank down on the side of the bed to take off her boots. "I can't keep my eyes open," she said, pulling her sweater off over her head.

Louise reached under the pillow and handed Faye her pajamas. "It must have been awful," she said, stricken by her own lack of reaction. It was like when Chuckie died, the same thing all over again. She couldn't cry. She knew it was awful, and she was shocked and upset, but it wasn't connecting with the feeling part of her, only the thinking part. Folding back the bedclothes, she said, "You go right to sleep, Faye. We'll talk about it in the morning."

Not even bothering to turn her back the way she usually did when she undressed, Faye stripped off her clothes, and Louise looked at her, abstractedly thinking that soon now she'd have a nice chest like Faye's. Clumsily Faye climbed into her pajama bottoms, then fitted her arms into the sleeves while Louise held the top for her. Swaying, eyes half closed, she allowed Louise to do up the buttons, then turned, lay down on her side, tucked her hands under the pillow, and drew her knees up.

"Poor Faye," Louise whispered, covering her. "What an awful thing to have happen." Faye didn't even hear her. She was already asleep. That fast. Louise watched her for a time, then sighed and started getting undressed.

On her way back from the bathroom, she paused outside her mother's door. Ma was still crying, making that strange squeaking noise, like some mechanical thing that needed oiling. She had a vision of wheels and gears inside Ma's chest, all turning, clanking, and rattling. Louise didn't feel a bit sorry for her, didn't believe for one second she was crying over Blanche. And what the heck was she supposed to have done to have made her so angry before? Nuts. The woman was nuts. She went through the house turning out the lights, then slipped into the bedroom. Faye was deeply asleep, her breathing slow and silent, her eyes moving under the lids. Dreaming. Louise wondered what she was dreaming about.

Getting her journal from the drawer, she sat at the desk, uncapped her pen, thought for a time, and began to write. She looked over at the door. Ma really had to be crazy. Only a crazy person would do the things she did.

Chewing on the end of her pen, Louise imagined herself giving an interview, talking calmly about what it was like living with someone who was crazy. Then people were congratulating her and Faye on turning out to be such nice normal girls. And Louise solemnly accepted their congrat-ulations, saying, "It was hard, but my sister and I have always looked out for each other." Front-page news. SISTERS SURVIVE LIFE WITH LUNATIC. She smiled, then felt a pang. This wasn't a time for making up dumb stories. Blanche had died. They'd never see her again. Faye was the very last person to see her alive. Her sister had actually seen someone die. It was terrible, tragic. Even Ma was broken up over it. So why couldn't she cry?

⤙

Maggie sat in bed in the dark with a cigarette, thinking about her last visit with Blanche.

She'd been stretched out on the sofa with a cold cloth over her eyes, but she sat up with a pained smile when Maggie walked in. "It's so nice of you to come see me," she'd said. "Come sit down and talk to me. How are you? How's everything?"

"The same old crap," Maggie had answered. "Just more of it."

"That's too bad." Blanche let her head rest against the back of the sofa. "It's always been hard for you, hasn't it?"

"Isn't that the truth. That damned factory's driving me crazy. I'm sick of that lousy job."

"I know," Blanche sympathized.

"One of these days I'm going to have to quit that dump. How much is a person supposed to take anyway?"

"I'm sure you could get another job," Blanche said softly. "You're such a good worker."

"Damn right I am. How're the headaches? Any better?"

"They're such a nuisance. But the boys and Frankie have been so good, looking after me. How was your mother's wedding? I imagine it was a lovely affair.''

''It was quite a shindig, all right,'' Maggie said. ''Big party in Rosedale with hot and cold running caterers and a band. Those houses are so *cold,* though, you know. Too many rooms, no nice homey touches. Give me a cozy apartment any day over one of those big barns.''

''I know what you mean,'' Blanche said. ''You look very well, Maggie. I like your hair that way.''

Maggie smiled and touched a hand to her side-parted hairdo. ''Yeah,'' she said, ''it's okay this way.''

''The girls are getting so grown-up,'' Blanche smiled. ''They stop by now and then on their way home from school.''

''They're a handful, believe you me.''

''Oh, but you've done such a good job with them. They're fine girls.''

''As long as you don't have to live with them. I spend my life picking up after those two.''

''I know. You work so hard.''

''That's old news,'' Maggie said airily. ''I sure wish you felt better. We haven't been to a bingo game in ages.''

''We'll have to go, as soon as I'm over these headaches.''

''Yeah,'' Maggie said. ''We gotta get you back on your feet again.''

So goddamned unfair, she thought, crushing out her cigarette. Now she was on her own, without a living soul to tell her troubles to. Why the hell couldn't goddamned Frankie have found a decent doctor for his wife? Men. They were all useless.

The evening before the funeral, Maggie, very subdued, announced she'd take the girls to the funeral parlor. Since learning of Blanche's death she'd been quiet and listless. She even talked differently, as if she didn't have the strength to raise her voice. She made no further mention of whatever had made her mad the night of the storm, and it seemed to Louise as if she'd forgotten all about it. She was silent during the streetcar ride, staring out the window, hardly even blinking.

Respectful of what they could only view as their mother's grief, the girls periodically exchanged puzzled looks. For the past four nights they'd discussed her in bed at night, arguing about whether Ma's ongoing despondency heralded a new era in their lives. Louise insisted Ma was only feeling sorry for herself. And Faye said she was being too hard on Ma, that

Ma had feelings like everybody else. But even as she was loyally supporting Ma's case, Faye kept remembering how she'd gone to hug her, and Ma had shoved her away. Maybe Ma wasn't like everybody else, but she had feelings nevertheless. "She's never in a million years going to change!" Louise declared. "Your problem is you're too softhearted. You forgive too easily."

"Maybe that's true," Faye had allowed. "But maybe you're being too hard-hearted, Lou. She's our *mother,* after all."

"She was ready to pound the daylights out of me that night, probably 'cause Gramma wanted me to sleep over. Some lovely mother."

They just couldn't imagine what their mother was thinking or feeling, and finally gave up trying. Sooner or later, they'd find out.

Blanche was in a white satin-lined coffin with the upper half of the lid raised. People filed past to look at her, a few saying a little prayer and crossing themselves, then went to talk to the family. Louise got behind Ma and Faye and waited, feeling kind of spooked. She'd never seen a dead person and wasn't sure she wanted to now. When her turn came, Faye looked down at Blanche, erupted into tears, and ran out. Louise saw Raffie go after her, and hoped Ma hadn't noticed. Fortunately, Ma was talking to Blanche's mother. It was Louise's turn at the casket.

Blanche didn't look dead. She lay with her head on a little satin pillow, with her beautiful hands folded peacefully on her chest. Her hair was spread on the pillow, and somebody had put makeup on her. It didn't look right. Blanche had never worn makeup. Sit up and smile! Louise silently told her. Don't be dead. Get up, climb out of that box, and go home. It'll be okay. Nobody'll be mad. She stood holding her breath, waiting for it to happen. But Blanche just lay there with her eyes closed, pink rouge on her cheeks and bright red lipstick. Louise tried to take in every detail, realizing this was the very last time she'd ever see her.

Finally, becoming aware of the people waiting patiently behind her, she stepped away and looked around. Sympathetic murmurs like a kind of low music filled the room. Over by the door was Aldo, in a suit, with a shirt and tie, looking like a normal guy for a change instead of a complete delinquent. Of course his hair was greased back, as usual, with a pompadour in the front, one greasy lock hanging down over his forehead, and his skin was covered with pimples. If he washed once in a while his complexion would clear up and he'd at least look okay. He'd still be a creep, though.

What was she doing? His mother had just died and she was thinking rotten thoughts about him. Disgusted with herself, she decided to go over and tell him how sorry she was. She worked her way through the jam-packed room, wrinkling her nose at the overpowering, sickly sweet smell of carnations. Steeling herself to do the right thing, she approached the doorway. "Hi, Aldo."

He turned and looked at her with a little boy's desolate expression, not a trace of his usual nastiness. His voice hoarse, he said, "Hi, Lou."

"I'm really sorry about your mother."

"Yeah," he said. "Thanks."

"She was wonderful. Everybody loved her."

"Yeah," he said soberly. "I know." He swallowed hard. "This is rough, you know."

"I'm sure it must be," she said, remembering what good friends they'd been, how much she'd liked him. What had made him change? Would he go back now to the way he used to be, because of his mother's death?

He looked down, saw his bitten fingernails, and folded his hands over each other so no one would see. "I still can't believe it," he said, looking up at the ceiling, working hard at not crying.

"Me, neither." She couldn't think of what else to say and glanced around, spotting her mother now sitting with Frankie, holding his hand. "Well," she said. "I guess I should go talk to your dad."

"Sure. Thanks a lot for coming," he said, as if he'd rehearsed the line for ages and had repeated it dozens of times.

"I'm going to miss her," she said.

"Yeah. Me, too."

She wanted so badly to make peace with him that, as kindly as she could, she said, "You know, if you wash your face three times a day with lots of soap and rinse it really well, your skin'll clear up."

His eyes went hard. Dropping his voice, he said, "Hey, fuck you, Louise!" and turned away.

Wanting to explain that she'd meant well, she put her hand on his arm. "Don't get mad, Aldo. I only wanted to help."

He turned, looked at her, saw she hadn't been insulting him, and said, "Okay. We'll forget it."

A group of people came in just then and he went to greet them, leaving her feeling like a jerk. Why'd she have to say that about his skin? Brother!

She started walking around the perimeter of the room, observing. People in tears all over the place, except for Blanche's mother. With aristocratic bearing, she accepted condolences, nodding her handsome head in acknowledgement, utterly self-contained. Louise leaned against the wall and watched the woman, noticing she had beautiful hands just like her daughter. She must feel awful, Louise thought. But her eyes were dry. Maybe it was all right not to cry.

Raffie and Faye stood in the shadows by the wall behind the funeral parlor. A long black hearse was parked outside the big double doors, and the sight of it gave Faye the creeps.

"This is so awful," she said. "I can't stop crying."

"I've been kind of holding it in," he said, resting his cheek against the top of her head. "I know if I start I'll never stop. It's so hard to believe. You know?" She nodded, and he went on. "None of the doctors did a damned thing for her, just kept giving her more and more pills that only upset her stomach and made her nauseated. And all that time she had this *thing* growing in her brain, this *tumor*. Why didn't they find it? That's what I want to know. If they'd taken a little trouble, they might've found it and she'd be alive right now. She'd be alive and things wouldn't be falling apart."

"I'm sorry, Raffie." She held him more tightly, wishing there were something she could say or do. "I know how much you loved her."

"And what about you?" he said. "You're the one who was there with her when she needed somebody."

"Are you mad you weren't there?" she asked. "You couldn't have known what was going to happen. Don't be mad at yourself." She searched his eyes, then kissed him. "Don't take it out on yourself. It's nobody's fault."

"I'm so glad I've got you," he told her, his hold on her suddenly fierce. "I love you so much, Faye. You're the only one I can really talk to now that Mom's gone. I mean, I love Pop, and we talk. But it's not the same. He's saying now he wants me to quit school and work with him in the store."

"But you *can't!*" she cried, horrified. "You're going to finish and go on to university, become an engineer. Doesn't he understand that?"

"He keeps saying everything's changed now. He needs me in the store.'' He closed his eyes and tears squeezed from beneath the lids. ''I don't *want* to spend the rest of my life working in the store!''

''You won't,'' she said, wiping his face, then kissing his cheeks. ''It'll all work out, I know.''

''We'd better get back in there,'' he said, looking over at the hearse, then quickly away.

''Don't worry, Raffie. I know everything'll work out all right.''

''From your mouth to God's ear, Faye,'' he said, then his face contorted and he sobbed painfully. ''That's what Mom always used to say. Jesus! How're we *ever* going to get through this? It feels like the end of the world.''

''Things'll work out,'' she told him, drying his face with a tissue. ''They will. You'll see.''

He took hold of her again in that same fierce embrace, saying, ''I don't know what I'd do if I didn't have you.''

''You'll always have me, Raffie. Now come on. You go back in first. I don't want Ma catching us together.''

He kissed her, then released her and started down the driveway to the entrance. Faye remained outside a few minutes more, unable to stop looking at the hearse. Then, suddenly scared to be out there alone, she hurried inside.

CHAPTER
TWENTY-TWO

STUNNED BY BLANCHE'S DEATH, MAGGIE SEEMED TO LOSE interest in her vendetta against Nolan and the Rosedale bitch. It required more energy and concentration than she had to spare. Besides, the bitch would probably dump Nolan first chance she got. He wasn't in her class, for one thing, and for another he couldn't afford her expensive tastes. So, to hell with them both.

When she went down to his office to tell him she was taking the day off to go to Blanche's funeral, she was prepared, if he gave her any argument, to quit on the spot. But he looked sad, his eyes brightly blue and very direct, saying, "Of course. Take the whole day. I'm sorry for your loss." And for a moment she wondered if she hadn't made the biggest mistake of her life in playing him the way she had. Then she dismissed the notion, said, "Thanks, I appreciate it," and went back upstairs. It wasn't as if she didn't have options. Maybe once the funeral was out of the way she'd make a few changes in her life. She'd start with giving Craig McCutcheon a call. Who knew where that could lead? If nothing else, the man had plenty of money and was generous with it.

On the morning of the funeral, as she got dressed in dark clothes suitable to the occasion, she found she was almost enjoying the ongoing drama. Perhaps not actually enjoying any of it, but the death gave her a certain focus. Her best friend had died, and each day was now emotionally shaped by that event. Once again she'd suffered a great loss. It heightened her perception of herself as a woman constantly battling adversity.

The only irritant—a distraction from her focus—was the fact that the girls insisted on going to the funeral. She couldn't very well refuse permission, and besides, it would be a show of respect if all three of them attended. It demonstrated publicly that she was a mother who'd instilled proper values in her daughters, had taught them how to behave. Still, it did spoil her image of herself as an intriguing, solitary figure in black, seated alone during the service.

As it turned out, she did wind up seated alone. Frankie and the boys insisted Faye sit with them. And, spotting her grandmother, Louise said, "There's Gramma. We should all sit together, don't you think?"

Maggie said, "Go ahead and sit with my mother. I'm staying put."

Louise didn't even question it. She said, "Okay," and walked back up the aisle to slide into the pew next to Ellen, who, to Maggie's irritation, seemed to be drawing the kind of quiet curious attention Maggie had imagined receiving herself. Never mind, she decided, her eyes on the closed, flower-draped coffin at the front of the church. Her heart seemed to settle heavily in her chest as she let her mind roam through the nearly seventeen years of her friendship with Blanche.

She and Blanche had both been newly married when they met. Blanche and Frankie had already been living upstairs for several months when Maggie moved in with John Parker, and Blanche was already pregnant with Raffie. The very first day Blanche had come down with a potful of spaghetti sauce, saying, "I thought you'd probably be worn out from the move so I brought you some supper."

Maggie never could understand what someone like Blanche, who came from a good family with money, saw in Frankie DiStasio. The two of them didn't even look right together. Blanche was tall and innately elegant while Frankie was stocky, peasantlike by comparison. When Maggie had circuitously worked around to asking how the two of them had managed to get together, Blanche had said, with her typical openness and enthusiastic warmth, "He's the only man I ever dated who didn't try to impress my parents. He was only interested in me. He didn't care about my father's construction business, didn't care about anything but me. He can always make me laugh, and he's such a kind man, so considerate. I'm very lucky to have him, Maggie. And I know he'll be a wonderful father."

Initially, Maggie was skeptical. Someone with as little as Frankie had to be looking to the main chance, marrying a girl like Blanche. But as time passed, she could see that every word Blanche had said was true. Frankie had worked like a slave, had refused to take a penny from Blanche's parents, and was so plainly devoted that Maggie was almost jealous. By comparison, John Parker was the real peasant, a fast-talking lowlife whose primary interest in Maggie was sexual. He had no time for conversation, wasn't interested in the one baby they had or the one on the way. And when she confronted him with his failings, he'd say, "Listen, kiddo. You want dialogue, go to the movies. I never promised you I'd sit around talking."

Jesus! This was getting her mad. The service was beginning. She saw Blanche's mother, sitting like a queen in the midst of the family. If she'd lived, eventually Blanche would've looked just like that: straight-backed, dignified, austerely beautiful. It was so unfair. Maggie opened her purse for a Kleenex, feeling as if she might start crying again. She wondered if any of these people knew what close friends she and Blanche had been.

—✦—

Raffie didn't know how he'd have managed to get through the ordeal if it hadn't been for Faye. Knowing she loved and believed in him gave him additional strength, enabled him to put Pop off when, the morning of the funeral, he again raised the subject of Raffie's dropping out of school to help in the store.

Faye had told him what to say and it had worked. How had she known? He was impressed by her instincts and could only believe she'd learned how to deal with people as a result of having had to handle her mother. He felt as if he was holding himself tightly together. The only time he'd let go, even a little, had been the night before, out in back of the funeral parlor with Faye. He didn't dare let go of his emotions now. There was too much going on. Pop was heartbroken over Mom. On top of that, it was eating him up that Grandmama was paying for the funeral because Pop's money was tied up in the truck he'd had to have to keep the business growing. With the truck he could pick up produce direct from the wholesalers; he could even offer a few local customers delivery service. There was no question he needed it. And he couldn't have known Mom was going to die. Nevertheless, his pride was taking a beating because Grandmama was footing the bill. He kept saying, "I'ma gonna pay her back every penny. But I gotta expand, do more business. I need you help for that, Rafael." Pop was obsessed. All he could think about was the store and repaying his mother-in-law.

When it was finally over and his mother's coffin was lowered into the raw-looking cut in the frozen earth, Raffie felt a misery so hopelessly deep and dark he was scarcely aware of the people who filed past to offer their condolences. His hand was shaken or held, he was spoken to, embraced, and kissed on both cheeks, but he saw no one, heard nothing that was said. His eyes kept seeking Faye, settling on her for precious, reaffirming seconds before being drawn back to the next handshake, the next embrace, the next murmured expression of sympathy. At one point when he looked up, he saw her and Louise moving toward the row of waiting cars, and underwent a moment of terror at the thought that she was leaving. Then he remembered that she'd be at his place, along with a few dozen others who were coming back to eat and drink, to cry some more and reminisce about Mom. The aunts and cousins had been cooking for days, right up until they'd had to leave for the church that morning. Why, he wondered, did they think anyone would want to eat? But they'd been heaping food on the table since the night Mom died, and somehow every bit of it got eaten, although not by him. All he wanted, all he could think of, was being with Faye and letting go of even a little of his agonizing pain.

Someone stood in front of him, softly spoke his name, and he collected himself, pulling in his attention to see Faye's grandmother giving him a sad, sweet smile. Maybe it was because she was a part of Faye, or maybe it was because she'd always been so nice to him, especially lately when she invited him to come over if Faye was going to be there so they could be together. Whatever the reason, the sight of her stirred him, and he put his arms around her, so close to breaking down that he couldn't get a word out.

She seemed to understand, and hugged him back for a long, long time. Then very gently she eased away and looked into his eyes. "I know," she said meaningfully. "I wish there was something to say that would make you feel better." Then she put her gloved hand on his cheek, gave him another sad, sweet smile, and slipped away. He had to take deep breaths, one after another, as if taking in enough air would keep him upright, hold him in place until somehow he got through this.

The apartment was packed with relatives and friends, everyone eating and drinking, helping themselves from the huge platters of food Frankie's cousins and nieces kept refilling from enormous pots on the kitchen stove. Louise sat down beside her sister with a plate of manicotti.

"Are you sure you don't want anything?" Louise asked her, watching Faye sipping red wine from a chunky glass.

Faye shook her head and looked down. "Did Ma leave?"

"Yup," Louise answered, her mouth full. She swallowed, then said, "Just have a bite of this. It's sensational."

Faye shook her head again. "No, thanks. I'm not hungry."

"She said she had something to do," Louise said, "so she might not be home till late. Sounds fishy to me. What could she possibly have to do tonight, of all nights?"

Faye shrugged. She could hear Raffie's voice in the other room, was able to pick it out from all the others, as if she had studied a sturdy rope and unerringly pulled free the one slender strand of spun gold at its core. She was so finely attuned to him that she knew instantly when he was nearby. She even knew from the way the telephone rang if it was Raffie calling. Sometimes when she walked into the store she could tell at once if he'd just been there, could almost touch the traces of energy left by his passage. He regularly told her he had the same reactions, that he knew as soon as his hand closed around the handle of the downstairs door whether or not she was inside, waiting for him.

Louise looked around as she worked quickly through her food. She recognized people she'd seen at the funeral parlor and again at the service today, and wondered who they all were. "Frankie's got a big family," she observed. "I never knew before how big. Don't you wish you could speak Italian? I'd *love* to speak it. Maybe after I'm done with French, I'll take Italian. Or Spanish. Spanish is even more romantic than Italian." She turned to see that Faye hadn't heard a word she'd said. Giving her sister a slight nudge, she said, "I've got something to tell you, Faye."

Faye roused herself. Sitting back on the sofa, she turned to ask, "What?"

"I've been trying to tell you for days, but there's been too much going on." Louise took another quick look around to make sure no one was listening, then, lowering her voice, she said, "I got it!"

"Got what?" Faye frowned.

"You know. *It!*"

"What?"

Putting her lips next to Faye's ear, she whispered, "My period. I got it."

Faye's eyes widened. "When? How come you didn't tell me?"

"I couldn't. It was the day Blanche died. Isn't it great?"

Faye hooked her arm around Louise's neck and laid her cheek against her little sister's. "It's terrific," she whispered, her sadness somehow compounded by this news so that she was yet again very close to tears. "I know you were worried it'd never happen. I'm glad for you." She unwound her arm to sit away and take another look at Louise.

"Now I'm finally going to get a chest," Louise said happily.

Faye nodded, then found herself in tears. Neither one of them was a child any longer. They were moving inexorably forward into their futures as women. And while it seemed right and reasonable for herself, Faye was sad because she would have preferred Louise to enjoy her childhood for a while longer.

"What're you crying for?" Louise asked, putting her empty plate down on the floor and using her napkin to blot Faye's eyes.

"I don't know. Everything. Blanche, Raffie, you and me, even Ma. I just feel so *sad.*"

"Don't be sad about me, Faye. I'm really fine. And for Pete's sake, don't waste your energy being sad about Ma. That's as silly as complaining about the weather. Why don't you go find Raffie, cheer each other up for a while? I'll keep a lookout, if you want."

At this suggestion Faye perked up. "You wouldn't mind?"

"Heck, no. I offered, didn't I? Come on." Louise retrieved her plate and got up saying, "He's in the kitchen. I'll take my plate back and tell him to meet you in the cellar."

Faye grabbed hold of her hand, whispering, "Don't let anybody hear you."

"I know," Louise said impatiently. "It's not like I've never done this before. Go on ahead and I'll give Raffie the message."

⊥

It wasn't planned. He couldn't have planned it, even though he thought about it all the time—or at least until his mother's death seemed to put a stop to almost everything. It just happened. He and Faye were finally alone. It felt like years since they'd been able to get down to their secret place in the cellar. And almost the instant they got to the bottom of the rickety steps they were kissing with a kind of crazed urgency.

They'd already come so far in the course of their stolen moments that there was nothing out of the ordinary in their working at each other's clothes, their hands seeking to meet warm flesh. He unzipped her dress to the waist and unhooked her bra, then lowered her slip and the dress so he could feel her naked breasts pressing against his chest while he kissed her. And she automatically unzipped him, stroking, shifting to accommodate his hand between her legs. They'd long since perfected their play, facing each other straddling the bench, kissing while they used their hands to bring each other off. They'd become so adept, so closely attuned to one another's reactions, that they could slip down to the cellar, make each other come, and be dressed and back upstairs in ten minutes.

But this time it changed. This time he eased her back on the bench and drew her underpants all the way off, then slid forward, closer and closer until he was halfway into her. For a moment he held back, knowing it was wrong, a mistake. But he simply couldn't stop himself. He kept going, pushing cautiously forward, with the sense that he'd become an explorer investigating previously unmapped terrain; progressing onward until he was all the way inside her, buried utterly in the dense cushioning heat of her body. Then, in a sudden frenzy, forgetting her while at the same time more aware of her than ever before, he began driving toward the point where he'd at last be free of his pain and fear and sorrow. He poured it all into her body, in one final rational moment before a brief oblivion, understanding fully what it was his father had lost with his mother's death.

⊥

Initially, Faye was so anxious to comfort him and so anxious to be comforted that the new dimension Raffie was adding to their lovemaking seemed only right and logical. She wanted to go wherever he chose to take her, believing their continuing closeness, and now this extension of it, might somehow compensate both of them for the loss they'd sustained. So for several long moments she luxuriated in the unparalleled nakedness they were revealing to each other, feeling a current of madness traveling between them. They were stealing precious minutes in which to be alone, in which to demonstrate to each other the boundlessness of their commitment. She allowed him this unique access to her body with a sense of frantic compassion, knowing how badly he needed her.

But when he began pushing his way inside her, her body reluctantly giving way to accommodate him, she was seized by panic at the realization of how dangerous this was. Yet she was powerless to stop him, hadn't the heart to push him away. The interior yielding, the slow, steady rending of tender tissues, the blunted pain, seemed to still her heart and paralyze her lungs. Suspended, pierced, she stared at twin blinding circles of light on her closed eyelids, watching them expand and contract in syncopation with the contraction and sudden expansion at the very center of her body.

There was no pleasure in this exercise, except in the knowledge of what she was giving and how much it meant to him. She remained detached from him, forced more firmly into herself by something that clearly gave him pleasure while it stunned her with pain. Her brain recorded every nuance of sensation while she assured herself that this experience could only be an indignity if she thought of it in those terms. If she considered the grim graphics—her legs sprawled on either side of the narrow bench while she lay half suffocated beneath Raffie's weight as he drove endlessly in and out of her—she'd never forgive either of them. So she concentrated on the significance of the gesture, its meaning and intent. And when it was finally over and Raffie was lying gasping and spent on her breast, she held and stroked him, suppressing her horror at discovering that an act she'd for some time imagined would be blissful was in reality excruciating. And on top of that, the possible repercussions were fairly terrifying.

After a few minutes he lifted himself and drew out of her body. A short, sharp involuntary cry flew from her throat at the pain that seemed greater upon his withdrawal than it had been on his measured entry. They both looked with dismay at the blood, and Raffie began to cry, terrible

racking sobs that robbed him of the ability to speak. She, astonishingly
dry-eyed, locked in continuing shock at what her body had undergone,
said, "It's okay, Raffie," and reached into her pocket for some tissues.
"It's okay," she repeated over and over— Reassuring him, or herself?
She didn't know—as she got herself cleaned up as best she was able and
back into her clothes. Then she set about getting him buttoned and zipped
and fastened into his suit, securing the black mourning band around his
sleeve.

By the time they were both dressed he'd managed to regain some
degree of control, and clutching her hand he searched her eyes. "I'm
sorry. I'm honest to God sorry. I didn't know that was going to happen.
Please tell me you forgive me. Tell me you don't hate me."

"I don't hate you. But God, Raffie!" She had to sit down again. "What
if I get pregnant?"

"I'd marry you," he said quickly.

She shook her head, amazed at the clarity of her thoughts. "That'd be
impossible," she said, able to see like a series of black and white photographs the many reasons why. "Let's just pray I don't. Raffie," she
complained softly, "you're hurting my hand."

"Jesus!" At once he released her. "I'm sorry. I don't know what I'm
doing."

"It's all right," she said with her new clearheaded logic. "But we can't
ever, ever take another chance like this."

"It'll never happen again, I swear."

She managed a small smile that eased him greatly. "From now on,"
she said, "we'll have to be very careful. We'd better get back upstairs
before people start wondering where you are." She stood up, her insides
in chaos, burning, pulsing. She turned slowly in a circle. "Am I all put
together?"

He threw his arms around her hips and pressed his face into her belly,
murmuring, "I love you so much."

"I know." She smoothed his hair, feeling decades older than she had
less than half an hour before. "Come on." She tugged at his arms, freeing
herself. "You've got to get back upstairs."

"Okay," he said, wiping his face with the backs of his hands. "Okay.
You're right. Okay." He rose and walked unsteadily ahead of her.

✝

Louise had been sitting on the stool by the cash register, keeping watch. A couple of people had glanced over at her on their way out.

"Just cooling off," she'd explained. "It's kind of hot upstairs, with so many people."

Satisfied, they'd gone on their way.

She kept an eye on the clock, thinking they were taking a long time down there, longer than usual. After fifteen minutes she started getting jittery, certain Mr. DiStasio would come down any minute asking if she'd seen Raffie. She was prepared to say he'd gone out to get some air, but luckily Mr. DiStasio didn't come down.

Finally, the door opened and Raffie appeared, obviously distraught. Louise could tell he'd been crying. He looked over at Louise, and she waggled her fingers at him. He seemed preoccupied, but she didn't find that surprising. He started up the stairs to the apartment, and was almost to the top when Faye came through the cellar door.

Louise took one look at Faye's dazed expression and knew what had happened. Her eyes were round, as if she'd seen something too astonishing to believe, like a pterodactyl or a unicorn. Moving like a windup toy, she closed the cellar door. Then, her arm dropping, she came over to Louise, opened her mouth to say something, and instead started to cry.

Jumping up from the stool, Louise said, "Sit down and wait here. I'll go get our coats and stuff."

Faye obeyed—another sure sign Louise had guessed right. She took the stairs two at a time, collected their coats and boots and purses, and went to tell Mr. DiStasio they were leaving. "Faye's not feeling too well," she told him. Giving him a kiss on the cheek, she looked over at Raffie, who guiltily averted his eyes. Then, both purses over her shoulder, the coats in one arm, the boots in the other, she charged back down to the store.

After getting her own stuff on, she helped Faye, then ushered her out, announcing, "We'll go over to the Mars for a coffee and talk."

Settled in one of the booths-for-two at the rear, Louise ordered two coffees—feeling very decisive and mature—then leaned across the table and asked in an undertone, "Did he make you, or did you want to do it?"

Startled, Faye's head jerked up. "Of course he didn't *make* me."

"Yeah, but did you *want* to?"

In such a state of shock that the conversation didn't seem the least unreasonable, Faye didn't bother pretending. She sighed and said, "I don't know. At first I did. Then I didn't. It doesn't matter. It's too late now.''

"Brother!" Louise sat back as the waitress set down their cups. "This is really something," she said, unsure of her feelings. Then, once more leaning forward, she said, "I hope you used something."

Faye started to cry again, covering her face with both hands.

"Oh boy!" Louise let out a low whistle. "Boy oh boy oh boy! What if . . ."

"Don't *say* it!" Faye warned, revealing her wet face. Grabbing several napkins from the dispenser, she mopped her eyes, then reached for the sugar. "I'm going to be praying nothing happens."

"Wow!" Louise drew the word out on a sigh. "Did you at least *like* it?"

Faye's eyes got that dazed look again. "I wouldn't want to go through it again, that's for sure," she admitted. "I never knew anything could hurt that much." Her eyes returned to Louise and she wrapped her hand hard around her sister's wrist. "Swear you'll never tell a living soul! Swear it!"

"Of course I won't!" Louise said huffily. "What d'you think I am, anyway? And let go of my arm, if you don't mind."

Faye did, and saw the whitened impressions of her grip on Louise's arm. "Sorry," she said quietly. "I'm kind of upset."

"I guess so!" Louise snapped, rubbing her wrist. "Jeez! You practically broke my arm."

"I said I'm sorry," Faye snapped back.

"Why're we being mad at each other?" Louise asked. "This is stupid. I'm not mad at you. Are you mad at me?"

Faye shook her head, absently stirring cream into her cup. "I don't know *how* I feel. It happened so fast. It's only starting to hit me now. God, Lou! Keep your fingers crossed. Okay? *God!*"

"Believe me, I will," Louise said zealously. "It gives me the willies just *thinking* what Ma would do. Gramma would probably be okay, but Ma . . ."

"Will you *stop,* please!"

"Right. Sorry." Louise poured sugar and cream into her cup. "You guys better buy some whatchamacallits if you're going to be doing this all the time now."

Faye's face turned very red. She clapped a hand over her mouth and started to laugh. Louise laughed with her, asking, "What's so funny?"

"You. Me. Us. Everything," Faye sputtered, the laughter ebbing. "You're so great, Lou. You really are."

"Yeah, I'm pretty good," Louise agreed.

"I really am sorry about hurting you."

"Oh, that's okay." Louise drank some of the coffee, then sat chin in hand, thinking. "So, it hurts, huh? Do you think that's only the first time, or what?"

"I'll let you know," Faye said.

Rolling her eyes over to her sister, Louise said, "Hah! I *knew* it! Just you make sure you guys get some of those doodads. If I have to, I'll buy them *for* you."

"You wouldn't dare!"

"Are you *kidding?* Sure I would."

"You wouldn't dare!" Faye repeated.

"Okay, fine! How much money've you got?"

"What for?"

"How much d'you have?" Louise got out her change purse and counted quickly. "I've got ninety-two cents. What about you?"

"A dollar fourteen."

"Fine. Give it to me!"

"Not a chance!"

"Give me the money, Faye!"

Faye handed it over. Louise lifted her coat from the stand and said, "You sit there. I'll be right back." Eyes bright with purpose, she marched out of the restaurant.

Faye drank her coffee hoping there'd be enough money left to pay for it. She could picture herself having to run back to the store to borrow some from Raffie, and she really wasn't in the mood to see him at the moment.

In under five minutes Louise was back. She hung up her coat, slid back into the booth, and slapped a small package down on the table. "So there!" she declared. "Hah!"

"Oh, my God!" Blushing again, Faye snatched the package off the table and pushed it into her purse. "I can't believe you did it! What did you *say?*"

"I went over to the pharmacist and said, 'I'd like a package of Trojans, please. They're for my mother.' "

Faye let out a shriek of laughter. "You didn't!"

"I most certainly did!" Louise grinned wickedly.

"How'd you know what to ask for?"

"I know about these things. I've seen guys buying them. I'm not a *child,* you know. Just don't let Ma find them in your purse or you're dead."

"You take the cake!" Faye said admiringly.

"Yeah, I do," Louise said proudly. "And make sure you use them, for Pete's sake."

Covering Louise's hand with her own, Faye said huskily, "I love you, Lou."

"I know. I love you, too. Oh! Here's the change." She reached into her coat pocket and dropped a handful of coins on the table.

Faye laughed again, saying, "You think of everything, don't you?" She felt so much better, thanks to Louise. Watching her sister take a swallow of coffee, she said fondly, "What would I do without you?"

"Don't get mushy on me now," Louise said, pleased nonetheless. "We've got to look out for each other. That's what sisters are for. Right?"

"Right."

"So, okay. Tell me the truth. Did you like it even a teensy-weensy bit?"

"You know something?" Faye said. "For a minute or two, I felt as if I hated him for enjoying something that hurt me so much."

"God!" Louise whispered.

"But then," Faye went on, "I didn't try to stop him. And in a funny way, you know, I think he was more upset about it than I was. All I know is, I feel entirely different now. No matter what happens, I can't ever go back to being the way I was before. I wish I smoked," she said. "I'd really love to have a cigarette right now."

"Really?"

"Honest to God."

"Okay." Louise turned, looked around the restaurant, and saw a man sitting alone at the counter, a pack of Players close at hand. Sliding out of the booth she went over to him, said, "Excuse me. Could I please have one of your cigarettes?"

The man turned to look at her, smiled, said, "Sure. Help yourself," and pushed the pack toward her.

Louise took a cigarette, got it lit, said, "Thank you very much," and went back to the table to give it to Faye. "Just don't make a habit of this," she said, positioning the ashtray between them.

"How do you *do* these things?" Faye asked her, bowled over.

"Most people want to be nice," Louise replied. "They want to be asked. It makes them feel good to be able to help someone out."

"You think so?" Faye said doubtfully.

"I *know* it!" Louise declared with typical conviction. "And it's all right to ask, as long as you don't ever take advantage."

"You really do take the cake," Faye said, taking an experimental puff of the cigarette.

"Yup. Want some more coffee?" Louise asked, and without waiting for her sister's answer, she turned to signal to the waitress.

CHAPTER

TWENTY-THREE

MAGGIE WANTED TO BE SURE MCCUTCHEON UNDERSTOOD she wasn't some kind of chippy, but without discouraging him from giving her more gifts of money. She rehearsed what she wanted to say before sitting down at the kitchen table to phone.

A woman answered, giving a company name. For some reason Maggie had expected McCutcheon to answer himself. It threw off her rehearsed strategy to have to ask to speak to him.

"May I say who's calling, please?"

"Tell him it's Margaret."

"And what company are you with?"

Annoyed, Maggie snapped, "I'm not with any company. It's a personal call."

"One moment, please."

Jesus, she hated being put through the third degree. She got a cigarette lit while she waited for McCutcheon to come on the line. Finally hearing his voice, she said, "It's Margaret."

"Yes?" He didn't even sound as if he knew her, and that threw her even farther off the prepared script.

"You did say to call," she said, thinking he'd probably tell her to get lost. A man with his kind of money likely had women crawling all over him. "I'm going to be in your area this evening and I thought you might be interested in getting together."

"Are you free for dinner?" he asked in the same chilly tone, as if he was proposing something he'd rather not do.

"I might be."

"Let's say seven at the Chez Paree on Bloor. Do you know where it is?"

"I'll find it."

"Good. See you there," he said, and hung up, not having given her a chance to say any of the things she'd planned.

Deciding she'd have to clarify matters later, she got up to look through her closet for something appropriate to wear to the expensive restaurant she'd passed many times.

Toweling dry after her bath, she heard the girls come in and was immediately irked. What the hell were they doing home so soon? She'd been counting on them hanging around at the DiStasios' for a few more hours. Now they'd see her dressed up for an evening out and start asking questions. Damn it! She shouldn't have to answer to anyone. One foot propped on the edge of the sink, she inserted her diaphragm, then washed the jelly off her hands.

Studying herself in the mirror, she considered what she'd tell the girls, then thought, to hell with them. She didn't have to explain a damned thing. It was none of their business where she went, what she did. Pulling on her robe, she left the bathroom, saw the door to their room was closed, and thought, Good. Let them stay in there until she was gone.

"I'm in no mood to see Ma," Faye said in an undertone.

"Fine. We'll stay in here until she's gone. It's almost six-thirty. She'll probably be leaving any minute. You want me to make you a sandwich or something? You should eat."

"I'm not hungry."

"You've got to eat, Faye, or you'll get sick. I'll make you a sandwich. You want milk or tea with it?"

"Tea, I think. Thanks, Lou." Faye stepped out of her dress and walked to the closet to hang it up. "I hope she goes soon. I really need to take a bath."

Louise listened at her mother's door for a moment before going to the kitchen. Ma was already dressed. Louise had smelled perfume, which was always the last thing Ma put on before going out. She'd be on her way any minute now.

Louise filled the kettle, got bread, then opened the fridge to see what they had. Leftover meat loaf. Perfect. She buttered one slice of bread, poured ketchup on the other, put a half-inch slice of meat loaf between them, cut the sandwich on the diagonal to make it more appealing, slid it onto a plate, and stood waiting for the kettle to boil.

She was pouring hot water into a cup when Ma came out of the bedroom in a sharp black sheath Louise had never seen before. She looked down the hall, saw Louise, and said, "Where's your sister? I want to borrow my mother's pearls."

"I'll get them for you," Louise said quickly, returning the kettle to the burner.

Standing by the chest of drawers in just her bra, garter belt, and stockings, Faye looked up sharply as Louise barreled into the room.

"Ma wants to borrow your pearls."

"What for?"

"She's all dressed up for something. Just give them to me, Faye. I don't want to get into a fight with her now, and neither do you."

Faye opened the drawer and got out the Birk's box.

Louise grabbed it, whispered, "She'll be gone in five minutes," and slipped out.

Faye quickly finished undressing, pulled on her robe, then examined her underpants. They were soaked with bloodied semen. The sight of it generated a low-grade revulsion that made her stomach constrict. *Why* hadn't she stopped him? She'd known what was going to happen the instant he'd urged her down on her back on the bench. But she'd felt so sorry for him, she hadn't had the heart to refuse him. And besides, at the beginning she'd been excited, and curious too. She'd always trusted him, and they'd agreed they wouldn't go all the way until they were at least officially engaged. Even while it was happening she kept thinking he'd stop any moment. But he hadn't stopped.

She thought of Gramma telling her to hold a little back for herself, and understood now what she'd meant. But how did you decide how much of yourself you were willing to give? Closing her eyes, she saw herself in the cellar with Raffie on top of her. When it had reached the point where it seemed as if he was going to go on forever, she'd looked at him and hadn't recognized him, his eyes squeezed shut, his teeth bared as if in a state of agony. It should never have happened. And now that she knew what was involved, she doubted she'd ever allow it to happen again. The more she thought about it, the greater her aversion became, the act assuming ever more repellent dimensions.

"Where you going, Ma?" Louise asked casually, handing over the box with the pearls.

"Out." Maggie turned, opening the box as she did, and went back into her bedroom.

"Nice dress, Ma," Louise said, and returned to the kitchen to remove the tea bag from the cup before adding milk and sugar. "She's got a date," she said to herself, getting the tray from beside the stove. "Which means she's got a new boyfriend."

"I'll probably be late," Maggie said from the front door. "Don't leave that kitchen in a mess, if you know what's good for you."

"I won't," Louise sang out, lifting the tray with the sandwich and tea. "Have a nice time."

Maggie said a clipped "Thanks," and left.

"I can't eat this," Faye said, looking at the ketchup-drenched meat loaf sandwich, normally one of her favorites. The sight of it made her stomach give a slight heave.

"You've got to eat *something*," Louise insisted, exasperated. "If not this, what?"

"Do we have any arrowroot cookies?"

"I'll go see."

Faye picked up the tea and carried it to the bathroom, setting it down on the lid of the toilet seat while she got the water started in the tub. Louise appeared in the doorway with the box of cookies. "Want me to keep you company?"

"No, thanks. I won't be long."

"What about your cookies?"

"I'll eat them in the bath."

Louise shrugged and left the box on the side of the sink. "I'm gonna call Kath."

With the hot water easing the rawness between her legs, her elbows propped on the rim of the tub, she bit into one of the cookies. A tear slid irritatingly down the side of her nose. She rubbed it away with a knuckle, chewed, swallowed, then drank some of the tea. Why did it feel, on one level, as if she loved Raffie with all her heart, and on another level as if she didn't care if she ever saw him again? She'd never been so confused. She pulled the underpants from the pocket of her robe and immersed them in the water, then got the soap and the nailbrush and began scrubbing away.

With each passing minute Raffie felt more terrible, until some three hours after their encounter in the cellar he was nearly sick with guilt. How could he have taken advantage of Faye that way? For the sake of making himself feel better for a couple of minutes he'd hurt the girl he loved. And not only hurt her but put her at risk. What kind of guy was he, to do something like that? Only a jerk wouldn't bother protecting his girl. He knew she had to be very upset. She hadn't even said goodbye, but had just left with Louise. Maybe she'd never forgive him. Jesus! He had to see her, talk to her, apologize, make things right.

He went to find his father, pushing through the crush of people crammed into the apartment, getting stopped every few seconds by someone else wanting to tell him how sorry they were about his loss. It was starting to make him claustrophobic, so it was no lie when he finally found Pop in a corner of the living room and whispered, "I've got to get out of here for a while, get some air. Okay?"

"Sure, okay."

He kissed his father and said, "I'll be back in a couple of hours. Okay, Pop? Will you be all right?"

"Sure, you go. It's okay. I wouldn't mind myself some fresh air. But alla these people, they come to pay respect. I gotta say thank you. Take you time, Raffie. You bin a good boy."

His father's remark compounded his guilt. He'd been anything but good, and if he didn't fix things right away, he'd find himself with nothing left—no mother, no Faye; just a battle on his hands with Pop for his need to stay in school.

Once outside, he filled his lungs with the reviving cold air, taking slow deep breaths in and out as he headed for the pay phone at the variety store. If Mrs. Parker answered, he'd tell her Faye had forgotten something and he needed to talk to her. But it was Louise who said hello and, relieved, he said, "It's Raffie, Lou. I really need to talk to Faye."

"I'll bet you do," she said sarcastically, unable to hold back her annoyance. "Hold on. I'll go get her."

He waited, praying she wouldn't refuse to talk to him. It was for sure she'd confided in Louise, otherwise Lou wouldn't have made that crack. At the other end of the line he could hear Lou's footsteps as she went down the hall. He heard her call, "Raffie's on the phone," and then there was a long silence that made him start to sweat. Footsteps approached. The receiver was picked up and he was certain it would be Louise saying, She doesn't want to talk to you or see you ever again. But it was Faye, saying a subdued hello.

"Faye, I need to see you. We've got to talk about what happened. Can I come over?"

"I don't know," she hesitated.

"What? Is your mother there?"

"No."

"What, then? *Please* let me talk to you, Faye. We've got to get this straightened out. I feel so bad."

She sighed tiredly. "Okay. Come over."

"I'm on my way right now." He hung up, hearing his nickel drop into the box at the bottom of the pay phone. She was willing to see him. Thank God for that! Now all he had to do was let her know how rotten he felt about what he'd done, try to find some way to make it up to her.

✢

"That's an attractive dress," Craig McCutcheon said, offering her a cigarette from a slim silver case.

"I'm glad you like it." She accepted one of his cigarettes, then waited for him to light it with his heavy silver lighter. "You bought it."

"Did I?" Eyebrows raised, he waited for an explanation.

"I don't know what you think I am," she said, with a smile to take any sting out of the words, "but I'm not in the habit of taking money from men."

"Ah!" He nodded and lit his own cigarette. "I apologize if I offended you."

"Actually, I wasn't offended. I just thought we should set things straight. It was very generous of you."

"I see. Well, since we're getting our facts straight, why did you tell me you're a nurse?" He positioned the lighter beside the cigarette case before looking at her.

"What makes you think I'm not?"

"Let's accept as a given that I know you're not."

"All right, I'm not."

"So, why tell me you are?"

"It seemed sensible at the time," she said offhandedly.

"You have a point," he said. "Obtuse, but a point."

"Of course I do."

"Divorced?"

"That's right. What about you?"

"I've never had the need for a wife," he said, and looked at his thin gold wristwatch.

"I see," she said, although she didn't, at all.

He drank some of his seven-and-seven, then asked, "How old are you?"

"How old do you want me to be?"

He laughed and said, "Your age, whatever it is."

"I'll be thirty-five in a few months."

"A perfectly good age."

"What about you?" she asked.

"Guess!"

She looked him over, taking note of his thinning brown hair, silver at the sides and back, his rather tired-looking eyes, longish upper lip, and the slightly slackened skin beneath his chin, and said, "Forty-five."

He laughed again and raised his glass to her. "You're either a consummate diplomat or very kind. I'm fifty-three."

"You don't look it."

"Thank you."

"You don't act it, either."

"Margaret, you're doing wonders for my ego."

"I'm being truthful."

"So," he said. "Let's be sure I have this right. You're not accustomed to selling your favors, but you're not averse to the notion. Have I got that correct?"

She narrowed her eyes, trying to determine if she was being insulted. He'd summed matters up accurately enough. She just wasn't sure if she cared for the way he put it. "I'm not sure I care for the way that sounds."

"Ah, let's not shilly-shally, my dear. You enjoyed the enterprise and you enjoyed the little reward. It seems clear enough to me and perfectly fair. After all, you're a divorced working woman. With children, I presume."

"What makes you think that?"

"I can tell," he said simply. "Shall we cut to the chase, Margaret? We've established terms, and I find them acceptable. Fridays suit me. So shall we say every other Friday, to begin with?"

She had to make an effort to keep her tone casual. "I think that could be arranged." The man was proposing to meet her on a regular basis and was willing to pay her for her time. It was too good to be true. She'd be able to quit the diner. She might even be able to put enough by to quit Raymar and get a respectable job. For once, things were actually going her way. "It can definitely be arranged," she said, giving him a wide smile.

"Good," he said, as if satisfied with the settlement of a business deal. "Now, shall we order?"

Right after Faye got off the phone, Kath called to ask if Louise could sleep over.

"I don't know," Louise said. "Let me check with my sister." Putting the receiver down she went to the bedroom, catching Faye in the act of removing her robe. Faye quickly pulled it closed. "What?" she asked.

"Kath wants me to sleep over. What d'you think?"

"I think Ma will have six fits."

"I'll leave her a note," Louise said. "Do you mind? I won't go if you want me to keep you company."

"I don't mind, Lou. Raffie's on his way over. If you go to Kath's it'll give the two of us a chance to talk."

"You're absolutely positive you don't mind?"

"I don't mind," Faye repeated. "Just don't forget to leave Ma a note."

"Great!" Louise ran back to the kitchen. "I'll sleep over," she told Kath.

"Oh, fantastic! Come right away and we can have dinner together."

"I'll be there as fast as I can."

"And don't worry about Pj's or anything. You can borrow some of mine. *Hurry!*"

"Okay, 'bye!"

Louise flew into the bedroom to get changed, then grabbed her toothbrush from the bathroom and pushed it into her shoulder bag. "Can you lend me two streetcar tickets?" she asked Faye as she wound a scarf around her neck and pulled on her coat.

"Take some from my purse," Faye said.

"Oh, brother!" Louise exclaimed. "We spent all our money on those thingamadoodles. I can't go out without even a dime."

"There's a couple of cartons of pop bottles in the kitchen," Faye said. "You could take them back to the store on your way to the streetcar."

"Brilliant!" Louise went over to give her a noisy kiss on the cheek. "You're a genius."

"You might as well take the rest of my change," Faye told her. "I won't be going anywhere tomorrow, and Sunday Gramma'll give us our allowances."

"You sure? What if you and Raffie want to go out for a coffee or something?"

"We can have coffee right here."

"Okay. Thanks a lot." Louise took two student tickets and twenty-eight cents from Faye's change purse, and said, "I'll call you later to make sure everything's okay."

"You don't have to do that, Lou."

"I know. But I will." Seeing how distracted her sister was, she suddenly wondered if it was such a good idea for her to be going out. "Faye," she said quietly, "if you'd rather have me stay home I honestly truly won't mind."

"Go on, Lou," Faye said. "I'll be fine."

Louise backed toward the door. "You're absototally certain?"

Faye laughed and said, "For heaven's sake, go!"

"Okay. 'Bye."

⊱

Raffie ran most of the way, twice almost falling on the ice. By the time he got to Faye's house, he was out of breath and sweating.

She came to the door and said, "Come in. Let me take your coat."

Raffie got his coat off, unnerved by the formalities.

"You'd better leave your boots on the mat," she told him, starting down the hall to the kitchen. "Would you like some tea or coffee?"

"Coffee'd be great," he said, watching her as he removed his boots. "If it's no trouble."

"It's no trouble." Faye got the percolator, pulled out the basket, filled it with cold water, put the basket back, and scooped some of Ma's Pride of Arabia grounds into it. "Come sit down," she said, glancing over at him in the doorway.

"Did I wreck everything?" he asked anxiously, one hand on the door frame. "You're acting like I'm a complete stranger."

"I'm very upset," she said, setting the percolator on the front burner and adjusting the flame underneath it. "Come sit down with me."

"It's been a long time since I've been in here," he said, looking around the kitchen nervously as he crossed the room to sit opposite her. "Years. It looks the same. You have every right to be mad at me, Faye. But do you believe I'm sorry?"

"I believe you." She traced the pattern on the oilcloth with the tip of one finger.

"No, you don't," he said. "I can tell. You won't even look at me. Please don't break up with me over this. What can I do to prove to you how sorry I am? Tell me and I'll do it."

"I don't know what I want you to do, Raffie. It's my fault as much as yours. It's just . . . it was so . . ." She shook her head. "It was as if I wasn't even there. I know it's been a terrible time for you. It has for me, too. I'm never going to forget what happened . . . your mother . . . God! I don't know. You *hurt* me!" she said, fixing her stricken eyes on his.

"I didn't mean to. You know I'd never intentionally do anything to hurt you, Faye. I don't even know how it happened. As God is my witness, I didn't plan it. I think it's always pretty bad for girls the first time. At least that's what I've heard. But only the first time. After that, it's supposed to be okay. Not that I'm saying there has to be a next time. That's not what I mean at all. Please tell me you forgive me," he begged. "I'll do anything to make it up to you."

She looked at him, saw his misery, and couldn't bear to add to it. "I forgive you, Raffie. But that's never going to happen again unless I say it's all right, and unless we use something. I'm going to be a wreck, worrying, until I get my period.''

"Whatever you want," he said. "So long as you don't break up with me. I love you, Faye." His eyes filled and he covered them with one hand. "I hate myself for what I did. I just couldn't help it."

Getting up, she went around and tugged his hand away from his eyes, then slid into his lap and held his head to her breasts. "I love you, too," she said, stroking his hair. "But it's a lot harder, a lot more complicated than I knew, loving someone. I always thought it would be so easy, like tobogganing or something; you'd just slide along feeling wonderful."

He lifted his head to give her a bleary-eyed smile. "Tobogganing?"

"You know what I mean. Something effortless. But it isn't."

"No," he agreed. "It isn't." Holding her cautiously, he said, "I wouldn't want to live my life without you in it, Faye. I really mean that. I'm always going to love you, and age doesn't have a thing to do with it. I'm going to feel the same way at fifty as I do at fifteen."

"Sometimes," she said, "it scares me when you say things like that."

"But why?"

"Because I feel exactly the same way, and I know we'll hurt each other lots more times. Why does it have to hurt?"

"I don't know," he said forlornly. "But it has to be worth it. When we did it—I know it was awful for you and I swear to God I'm sorry— but when it was happening, all of a sudden I really knew what love was. And I knew why Pop was so torn up. So're Aldo and I, but not the way Pop is. And it's because he and Mama were so close, the way you and I were this afternoon. And if it was something that hurt every time, people wouldn't do it."

"I suppose not."

"It was kind of like a miracle in a way, Faye. But it'll never happen again unless you say the word."

Bending her head to his shoulder, burrowing into the silky warmth of his neck, she clung to him, and he held her in silence until the sound of the percolator boiling over roused her. Climbing off his lap she said, "We'll have our coffee in the living room. Okay?"

"Whatever you say."

Reaching for the cups, she smiled over her shoulder at him. "You don't have to agree with every word I say, Raffie."

"Okay," he said, then smiled diffidently.

"It's nice having the place to ourselves," she observed.

"Yeah," he agreed. He was so relieved, he felt exhausted.

Craig lifted his head and studied the flush that rose from the tops of Maggie's breasts right to her hairline. "You love all of it, don't you?" he said, placing one hand flat on her chest, feeling the heat rush into his palm.

"I like it," she admitted, her heart still hammering, her limbs wonderfully heavy.

"Yes, I can tell." He brought his hand down the length of her body, applying a slight pressure with his fingertips. Her torso jerked in response. Sitting up on his knees, he pulled her forward until her legs lay on either side of his lap.

Raising herself up on her elbows, she bent her knees and held steady as he eased into her. He held her from underneath and she wrapped her legs around him, fell back, gripped handfuls of the sheet and gave herself up to his rhythm. Neither John Parker nor Jerry Nolan had had this man's inventiveness or skill. And the fact that she'd be paid, to boot, added to her excitement. Closing her eyes, she concentrated on the pleasure, feeling it mount with each measured thrust. Christ! It was perfect.

𝒞HAPTER
TWENTY-FOUR

FAYE PRAYED EVERY DAY THAT SHE WASN'T PREGNANT. BEcause if she was, her life would be over. Ma would find out somehow and throw her out of the house. And it'd be all her own fault for not stopping Raffie when she should have. She was in such an ongoing state of anxious distraction that Miss Giddings held her back one morning after class to ask if anything was the matter.

"Oh, everything's all right, Miss Giddings," Faye answered, plastering a smile on her face. "It's just that I've got so much schoolwork and it's hard keeping up. That's all."

Miss Giddings seemed reluctant to accept her explanation, but said, "Well, as long as you're sure nothing's wrong."

"Honestly, I'm fine," Faye assured her, wishing she could tell the truth.

"All right, then, dear. You'd better run along now."

Faye went off, and Ella Giddings sat down at her desk, her eyes on the rows of silent typewriters. It was, she decided, probably only one of those teenage moods. She hadn't seen any hint of a similar preoccupation in Louise, whose class preceded her sister's. Louise was as bright and charming as ever. The personality differences between the two girls struck her as extraordinary: Louise outgoing and exuberant, Faye introspective and soft-spoken. She reasoned that if there were some problem at home both girls would have been displaying the symptoms. So she put the matter out of her mind and turned her attention to the typing tests the class had handed in.

That same afternoon, during her history class, Faye had a sudden cramping at the base of her belly and felt almost giddy with relief. She got permission to leave the class and went to the girls' room, almost euphoric at being able to set her worst fears aside. It was as if she'd been staggering along through a maddeningly complex labyrinth and at the point when she'd all but given up hope of escape, she looked up to find herself standing in front of an exit. Her anxiety was gone and life was once again rich with potential.

In the nurse's office she got a note, then collected her things from her locker, handed the note in to the front office, and went out into the glaring brilliance of sunlight reflected off old snow. Her affection for Raffie rushing back, she walked along Harbord, headed for the hole-in-the-wall restaurant at the corner of Bathurst. There she sat for an hour doing her homework over a cup of acidic coffee. Then she went to wait by Raffie's locker at Central Tech, eager to tell him the good news.

She was moved by the way his face changed at the sight of her, his eyes widening, a smile automatically reshaping his lips. He loved her. It was something she'd forgotten she could count on.

"Hey, Faye! This is great! D'you cut school?"

"Only two classes. I wanted to see you. I've got good news."

"Yeah?" He grabbed his jacket and pulled it on, slung his books under his arm, and slammed the locker shut. "What?"

"I'll tell you outside," she said, conscious of all the kids moving in the echoing hallway.

Once they were beyond the immediate environs of the school, Faye looped her arm through his and said, "We can both stop worrying. I'm not pregnant."

He looked into her eyes for several seconds, then exhaled mightily, threw his head back to look straight up into the sky, then looked at her again. "Thank God," he said feelingly. Ever since the day of his mother's funeral he'd felt as if he were on probation, apprehensive of touching her in even the most innocent fashion. Each time he'd seen her, the guilt had doubled and tripled, until he'd felt most days as if he were carrying a load of cement around with him everywhere he went. "Thank God," he repeated. "I swear I'll never put you through anything like that ever again."

"We were both responsible," she corrected him. "I was as much to blame as you."

"No," he said, having thought it over time and again. "I'm supposed to look out for you, Faye, and I didn't. I'll never let you down again." He gave her another smile. "Maybe things'll work out after all."

"They will, Raffie. You'll see."

"I don't know. Pop won't let up. He starts in first thing in the morning and picks up again the minute I come through the door after school. It's starting to wear me down. I'm sick of the whole subject. Want to stop for a Coke or something at the Mars?"

"Sure."

"Oh yeah," he said. "Wait'll you hear the latest! It's Aldo's birthday in two weeks, right? So Pop's trying to be nice, and he says the three of us'll do something special to celebrate. Mom always used to make a big supper on our birthdays, with a cake, and lots of little presents, you know? Anyway, so Pop's really trying to do something decent for him, and what does Aldo say? He goes, 'Jeez, Pop, I already made plans to go for pizza and five-pin bowling with the twins that night.' You should've seen Pop's face. He goes, 'You gonna go *bowlin'* ona you *birthday?*' And Aldo says yeah. He's such an idiot! Anyway Pop's all disappointed, and I don't know what to say. So Pop thinks for a couple of minutes, then he says, 'Okay. Me and Raffie, we go out to Old Angelo's, and you go on bowlin' with them two *buffones.*" He laughed, shaking his head, then said, "Pop told me to ask if you'd like to come with us."

"Sure, I'd love it," she said. "God! Aldo's such a jerk."

"Isn't he? Unbelievable. Going to play five-pin instead of out to a restaurant." He shook his head again, then put his arm around her shoulders. "I'm so glad you're okay, Faye. I've been worried sick."

"I know you have," she said. Ever since it had happened he'd been treating her the same careful way he'd treated his mother all the time she'd been sick. "You'll be okay, too, Raffie. I feel it in my bones."

"I hope to God you're right, because if I have to drop out to work in that store . . ." He shook his head, lost for a way to describe how much of a disaster he knew leaving school would be.

"I love you so much," she told him. Somehow, now that the worst was behind them, her feelings for him were even greater than before.

Aldo had been listening to his father and brother arguing for over an hour. Every night it was the same damned thing. He wished they'd quit. He was hungry. The sauce was simmering on the stove; the water had already boiled for the pasta, but Pop wanted to keep on arguing, so Raffie had turned off the burner. The salad was sitting on the table; the bread was sliced, waiting. Aldo could almost taste everything, but nobody was going to get to eat one mouthful until their stupid argument was over. Day in, day out, it went on and on: Pop saying his stuff, then Raffie saying his stuff, back and forth, over and over. It was giving him a headache. He was supposed to meet the twins at the pool hall at eight. At the rate things were going he'd probably be late. Swell. He groaned inwardly.

"Listen," he said, fed up with sitting there every single night, his stomach growling, while Pop insisted he had to build up the business so he could make more bucks to repay Grandmama, and Raffie moaned about how he had to stay in school so he could become an engineer— Who ever heard of anything more boring? "I got an idea, you guys."

"Aldo," his father said, "me and Rafael, we're havin' a serious discussion here."

"Yeah, I *know* that. I been listening to this 'serious discussion' for weeks now. I'm fed up with listening to this every night before we can eat. I'm *hungry.*" He directed this to Raffie. "Could we maybe eat sometime this year, eh?" he asked his father.

"Why don't I cook the pasta now, Pop? Okay?" Raffie asked.

Frankie sighed. "Yeah, go on. So, Aldo. What'sa you big idea?"

"Look," Aldo said, almost certain his father wouldn't go for it. "Raffie wants to stay in school; he's got his heart set on it. Right?"

With a frown, Frankie said, "Right."

"And you need help with the store. Right?"

The frown holding, Frankie said, "Atsa right."

"So, okay," Aldo said with a smile, enjoying having center stage for a change. "I could care less about school. I'm not learning one thing I'm ever gonna use. So here's my idea: *I'll* drop out and help you in the store." Beaming, he sat back and folded his arms across his chest.

Raffie, wooden spoon in hand, turned from the stove. This was an unexpected solution. He watched his father closely, praying Pop would see the sense of it.

"Fourteen you gonna be. You can't even make change right, can't even drive," Frankie said dismissively.

"Hey! I can too make change," Aldo pointed out, his pride stung. "Plus, I can get a learner's permit next year. And you'll give me lessons like you do Raffie. In two years I'll have my license. In the meantime I can work in the store, look after things while you make the pickups and deliveries."

"It's a pretty good idea, Pop," Raffie said, trying not to come across overly enthusiastic so Pop wouldn't think the two of them had cooked up Aldo's plan together. "Once I've got my license I'll be able to drive for you after school and on the weekends."

"I dunno," Frankie said doubtfully, frowning again. "You be alla the time runnin' with Bruno and Anthony, Aldo. I gotta have help I can count on. You alla time lettin' people down."

"The twins'll still be in school," Aldo said. "I won't be running anywhere. I'll be here every day to work in the store."

"I wanna think about this," Frankie said. "I let you know. Let's eat, eh, Raffie?"

"Five minutes, Pop," Raffie said, holding down his excitement as he poured a few drops of olive oil into the boiling water and dropped in a handful of pasta. He and Faye had come through one crisis, and now they were even closer than before. With Aldo volunteering to quit school and help in the store, he'd be able to keep working on his math and science, aiming for the engineering school at the U of T. He and Faye would be another step closer to having the life together they'd been planning for years. "It really is an answer, you know, Pop." He turned back to look again at his father.

"I'll think about it," Frankie told him. "But I tell you one thing, Renaldo." He shook a finger under Aldo's nose. "If I decide to let you come work with me, you gonna *work.* You gonna be polite to the customers, you gonna stop all the foolin' around. You don't go botherin' nobody. You come down to the store eight in the mornin' and you *stay* in the store until I'ma sayin' it's okay you go. Cause I wanna keep open every night late. *Capisch?"*

"I understand, Pop," Aldo said. "And I'll do everything you want. I will, I swear. See, the beauty of this deal is everybody gets what they want. Raff stays in school; I get to quit; and you get help so you can keep the store open late. It's perfect." Plus, Aldo would be able to lift a buck or two now and then with nobody the wiser. On top of which, Pop would probably pay him a little something. He might actually have enough dough in his pocket to get himself a steady and treat her good, butter her up with stuff so she'd put out. A goddamned beautiful deal, if he could get the old man to go along.

"We'll see," Frankie said, and reached for the bread.

Faye was sitting in bed reading and Louise was at the desk bringing her journal up to date. Turning to look over at her sister, Louise said, "What d'you think's going on with Ma?"

"In what way?" Faye asked without taking her eyes from the page.

"It's been a couple of months since she quit her job at the diner, but she's not complaining about money all the time; she's even been almost *pleasant* lately. It doesn't make sense. I'd like to know what's going on."

Faye turned her book face down. "You're right, it doesn't make sense. And she's been buying new clothes. Three dresses that I know of, anyway, and expensive ones at that."

"Where's she getting the money?" Louise wondered.

"Somebody's giving it to her, that's for sure."

"Maybe she's blackmailing Mr. Nolan, or Kath's mom."

"Come *on,* Lou!" Faye chided. "Blackmailing them for what?"

"I don't know. Maybe she's threatening to tell the owners of Raymar something bad about Mr. Nolan."

"What could she possibly tell them? Mr. Nolan's divorced and so's Kath's mom. It's not like they're doing anything illegal."

"Maybe *Ma's* doing something illegal," Louise suggested, making a wicked face. "Maybe she's stealing umbrellas and selling them."

"Oh, please! How would she get them out of the factory, and where would she sell them, for Pete's sake?"

"She'd hide them under her coat. She could sort of hook them inside the sleeves, and walk out with five or six at a time, with nobody noticing."

Faye laughed. "Sure, I can just see it: Ma sailing out of the factory with her armpits full of umbrellas. That's hilarious! Besides, she'd have to steal dozens to get the kind of money she's been laying out for those dresses. Did you *see* that blue one? It's gorgeous. I bet it cost at least seventy-five dollars. She only makes fifty-two fifty a week at the factory."

"Okay, so she's not stealing umbrellas," Louise relented. "But she's doing *something*. She didn't go right out and get another waitressing job, so where's the money coming from? Gramma certainly isn't giving it to her."

"You don't know that for sure, Lou."

"Course I do. Gramma doesn't *have* that kind of money."

"No, but Uncle Bob does."

"Uncle Bob *hates* Ma. He wouldn't give her a nickel to call the fire department if she was going up in flames."

"You're terrible!" Faye grinned, amused as always by Lou's audacity. "He does not hate her."

"Okay, he loathes, detests, and despises her. He still wouldn't let Gramma give his money to Ma, especially not to buy herself a bunch of expensive dresses. So where's she *getting* it?"

"I don't know. Why don't you ask her."

"What a good idea, Faye. I'll go knock on her door right now and say, 'Oh, by the way, Ma. Who's been giving you all the money you're spending lately?' And she'll say, 'Please come in and sit down, Louise. I've been meaning to discuss this with you and your sister but I simply haven't had a moment. My dear, I've inherited a million dollars, and I've been waiting for the right time to tell the two of you the great news. I'm giving up my job at the factory and we'll be moving into a mansion in Rosedale. From now on I intend to be a perfect mother. I'm hiring a cook, a butler, and a maid, and you girls will never have to lift a finger again. You have every right to despise me, but I'm begging your forgiveness and I hope you'll learn to love me in time.' "

Her face bright red, tears running down her cheeks, Faye was howling by the time Louise finished.

Louise chuckled. "Do you realize she's never given you back the pearls?"

"Holy cow! That's right. What'll I do?"

"Ask for them back."

"She'll want to know why."

"Just say you want them back, Faye. They are *yours,* after all."

"Not really. Gramma only gave them to me because Ma was doing that Joan Crawford routine and it got on Gramma's nerves."

"Ask for them back, Faye, or else I will."

"Okay. You ask her. I want to keep out of her way."

"Fine. I'll do it tomorrow." Louise swung around and picked up her pen. She wrote for a minute or two then said, "I don't have any chest at all yet. *Pas de poitrine, pauvre moi.*"

Retrieving her book, Faye said, "You can't expect to grow one overnight."

"I thought once you started getting periods you got a chest right away."

"You've only had three periods so far, for heaven's sake."

"I'm growing hair. Argh! I'd rather have a chest."

"You'll get both. Okay? You can't have one without the other."

"I don't see why not. A person should be able to have a chest without turning into a werewolf." She jumped up and held out her hands, whispering, "Hair on zee palms of my hands, my dear. At meednight, zee transformation vill be complete." Launching herself from the foot of the bed, she leaped onto her sister. "I hunger for zee taste of human flesh." She growled. "Let me bite you a leetle."

"Get off, you lunatic!" Faye pushed at her, giggling.

"Only a leetle bite. Zen you, too, vill be immortal." Grabbing her sister's arm, she opened her mouth wide and made as if to sink her teeth into the meat of Faye's upper arm.

"I'll immortal you, you loon!" Faye said, starting to tickle Louise in the rib cage. "You'll be sorry you ever tried to sink your nasty fangs into me!"

Louise wriggled, squealing. "I give up! You win! You win!"

Drawing her lips back, her fingers digging into Louise's ribs, Faye clicked her teeth together, having fun. She felt a splendid lightness inside.

Raffie was staying in school, and things were back to the way they used to be when they sneaked down to the cellar. Ma wasn't after them all the time lately, even if it was kind of strange that she seemed to have so much money suddenly. Aside from having trouble keeping up with her school-work, Faye had never been happier.

Maggie's savings account was swelling very nicely. She'd already put away more than two hundred of what McCutcheon had given her and, according to her calculations, if she kept seeing him for a year she'd be able to save close to a thousand dollars. If he stayed interested, she might, in time, get him to be even more generous. The situation's potential was practically unlimited, and he showed no sign of losing interest in her. Meanwhile, she was being wined and dined in some of the city's best restaurants. Aside from the Chez Paree, they'd gone to the Club Top Hat, La Chaumiere, the Victoria Room at the King Edward, the Lichee Gardens, and the Town and Country. Tonight she was meeting him at Winston's, a place so hoity-toity you had to have a membership key to get in.

Upon being shown to the table, she was taken aback to find Craig sitting with another man, and wondered if this third person's presence meant she wouldn't be going back later to the house on Collier Street. She certainly hoped that wasn't going to be the case.

"Margaret." Craig and his friend stood while the maître d' seated her. Then, sitting again, he said, "I'd like you to meet my old friend, Elliot Neville."

Neville, who appeared to be about McCutcheon's age, shook her hand and offered a pleasant smile. "Good to meet you. Craig's spoken very highly of you."

Flattered, Maggie returned his smile.

"Elliot's an old friend," Craig explained, "in from London for a visit."

"London, Ontario?" she asked politely.

"England, actually," said Neville, still smiling. "Craig very kindly invited me to join the two of you for dinner. I do hope you don't find it an imposition."

"Oh, no," she said, getting her cigarettes from her bag. She wouldn't know whether or not it was an imposition until later. So during the drinks beforehand and during the dinner itself she made an effort to be charming to Craig's friend, hoping his presence wasn't going to wind up costing her money. She'd been counting on using half this evening's money to buy a pair of shoes she'd spotted in Eaton's.

When the table had been cleared Neville excused himself to go to the men's room. At once, Craig said, "So, Margaret, what do you think of my old friend?"

"He seems very nice," she said neutrally, hating that sort of question. Her immediate instinct was always to say, How the hell should I know?

"Elliot's a decent fellow. We go back many years. We were both at school in Paris. I was doing post-graduate studies in art history and he was doing a year at the Sorbonne, perfecting his French. Elliot's bilingual, does quite a lot of business in Quebec."

"You went to school in France?" she asked, ever more impressed by him. She'd never known anyone else who'd been rich all his life. She was fascinated by his wallet full of cash and credit cards, by his clothes, his lifestyle, and by his occasional references to the Granite Club, about which she'd been hearing all her life. With enough money, you could do anything, go anywhere.

"And in England," he said matter-of-factly. "Would you have any strenuous objections to Elliot's joining us at the house?"

"What exactly do you mean by that?" she asked warily.

"I mean it literally." Lowering his voice, he said, "We'd certainly make it worth your while. But of course if you object we'll forget all about it."

She gazed at him. He was asking her to take them both on, to sleep with the two of them. What the hell did he take her for anyway? "I don't know about that," she said, wondering just how much worth her while they were willing to make it. Logically, it should have been twice what he usually gave her. The thought of a hundred dollars was definitely enticing. But two of them? "Both of you together," she asked in an undertone, "or one at a time? What are you asking exactly?"

"I thought we'd simply play it by ear, if you're willing."

"I don't know," she repeated. Would two men make it twice as exciting? Neville was attractive enough, and he did have a very upper-crust accent. They weren't exactly bums, these two.

"Let's see how it goes, shall we? If at any point you find it's more than you can handle, we'll stop at once."

"Is this something you've done before?" she asked, her eyes narrowing slightly.

"No, but it is something I've thought about. Haven't you?" he asked with a smile.

"No," she said flatly, "I haven't."

"But you'll give it a try?"

"I suppose we can see how it goes," she allowed.

"Good girl! Dessert?" he asked as both Neville and the waiter returned to the table.

When they got back to his house, Craig poured more drinks. He and Neville had Drambuie; she took Cointreau, having lately developed a taste for the clear, potent orange liqueur. He put an LP on the turntable of his hi-fi, which was discreetly housed in an antique armoire, and the three of them sat in the dimly lit living room with the swagged dark gray velvet draperies and lace curtains, the old-fashioned wallpaper and marble fireplace, the portrait over the mantel of the woman in the red dress, while boring violin music played in the background. Nothing appeared to have been planned. The men sat with their suit jackets unbuttoned, their legs comfortably crossed, sipping their Drambuie and chatting with Maggie, who drank her Cointreau in half a dozen swallows, perspiring as she imagined the possible combinations and permutations of lovemaking as a trio, and trying not to let her nervousness show.

By the time she'd finished a second tiny glass of the liqueur, she was becoming fairly agitated, wondering how and where and when this was supposed to happen. The longer they sat there, the more doubtful she became.

Then, just when she was beginning to think it might be a good idea to go home and forget the whole business, Craig refilled his and Neville's glasses, then said casually, as if he'd done this many times before, "Shall we go upstairs?" and both men turned expectantly to her.

She excused herself and went upstairs to the old-fashioned bathroom with the lion's-paw tub and marble-topped basin. As had become her custom on these evenings with Craig, she'd inserted her diaphragm before leaving the house. This trip was merely a stalling tactic, a chance to inspect herself in the broad framed mirror over the sink while she asked herself if she really wanted to go through with it. Not only was the additional money an inducement, but the idea of two pairs of hands on her body was, finally, quite thrilling.

They were waiting for her in the bedroom, smiling hungrily, like greedy little boys dressed up in costly hand-tailored suits. "Well," she said, smiling back at them, the liqueur sending heat through her belly and short-circuiting the last of her inhibitions, "what happens now?" And she really did have to laugh at just how greedy the two of them became once they'd got her clothes off.

✝

She fell asleep sprawled on the damp, rumpled sheet of McCutcheon's ornate four-poster bed. Awakened by a hand on her shoulder, she opened her eyes to see Craig in his burgundy silk dressing gown.

"It's getting late, Margaret. I thought I'd phone for a cab."

"Oh," she said groggily, sitting up. "Okay. Where's your friend?"

"Elliot's gone back to his hotel. Take your time," he said, "and come down when you're ready." In his leather slippers, one hand in his pocket, he went padding out, and she listened to him going down the stairs as she reached for her underwear. She'd never felt so thoroughly sated, so luxuriously depleted. Her hands were clumsy, her body sluggish and sore as she dragged on her clothes.

Craig was waiting at the foot of the stairs to help her into her coat. "I think the evening was a great success," he said contentedly. "Don't you?"

"It was different, that's for sure."

"Ah," he smiled. "But you enjoyed yourself tremendously, didn't you, Margaret?"

"It was different," she repeated noncommittally. She didn't want him getting the idea that she was game for absolutely anything. For all she knew, if he thought she was a pushover, he'd show up next time with two friends, or three, and expect her to take them all on. And she was no whore!

"You're a veritable treasure, my dear," he said, giving her a kiss and her handbag as the doorbell rang. "By the way, could you let me have your phone number?"

"Why?"

"In case I need to reach you," he said patiently. "Would you mind?"

"I guess not," she said, and recited it for him. "A week from Friday, as usual?"

"Absolutely. We'll talk Friday morning to confirm."

"Fine," she said, following him to the door.

He handed the driver a folded bill, said a seemingly fond good-night to her, then waited to see she was safely inside the cab before he stepped back into the house and closed the door. The front light blinked off a moment later.

After getting a cigarette lit, she opened her bag to see what Craig considered "making it worth her while." Out of the driver's viewing range, she unfolded the notes he'd tucked into her bag to discover she was holding three fifty dollar bills. Jubilant, she tucked them into her change purse, then sat back to enjoy the ride. Tomorrow she'd treat herself to the new shoes and maybe some lingerie, and Monday another hundred would go into the savings account. She'd have the whole weekend to relax and soak away her various aches and chafes. And while the girls were out, she'd get caught up on Louise's journal. The little bitches never told her a thing. She had to keep tabs on them by deciphering what she could of Louise's coded comments.

Closing her eyes, she reviewed some of the scenes from Craig's bedroom, shuffling through them like photographs, pausing when one or another particularly graphic, especially arousing image captured her attention. Six hands, three mouths, three pairs of legs; a trio of bodies contorting to make connections. Jesus! The recollection sizzled along her nerve ends. She wouldn't mind at all doing that again. Especially when this kind of money was involved.

CHAPTER
TWENTY-FIVE

"WHAT D'YOU *MEAN* YOU GAVE MY NUMBER TO A FRIEND of yours?" Maggie demanded. "Since when do you go giving out my phone number?"

"I thought you wouldn't mind," Craig McCutcheon said, unruffled. "Jim Stewart's a good friend, a highly respected banker. He's in town from Calgary for four days and wanted someone to have dinner with him. If you're not interested, Margaret, all you have to do is tell him so."

"What exactly have you told this person about me?"

"Simply that you're a friend, and that we have a certain . . . arrangement."

"I see. So now this man's going to be phoning, expecting me to have dinner with him. And what else?"

"That's entirely up to you, Margaret. He is, shall we say, aware of the terms."

"What *terms?*"

"He's very generous, my dear. What you do or don't do is your decision." There was a moment's silence before he said, "I had no idea you'd be so offended. Perhaps it would be best if I call him right back and tell him not to bother."

"Wait a minute, Craig. Could I have a minute to think about this, if you don't mind?"

"Take all the time you like. I do realize tomorrow's Sunday, and it's very short notice. But I assure you Stewart's a delightful fellow. At the worst, you'll have a pleasant dinner at his hotel."

"I'll see how I feel. In the meantime, I'd appreciate it if you didn't go giving my number to total strangers without even bothering to ask permission."

"My apologies. There's no obligation, as I've said. We'll discuss it further on Friday, clarify matters for future contingencies. Fair enough?"

Disgruntled, wondering what he could mean by "future contingencies," she said, "I suppose so."

They exchanged goodbyes and she hung up to pace the kitchen with a cigarette, thinking. On the minus side, Craig had discussed her with one of his friends, and given out her number. Where did he get the nerve? On the plus side, for almost five months he'd been taking her to places she'd always wanted to go as well as giving her more money than she'd ever imagined having. As he'd pointed out, she wasn't obligated to *do* anything. If she did decide to have dinner with this Stewart person, she might come out ahead by fifty dollars, maybe even more. Craig did say the man was very generous. And if Neville was anything to go by, she might even come out ahead by as much as a hundred. Still, where did Craig get off, giving out her number that way, telling people about her? They were going to iron out a few matters on Friday, that was for damned sure.

Her temper subsiding, she thought she'd just have to wait and see what this Stewart was like. It wouldn't kill her to eat at a hotel. At least she wouldn't have to sit around her mother's place, with Bob pretending he was interested in what she had to say, pretending he liked her. She went back to the telephone to call her mother.

✦

"I had an idea your mother wouldn't be coming," Ellen told the girls. "So when she phoned last night to cancel, I asked Nancy, Katharine, and Jerry to join us instead."

"Oh, great!" Louise said happily.

"And," Ellen told Faye, "I spoke to Raffie and he'll drop by later for dessert. He has to fix lunch for his father and brother, and then he'll be over."

Faye gave her grandmother a kiss. "I'll go call him, okay?"

"Of course. Use the extension in the bedroom."

Faye hurried down the hall as Louise asked, "Can I help you in the kitchen? Where's Uncle Bob?"

"He went out to get some cream. He'll be right back. Come on." Ellen put an arm around her granddaughter's waist. "You can make the salad while I do the potatoes."

"You know what? Faye got herself a job for the summer."

"But school's not out for another three weeks." Ellen handed Louise an apron.

"I know. She was afraid if she didn't apply right away all the jobs would be gone. So she went to this Manpower agency and told them she was sixteen. They gave her a typing test, and she did *seventy-seven* words a minute."

"Oh, that's excellent."

"It sure is. I only got sixty-three words a minute on my last test."

"That's very good, too, Lulu."

"I know, but not as good as Faye. Anyway, they said they've got tons of work for her. So she'll be starting the minute school's out at the end of the month. *And* they'll pay her one seventy-five an hour! Isn't that fantastic?"

"It certainly is."

Faye returned and said, "Raffie will be here by three, Gramma."

"That'll be fine, dear."

"It was so nice of you to ask him. Can I do anything to help?"

"Keep us company while we finish. Lulu tells me you've signed on with Manpower."

"Uh-huh. I'm so excited, Gramma. If I work thirty-five hours, not counting time out for lunch, I can make sixty-one dollars a week. That's more than Ma makes at the factory.''

"I'm very proud of you, Faye.'' Ellen opened the oven door to check the roast, then straightened. "That's top dollar for a typist.''

"I'll be doing Dictaphone typing. It pays more.''

"When did you learn how to do that?'' Louise asked, carefully cutting a tomato into wedges.

"I didn't. They asked if I wanted to test for it, and I said sure. It's so easy. You run the machine with a foot pedal and type what you hear. I did sixty-eight words a minute.''

"You're a wonder,'' Ellen said. "What will you do with all that money?''

"Buy some decent clothes for me and Lou, save up. If I work the whole summer I can save at least three hundred dollars. And if I do overtime, I can save even more. I figured it all out, including car fare and everything. So you won't have to give me an allowance anymore.''

With a smile Ellen said, "You can just add it to your savings.''

"Honestly?''

"Honestly.''

"Thank you, Gramma. I could set the table,'' Faye offered.

"We have to wait for Bob to get back so we can put in the extra leaf. Then, I'd love you to do the setting. What are you doing this summer, Lulu?''

"I don't know.'' Louise paused, holding a handful of lettuce. "Maybe I'll say I'm fifteen and try for a job, too. You think that agency would take me, Faye?''

"You've got to be sixteen.''

"Oh! Well, I'll try somewhere else. Sixty-three's not so bad, is it, Gramma?''

"It's not bad at all. Let me talk to Bob. We always need help at the office. Maybe we can find something for you.''

"Wow! You mean I could come work with the two of you?''

"I don't see why not. You can type, and I know you could handle the filing. Let's see what Bob says.''

"Okay! Great!''

"I don't think they'll pay you more than forty, though, Lulu.''

"Forty dollars a week? That'd be incredible, fantastic! I'll have a job too, Faye!'' Louise crowed. "We'll be rich!''

"Not on forty a week," Ellen laughed. "But it'll be a treat to see you every day."

"For me, too. Oh, boy!" Louise tore the lettuce with renewed enthusiasm.

Jim Stewart was polite, paunchy, and boring. Maggie sat back and let him talk. He enjoyed the sound of his own voice, and went on and on about the prime minister—St. Laurent this and St. Laurent that—until she stopped trying to follow whatever the hell it was he was saying and looked around at the other diners, her foot keeping time under the table to the music of the dance band.

Every so often she glanced over and smiled to show she was listening, but she was really trying to decide if she wanted to go to bed with the man. He wasn't unattractive, but she imagined that if she did go to bed with him he'd probably talk all the way through it. She lit a cigarette and sipped her Tom Collins, noting his dainty hands and scrupulously clean fingernails. He didn't do a thing for her. Maybe he wouldn't even ask her to go upstairs with him. She didn't care one way or the other, although she'd come out to meet him with the idea in mind of going home with an extra fifty in her purse.

"An amazing number of successful—even famous—people are Canadian," he was saying.

"Is that so?"

He smiled and said, "Let's see how many you can name."

"What, famous Canadians?" She laughed. "You mean politicians, businessmen, and so forth?"

"Anyone at all." He wrapped both of his slightly chubby little hands around a squat glass of scotch and water.

"Okay," she said. "Let's see. E. P. Taylor and Jack Kent Cook."

"Very good."

"Then there's Raymond Massey and Jack Carson."

"Good, good."

"Who else?" she asked herself, finally having fun. "Mary Pickford and Robert Beatty. Beatrice Lillie. Oh, and Raymond Burr."

"Let's stay with movie people," he said. "Can you think of any others?"

"Hang on," she said. "What about the Four Lads and the Diamonds? They're Canadian groups."

"A point for you, my dear. I'm not up on popular music."

"Come on. You've heard 'No, Not Much,' and 'Little Darlin'.'" *Everybody* has." She sang, " 'I don't want my arms around you, no not much.' You've *heard* that on the radio."

He shook his head. "Afraid not, but I do know that Percy Faith is one of our own. And were you aware that Pablum was invented by Dr. Fred Tisdall right here at Sick Children's Hospital? He took the name from the Greek word *pabulum,* which means food."

"For Pete's sake," she said. "Both my girls grew up on that stuff. I had no idea."

"There you go, Margaret. We learn something new every day. Did you know there are two famous actresses from Canada who both have the same real name?"

"Who?"

"Both born Gladys Smith: Mary Pickford and Alexis Smith." He beamed proudly. "What d'you think of that?"

"You're joking! I didn't know that. Who else do I know?" she wondered, enjoying the game. "Hume Cronyn! And . . . I can't think."

"Walter Pidgeon," he said.

"Right! I forgot him."

"And Walter Huston, Rod Cameron, Norma Shearer, Gene Lockhart, Ruby Keeler."

"Ruby *Keeler?*"

"Absolutely. Born in Halifax, lived there until she was three."

"Well, I'll be," she said, impressed.

"There are dozens," he told her. "Marie Dressler, Deanna Durbin, Glenn Ford, and John Ireland. And I'll bet you didn't know John L. Warner, the head of Warner Brothers, was born in London, Ontario."

"For God's sake!" she exclaimed. "That's unbelievable. How do you know all that?"

"It's a kind of hobby of mine. And it makes me proud to see one of our people do well."

"It seems to me the only time 'our people' do well is when they leave and go somewhere else."

"A not invalid point," he conceded. "It's always been a disappointment to me that we don't have our own movie industry, with our own stars."

She laughed. "Are you joking? We'd be too embarrassed. It'd call attention to us."

"Sad but true. Would you care to dance, Margaret?"

She thought he'd probably step all over her feet but said, "All right," and got up to walk out onto the dance floor with him. To her considerable surprise, he danced extremely well, with a light step and a firm but not hard grip on her waist. "You're a good dancer," she told him.

He smiled again and said, "So are you." And she thought she probably would go to bed with him after all.

During lunch, Nancy announced, "Jerry has some wonderful news."

She and everyone else turned to look at him.

With a slightly shy grin, Nolan said, "I've been offered another job. I get offers now and then, but this one seemed too good to pass up."

"What is it?" Louise asked with interest.

He turned his grin on her, saying, "The previous offers have been for other manufacturing outfits, you see. And it always seemed fairly much of a trade-off. But a few weeks ago I was asked if I'd be interested in a corporate position."

"What's that?" Louise wanted to know.

"Business, Lulu," Bob interjected, "as against manufacturing."

"Oh!"

"It's a considerable step up. After talking it over with Nancy," he said, glancing in Nancy's direction, "we've decided I should make the move."

"What's the position, Jerry?" Bob asked.

"I'll be taking over as manager of the Canadian headquarters for a British import/export group, in charge of a staff of sixty-odd. Which is only a dozen or so more than I'm dealing with now. The offices are on Bloor between Church and Jarvis, and that means I'll be able to walk to work."

"It's a very good move for him," Nancy put in.

"I won't miss the noise of machinery, although the people at Raymar are a decent bunch and I will miss them."

Louise thought to herself that he probably wouldn't miss Ma, and catching Faye's eye, she knew Faye was thinking the same thing.

After lunch, Louise volunteered to do the cleaning up.

Kath at once said, "I'll help," and the two girls busied themselves clearing the table while the others moved to the living room.

"You want to wash or dry?" Louise asked her friend.

"I'm so spoiled," Kath said. "At home, if it's the housekeeper's day off, Mom and I just throw everything into the dishwasher. I'd better dry. I'm not too good at the washing."

"Okay. The dish towels are in that drawer."

Getting the twin sinks filled, Louise began with the glassware while Kath stood by holding the towel. In a whisper, she said, "I think Mom and Jerry are gonna get married."

"No kidding!" Louise said. "Fantastic! When?"

"Oh, not for a long time yet. Maybe next spring."

"How come they're waiting so long?"

"I think they want to be sure. You know?"

"Are you glad?" Louise asked.

"Yeah. Jerry's way nicer to me than my dad. I hardly ever see Dad these days, and he didn't even remember my birthday, didn't send a card or anything."

"That stinks," Louise commiserated. "If I hadn't reminded Ma, she'd have forgotten Faye's birthday, too. Mr. Nolan's a nice man," she said seriously. "I bet he'll be a really good father."

"Well, it's not as if I'm a little kid. But he always takes Mom and me both out. And he's actually got her started painting again. She hasn't done any of that since I was about six."

"Really? What's she painting?"

"Me," Kath laughed. "Isn't that a hoot? I've been sitting for her on the weekends. Makes me feel like such a dodo, but it's kind of nice too. We talk about all kinds of stuff while she works. She's *crazy* about Jerry. You should hear the way she talks about him. Sounds just like the girls at school. It's cute, really. And I have to help her decide what to wear when they're going out."

"You're so lucky, Kath," Louise said wistfully. "Your mother *talks* to you, she cares about you. Me and Faye, we've probably got the worst mother in the entire western hemisphere."

"I know," Kath agreed. "But your grandmother's *wonderful*. I love her to death."

"Isn't she great? And isn't Bob *dreamy?*"

"He's *divine*," Kath agreed again. "I want to marry someone exactly like him. Don't you?"

For some reason, Louise suddenly thought of Mr. Craven. Daniel, with his dark good looks. "Yeah," she said, thinking of his dimpled chin and his long attractive hands.

For the first time ever, Maggie got absolutely nothing out of going to bed with a man. Jim Stewart was one of those types she'd heard the girls at the factory talk about for years, a wham-bam guy who was finished before she'd even started getting in the mood.

But he was not only grateful, he was, as Craig had said, very generous. When she was dressed and ready to leave, he pressed an envelope into her hand, and asked, "May I call you again, next time I'm in town?"

"Sure. You do that," she said.

Before opening the door to his room he gave her an affectionate kiss on the cheek and said, "Thank you for a pleasurable evening, Margaret."

"You're welcome. And don't forget to call me."

"I certainly won't."

She waited until she was in the back of the taxi before opening the envelope. Five twenties, the easiest, fastest money she'd ever made. Gratified, she lit a cigarette and sat back to enjoy the ride.

The following day, on a whim, she went home at noon. It wasn't something she usually did, but she was in no mood to sit around the lunchroom listening to the other workers yacking. She also wanted a look at Louise's journal, curious to know what had gone on at her mother's the previous day.

G invited K, N, J and R. cuz M. cncld. G says maybe I'll be able to work for Uncle B this sum. in the off. *$40/wk!!!* Amazing! J has new job, and K says nxt yr. J & N to get mrd! Fantastic! K tlkg and I thought of Mr. C. He's so nice. Might work on HR nxt yr. We'll see.

It took Maggie a few minutes to decipher it all. Then she sat with her heart racing, absorbing the shock. Nolan was leaving Raymar. *And* he was going to marry the Rosedale bitch! She was so stunned she could hardly breathe.

Getting up, she put on the kettle, then munched some saltines while trying to decide what to do. A sudden inspiration set her pulse racing again and she phoned the factory.

"It's Maggie Parker," she told the receptionist. "I'm feeling lousy, so

I won't be back this afternoon. Let the foreman know, will you, so he can clock me out."

While the tea was brewing she went to the bedroom to look through her closet. Why the hell not? she thought, reaching for one of her new day dresses. She'd steal Nolan's thunder, make a little announcement of her own, beat him to the punch.

⤚

She filled out an application, then waited to be interviewed, hoping it wouldn't be by one of the brittle-looking women who came out to call this name or that.

She was in luck. It was one of the men, and he smiled when she stood up in response to his call.

"Come in, Mrs. Parker," he said, leading the way to his office and closing the door. Seating himself behind the desk, he scanned her application then smiled at her again. "May I ask why you're looking to change jobs? You've been with"—he glanced down at the clipboard—"Raymar for a good many years."

"Too many," she said, giving him back a great big smile and crossing her legs. "It's time for a change. I've always shopped at Eaton's and I thought it might be nice to be on the other side of the counter."

"I see that you're interested in"—again his eyes went to the board—"fashion, cosmetics, and jewelry. No need to ask why," he said, giving her an admiring once-over. "Let's have a little look-see." He pulled over a box of index cards and began fingering through them. "As it happens, we've got openings in better dresses and in cosmetics. Have you a preference?"

"Better dresses," she said at once.

"Uh-huh. Now I see here"—yet again he referred to the application—"you're presently at fifty-two fifty. I think for someone with such a stable background we could probably come close to that. And, of course, you'd have a staff discount."

"Of course," she smiled.

"When would you be free to start?" he asked, reaching for his pen and holding it poised over the application.

"I'd have to give two weeks' notice. Today's only Monday. I'd have to wait until Friday. So, say, three weeks from today?"

"I think that would work out splendidly. You'll be shown how to write up the orders, how to take CODs, how to do credits and refunds, and so forth. We instruct all new employees in the store policies on their first day, which is also when we take care of the paperwork. You'll also be introduced to your supervisor, the floor manager, and the others in your department. So,'' he took a deep breath, studied her crossed legs for a second or two, then showed his teeth in another wide smile, ''I'd say that about covers it. I'm Fred Brundage. You'll come back up to Personnel Monday, three weeks from today, and we'll get you squared away.''

''Wonderful.'' She stood up and extended her hand, saying, ''Thank you, Fred.''

''You're very welcome. A pleasure meeting you, Margaret. I'll be looking forward to seeing you again in three weeks' time. And welcome to Eaton's.''

''I'll be looking forward to that, too,'' she said, finding him quite attractive.

To celebrate, she stopped at the perfume counter on the main floor and, after some deliberation, bought herself a bottle of White Shoulders. Not the cologne or toilet water, but the actual perfume. She handed over the cash thinking next time she'd be able to use her employee's discount. And with the girls working now, buying their own clothes, they'd be able to take advantage of her discount, too. A little something they'd have to thank her for.

On the streetcar going home she marveled over how easy it had been, and wondered why she hadn't made the change years ago. Never mind. No more Mack's diner, and now no more goddamned umbrellas. At least working at Eaton's wasn't anything she'd have to be embarrassed to admit to people. And she'd get back her pension contributions from Raymar as well as whatever vacation pay she had due, which would be a nice chunk of change to add to her savings account. How d'you like that, Nolan! she thought, running a hand over her hair. He could take that sewing machine and shove it straight up his keister! Between her new job and the money she was receiving from Craig and his friends, she'd be in fine shape. In fact, she might be able to quit work altogether, if Craig kept coming up with such generous friends. With both girls working, her expenses would be down to practically nothing, just the rent, phone, and hydro bills. She wouldn't have minded moving to someplace a bit classier, but that could wait. She felt positively exultant. Things were going better than she'd ever dreamed possible.

☨

"Faye, look!"

Faye raised her eyes from her book to see Louise standing, hands on hips, wearing only her pajama bottoms. "What?"

"Are you blind or something? My *chest!*"

"Oh, right." Faye smiled, touched by Lou's pride in the slight swelling of her breasts, the nipples just taking shape; awed by her sister's narrow little body. Louise still looked about ten or eleven. "Congratulations, kiddo. Nice going."

"It's about *time,* eh?" Louise tried to lift them from underneath, then to push them together; she failed. "Think I need a bra yet?"

"Not yet. Soon, though," Faye said encouragingly.

"Yeah. Soon, boy. Now if I could just grow a few inches taller. I haven't grown even one single inch." Touching herself gingerly now, she said, "Do they ever hurt! Did yours hurt when they started growing?"

"Uh-huh. Everybody's does."

"Oh! Well, that's okay, then."

"Put your top on and come to bed," Faye said, wishing she could be as unselfconscious. There were so many things Louise could do that Faye didn't dare even think of—like buying the safes that time, and asking that man in the restaurant for a cigarette; like standing in front of someone, half naked, showing off her tiny new bosom.

Louise buttoned on her pajama top and bounced into bed, getting *Beautiful Joe* from the night table.

"How come you're reading that again?"

"I *love* this book," Louise said defensively. "It's my all-time favorite. Marshall Saunders is a genius. He's a wonderful, wonderful writer, and Joe is the best and bravest, smartest dog ever."

"Marshall Saunders happens to be a woman, Lou."

"Don't be silly! Marshall's a *man's* name."

"Maybe so. But she's a woman."

"How do you know that?"

"Because I did a book report on it in grade seven, for Pete's sake. And she was a woman."

"What d'you mean *was?*"

"She died, about ten years ago. I'd like to remind you who gave you the book, anyway."

"You did. Oh, poop. Now I'm all sad. I don't think I'll read it again after all."

"Why not? It shouldn't make any difference."

"I know, but it does." Louise got out of bed and went over to the desk to pick up one of her new batch of library books. "Is Ernest Hemingway dead, too?"

"I don't think so."

"Okay, good." Louise looked at the front, then the back covers of *A Farewell to Arms.* "Do you realize we're in grade ten? Don't you feel incredibly grown-up? I do. I mean, I worked the entire summer and saved almost two hundred dollars. I'm a *responsible* person. Uncle Bob and Gramma said so. So how come I still look like a dwarf? Things better be different this year, boy. I'm going to that sock hop tomorrow for exactly fifteen minutes. If nobody asks me to dance, I'm *leaving.* So," she took a breath, puffed it out, then asked, "How was good old Raff tonight?"

"Just fine," Faye said quietly, pretending to be absorbed in her reading. She wasn't in the mood to talk about what had happened that evening.

She'd actually been so excited down in the cellar that she'd told him it was okay, they could go all the way; she wanted to do it. So they got out one of the Trojans, but as soon as he started pushing into her she got so scared, went so tight, she had to tell him to stop. And he did, right away. He said it didn't matter, and after a while they did it the usual way, rubbing each other until they both came. But it had actually hurt when he'd started pushing, and she'd felt this awful panic as if she was going to be killed. Raffie kept saying, "It's okay, sweetheart. Honest to God. It doesn't matter. We don't have to do it." He'd been great about it, really sweet and kind. But it'd scared her. And it scared her again, thinking about it now.

"What's the matter, Faye?"

"Nothing. I'm just tired."

Louise gave her a naughty smile. "All that sex wears you out, eh?"

"Right!" Faye managed a smile and gave her a punch on the arm. "That's it exactly. Shut up now and let me get back to this."

Louise opened her book and Faye went back to pretending to read *Saratoga Trunk,* wondering if there was something wrong with her. It didn't seem right that they could make each other feel so good, that he could get her so excited that she actually wanted to go all the way. But the moment he tried to enter her the excitement died completely. She turned cold and had to close her legs, get him off her right away. She'd been terrified, and it had taken her a good fifteen minutes to get over it. She wished there was someone she could talk to. But there wasn't. And anyway, if it came right down to it, she knew she couldn't. It'd be too embarrassing, for one thing. And for another, she and Raffie weren't even supposed to be doing the things they were, let alone going all the way.

CHAPTER
TWENTY-SIX

THEY HAD A LIVE GROUP, NOT JUST RECORDS, FOR THE sock hop—Bert Niosi and his band—and they were really good. Louise was always thrilled by the sound of live music, by the thrum of a bass and the lure of the drums' solid rhythm, the driving melody line of a piano. She stood by the wall just inside the gym, watching the kids dance in the cavernous, dimly lit room that was, no matter how hard they tried to disguise or dress it up for dances, inescapably a gym. Smelling faintly of sweat and rubber, it seemed to echo at ceiling height with the squeak of sneakers and the grunt of tall, lean teenage boys playing basketball. Her body moved gently of its own accord to the music. She checked the time: four-fifteen. She'd give it exactly fifteen minutes, then get her books and go home. She hated hanging around on the sidelines, with the girls on either side in their straight skirts, sweater sets, and pearls, their page boys and Tangee Natural lipstick, giggling and whispering, whooping with sudden laughter if some boy cruising the row of candidates broke stride and came over to ask one of them to dance. As an admittedly pointless gesture of defiance, Louise kept her shoes on.

Someone approached her but she purposely didn't look up. What she hated more than anything else was being a wallflower and looking all wide-eyed and hopeful every time some guy walked by. If it were the other way around, she'd simply march over and ask someone to dance. She wouldn't cruise the lineup by the wall as if she were in a grocery store looking for bargains.

"Would you care to dance, Miss Parker?"

Her stomach giving a leap, she looked up. Holy Pete! Mr. Craven was asking her to dance. She thought she might drop dead on the spot. But she said, "Sure," and followed him into the middle of the gym, glad to see he had his shoes on, too. It struck her as symbolic, although she couldn't have said why.

He put his arm around her waist and took her hand. They were playing "Since I Met You, Baby," Ivory Joe Hunter's song, which she loved, and she felt as if her breathing might stop altogether—she was actually dancing with Mr. Craven, Daniel. The girls on the wall were probably gawking, whispering urgently; all of them talking about it. She didn't care. He smelled wonderful, that cool lemony scent, and his hands weren't a bit sweaty. They were warm and dry and he was holding her perfectly—close, but not too close.

"You're a good dancer, Miss Parker." He smiled at her.

"So are you, Mr. Craven."

Up this close she could see how long his eyelashes were; black and thick like little fans. And his eyes were so dark and shiny he looked almost as if he might be about to cry. Which was so silly, she could hardly believe she'd even thought it, but those eyes gleamed like inky liquid.

"We still have some openings on the *Review* this year," he said. "Would you consider working on the yearbook?"

"Sure," she said without thinking, at this point prepared to agree to anything he said. "That'd be fun."

"Good." He gave her another smile, and something happened low in her belly; a twisting sensation that made her want to close her eyes and let her head rest against his chest. "Stop by the *Review* office and see me after school tomorrow. We'll put you to work."

She said, "Okay." Her mouth was suddenly so dry her upper lip stuck to her teeth and she was unable to smile back at him.

"I miss having you in my class this year, Louise."

"You do? How come?" she asked stupidly. Kids were invisible and they all knew it. Teachers could never remember their names without referring to the attendance sheets at least until Christmas, and sometimes until Easter.

"You brighten things up, get things going. You're hardly a typical student."

"I'm not?"

"No," he said. "You're not. It was a pleasure having you in my class last year."

"It was? Gosh!" She wanted to say it had been a pleasure for her seeing him every day, but didn't think that would sound right. He was only being kind, after all. The last thing he wanted or needed was to have her turn gorpy, like the girls lining the wall. Again she had that feeling of wanting to close her eyes and let herself lean against him. Her legs were wobbly, and that twisting sensation reminded her of how, during her first couple of years in public school, she used to wrap her legs very, very tightly around one of the metal struts of the swings in the schoolyard, then hold on loosely with her hands, lean way back, and rock back and forth. She used to do it every day, at recess in the morning, at lunchtime, and at recess in the afternoon, because it felt so good. Lots of the kids did it. But one morning Miss Dorrance came up, saying, "Stop that this instant!" and chased all the kids away from the swings, except those actually riding them. She thought Miss Dorrance knew about the good feeling she got rubbing on the swing leg, and decided that it must be wrong, because the woman looked so angry and offended. Miss Dorrance made her feel so guilty and even evil, somehow, that Louise never did it again after that. The following year they took the swings away, patched over the holes in the concrete where the struts had been anchored, and Louise was convinced it was her fault. She'd been doing something bad and was caught, so they took the swings away. Occasionally she had twinges of that remembered pleasure, but at once she'd think of Miss Dorrance and feel vaguely wicked. Dancing with Mr. Craven now gave her the exact same sensation, like a pleasant, faintly irritating and persistent itch between the legs that she badly wanted to scratch because she knew it would feel wonderful.

The music ended. Everyone clapped. Mr. Craven said, "Thank you, Louise," and escorted her back to the sidelines. "See you after school tomorrow," he said, then walked over to talk to tall, elegant, silver-haired Mademoiselle Castle, who smiled suddenly, brilliantly, at his approach.

Louise sagged against the wall, trying to catch her breath.

"God, Louise!" The girls crowded around her, all talking at once.

"You danced with Mr. *Craven!* What was it *like?*"

"Isn't he *dreamy?*"

"I'd *kill* to dance with him. He's so gorgeous."

"After parents' day last year my mother said he's a *baby!* She found out he's only *twenty-three!*"

"Is that *all?* Oh my God!"

"My sister who's in grade twelve dates a guy who's twenty-three. Course my mother doesn't know or she'd kill her."

"Yeah, well, I've gotta go now," Louise said, in no mood to discuss the experience. If she talked about it, she'd lose the ecstatic feeling she'd had being so close to him. "See you guys tomorrow." She headed out of the gym, knowing they were all watching her.

Boy! She could scarcely walk. Little electric shocks were going off in her brain. Daniel Craven had asked her to dance; he'd held her in his arms; he wanted her to work on the yearbook with him. He thought she was special. Her lungs were struggling like living things crowded into her chest, and she had to swallow hard in order not to cry. Yet she was oddly happy.

Aldo liked working in the store. It made him feel good to be left in charge to look after things when Pop had to go out with the truck. During the day Aldo waited on the customers, and restocked the shelves when things were quiet; he restacked the fruits and vegetables into shining pyramids, he swept the floor and the sidewalk out front; and once a week he cleaned the plate glass window inside and out with a sponge and a pailful of water cut with white vinegar. He didn't mind any of it. One of these days the place'd be his, and the way Pop was working to build up the business, it'd be worth a few bucks.

When it was slow, usually first thing in the morning and for a couple of hours in the middle of the afternoon, if he had nothing else to do, Aldo sat on the stool by the cash register. Every so often he'd count the till, pocket a couple of quarters, maybe a dollar; just a little, so the old man wouldn't notice. Then he'd have a smoke, look through *Hush,* a real sleazy rag that gave the dirt on what was going on in the city, or sneak a look at *Playboy,* which he had to keep hidden 'cause if Pop ever caught him with it he'd break every bone in Aldo's body.

All those naked broads got him so hot he'd have to put the CLOSED sign on the door for ten minutes and whip up to the can to whack off. Then he'd hide the magazine and zip back downstairs to flip the sign to OPEN, sit again by the register, and fire up a smoke with shaky hands. Slowly calming down, he'd sit there wishing he could actually put it to some girl instead of forever having to shake hands with Mister Meat.

He kept asking chicks out but couldn't get anywhere with them, not even the ones he knew for a fact put out for half the guys he'd been in school with. Mary-Lou Slovitski didn't mind hanging around with him and the twins at the bowling alley or down at the rink, but she had the hots for Bruno. The one time he'd asked her out to a show she'd simply looked at him blankly before saying, "I couldn't do that. Bruno'd be mad." Which, of course, was absolute bullshit, because Bruno was dying to get rid of her. He said it gave him the creeps, having her hanging around him all the time, making out like they were an item.

Rita Morelli was forever chasing after Anthony, who wanted nothing to do with her, and she wouldn't even give Aldo the time of day. One evening when they were all sitting around at the Mars, he said, "Whyn't you give Anthony a rest and hit the sheets with me one time, eh?" And she shot him a look. "Call me up," she snapped, "when you've got some hair on your balls, little boy."

The twins thought that was a riot, laughing fit to beat the band until he said, "You two goons think that's so fucking funny, you can pay for your own fuckin' burgers." That shut them right up. "And you, you scummy slag." He'd rounded on Rita. "Get the fuck away from my table. You want to eat, find somebody else to pay for it."

"Hey! I was just kiddin'," Rita protested.

"Fuck you, cooze!"

"You better go," Anthony had told her. "You shouldn't talk that way to Aldo."

"Yeah," Bruno had chimed in. "You don't go talkin' like that to no frienda mine."

Sliding out of the booth, Rita's wedge-shaped face sharp with anger, she bent down and whispered right into Aldo's ear, "I hear you got a teeny-tiny eeny-weeny little cock, you scuzzy punk." Then she'd marched right out of the restaurant.

His ears afire, Aldo said, "What're you always lettin' her hang around for? I hate that bitch."

"She ain't so bad," Bruno said. "She blows me'n Anthony anytime we want."

"Hey!" Aldo pointed a finger at Bruno's big lumpy nose. "You're so crazy about her and her big dirty mouth, you can get the fuck out, too."

"Take it easy, man," said Anthony. "Let's get something to eat and forget it, eh?"

Those two gorillas had girls crawling all over them, but Aldo, even with a pocketful of money, couldn't get a broad to give him the time of day. On top of which he had to take a lot of lip from slags like goddamned Rita. He couldn't figure it out.

After what Lou had said at the funeral parlor, he'd started washing his face three times a day, lathering up with a shitload of soap, and sure enough his skin cleared up right away. So he was looking sharp these days, even with the gooney white apron Pop made him wear in the store. He had some cool shirts and jeans he'd bought with the money the old man was paying him and with what he'd nicked from the till. He checked himself in the Coca Cola mirror five, six times a day, and he looked damned good. If the mirror didn't prove it, he could tell by the way the old broads laughed and teased him when they came in, and he said, "Eh, Mrs. Scaffone," or, "Eh, Mrs. Morelli, you're lookin' real good. Bet you drive your old man nuts." They loved it; they thought he was A-OK. He wondered if maybe he wasn't wasting his time going after the young chicks, if he shouldn't work on putting it to one of the housewives who ate it up when he started laying on the charm.

Raffie was still going steady with Faye. She was always showing up to eat with them, or to work a couple of hours on a Saturday. The old man was crazy for the Parker sisters. He'd light up every time Faye came through the door, and start giving her fruit, asking how was she, how was her Ma and her sister. Pop loved that Faye. Aldo thought she was a prude; he liked to scare her, fake a move just to see her jump. And Faye fell for it every time, jumping a mile then looking at him with those big reproachful gray eyes. But he kept it innocent so she wouldn't go ratting him out to Raffie, who'd pulverize him for messing with Miss Priss.

Louise was something else altogether. That night at the funeral parlor she'd been real nice—until she had to go make that wiseass crack about his skin. Otherwise, she'd been so nice he'd thought he might actually have a shot at getting her to go out one night. But after the funeral things were right back to the way they'd always been. He couldn't say a word without her firing back some crack. Nothing disgusting like that slag, Rita. But cracks to let him know he didn't stand a chance in hell with her. Not that he gave a damn, although it'd been strange last summer without one of the Parker girls dropping by all the time. The two of them working office jobs made them think they were too good to hang around the store. Even so, he'd actually kind of missed them. But once school started up again, there was Faye, coming in almost every day on her way home, and staying for supper a couple, three times a week, keeping Raff company upstairs while he did the cooking.

It was in February, about a week after his birthday, on one of her regular Friday nights with them that Aldo finally got the lowdown on her and Raff. Afterward, he couldn't believe he hadn't figured it out before. It absolutely amazed him, how dumb he'd been.

Raffie laid out a really good spread that night, as usual, with lasagna, a big salad, and a crusty loaf of bread he'd split down the middle, covered with butter and garlic and oregano and warmed up in the oven. Pop got out a big bottle of Chianti and poured them all glasses. Then they went to work on the food. One thing Aldo had to say for his brother, Raffie could cook as good as Mom. If he knew he'd be late home or something, he'd fix food the night before so all Aldo and Pop had to do was heat it up. It was kind of like Mom was still around, and sometimes Aldo would move to get up from his chair to go check on her in the living room, see maybe did she want anything. Then he remembered Mom was dead, buried and gone for all time, and he sat back down, feeling like a jerk, and hoping nobody'd noticed his move.

After supper that Friday Pop announced he was going over to see Grandmama, he had a check to give her. "This's the lasta what I owe her," he told them. "Now, we free an' clear, an' I go ahead order you Mama's headstone."

"That's great, Pop," Raffie said.

"Yeah, great," Aldo chorused.

"Tonight," Pop said, "we closea the store early. You ben good, Aldo, you go see you friends, takea the night off."

"Hey! Thanks, Pop." Aldo jumped up to go call the twins.

Faye and Raffie started cleaning the kitchen, and Aldo heard them talking about going to the show to see *Giant;* Faye raving about James Dean, and Raffie saying he'd kind of prefer going to see *Around The World in 80 Days.* Aldo finished on the phone and went into the bathroom to get washed up.

By the time he was changed and ready to go meet the twins, the lights were out in the kitchen; there was no sign of Raffie and Faye. Thinking they'd taken off pretty damned fast, he stood listening for a moment, thinking he heard a sound from downstairs. Deciding he was mistaken, he got his coat and went down to the store, where he stood looking out the window, trying to make up his mind if he should bother with his boots. The snow was hard packed and dry. No boots. He went to check the till but the old man had already cleaned it out, probably making a night deposit on his way to see Grandmama. He turned to go when he noticed the door to the cellar wasn't quite closed and the light was on down there.

What the hell? Easing the door open, he tiptoed down the wood stairs. Halfway down, he ducked to take a look around, didn't see a thing. The old man must've forgotten to turn off the light. He turned to go, heard a faint sound, and stopped. Was the old man down here after all? Did he have some secret hiding place for his dough? Man! It'd be great to know about, if he did.

Keeping silent, Aldo got down to the cellar and looked around. Another faint sound, like a whisper, but not quite, came from over behind the furnace. Moving very slowly and, for some reason, keeping low, he crept toward the furnace, slid cautiously around its dangerously hot perimeter, and peeked behind it, discovering a small space he'd never before noticed.

He was so astonished, so instantly a captive to the scene taking place in the dimly lit corner, that he remained rooted to the spot. Not even daring to breathe, his eyes somehow suddenly too large for their sockets, he absorbed the sight of Faye all but naked, her clothes puddled around her waist, legs widely straddling the narrow bench, and his brother, naked from the waist down, facing her, the two of them silently grappling in that little airless space.

Jesus! Aldo gaped at them, watching, getting an acutely painful hard-on from what he was seeing. Then he jerked back out of sight, realizing that if either of them looked up they'd see him. Turning, their gasping sighs loud now in his ears, he crept away. It took him forever to climb back up the stairs, all the while certain Raffie's big hands would grab him from behind and throw him down to the cement floor where he'd proceed to kick the living shit out of Aldo for having caught them in the act. But it didn't happen. He made it to the top and out, pushed the door to, the way he'd found it, and went over to stand by the register for a minute pulling himself together. Fear had killed his hard-on deader than dead.

Lighting a cigarette, he wondered how the hell long the two of them had been fucking down in the cellar. Had to have been years, he reasoned, and couldn't understand why it'd taken him so long to twig to what the two of them were up to. How goddamned dumb could you get? he asked himself, once again wide-eyed at the fresh and very vividly detailed mental picture of prissy Faye Parker bare-assed naked down in *his* cellar, and Raffie with one hand up her muff and the other closed over one very good-looking tit. The last girl in the world he'd have pegged to be putting out, but he'd just seen with his own eyes little Miss Parker in action, and loving it. Jesus H. Christ! That sneaky stuck-up slag!

All at once remembering, he hurried to the front door. The twins would be waiting for him. Tossing his cigarette into the snow, he went skidding along the icy sidewalk toward the streetcar stop. His head felt like a pocketful of loose change, ideas jangling around, weighing his brain down. But like a pocketful of coins, it felt all right. He was in on the big secret now; he knew what Faye Parker was. He had himself some serious ammunition. The only question was how and when he'd use it.

Faye stiffened and whispered, "I heard something."

Raffie held still, listening, then said, "It's only Aldo, going out."

"Oh, God! That scared me."

"It's okay," he assured her, his fingers slipping over her, causing her to jump.

Pushing forward, lifting to heighten the pleasure, she whispered, "I feel as if I want to try again."

"Are you sure, Faye?" He ran his tongue along the top of her shoulder, up the side of her neck, circled behind her ear.

She shivered, tightening her hand around him. "I want to try. I've got the safes in my purse."

Quickly, he got one of the Trojans from her bag. While she watched him put it on she could feel herself starting to cool, and whispered, "Hurry," shifting forward, closer to him, spreading her legs even more as she lay back, the top of her head over the end of the bench. "Hurry."

He didn't try to enter her right away but went back to stroking her, taking his time, not wanting it if it wasn't going to be good for both of them. It certainly was no hardship waiting. He loved the feel of her, the softness of her breasts and belly, the slippery insides of her thighs. He could never get enough of touching her.

When he felt her lifting, her hips rolling slowly from side to side, he began very gently fitting himself into her, encouraged by the way she seemed to be holding herself open and still to receive him. He was better than halfway there and beginning to think this time they might actually make it, when she put her hand on his chest, whispering, "I can't! Stop, Raffie! I can't!"

She looked so scared, her eyes were so flattened and glazed with fear, that he stopped at once and quickly withdrew.

"I can't do it!" she cried. "Why can't I *do* it? I feel as if I want to, but the minute we start, it's as if I'm having a heart attack, as if I'm dying." Tears leaked down the sides of her face and she covered her breasts with her arm.

"Faye, we don't *have* to do *anything*. Don't cry, okay, honey? Let's forget it." Pulling her up, he wrapped his arms around her and held her close to his chest, murmuring, "Please don't cry, okay? Please don't. It doesn't matter. It's nothing we have to do."

"But I *want* to. *Why* can't I?"

"You're just scared," he said, although he was starting to believe it was more than that. This had happened half a dozen times in the year or so since his mother died, and it was the same every time. He could feel how excited she was, then, wham, she was scared. He felt her muscles inside slam closed, shutting him out, felt the way her body suddenly went cold. Her eyes went round and flat, and the fear would shine out at him like some strange entity that lived in her eye sockets and looked out through the darkened windows of her pupils. "It'll be all right in a minute. It's okay, okay," he comforted her, his hands soothing the rigidity out of her naked spine. "There's nothing to be afraid of. I'll never hurt you. I love you, Faye, I love you."

Gradually the heat returned to her body and the stiffness eased away. That creature who lived behind her eyes retreated, the natural roundness and color returning. Sinuous again in his arms, aroused by their closeness, her nipples stiffened. She lifted her legs over his and rubbed herself against him. "We'll do it this way, okay?" she whispered, sliding up and down against his belly, hands pressing him closer.

It was almost as good as the real thing, he told himself, succumbing to her heat and the maddening friction as she slid up and down with him trapped hard between them. His hands under her buttocks, his mouth on hers, he moved with her, telling himself it didn't matter he loved her he'd never hurt her it didn't matter this was just as good better safer good.

The whole evening all Aldo could think about was Faye naked on that bench, with her head arched back, moaning. The bitch loved it! Man! Were both the sisters hot numbers? Maybe Louise liked to put out as much as her big sister. Maybe if he went at her the right way she'd let him lay her. Jesus, but he could make big trouble for Raff! A word in the old man's ear and Pop would ship Raff off to confession, have him into the priesthood so fast he wouldn't know what'd hit him. Or maybe he'd toss Raff out on his ear, driver's license or no. He needed to think about this, go one step at a time.

CHAPTER
TWENTY-SEVEN

SOME OF THE CUSTOMERS DROVE MAGGIE WILD. THEY tried on every dress in the department, then decided they didn't want anything after all. They had no regard for the clothes and regularly got makeup or lipstick on light-colored fabrics, then asked to have the item marked down because it was soiled. They bought a dress, then came back the next day to return it, even though it had plainly been worn. Unlike the dress she'd worn to her mother's wedding at city hall which hadn't had a mark on it, customers came in carrying dresses that had actual food or perspiration stains, yet insisted they hadn't had the damned thing on. But company policy was to accept returns and issue refunds or credits, so she wrote up the credit slips even though it galled her to see these women getting away with murder.

Being a salesgirl was anything but glamorous and, in many ways, a lot harder work than her old job. Standing on her feet all day in high heels made her legs and back ache. Often she had to miss a coffee break because one of the other girls was out, or late returning from her break. Lunch in the employees' cafeteria was bedlam. Tallying her cash, charge, COD, and credit slips at day's end was a time-consuming nuisance, as was balancing her cash drawer. She disliked the majority of the other girls in the department, especially the section buyer. A tall, thin woman in her late thirties, who invariably wore black and did her face up in dead white makeup and dark red lipstick, she looked like a vampire, and was bitchy to everyone. But, grudgingly, Maggie had to admit the woman knew what to buy. Every time a fresh shipment of garments came in there was something Maggie coveted and often used her employee discount to purchase.

The discount was the only good thing about the job. After nine months of taking crap from snotty customers, and more crap from her female superiors in the department, she was sick to death of the store. She thought constantly about quitting, but without specific skills the best she'd wind up with would be another selling job. She was *never* going back to factory work, and since selling would be more or less the same wherever she went, she wasn't yet ready to leave Eaton's.

She was going out on dates at least twice a week. Aside from her alternate Fridays with McCutcheon, several of his friends had taken to calling her on an average of once a month. And a few of those men had asked if she'd mind their giving her number to a particular friend. She permitted it in a couple of instances, with the result that she was building an ever-widening circle of men friends. She slept with the majority of them, although there were some who simply wanted company for an evening. They all paid for the pleasure of her company, and in the fifteen months since she'd met McCutcheon she'd managed to save more than two thousand dollars. She had a standing appointment with the hairdresser, and she'd purchased an entirely new wardrobe as well as a Sylvania television set with halo-light she'd seen on sale when passing through the appliances department one afternoon.

The girls went wild upon seeing the set.

"I thought it was about time we had one," she told them casually. "Just don't let me find you glued to that thing instead of doing your work."

In fact it was Maggie herself who spent the most time watching. She loved everything from *Tabloid* to Lawrence Welk. She watched *The Arthur Godfrey Show, Kraft Television Theatre, The Millionaire, The $64,000 Question, You Bet Your Life* with Groucho, whose sarcasm gave her a kick; *Dragnet, The Life of Riley,* and the Loretta Young and Perry Como shows. There was rarely an evening when she didn't catch at least an hour's worth of

TV, while the girls only occasionally sat down to see *Father Knows Best* or *I Love Lucy*.

When she found herself out with some man who bored her to tears, she thought longingly of the TV fare she was missing. And sometimes upon entering a date's hotel room, if there was a set, she'd find some way to convince him to keep it on.

She went out a few times with Fred Brundage from personnel but didn't sleep with him even though she found him quite attractive. It seemed too risky, after her experiences with Nolan, to start up with someone from work. She'd also become accustomed to receiving gifts of money in return for sleeping with a man, and it didn't make sense to go back to giving it away for free. Also, she had the idea that Fred might one day prove useful to her, so it was best to keep things on a purely friendly basis.

Her evolving dilemma seemed to be whether or not she should quit working altogether and live on the gifts of money that regularly found their way into her hands. Certainly she deserved a chance to take things easy after so many years of daily labor. But she couldn't think of any acceptable explanation to offer her mother or the girls. She could hardly tell them—and never mind how it maddened her to have to explain herself to *anyone*—she was making a small fortune simply by having a good time. She didn't really give a damn what the girls thought, but her mother was another matter. She'd see it all wrong and then, shocked and offended, she'd slam the door in Maggie's face for good and always. On the surface she didn't care particularly, but on another, deeper, level she didn't want to be cut off from her only living relative aside from the girls. After all, when things had been tough in the past her mother had always come through for her. So for the time being it seemed best to let things ride. It wouldn't be long before the girls were out on their own. Faye was already sixteen and, according to Louise's journal, talking about quitting school to take a full-time job. In another year, Louise would be sixteen, too, but she had hopes of going to university, which meant Maggie might be saddled with her for years.

Her fantasy was that Faye would get a job and move out, taking Louise with her. Then she'd be able to move into a decent apartment and live whatever damned way she chose, without having to answer to anyone. It would be the ideal situation, and she wanted it more every day.

Working on the *Review* was more fun than Louise had thought it would be. She enjoyed reading the articles and selecting photos with the other editors, but the best part was seeing Mr. Craven on a regular basis. She could tell he liked her. He always broke into a big smile at the sight of her, and those smiles worked like a narcotic on her central nervous system. She tried hard not to be gorpy and to act as if they were friends, but sometimes he'd put a hand on her arm or come to read over her shoulder and her body would undergo what felt like oxygen deprivation. Her lungs would come alive and start pushing against her ribs, her eyes wanted to go out of focus, and a deep aching would begin at the apex of her thighs. Being close to him was the high point of any school day. None of the boys interested her romantically. Some were good to be with, like Leo Cohen, the yearbook's editor-in-chief. He was tall and very fat but appealing in spite of his weight; a shoe-in for valedictorian, he'd already been accepted by Harvard, and his steady girlfriend had been Miss Harbord the previous year. Soft-spoken but not at all shy, he had a wonderful sense of humor. It showed in the double-page photo montage he'd created as the book's centerpiece. He'd cut and cropped pictures so that people seemed to be growing out of each other's bodies; girls in full-skirted formal dresses (minus their legs) became bizarre hats crowning the heads of several basketball players. It was a clever and witty view of the year's highlights, and Louise had watched with intense interest the meticulous manner in which he'd juxtaposed the photographs. She loved working with him. He was patient and charming and during cut-and-paste sessions he explained to Louise the nuances of the classical music he played constantly on his portable hi-fi.

There were also two boys in her class with whom she was friendly, Lefty Liebowitz and Ernie Knight. At thirteen, Lefty was the youngest grade ten student, and Ernie was one of the four Negroes in the school, and therefore treated with great respect. There were so few Negroes in the city that the kids seemed to view it as something of an honor to have Ernie in the class. The two boys were not only best friends but also the top students in the grade. Louise ranked right behind them, with the third-best marks. They regularly invited her to sit with them in the lunch room, and she went to the show with them at least once a month.

At fifteen, Ernie was small, only an inch or two taller than Louise; a mathematical wizard who could do amazingly complicated calculations in his head, he regaled Lefty and Louise with tales of his father's adventures as a porter on the CNR. Lefty was the youngest-ever student council president, and Ernie had the distinction of being the only boy in the typing class, and far and away the fastest. He was even faster than Faye, and the two of them were always having impromptu contests, with Faye trying and failing to better his score.

While Louise took pleasure in the company of these boys, no one had remotely the effect on her that Mr. Craven did. She wondered sometimes if she was in love with him. But since she didn't behave or feel the way Lucy or Kath or any of her other girlfriends did about the boys they claimed to love, she thought she probably wasn't. She didn't want to talk about him all the time, discussing in the minutest detail every last thing he said and did. She simply wanted to be near him. Of course that was the way Faye felt about Raffie. So maybe she did love him. It was horribly confusing, and completely impossible, so she tried not to think about it at all. Daniel Craven was a teacher; he was twenty-four years old (his homeroom class had bought him a chocolate cupcake with a candle in it on his birthday the month before), nine years older than she was, and probably had scads of gorgeous, sophisticated girlfriends.

One afternoon in mid May she was heading up to the Kresge's on Bloor for lunch when she heard running footsteps behind her. Turning, she saw Mr. Craven, who waved and called, "Wait up!"

Catching up to her, he asked, "Where're you off to, Louise?"

"To Kresge's, for lunch."

"Oh, good," he said. "Me, too. We'll go together."

"How come you're not with Mademoiselle Castle? I thought you always had lunch with her."

"Lillian had an appointment. And we don't *always* have lunch together, just a couple of times a week."

"Oh! I thought you did."

"*I* thought *you* always brought your lunch to school," he teased.

"I do, usually. But today I didn't feel like it."

"You see!" he said. "Everything's subject to change."

As they settled on stools at the lunch counter, Louise felt self-conscious. She didn't know what to do with her hands, and her shoulder bag kept falling off her lap. She finally put it down between her feet, then laughed edgily, saying, "I never know what to do with my stuff when I sit at counters."

"Am I making you nervous?" he asked with a smile.

"Kind of, I guess. I'm not used to eating with teachers."

At this he laughed and said, "Neither am I, especially. Last year I kind of ate on the run. I'd go for walks at noon because I was so intimidated by the staff room. This year, Lillian took pity and started inviting me to join her for lunch."

"Took pity on you?" She was flabbergasted by the idea that anything could intimidate him.

"Sure. I'm the baby on staff, you know."

Starting to smile, she said, "I know how that feels, all right."

"Some of those grade thirteen guys make me feel like a ninety-eight-pound weakling," he said. "I have this idea now and then that they'll rise up en masse and wipe the floor with me. I figure by the start of next year I'll finally be getting the hang of it."

"I never thought teachers got nervous."

"We're just people, Louise," he chided gently. "We get the same feelings kids do."

The waitress came. Louise ordered an egg salad sandwich and a coke. Daniel Craven said, "That sounds good. Make it two." The waitress moved off to get their sandwiches, and he picked up where he'd left off. "When I was in school I always thought teachers were even worse than parents, as far as authority figures go. Mine were," he confided. "If you think some of these people are tough, you should've been at my school."

"Where did you go?" she asked, leaning on her elbow on the counter.

"Forest Hill."

"No, kidding. I can't even imagine you as a student."

"Don't tell me I look *that* old."

"You don't look old at all," she said. "I guess I just never thought about teachers being real people."

"We are," he said. "Honestly. We eat egg salad sandwiches and suffer from anxiety and everything, like the rest of the population."

She laughed, and again had that feeling of wanting to close her eyes and let her head rest on his shoulder. Suddenly, with rare clarity, she knew exactly how she felt about Mr. Craven. For a few moments she wasn't just fifteen, still five feet one, and only about halfway to having a decent chest. Her brain was fully developed, completely functional, and it made direct contact with an emotional truth. She understood that she loved him, and marveled at this fact. It was much more than a schoolgirl crush, or playing at being in love with some unattainable guy in grade eleven. It was a boundless yet solid emotion that was firmly rooted in reality. She loved everything about him: his looks, his personality, his kindness and humor and intelligence, the sound of his voice and the things he said, the clothes he wore and even the way he danced. For perhaps thirty seconds she gazed into his deep liquid eyes and understood the true nature of love, knowing that it had to do with respect and admiration and a profound desire that the object of one's caring should be happy. It was a dazzling insight that came to her whole. Then, losing her hold on this elusive comprehension, she returned to herself. Realizing she was staring, she laughed, blushing, and said, "You're a really good teacher, you know."

"Thank you, Louise. That's very nice to hear."

"No, I mean it. You make things exciting, make kids want to learn. The only other teacher I've had who's even halfway as good is Mademoiselle Castle. But that's partly because I really wanted to learn French. You're not like the others. I mean, you're sort of more in touch with us. You know?"

"I try very hard to be."

Her throat starting to close, she said, "You're a really nice man, Mr. Craven."

"You're a really nice girl," he replied, without a hint of condescension.

Awkward now, she said, "I'm okay, but I have a terrible tendency to exaggerate."

Breaking into laughter, he chucked her under the chin, saying, "You're a delight." He studied her deep blue eyes, noting the flush of color in her cheeks, the tidy set of her ears and the dainty dimpled point of her chin, and said, "And you're very pretty, too. Ah! Here's our food."

She gazed at him a moment longer, then straightened and looked down at her plate. She couldn't help thinking that another conversation was taking place beneath the words they were saying. But she was unable to decipher it. She hadn't yet learned that language or how to hear it correctly. And all at once she felt as if she were being suffocated by her youth. Like some unbearably heavy blanket, she longed to throw it off and be once and forever past the uncertainties of childhood. She could almost reach out to touch the edges of that burdensome load, but she was still a little too small to lift it. She'd do it, though, someday soon. It was such a pity, she thought, that things always took so long to happen. You couldn't be a grown-up just because you thought it was time. You had to wait, and wait.

✢

Faye was falling further and further behind at school, and talking more and more about quitting to get a job. Louise kept telling her to stick with it for at least another year, but Faye was determined.

"Three of the places I worked for last summer said to let them know if I ever wanted a job," she said. "I don't think I'd want to work full-time for the insurance company. But I loved Haley Associates, and Sue said all I have to do is phone her if I want to come back."

"But if you drop out and go to work I'll never see you," Louise argued.

"Don't be silly. Of course you will. I'm not leaving town. I'd just be going to work every day instead of school."

"Ma will never let you."

"She could give a care," Faye said. "The two of us could quit school tomorrow and she wouldn't give a damn. No, I've made up my mind, Lou. I'm going to do it."

"What, now?"

"Why not? I don't want to sit through all those exams next month. I'll fail everything anyway, so what's the point?"

"Maybe you should talk it over with Gramma."

"I've *already* talked it over with Gramma, and she agrees with me."

"She does?" Lou was taken aback. "You never told me that."

"I don't tell you everything."

"You do too. Mostly everything, anyway."

"Why're you arguing with me, Lou? I hate school. I'm not smart like you."

Hurt by this statement, Louise said, "You are so. You're very smart. I don't like it when you talk about yourself that way."

Faye smiled. "I'm good at office work, kiddo. And that's what I intend to do. I'm going to call Sue, see what she says. Then I'll talk to Ma."

"You're too young!" Louise played her final card.

With a laugh, Faye said, "I'm sixteen, for Pete's sake. Lots of girls my age are out working."

"Okay. *I'm* too young."

"For what?"

"I need you at school."

"For *what?*"

"I don't know for what. I just need you there, Faye."

"You'll be fine. I hardly see you these days as it is, what with you working on the *Review* all the time, and going off with Ernie and Lefty. And, besides, you'll see me every night."

"Sure. You'll be over at the DiStasios' every night."

"No, I won't. Stop this. Okay? You're getting me upset."

"No," Louise said stubbornly. "I don't *believe* Gramma said she thinks it's a good idea."

"Well, she didn't exactly say that. She said she understands."

"Hah! I knew it."

"She *said* if it was what I wanted, I should *do* it, Lou!"

"Oh!" Deflated, Louise looked down at her lap, trying to understand why she was so upset. She'd known this was coming, yet she wasn't at all prepared.

"You'll be fine."

"Yeah," Louise said glumly.

Faye gave her a punch in the arm, saying, "Stop it. In a week, you'll forget it was ever any other way."

"I'm *used* to doing things with you."

"So you'll get used to doing them without me. I don't know why you're making such a big deal about it."

"I don't know why, either," Louise admitted. "You'll see," she said, giving it one last lame try, "Ma won't let you do it."

"She'll jump for joy," Faye said confidently. "Don't you realize she wants to be rid of us, Lou? Wait and see."

Maggie sat half watching Percy Saltzman doing the weather report and half listening to Faye.

"Anyway," Faye wound down, well aware she didn't have her mother's complete attention, "I spoke to Sue and she said I could start full-time on Monday. I said I'd talk to you and call her back to let her know."

Percy threw his chalk in the air and caught it, his trademark ending of the report, and Maggie looked over at Louise, then at Faye.

"What're these people going to pay you?" she asked at last.

"Sixty a week," Faye said proudly.

"They're going to pay a *sixteen-year-old* that kind of money?"

"That's what I was making this summer, when I worked through my lunch hours."

"Well," Maggie said, looking at her watch, "if you're going to be working, you'll have to start paying your way around here."

"What?" Faye and Louise said in unison.

"You heard me. From now on you'll pay me fifteen dollars a week for your room and board."

"That's not fair!" Louise protested. "Why should she have to pay to live in her own home?"

"I can't pay you that kind of money, Ma," Faye said weakly, feeling sick. "After the deductions, I'll hardly have anything left."

Getting up from the sofa and smoothing her skirt, Maggie said, "Fine. We'll settle for ten. Make sure you don't leave every light in the house on if you go out." With that, she picked up her bag, checked to make sure she had her keys, and started for the door.

"That is completely unfair!" Louise said loudly. "She shouldn't have to pay you anything!"

"It's fair, Lou," Faye said quietly.

"No, it's not right!"

Turning back, her face going red and her mouth thinning, Maggie said, "It bloody well *is* right! I've fed and clothed you and kept a roof over your heads for sixteen years. Now you can start paying some of it back. And *you,*" she pointed at Louise, "watch your p's and q's, miss."

"What'll you do," Louise challenged, "stop feeding and clothing me? Faye and I've been buying our own clothes and making our own meals for *ages.* All you pay is the rent."

"If you don't like it," Maggie said, "the two of you can move out." She turned again and marched out the door.

Louise burst into angry tears. "She's such a *bitch!*" she cried, her hands curled into fists. "God, I hate her."

"Never mind, Lou." Faye handed her a Kleenex. "When I get enough saved, we'll get our own place and move out."

"You'll never be able to save enough if you have to give her ten dollars every week. She doesn't *need* the money. She just wants to hurt you."

"It's okay. I should contribute. It's only fair," Faye said. "Anyway, I get a salary review after three months. If they're happy with me, I go up to sixty-five."

Throwing herself into one of the armchairs, Louise mopped her face.

Faye came to sit on the arm of the chair and ran a hand over her sister's hair. "Thanks for standing up for me, kiddo."

"You're welcome," Louise said grimly. "You know what I just realized?"

"What?"

"I'm never going to be able to go to university."

"Of course you will. You're forgetting the money Gramma put aside."

"You're right. I forgot," Louise admitted. Then, still angry, she said, "God, I hate her! And where the hell does she keep meeting all these men who're always phoning?"

Faye shrugged. "Beats me. At least she's not home every night."

"Yeah, thank heavens for small mercies."

"I think we should celebrate. Want to go out for something to eat?"

"I'd love it. Is Raffie coming too?" she asked with a sly smile.

"D'you mind?"

"Heck, no. Why should I mind?"

"Okay. Go wash your face and we'll walk up and meet him at the store."

"Okay." Louise jumped up and raced to the bathroom.

Louise waited downstairs while Faye went up to get Raffie. Aldo got up from the stool by the cash register and came over saying, "Hey, Louise. How's things?"

"Fine. How's everything with you?"

"Can't complain." He stood a few feet away, picked an apple off the top of the pile and began polishing it on his apron. "I was thinking," he said, "you and me should maybe go to the show one night."

She opened her mouth to fire off a smart reply then thought better of it. She could tell he'd been working up to asking her out and she didn't want to be cruel. "I'm kind of dating this guy at school," she lied. "Otherwise, that'd be nice."

"Oh, yeah? What guy?"

"Just this guy," she hedged.

"What's his name?" he asked pleasantly.

"Ernie Knight," she answered, giving the first name that popped into her head.

"Ernie? He go to Charles G. Fraser with us?"

"No. He went to Jesse Ketchum."

"Oh! How long you two been goin' out?"

"Most of this year. We're practically going steady. So it wouldn't be a good idea for me to start dating someone else."

"Sure. I getcha."

"But thanks for asking, Aldo."

"Sure. No big deal." Absently, he kept rubbing the apple down the side of his apron.

She was relieved to see Faye and Raffie coming down the stairs, and went to the door saying, "See you around, Aldo." But he didn't seem to hear her. He was looking at Faye. Then he quickly turned, gave Louise a sudden smile and said, "Yeah. See you around."

She stared at him for a moment, wanting to say something, but unable to think of anything to say. So she waved and went out onto the sidewalk where she stood watching through the window as Raffie paused to talk for a moment to his brother. Faye came out to wait beside her on the sidewalk.

"Aldo just asked me out," Louise whispered.

"What'd you say?"

"I told him Ernie Knight and I were going steady."

Faye laughed. "Does Ernie's girlfriend know?"

Louise took her by the arm and walked her away from the window, saying, "I don't want Aldo to think we're laughing at him, for Pete's sake."

"Have you told *Ernie* the two of you are going steady?"

"I had to say *something*," Louise defended herself. "Aldo's the last guy on earth I'd go out with. And I *do* go out with Ernie. His girlfriend even comes along sometimes. It's not entirely a lie."

"Okay, girls!" Raffie said, linking arms with both of them. "Let's go celebrate Faye's new job."

Louise glanced back over her shoulder, wondering why all of a sudden Aldo had decided to ask her for a date. Then, putting it out of her mind, she said, "I'm starving. Who's paying?"

"My treat," Raffie said. "Anything you want, Lou, up to a dollar." He laughed at the look on her face. "Just kidding. Pop gave me money. You really can have anything you want."

"Great! Just for that I'll have a hot hamburger sandwich with double chips and a large Coke."

"Wait till you get to the restaurant to order," he told her, then turned to kiss Faye's cheek. "So," he said, "tell me what your mother said."

CHAPTER
TWENTY-EIGHT

Every morning as she stepped through the front door in her business clothes and high heels, Faye felt enthusiastic and in charge of herself. She was an adult, who held down a good job and paid her own way. No two days were the same at Haley Associates, the advertising agency where she now spent eight hours daily. The only really traditional type of employee was Sue Shaver, her immediate superior, a no-nonsense woman in her late twenties who ran the office with a good-natured but slightly military zeal. Everyone relied on Sue. She kept track of everything from phoned-out lunch orders to the whereabouts of the thirty-odd staff members. Even her appearance was somehow military: short brushed-back hair, slim skirts with man-tailored shirts, not a trace of makeup. Her only visible vanity showed in the three-inch spike heels she wore to show off her long slim legs.

Everyone else was eccentric to some degree, particularly Ned Haley, the president. Ned was a small, dapper man who seemed to run on his own limitless supply of supercharged energy. And he did run. In the course of any given day he made dozens of trips, darting in and out of the partners' offices, flying through the sundry cubicles that housed the graphic designers, the secretaries, the copywriters, the illustrators. Carrying a storyboard, he'd rush into the boardroom for a meeting. Half an hour later, minus the storyboard, he'd burst through the door and run to Sue's office, or to his own, only to reappear five minutes later stuffing papers and drawings into his portfolio as he shouted to Sue to call a taxi, he was on his way to see a client.

Ned's personal energy fueled the entire office. Everyone moved at a good clip. People popped in and out of offices to swap ideas, or went off in small groups to grab a bite to eat and swap more ideas. The place was lively and full of color, and Faye loved going to work each day.

True to their promise, her salary had been reviewed and raised after three months. At Christmas she got another raise as well as a bonus of a week's pay. She took Raffie to the staff Christmas party at the Savarin and felt very proud, both of him and of herself. Life was proceeding according to the plans the two of them had begun mapping out more than three years before, when they'd go down to their tiny private beach on the lakefront and discuss their combined futures as they cleared rocks to widen their domain.

Aside from her and Louise's ongoing battles with Ma, all that truly bothered her was her inability to make love properly with Raffie. Although they'd given up attempting to complete the act and rarely discussed it any more, she viewed this as a terrible personal failure. They loved each other; therefore she should have been able to demonstrate her love by taking him into herself. But she couldn't, and it distressed her. Every time they went down to the cellar she felt ready to commit herself in the ultimate fashion, yet merely contemplating the act caused her to seize up inside. She told herself it would change once they were married and could sleep together in a bed; she was convinced that the illicit nature of their lovemaking was responsible for her continuing apprehensions. Within the bounds of a sanctioned union, she'd undoubtedly be able to give herself without reservation or fear.

In the meantime, they devised new and different ways to stimulate each other, and seemed to draw closer even though they saw each other less often. With her working five days a week and Raffie driving after school and on Saturdays for his father, they managed to get together only a couple of times a week—usually on Friday nights, when she went to the store for supper, always on Saturday nights, and occasionally on Sunday afternoons when Ma announced at the last minute she wouldn't be coming to Gramma's and Raffie would come in her place.

On her lunch hours Faye read the real estate section of the *Globe,* scanning the columns of apartments to rent. Her immediate goal was to get herself and Lou away from Ma. She felt was paying too dearly for the privilege of sharing a bed with her sister and using the kitchen and bathroom. Not in money so much as in emotional wear and tear. Ma was out on dates three or four nights a week. But when she was home she still had her eternal demands and complaints. Lou had forgotten to take out the garbage or to take in the laundry. Neither of them had remembered to defrost the refrigerator; one of them had neglected to clean the bathroom. And it struck Faye hard every evening when she walked back into the house that her freedom and maturity were wiped out in the space of time it took Ma to list her orders or grievances.

Louise was fed up with it, too. "How'm I supposed to get any work done around here?" she railed, forced to scrub the bathroom from top to bottom when she had an English essay to write. "She's got two servants, one unpaid and one who's paying for the privilege, while she goes waltzing off with another one of her boyfriends. And would somebody explain to me, please, how come none of them ever comes here to pick her up? All these guys and we've never met one of them. Doesn't that strike you as a little strange?"

"Uh-huh. Listen, a few more months and I'll have enough saved to put money down on an apartment. Then we'll be away from her for good and always."

"Can't come soon enough to suit me. If I don't get that damned essay done I'll only be able to stay an hour or two at Kath's mom's wedding party on Friday night. I'll have to come home early and work all weekend so I can hand the thing in on time."

"Look," Faye said. "It's only Monday. You've got plenty of time. Go work on it and I'll finish up in here."

"I don't want you to do that. You work all day. You shouldn't have to come home and work here, too."

"Go on and let me do it. I want to have a good time at that party, too. And I won't if I know you're home writing an essay."

"Thanks, Faye." Louise hugged her, surrendering the scrubbing brush. "I'll pay you back."

"You'll pay me back by keeping up your grades. Go on now. I really don't mind."

Louise hung in the doorway for a moment, then said, "I'm still not used to going to school alone. And Miss Giddings asks about you all the time."

"She does? That's sweet. Send her my best, okay?"

"It's going to be a great party, just like Gramma's, with a band and caterers and everything."

"Yup. Go *on,* Lou. Get working on your essay."

"Yeah." Louise drifted across the hall and sat down at the desk. Reaching for her pen, she wished she could be going to the party with Daniel Craven. She imagined the two of them dancing together, and sighed. The only place she'd ever dance with him would be in the gym, surrounded by five hundred other kids. And why would a grown man be interested in a kid like her? She wished she'd meet some boy who'd take her mind off Mr. Craven.

The balance in Maggie's savings account was climbing higher and higher as her circle of men friends gradually grew wider. She was out on dates an average of four nights out of seven, and banking roughly three hundred dollars a week. The higher her balance became, the more potent she felt. Her only regret was that she hadn't met Craig a decade earlier. If she had, she'd have been able to retire in comfort by now. But better late than never, she told herself every time she filled out another deposit slip. If she could keep on for three more years she'd never have to work again. She'd be able to sit back and live very nicely on the interest accrued from her savings. Craig had provided her with an annuity of sorts, and she never failed to demonstrate her gratitude for that. Of all the men, she enjoyed him most.

He never asked about her nightlife, even when she volunteered tidbits, dropping a name or two she thought might spark his curiosity.

"What you do on your own time, my dear, is entirely your own business. If things are going well for you, I'm delighted, naturally. When the occasion arises, I do recommend you highly."

"Recommend?" She didn't know if she cared for that. It made her sound like a brand of liquor or some dish on a menu.

"I *speak* well of you. Better, Margaret?"

"Yes."

Only three times did he ever cancel one of their standing Friday dates. On two of those occasions he telephoned to ask if she'd mind his sending along a substitute. Once she agreed. Once, being in the middle of her period, she declined. While her menstruating didn't at all discomfit Craig, she suspected his friends might not be quite so liberal. And on the third occasion, when he telephoned just as she was leaving the house to meet him, he sounded so ill, his voice thick and raspy with bronchitis, she said, "Don't worry about it. If you're better, we'll make it next week instead." She was actually quite happy to settle on the sofa in her robe with a cup of tea and a piece of pound cake and watch the *Schlitz Playhouse of the Stars,* followed by *The Lineup* and *Person to Person* with Edward R. Murrow. She didn't even mind missing out on the money. Television was her refuge. She could watch it for hours on end, curled up contentedly with an ashtray near to hand and cups of tea she replenished during the commercials. There were nights when she had to force herself to turn off the set and go to bed, so reluctant was she to miss anything. The Sylvania was, next to poor Blanche, the best friend she'd ever had. She washed the screen faithfully twice a week, and frequently polished the blond wood cabinet. Sometimes she even talked to the set, commenting aloud on commercials that irked her—like that irritating jingle for Bosco. Pushing out a nasal sound, she'd sing along: "I love Bosco, it's rich and choco-latey. Chocolate-flavored Bosco is mighty good for me." Then she'd laugh derisively. She knew all the commercials and now and again caught herself humming, "Chock full o'Nuts is the heavenly coffee, heavenly coffee, the finest coffee anyone's money can buy."

Between shows she'd get caught up on Louise's journal, frowning as she struggled to make sense of the cryptic, fragmented entries. Several times she went back through three or four of the notebooks now in the drawer, puzzling over some old entry she'd never been able to compre-hend. She was doing this on the evening of—according to Louise's most recent entries—Nolan's wedding to the Rosedale bitch (no one had even bothered to tell her, and naturally she hadn't been invited to the party), when suddenly she was able to make sense of references that had previ-ously eluded her.

In a frenzy, she went back to the very beginning and read through each of the books, then slammed the last of them down on the table and marched into the kitchen for her cigarettes. The little sluts! Faye seeing Raffie on the sly all this time. And Louise taking up with a *teacher!* Well, they'd see about that! The lying chippies! The two of them sneaking off to the party, not saying a single word about it. Getting changed into their dress-up clothes at their grandmother's. *"Nbdy wants to upst Ma, so chg at G's."* She'd be waiting when those two got home, even if she had to stay up all night. Raffie, for God's sake! A useless teenager. And a teacher! She had a good mind to phone that school first thing Monday morning and get the scummy child molester arrested.

✝

Louise danced with Bob junior, with Mike, and with Uncle Bob. She and Kath jived together a couple of times. Then the two of them went to line up at the buffet to get something to eat.

"Was the wedding nice?" Louise was finally able to ask her.

"It was really sweet. Mom was so nervous, but Jerry was fine. He held her hand the whole time and kept giving her these little smiles. Afterward, the judge signed the papers, so now I'm Katharine Vickers Nolan."

"You're taking Mr. Nolan's name, too?"

"He's my legal father now," Kath said, pulling herself up to her full five foot eleven inches and squaring her shoulders. "He adopted me."

"Holy cow! Did you want to do that?"

"Yup. The whole thing was my idea. He's better to me than Vickers ever was. I haven't *seen* that ratbag in over a year. He never even phones. He signed the papers without even batting an eye. I *love* Jerry, Lou. He's so good to Mom, and he's so much fun. He *does* things with us, wants to take us places. He brought me this fabulous tote bag from London that his company's importing. He buys me little things all the time. Do you know what he gave me last night? A teddy bear! Isn't that *darling?* And all because I told him one time I'd never had one. At the March break the three of us are going to Barbados for a belated honeymoon."

"You're going along on the honeymoon?"

"That's what *I* said. But he wants all three of us to go. He says we're a family and families go places together." Dropping her voice, she said, "His hand started shaking when he signed the adoption papers. I was so touched, Lou. My own father never cared as much about me as Jerry does. Then he gave me a big hug, and he actually *cried*. Said it was the proudest day of his life. I got kind of weepy myself, and Mom couldn't stop smiling. It was *very* mushy."

"It sounds so nice."

"Your grandmother was great. She opened her bag and started handing out tissues. Uncle Bob laughed and said it was the wettest wedding he'd ever seen. But he got kind of misty, too. The judge asked to kiss the bride, then he shook hands with Jerry and gave me a kiss on the cheek. He said we made a lovely family."

"I wish I could've been there."

"Me, too. Except we agreed it'd just be the five of us."

"I understand, Kath. It's okay. I meant it would've been great to see it. So, where's Mr. Upper Canada College tonight? Isn't he coming?"

"We broke up," Kath said flatly, her squared chin jutting.

"When? How come?"

Kath led the way to a far corner of the living room. And once they were settled, she leaned close to Louise to whisper, "He wanted to go all the way, kept saying if I really cared about him I would. And I said if he really cared about *me* he'd respect me and not keep asking me to do something I didn't want to do. We went around and around and finally I said that if all he cared about was getting laid he'd better get himself another girlfriend. He said, Fine, then. He would. So that's that."

"What a creep!"

"Yeah," Kath agreed morosely. "But I really liked him. I just don't see why I should have to do something if I don't want to."

"Did you think you might want to?"

"I thought about it," Kath admitted. "A lot, to be honest. We went pretty far, you know. We almost did it in the den one night. Mom and Jerry were out, and Ken came over to watch TV. We started necking, and it got kind of out of hand. We had most of our clothes off and everything and I thought, Why not? Why shouldn't I do it? But then I thought, What if I get pregnant? He didn't have a safe or anything, otherwise I probably would've. But at the last minute I said we had to stop. It was too risky. Boy, was he mad! He said I was giving him a terminal case of blue balls."

"Blue balls? What the heck's that?"

"I don't know. Some guff about how if a guy doesn't get laid his balls turn blue or something."

Louise started laughing. "That's hilarious! Blue balls. It's the stupidest thing I've ever heard."

"It's pretty stupid, all right. Except he wasn't joking. He was doubled over with his hands between his legs, moaning and groaning about how I was killing him."

"Holy cow!" Louise thought for a few moments as they both began eating. "Did you like it, Kath?"

Smiling, she said, "Yeah. It was really hard to say no. But I had to."

"Sure you did. I would've too," Louise said supportively.

In the ensuing silence while they went on eating, Louise pictured herself with Daniel Craven, the two of them kissing, naked. It was a blurry image, with diffused edges. She was going to be sixteen in April and she'd never even kissed a boy, had no idea what two naked people might actually do together. But she had the feeling she'd let Daniel Craven do anything he wanted to her.

They took a taxi and dropped Raffie at the store before going home.

"Wasn't it a great party?" Louise said, happily tired.

"Fabulous," Faye agreed. "I'm so happy for them. I've always liked Mr. Nolan, and Kath's mom's so stunning. Wouldn't you love to be that tall?"

"Are you kidding? At least you're five three. I'm still only five one and a half. I'm practically a dwarf, for Pete's sake."

"You are not. And lots of kids keep growing until they're eighteen."

"I'd *better* keep growing. I still can't even fit into a 32A."

"You worry too much about it. If you keep watching, you'll never notice that you're actually developing."

"D'you really think I am?" Louise asked eagerly. "Do I look any bigger to you?"

"A bit. You're really fixated, you know that?"

"No, I'm not. I'm just anxious to be normal."

"Maybe for you, the way you are right now *is* normal."

"It better not be, kiddo."

Louise waited on the sidewalk while Faye paid the cabdriver. Then they went up the front walk together.

"Ma left the lights on for us," Louise whispered. "That's a novelty."

"Maybe she's still up."

"It's almost two in the morning," Louise reminded her. "She never stays up this late."

Faye fitted her key into the lock, opened the door, and Ma came flying out of the kitchen down the hallway toward them. With her brown robe billowing out around her she looked like some kind of winged creature, Louise thought, like something right out of *Grass of Parnassus,* her grade nine book of Greek mythology. Startled, both girls jumped.

Her face contorted, Maggie growled, "Get in here, the two of you," and pushed Faye, who was nearest, into the living room.

"What're you doing?" Louise asked. "Stop pushing."

"Don't open your mouth to me, you lying tramp."

"Tramp?"

"The two of you," Maggie raged, "carrying on behind my back, thinking I wouldn't find out."

"We didn't want to tell you about the wedding—" Faye began.

"Shut up!" Maggie's hand shot out and she slapped Faye across the face.

Louise at once grabbed her arm with both hands. Maggie simply shook free and whacked Louise across the side of the head.

"Are you *crazy?*" Faye put her arms around Louise. "What the hell's the matter with you?"

"Two sluts, that's what you are. You think I don't know about the two of you? You think I don't know what you and Raffie have been up to? And you"—she jabbed a finger at Louise, who shrank away—"with that teacher. Who d'you think you're playing with here? I'm no fool. I know what you two sluts've been up to."

"What're you *talking* about?" Louise asked, horrified. "What teacher?"

Ignoring her, Maggie now focused on Faye. "What did I *tell* you? Haven't I warned you? I've told you over and over: You let some boy take advantage of you and he'll leave you high and dry. But do you listen? No. You sneak off and let that boy do whatever he wants to you."

"You're crazy," Faye whispered, trying to think how Ma could've found out.

"Oh, I'm not crazy!" Maggie smiled malevolently, reaching into the pocket of her robe. "It's all here in black and white."

"*My diary!*" Louise cried, grabbing for it. "How *dare* you go through my personal things!"

"This is *my* house!" Maggie held the book out of Louise's reach.

"You had no *right* to read my diary!" Louise again grabbed for it.

"I do as I damned well please in my own house."

"Come on, Louise," Faye said, taking her sister by the arm. "We're getting out of here."

"You're not going *anywhere!*" Maggie blocked the doorway with her body. "We're not finished yet, not by a long shot."

"Get out of the way!" Faye said coldly, still holding Louise's arm. "We're going."

"Over my dead body!"

"If I have to," Faye said, in a voice unrecognizable to her mother and sister, "I'll kill you. Lou and I are leaving."

"Just where the hell d'you think the two of you're going?" Maggie asked, holding her ground.

"Away from you. Get *out* of the *way!*"

"Oh, no you don't!" Maggie's hand shot out and she slapped Faye again.

At that moment something inside Faye seemed to shatter. Suddenly she didn't care about anything except getting herself and Louise out of that house. She felt violence pour through her body, felt the rightness of its force. If she had to, she'd rip this woman into bloody pieces. Releasing Louise, she began slapping her mother back, hitting her as hard as she was able. Maggie was so stunned she dropped the book to raise her arms over her face. Louise darted over to pick it up, then grabbed Faye's coat sleeve, saying, *"Come on! Just come on!"*

The two of them ran out of the house and down the sidewalk as fast as they could. They ran until they got to Queen Street, where Faye suddenly sagged against the side of a building and sobbed, holding a trembling hand over her eyes.

"It's all my fault," Louise gasped, trying to catch her breath. "I'm sorry, Faye. It's *all* my fault."

"It isn't," Faye got out, shaking from the cold and her emotion. "She had no right to read your diary. God! Where're we going to go? We can't stand on the street all night."

"We could go back to Kath's. They've got plenty of room."

"We can't do that." Faye fished in her pocket for a Kleenex. "The party's still going on. There were tons of people there when we left."

"We'll go to Gramma's," Louise said. "They went home at least an hour ago."

Blotting her face, Faye said, "Okay," and let out a tremulous breath as she straightened. Looking up and down the deserted street, she said, "We'd better see if we can get a cab."

"We'll phone for one from the booth across the road." Louise took her sister's hand and directed her across the icy street. "It *is* all my fault," she said, half to herself. "I never thought she'd *read* my *diary.* Faye! What if she tries to get Mr. Craven in trouble?"

"He hasn't done anything," Faye sniffed.

"No, but she could make it seem like he did. *God!* If she gets him in trouble . . . Give me a nickel for the phone."

Faye gave it to her, saying, "What if she makes trouble for Raffie? This is the worst nightmare."

"Uncle Bob will know what to do," Louise said, suddenly able to see some hope in the situation. She stepped into the booth and dialed the Diamond Cab number from memory. Empire 6-6868. If Ma got Mr. Craven in trouble, she'd take the bread knife from the kitchen and stab her. She could see herself doing it, and felt a savage sense of satisfaction.

✝

The sound of the intercom jolted Ellen and Bob awake. "Who could that be?" she said, sitting up, her heart racing.

"Probably someone buzzing the wrong apartment again. I'll go, Ellie. You go back to sleep."

She sat listening, sensing it wasn't someone ringing them by mistake. Bob was back in a minute, his fine high forehead furrowed. "Something's wrong," he said, slipping on his robe. "It's the girls. They're on their way up."

"What's happened?" she asked anxiously, reaching for her own robe while feeling about on the floor for her slippers.

"Faye was crying, a little incoherent. She said something about their mother going crazy."

"Oh, Lord! What's Marg done now?"

"She asked if they could spend the night. I said of course."

"What has she done this time?" Ellen repeated, hurriedly belting her robe as she went to the door. Dread, like alum, dried the inside of her mouth.

Coming down the hall, Bob said, "I'll put on some coffee."

She turned to look at him.

Halting, he said, "What, Ellie?"

"I have a terrible feeling about this." She put one hand to her mouth, as if to prevent herself from saying anything further.

He kissed her on the forehead, then lifted her chin. "There's nothing we can't handle. Go easy. All right?"

She nodded. The doorbell rang, causing her to start.

"Let the girls in, dear heart. I'll put on the coffee."

She nodded again and turned back to the door.

Chapter
TWENTY-NINE

"You SEND THEM HOME AT ONCE!" MAGGIE SHRIEKED.

Bob ignored this, saying in an even tone, "They'll be staying the night."

"You send them home or I'll come there and get them."

"If you set one foot anywhere near this building, I'll swear out a complaint against you for everything from harassment to assault."

"You can't threaten me! I'll have you charged with . . . with kidnapping."

"I suggest you do that. In the meantime, the girls are staying here and you are staying precisely where you are. Good night, Margaret." He put the receiver down, cutting off the squawk of her ongoing threats. Then he returned to the kitchen to get out cups and a tray. His dislike of the woman was such that he had to stop and wash his hands at the sink before pouring the coffee.

"You've got a change of clothes. Somehow we'll arrange to get things for you both to wear," Ellen was telling the girls, "and you'll both go off from here on Monday."

"But I need my books," Louise said.

"I think you'll be able to manage for one day without them, don't you, Lulu?"

"I guess so," Louise conceded, "but I've got homework to do, Gramma."

Bob brought in the tray and set it down on the coffee table.

"Ma's going to make trouble for everyone," Faye said despairingly.

"No, she isn't," Bob said. "You have my word on that. Have some coffee, girls."

"Are you hungry?" Ellen asked. "Would you like something to eat?"

Both girls said, "No, thank you, Gramma," and sat forward to add cream and sugar to their coffee.

"What are we going to do about this?" Ellen looked over at Bob. "This can't go on."

"No," Bob agreed soberly, "it can't. Until we get matters straightened out, I think it'd be a good idea for you girls to stay here with us. Tomorrow your grandmother and I will drive you home and pick up some of your things."

"Marg's not just going to sit back and allow us to do that," Ellen said doubtfully, lighting a cigarette. "She'll create a terrible scene, make it into a full-scale battle."

"You're probably right," he said, and took a sip of his coffee.

"And besides," Louise said, "we can't stay here forever. It wouldn't be fair to the two of you. Which means that eventually we'll have to go home."

"Let's take it one step at a time," Bob said. "I've got an idea how we can get the girls' things and avoid seeing Marg altogether. Ellie, you'll call her in the morning and say you'd like to see her, tell her to come here. The girls and I will wait downstairs in the car and when we see her coming, we'll head over there, pack up a few days' worth of clothes and so forth, then come home. It shouldn't take us more than an hour. We'll leave everything in the car, have a little meeting with Marg and try to come to some sort of meeting of minds, and then, after she's gone, we can unload the car. How does that sound to everyone?"

Louise smiled for what felt like the first time in weeks. "You're pretty smart, Uncle Bob."

He smiled back at her. "I'm no shmoe, Lulu."

"The thought of trying to talk to her makes my stomach turn," Faye said. "She's not going to listen to a thing anyone has to say. She'll only shout and make accusations and upset everybody."

"We'll see," Bob told her. "At least it'll give us a chance to get you girls a change of clothes. One step at a time, okay?"

"Okay," Faye said quietly.

After the girls had settled for the night in one of the guest rooms, Bob carried the tray back to the kitchen. Ellen moved automatically to rinse the cups, and he said, "Leave them, Ellie. Come to bed."

Taking hold of the hand he held out to her, she switched off the light and went with him to the bedroom. "How could she say things like that to them?'' she asked sadly. ''What kind of woman calls her children sluts?''

''Marg does,'' he said, running his hand over the heavy hair that hung halfway down her back. ''We're going to have to do something about putting a stop to her abuse once and for all.''

''Yes, but what?''

''I have a few ideas, but now's not the time to discuss them.'' He unbelted her robe, saying, ''We'll thrash it out tomorrow.''

Slipping off the robe and her slippers, she sat down on the side of the bed and turned to look over her shoulder at him. ''I'm too upset to sleep,'' she said. ''Marg's going to turn all our lives upside down. I feel it in my bones.''

He reached to turn off the light. ''I hate having you upset,'' he said, looking at her in the glow of the streetlights.

''I hate *being* upset. I hate walking around all the time waiting for the other shoe to drop. And I *know* there'll be something else. There always is, always has been.'' She stood up and took off her nightgown. Her body looked silvery, polished in the thin light; her breasts seemed to glow faintly, shimmering. Sliding beneath the bedclothes, she asked, almost as an afterthought, ''Are you too tired?''

''I might be when I'm seventy,'' he murmured, bending to kiss the side of her throat, one hand cupping her breast.

She was grateful to be able to put aside all thought and surrender to sensation, filled with wonder as always at his ardent absorption in her flesh and her perennial need to reciprocate, stroke for stroke, caress for caress, the attention he paid her.

The full horror of the situation hit Louise once she and Faye were in their beds with the light out. She lay staring at the ceiling, recoiling from projected scenes of Ma calling the school, creating a scandal that would get Mr. Craven fired. He'd lose a job he loved because some silly girl's insane mother had read her diary and misconstrued every last thing in it. Fear held the outside of her body rigid while everything inside was sent into chaos. She felt as if she was going to wet herself, or bring up the food she'd eaten earlier at the party. Her heart seemed scarcely to be beating, lifting itself sluggishly every so often in a reflexive contraction. Her breath came slowly, painfully, from the depths of her chest. Now and then she raised one leaden arm to blot her face on the sleeve of Gramma's nightgown. Ma was going to destroy their lives now, hers and Faye's. And it was all because Louise had been stupid enough to believe no one, not even Ma at her worst, would violate her privacy by reading her diary.

Ma hated them. She always had. But until tonight Louise had never truly believed that. Despite the beatings, despite the accusations and orders and various forms of punishment, she'd believed that somehow Ma loved them, in her own fashion. Maybe she was mean and unreasonable and cruel, but she did care for them.

"Ha!" She gave a brief, bitter little laugh. "I was so stupid!"

"I don't blame you, Lou," Faye whispered. "It's really not your fault."

"I know you don't." Louise again wiped her face on her sleeve. "What's stupid is my thinking all this time that she had some feeling for us. That's so stupid, it's pathetic. How could I *ever* have thought that?"

"I did, too," Faye admitted. Then, overcome by renewed sobbing, she choked out, "She'll ruin *everything*."

"That's what I'm scared of, too."

Faye put out her hand and Louise reached over to take hold. "If she ruins things between me and Raffie, Lou, I'll die. I love him so much."

"We won't let her," Louise whispered heatedly. "We won't."

Maggie refused to come to the apartment.

"I have nothing to say to you," she told her mother. "Anyway I have things to do around here this afternoon, since I happen to be going out tonight."

"I see," Ellen said, indicating to Bob that his plan wasn't going to work. "Well," she said, "the girls will be staying here until you decide you can find time to discuss the situation, Marg."

"You're trying to turn them against me," Maggie accused.

"You've done that all by yourself," Ellen said, "without help from me or anyone else."

"I want them home!"

"You don't want them home, Marg. You just don't want them *here*. And the answer is no. I'm sorry, but I couldn't possibly allow that."

"What d'you *mean* you couldn't *allow* that? They're *my* goddamned children, not yours."

"They're staying," Ellen insisted, and put down the receiver.

"What did she say?" Louise asked apprehensively.

"She's going out this evening. We'll be able to go over then and get your things."

"Another *date*," Louise said contemptuously. "God forbid anything should interfere with her social life."

"Gramma, would you mind if I call Raffie on your extension?"

"No, dear. Go ahead."

On the sofa, Louise pulled her knees up under the nightgown and sat morosely, chin propped on her knees. Looking at her, Bob felt a pang of sympathy. She was so young, so palpably vulnerable, and so undeserving of the treatment she received almost as a daily diet. "Lulu," he said, "why don't you and I make breakfast for everyone? How would you feel about some pancakes?"

"Okay," she said. "Sure." Unwinding her arms from around her knees, she got up and went to give him a hug. "I love you, Uncle Bob."

"I love you, too," he said, looking at Ellen over the top of Louise's head. "Ever made pancakes?" he asked, taking hold of Louise's tiny hand to direct her into the kitchen, eyes still on Ellen, who gave him a grateful smile.

"I'll go get dressed," Ellen said, and got up to go to the bedroom where Faye was talking in low urgent tones into the telephone.

"You want me to get off, Gramma?" Faye asked.

"No, no. I'll only be a moment." Ellen collected underwear from the dresser drawer and closed herself into the bathroom. While the tub filled, she considered the complications that would be created by having the girls live with them. There wasn't anything she and Bob couldn't cope with, she decided. What mattered was that Faye and Lulu had some peace in their lives, some sort of orderly routine. And if that meant sacrificing a minor degree of privacy, it was a small price to pay.

He came in while she was still in the tub and gave her a smile, saying, "Would you like me to do your back?"

In answer, she handed him the washcloth and soap.

Dropping to his knees, he lathered up the cloth. "I know you want them to stay with us, Ellie. I have no objections."

"You read my mind again. How do you *do* that?"

"You read mine at least twenty times a day. Why shouldn't I make an equal effort for the woman I love?" He leaned around to look at her and she lifted her mouth for a kiss.

"If we didn't have pancakes already on the griddle, I'd climb right in

there with you,'' he said, rinsing the soap from her lean, tapering back.
''The sight of you in a bathtub is completely irresistible.''

''What time are the boys coming over?''

''They said noon, but knowing them it'll be more like one-thirty or
two.''

''It's lucky Nancy invited them to stay there. Otherwise it would've
been a three-ring circus here last night.''

Returning the washcloth and soap to her, he said, ''Things have a way
of working out. But I'll promise you one thing, Ellie. This is the *last time*
Marg's going to disrupt us or exercise herself at the expense of those girls.
I just won't have it.'' With his arms crossed on the side of the tub, he
said, ''The time has come for you to write her off, make a break. I know
you're grieved by the idea, but I think for the sake of all concerned it's for
the best.''

''I know,'' she said soberly. ''I've been hoping it wouldn't come to
this, but I don't see that I have any choice.''

''I don't see that you do, either.'' He gave her another kiss and got to
his feet. ''You're not alone, Ellie. Don't forget that.''

''No,'' she said, ''I could never forget that.''

''Okay. Breakfast in ten minutes.'' He went out and closed the door
quietly.

✝

Maggie was in a foul temper when she left to meet her date, Charles
Sherman, at the Royal York. He was a friend of Jim Stewart's whom
she'd dated twice before, and, fortunately, she found him attractive. In
fact, halfway through the meal, she was suddenly anxious to get upstairs
to his room to work off some of the weekend's tension. She was in no
mood for the polite chitchat these evenings entailed. She just wanted to
get on with it. But she had to play it out according to what her date
wanted, so she tried to slow herself down, realizing she was eating far too
quickly.

''Hungry, eh?'' Sherman observed.

''Very.'' She blotted her mouth with her napkin and, looking at his
mouth, gave him a smile. Last time he'd been in town they'd done it in
the bathtub, then again in the bed, and a third time standing against the
wall. ''I can't wait to get upstairs with you,'' she said in a low voice. ''I
was just thinking about the last time I saw you.''

Flattered—naturally, she thought; every man she met liked to claim he was oversexed—he grinned lasciviously. "I was thinking about it myself. Had me going like a teenager that night, Margaret."

He was somewhat younger than most of the men she saw, perhaps in his late thirties, well built, very well endowed, and possibly the only one who actually *was* oversexed. Remembering herself on her hands and knees in the bathtub sent heat into her face. "Better than any teenager," she said, and licked her lips.

"Jesus! What d'you think? Want to pass on dessert?"

"Definitely," she said, pleased he'd got the message.

"Then let's finish and get the hell out of here." He went back to his food, his eyes on her as he diligently consumed the last of his steak.

By the time they were riding up in the elevator she was so wet she could feel the seepage at the tops of her thighs. He had an arm draped casually around her waist, his hand resting on her hip. "If we feel like it," he said, "we can always order dessert from room service."

"If we feel like it," she said, and looked again at his mouth.

She didn't even give a thought to the TV set. While he locked the door she began undressing, stepping out of her shoes and putting her bag down on the desk near the door.

Sherman was a man who liked to use the furniture. They did it first in the armchair, with her straddling his lap. Then, reminiscent of her encounters with Nolan, he sat her on the side of the desk and held her hands over her head with both of his as he drove into her. And finally, allowing her to lead, they did it on the floor, their bodies reversed, heads resting on each other's thighs. He was good, and she came, at last, in a series of spasms so explosive she all but choked as he let go at the same time.

By a quarter to ten when she went into the bathroom to get washed, she felt thoroughly eased and ready to go home to sleep. Sherman, in his shorts and shirt, handed her her purse, gave her a wet kiss she could well have done without, and opened the door, promising to call her soon. She thanked him for a lovely evening and slipped outside.

As she turned the corner, headed for the elevator, two men stepped away from the wall and approached her, one of them saying, "Come with us, please."

"I will not," she said, moving to sidestep them.

The second man grasped her firmly by the upper arm, saying in a low voice, "We'd prefer not to have a scene. You're under arrest. When we get to the station you'll be given a chance to call your lawyer."

"Arrest? For what? What the hell're you talking about?"

"We're arresting you for prostitution," the first one said, flashing his badge as the other pressed the call button for the elevator.

"Are you *crazy?*" she exclaimed. "I most certainly am *not* a common prostitute. How dare you?"

The first man smiled. "Nobody said you were common, lady. Now, let's go."

+

No one would listen to a word she said. When they finally allowed her to make a call it was after midnight. She went to the pay phone, trembling with outrage, to call Craig. Luckily he was home.

"It's Margaret," she said, her voice vibrating with humiliation. "I've been arrested. You've got to help me."

"Arrested? Whatever for?"

"Prostitution," she hissed. "You've *got* to help me, Craig. It's all a ridiculous mistake. They were waiting for me when I came out of Sherman's room at the Royal York."

"Damnation! Look, I'll call my lawyer. Don't say a word until he, or someone, gets there. How on *earth* did this happen?" he was saying as he hung up.

+

Craig looked up the number, then dialed and waited. What a hell of a thing this was! he thought, distressed. How could she have been so stupid as to get herself arrested? What had she been *doing?* The phone at the other end was picked up and, relieved, Craig said, "It's Craig McCutcheon. I'm sorrier than I can say to be calling you at home this late on a Sunday night but a friend of mine's in some trouble and needs a lawyer."

"What's the problem?"

"It's got to be a silly mistake, but she's been arrested for prostitution. She needs someone to bail her out, or get the charges dismissed. Something. I don't know."

"A friend of yours, Craig?"

"I know," Craig said apologetically. "It's a mistake, I'm sure. *Would* you go down to the jail and get her out? I'd consider it a great personal favor."

"It's not really my line of expertise, Craig. But I suppose I could. What's your friend's name?"

"Parker, Margaret Parker. I do appreciate this enormously."

"What was that name again?"

Craig repeated it. There followed a silence.

Then, "Leave it with me, Craig. I'll take care of it."

"I'm very grateful. We'll talk tomorrow, shall we?"

"Definitely."

Craig hung up and went downstairs to pour himself a drink. Then, glass in hand, he stood looking at his mother's portrait over the fireplace, thinking it was a pity, but he'd have to stop seeing Margaret. He didn't dare risk having it known he was involved with a woman who'd been foolish enough to get herself arrested like some cheap streetwalker.

"What is it?" Ellen asked as Bob put down the phone.

"I'm not entirely sure," he said, shaken but unwilling to discuss it with Ellen until he knew for a fact it wasn't some other Margaret Parker. It wasn't an uncommon name. Possibly it wasn't Marg, although somehow he knew it was. "I've got to go down to the jail and arrange the release of a friend of one of my clients." Was this what Louise had been referring to when she'd talked so disparagingly of her mother's dates? Did the girls know what Marg was up to? No, he thought. They'd never have reacted as they had to her accusations had they known their mother was engaged in prostitution. *If* it was she.

"At this time of night?"

"Afraid so." He opened the closet and reached for a shirt. "It shouldn't take too long." Christ almighty! This would devastate Ellen. He knew in advance how upset she'd be. Was this never going to end? How much was Ellen supposed to take?

"But that isn't your bailiwick, Bob."

"It's strictly a one-time-only favor, dear heart," he said, pulling the cardboard from the shirt.

"What aren't you telling me?" she asked cannily.

Fitting his arms into the sleeves he said, "I'll tell you everything when I get back. Right now, I can't say. I'm sorry. But it isn't anything for you to get worried about, Ellie." Goddamnit! Bloody Marg had him lying now to his wife. Maybe, *maybe* it was some other Margaret Parker.

"This doesn't feel right," she said, getting out of bed. "Is this about Marg?"

"I honestly don't know," he answered, looking directly into her eyes. "I'll be able to tell you that when I get home." Quickly he finished dressing, then stepped into his shoes and reached for his keys. "I'll be back as quickly as I possibly can." Hoping to allay her fears, he smiled, gave her a kiss, and said, "Now I know why I didn't go into criminal law. The hours are rotten. You don't have to wait up for me, love."

"I couldn't possibly sleep now," she frowned, walking with him to the front hall where he stopped to get his topcoat.

Maggie had been fingerprinted and photographed and put into a holding cell, where she had to sit waiting, without even her cigarettes. They'd taken her purse. Fuming, ignoring the several other unkempt women, she stood in a corner, her arms folded tightly across her chest, and waited for Craig to send help. Someone was going to pay dearly for this mess, she vowed silently. Someone was going to get hung out to dry, if she had anything to say about it. Those stupid pricks, arresting her like some kind of criminal!

Bob was directed to the arresting officers, and sat down with them to hear their case. It was circumstantial, and clearly without any supporting evidence except for what they'd seen and overheard, and the statement of the house detective who'd become suspicious after seeing the same woman leaving the rooms of various male guests.

"How often?" Bob asked, still unaware of whether this particular Margaret Parker was his Ellen's daughter.

"Half a dozen times in the last few months."

"They take note of this kinda thing," the second detective put in.

"Indeed," Bob said. "I'm sure they do. But you have nothing I can see to warrant holding the woman."

"We pegged her right off for an amateur," the first officer said. "But that don't alter the fact she was working her trade in the hotel. We know what we saw and heard, that's for sure. And you know how it is, once the complaint's been made, we have no choice but to make the arrest if it looks like it'll stick."

"I see. Well, I'd like to speak to my client now, if I may."

"Yup." The second cop said, "I'll get her brought up from the holding tank. You can talk to her."

It took perhaps fifteen minutes before Maggie was brought in. And even though he'd geared himself up for the worst, Bob was still badly jolted by the sight of Ellen's daughter being led in by a police matron.

Automatically he got to his feet, and the first officer said, "I'll leave you to talk privately to your client."

Maggie's stomach turned over at the sight of Bob. "What're *you* doing here?" she asked in a voice without volume, sitting down abruptly on one of the hard wooden chairs.

"My client, Craig McCutcheon, called and asked me to do him a favor. You're it," he said coldly, sickened by the discovery of this latest facet of his stepdaughter's character. The woman really was capable of absolutely anything.

"It's a mistake!" she said flatly. "I'm going to sue them for false arrest and—"

"Shut up, Margaret. We all know it's no mistake, so stop trying to bluff your way out of this. My job is to get you out of here. Now, tell me exactly what's been going on, and specifically what happened tonight."

"I had a *date,* for God's sake! I went up to his room for a nightcap and when I came out to go home those two *morons* arrested me."

Bob sighed tiredly and said, "You didn't go up to his room for any nightcap. You've been seen in the hotel in the company of male guests at least half a dozen times in the past few months. Your presence has been noted. On top of that, the arresting officers found a hotel envelope in your purse containing a hundred and fifty dollars."

Maggie almost smiled at hearing how much Sherman had given her. Then, remembering her circumstances, her thoughts racing, she said, "It's not against any law that I know of to have an envelope with money in it."

"For the sake of argument, that's true. However, hotel detectives aren't stupid. It's their job to know what's going on. And you've been seen too many times. The man made calls to several other hotels downtown. He described you and asked if any of his associates had spotted you. Two had. The house detectives at the King Edward and the Park Plaza both recognized you from his description. Now stop waltzing me around and tell me *exactly* what happened down there tonight, so I can do something about getting both of us out of here. I'm not particularly fond of this place."

"You think you're so smart, don't you?" she said unpleasantly, her mouth curling. "You think you're pulling all the strings now just because those two cops made a mistake."

Again he sighed. "It's late and I'm tired. If you want to spend the night here, that's fine. Otherwise, stop all this bullshit and tell me what happened."

"They made a *mistake!*" she insisted. "I'm not going to admit to something I didn't do."

"So you didn't go up to your 'date's' room and spend an hour and forty minutes there engaged in various forms of sexual play? The detectives who followed you from the dining room and clocked you upstairs can't count, can't hear, and have the wrong woman. Is that it?"

"They *spied* on me?" she asked, appalled.

"Yes, indeed, they listened in from the vacant adjoining room. Evidently you're quite the athlete. Now you *listen* to me! It is *not* illegal for consenting adults to have sexual relations in a hotel room. And the police haven't any hard evidence. Frankly, I think the hotel just wanted you scared off. So you're going to keep your mouth shut and I'm going to try to get the charges dismissed. But your activities during your 'dates' had better be open and aboveboard from now on, because I have no intention of defending you ever again. If it were up to me, I'd let you rot in here for the rest of your life."

Suddenly losing her composure, she grabbed his arm, saying, "Don't tell my mother! I'll do whatever you like, *anything* you like, but don't tell her about this."

"I'll disregard that remark," he said, not bothering to mask his distaste for her. "You're not in a bargaining position." Removing her hand from his arm, he said, "You won't be in any position at all if there are journalists hanging around downstairs."

Paling, she whispered, "It's going to be in the papers, even if you get me off?"

He shrugged. "Maybe."

"Can't you do something about that, stop it from happening?"

"There are only a few things about which I can do anything, Margaret. For Craig's sake, and for your mother's, I'm going to get you out of this mess, if it's humanly possible, which I believe it is. Then I'm going to see to it that Ellen gets custody of the girls. You're a deplorable excuse for a mother, and you're never going to get another chance to hurt Faye and Louise."

"You can't do that!" she said, unbelieving.

He had to laugh. "Come down to earth!" he said scornfully. "I not only can do that, I will. Those girls mean nothing to you, except as a bargaining tool. And that's all over as of tonight. Now," he said, getting to his feet, "come on. The sooner I'm rid of you, the happier I'll be."

"You fucking bastard! You rotten fucking bastard!"

He gazed at her for several seconds, battling down an urge to strike her. He found her so odious, he was so repelled by her, that he couldn't bring himself to respond to her invective. Taking hold of her arm, he yanked her forcibly out of the chair, and gave her a push that propelled her out through the door. "Keep your mouth shut," he warned, "or I will let you rot in here. It'd probably be the best thing that ever happened to your mother and the girls. God knows, they don't deserve to be saddled with a piece of walking, talking vermin like you. Just," he repeated, "keep your mouth *shut,* and let me do the talking. Don't say one more word."

CHAPTER
THIRTY

FEELING CHILLED, ELLEN SAT BESIDE HER HUSBAND ON THE sofa, gazing at his face as he told her what had happened. She couldn't seem to absorb what he was saying.

"She denied it until she was blue in the face," Bob wound down. "And when she was let off with a warning, she all but gloated, giving me this look that was part preening vindication and part pure loathing. I offered to drive her home. She told me to go fuck myself." He gave Ellen a wry, tired smile. "She's unbelievable, *unbelievable.*" He moved to pick up his coffee cup, changed his mind, and said, "What we both need is a drink." He got the brandy and poured some in each of their cups.

Ellen lit a cigarette. "We can't let the girls go back to her now," she said, amazed by how calm she sounded when inside her all was chaos: voices screaming, crashing noises; her body was as busily active as an ant colony under attack, everything rushing wildly in a futile search for shelter.

"No question of it," he agreed, taking a swallow of the brandy-laced coffee. "I was mulling it over on the way home, and I think I may have a workable solution."

Her eyes, which had been fixed on a vague point in space, now returned to him. "My daughter's been prostituting herself," she said, her lips very dry. "I don't want to believe it, but I do. It explains so much."

"She'll never admit to it," he said.

"But all those hotel detectives saw her coming out of men's rooms." The details were belatedly catching up to her, heightening the internal chaos.

"I'm afraid so. I'll talk to Craig tomorrow but I can pretty well predict what he'll say."

"She didn't even thank you for coming out in the middle of the night to help her?"

He laughed softly and took her hand. "Marg thank me? Never. She's made me the villain of the piece, accusing me of working with the police to deprive her of her rights. She wants to sue the police department. Unbelievable," he said again, on a certain level impressed by her talent for self-delusion. "Try not to let this upset you too much, Ellie. We've got to concentrate on the girls and what's best for them."

"Yes," she said, at last tasting the coffee, her chill relieved somewhat by the gentle burn of the brandy. It was over, she thought. Her active role as Marg's mother had ended. Years and years of effort and worry, of caretaking and counseling, all fruitless, all finally finished. You did your best, you hoped like hell, and in the end it didn't matter, because your child's destiny was never in your control. Not *that* child's anyway, not Marg's.

"First," Bob said, "we'll petition the court to have you appointed guardian. Marg won't dare fight it. But if she does, she'll lose, given the circumstances. Then, I don't think that bachelor apartment down the hall has been rented yet." He held her hand firmly as if to anchor her, as if he knew she felt in danger of drifting off into space. "I was thinking we'd rent it for the girls. That way we'd all have privacy but they'd be right nearby. We'd get them whatever furniture they need, and so forth. What do you think?"

"I think . . ." She stopped, moistened her lips, and began again. "I think it's a good idea. The girls are old enough to have a place of their own, and much as I love them, we do all need some privacy."

"I'll talk to the super first thing in the morning, make arrangements for a lease.'' He drank some more of the coffee, studying Ellen over the rim of the cup. ''Am I riding roughshod over your feelings, Ellie?'' he asked with concern.

She shook her head and leaned to one side to put out her cigarette. Straightening, she managed a slight smile. ''Marg's been doing that to me for years. But you, never. You're tired, Bob. We should go to bed.'' She doubted she'd sleep, but she longed to lie down, ease some of the tension in her body.

''You're sure? Don't let it slide if I'm out of line.''

Again she shook her head. ''After the appalling things she said to you, I'm surprised you're not angrier than you are.''

''Oh, I'm angry all right. Believe me, I'm livid. But I won't allow it to cloud my judgment. She can do whatever the hell she likes with her life, but she's never going to have another chance to cause you or the girls more pain. It's time to write her off, Ellie. You do see that, don't you?''

''I see it, but that doesn't make it easy. One part of me wants more than anything else to have done with her. But another part still feels guilty, still thinks there must have been something I could've done. I'm staggered to think that Marg, of all people, would sell herself.''

''To me, you know, it has a kind of horrible logic. One way or another, she's been making people pay all her life. This is simply an extension of her attitude that people *owe* her. I might have respected her if she'd owned up to the truth. But of course she could never do that.''

''No, and she never will. She'll turn everything around to suit her interpretation of the situation. And she'll fight me for the girls,'' she said worriedly. ''Not out of any love for them, but simply because she won't want me to have them. It exhausts me just thinking about it.''

''Then don't think about it,'' he advised. ''At least not now. It's almost four and we've got to be up in a few hours. Come on, Ellie,'' he said solicitously, ''let's go to bed.''

''That's a *fantastic* idea!'' Louise declared. ''Fabulous, terrific!''

''Could we really do it?'' Faye asked uncertainly. ''How much would the rent be? And how would we pay for the furniture?''

''We've discussed it,'' Ellen said, glancing over at Bob. ''We thought we'd use some of the money from the sale of my old house. A year's rent and the basic furniture would still leave enough to pay Lulu's way through university and give you a nest egg, Faye. Next year you could start paying half the rent.''

"That sounds very fair," Faye said judiciously.

"Great! Can we go see it?" Louise asked.

"I've got the key," Bob told them. "Let's all go take a look."

The main portion of the apartment was a reversed L. North-facing windows ran the entire length of the main room, flooding the place with light.

"It's a good size," Bob said, pacing off the dimensions. "I'd say fourteen by twenty-two, and this L's a good ten by twelve."

"I love it!" Louise crowed. "It's wonderful."

"What do you think, Faye?" Ellen asked.

"It's the kind of place I've always dreamed of," Faye said, scarcely daring to believe this could actually be happening.

Louise went spinning in circles across the carpeted floor, flinging her arms out, singing, "I love it, love it, love it. It's even got wall-to-wall carpeting and drapes on the windows, our own stove and fridge and everything."

Faye extended one arm around her grandmother's waist, letting her head rest on Ellen's shoulder. "It's like a dream, Gramma." She and Raffie would finally have a place to meet instead of always having to go to coffee shops or movies.

"No more Ma!" Louise said gleefully. "When can we move in?"

"As soon as we can get you girls some furniture," Bob said. "The lease has been signed. We'll have to get the hydro turned on and a phone installed, but that's about it."

"Gramma," Louise said, brimming with excitement, "we've got to go shopping right away."

"We'll have to sit down first and make a list of everything we need," Faye said sensibly.

"I think the two of you will be very comfortable here," Bob said.

Louise ran over and threw her arms around him. "You're a genius, Uncle Bob. This is a brilliant idea. Oh, it's going to be so fabulous! I could just die!"

He laughed and hugged her. "It'll be a treat for us having you right down the hall." Turning to look over at Faye and Ellen, he said, "Next on the agenda will be getting your things from the house."

"Does Ma know about this?" Louise asked, abruptly grounded by apprehensions.

"Your grandmother and I are seeing her this evening."

"Oh, groan," Louise said.

"Don't worry," he said. "The two of you needn't come if you don't want to."

"We should get some more clothes," Faye said.

"All right then," he said, his eyes again on Ellen. "We'll all go."

Maggie couldn't get hold of Craig. She left several messages on Monday and tried his house for hours that evening with no luck. Tuesday she left more messages at the office, then tried his house again. Finally, she called him at home at seven on Wednesday morning. This time he answered.

"Are you avoiding me?" she asked accusingly, dispensing with formalities and driving straight to the point.

"Not at all. I've simply been very busy. I do have a business to run, Margaret."

"We need to talk, Craig. Why the hell did you have to call Bob Wolford, of all people?"

"You know Bob?" He sounded surprised.

"He happens to be married to my mother."

"Good heavens! I had no idea."

"Obviously," she snapped. "Now, thanks to you, I'm up to my ears in problems."

"That is too bad," he said carefully, bridling at the suggestion that her problems were his responsibility.

"You're damned right it's too bad," she said, then remembered who he was and softened her tone. "Sorry to bark at you, but this is a mess. Could we get together to talk? I really need to see you." What she wanted was his assurance that they'd continue as before, but she had a hunch that wasn't going to happen. She shouldn't have started out by attacking him, and she wouldn't have if he hadn't been avoiding her. She'd make it up to him when she saw him.

"Well," he hedged, "let me think a minute. All right. I'll meet you Friday at the Park Plaza at seven. But I honestly don't think there's anything I can do. It's simply an unfortunate situation."

"We'll talk about it Friday," she said pleasantly.

They exchanged goodbyes, and she hung up knowing the son of a bitch was going to dump her. It was his fault the walls were caving in on her, but he'd try to weasel his way out of it. She knew it, could feel it in her bones.

She hurried to get ready for work, trying to sort things out. Her mother and that pompous bastard she'd married were coming over to-night to talk about the girls. They were hatching some plot against her. Bob had probably rushed right home to tell her mother about her getting arrested. Never mind that it was a mistake, that she'd been treated like some kind of criminal. She had a good mind to go ahead and sue that hotel detective and those two idiot cops, and never mind what Bob said. Telling her to consider herself lucky to get off with only a warning when she hadn't done a damned thing wrong. He'd been trying to turn her mother against her from the start. She could see right through him. Maybe he could fool her mother with his fancy airs, but he wasn't fooling her.

The girls wanted to stay out of it. They went into the bedroom with the half dozen cartons Mr. DiStasio had given them, and began emptying the closet and the chest of drawers. As they worked, they could hear Ma ranting and raving in the living room.

"She'll never let us do this," Faye whispered, scared.

"It's not up to her anymore," Louise whispered back. "No matter what Ma says, Gramma and Uncle Bob won't let us stay here."

Louise tiptoed down to the kitchen for a couple of shopping bags to carry the excess. Fifteen minutes later they were done. "We sure don't have much," Louise observed, eyeing their possessions.

"Better check the bathroom," Faye told her. "Don't forget our shower caps and toothbrushes."

"Okay." Louise ducked across the hall and returned in seconds to dump these last items into one of the shopping bags. Faye was sitting on the side of the bed staring at the floor. "I'm gonna find out what they're saying," Louise said.

"Don't, Lou. Just stay here."

"No. I want to know." She crept out to stand by the living room door, listening.

". . . you were arrested for prostitution, for God's sake, Marg," Gramma was saying, sounding distressed and angry.

Holy cow! *Prostitution?*

"And they let me go because they made a *mistake!*" Maggie argued.

"You're always willing to believe the worst about me. Why should this time be any different?"

Prostitution? Louise couldn't get over it. Ma, who hated men, sleeping with them for money? Wait till she told Faye!

"I'll ignore that," Ellen said. "But the girls are coming with us."

"Oh, for Chrissake! I'm sick to death of your crap! You marry this, this phony stuffed shirt and all of a sudden you're queen mucky-muck."

Louise held her breath, shocked to hear Ma attacking Uncle Bob.

"You're in no position to be calling anyone names," Ellen said flatly. "And you're not getting another chance to harm the girls."

"Harm? What harm? What the hell're you *talking* about? I'm the one who's kept them fed and clothed all their lives, kept a goddamned roof over their heads."

"And made them pay for it," Ellen said. "You sicken me, Marg. The only person you care about is yourself. You don't love those girls. You never have."

"Oh, and you're such a paragon of virtue!" Maggie attacked. "You never gave a *damn* for me."

"That is not true," Ellen said evenly.

"This is completely unproductive," Bob interjected quietly. "We're applying for custody of Faye and Louise, and we'll get it."

"You *want* them, *take* them!" Maggie shouted. "They're not grateful for a single thing I've done for them. If you think they'll appreciate anything the two of *you* do, you're dreaming. Go ahead! Take them! I'm fed up with the ungrateful little bitches."

"Charming," Bob said.

Louise could hear him getting to his feet. She raced back to the bedroom to sit beside Faye, murmuring, "She's not going to stop us. Wait'll I *tell* you!"

"All set, girls?" Bob asked from the doorway.

"We're ready, Uncle Bob." Faye went to pick up one of the cartons, saying, "Come on, Lou. Let's get this stuff out to the car."

As they were passing the living room, Maggie jumped up from the sofa, yelling, "Make sure you take every last damned thing with you! Whatever's left goes straight into the garbage. I don't want you two coming around, whining you forgot this or that."

"Don't worry, Ma," Louise said. "We won't be coming around."

"Ever," Faye added under her breath.

As they were loading the boxes in the trunk, Louise said, "Uncle Bob, did Ma really get arrested for prostitution?"

"*What?*" Faye gasped.

"Lulu," he said, tapping the tip of her nose with one finger, "eavesdropping is a dangerous way to get information."

"I know," she said sheepishly. "But is it true?"

"Essentially, yes. It wasn't proved, though, Lulu."

"Ma did get arrested, though, right?"

"Technically, she did. The matter was dropped. And that's what I'd like you to do now. I don't feel comfortable discussing this with you, sweetheart. You can talk about it later with your grandmother."

"Okay, Uncle Bob. I understand."

"They wouldn't have arrested her if they hadn't caught her at it, would they?" Faye asked.

Sadly, he said, "No, they wouldn't have. May we discuss this later, please?"

"Sure," said Louise.

"All right," said Faye.

He preceded them back into the house and Faye took hold of Louise's arm, saying, "And she had the nerve to call *us* sluts."

"You should've *heard* what she said about Gramma and Uncle Bob! She's completely out of her mind."

"My God," Faye said softly. "What a rotten hypocrite!"

"Let's go get the rest of the stuff," Louise said. "I can't *wait* to get out of here."

⊁

Faye got permission from Sue to take the next afternoon off to go furniture shopping. They bought twin beds, a sofa and coffee table, a desk for Louise, a small round dining table with four chairs, a coffee table, two low chests of drawers that would serve double duty as night tables, a telephone table with an attached seat and a shelf underneath to hold phone books, a shower curtain, towels, sheets, pillows and blankets, a twenty-piece set of dishes, pots and pans, and some inexpensive cutlery and utility knives.

"I'll be able to give you bits and pieces," Ellen told the girls. "I've got quite a few things down in the locker in the basement, lamps and knick-knacks, some pictures you might like. We'll get whatever else you need as we go along."

"I've never had so much fun. Have you, Faye?" Louise said.

"Once we're moved in, Gramma, Lou and I will cook supper for you and Uncle Bob."

"Yeah!" Louise jumped in enthusiastically. "We'll have you over to *our place* for a change. Thank you for everything, Gramma." She gave her grandmother a noisy kiss, then said, "I've gotta get caught up on my homework. But I'll come help you make supper. Okay?"

"I'll help Gramma, Lou," Faye said. "You get your work done."

"Really? Thanks, Faye."

After Louise had gone, Ellen said, "I've been wanting to have a little chat with you, Faye, about Raffie."

"Is there something the matter?" she asked, at once on guard.

"I didn't want to bring it up before, and I really don't want to go into all the details now, but there had to be something in Lulu's diary to send your mother jumping to conclusions. Are you and Raffie . . . intimately involved, Faye?"

Her face coloring, Faye said, "Kind of."

"I'm not here to judge you, dear. But I do hope you're being careful."

"Oh, we *are,* Gramma. Honestly! Do you think I'm a slut?"

"Faye, I think you're human. You're a little young to be as serious as you are about a boy, but it's not up to anyone else to make your decisions. Raffie's a sweet boy. It's just that you're both very young."

"I know we are, but we love each other, Gramma. And once Raffie's got his engineering degree, we're going to get married."

"That's still a good five years away, Faye. A lot can happen in five years."

Faye nodded. "I know that too. And I know you're only saying this because you care about me. But I'm always going to love him, and I know he'll always love me."

"All right, dear. Only promise me you'll keep on being careful."

"I promise, Gramma. Swear to God."

Maggie was so angry and, underneath, so scared that she could barely be civil to the customers. In some ways she wished she'd never left Raymar. At least at the sewing machine she hadn't had to bother with a bunch of silly women trying to look smart in dresses that didn't suit them, or looking to get a bargain on an expensive garment. She hadn't had to waste her time being polite to overweight pampered ninnies with nothing better to do than go shopping with their husbands' money; arrogant fatties insisting they wore a size ten when they'd never worn anything less than a fourteen.

Her phone hadn't rung once all week, and she had to wonder if Craig had scared off all his friends by telling them she'd been arrested. She hoped he hadn't done that. He hadn't even heard her side of the story yet.

She'd become accustomed to having a wallet full of money, to banking a tidy sum every week. She relied on her dates. She enjoyed most of them too. If she had to depend only on her Eaton's salary she'd be back to where she'd started before she met Craig, back to making do with maybe two new dresses a year and no little luxuries.

She had to know what he'd said and done, and set off on Friday evening to meet him, prepared to be sweet as pie. She'd go home with him and ten of his friends, if that's what he wanted.

When she gave Craig's name to the maître d', he said, "Oh, yes. You're Miss Parker?"

"That's right." What was going on? Why didn't he pick up a menu and show her to the table?

"Mr. McCutcheon asked me to convey his apologies and to tell you he's unable to join you this evening."

"What?" She looked around the dining room, unwilling to believe what was happening.

"And he asked me to give you this," the man said, handing her an envelope. "He said to say he's very sorry and he'll talk to you soon."

"I see," she said, looking at the envelope as she drifted back out into the corridor.

In the ladies room she opened the envelope. Inside was a note and some bills. The note read:

Dear Margaret,
I did try to telephone but couldn't reach you. I'm sorry to have to cancel this evening but under the circumstances I think it's best if we don't see one another again.
I wish you well.
Sincerely,
Craig.

That son of a bitch! Two hundred dollars and a kiss-off. He wasn't getting off that easily. Marching over to the telephone, she dropped in a nickle and dialed his home number. It rang twice, then a recorded voice said, "We're sorry. The number you have reached is no longer in service."

She called the operator, who checked and said, "There is a new number, but I'm afraid it's unlisted."

Maggie hung up, enraged. She'd wait until Monday and call him at the office. He'd started this whole thing. Now he'd finish it properly, or by God she'd make him rue the day he'd been born.

*C*HAPTER
T H I R T Y - O N E

EVERY DAY, FAYE STOPPED ON HER WAY HOME FROM WORK to deliberate over what to buy for their supper. It was a small daily delight, as was the moment when she came through the front door and stopped to admire the brightness and charm of their new home. Her lungs' capacity seemed to have become progressively greater each month of their newfound freedom, and nightly she drew a deep contented breath as she surveyed the appealing environment she and Louise had created for themselves. They took turns at everything from doing the laundry to washing the dishes. Each morning, they made their beds and tidied up before going off with the lunch bags they'd prepared the night before.

For the first time they were able to entertain friends, to make and receive telephone calls at their leisure, to accept spur-of-the-moment invitations, to do, in fact, all the things most people they knew had been doing throughout their lives. Once a week they dined with Gramma and Uncle Bob, and every other week or so they returned the invitation. Raffie stopped by for an hour when he could get away from the store, and, as always, saw Faye Saturday nights and Sunday afternoons. All their friends exclaimed enviously over the apartment, saying they couldn't wait to leave home and have places just like it.

From time to time when she was home alone for an evening—Faye being off with Raffie or Sue or one of her other friends from the office—Louise imagined Mr. Craven dropping by for a visit. She pictured him admiring the apartment and revising his view of her, at last seeing her not as a schoolgirl but as a grown-up in charge of her own household. She had to laugh at herself. She hadn't the faintest idea what Mr. Craven thought of her. Yet whenever she ran into him at one of the after-school dances or at the lunch counter at Kresge's, she wondered how he'd respond if she casually said, "Oh, by the way, we're having a few people over on Friday night. Why don't you drop by and join us?"

When he caught up with her on her way up Euclid one day in early May, he said, "I hardly ever see you these days, Louise. Are you going up to Kresge's for lunch?"

"Uh-huh."

"Good. I'll join you, if you don't mind. It'll give us a chance to get caught up."

"Sure." She smiled, feeling elevated as always by his interest.

"I wish you'd consider working on the *Review* again next year."

"But I'll have an even bigger workload," she said. "It's my junior matriculation year."

He smiled. "I know. I don't suppose you'd consider being editor?"

"Oh, I couldn't," she said, very flattered. "I'd have no idea how to do it."

"You could, you know. And you'd do a terrific job of it too."

"I honestly couldn't, but thanks a lot for asking."

He gazed at her for a moment then asked, "Have I done something to offend you, Louise?"

"Oh, no," she answered, taken aback by the question. "You've always been really nice to me."

"Well, good," he said, his handsome features clearing. "You're one of my favorite students, you know."

It had been more than two years since she'd been in his class and well over a year since she'd worked on the yearbook. Every few weeks they saw each other for forty minutes or so at lunch. So why did he claim she was one of his favorite students? Bemused, she walked at his side, trying to decipher what he was really saying. Consistently she got the impression their conversations were somehow coded.

"How are things going?" he asked, breaking several minutes' silence as they pushed into the store. "Are you enjoying being an independent woman?"

"I'm hardly that," she laughed, more at ease with his good-natured teasing. "But things are great." It was on the tip of her tongue to invite him to come for supper. He could only say no. All she had to do was ask. He might surprise her. "Faye and I share all the work, take turns cleaning and cooking. It's really terrific."

"Do you see your mother?"

"We haven't seen or heard a word from her since January," she told him, unable to keep her tone as light as she'd have liked. Ma's complete silence was further proof—not that they needed it—of how little she cared about them.

"Does that bother you?" he asked.

"Nope. It's a treat, to tell you the truth."

He looked somewhat dismayed, and she said, "You probably have a really nice family, so it's hard for you to imagine anyone not being glad to see her mother. But then you never met my mother. She never went to a parents' night in her life." With a slightly wild laugh, she said, "I think our teachers assumed we were orphans."

The waitress came over and Louise ordered a chicken sandwich on white bread with lettuce and mayonnaise, and a coffee. As he usually did, Mr. Craven said, "That sounds good. Make it two." Then, turning back to Louise, he leaned one arm on the counter. "You're right. I come from a very close family. Whenever I hear someone speak disparagingly of a parent my initial reaction is disapproval. Which isn't wise. There are people who shouldn't be allowed to have children."

"My mother's one of them," she asserted. "You'll have to take my word for that."

"That's a shame," he said soberly. "I'm sorry you and your sister have had such a rough time."

"Oh, we're fine," she said, hating the idea that he'd feel sorry for her.

"Well, for future reference," he said, "if you ever need help, with anything, just let me know."

She nodded and directed her eyes to the big color photographs of fancy sandwiches on the far wall. She wished suddenly, fervently, that some boy would ask her out, so she could stop fantasizing about this man. But the only one who ever called her was Lefty. And they were just pals. She always got asked to dance at the sock hops and tea dances but only because everybody knew she was a good dancer. Not one of the boys who asked her to dance even so much as glanced at her in the hallways between classes. Sixteen years old, for Pete's sake, and she'd never been out on an actual date. It was positively pathetic.

"Now I *have* said something to offend you," Mr. Craven said, studying the set of her profile.

She turned to look at him, saying, "You don't have to feel sorry for me, Mr. Craven. My sister and I are doing really well. We're way better off on our own than we ever were with our mother. We're not helpless little kids, you know. We've been looking after each other all our lives."

"I don't feel sorry for you, Louise. Not at all. I apologize if I gave you that impression. As a matter of fact," he said, "I admire you. You have remarkable aplomb for someone your age."

"Aplomb?"

"Poise, self-assurance," he elaborated.

"Really?" she asked, starting to smile.

"Categorically. You're reliable and responsible and highly imaginative. I think you're going to be a very interesting woman."

Feeling very much better, she grinned and said, "I intend to be."

He laughed and patted her on the arm. "That's more like the Louise I know."

You don't know me, she thought, her arm burning where he'd touched it. Maybe she looked like a kid because she was still small for her age, but she wasn't a kid, had never been one. You didn't get a mother like hers and stay a kid for very long. "Nobody knows anyone," she said quietly, the pulse in her throat beating hard. "We only think we do. But we only know the surface and what people decide they want to show us."

"No," he disagreed soberly. "Some of us look and actually *see*, Louise. Ah, here's our food." He smiled at the waitress as she set the plates down.

Louise desperately wanted to ask him what it was he saw, but the moment was gone.

↟

Maggie left dozens of messages at Craig's office but he never called back. Short of going there or waiting outside his house, which she refused to lower herself to do, she had no choice, finally, but to give up. It galled her, and she found it increasingly difficult to control her temper, particularly when dealing with her customers. She was tempted a dozen times a day to tell these women to go to hell and stop wasting her time. They drove her crazy with their vacilating, their lack of taste, and their excesses —of perfume, of makeup, and of money.

For two solid weeks after the girls left she sat home every night watching the Sylvania, becoming progressively more depressed as the telephone failed to ring. But then, on the Monday of the third week, one of her out-of-town regulars called and, elated, she agreed to meet him for dinner. Luckily, he was staying at the new Westbury Hotel. She'd never been inside the place, so there was no possibility of some moronic hotel detective making trouble for her.

In very high spirits, she took extra care dressing and making up, and had a most satisfactory evening that not only allowed her to work off a considerable amount of pent-up anger and energy, but also netted her a hundred dollars. It started her thinking too.

Since it was now risky to meet her dates at their hotels, it would be wiser, not to mention safer, to bring them home. Except that she'd be embarrassed to have these men see where she lived. She went to considerable pains to give the impression that she was a woman of some means. She'd never given even the slightest hint that she accepted dates strictly for the money, but one look at that house and men would think twice about calling her again. The damned place had "low class" written all over it, with its sagging front steps and cramped rooms filled with shabby furniture. If she wanted to continue going out once or twice a week, her only option was to move.

She had enough saved to cover the cost of some decent new furniture, and now that she no longer had the expense of the girls, she didn't need more than a one-bedroom apartment. When she got a call the following week from one of her occasional dates who was in from Calgary, she decided it was time to take action. She started apartment hunting the very next day.

The place she rented was in a fairly new high rise on Isabella Street just east of Yonge. It was only a three-block walk from the subway at Wellesley, which meant that her traveling time to and from work would be shortened considerably, and it was situated within easy walking distance of the nicer stores on Bloor. The only disadvantages were the kitchen, which had no room for a table and chairs, and the rent, which, at seventy-two fifty, was more than she'd wanted to pay. Otherwise, she was crazy about the place. It had a big living room with a dining ell, and a good-sized bedroom with plenty of closet space. There was a south-facing balcony running the width of the apartment, and an entry-phone system in the lobby, which meant that people couldn't just wander in off the street. She signed a two-year lease, then, using her employee discount, shopped for new furniture.

It was the first time in her life she actually got to choose what she wanted. When she'd married John Parker he'd already had furniture, and her parents had contributed extras from the attic of the old St. George Street house. The hours she spent making her purchases were among the happiest she'd ever known. Of course she looked for sale items where possible, but the extra savings only added to her pleasure.

She bought a smart walnut dining set, a sleek modern sofa upholstered in charcoal gray wool with a pair of matching armchairs, two low square end tables, and a new stand for the TV set. Then, to top off her pleasure, she phoned Mr. Silverman to inform him of her plans. She had the Salvation Army come to collect most of the old furniture, and spent her final week in the denuded house on Manning Avenue packing. It was a week that brought two dates, which netted two hundred dollars. So much for you, Craig! she thought, as she made out her savings deposit slip, already well on her way to recouping what she'd had to lay out.

She transferred her bank accounts to a branch close to the new apartment; she put in a change of address with the post office, notified Ontario Hydro and the Bell and, of course, Fred Brundage up in personnel.

"Moving, eh?" He smiled. "You'll have to invite me over sometime to see the new place."

"We'll see," she said, returning his smile, anxious to keep on good terms with him. Her dates were still sporadic, and she needed the job.

At last, on her lunch hour the day after the move, she went to the pay phone by the employees' cafeteria to call her mother.

"I wanted to let you know my new number," Maggie told her coldly.

"Oh? Are you moving, Marg?"

"I've already moved, for your information." She rhymed off the address and phone number, then said, "Now you know where to find me."

"Are you well?" Ellen asked.

"A fat lot you care," Maggie said, and hung up. *Are you well?* What a phony! Jesus! She hadn't heard a word from one of them in weeks. She was glad to be rid of the whole bunch—her mother and that snotty stuffed shirt, and those two conniving little sluts. Good riddance to all of them, including that son of a bitch Craig. She hadn't forgotten him, not by a long shot. And one of these days she'd fix his wagon but good. Maybe she wasn't dating as much as before, but they'd all come around again eventually. And her out-of-town dates were always asking if they could give her number to a friend. She'd be back to dating three or four times a week in no time, and banking the gifts. She'd show them all! Nobody got the better of her.

✦

Faye was beginning to think there might be something wrong with her. She'd thought that once she and Raffie actually had someplace private where they could be alone everything would be different. But it wasn't. Once or twice a month when they had the apartment entirely to themselves on a Saturday night, she'd lock the door and put the chain on, then, with the radio playing nice music, the two of them would undress and lie down together on her bed. Very quickly they'd both become excited, and several times she wanted to go all the way. She'd get one of the safes from the back of her night table drawer and they'd start, but she couldn't go through with it. Each time she'd hold very still, but as soon as Raffie started to push into her she'd panic. Twice she managed to let him all the way inside of her but the moment he began to move she had to stop him. It scared her. It hurt. She simply couldn't go through with it.

Each time, Raffie sought to reassure her by saying, "It'll be all right once we're married. I know you're scared. I hear stories all the time about girls getting pregnant because the safe broke. I understand, so don't worry about it."

But he was beginning to wonder. He'd gone out for the football team at the start of grade eleven and all of a sudden girls were saying hi, smiling at him in the hallways. Some of them were damned good-looking too. Of course he was crazy about Faye and always had been, so it made him feel guilty when he found himself smiling back at girls. He just wished they could settle the sex business once and for all so he didn't have to spend most of their time together trying to make her feel better for not being able to do it. It seemed as if she were trying to prove something—not to him, but to herself.

"Let's make a deal," he said that August, on a night when they'd been to the Ex. "Let's forget about it for the time being. Okay, Faye? It seems to matter more to you than it does to me. And it upsets me to see you get so worked up. It's not worth it."

"What d'you mean?" she asked fearfully.

"I mean, let's leave the safes in the back of the drawer and just enjoy each other. It's not as if we don't have a great time otherwise."

"You really don't mind, Raffie? You're not just saying that?"

"The only thing I mind is how it upsets you. So let's forget it for now. Later on, when we're married, if it's still a problem, we'll worry about it. You don't have to prove anything to me, Faye. I know you love me. And you know I love you. Let's not do this anymore. Okay?"

"You mean it, honestly?" she asked, holding him tightly.

"Swear to God, Faye. Let's forget it for the time being."

"I love you so much," she said gratefully. "Once we're married, I'll make it all up to you."

"There's nothing to make up. I love you the way you are." He kissed the side of her arm, then sat up, saying, "I'd better get going. Lou'll be home soon."

The timing was very close. Louise arrived home not five minutes after Raffie left. She sailed in carrying a huge black-and-white teddy bear, saying, "Look what Lefty won for me at the ringtoss! He's so cute. If only he was older."

"He's not that young," Faye said, concealing the abandoned condom in a tissue.

"He's going into grade twelve and he's not even fifteen yet, for Pete's sake. I feel positively *ancient* compared to him."

"You make it sound like you're so much older."

"A year and a half is a *great* difference," Louise insisted, pulling off her clothes. "Did you and Raff have fun at the Ex? I thought it was pretty crummy, nowhere near as much fun as it used to be."

"We didn't stay that long," Faye answered. "It was too crowded. I'll just take a quick shower, okay?"

"Sure. Want a cup of tea?"

"No, thanks. I'm going to have my shower and go straight to sleep."

"Okeydokey," Louise said, padding nude into the kitchen. "I want some tea."

"Don't you think you should put something on?" Faye asked.

"What for?" Louise looked over in surprise. "It's hot, and besides, who's going to see me?" She glanced over to confirm that the drapes were closed.

"Never mind," Faye said, and closed herself into the bathroom.

While waiting for the kettle to boil, Louise wandered into the living room and flopped down on the sofa, dragging the teddy bear into her lap. Lefty had actually kissed her good night. He'd pushed his mouth against hers, then, his face flaming, had said, "See ya, Lou," and went off whistling. Her first kiss, and she hadn't felt a thing, probably because Lefty didn't know how to kiss. Not that she did, but she knew he definitely didn't. Daniel Craven would know how to kiss, she thought, cuddling the itchy bear. He probably took his girlfriends to romantic candlelight dinners, then drove them home in his Triumph sports car, and kissed them so well their bones melted. The kettle started whistling and with a sigh she abandoned the stuffed toy and went to make her tea.

"So when're you going to invite me over to see the new apartment?" Fred Brundage asked, sliding into the empty seat opposite hers in the employees' cafeteria.

"One of these nights," Maggie answered. "I'm pretty busy, you know."

"The store's going to start staying open late a couple of evenings a week," he said, lighting a cigarette.

"That's nice," she said disinterestedly, wishing she'd gone out for lunch. She wasn't in the mood for chitchat. It had been months and she still wasn't having the number of dates she'd had before those jerks had arrested her at the Royal York. She even had an answering service now, so she wouldn't miss any calls. But she was lucky to be out one night a week. She was considering canceling the answering service and saving herself twenty dollars a month.

"We'll have to stagger the staff hours," Fred went on.

"So?"

"So, you'll probably have two days a week when you come in at noon and work till nine."

"Uh-uh," she said, shaking her head. "Impossible. I can't work evenings."

"Why don't we get together after work, have a drink, grab a bite to eat, and we'll talk about it."

"Don't you have a wife or something?" she asked with a smile, to keep things light.

"Doesn't everybody?" He shrugged this off. "I still have to eat. You free Friday?"

"I might be. Could you see to it that I don't have to work evenings?"

"All things are possible, Maggie, my dear," he said cheerfully. "We'll discuss it Friday night. I'll meet you up the street at the Silver Rail at, say, seven?"

"All right."

"Good!" He put out his cigarette, saying, "We'll celebrate my promotion to assistant manager." With a smile, he got up and left.

That Friday evening, Maggie started sleeping with Fred Brundage.

CHAPTER

THIRTY-TWO

ALDO WAS WAITING, KEEPING HIS EYES OPEN AND WAITING. He wanted a crack at proving he was more than just some teenage kid who worked in his father's grocery store. He had plenty of ideas for expanding the business, but Pop would never take him seriously. Of course, if *Raffie* had something to say, that was something else entirely. Pop would practically beg when Raffie said, "I've got an idea." But Aldo could say he had an idea and Pop would say, "Aldo, don't wastea my time, eh? Be a good boy an' go helpa the customers," or "Aldo, I ask you fifty times now to dust what's ona the shelves." He didn't want to hear anything Aldo had to say. Where the old man was concerned, Aldo couldn't do one thing right. Raffie, though, was golden; Raffie could walk on water. He'd be graduating soon, and he'd already been accepted into the U of T school of engineering. And despite Pop's having fought it like a bastard, wanting Raffie to drop out after Mom died, now the old man was forever bragging to his customers about his son, the future engineer. It made Aldo sick.

Most of the time Aldo couldn't get near the truck, even though he'd had his license for more than a year. Only if Raffie wasn't around and things had to be picked up or delivered and Pop couldn't do it himself would he let Aldo get behind the wheel of the rusting old heap. That was just one thing. When Aldo suggested putting in a cooler so they could sell dairy products, give the variety store up the street a little competition, the old man practically laughed in his face. But when Raffie said maybe Pop should think about it, the idea of carrying milk in the store was suddenly a stroke of pure genius. It was the same when Aldo said they should maybe start carrying some imported cheese and sausage. "You think I'ma made a money?" Pop rounded on him. Raffie said, "You know, Pop, that's not such a bad idea," and Pop went for it, but only in a small way. Instead of getting in a refrigerated display case and offering a decent selection, the way Aldo had wanted, Pop got some provolone and mozzarella and a few crummy sticks of pepperoni. He might as well not have bothered. Hardly anybody even noticed the little hand-printed sign on the wall by the register: IMPORTED CHEESE AND SAUSAGE. So the sausage dried out, the lousy cheese turned green, and Raffie had to cook with the stuff every day for weeks before Pop was satisfied and they could throw what was left in the trash.

Pop would never go whole hog on anything, so none of the ideas came to much. Keeping a few quarts of milk and half-and-half in the fridge at the back of the store didn't hurt the variety store's late-night business at all. And delivering seven or eight bucks' of stuff to little old ladies in the neighborhood wasn't worth the time or trouble. But Pop saw those deliveries as personalized service. He wouldn't go after local restaurant business the way Aldo told him he should, cutting deals on the prices to do some real volume selling. The old man just couldn't *see* it. It frustrated the hell out of Aldo. Even Raffie couldn't get Pop to see the sense of expanding in a serious way, of making the business into more than the local fruit market.

Outside of the store, things weren't too bad. Every month or so, he and the twins would pool their money and cruise Jarvis Street, pick up one of the whores and have a party, get their ashes hauled. The twins had finally quit school. It was either get jobs or spend a third year in grade nine. And while Bruno and Anthony didn't care one way or the other, their old lady slapped a newspaper down on the breakfast table one morning and said, "Go to work, you bums." So they got jobs on the loading dock of a factory down on Adelaide. From eight to four Monday to Friday and eight to noon Saturdays they loaded and unloaded semis full of machine-tooled parts. Lunchtimes they sat with their work-booted feet hanging over the side of the dock to eat the sandwiches their old lady packed every morning. They actually liked working, and didn't mind forking over ten bucks a week each to their mother. They still had plenty left—more, in fact, than Aldo ever would've had if he didn't help himself to sales he didn't bother to ring up, and without the odd couple of bucks he lifted from the till.

Aldo wouldn't have minded working in the store if Pop just let him try a few things, if he'd only be willing to listen once in a while to something he had to say. But no. Aldo couldn't do anything right, and Raffie could do no wrong. Raffie was going to be the first on Pop's side of the family to go to university, the first to have a *career*. Raffie could use the truck any goddamned time he wanted to grab a piece of ass from his prissy slut girlfriend, Faye. But Aldo had to get down on his knees and beg and still the old man said no, he couldn't drive the truck. And Aldo had to fork over his hard-earned money to some slag so he could get laid.

All goddamned Faye had to do was walk into the store and Pop went gaga. She'd come clicking in in her high heels, decked out in the fancy clothes she wore to work, and the old man would fall all over himself like it was a visit from the goddamned queen or something.

"How you, cara?" he'd ask, beaming. "How's your sister? Everything good? You want some nice fruit, Faye? Here, you take somea these nice Clementines home."

She always played it so sweet and proper, but she didn't fool Aldo. He had her number. And every time she came through the door he itched to teach her a lesson, let her know she could maybe fool the old man, but she didn't fool him. He was fed up with everybody treating him like garbage—the old man never listening to a word he had to say while he sucked up to Raffie; the customers always wanting Pop to serve them, acting like Aldo wasn't good enough to weigh their stinking eggplants, or like maybe Aldo was gonna steal their crummy purses; and Faye pretending to be so nice, saying hello and asking how're you Aldo when she could've cared less if he dropped dead on the spot in front of her. Every time he saw her he thought about how good it'd feel to take her down a few pegs, show her who she was dealing with.

So on a late Saturday afternoon in April when Raffie phoned to say the truck had broken down and he and Pop were stuck out in Port Credit waiting for the Ontario Motor League to send someone to give them a tow, Aldo at once began seeing possibilities in the situation.

"Faye's supposed to meet me at the store at seven," Raffie said. "But we're never going to make it back by then. Do me a favor, Aldo, and tell her to go ahead to the party. Tell her I'll meet her there. Okay?"

"Sure," Aldo said, the possibilities widening enticingly. "No sweat. What's wrong with the truck?"

"It looks like the clutch is gone. They'll have to tow it. Then Pop and I will catch a bus back into town. It'll be hours. Be sure to tell Faye, okay? I tried to call her place but she's probably still downtown with Lou."

"Will do," Aldo said happily. "You guys take it easy, and don't worry about a thing. I'll take care of everything."

"Thanks a lot. See you later."

The instant Raffie hung up, Aldo called the twins, keeping his fingers crossed they'd be home.

They were. Bruno came clumping down the stairs—Aldo could actually hear him through the receiver, that's what a bruiser the guy was— and when he came on the line, Aldo said, "You guys get over here before seven. We're gonna have some fun."

"Yeah? What?"

"Never mind. I'll tell you when you get here. Just don't be later than a quarter to seven."

The girls had a good day. They got downtown by ten, shopped for a couple of hours—Louise used some of the birthday money Uncle Bob had given her to buy new high heels for the party Kath's mom and Mr. Nolan were giving that night, and Faye bought some slips and a blouse. Then, Faye's treat, they had lunch at Diana Sweets before catching a matinee of *Vertigo,* which they both loved. On the way home, Louise speculated on the interesting people who might be at the party. Kath's mom had lots of artist and writer friends, and her parties were always terrific. Kath had said that her new boyfriend, Rollie, was going to bring along a friend for Louise, which had put something of a damper on Louise's enthusiasm for the evening.

"I hate blind dates," she'd protested, although she'd never actually had one. It was the idea of having a total stranger foisted on her that she really didn't like. "I wish you'd told me he was going to do that. I'd have said not to bother."

"It's not a blind date. It's just an extra man for the party," Kath had said. "You don't have to *marry* the guy, Lou, but he might be nice."

"Well, as long as he doesn't think I'm his date," Louise relented.

"You might like him, you know. Boy! You're so *choosy!*"

"So're you," Louise had countered.

"I know. Never mind. It'll be fun."

When they got home, Faye said, "Let me use the bathroom first, okay, Lou? I have to leave earlier than you do."

"Sure. I'm going to run down the hall to show Gramma my new shoes and see what she's wearing tonight."

"Take your keys and lock the door, will you?" Faye said. "I don't like the idea of being in the bath with the front door wide open."

"The bogeyman's gonna come in and get you in the tub, eh?" Louise laughed. "Don't worry, kiddo. I'll lock the door."

Faye was looking forward to the party. It was one of the last chances she and Raffie would have to be together for an entire evening before he knuckled down to studying for finals. For the next month or so he'd be home every night with his books.

⸸

The twins were hanging around the store with Aldo, which wasn't unusual. Faye thought nothing of it when she arrived promptly at seven. She said, "Hi, Aldo. Hi Bruno, Anthony. Where's Raffie, upstairs?" She looked around, wondering what she'd said to make the three of them smile in unison.

Aldo rose from the stool by the cash register, saying, "Come on up, Faye," as he crossed over to her. "He called to say he'll be a little late. He wants you to wait." He put a hand on her elbow, directing her toward the stairs.

"How late? Where is he?" She hoped they weren't going to miss the party. She'd really been looking forward to it.

"Just a little," Aldo said, giving her another smile as he moved her up the stairs. "They got delayed, trouble with the truck, but they're on their way."

Something didn't feel quite right but she couldn't think what, and Aldo distracted her, saying, "Beautiful day today, eh, Faye? Gorgeous weather. You look real nice. New dress? Must be going to a big party. Lucky old Raffie."

"It's not new," she said, wishing he'd take his hand off her arm. Something was wrong here. She looked back. The twins were standing by the front display watching her and Aldo go up the stairs.

"You guys hang on a minute," Aldo said. "We're going out," he explained to Faye as they reached the landing. "Got a big night of our own lined up. Hey! While you're here, there's something I want to show you. Come in here for a sec, Faye," he said excitedly, directing her down the hall. "Wait'll you see this! You won't believe it."

Gently pulling free of his hand, she said, "Maybe I'll wait downstairs . . . or better yet, I think I'll go on ahead to the party and Raffie can meet me there." She didn't like being alone with Aldo and the twins. The air seemed heavy, ominous. In spite of the warmth of the evening, she felt suddenly chilled.

"Okay, Faye. Sure. But before you go, let me show you. It'll only take a second." He smiled pleasantly, his hand now in the small of her back as they arrived at the door to his bedroom.

"No, I think I'd better go." She started to turn back toward the stairs. "Lou's waiting for me," she lied. "We're supposed to be there by seven-thirty, and I'd hate to be late. Maybe another time. . . ."

"Just get the hell in here!" he said, and gave her a shove that sent her flying into the room. The force of the gesture was such that she very nearly fell and had to throw out her arms for balance, dropping her purse in the process. "You and me, we're gonna have some fun, Faye." He shut the door and approached her.

"What d'you think you're doing?" she said, badly frightened now, her heart pumping hard, a rushing in her ears. "Stop this right now, Aldo, and we'll forget all about it. I'm really in no mood to play games with you. People are waiting for me."

"Hey!" he said softly, his smile menacing now. "We haven't even started yet." He put out a hand to touch her hair and she swatted it away.

"You lay a finger on me and Raffie'll kill you. Are you crazy? I'm walking out of here right now." She tried to push past him but he grabbed her by the arm and threw her down on the bed. Her fear skyrocketed. He was twice her size and could easily hurt her. She sat up and struggled to get past him to the door. On one level she couldn't believe this was happening. This was Raffie's little brother, a boy she'd known all her life. Surely he couldn't really want to hurt her. They were friends! She'd never done anything to cause him to look at her the way he was looking at her now, with such hatred. But on another level, she knew exactly what was going to happen, and she was terrified. Almost lazily, he held her down. The more she struggled, the more his weight bore down on her. She could feel the strength of his determination collecting in his arms.

"You don't want to do this," she pleaded. "You don't really want to hurt me. When Raffie finds out, he'll kill you, and you know it. You're not *thinking*."

"Raffie's never gonna know," he said confidently, one hand on her shoulder keeping her down, the other lifting her skirt. "We're just gonna have a little fun, with no one the wiser."

"Don't *touch* me!" she cried, kicking out.

"I don't wanna have to hit you, Faye," he warned. "Stop making out like you're some kinda virgin. You've been fucking my brother down in the cellar for years. Now it's my turn."

She threw out her hand and smacked him across the face, her legs thrashing, wanting to kill him for scaring her this way, for saying these obscene things to her. "Let me up or I'll scream," she warned tremulously, tears in her eyes. "Stop this right now! I mean it, Aldo."

"Go ahead and scream. I told the guys you might."

She screamed. The sound was shattering inside her head. Aldo laughed. Nothing happened. Nobody came to help her. She was trapped.

Downstairs Bruno winced and looked at his brother.

"Forget it," Anthony smiled. "Aldo said she'd probably scream."

"I don't like it," Bruno said. "I'm goin' for a Creamsicle."

"Hey! You can't leave. Aldo said to wait."

"I'm *goin'* for a *Creamsicle*," Bruno repeated. "I don't give a shit what Aldo said. I don't like this." He went over to the door. "I'll be back in a while."

Anthony shrugged, flipped the sign on the door from OPEN to CLOSED, and looked over at the stairs. Aldo had said they could all have a turn, and they wouldn't even have to pay, not like with the shag-bags on Jarvis.

⤙

Bruno bought a Fudgesicle instead, bit into the thick chocolate ice thoughtfully, then wandered over to the racks to look at the magazines. He didn't even bother picking one up. He kept hearing Faye scream. He didn't like what was going on. This wasn't fun; it wasn't right. Aldo didn't say nothing about hurting her, and nobody screamed like that who wasn't getting hurt.

He stared at the cover of *Popular Mechanics,* finishing the Fudgesicle in half a dozen bites. The store owner was watching him. He could feel the guy's eyes on his back. This was bad. He turned and went back to the counter, fishing in his pocket for a buck as he said, "Pack of Export A's, eh?"

The owner reached behind him, got the cigarettes, took Bruno's dollar and gave him change, saying, "Want matches?"

"Nah, that's okay." Bruno stripped the cellophane and let it drop on the floor.

"Hey, pick that up!" said the owner. "What're you, raised in a barn?"

Bruno said, "Sorry," grabbed the wrappings, and put them on the counter. "Throw that away, eh?" He turned and got out a cigarette, lighting it with his Zippo as he went out the door, hearing the owner muttering something about punks at his back. Bruno was thinking how it didn't feel right. He started back to the store. That Aldo, some of the stuff he thought was fun wasn't no fun at all. Going with the pros was okay, but a couple of times Aldo got pretty rough, and Bruno and Anthony had had to tell him to take it easy. It was like Aldo hated the girls, wanted to do mean stuff, hurt them. Him and Anthony, they had to make it like a joke, smiling, telling Aldo to lay off, eh, what was he trying to do, kill the poor bitch? But it wasn't right. Like the way Aldo always treated old Mary-Lou and that Rita. So, okay, they were a pain, hanging around all the time, but he didn't have to go talking rotten to them, calling them names like he did.

Bruno started walking faster. Faye wasn't like them others. For one thing, her and Louise were practically family. Faye was always nice to them, and real pretty. And she was Raffie's girl. He'd break Aldo's hands for touching Faye, break *their* hands if they touched her. How'd Aldo figure he could go hurting her without Raffie finding out? No, he didn't like it one bit. He threw the cigarette into the gutter and ran the last yards back to the store.

The door had the CLOSED sign on but wasn't locked. Anthony was gone. What the hell? Bruno glanced around, then took the stairs three at a time, ran down the hall, and burst into the room to see Aldo pulling up his pants and Anthony ready to take his down.

"Hey, Tone!" Bruno yelled, mad, seeing Faye curled up in a knot on the bed, crying so hard the whole bed was shaking. "Don't you touch her, Tone!"

"What's with you?" Aldo demanded, red in the face. "It's Anthony's turn, then it's yours."

"I'm telling you, Tone, leave her alone!" Bruno said. "What're you? *Stronzo! Tèsta di cazzo!*" He yanked his brother away from the bed. "You crazy, Tone?" he whispered. "That's *Raffie's* girl. That's not some piece of trash from Jarvis Street. That's *Faye.* What're you *doing?*"

Anthony blinked, nodded slowly, then turned to Aldo saying, "You crazy, Aldo?"

"What the hell's the *matter* with you two assholes?" Aldo hissed. "You chickening out?"

Bruno shoved him aside and looked down at Faye, then over at Aldo. "What'sa matter with *you?*" Then more softly, he said, "You okay, Faye?" and went to touch her arm. She cringed, curling more tightly into a knot. "Shit!" Bruno said quietly. "Why'd you go do this, Aldo? Come on, Faye," he said, trying to get her to sit up. She was shaking and crying so bad, Bruno thought Aldo probably pounded her some, the way he'd started hitting that pro the last time, whomping her in the ribs, kicking her in the butt like she was a dog or something. The pro started crying and shaking just like Faye was doing. "You okay, Faye?" he asked again, awkwardly trying to straighten her clothes, cover her up decent. "Tone," he said over his shoulder, real mad now, "go down get a cab."

"Hey," Anthony protested. "You go."

"Vai fa'te in culo! Go get a cab!"

Anthony went.

Aldo said, "What're you doing, eh, asshole? Let the bitch *walk* home!"

"You're makin' me mad," Bruno warned, eyes narrowed. "Faye don't tell Raffie, maybe I will."

Aldo suddenly had a knife in his hand and waved it threateningly under Bruno's nose. "Open your mouth and I'll cut your fucking tongue out!"

Bruno stared at him. Aldo was crazy enough to do it, and Bruno hated knives. "Okay," he backed down. "But I'm putting her in a cab and Faye's goin' home."

"Who gives a shit! She's a lousy lay anyway, like humping rubber. Get her the hell outa here. I gotta take a crap."

Bruno thought, Pig. Guy's a stinking pig. "Come on, Faye," he said, patting her on the arm with one big clumsy hand. She was in even worse shape than the pro that time. "It's all over now." He found her shoes and purse, got the shoes on her, then lifted her off the bed. She was crying like a little kid, her hair hanging all over the place, black stuff from her eyes running down her face, gulping and sobbing. "You'll be okay now, Faye," he said, carrying her down the stairs. Outside, Anthony had a taxi waiting and was leaning on the side of the car talking to the driver. "You're goin' home now, Faye," Bruno said, thinking she didn't weigh any more than his kid sister, Felice, who was only nine, and talking to her the same way he did to Felice when she got bad dreams and he had to rock her back to sleep. This was very bad.

"Hey, what'sa matter with her? She sick?" the cabdriver wanted to know. "I'm not taking no sick broad in my cab."

"She's okay," Bruno said. "You take her home." He got Faye into the back of the car, put the purse in her lap, saying, "You'll be okay now, Faye. You're goin' home," then closed the door and stepped back onto the sidewalk, worried. This was the worst thing Aldo'd ever done. Raffie would find out and come kill them. He whirled around and backhanded Anthony across the chops. *"Imbecile!* You're gonna get us killed. Come on! I'm not hanging around here."

"Hey! Watch who you're hitting!" Stunned, Anthony held a hand to his bruised cheek. "We're goin' to the pool hall," he said, turning to look over at the store.

"Not me," Bruno said. "I'm goin' somewhere quiet for a beer. You comin'? Or you wanna hang around with that . . . that *garbage.*"

Anthony looked at his twin, at the store, then back at Bruno. He shrugged and said, "Okay. Maybe you're right. Let's go for a beer."

They started off along the street, Bruno saying, "I had enougha Aldo, eh? And you! What're you thinking, you're gonna go put it to a nice girl like Faye when she doesn't want to. You don't get enough from Rita? You gotta do everything Aldo says?"

"I do what I want," Anthony defended himself.

"It's bad, what he did," Bruno said darkly. "I'm not goin' there no more."

"Me, neither," Anthony said.

"Yeah. From now on we stay away from Aldo. That guy's trouble."

"Trouble," Anthony repeated. "Yeah."

"Where to, miss?" The cabdriver extended his arm along the back of the seat and swiveled to look at Faye suspiciously.

She managed to choke out her address, then slumped back, shivering.

Oh God! What time was it? She looked at her watch. A quarter to eight. Everyone would be gone by now to the party, so it was safe to go home. *God!* He'd hurt her so horribly. And it was all her own fault. How could she have been so *stupid?* She should've known better than to believe anything Aldo said. But where was Raffie? Why hadn't he come to stop it? And why why *why* had she gone upstairs? Her own fault, stupid. She should've said she'd wait in the store, shouldn't have gone upstairs. If it wasn't for Bruno . . . Anthony would have raped her, too. If not for Bruno . . . She couldn't stop shaking. Her clothes were ripped. It felt as if she might be bleeding. It hurt so badly. Stupid, she'd been so incredibly stupid!

Luckily she made it up to the apartment without seeing anyone. Trembling, she leaned against the inside of the locked door and tried to think what to do. They'd be looking for her at the party. She'd better phone, say she wasn't coming. Yes. She went to the telephone.

Mr. Nolan answered.

"Hi, Mr. Nolan, it's Faye."

"Ah, hello Faye. We've been wondering where you are."

"I'm afraid I'm not feeling very well, Mr. Nolan. I'm not going to be able to come."

"That's a pity, Faye. We were looking forward to seeing you."

"I'm really sorry. I was wondering if I could speak to my sister."

"Of course. I'll fetch her. Hold on a moment, Faye." He put the receiver down and she sat with one arm wrapped tightly around her middle, hearing the party noises, the music, people laughing. She couldn't stop crying. At last Louise came to the phone.

"Hey! Where are you guys?" Louise said.

"Lou, I'm not coming. I don't feel well. I'm going to stay home, go to bed."

"What's the matter? You sound awful."

"I think maybe it's food poisoning."

"Where's Raffie?"

"I don't know. He and his dad got delayed or something. If he shows up will you explain?"

"Sure. Listen, do you want me to come home? I don't mind if you're sick."

"No, stay there. Have a good time. Say hi to everybody for me. Okay?"

"Are you throwing up and everything?"

"I feel as if I might. I'm going to bed now, Lou. I'll see you later, or in the morning."

"I'm really sorry. You're missing a great party. And Rollie brought along this friend of his, Terry. He's a *terrific* dancer."

"That's great, Lou. Have fun."

Her stockings were in shreds, her underpants were gone, her slip was torn and wet with blood, slimy with semen. Sickened, she threw her clothes and shoes in a pile in the foyer, then backed away into the bathroom. The sight of herself in the mirror was unbearable. She turned off the light, leaving the door open so she could see what she was doing as she got the shower going and climbed beneath the scalding spray.

She couldn't wash it away. It kept happening over and over as she scrubbed herself, soaping and rinsing, soaping and rinsing. The pain inside had her bent forward and her legs kept wanting to buckle. How *could* she have been so *stupid?* She berated herself nonstop, lips moving, whispering to herself as she shampooed her hair three, four, five times. Raffie would never forgive her. She could never tell him, never tell anyone. She'd be too ashamed to admit what a fool she'd been, letting herself get tricked that way. Three of them in the store, but she went in anyway when she should've known better. It was her own damned fault. She was too stupid to live. But *how* could she have known? How was she supposed to know Aldo was capable of doing something like that? It wasn't her fault. But it was, it was. Shame was a knife in her abdomen, a steady ringing in her ears. She felt unutterably dirty, hopelessly soiled. The scrubbing only cleaned the surface. Underneath she was crawling with maggots.

In her robe and pajamas, with heavy socks on, she bundled all the clothes into a shopping bag then darted down the hall to the incinerator room and pushed the bag into the chute. She listened to it fall to the furnace in the basement. Then, heart hammering, she flew back to the apartment and locked the door. She wanted to put the chain on, but then Lou wouldn't be able to get in. So she had to leave the chain off, and went to sit on the sofa, terrified Aldo would come pounding at the door, break it in, and hurt her again.

When the telephone rang, she leaped off the sofa and ran several steps, then stopped, afraid to answer. But what if it was important? Scared, she lifted the receiver. It was Raffie.

"What's the matter, honey? Louise says you're sick."

Her mouth dry, she had to wet her lips before answering. "I think it's food poisoning."

"That's a rotten break. I'll come over, take care of you."

"No!" she cried. Then getting hold of herself, she said, "Raffie, no. I'm a mess. I'm throwing up. I've got diarrhea. I'd rather be alone. You stay at the party and have a good time."

"I'm not going to have a good time without you," he said, mildly reproachful. "You know that."

"I'm sorry," she said, struggling not to let him hear her crying. "I feel lousy. I'm going to bed. We'll talk tomorrow. Okay?"

"Aren't you going to be at your grandmother's for lunch?"

"Oh, that's right. I forgot. I'll see how I feel," she told him, panicked at the idea of having to see and talk to him, of having to pretend nothing was wrong. "Call me in the morning. Okay?"

"You're sure you don't want me to come over? I was really counting on seeing you. It's the last chance we'll have to be together for ages, what with exams and everything."

"Positive, honestly. I'm really sorry. I was counting on seeing you too. But I wouldn't want anyone to see me now. Try to enjoy yourself, and we'll talk in the morning."

"Okay," he said, sounding doubtful. "I love you, Faye."

"I love you too."

For quite some time after the call she stood in the kitchen and stared at the knives in the drawer, torn between wanting to die and wanting to kill Aldo DiStasio. She felt sickeningly guilty and dumb; she wanted to scream out the window, tell the entire world it wasn't her fault. She couldn't stop crying, couldn't stop shaking. And the pain burned away inside her like something alive and evil.

*C*HAPTER

THIRTY-THREE

FAYE PRETENDED TO BE ASLEEP WHEN LOUISE ARRIVED home from the party just after 2 A.M. She didn't want to have to talk, not to anyone. She just wanted to sink into unconsciousness, then awaken to discover that what had happened had been only a monstrous fantasy. But she couldn't sleep and had to lie, stiffly unmoving, for what felt like a very long time before Louise slipped into the adjoining bed and, with enviable ease, went quickly to sleep.

Faye did finally succumb to sleep, only to suffer through endless slow-motion reenactments of the attack, which revived the pain and left her body knotted with tension. In the morning Louise brought her a cup of tea, then sat cross-legged on her bed and reviewed the highlights of the party.

"Raffie only stayed about an hour," she wound down. "Gramma insisted he have something to eat, so he did. But it was easy to tell he wasn't having a good time, and he went home right after he ate. So, how d'you feel? Any better? You look sick."

"I feel sick," Faye admitted. "I don't think I'll be able to come to Gramma's for lunch. I'm going to stay in bed."

"It's funny I didn't get it, too," Louise said. "I mean, we ate the same thing. But I feel fine. Your tea's getting cold."

"Maybe you've got a stronger stomach," Faye said, and forced herself to take a sip of the tea. She thought the milk tasted slightly sour but didn't say anything.

"Maybe," Louise allowed, studying her sister's face. Faye really did look awful. The pockets under her eyes looked bruised; her skin was so pale Louise could see the blue veins in her temples. For the first time she was aware of her sister's delicacy; the translucency of her skin and the vulnerability of her size. Altogether, she looked very frail; her hands were so small and her wrists so thin. Looking at her own wrist, Louise felt

positively robust by comparison, especially since she'd finally grown another inch and a half and had gained nearly six pounds. "God, you're
puny," she said with fond protectiveness. "I feel like King Kong compared to you. I'm going to make you some toast."

"I couldn't eat it," Faye told her. "Don't bother."

"You sure? You really should try to eat something, even if it makes
you sick. It's bad for you to bring up on an empty stomach."

Faye was being very careful. She didn't want to give any hint that she
might be suffering from anything other than some sort of bug. But she
couldn't seem to remember how she usually behaved when she was sick.
Her brain felt sluggish, her thoughts syrupy, thick. "Okay," she said.
"Maybe you're right."

For the remainder of that morning she took her cues from Louise. It
amazed her how her sister was able to describe symptoms and even
emotions she believed Faye must have. Louise actually made it quite easy
for Faye to play ill. She brought toast and Faye ate one piece, the crumbs
like sawdust in her mouth, the butter leaving a faintly rancid slick on her
tongue. She tried, but failed, to wash it away with the slightly sour-tasting
tea. She locked herself into the bathroom and brushed her teeth vigor-
ously but couldn't get rid of the foul taste in her mouth, the nasty coating
on her tongue. She was convinced her breath was bad, even after gargling
twice with Listerine.

Stripping off her nightgown, she saw that there were bruises on her
thighs, on her belly, hips, and upper arms. She'd have to make sure no
one—especially not Raffie—saw them. One look and anyone would
know what she'd been dumb enough to let happen to her; they'd know
she was a fool, a pushover who'd got herself viciously attacked by her
boyfriend's kid brother. God! The shaking started up again. She stood
under the shower, scared she wouldn't be able to keep people from
finding out. They'd shake their heads scornfully at her pathetic gullibility.

When she came out of the bathroom Louise was on the phone with
Kath, engaged in a typical postmortem of the party.

"Rollie says Terry really liked you," Kath was saying. "Maybe he'll
ask you out."

"I doubt it," Louise said, watching Faye walk back to her bed. She was
moving like an old woman, all hunched over, her towel-dried hair
curtaining her face. "Listen, I'd better go. Faye's still sick and I shouldn't
stay on the phone."

"Okay. I've got to go start cramming, anyway," Kath said unhappily. "Boy, will I be glad when this year's over. I'm sick of Branksome and bitchy girls and kilts and clans and carol services and mother-daughter teas. The only decent thing this entire year was the father-daughter dance. Jerry was so darling. Okay. I'll talk to you later."

Louise put the receiver down, her eyes still on Faye, who was sitting now on the side of the bed with her hands folded in her lap.

"Maybe we should call a doctor," Louise suggested.

Faye's head shot up. "No! I don't need a doctor!"

"Okay. Don't take my head off. I'm only trying to help."

"I know." Faye softened her tone. "The bathroom's all yours."

"Want me to make you some more tea or something?"

"No, thanks." Robe and all, Faye lay down and pulled the blankets over her.

Louise crossed the room to touch the back of her hand to Faye's forehead. Startled, Faye jumped.

"Sorry. Didn't mean to scare you. You're not hot. That's good, at least."

"I'm going to try to sleep."

"Sure. I'll be really quiet." Louise crept away and went into the bathroom.

When Raffie called about ten minutes later, Faye said, "I'm not any better."

"Gee, that's rough," he said. "I'll come keep you company. Anything you want me to pick up on the way?"

"You'd better not. It might be catching. I mean, it could be flu or something and I'd hate to have you get sick with the finals coming up."

"You've got a point," he conceded a bit sadly. "Maybe I should call your grandmother and cancel."

"Don't do that, Raffie. She's counting on you. You know she likes having you there. Besides, I know she's got a lot of food. It'd be awful to waste it."

"I guess you're right. Look, I'll stop in for five minutes to see how you're doing. Okay?"

"Okay. See you later," she said listlessly, her eyes already starting to close. It was safe to sleep now, she told herself. Louise was home. The sun was shining. Nothing bad could happen. She plunged into a sleep that was finally free of horror. It took her down into a place that was bright and warm, a glowing, pillowy place where her body was cushioned by weightless clouds and there was no pain, no sound, just perfect rest. Eased, relieved, she burrowed deep into the feathery clouds and allowed them to comfort her.

They wouldn't leave her alone. First Louise fussed over her, then Gramma came down the hall to see for herself how Faye was and if there was anything she needed. After that, Raffie came. She didn't want to see anyone, didn't want to have to talk. All she wanted was to turn on her side and go back into that wonderful sleep. But she couldn't. People would become suspicious if she refused to see or talk to them. And it was so hard to talk, especially to Gramma. She had to fight not to cry, not to fling herself into her grandmother's arms and tell her about the abominable things Aldo had done to her, about the horrendous pain he'd caused her. She didn't dare say a word about any of it. She could just picture Gramma's disgust. Gramma would tell Uncle Bob. The two of them would whisper together, discussing the trouble their idiotic granddaughter had managed to get herself into. They'd tell her she should've known better than to put herself into such a dangerous position—alone in an empty building with three young men. They'd tell her it was unfortunate, but really she'd brought it on herself. She felt bad enough as it was, sick and diseased and utterly ashamed. She couldn't bear even the idea of what Gramma might say. There was right and there was wrong. Her unspeakable stupidity had put her squarely in the wrong. So she held brief, innocuous conversations with Louise, with Raffie, with her grandmother, and swallowed down her overwhelming indignation, her self-loathing, her hatred. She was afraid even physically to allow her lips to open for fear that words might start spewing out of their own accord. So she kept her jaws clamped shut, and felt the resulting ache in her head spread to become a fierce additional pain.

Finally, when she was alone again, she pulled the covers over her head, closed her eyes tightly, and willed herself back to that wonderfully soothing place. But instead she was transported to Aldo's cramped bedroom and the knife was in his hand. Abruptly, she threw herself off the bed and ran to sit on the sofa, her arms wound hard around her drawn-up knees.

After a time she tried to read but couldn't concentrate. Then she turned on the radio, but everything she heard was grating, raucous noise. She turned it off and walked several times back and forth the length of the apartment. It was only two-thirty. If she couldn't even get through one day, how was she going to get through the rest of her life? How was she going to live with the memory of what had happened?

She told herself she'd forget it. She'd put it out of her mind, pretend it never happened. But how, when her head throbbed, and she still hurt so terribly inside, when she was bruised all over? Get dressed! she told herself. Get dressed, then eat something. Go on as usual. She pulled on some old, comfortably worn jeans, a long-sleeved shirt, socks, and loafers. Then she put her hair up in a ponytail and went to open the curtains.

The flood of light scalded her eyes, but she blinked defiantly, directly into the sun-filled windows. Suddenly, she wished they had a TV set. It would have been so good to sit down and fill up the hours staring at the screen, watching one show after another, the way Ma did. She could understand, all at once, the appeal of television. It was something you could do that took your mind away, distanced it from things you didn't want to think about. Maybe after work tomorrow she'd check on the prices. She had almost seven hundred dollars saved. It was supposed to be for the down payment on a house for her and Raffie, but that was years away and right now she really needed a TV set. She had no idea what they cost, but maybe she could get a small one that wouldn't be too expensive.

She paced for a while longer, thinking that what she wanted most, next to a TV set, was a cigarette and some coffee. Grabbing her purse and keys she let herself out, glanced furtively down the hall, then ran to the fire stairs, unwilling to risk waiting for the elevator.

She walked several blocks to a coffee shop and bought a pack of Rothman's and a regular coffee to go, then she returned home, rode the elevator upstairs, again checked that the hallway was clear, and dashed back into the apartment. With a sense of ceremony, she removed the lid from the coffee container, got a cigarette lit, and settled on the sofa to sip the coffee between puffs of the dizzying tobacco. By the time she'd finished, she actually did feel sick. Pushing off her shoes, she crawled back into bed, tentatively closed her eyes, and willed herself down to that comforting place. She felt herself sliding gratifyingly into the beckoning billowy depths and surrendered, very glad to go.

✦

Like Raffie, Louise was studying hard for her grade twelve finals. It meant that she was home every night, so Faye had no time to herself. And it would've been pointless buying a television set when watching it would only have disturbed her sister. But she found the long quiet hours unbearable.

After a week of sitting in silence and trying to suppress the horror of her thoughts, she interrupted Louise at her studies to say, "I'm going to the show. I'll be back in a couple of hours."

Preoccupied, Louise looked up from her French vocabulary to say, "Oh. Okay. Have fun."

Faye walked down to Bloor Street, headed west, and found herself with a choice of three movies—at the Alhambra, the Bloor, or the Midtown. She chose the Alhambra, which had *Some Like It Hot*. She sat through *News of the World,* a cartoon, three previews, and one hundred and twenty-one minutes of a delightful film, worlds removed from the horrible reality of her life. By the time she got home she was sufficiently relaxed to be able to sleep. And she had no nightmares. So, two nights later she went again, this time to see *Anatomy of a Murder,* and again she was able to sleep relatively well. In the weeks that followed, she saw *North by Northwest, Ben-Hur, The Diary of Anne Frank,* an English comedy called *I'm All Right, Jack;* a profoundly moving French film, *The Four Hundred Blows;* and two more French films she didn't entirely understand but that were reasonably engrossing, *Hiroshima, Mon Amour,* and *Breathless.* She saw the full-length cartoon *Sleeping Beauty,* which she liked so much she sat through it twice. She also saw *A Night to Remember, The Horse Soldiers, Separate Tables, The Young Lions,* and *The Defiant Ones.*

As a result of her seeing so many movies, her dreams began to be populated with characters she'd seen on the screen: a blond Marlon Brando in his uniform talked with escaping prisoner Sidney Poitier. Jean Seberg became Louise, Deborah Kerr was Gramma, Kenneth More was Uncle Bob, James Stewart was Mr. Nolan, Peter Sellers was Mr. DiStasio, Lee Remick turned into Kath. Everything became intriguingly confused in the nightly dream-scenes of her sleeping hours. People she'd always known looked and sounded different, yet were otherwise the same. Even in waking, every person she encountered, including herself, seemed to have evolved into an actor playing out some role—although she couldn't seem to decide who was playing the part of Faye Parker.

At the office, Sue definitely qualified as an actress, with her short severe haircut and man-tailored shirts, her spike-heeled shoes accentuating her long shapely legs. Ned Haley, the boss, had to be performing, with his booming laugh, his perpetual rushing here, there, and everywhere, and his primary-colored bow ties and matching handkerchiefs. The other secretaries, the copywriters, the designers and illustrators, even Nellie, the file clerk, were all playing out assigned parts. Faye became increasingly intrigued by Nellie, a very pretty girl only a few months older than she, who always wore long-sleeved clothes because, she confided one afternoon over lunch, her boyfriend liked to have her demonstrate her love for him by allowing him to put out his cigarettes in the bends of her arms. This girl had to be acting, Faye reasoned. Otherwise why would she allow herself to be tortured for the sake of love? She was so innocent somehow, and so pretty, with long black hair and wide blue eyes, freckles on the bridge of her nose; she was Millie Perkins, suffering stoically in *The Diary of Anne Frank.*

Faye looked at the crusted, overlapping circular burns on the girl's arms, saw the crinkly scar tissue of old injuries surrounded by the angry inflammation of new ones, and had to ask softly, "How can you let him *do* that to you, Nellie?"

Nellie appeared momentarily confused, as if no one had ever questioned her motives. "It's 'cause he loves me," she said. "It proves it. If we didn't love each other, he wouldn't do it and I wouldn't let him."

"But it has to hurt," Faye argued.

Nellie gave a half shrug. "You get used to it. I hardly even feel it now when he does it. But," she admitted, "they are kind of sore."

After lunch Faye stopped off at the drugstore to buy a tube of ointment and some gauze. When she gave these things to Nellie, the girl looked at her in amazement. "How come you did this?"

"They're infected," Faye said quietly. "They need looking after."

"Wait a sec and I'll pay you back," Nellie said, prepared to get her purse.

Faye shook her head. "Pay me back by not letting him burn you anymore."

"It's none of your business," the girl said, more surprised than offended.

"I know. But I don't like to see anybody getting hurt."

Thrown by this kindness, Nellie asked, "How d'you prove to *your* boyfriend that you love him then, eh?"

Her throat going tight, Faye said, "By being nice. He'd never *want* to hurt me. I've got to get back to work." She turned to go to her desk.

"Thanks, Faye," Nellie said, awed. "I'll go put some of this on right now."

"Good," Faye said, and walked across the office wondering what kind of monster Nellie's boyfriend was. Maybe he was like one of the motorcycle gang members in *The Wild One,* vicious and crazy. Like Aldo . . . She shuddered and grabbed for her earphones, sliding one of the red belts into the Dictaphone. She *wouldn't* think about it. It had never happened. It was a movie she'd seen, just something awful she'd seen one night at the show.

⥊

Raffie telephoned almost every evening and they spoke briefly before he went back to his books and she went off to see another movie. Sunday afternoons Raffie came to lunch. He apologized constantly for not being able to see her more often. And she said, over and over, "I understand, Raffie. You don't have to keep apologizing."

In fact, she was relieved not to have to see him. If she didn't see him she didn't have to kiss him or hold his hand. She didn't have to touch him, and she was glad. When they were together, each time he moved to embrace or kiss her she had to stifle the repugnance she felt, to endure it while pretending she didn't mind the feeling she had of being suffocated by his enclosing arms and powerful body, the nausea that swept through her when his mouth closed over hers. Without fail when he kissed her she thought of squirming earthworms, of writhing snakes, of vile slithering creatures pushing their way into her mouth. She was nearly sick with relief each time the doors closed and the elevator bore him away.

Four weeks after that frightful Saturday night, she saw Raffie off at the elevator following a particularly long lunch at Gramma's, and was suddenly gripped by an abdominal spasm. Flying back to her own place, she ran into the bathroom and heaved into the toilet. When the spasm ended, she drank some water and, feeling shaky, went into the living room to sit down, convinced she'd picked up a virus after all. She decided she'd tell everyone it was a recurrence of last month's sickness, and felt grimly satisfied with this turn of events. Not only would it validate her spending so much time in bed when she wasn't off at the movies, it would also allow her to go on keeping Raffie at a distance. She needed more time to get back to herself, and this bout of flu or whatever it was would provide that. She telephoned down the hall to explain she'd been taken sick again and to say she was going to bed.

The next morning, however, she felt perfectly well and saw no reason to take any time off work. It was her turn, and she made the tea and toast while Louise was in the bathroom, then ate with her sister before they rode downstairs together in the elevator.

"It couldn't have been food poisoning again," Louise said, eyes on the floor indicator, "or you'd still be sick."

"I don't know what it was," Faye admitted. "I'm just glad it's over."

But it wasn't. That afternoon, another wave of nausea overcame her and she had to run across the hall to the ladies' room to be sick. As she was drinking water at the sink from her cupped hands, Nellie emerged from the second stall, saying, "Oh, it's you. Sounds like you're sick as a dog."

"I've caught some kind of bug, I think."

"Say," Nellie said with a sudden smile, "that stuff you gave me helped a lot. My burns are way better." She rolled up her sleeves to show Faye the healing wounds. There didn't appear to be any new ones.

"That's great," Faye said, managing a thin smile. Her throat and stomach ached from retching.

"I told him he couldn't burn me no more," Nellie said proudly.

"Good for you, Nellie."

"Yeah." The girl's smile collapsed. Eyes flicking to the door and back, she whispered, "He said if he couldn't burn me, would I let him do it to me in the bum."

Horrified, Faye gazed at her round-eyed. "Did you let him?"

"I'm no pervert," Nellie declared. "I told him no. So he pinched me, hard, right here." She put one nail-bitten hand to her breast. "And when I cried 'cause it hurt, he said he didn't want to go with me no more. I said, fine. So that's that."

"He sounds *awful*," Faye said sympathetically.

"Yeah," Nellie agreed rather wistfully. "I don't care. There's lots of other guys." She looked closely at Faye for a moment, then said, "You're all green around the mouth. You know that?"

Faye turned to look at herself in the mirror.

"That's how my sister Gert looks every time she gets in the family way. You in the family way?"

Faye automatically shook her head, but she was suddenly frantically tracking backward, counting weeks. Her period was overdue. Almost two weeks. It couldn't be! she thought, starting to sweat. To mask her sudden horror, she turned back to Nellie, asking, "Your sister has a lot of children?"

Nellie laughed. "Nah. Gets herself knocked up all the time. But she don't have no kids, says she's not ready to settle down. Gert's twenty," she said, as if that explained everything.

"So what does she do?" Faye asked faintly.

Disposing of her fistful of paper towels, Nellie said blithely, "She gets rid of them. I keep telling her she oughta use rubbers, but she says it don't feel as good with a rubber. I don't know about that. It never bothered me none. See ya later, Faye."

That evening Faye couldn't concentrate on the movie. She sat through the entire program counting and recounting, telling herself it simply couldn't be, but unable to accept this particular bit of self-deception. Aldo had made her pregnant. All the evidence pointed to that. But in case she was wrong, praying she was wrong, she decided to wait two more weeks. Then, if she still didn't get her period, she'd have to do something drastic.

She was pregnant. There could be no doubt. And her dreams turned back to nightmares that roused her several times a night. While Louise slept, she'd pace barefoot, smoking a cigarette, trying to think what to do. She couldn't tell anyone. If she did, they'd demand to know why she hadn't told about Aldo right away instead of waiting a month and a half. No one would believe her. She couldn't keep any food down and could feel herself shrinking, her skirts beginning to hang from her jutting hipbones. She couldn't stand the thought of seeing Raffie. She was certain he'd take one look at her and guess the truth. She had no alternative but to find some way to get rid of the baby. If she didn't, she might as well die. Her life would be over anyway. The moment she started to show, Sue would fire her, so she'd have no money to live on. And even though she'd read stories about girls going away to have their babies, then coming back and getting on with their lives as if nothing had happened, it cost a lot to do something like that. And how would she explain it? Where would she go?

There was only one person she knew who could conceivably help her: Nellie. It was risky. She hadn't known the girl long enough or well enough to know if she could keep a secret. But she had no choice. She

invited Nellie to come out to lunch with her, and once their orders had
been taken, she leaned across the table to say, "I need your help, Nellie."

"Oh, yeah?" Nellie looked flattered by the notion. "How
come?"

"You know you were talking a few days back about your sister?"

"Gert?"

"That's right."

"What about her?"

"You know, you were saying how she keeps getting pregnant then gets
rid of the babies?"

"Uh-huh."

"Well," Faye said, "she must know someone. I mean, there must be
someplace she goes, you know, to get it done."

"Ooooh!" Nellie said slowly. "So you *are* in the family way. I *thought*
so."

Her face turning very hot, Faye kept her eyes on Nellie's. "I've *got* to
get rid of it. Could you find out who your sister goes to and how much it
costs?"

"Oh, sure," Nellie said readily. "I'll ask her tonight, let you know
tomorrow."

"Thank you," Faye said fervently. "You'll never know how much it
means to me."

Nellie laughed. "I know for sure how much it means to Gert, eh?
She'd have about five kids by now, otherwise. I'll let you know first thing.
Unless you want me to phone you at home later."

"No, no," Faye said quickly. "Tomorrow'll be fine. I really appreciate
it, Nellie."

"Oh, that's okay. You were real nice, getting me that burn cream and
telling me I shouldn't let Rick do that to me with his cigarettes. Nobody
ever talked to me the way you do, Faye. I'll find out for you for sure. And
don't worry, I won't tell nobody. You can trust me. I know how to keep
a secret."

"Thank you," Faye said again. "I'm very grateful."

Faye was so distracted that evening she couldn't sit still, and she'd
already seen every movie in town. But finally she knew she had to get out,
even if it was just for a walk. She'd be so glad when Lou was finally
finished with exams and she could have the apartment to herself now and
then.

"I'm going out for some air," she told Louise. "You want anything from the store while I'm out?"

"Uh-uh, no thanks," Louise answered, winding one strand of hair around her finger as she gazed at the wall whispering Latin declensions. "Will you help me with this when you get back?" She swiveled around to look at Faye.

"Sure, okay," Faye said, agitated and anxious to get out of doors. "I'll be back in an hour or so."

Louise gave her a slow smile. "I'll bet you'll be glad when exams are over and you can see Raff again."

Faye's first instinct was to say she didn't care if she never saw him or any other boy ever again. The thought of having Raffie touch her made her cringe. But she returned her sister's smile and said, "I sure will. Get back to work now. I'll see you in a little while."

"Lack of nooky," Louise teased. "You're acting just like Liz in *Cat on a Hot Tin Roof.*"

"Right. Exactly." Faye forced a laugh and escaped. Rage was simmering in her blood, heating her body and making her sweat. She wanted to go wait near the store on College Street and stab Aldo through the heart when he came out the door. But soon now she'd be rid of the evidence of what he'd done to her. Then she'd be able to start her life all over again.

CHAPTER
THIRTY-FOUR

THE "REPAIR" WOULD COST THREE HUNDRED DOLLARS, Faye was told. The woman she spoke to wanted to know when Faye wished to "have the work done."

"Friday," Faye answered, having already determined that Louise would be out for the evening with Kath, now that exams were over and school had ended for another year.

"Six-thirty," the gravel-voiced woman said. "Please bring cash."

Faye made a note of the address and hung up, her palms wet. This was all so furtive and bewildering. What she planned to do was illegal, so she understood there was a real need for secrecy. But it merely heightened her confusion and anxiety. If she got caught, she could be arrested, even sent to jail—all for something that wasn't really her fault.

It was Wednesday. Two days from now the nightmare would finally be over. She and Raffie were going out Saturday night to celebrate his graduation. All she had to do was get through the intervening hours. There was plenty of dictation to transcribe, as well as a rush presentation to type for Sue, but it was very difficult for Faye to focus. Like an unruly puppy straining against its leash, her mind wanted to go over there, to look at the possibilities beyond the immediate present. Would it hurt? How was it done? How long would it take? She had a brand new fear to contemplate and it howled for her attention. She had to fight it off, urging her eyes back to the letter she was typing, the words funneling into her ears through the headset and bouncing around inside her skull like exploding firecrackers. It wouldn't hurt. Would it? God, she was so scared! Why was this happening to her? One horrible thing after another. She longed to have her former quiet life back, to be able to stop pretending nothing was wrong. It was so exhausting, playing out the role of Faye Parker for the benefit of her family and coworkers. She wanted simply to *be* Faye Parker. But she might never be able to go back to being that girl. Maybe Aldo had killed that Faye Parker, and for the rest of her life she'd be performing the role from an ever-fading memory of what she'd been like, that unsullied girl, that innocent idiot. How was she going to make it through to Friday? It was taking forever, as she watched, for the hand on the wall clock to tick forward from one second to the next.

"We're going to go to George's Spaghetti House," Kath said. "It'll be great. They've got *live jazz.*"

"How come if Terry wanted to see me again he didn't call me, instead of telling Rollie?"

"Maybe he's shy, Lou. I don't know. What difference does it make?"

"It does, that's all." Louise couldn't articulate her feeling that it wasn't really a date unless the boy took the trouble to phone and make the arrangements himself. He hadn't, and her potential pleasure in the evening was considerably reduced. "Never mind," she said, giving in. "What time should I be there?"

"Get here by six. That way we'll have some time before the guys arrive. What're you wearing?"

"What're *you* wearing?"

"That depends on what *you're* wearing. I'm not going to get all dressed up if you're not."

"I wasn't planning to get *all* dressed up. Just a skirt and sweater."

"Heels?"

"Are you?"

"Only if you are," Kath said.

"Jeez, Kath! This is ridiculous. I'm wearing flats. Okay? You wear whatever you want. I'll see you at six."

After the call Louise was annoyed with herself for being so peevish with her best friend. It was because she was lonely in advance of Kath's going off to university in British Columbia at the end of August. It meant they wouldn't see each other again, and never mind what Kath said about getting together on school breaks and during the summer. They wouldn't, in fact, see one another much at all after tonight, with Louise working for Uncle Bob again and Kath going off with her Mom and Mr. Nolan to Ireland. It would be his first trip home since childhood.

She felt unusually blue. Faye had been going to movies nonstop, the way Ma used to watch TV. And she'd started smoking, maybe four or five a day tops, but it seemed somehow out of character. She'd be glad when Raffie was back on the scene. The two of them had a big night planned tomorrow, and Louise was happy her sister would be getting back into a more normal routine. If she had her way, things would simply stay the same, but of course that was stupid, childish. They were seventeen and eighteen years old now, adults to all intents and purposes. Things changed. The problem was they seemed to be changing for everyone but her. She never got asked out on dates, and she still daydreamed about Daniel Craven. He seemed to have taken up a permanent place in the part of her that dreamed. She saw him occasionally in the hallways and once in a while they ran into each other at Kresge's for lunch. He'd ask how she was getting along; they'd discuss movies they'd both seen; he'd talk about taking his class to Stratford to see *Othello*. Some mornings she'd see him drive through the gates at the rear of the school to park his Triumph next to the Chevrolets and Buicks and Oldsmobiles belonging to the other teachers—a little blue bullet sitting next to those staid sedans. And some afternoons she'd pass by the *Review* office and see him at work on the yearbook with half a dozen kids. Dark, elegant, he perched on the edge of a desk, one foot planted firmly on the floor, the other gracefully dangling. Each time, the sight of him gave her something of a small heart seizure, and she hurried on her way, wondering when, if ever, she was going to get a boyfriend and stop lollygagging over a teacher like some dreary grade niner. It would've been great, she thought, to have someone who adored her, the way Raffie did Faye. After all, she was finally beginning to look her age. She'd actually passed the five foot three mark, and her chest, while not as perfect as Gramma's or Faye's, was at least an honest-to-God chest. So how come nobody but Lefty ever phoned to ask her out?

Friday, midmorning, Sue paused at Faye's desk to ask, "You all right?"

"Oh, I'm fine." Faye dredged up a smile. "Why?"

"You seem a little edgy lately, that's all."

"No, I'm fine," Faye repeated, wondering if she was actually behaving differently. She'd have to keep a closer watch on herself. Sue was very aware of everything that went on in the office. Her sharp-pointed nose seemed to pick up the faintest scent of trouble.

"How about lunch today?" the woman asked somewhat brusquely, as was her style.

"I'd love to, but I said I'd go with Nellie. We could do it Monday, though, if you like."

Sue looked around the office, then bent close to Faye to whisper, "You've been very sweet to that girl," she said, "especially under the circumstances."

"What circumstances?"

"Didn't she tell you?" Sue looked taken aback. "Today's her last day. I had to give her notice. She's a nice kid, but too slow, makes too many mistakes. It was starting to drive Ned wild. Every time he went to look for something it was filed incorrectly."

"That's too bad," Faye said. "Thanks for telling me. Maybe I'll get her a card or something."

Sue straightened and gave Faye a pat on the shoulder. "I'm going to buy her a small gift at lunchtime. All the girls are chipping in."

"Okay. I will, too."

"Two dollars," Sue said, moving off. "Give it to me later."

Nellie had been fired and hadn't said a word. Faye felt sorry for her but glad in a way that she was going. Nellie was the only one who knew her secret. With Nellie gone there was no chance of anyone else finding out.

At lunch, Nellie asked, "D'you call those people?"

Faye nodded, the bite of salmon salad sandwich lodging in her throat.

"When're you gonna do it?" Nellie asked.

Faye swallowed, then drank some coffee to wash the food down. It was a pointless exercise, eating. She'd probably bring it all up in an hour. "Tonight, after work," she answered, gripped by renewed fear.

"I'll come with you if you want," Nellie offered. "I've gone twice with Gert."

Faye was touched, but said, "No, that's okay. I just want to get it done and forget it."

"Yeah," Nellie said. "That's how I'd be, too."

"Why didn't you tell me today's your last day?"

Nellie gave one of her half shrugs. "I don't know," she said, gazing off into space. "Embarrassed, I guess."

"But why?"

Nellie returned her eyes to Faye. "I know I'm not very smart," she said without a trace of self-pity. "You're younger than me and you're one of the *secretaries,* but I can't even do filing right. I didn't want you feeling sorry for me or anything. I've got another job," she said with energy. "On the reception desk for a company downtown. It pays more too."

"Well, that's good. I'll miss you."

"You've been real nice to me, Faye. Nicer than any of them. You sure you don't want me to come with you tonight? You might feel sort of wobbly after it's over."

"Wobbly?" This was the first hint she'd had of possible aftereffects.

"Gert was," Nellie said. "And there's a lot of bleeding, so you better get some extra pads."

"I will," Faye said soberly. "What else?"

"That's about it. Gert says it's like a heavy period with some cramps."

"Oh! That doesn't sound too bad."

"It's a snap," Nellie said. "Don't worry about a thing. Maybe we'll meet up for lunch sometime."

"Sure," Faye said, thinking she'd miss Nellie. There was something so very childlike about her, so very needy. She put a hand over Nellie's, saying, "We'll definitely do that. We'll keep in touch." They never would, though. Faye doubted they'd ever get together or even see each other again after today.

✦

It looked like a regular doctor's office, Faye thought. And the gravelly voice belonged to a pleasant-looking woman in her forties who wore a white uniform and sat behind a desk. There were no other patients in the small waiting room. Faye handed over an envelope containing six fifty-dollar bills and the woman slipped it into a drawer, locked it, then said, "Have a seat. Be with you in a minute." She got up and went through a door behind the desk.

Faye sat down, her eyes on the door, her hands wet and her heart skipping fast, an insistent tattoo in her chest. She was reassured by the office, even by the magazines on the table. It looked and felt like a regular doctor's office, right down to the nameplate on the outside door: Dr. Henry Harris, Ob-Gyn. There was a real doctor practicing here, someone who knew what he was doing.

The nurse returned after about five minutes and beckoned to Faye, who followed her into an examining room that looked like every other such room Faye had ever seen. Except that at the end of the examining table were metal stirrups, and what looked like straps dangled from padded boards. A stainless steel tray of instruments sat on a small table to one side.

"Take off everything from the waist down and put this on," the woman said, handing her a white cotton hospital gown that tied in the back. "If you have to use the toilet, it's through that door. We'll be with you in a minute."

There was no "we," Faye discovered. There was only the woman with her white uniform over which she'd pulled on a blousy white smock. She covered her hair with some kind of cloth cap, tied a surgical mask over her face, and instructed Faye to lie down on the table. In a few practiced moves, she lifted Faye's feet into the stirrups and secured her knees to the padded boards.

"Try to relax." The gravelly voice sounded disembodied now. "What's your first name?"

"Faye. Are you a doctor?" she asked fearfully.

"Nurse," the woman replied curtly.

Faye gazed at the acoustic-tiled ceiling, mortified as the woman adjusted a light aimed directly between Faye's wide-spread legs.

"If you relax, it won't be especially painful." The woman pressed one hand flat into Faye's belly, saying, *"Relax!"* Then she seated herself on a stool and reached for one of the instruments on the tray.

"Hmmmn," the woman murmured. "Find sex painful, do you, Faye?"

"Why do you say that?"

"You've got a very short vagina. Straightforward sex means your cervix takes a pounding. It can't feel good. Hmmmn," she said again. "Recent scarring." She looked up at Faye, her eyes wide and unblinking above the mask. Faye looked back at her, trying not to cry. Mercifully, the woman didn't say anything but merely blinked slowly, knowingly. She again pressed her hand into Faye's belly, saying, "Try to let these muscles go. I know you're scared, but try."

At the first inner probing, Faye's body jerked involuntarily, and there was a sudden, fiercely biting pain. *"Damn!"* the woman exclaimed. "Stay *still,* Faye! Damn, damn! *Don't* make another move, no matter what!"

Faye bit down hard on her lower lip and gazed at the ceiling, tears leaking down the sides of her face as sharp metal objects expanded inside her, as they poked and scraped at her, on and on. The pain was white hot, hungry, eating upward and sideways, spreading through her body.

Finally, the instruments clattered on the metal tray and the woman said, "That's it. All done," and stripped off the rubber gloves, dropping them into a basin. She released Faye's knees from the padded boards, lifted her feet from the stirrups. "Rest for a couple of minutes, then get dressed. I'll leave a pad here for you. When you're ready, come out." Pulling off her mask and gown, and mopping her face with the gown, the woman left the room.

Faye slowly unbent her legs and lay still for several minutes, a red sun searing inside her lower belly. Then she sat up cautiously and slipped off the table, the linoleum floor a cold shock to her bare feet. Turning her back on the table and the equipment, very shaky, she positioned the pad between her legs and got dressed. All she wanted was to get her molten body out of there, to go home and go to sleep. It was over now. She'd sleep, and when she awakened, she'd begin the journey back to herself.

"You'll have a heavy flow for a few days," the woman told her. "It's perfectly normal. Don't worry about it. But if there's any problem, go to the emergency room of the nearest hospital. *Don't* come back here! Understand that?"

Faye nodded.

"They'll take care of you, because the job's already been done and they can't be held responsible. Under no circumstances do you call or come back here unless you find yourself pregnant again. Got that?"

Again Faye nodded.

"Okay. There's a cab waiting out front. Have you got money for the fare?"

"Yes."

"Good. One more thing, Faye. From now on, use a condom, or get yourself a diaphragm. And try some different positions with your boyfriend. Going at it missionary fashion's only going to be painful. You'll find reversing positions, with you on top, makes all the difference. Unless," she said, "it was the boyfriend who raped you."

Faye gasped out, "No," and shook her head.

"Then report the son of a bitch who did. That scarring's serious. Whoever it was, he did damage. It could mean problems later on when you want children. If it was me, I'd make a visit to the police station. Any doctor worth his salt'll verify the damage. But of course it's up to you. And you're probably too ashamed even to admit it happened. Think about it. Now, go on home and take it easy for a few days. And remember, if anything goes wrong, *don't* contact me. It's after the fact now, and the medical society will be more than happy to take care of you."

Confused, in pain, Faye thanked the woman and made her way out of the building to the waiting taxi.

⨤

During the cab ride home she thought about that French film *The Four Hundred Blows*. She thought about the very young hero and how he and his friend shook hands each time they parted. In particular, she thought of the scene when he was arrested and gazed out through the rear window of the police van at the nighttime Paris streets. She'd cried seeing the film, and she cried now remembering it, recalling the resignation and sadness in the boy's eyes. He'd been so young and so lost, so uncared-for. Consigned to sleep in what amounted to a closet by his mother, whose only emotion for him seemed to be impatience. A pretty blond mother who strongly reminded Faye of Ma. And a sweet, mischievous boy, riding in the back of a police van.

By the time she got home the pad was soaked through. And while she was changing it, blood streamed down her legs. Was this what was meant by a heavy flow? Wearily, she got out of her clothes and into a nightgown. Not five minutes and she could feel the blood oozing past the sides of the pad. She returned to the bathroom. Bright red blood splattered on the tiled floor as she reached for a second pad to go beneath the one she already had on. She pulled on a pair of underpants to hold them in place. She cleaned the floor with a handful of wet tissues, and flushed the tissues down the toilet.

The heat blazed away at her core, while the rest of her body was cold, her feet almost numb with it. She closed the windows, got a sweater, and moved to sit on the sofa, but stopped. Afraid of soiling the upholstery, she brought a towel from the bathroom, spread it over the sofa cushion, then sat down gingerly, with a tired sigh.

A few days of bleeding, then she'd gather up the threads of her life, find the pattern again, begin working the threads back into a whole. Raffie would be starting university in the autumn. All their dreams would come true. They'd marry in four years, and two years after that they'd start their family. *Any doctor worth his salt'll verify the damage.* Did that mean she wouldn't be able to have babies? Did it mean any doctor would be able to take one look at her and know what Aldo had done? If she was scarred, that meant this would never end. No, no. Scars faded, went away. No one would ever know.

She was so sleepy her eyes wanted to close. And cold. The bottom of her nightgown felt sticky. The blood couldn't have gone through two pads already. She stood up to look. It had. The towel was stained, too. Quickly she snatched it up. It hadn't penetrated to the upholstery. She plodded into the bathroom, put the towel and the nightgown in the sink and started the cold water running. A fresh nightgown, two fresh pads. The small wastebasket was full. She removed the bag, set it by the front door, and got a fresh bag from the kitchen before pulling on her robe and darting across to the garbage chute. Back inside, she locked the door, wrung out the towel and nightgown, and hung them from the shower curtain rod to dry.

Dizzy, she covered the sofa cushion with a clean towel and sat down again, letting her head rest on the arm. She was so cold she was shivering, and curled into herself, too sleepy to go for a blanket. Her eyes closing, she went back to the movie, to the boy running away from the reform school. Running and running until he arrived at the seashore. And he kept going right to the water's edge. Then he stopped, turned, gazed into the camera, and the picture froze. Did it mean he died? Or did it mean he couldn't go any further?

She rewound the film, then ran alongside him. They ran and ran, along the country roads. Together, running. Ahead was the beach, and she reached out to take his hand—slightly pudgy, a little boy's hand with dirty fingernails. She could smell the dead seaweed, the cold salty wind; she could feel the give of the hard-packed sand under her feet. They ran right to the water's edge. But this time they didn't stop, didn't turn back to look into the camera's eye; the picture didn't freeze. They raced together into the stinging surf, the water warm after the initial shock. The bottom sloped away but their feet held, and they ran down, down, following the line of the earth beneath the water. She was crying, but the wonderful thing about being underwater was that nobody would ever know.

Louise couldn't believe it. Right in the middle of dinner her period started. She didn't have anything with her, and there wasn't a sanitary napkin dispenser in the ladies' room. She pushed a thick wad of toilet paper into the crotch of her underpants and returned to the table where Kath was, miraculously, sitting alone.

"Where're the guys?" Louise asked.

"Went to the john."

"Listen, Kath, I've got to stop by my place for a minute when we leave."

"Why?"

"Period, and I don't have anything with me."

"Oh, okay. Sure. Good thing Rollie's got the car."

"Thanks a lot," Louise said gratefully. "It won't take five minutes. Then we can go on to that party. Who's giving it anyway?"

"Beats me. There are parties all over town tonight. This is some girl from Forest Hill. *Big* place on Russell Hill Road. Ought to be quite a bash."

"You mean we're crashing?"

"Nope. Rollie was invited. We'll see how it is. If we don't like it, we'll head somewhere else."

"I'm really not dressed for a party," Louise said doubtfully.

"Who is? Don't worry about it. Hey, Roll," Kath grinned as the boys returned to the table. "Louise has to stop home for a couple of minutes on the way. Okay?"

"Sure, no problem."

"Great. Thanks a lot. I forgot something," Louise explained.

"No problem," Rollie repeated.

Rollie parked at the top of the circular driveway out front and Louise slipped out of the car saying, "Five minutes tops."

"Take your time," Rollie said good-naturedly.

"Want me to come with you?" Kath offered.

"Sure, if you want."

Kath got out, bent down to say something to Rollie, then followed Louise inside.

"I hate it when this happens," Louise said in the elevator. "I'll be glad when I can start using Tampax."

"Why can't you use them now?"

"You can't if you're a virgin, can you?"

Kath laughed loudly. "Whoever told you that? I've been using them from day one. My mom showed me how."

"You're joking! You mean I could've been using them all this time?"

"Sure. Next time you're over, I'll show you how. It's a cinch."

"For Pete's sake," Louise said, annoyed. "If that doesn't beat all."

"Where'd you ever *get* such an idea?"

"I don't know. From the instructions, I guess."

Louise unlocked the door and made a dash for the bathroom, saying, "Grab a seat. I won't be two minutes."

Kath went into the living room and stopped at the sight of Faye. She stood, very aware of the sound of her own breathing, then turned and ran to knock on the bathroom door. "Louise! You better come out here. Something's wrong with your sister."

"What?" Louise flushed the toilet, then moved to the sink to wash her hands.

Kath knocked harder on the door, saying, "I *mean* it! Come out!"

Thinking it was a joke, Louise opened the door and followed a wildly beckoning Kath to the living room where Faye, her face bleached of color, lay slumped against the arm of the sofa. Kath backed away, grinding her hands together, as Louise touched her sister's arm, saying, "Faye? Faye?"

Faye didn't move. Her breathing was very faint, her hands icy.

"What's the matter?" Louise said, very frightened. "What's the matter with her?" She looked over at Kath.

"I don't know! You'd better call an ambulance."

"Oh God!" Louise whispered, patting Faye's cheek, saying her name again. "She's so cold."

Kath ran and grabbed a blanket from one of the beds, came back and pushed it at Louise, saying, "Call an ambulance, Louise! Something's really wrong with her!"

Louise ran to the phone. Kath tucked the blanket around Faye, then backed away several steps. "I'm going to see if your grandmother's home," she said, and flew down the hall to pound on the door. No one came. She raced back. Louise was talking urgently into the telephone, giving her address, saying, "Hurry, hurry!"

Wetting her lips, feeling horribly helpless, Kath stood watching, and suddenly remembered the boys sitting in the car downstairs. "I'd better go tell Rollie to go on without us."

"Go with them!" Louise said.

"I'm not *leaving* you! Are you crazy?"

"I want you to go with them!" Louise insisted. "Please, *go* with them! I'll talk to you later, when everything's all right."

"Lou, I'll stay. You can't do this alone."

Louise was kneeling on the floor, rubbing Faye's hand, trying to warm it. "Just go, Kath! I've got to take care of Faye now. I can't . . . Go! Okay?"

In tears, Kath started for the door. "Promise you'll call me, let me know how she is!"

Louise didn't seem to hear. She was massaging her sister's hand and whispering to her.

"Promise you'll call me!" Kath repeated, more afraid than she'd ever been in her life. Something terrible was happening, and she was being sent away like a child. Yet she had no choice but to go. Wiping her eyes on her sleeve, she pressed the elevator call button, then turned back to stare at the closed apartment door. "God!" she said softly. "Please let everything be all right."

CHAPTER
THIRTY-FIVE

LOUISE DIDN'T SEE THE BLOOD UNTIL THE AMBULANCE AT-tendants lifted Faye off the sofa. Then the sight of it froze her in place. Everything was all at once a hundred, a thousand times more serious. So transfixed was she that one of the attendants had to touch her on the arm to get her attention, gently saying, "Lock the place up and come with your sister."

Louise turned, saw them already pushing the stretcher out through the door, and shot into action. Snatching up her bag and keys, she raced after them and stood gazing down at Faye's too-white features, urging everything to hurry: the elevator, the attendants, time. They had to save her sister, somehow put back all that blood.

In the ambulance she watched the attendants positioning an oxygen mask on Faye's face, taking her blood pressure, her pulse, murmuring to each other. Louise felt small, invisible, particularly when they arrived at the hospital and people came on the run to wheel Faye away. A swirl and flurry of white, voices snapping orders, the stretcher propelled down the corridor by urgent hands. She knew she couldn't follow. The double doors swung closed. NO ADMITTANCE. She looked through the round port-hole-like windows and saw one nurse using scissors to cut away Faye's nightgown and sweater while another fed a needle into a vein on the back of Faye's hand. Then people closed in, blocking Louise's view, and she backed away, turning to take in the empty corridor, the waiting area opposite the nurses' station, an elderly man smoking a cigarette.

Louise went to the station, got the attention of the nurse, and asked, "What do I do now?" She felt like a five-year-old, helpless and terrorized by the circumstances, by the sterile surroundings.

The nurse looked up. "We'll fill out this form," she said, studying Louise's face, then offering a smile of sympathy and encouragement. "We need some information on—your sister, is it?"

"That's right." Louise's voice sounded rusted, squeaky, like some mechanical toy that had been left out in the rain.

"It'll only take a couple of minutes. Then you can sit over there and wait. There's a coffee machine around the corner. Okay?"

Louise nodded, and began to supply answers as best she was able to the many questions. It was hard to pay attention. She kept wanting to go back down the hall, to look again through the round windows. She had the arbitrary idea that if she remained close by Faye would be all right. Her body of its own accord turned toward the double doors. Still, she reasoned, by the time all the questions were answered Faye might be ready to go home. So she listened and responded. Initially, the questions were simple. Age, place of birth, address, childhood illnesses, and so forth. Then they became complicated.

She couldn't say what her sister's symptoms were. All she could tell about was the blood. And she couldn't bring herself to say more than, "She was bleeding. But I didn't know that until they lifted her . . ." Her eyes drifted away; she saw again the saturated towel on the sofa, and shuddered.

"We'll skip that part," the nurse said, drawing Louise's eyes back to her. "Next of kin?"

"I am. Put down sister."

"What about your parents?"

"We don't have parents," Louise said, stricken by a sudden immense bitterness toward Ma. A mother was someone who took the trouble to find out how her children were; she stayed in touch, she visited; she cooked special food when her children were ill. The only mother they'd had as little kids was Blanche. And Gramma. "We have grandparents," she said, and gave Gramma's name and number.

"Okay. That'll do for now. You go sit down, hon. As soon as they know anything, you'll be informed."

"What does that mean?"

"It means when they have an update on your sister's condition one of the doctors will be out to speak to you."

"Oh!" Louise turned and looked over at the waiting area. The elderly man was gone. The area was empty. She turned back to the nurse. "Is there a telephone?"

"Pay phone's around the corner, near the coffee machine."

"Thank you." Louise went along the corridor, stricken by the sight of empty gurneys, wheelchairs, examining cubicles, unadorned light green walls, highly polished linoleum floors, closed doors, the pungent reek of powerful disinfectant. Eerie, disembodied voices made cryptic announcements over the PA system. She found a nickel, but could only remember the first three digits of Gramma's number. After several anxious moments, she looked it up in the telephone book. She let it ring twelve times before she hung up, retrieved her coin, and trudged back to the waiting area.

⤙

Every half hour she walked down the hall and tried her grandmother's number again. When, at eleven-twenty, Bob finally answered, Louise couldn't get herself to speak. Then everything came spilling out. In a gush of tumbling words she told about coming home with Kath to find Faye unconscious, about calling the ambulance, about Faye's being wheeled into a room marked NO ADMITTANCE, where her clothes were sliced off her unmoving body. At last, she said in her new tinny little voice, "I've been here for over three hours and nobody'll tell me a thing. I don't know what's *happening!*"

"We'll be there in fifteen minutes," he said firmly, decisively. "Sit tight, Lulu."

Marginally eased by the knowledge that shortly she wouldn't be so terrifyingly alone, she went back to the waiting area where she sat, eyes on the closed doors, NO ADMITTANCE, and wondered why it was taking so long and what they were doing to Faye. The peculiar silence drilled into her eardrums. Only a handful of people had come and gone in all the time she'd been waiting. Now she was again by herself, surrounded by empty black chairs. Fragmented thoughts and unanswerable questions filtered unbidden into her brain. She didn't want to deal with any of them, and had to use all her willpower just to censor her own thoughts.

When she looked up again, there was a doctor in surgical clothes talking to the woman at the nurse's station. The nurse indicated Louise, he nodded, and started in Louise's direction.

Jumping up, Louise hurried over to him, asking, "How is she? What's wrong with her? Why is it taking so long? It's been *hours.* Why won't anybody tell me anything?"

He didn't answer for a moment, but studied her with his head tilted slightly to one side. "Don't I know you?" he said. "You look awfully familiar."

Now she took a few seconds to look at him. He was quite young, with dark, very curly hair, and with a pang she remembered him. "You took a piece of glass out of my foot at Sick Kids years ago."

"That's right. Now I remember." He started to smile. "You wanted to be a Canadette but couldn't do the splits."

Being reminded of that sent time spinning backward, making her smile at the whimsy of her twelve-year-old self. "I can't believe you remember that."

"Oh, sure. You were with your sister . . ." His smile melted away, and he repeated, "Your sister," as if just now making the connection. "Let's sit down. What's your name again?"

"Louise."

"Right. Lulu. I remember you like it was yesterday. I was doing my residency. You were the spunkiest little kid . . ."

Clutching at his arm, her stomach giving a threatening heave, she asked, "How's Faye? What's wrong with her? Please tell me what's going on. No one will *talk* to me."

"Come on over here," he said, and with an arm around her shoulders directed her to a couple of chairs in a corner of the waiting room. Taking hold of her hand, he looked directly into her eyes. "Did you know your sister was pregnant?" he asked.

Louise shook her head, dread flooding her system. Her entire body seemed filled with electric sparks.

"She had an abortion. Whoever did it perforated your sister's uterus. Tore it, actually."

Louise gasped, her grip going tight on his hand.

"We did everything we possibly could, but she'd lost too much blood."

"What d'you *mean?* What're you *saying?*"

"We couldn't save her, Lulu," he said sadly, his eyes never leaving hers. "We tried our damnedest. We transfused her, we repaired the damage, but she was too weak. Her heart simply stopped. I'm terribly, terribly sorry. If she'd just come in sooner . . ."

"I want to see her! Let me see her!"

"You're all alone here?" he asked disbelievingly, finally taking his eyes from hers to survey the deserted waiting area.

"I have to *see* her!"

He turned back to examine the grimly determined set of her features and said, "I don't see why not. Maybe it's the best idea under the circumstances. Come on, Lulu." He addressed her as if she were a precociously clever child, his hold on her hand directing her out of the chair and along the corridor. "You're sure you want to do this?" he asked, although her determination was tangible. He recalled very clearly the closeness of the two little girls, the way the older one had given strength to her sister. There'd been no parent with them that night, and there was none present now. These were children who'd obviously parented each other. He'd seen too many kids like them, valiantly providing for themselves what absent or neglectful parents failed to give; sober, sensible kids pushed into premature responsibility. Some of them, like these two, had torn hunks out of his equilibrium with their interdependency, their stoicism, and their resignation. It was why he'd opted out of pediatrics and switched over to internal medicine.

"I want to see her," she repeated. She'd never believe Faye was dead until she saw for herself.

"Okay, Lulu," he said consolingly. "You'll see her."

Upon entering the emergency room, Louise took in the people moving about, doctors and nurses, perhaps six or seven people altogether. They seemed to be doing final things, cleaning up, talking in tired sighing voices. There was an abrupt silence when they saw her. She was only peripherally aware of the doctor signaling them to leave. Her eyes were locked on the sheet-draped stretcher to one side of the operating room toward which she was being led. She opened her mouth, breathing hard, as the doctor released her hand and went to the head of the stretcher to fold back the sheet. His movements seemed reverential, as if he were contemplating something beyond mortal comprehension, something miraculous; distressing, but miraculous nonetheless. Louise kept her eyes on his face—a kind, caring face with good-humored brown eyes, laugh lines bracketing a generous mouth—until he looked down and, following his eyes, Louise looked, too.

It was Faye. She'd known all along he'd told the truth. He had no cause to lie to her. Now she believed it. Her sister looked like a pencil drawing, all pale lines on a white background. Louise put out a hand to touch Faye's cold cheek, ran the tip of one finger over her eyebrow, across her lips. Then slowly she pulled back her hand. There was no life here. Its absence was manifest in Faye's impossible stillness. Even in sleep her sister had never looked this way, like a fine marble statue, something too beautiful to be real.

As if reading her thoughts, the doctor said softly, ''Such a beautiful girl.''

''Beautiful,'' Louise echoed, awed by this singular viewing of someone she'd known all her life but hadn't ever truly seen until this moment. Beautiful beautiful. The squared jaw, the elegant patrician nose, the dainty pointed chin, the flawless skin and long sweeping eyelashes; arching cheekbones, long slender neck, the thick dark blond hair massed around the exquisitely shaped skull. Beneath those delicately veined closed eyelids, sightless forever now, were lake-water gray eyes, depthless, dead.

The pain struck suddenly in her solar plexus and she began doubling over on it. How could this be? How could she and Faye have said goodbye that morning only to be parted for always tonight? How did that happen? Where did the life go? The doctor moved to cover Faye's face again with the sheet but Louise whispered, ''No. Don't cover her. She always hated having anything over her face.''

He said, ''Sure. Okay,'' and an arm around her shoulders, he led her out, again saying, ''I'm so sorry. Is there someone we can call?''

The pain made it hard to walk, but she moved along beside him down the corridor toward the waiting area. What did you do when your sister died? Who was she supposed to talk to now? Just then the doors pushed open and Gramma and Uncle Bob came hurrying in. Louise looked at their faces, saw their fear, and broke away from the doctor to go running to her grandmother, whose eyes read everything in Louise's flight. She knew in an instant what it had taken Louise long minutes to accept, and her arms opened then closed hard, almost frantically, around Louise.

Bob went to speak to the doctor while Louise stood inside the circle of her grandmother's arms, thinking it was the same as when Chuckie died, and when Blanche died. She couldn't cry. Her sister was dead and she couldn't cry. She had this unbearable pain, this incapacitating internal injury, but she couldn't cry. No one even had to say a word to Gramma. She simply picked the truth out of the air, bent her head to Louise's shoulder and wept convulsively. Stricken by her grandmother's tears, Louise held and instinctively comforted her. But she herself was desiccated, so utterly dehydrated that her upper lip split when she opened her mouth to speak. She licked her lip and tasted blood. ''Faye's dead,'' she whispered, and her grandmother cried harder. ''Faye's dead,'' she repeated. "Dead." It was all Raffie's fault, she thought, her brain fusing to this notion. Faye had loved Raffie; she'd taken him into her body, and now she was dead. He'd vowed always to love and protect her, to ensure that no harm ever came to her. I love you, he'd said over and over. Louise had heard him say it with her own ears. He'd killed Faye with his love. He deserved to die.

✝

Maggie's date left at eleven-thirty. She stood at the kitchen counter sipping some Cointreau while she divided the money. Twenty-five went into her wallet. The remaining seventy-five would be deposited into the savings account on Monday.

Carrying the Cointreau she went out onto the balcony for some fresh air. It was a muggy night and she thought again about buying an air conditioner. There were times when it was too hot almost to breathe let alone get into bed with a date. On a night like tonight, even after changing the sheets, the bedroom reeked of sex. It was one thing to enjoy herself for an hour or two, but that didn't mean she wanted to smell it for the rest of the night. No. Tomorrow on her break she'd price the units, use her employee discount to buy something that'd keep the apartment cool. Her dates would appreciate it. Not that she had that many now, five or six a month on average, not counting that son of a bitch Fred Brundage. It wasn't enough that he summoned her up to his office on some pretext or other a couple of times a week, then locked the door so they could go at it for ten or fifteen minutes, he also had to stop by the apartment every Wednesday evening. Fred was without question one of the oversexed ones, and proud of it.

She'd have given her eyeteeth to have him out of her life, and wished she'd never become involved with him in the first place. But her job depended on it. He never came right out and said it in so many words, but they both knew. The only good thing was he never stayed long. He liked to get right down to it, grab a shower, then head on home. And he usually brought a bottle, wine or the Tanqueray gin he liked, or some Cointreau. She just hated his attitude, the way he came swaggering in as if he owned the place and everything in it, including her. One of these days she'd slam the door in his goddamned face and get herself another job. But not before she had enough in the bank to keep her going for a good long time. Jesus, it was hot! She finished the liqueur and stepped back inside. She'd take a cold shower and go to bed.

When the phone rang she assumed it was one of her out-of-towners, calling to set up a date, so she let it ring a second time before answering in her friendliest, sexiest voice.

"It's Bob Wolford, Margaret. I apologize for calling so late."

"And to what do I owe the pleasure?" she asked archly, despising him more with each passing month. He'd stolen away her mother's affection, installed himself in Maggie's place in her mother's heart.

"I'm afraid I have some bad news," he said, and at once she thought something had happened to her mother. She'd had a heart attack or a stroke.

"What?" she asked, wondering how bad it was going to be. Was her mother dead? She hoped not. She'd been waiting for the marriage to fall apart, for her mother to welcome her back into her life. And aside from that she was used to living without the girls now. The last thing she wanted was to have them back on her hands.

"It's about Faye," he said somewhat hesitantly.

"What about her?" she asked impatiently, wishing he'd get on with it.

"She's dead," he said bluntly.

"She's what?"

"She died tonight at Mt. Sinai."

"What of, for God's sake?"

"A botched abortion, I'm afraid," Bob said.

"The stupid bitch," Maggie said. "Why the hell did she go to some butcher?"

"We'll be in touch about the arrangements," Bob said coldly. "I just wanted to let you know."

"What d'you mean? I should be making the arrangements, not you. *I'm* her mother."

"You quite happily abandoned that role some time ago. As I said, we'll be in touch. Good night, Margaret," he said, and hung up.

"Arrogant bastard," she swore, and slammed down the receiver. Bad enough he'd turned her mother against her, now he wasn't going to allow her to bury her own child.

✝

Bob had to take a few minutes to compose himself. Tears filled his eyes and he went into the bathroom to blow his nose and splash cold water on his face before going back to the living room where Louise and Ellen sat huddled together on the sofa. He perched on the edge of a chair and looked at his wife. Eyes reddened from weeping, she gazed inward while one hand automatically, rhythmically stroked Louise's hair. Dry-eyed, Louise stared into space, breathing asthmatically through slightly parted lips.

"It might be a good idea," he said quietly, "to try to get some sleep. It's past midnight."

Louise turned her head and looked at the door, then grimaced, saying, "I can't go in there." She had a vision of that blood-drenched sofa and knew she couldn't face it.

"You'll stay here," Ellen said, her hand continuing to smooth her granddaughter's hair. "We wouldn't dream of letting you spend the night alone."

Louise now looked at her grandmother, envious of her ability to shed tears for Faye. Gramma was human. Louise doubted her own humanity. Her sister was dead, but she hadn't shed a single tear. That wasn't human. There was something lacking in her nature, some fundamental element missing. She put a hand to her grandmother's cheek, touching with her fingertips the dampness beneath Ellen's eyes, then, turning slightly aside, she put her fingers to her own lips to taste the salty evidence of her grandmother's caring. "It's all Raffie's fault," Louise whispered. "All his fault."

"Don't place blame, Lulu," Ellen said. "It doesn't solve anything, doesn't help. These things happen. Girls accidentally get pregnant every day of the world."

"Yeah. But they don't die because of it."

"Some do," Ellen said sadly. "Quite a few do. One of my best friends in high school died just this way."

"No matter what you say, it's his fault."

"It can't make you feel any better to blame him, does it?" Ellen asked her.

"No," Louise admitted. "But it's his fault," she insisted.

"I have to go to bed, Lulu," her grandmother said. "And so do you. It's impossible to think straight at a time like this." Looking over at him, she asked Bob, "Did you reach Marg?"

He nodded. "I reached her."

"How did she take it?"

"We'll discuss it later," he said.

Louise exclaimed furiously, "I'll bet she took it *personally*. I'll bet she treated it like something that happened to *her*. I'll bet she never even said she was sorry. I'm right, aren't I? God, I *hate* her!''

"Lulu," Bob said quietly. "Come here."

"What for?"

"Come here," he repeated, patting his knee.

Reluctantly, ready to fight everyone, she got up, crossed the room and sat on his knee. He wrapped both arms around her and drew her close so that when he spoke she could hear his voice vibrating deep in his chest. "You're distraught," he said. "We all are. Even though you might not think so, you need to rest. I'm going to get us each some drinks and something to help us sleep. Then we're all going to go to bed. The next few days are going to be very rough."

"The rest of my *life*'s going to be very rough," she said angrily, holding herself stiff in his embrace.

"I know that, Lulu," he sympathized. "Perhaps better than you realize."

Unbending, she wound her arms around his neck and hugged him. "I know you're right," she said. "I'm acting like a maniac. I'm sorry. I can't help it."

"You're acting human," he said, holding her away to look into her eyes. "Don't be so hard on yourself. Okay?"

"I can't help it," she said again. "I'm so *angry*."

"We're all angry. What's happened is a tragic waste. Tragic. There's no sense to it." Easing her off his knee, he got up saying, "I'll get those drinks."

Louise put a hand on his arm, asking, "Do you feel like crying?"

"I feel like screaming," he answered. "I feel like putting my fist through a wall. I feel like going completely crazy. And, yes," he admitted, "I feel like crying."

Louise let her hand drop and he went to pour brandy into three glasses.

Ellen was sitting with her legs pressed tightly together, elbows on her knees, head bent into her hands. Overwhelmed by sudden guilt, Louise went back to the sofa to stroke her grandmother's back. "I'm sorry, Gramma," she said miserably.

Ellen blotted her eyes with a handkerchief and turned to look at Louise. "Don't apologize," she said. "You don't have to do that. Excuse me for a minute." She got up and walked stiffly down the hall. A moment later Louise heard the bathroom door close. Unable to sit still, she got up and went to look out the window. In the near distance, on its hill overlooking the city, Casa Loma was all lit up, like something out of a fairy tale. The streets were deserted. The sky was perfectly clear, the full moon a deep yellow. Faye was dead. Every few seconds this reality shocked her consciousness like a blow to the head. Faye was dead, never coming home, dead. Tomorrow they'd cut her open, examine every part of her to give official reasons for her death. But Louise knew she'd died because she'd trusted Raffie.

Bob came to stand beside her, handing her a glass and a capsule. Louise swallowed the capsule with a mouthful of brandy, then gasped as the liquid scorched her throat. "I want her coffin closed. Okay, Uncle Bob? I don't want people staring at her. She'd have hated that. Faye was very shy."

"All right, Lulu," he said softly. "I personally find open caskets barbaric."

"Me, too," she said fervently. "Me, too."

He bent and kissed the top of her head, saying, "We'll have to take very, very good care of you."

"You always have," she said. "You took good care of Faye too. I just wish she'd *told* me. I'd have talked her out of it. Why didn't she *tell* me? We never kept secrets from each other."

"Maybe she was afraid, or embarrassed."

"But we told each other *everything.*"

"Sometimes things happen that we can't tell anyone else, no matter how close we are."

Had Raffie known about the baby? God, if he had! She could feel herself going tight again with rage, and made an effort to calm down. "I feel as if in a way *I* died, Uncle Bob." Looking up at him, she said, "What'm I going to do without her?"

"One step at a time, sweetheart. One step at a time." He looked out at the night sky thinking about Marg referring to Faye as a stupid bitch, and his own anger rushed back. Hearing Ellen approach, he moved to get her drink. Then, halfway there, he stopped to take his wife into his arms and hold her, not sure if he was seeking to comfort her or himself. He doubted anything would comfort Louise. She seemed so young, too slight to withstand the blow. Yet her spine was steely straight as she stood gazing out the window, her shoulders rigidly set as if to withstand further pain.

In the glass Louise saw the reflection of her grandmother and Uncle Bob embracing, and heard the sudden breaking of his breath as he began to cry. It sounded painful, as if shedding tears was against his nature. But at least he was able to cry. He was human. It was why Gramma loved him. Her own eyes remained dry, dry. She looked again at the castle, then back up at the moon. Faye was dead. *Dead.*

CHAPTER
THIRTY-SIX

SHE DIDN'T THINK SHE WOULD, BUT LOUISE ACTUALLY slept: a four-and-a-half-hour-long convoluted nightmare wherein she tried to return her sister to life. First she tried frantically to wring the blood from the sofa pillow, but managed only to collect a few drops, not nearly enough to be transfused into Faye's arm. Then she ran along slick empty corridors searching for those double doors, NO ADMITTANCE. When at last she found them, she pushed inside only to see two naked people writhing about on the examining table in the otherwise empty room. Fascinated and appalled, she watched their fevered coupling, wanting to turn away but held to the sight as if by force. Finally she tore free and ran from the room only to see a solitary white-clad figure pushing a stretcher through another pair of double doors.

A stitch in her side, she raced after, thrusting aside the orderly and pulling back the sheet. "Stop that!" said the fat, middle-aged woman beneath. "What d'you think you're doing? Do you want everyone to see me?"

"Sorry," Louise apologized, bewildered. "Sorry." Turning, she scanned the corridors leading off in all directions from the central hallway. Impossible to know which one to take. Her heart giving a resigned heave, her dreamself wept in despair.

At 6 A.M., while Gramma and Uncle Bob were still sleeping, she went silently barefoot to the kitchen to make a cup of tea. Her head ached. She found a bottle of aspirin in the hall bathroom and took three tablets, then carried her tea out to the balcony.

Sitting in one of the quartet of white chairs that surrounded a small round garden table, the sky gradually growing light, she considered what Gramma had said about placing blame. Maybe it wouldn't make things any better, but confronting Raffie with what he'd done would give her a certain real, if admittedly negative, satisfaction. If he had known about the baby and about Faye's plans, Louise thought she might very well kill him.

By seven-thirty, having left a note on the stove saying she'd be back shortly, she was on her way to the fruit market. She could have taken the streetcar but her body was so full of angry energy that she decided to work some of it off by going on foot. It wasn't that far, and she walked so quickly that she got to the store in twenty minutes. Mr. DiStasio was carrying bushel baskets of fruit and vegetables to the outside display.

At the sight of her he broke into a wide grin, as always, saying, "Eh, Louise. You up real early. How you, cara? We don't see you so much no more."

"I need to see Raffie, Mr. DiStasio. Is he up?"

"Sure," he said. "What'sa matter, Louise?"

"It's about Faye," she said.

Touched by the graveness of her manner, he said, "Come on in. I get him."

She stepped inside to breathe in the loamy fragrance of the potatoes and the citrous sweetness of overripe oranges as Mr. DiStasio went to the foot of the stairs and called up to Raffie to come down. Then he turned back to Louise. Wiping his hands down the sides of his apron, his heavy eyebrows drawing together, he said, "Something the matter with Faye, cara?"

"I'll tell you both when Raffie comes down," she said, trying hard not to be rude. It wasn't Mr. DiStasio's fault Faye was dead. He and Blanche had always been wonderful to her and her sister.

A minute or two later Raffie came loping down the stairs. Louise looked at him with new distance, a new objectivity. Tall, muscular, handsome, his eyes as clear and innocent as a newborn's. As he arrived at the bottom of the stairs, his face brightening at the sight of her just as his father's had done, she was gripped by doubt. She'd known Raffie all her life. She knew he'd never knowingly have harmed Faye. But he *had* harmed her, perhaps without knowing.

"Hey, Lou!" he said warmly. "What's up? This is a real surprise."
Behind him Mr. DiStasio stood waiting, his hands in his pockets.

"Did you know Faye was pregnant?" Louise asked bluntly.

"What?" Raffie was plainly astounded. "What're you talking about, Lou?"

"Did you *know?*" she repeated.

"No, I didn't know. And she couldn't be. What's this all about, Lou?"

"She *was.* Did you know she planned to have an abortion?"

"Louise, what is this? What're you trying to do here?" He cast an anxious look over at his father, then faced her again. "Where's Faye anyhow?"

"Faye's dead. She was pregnant. She had an abortion. Whoever did it tore her to pieces. She died last night in the emergency room at Mt. Sinai."

"What're you *saying?*" Raffie had gone pale, his eyes round, staring.

"Faye's dead?" Mr. DiStasio asked, hands hanging at his sides now, mouth agape.

"My sister's dead," Louise said coldly, killing Raffie with her eyes, "and it's your fault."

"Louise, listen!" Raffie cried, reaching to take her by the arm. "This is crazy. Is this some kind of sick joke or something? What're you talking about?" Louise stepped away from him. Raffie turned to appeal to his father. "Pop, this is crazy. I don't know what she's talking about."

Mr. DiStasio threw out his hand and caught Raffie hard across the face.

"Wait a minute!" Raffie exclaimed, turning back to Louise.

Having said what she'd come to say, Louise went to the door.

"Louise, wait!" Raffie hurried after her. "Where's Faye? Tell me what happened. This can't be!"

"They're performing an autopsy on her this morning," Louise told him. "Don't you *ever* again come anywhere near my family! My sister's dead because of you." With that, she marched away, Raffie's protests following her.

"It's a mistake, Louise. Listen to me! Wait a minute and listen! My God! Will you please *listen!* Stop and talk to me!"

Louise kept going. Behind her she heard Mr. DiStasio cursing in Italian and the sound of him going at Raffie with more blows.

Good! she thought, and put on speed, heading for home. I hope he beats you to death.

✦

"You pack up and get out!" Mr. DiStasio screamed. *"Go take what you can carry and get outa my sight, you scum!"*

"Pop, what're you doing? Why won't you to listen to me?"

Aldo came out of the kitchen, asking, "What's going on?"

"Get down to the store!" Mr. DiStasio shouted at him. *"Look after the customers!"* Then, to Raffie, his voice dropping menacingly: "Pack and go now!"

"But where'm I supposed to go? *Why* won't you listen?"

"You go, or I'ma gonna kill you!" his father ranted.

Fifteen minutes later, Raffie was out on the sidewalk with a duffel bag full of clothes and fourteen dollars he'd saved in his pocket. Pop wouldn't let him say a word, wouldn't even let him talk to Aldo. Raffie stood outside trying to make sense of this, trying to absorb the fact that Faye was dead. Pregnant. Abortion. Dead. It couldn't be. And where was he supposed to go, what was he supposed to do?

Through the front window he saw Pop go to the rear of the store and out to the truck. The front door opened and Aldo darted out, saying, "What the hell's going on, man?"

"Faye's dead," Raffie said through numbed lips. "What should I do?"

"Jesus H. Christ!" Aldo went wide-eyed. He glanced back to make sure Pop wasn't coming, then reached into his pocket and pulled out some bills. "Take this," he said, pushing the money at his brother. "And let me know where you are. I better get inside or he'll kill me."

Raffie pocketed the money, looked first one way up the street, then the other. Where to go? He started walking, the duffel bag dragging his arm down, straining his shoulder. Faye was dead? How could this be? It had to be true. Everything about Louise had screamed it was true. She believed he was guilty, that he'd made Faye pregnant. But he couldn't have. It wasn't possible. Unless by some freak accident . . . Could sperm travel from the outside of someone? Was that how Jesus got to be a virgin birth? His head ached. His eyes felt too large for their sockets. Where was he going?

He walked for miles, his legs moving him along the sidewalk, through intersections, while his brain tried to accept the idea that Faye no longer existed, that he'd never see her again. She was dead, and suddenly everyone blamed him. It wasn't his fault. Faye could have told them that. But he had to be guilty. Otherwise how did Faye wind up pregnant? There'd never been anyone else. So somehow he'd done it, made her pregnant. Why hadn't she told him? Okay, he'd been busy for weeks with his exams, but they'd talked every day, and she'd never said a word. Not a single word, not even a hint.

His arm ached from the weight of the bag. When he stopped to take stock of his surroundings he found he was on Bloor west of Dufferin. Maybe his legs knew where to take him after all, he thought, because there was only one place he could go, only one person who'd take him in and who'd listen to what he had to say: Grandmama. He was already more than halfway to her house on Indian Grove in High Park.

He lifted the bag again and kept walking.

"What's happened, Rafael?" Grandmama asked.

"I don't know, Mama. None of it makes sense."

The housekeeper brought coffee on a tray and set it down on the small table between the two wing chairs in the alcove of the living room. Raffie watched his grandmother, fascinated, as she said, "Thank you, Anna," and the woman who'd worked for his grandmother for almost thirty years nodded and left the room.

At fifty-nine, his grandmother looked the same to him as she always had. In contrast to the short meaty women in Pop's family, Grandmama was tall and slim, elegantly but austerely beautiful, and very like the ladies he sometimes saw on a Sunday morning filing into Timothy Eaton Church: very proper, meticulously put together, with expensive clothes and an aristocratic posture. "Now, Rafael," she said in her deep, commanding voice, "tell me everything."

He was consoled simply by his grandmother's powerful resemblance to his mother. But where his mother had been soft and light, Grandmama was dark and forceful. Pop and Aldo had always been scared of her, cowed by her innate authority, but Raffie had admired her all his life, had found her to be, more than anything else, uncompromisingly fair. His only hope was to tell her the complete truth. And so he did.

"It couldn't have been me, Mama," he wound down. "Faye and I only went all the way once, the night of Mom's funeral."

"Why only once?" she asked with a slight narrowing of her deep-set, very dark eyes.

"She didn't like it," he confessed, "said it hurt her. So we, uhm, did other things. It's the truth, Mama. We made love all the time, for years.

From the time we were fourteen. I admit that. But we did it without . . . you know.''

"Don't be embarrassed, Rafael. I haven't spent my life in a cave. I know about these things.''

"We didn't have intercourse, except that once.''

"I understand.'' She held the fragile porcelain cup with both hands and turned her strong profile to him as she gazed out the window.

"It's the God's honest truth, Mama. We tried maybe a dozen times, but she got scared, so we'd stop. And even then we always took precautions. But Pop wouldn't listen. He wouldn't let me say a word.'' Suddenly, it struck him: Faye was dead. He started to shake and had to put his coffee down, sobs breaking from deep in his chest. She was dead and everyone blamed him for something he hadn't done.

"I believe you, Rafael,'' she said, handing him a carefully ironed and folded man's handkerchief. "But the girl was pregnant. How do you explain that?''

"I can't,'' he sobbed. "But I swear on my mother's grave it wasn't me. Unless you can get pregnant without actually doing it.''

"Only in the Bible,'' his grandmother said with mild sarcasm, "and that is a book not meant to be taken literally. You'll stay here,'' she declared, "until we come to some decision.''

"About what?''

"About,'' she said patiently, "what you're to do with the rest of your life, Rafael. Your father will never have you back. You must realize that.''

"But when he knows the truth . . .''

She cut him off. "He'll never be willing to hear it. You know your father; you know how rigid he is. Think of how difficult he made it for your mother and me to see one another! I'm sure I don't have to remind you of all those years when I came to visit on Manning Avenue only during the afternoon when he was safely out of the house.''

"No, I remember.''

"Then you have to accept the fact that he'll never take you back.''

"Everything's ruined,'' he cried, blotting his face with the cool linen handkerchief that had been his grandfather's.

"Someone you loved has died,'' she said pragmatically. *"That* is ruined, and I'm sorry. Faye was lovely, frail but lovely.''

"She wasn't frail,'' Raffie disagreed.

"A frail spirit, Rafael, can sometimes be as debilitating as a physical illness. You're very young. You'll know other lovely women."

He shook his head. "I'll never love anyone the way I loved her."

"Perhaps not," she conceded. "But your life will go on. For now, you'll stay here, and we'll make plans for your future."

"Thank you, Mama."

"You did the right thing, coming to me. It's what your mother would have wanted."

Shattered, he wept uncontrollably.

Gramma was right, Louise thought as she walked exhaustedly up Bathurst. Placing blame didn't help. She wished now she hadn't done it the way she had, throwing it at Raffie like mud. She'd never forget the look on his face when she told him Faye was dead. He'd actually staggered, as if she'd struck him. She'd set out to hurt him and she had, but if anything, she felt worse now. And still she couldn't cry.

Bob awoke first and got up to put on a pot of coffee while he took a quick shower in one of the guest bathrooms so as not to disturb Ellen. It was going to be a hell of a long day.

He wondered where Louise had gone so early in the morning. Probably out to walk. The girl was devastated. She had the same look a lot of soldiers had during the war, that same glaze of incredulity. Death had a way of making old men out of eighteen-year-old boys, and it had a way of making one feel one's innards had just been scooped out with a rusty spoon. He'd felt it when his first wife died finally after the long months of her illness, and he felt it now.

When he emerged from the bathroom he tiptoed into the bedroom to get dressed only to hear the shower going and to see the master bathroom door ajar. He pushed open the door and went inside to peer around the end of the shower curtain, asking, "How are you?"

"Older," she answered, "by several decades. Did you sleep?"

"Some. I'll get you some coffee."

"Is Lulu still sleeping?"

"She went out. Back in a minute."

He returned to set her coffee on the counter, then leaned against the door and sipped his own, waiting for her to finish. The water went off, she reached for a towel to dry her hair, then wound it into a turban as she wrapped a larger towel around herself, pushed back the shower curtain with a clattering of the rings, and climbed out of the tub.

"Why did you use the guest bathroom?" she asked, reaching for her cup.

"Didn't want to disturb you. You were sleeping so peacefully."

"Sleeping, but not peacefully. What did Marg say?"

"I don't really think you want to know."

She studied him over the rim of her cup as she swallowed, then said, "You're right. Don't tell me. I can well imagine."

"I'll make breakfast," he offered.

"I couldn't eat."

"Toast."

"All right, but only toast."

"Ellen?"

She put the cup back on the counter, saying, "What?"

"I think it'd be best just to have a funeral service, nothing more."

She nodded slowly. "We'll discuss it with Lulu."

He turned to go and she came into his arms. "It never ends," she said unhappily. "You go along thinking things are finally settled, life is peaceful and good, then you get hit between the eyes. She was only *eighteen,* a baby. Faye never once in her life hurt anybody. Why did this have to happen?"

"I haven't an answer to my name. It's a goddamned tragic waste." He stood and held her, breathing in her damp warmth.

"Thank God I have you," she said, her arms tightening around him. "I don't know what I'd do without you."

"If I have anything to say or do about it, you never will."

"I think you can accept as a given," Bob was saying, "that your mother's going to try to kick up a fuss. Therefore, I suggest keeping everything as simple as possible."

"How?" Louise asked.

"This must seem so . . . cold to you," he said apologetically.

"No, it's okay, Uncle Bob. I understand."

"It's just that these things have to be discussed, arranged."

"Honestly, I understand. What do you think we should do?"

"I think a chapel service followed by cremation. No viewing. That way we avoid almost every possible opportunity your mother might have to make a difficult situation even more difficult.''

Louise turned her cup in its saucer. She could readily imagine Ma coming to the funeral parlor—in her mind she saw the one where Blanche had been on view—and demanding that the coffin be open. She could practically hear Ma shrieking, ''Who said it was to be closed? Who put these clothes on her? Why's she being buried with the pearls? Who did all this?''

''What happens to what's left of her after she's cremated?'' she asked, looking first at Bob, then at her grandmother.

''That's up to you,'' Ellen said, her throat threatening to close. ''The ashes can be buried, or dispersed, or you could even keep them.'' The conversation was making her ill. She got out a cigarette. At once Bob reached for her lighter and held it to the tip of her cigarette. ''Everything is your choice, Lulu,'' she said, then inhaled deeply. ''We'll abide by whatever decisions you make.''

''When will the notice be in the paper?''

''Monday, in all three papers,'' Bob answered.

''And when will they let us have Faye back?''

''They should release the body Monday,'' he said.

''What do they do with the report once it's done?'' she asked.

''File it. Why?''

''Could I have a copy?''

''I suppose that could be arranged. But why, Lulu?'' he asked, looking pained.

''I want to have it, that's all.'' She turned her cup in several full circles, then said, ''Okay. We'll do it the way you suggested. When?''

Bob turned to Ellen. ''Wednesday?''

''I think so,'' she agreed.

''Uncle Bob, could you get rid of that sofa?''

''What sofa?''

''Our sofa.''

''Why? What's wrong with it?''

In answer, Louise reached into her pocket and handed him her keys. ''I don't think you should go with him, Gramma.''

''My God!'' Ellen covered her mouth with one hand, then slowly closed her eyes.

"I'll be right back," Bob said, touching Ellen's shoulder briefly before moving away.

"What'll I do now?" Louise asked her grandmother. "I don't know what to do."

"Do you think you'll want to stay on in the apartment?" Ellen asked.

"I've been thinking about it. I guess I'll get a job and stay on. I can't move in on you and Uncle Bob. It wouldn't be fair."

"If you'd prefer to be here, then I want you here, Lulu."

"No, it wouldn't be good."

"I don't like the idea of your leaving school," Ellen said, thinking that she was grappling with too many things at once.

"I can't go back. That's the one thing I know for sure. God!" she said, suddenly remembering. "I'll have to call Sue, let her know. They'll be expecting Faye at work tomorrow." Pushing the coffee cup aside, Louise put her head down on the table with a sigh, saying, "I'm so tired, Gramma."

"Go lie down, take a nap," Ellen said. "Bob and I will take care of everything."

Sitting upright, Louise said angrily, "You shouldn't have to. I *hate* this! I don't understand! I want my sister back. They're cutting her up in little pieces."

"No, they're not," Ellen said softly, sickened by the image. "They have to establish a cause of death, but they won't cut her into little pieces."

"They already know the cause of death!"

"It's due process," Bob said, returning. "In all cases of suspicious death autopsies are performed. I'll have the Salvation Army come pick up the sofa, Lulu. I'll put it down on my list of calls."

"You'll have to call Faye's office," Ellen told him.

"I'd better call Kath," Louise said wearily.

"Then lie down for a while," Ellen said. "You're worn out."

"So're you." Louise came around the table and bent to rest her cheek on the top of her grandmother's head.

"She's right. Why don't you both take a nap while I take care of these calls?" Bob ran a hand over Louise's hair, his other hand taking hold of Ellen's. "Go on, both of you. I'll clear up the dishes, then make the calls."

"Can I use the extension in the bedroom?" Louise asked.

"Go ahead, honey," Bob said, and watched her walk through the kitchen and out.

"Tell me," Ellen said, keeping hold of his hand.

Sitting down heavily, he put the keys on the tabletop, saying, "I've never *seen* so much blood. I'll wrap up the pillow, take it down to the incinerator. The Salvation Army ought to be able to replace it. If Lulu wants to stay on in the apartment we'll get her another sofa."

"Why didn't Faye call someone for help? This makes less and less sense, and I'm so tired I can hardly think straight."

"When Lulu's finished her call, I think you should try to sleep for a while, Ellie."

"What about the office?"

"We won't be going in this week. I'll get Hugh's secretary to call around, cancel my appointments. One more item for my list."

"It's obscene," she said, her voice gone husky, "that my grandchild should die before me."

"It's obscene only because of her age," he said almost angrily. "Death has no fixed agenda, for God's sake, Ellie! I don't want to hear you talk about dying. I can't take it."

"You know what I meant."

"Of course, I do," he relented. "But I can't deal with the logistics of Faye's death and cope with having you refer, even in the most tangential fashion, to your own. I've lost one wife. Now I've lost one of my children. I just cannot contemplate losing you." His eyes filling, he sighed heavily, saying, "I've got to call the boys. This is unspeakably awful."

Ellen slipped from her chair onto his lap. "When you're finished the calls, come lie down with me. You're tired, too."

"Have you noticed Louise hasn't cried?" he said, his face in her neck. "She's holding herself together with steel bands."

"I've noticed. But she'll be all right. She's very strong."

"Maybe too strong. I worry about her."

"You and I see different things in Lulu," she said, holding him to her. "I can see her power. Perhaps you only see her as young. She's never been the one I worried about, not the way I worried about Faye. Faye always reminded me of a peony at full bloom. Exquisite but fragile, as if a strong breeze would cause all her petals to fall away. She cared so much, so deeply. Poor Raffie," she said softly. "He adored her. I wonder what'll become of him now."

"You make it sound as if you think of him in the same terms," he said, lifting his head to look at her.

"I do, Bob. He may be big, but underneath he's every bit as perishable as Faye. He's only superficially strong."

"You don't blame him?" he asked, surprised.

"I couldn't. I've never for a moment doubted he loved her. I don't think he knew she was pregnant. And that's what bothers me about all this. As close as they were, he was bound to have known. If he didn't, then there's more to this than maybe we'll ever know. I can't help feeling nobody knew because Faye didn't want anyone to know. That means something. I just don't know what. I keep remembering the morning Ron died, the way he fell. I was so frightened, not knowing what to do. By the time the ambulance came he was dead and I felt as if there should have been something I could have done. For days and weeks after I was terrified. He kept dying, falling to the floor, dying in front of my eyes. But at least I was *there;* he didn't die alone. Faye," she said, her voice breaking, "was all alone, bleeding to death all alone. And now I feel exactly the way I did when Ron died, as if there should've been something I could have done." She wiped her face with the back of one hand.

"There's nothing any of us could've done, Ellie, because we didn't *know.* Please don't think this way."

"I can't help it. Those great-grandchildren were so real to me, Bob. I could *see* them. I knew exactly how it'd be on Sundays when Raffie and Faye would bring them to visit. The little girl was dark like Raffie, and the boy was . . ." Choking, she fell silent.

"Come on, dear heart," he said, easing her off his lap. "I'll tuck you in and stay with you until you're asleep."

Kath couldn't stop crying. After talking to Louise, she went in search of her mother and Jerry. The housekeeper said they were in the garden.

"What's the matter, Kath?" the woman asked.

"A friend of mine died," Kath gulped out, opening the back door.

Her mom and Jerry were weeding the flower beds. Jerry loved the garden and spent all his free time out of doors, planting bulbs, pruning the rosebushes, keeping the beds pristine. Kath ran across the grass, crying out, "Faye died! Moooom! She died!"

Jerry got to his feet. "Oh no," he whispered, stricken, remembering those two little girls every year at the factory Christmas party; Louise's sweet mischief and Faye's shy grace. "Bloody hell!" he whispered, meeting Nancy's eyes. All his sympathy instantly directed itself toward Louise, Ellen, and Bob. Somehow he couldn't imagine that Mag would give a damn. But he felt a sudden inner aching. He'd loved those girls. He'd once even considered marrying Mag just to be a father to them.

"I'll telephone Bob," he said, pausing to embrace both his women, "see what sort of arrangements are being made." He stood for a moment watching the way the sunlight turned his wife's and daughter's hair to glowing copper. Then, pulling off his cotton gardening gloves, he made his way to the house.

CHAPTER

THIRTY-SEVEN

NONE OF IT SEEMED REAL TO LOUISE. THE COFFIN WAS surrounded by flowers, masses of them, so many that their scent was overpowering. She kept wondering who'd sent them all, and why she was so bothered by their fragrance. The coffin itself kept drawing her eyes. As she gazed at it she couldn't help doubting that Faye was actually in there, even though she and Gramma and Uncle Bob had been given a brief final viewing before the lid was closed. Louise had taken one quick look at Faye's unadorned lifeless face, had felt her stomach begin to turn, and had had to back away.

The dimensions of this event seemed dreamlike, contained somehow solely within her own mind. While she and Uncle Bob and Gramma went to the anteroom of the chapel in their somber clothes, even the movements of her own body had that cumbersome awkwardness of a dream. She longed to be light and quick but her body refused to comply. It was being held to the earth by an overwhelmingly powerful gravitational pull.

People began arriving well in advance of the scheduled service. Louise watched them enter, able to see the same gravitational pull affecting their faces as they came forward to express their condolences. She was touched. She thanked them for coming. An entire contingent from the factory arrived: Flo with her daughter, Cass; Mick and one of his three sons; Mrs. Theodopolus and her daughter, Christine. They swarmed over Louise, touching her with tentative consoling hands, kissing her cheeks, embracing her. The children of the factory workers looked discomfited, as if death were an invasion of their personal territory. She understood; she agreed; she knew how they felt. She felt the same way.

It seemed the entire staff of Faye's office had taken the afternoon off to attend. There was Sue with Ned Haley, and at least a dozen other employees all of whom made it a point to tell Louise how much they'd liked her sister. Sue in particular stood with Louise for a few moments to say, "She was one of the dearest people I've ever known. I cared very much for your sister. So did a lot of other people."

The words seemed to be entering Louise's head in layers, accumulating one atop the other like *mille-feuille* pastry dough, slowly filling the bottom of her mind.

Kath was real. So was Aunt Nancy and Mr. Nolan. The three of them enclosed her in the circle of their love, and she gave the expected responses, returning their hugs and kisses, thanking them most sincerely for their caring, for attending. More layers fluttered down atop those already there.

Lefty and Ernie came and stiffly shook her hand, saying how sorry they were. She thanked them. They moved on into the chapel. Others came to take their places. Whenever she looked around it was to see that Gramma and Uncle Bob were also being embraced, having their hands shaken, dealing with the flood of mourners who'd come to honor Faye.

A dream, a dream, whispered the voice inside her skull. How, when so many many people loved her, had Faye managed to die?

"She was so very special," said a small woman whose unremarkable features were made remarkable by the lurid lipstick shouting from her lips.

"Miss Giddings," Louise said, moved almost into reality by the presence of the typing teacher with her short wispy brown hair, her ugly Harris tweed suit, the tears glossy in her myopic blue eyes.

"I'll remember her always," said the teacher, holding both Louise's hands. "I . . ."—she choked, had to draw a deep faltering breath—"I *loved* your sister."

Dangerously close to reality, Louise leaned forward to kiss the woman's dry powdery cheek, murmuring, "Faye loved *you*, Miss Giddings. Thank you for coming."

Then, mercifully, the woman moved on. Louise heard her introducing herself to Gramma and Uncle Bob. God! she thought. This was becoming more and more difficult. Her gravity-bound feet and legs seemed to be sinking into the marble floor. Very much longer and she'd be swallowed by the cold stone. Suddenly she wondered where Ma was. A glance at her watch told her the service would be starting in ten minutes. Maybe Ma wasn't even going to come. She'd make herself felt by staying away.

Mr. DiStasio arrived looking uncertain, with a visibly reluctant Aldo in tow. Uncomfortable in his suit and tie, the man approached Louise, saying, "Cara, I'ma so sorry." He shook his head once, twice, while he tried for words, then said, "So sorry," again and moved on. Aldo looked at Louise, then at the floor, again at Louise, then followed his father. Louise hesitated a moment, then went after Mr. DiStasio to give him a hug.

Surprised, gratified, the man hugged her back. She thanked him for coming, then released him. Aldo kept his eyes on the floor as if fearful she might take it into her head to hug him too.

A very pretty girl arrived alone. Perhaps thirteen or fourteen, eyes round with uncertainty, she stepped inside and looked around. Then she saw Louise and worked her way through the new arrivals.

"You don't remember me, do you?" she said. And Louise tried to think who she could be, but her head was too full of those papery pastry layers of words. "I'm Sophie," she said. "Sophie Wisznowski. We lived upstairs, remember?"

"Sophie!" Louise studied the girl's face, looking for some resemblance to the good-natured toddler. "Thank you for coming. Faye loved you so much."

The girl's eyes overran. Louise was shocked to have this effect on her. "My parents are working," she explained, "but I wanted to come. Faye was my hero," she said with a wavering smile. "I always wanted to be just like her when I grew up."

Louise hugged her, feeling reality driving a wedge right into her belly. This was rough and getting rougher. "Thank you for coming," she told the girl again, and released her. "It means a lot."

"Are you okay, Louise?" she asked.

Surprising herself, she answered, "No. But I will be. Please say hello to my grandmother, Sophie. It'll mean a lot to her that you came."

"I will," Sophie said, and moved away.

Louise dragged air into her lungs, glanced again at her watch. Another five or six more minutes of this before the service started. She looked over at the doors, astonished to see Bruno and Anthony climbing the steps. With their hair wet-combed, in ill-fitting suits, they arrived at the top of the steps and filled the doorway with their bulk. Anthony hung back, but Bruno lumbered over to her, his mouth working as if he were physically shaping the words he wanted to say to her.

He stopped in front of her and in his rumbling voice said, "Hey, Lou. We come to say we're real sorry about Faye."

"That's very nice of you, Bruno."

He lowered his massive head, his mouth again working. He seemed to be struggling to say something and she wished she could help him. He appeared to be suffering, almost as if the words were sharp-edged and causing him pain. She was about to speak when a figure moved to one side of Bruno and a hand touched her arm. She looked up and all the air she'd carefully conserved in her lungs rushed out as she automatically reached to embrace him, whispering, "Daniel."

He held her very tenderly for a long moment, then eased away, holding both her hands, saying, "I'm so sorry, Louise."

Unable to think, she kept hold of his hand and whispered, "Stay with me, please."

He simply stepped to her left and allowed her to maintain her grip on his hand while Bruno, finally abandoning his attempt to say whatever it was he'd been trying so hard to get out, muttered, "I'm real sorry about Faye," and moved off. Anthony came forward to join him and the two of them entered the chapel.

Louise was about to speak to Daniel Craven when Raffie appeared arm-in-arm with his grandmother. She felt such an explosive mix of ancient fondness and recent anger that she was immobilized. How dare he come here! she thought furiously. Then she was overcome by admiration for his courage. Whatever else he'd done, there'd never been any question that he'd loved Faye. But she prayed he wouldn't try to speak to her. Her hand tightened around Daniel's.

Ellen went to meet them at the door. Extending her hand to Raffie's grandmother, she accepted the woman's kisses on each cheek, saying,

"It's so good of you to come, Leonora." Then she embraced Raffie, who broke into tears and was unable to speak at all.

"Please come sit with the family," Ellen said, directing the pair over to Bob.

Louise's eyes met her grandmother's for a moment. Gramma's look told her to set aside her anger. Louise wet her lips and lowered her eyes.

"I'd better go inside and find a seat," Daniel said.

Louise turned to him, consciously taking a mental step backward from the edge of reality. "Please don't leave without me," she said. "People will be going to Aunt Nancy's house after. Will you come?"

"Of course," he said. He put a hand to her cheek, then slipped away inside.

After a moment she turned to look into the chapel. It was full, with people standing in the aisles. Behind her an attendant was about to close the doors. Louise walked slowly down the aisle to the front pew and slid in beside Uncle Bob, reaching at once for his hand. Organ music was playing softly. The wood of the coffin gleamed beneath the flowers. She heard what sounded like a collective intake of breath and turned to see what was happening. It was Ma, making her entrance.

Louise knew she'd waited until the last possible moment in order to have the maximum effect. In a tailored black suit, black high heels, sheer black hose, a broad-brimmed, heavily veiled hat, clutching a handful of startlingly white tissues, she came down the aisle as everyone watched. Disgusted, Louise turned to face forward where the minister, standing behind a lectern, also watched Maggie advance. She took all the time in the world, nodding regally to the group from the factory, making the performance last.

There was nowhere for her to sit but next to Louise. Maggie slid into the pew, nodded to all of them, then turned to look at the minister, as if giving her permission for him to begin.

Louise was so enraged, and so sickened by her mother's overpowering perfume, she had to keep her fists clenched in order not to say or do anything that would ruin this farewell to Faye. She was so infuriated that the entire service passed without her hearing a word. All she saw—and that only peripherally—was her mother's expression of synthetic sorrow. The tissues were merely a prop. Maggie remained dry-eyed throughout. Louise wanted to go at her with her fists. Instead, she turned inward and thought about Faye, about the first time they met Bob when he took them to the Royal York for dinner, about Bob's dancing with Faye, about their hundreds of bedtime conversations. She saw Faye's life in her mind, and examined it until those layers and layers of words threatened to swamp her. Then she simply closed her eyes and waited for the dream to be over.

⤙

Daniel Craven sat through the service feeling Louise's phantom grip on his hand. From time to time he looked down, flexing his fingers slightly, as if fully expecting to feel her small soft hand still in his. She had a phantom grip as well on his emotions, but then she always had. From the first moment he'd seen her in the second seat of the second row in his classroom four years earlier he'd been enthralled by Louise.

Initially he'd been fascinated simply by her appearance, by the wisdom-filled eyes in the child's face. She'd looked no more than ten years old, her face and body small, unformed. But intelligence radiated in bright blue rings from those eyes, and a certain impossible knowledge governed her behavior. She merely *looked* like a child. Housed within that tiny body, within that well-shaped head, was an innate comprehension of life's dynamics. Her size and voice and playfulness were childlike, but her thoughts were fully adult, broad and comprehensive.

He'd watched her flower and grow, and saw too the way her peers were daunted by her directness, the quicksilver flare of her intellect. And he saw, perhaps most importantly, her isolation. Despite her vivacity, her affability, she was so alone it positively assaulted his sensibilities. Possibly he saw all this because he recognized in her the very qualities that had so successfully kept him apart from others all his life. Neither of them lacked the capacity for friendship; neither of them lacked for friends. But he'd always been alone and he knew he'd found a kindred soul. She was painfully attractive but completely unaware of how undermined people were, and always would be, by her compelling good looks and even more compelling intellect.

He watched her and found occasions when he could legitimately savor her company without risking either her innocence or his own position of trust. They sat together at the counter at Kresge's and chatted while they ate, but underneath there flowed a powerful tide he knew she seemed to sense but couldn't identify. He'd always taken pains not to presume on her innocence, but now and then, while he examined the purity of her profile, the sweetly stubborn thrust of her pointed chin, he'd suffered from the need to reassure her, to share with her his understanding of the solitary state. At those times he was overwhelmed by frustration. He was nine years older than she, and in a position of trust. He had no right to breach that trust by attempting to reassure her of her beauty, her desirability, her very lovability. Yet he yearned to do just that, to tell her in very specific terms how extraordinary he found her.

He'd read the obituary in that morning's *Globe & Mail* and felt her anguish. It leaped at him from the small block of newsprint and he trembled, reading of her sister's death: *Suddenly, at Mt. Sinai Hospital, Friday, June 30th.* For all her self-reliance, Louise had always been entirely involved with her sister. He'd seen them together in the corridors at the school, and the tremendous strength of their bond had been almost palpable. Without a moment's hesitation, he'd set aside the newspaper and telephoned to cancel the day's appointments. He could be only one place that day: at Louise's side.

When he entered the chapel and saw her in a prim black dress, he saw too that she'd been pushed well beyond childhood by her sister's death. It showed in the set of her head, the length of her neck exposed by the hair drawn back and clasped at the nape; it showed in her jawline and pulsed in her throat. It didn't surprise him that he should all at once no longer be Mr. Craven to her, but Daniel, or that she would offer herself into his arms for consolation. It was, after all, what he'd come to give.

After the service, when she came directly to him—again seeking his hands with hers—to give him the address, she needn't have elicited his promise to be there. He'd always intended to go.

The house was crowded with mourners, knots of dark-clothed, murmuring people. There was food and drink and the trio of Louise, her grandmother, and her step-grandfather accepting more declarations of sympathy, half-smiling through reminiscences rendered by old friends. Louise looked up. Her eyes fixed on him, a burning blue light. Then she looked away.

He got a drink and went to talk to Ella Giddings, who was sipping neat rye from a short glass and blinking back tears. Unlikely as it seemed, Ella was one of the few on staff he knew who formed deep and abiding attachments to her students. She'd always liked Louise, but she'd adored Faye, perhaps seeing a finer, more beautiful version of herself in the girl.

He said hello and Ella looked up at him, startled. "I didn't expect to see anyone else here from school," she said in her small voice with its faintly Irish Newfoundland accent.

"I've always been very fond of Louise," he explained. "I never taught her sister."

Ella took a large swallow of her rye, blinked rapidly several times, then said, "This is brutal. I've got to get out of here, go home and feed the cats. It's very decent of you to come, Dan."

Seeking to lighten her mood he gave her a smile and said, "I'm a decent sort of guy. Do you need a lift home?"

"No, no." She drained the glass, set it down on the table beside her and said, "I can't take this. I need to go home and have a good cry." Going up on her toes, she kissed his cheek, patted his chest, and said, "I'll see you in September." Then she toddled away in her ugly black lace-up shoes. He watched her go with renewed admiration. Inside that small nondescript body lived a lovely woman who, had life been remotely fair, would have had a loving husband and children.

He nursed his scotch and water, surveying the crowd. No sign of the mother. Mentally he whistled through his teeth, reliving that entrance she'd made into the chapel, like a fashion model swishing down a ramp. No wonder Louise spoke so disparagingly of the woman. Anyone who could time her arrival in order to make an entrance at her own daughter's funeral was something for the books. He found a quiet corner and sipped his drink, watching people drift past.

Louise found her grandmother temporarily alone and sat down beside her on the sofa. "Gramma, I'm going to leave. Do you mind?"

"I don't mind, Lulu. Where are you going?"

"I don't know. But don't wait up for me. I don't know how late I'll be. Okay?"

Ellen stroked back a stray wisp of hair from Louise's face. "If it gets to be late, call me. Otherwise, I'll worry."

"All right, Gramma. I'll call you. But don't worry. I'll be fine. I just can't handle any more of this."

Louise kissed her and slipped away.

Curious, Ellen got up and followed at a distance. When she saw Louise approach the English teacher, her heart was suddenly seized and she had to put a hand out to the wall for support. Louise took the man's hand. He put down his glass, and they began heading for the door.

"What is it?" Bob asked at her side.

Ellen indicated Louise, and Bob turned to look.

"I know what she's going to do," she whispered. "God! I know her too well."

"She'll be all right, Ellie."

"That's what she says," she mouthed, tracking Louise and the man as they made their way through the foyer to the door. "That's what she says."

"You said yourself she's strong."

"I know," she said, the front door closing. Turning to Bob she removed her hand from the wall. "Marg didn't come."

"She'd never come here and you know it."

"It's over," she said. "I think I need another drink."

"Let's get you one." Lacing his fingers through hers, he said, "I love you, Ellie. Don't ever forget that," and directed her toward the bar.

⅄

"Where would you like to go?" Daniel asked. "Are you hungry, Louise? Have you eaten anything?"

"Where do you live?"

"Me? Not too far from here, in Rosedale."

"Do you have food at your house?"

He smiled. "Yes, I have food at my house. I even know how to cook it."

"Then let's go to your house."

"I don't know if that's a very good idea."

"Why not?" She shifted in the low-slung bucket seat to look at him.

"I can't become . . . socially involved with a student, Louise."

"I'm not a student. I'm not coming back to school."

"Oh! I don't suppose I can talk you out of that."

"No, you can't. Let's go to your house," she said tiredly.

In answer, he put the Triumph in gear and pulled away from the curb.

She let her head fall back against the seat, saying, "I always knew someday I'd ride in this car."

"You could have asked me," he said. "I'd have been happy to take you for a spin any time."

"I couldn't have asked you," she said quietly. "But everything's changed now. I like the way you drive, fast but not too fast. Uncle Bob's car is very cushy. It's like riding on a pillow. He has a Cadillac," she said, turning in the seat to face him. "He gets a new one every year, at Addison's on Bay. Every year he trades in the old one and gets a new one exactly the same as the one from the year before. I love him for that. Does that sound ridiculous?"

"No. You like his constancy."

"Yes, I do. He and Gramma came to my last two parents' nights. They talked to my teachers. They went to every class. My mother never went to one, ever."

"I know. You told me that."

"Did I?" She watched him downshift. "Are we almost there?"

"Almost. I have the second floor of a house on Dale Avenue."

"Do you come from a wealthy family, Daniel?"

Unembarrassed, he replied, "Yes, I do. Are you all right, Louise?"

She didn't answer. He didn't press the matter, choosing to let it drop as he pulled into a long driveway and followed it to the rear of a large house where there was a four-car garage. He stopped in front of the last, vacant slot, and switched off the ignition.

"Come on in," he said, "and we'll see about some food."

"Could I take a shower?" she asked as they entered through the rear door of the apartment. "I feel very grubby." It was a large, attractive place, with a long central hallway. She liked its spaciousness.

"Sure," he said. "The bathroom's along here."

He opened the linen closet in the hall and removed an egg-yolk yellow bath sheet, saying, "This is a good color for you. Take your time. When you're finished we'll put together something to eat."

"Thank you," she said, and went into the old-fashioned but wonderfully elegant bathroom. Not only was there a very long tub, there was also a marble shower stall. The floor was done in octagonal black and white tiles, the walls in large glossy white tiles with a narrow black border. Leaving the door ajar, she undressed and stepped into the stall.

Her body felt altogether strange, unfamiliar, as if it belonged to someone else. She smoothed her soapy hands over her limbs, across her torso, with a profound sense of dislocation. Strange, strange. In a corner of the stall sat a bottle of shampoo. She picked it up, removed the lid, sniffed, then poured a little into the palm of her hand and began lathering her hair. This was helping. The hot water was washing away the strain of the day, easing the effervescing anger she'd felt since seeing Faye's body under the sheet. Feeling more than surface clean, she turned off the water and reached for the towel Daniel had said was a good color for her. What an odd thing to say! It was such a personal remark, as if he'd spent time considering what might or might not be suitable for her.

Dry, she used his comb, her sense of dislocation heightened by making use of his possessions. She looked at her clothes draped over the side of the tub and couldn't bear to put them on. Besides, she'd only have to take them off again. Fastening the towel around her, she went to look for him.

The living room ran the entire width of the house. To the left, built-in bookcases flanked a white marble fireplace. A pair of chairs sat on one side of the room, a sofa on the other. Daniel was sitting on the sofa with a book, and looked up when she came in, automatically placing a bookmark between the pages before setting the book aside.

"Is there something you need?" he asked, his stomach going tight at the sight of her clad only in a towel.

"No," she answered, coming to stand directly in front of him. "This is a beautiful place. You live all alone here?"

"All alone," he said, thinking he'd been right: The yellow was a very good color for her.

"Do you have a lot of girlfriends?" she asked, looking over at the tightly packed bookshelves.

"No."

"Not even one?" She looked back at him.

"There was someone I was seeing. It ended some months ago. Louise, I think you should get dressed."

"No, you don't," she said quietly.

"Yes, I do. I'm very fond of you, but . . ."

"That's not true," she said in that same quiet tone. "Don't be dishonest. You're not just fond of me, Daniel." She undid the towel and watched him look at her. "All those conversations we didn't have," she said, "all the time we were talking about movies, we were talking about how we feel about each other. It took me quite a long time to understand, but I did finally. Now we have to do this." She took a step closer to him, then looked down at herself. "My sister was very shy. I never have been. Do you think I'm all right? Faye had a much nicer chest, but I'm still growing. Isn't that amazing? I turned seventeen in April, but I'm still growing." She put the towel on the arm of the sofa and sat down beside him. "Have you made love to a lot of women?"

She was so earnest, he simply had to smile. "Not a lot," he replied, making a concerted effort to keep his hands in his lap. "And only one with any degree of proficiency."

"The someone you broke up with some months ago?"

"That's right."

"Who was it? What was she like?"

"I can't sit here with you naked and hold a rational conversation," he said softly, trying to keep his eyes on her face.

"We don't have to talk at all. Don't you want to touch me?" she asked, some doubt edging into her eyes.

He couldn't help himself. He had to look at her. The sight of her was like a fish bone stuck in his throat. He could scarcely swallow.

"As long as you have something we can use, I want to do this. I really do. And I'm not one of your students anymore. I don't have any experience to speak of, except for getting kissed good night one time by Lefty. But that wasn't real. I want to do the real thing, all of it."

He leaned forward, his hands still in his lap, and touched his mouth to hers, then sat back. Her eyes blinked open and she said, "Where is it? Is it down here?" as she got up and walked out of the room.

He rose and followed, stopping her when she was halfway down the hall, taking her by the arms and holding her still as he looked into her eyes. Then he clasped her to him, shocked by the cool resiliency of her flesh.

Her arms winding around him, she said, "You'll have to show me what to do. I don't know anything."

His bedroom had burgundy wallpaper with brilliant white trim. The bed was positioned at an angle, pointing toward the door. She walked over and sat down on the side of it as he removed his jacket and draped it over the back of the chair by the desk. She watched with interest as he undressed, and when he'd shed the last of his clothes, she got up to fold back the bedspread saying, "I like the way you look. Does it hurt for men the first time the way it does for women?"

"No," he said. "And it doesn't always hurt for women, so I'm told." He again took her into his arms, sighing deeply at the pleasure. "I like the way *you* look," he said. "You are so incredibly sweet."

"So are you. You don't seem very much older than me."

"I don't feel very much older. I've only caught up with myself in the past couple of years because of . . . the woman I was seeing."

"Who was she?" she asked, excited by the feel of his body aligned to hers. His skin was very dark against hers.

"Lillian," he confessed. "Lillian Castle."

"Mademoiselle Castle?" Louise thought of the tall, silver-haired woman with her impeccable clothes and found the concept of her being Daniel's lover wonderfully intriguing. "Isn't she very old?"

"She's twenty years older than I am. No one knew. We were together for just over two years. I didn't know *anything* until I became involved with Lillian."

"Why did it end?"

"She ended it. She said we had no future."

Neither do we, Louise thought, but didn't say it. "What do we do now?" she asked.

"Now," he said huskily, "I hope I'm going to make you feel very good," and put his hands over her breasts as he kissed her.

She kept waiting for the pain, but there was only pleasure. Each caress created yet another short circuit in her brain, so that finally it seemed to cease functioning. She returned each gesture in kind, attempting to touch him in the same gently probing fashion he touched her, stroking him precisely as he stroked her, kissing him exactly where he'd kissed her.

"It's all in the angles," he murmured, holding her astride his lap. "Something Lillian taught me. Does it bother you, my talking about her?"

"No, no. I'm glad you were with her. She's very beautiful. It makes it better, in a way."

"Everything's here," he said, pressing inward at the apex of her thighs so that her body of its own volition thrust forward, opening. "Right here," he said, pushing firmly, knowingly, so that she shuddered in response. "Please don't let me hurt you," he implored, holding her from beneath with both hands. "Stop me if I hurt you."

"Just don't let me get pregnant. Otherwise, I don't care. It feels so good." She looked down, watching him fit himself to her, feeling herself spreading inside. "It doesn't hurt," she whispered, stretching to contain him. Faye was mistaken, she thought. There was no pain. Only this inner elasticity, this astonishing ability to hold a man deep within herself.

His eyes acquired a different light, a new intensity once they were joined. "Now," he whispered, his lips against her ear, "we find the angle. You're all right?'' he asked anxiously, falling back with her locked to his chest.

"I'm fine. What do I do?"

"When it feels right, you move. You can't help yourself, you move."

His hands steadying her hips, he thrust upward, his hips rolling against hers. Tightening her knees against his thighs, she thrust down, seeking to relocate the sensation he'd created before. "I'm not very good at this," she said, feeling graceless, unable to find the feeling again.

"You're *very* good at this," he said, keeping hold of her and shifting so that they lay on their sides, facing. "We just have to find the angle."

Shifting, shifting, turning, they completed a full circle and suddenly his body meshed perfectly with hers. If she moved just so, a spark danced behind her eyes. Again, another spark. Again, again. She found his mouth, kissed him with desperate hunger, and the sparks became small electric shocks sizzling through her brain, reverberating the length of her body. She worked blindly at it, lunging downward after that gritty satisfaction, striving mindlessly to go deeper, harder into the very core of pleasure. It was suddenly that place her five-year-old self had tried to get to when she'd swung on the struts of the schoolyard swings. Frantic to get there, she writhed in concert with this man who'd always loved her; she'd known for such a long time that he loved her. Then her breath stopped in her throat, her heart leaping crazily as she was sent shaking into a frenzy of feeling that culminated in her emitting a sorrowing cry that evolved into wrenching sobs. Her body caught in a chaotic dance, she wept violently, helplessly.

"Oh, God!" he exclaimed. "What is it?" Seeking to console her, he held her tightly to him with his arms and legs, his hand cradling her head to his shoulder. "What is it, Louise? What?"

"*I want my sister!*" she cried. "Oh, please, I want my sister back. Please, please."

"Oh damn," he whispered, and, falling back, held her while she cried and cried. "I love you I'm sorry I love you I'm sorry. It's all right I'm sorry. Cry it's all right I'm so sorry I love you."

Part 2

LONDON,
1960–65

CHAPTER

THIRTY-EIGHT

A VOICE INSIDE THE HOUSE CALLED, "I'LL GET IT!" THEN came the sound of running footsteps. The door was opened by a small thin girl in her late teens dressed in black slacks with a black pullover, and white running shoes on bare feet. Set incongruously on her head, atop a mass of dark curly hair, was a vividly pink hat that looked like an inverted pot swathed in netting. She wore makeup so pale it was almost white, and thick black eyeliner, no lipstick. Once past her initial shock, Louise found the overall effect oddly appealing, primarily because the girl had such large dancing brown eyes and because her demeanor seemed to state that she didn't take herself seriously.

Louise smiled and said, "Hi. I've probably got the wrong address. I'm looking for Philip Townsend-Post."

The girl tilted her head to one side and studied Louise for a moment, then grinned, revealing a mouthful of large perfect teeth. "I know you!" she declared merrily. "You're the Canadian girl Philip took such a fancy to when we visited Canada."

"That's right. I'm Louise Parker. I'm amazed you remember."

"Oh, I recall the evening perfectly, even the super frock you wore. Do come in. I don't expect you remember me, but I'm Rachel, Philip's sister." She extended a small hand to Louise, eagerly drawing her inside. "Come in, come in. Are you over on holiday? How super to see you again!"

"Actually I've come to stay. And I do remember you, although you've changed a lot," Louise said tactfully, liking the girl immediately.

"I know!" Rachel said, as if greatly pleased. "Let's have some tea!" She directed Louise toward an enormous living room full of overstuffed furniture and gleaming antiques. "You would like some tea, wouldn't you?"

"That'd be very nice."

"Super! Have a seat. I don't be a tick."

Rachel went off and Louise looked around the lovely room. The walls were painted a pale green, the high ceiling and trim in matte white. Separated by a massive wood coffee table with brass trim, a pair of sofas faced each other before an ornate white marble fireplace. A grand piano was angled into the bay of the three front windows overlooking the street, its top crowded with silver-framed photographs of varying sizes. Impressed, Louise seated herself in the center of one of the sofas and looked over at the array of magazines fanned on one end table, then at the crystal jug of fresh flowers on the table opposite. Everything was immaculate, yet inviting. It was a room not meant merely for show.

"Tea will be along momentarily," Rachel said, returning to sit directly beside Louise. "It's such a pity Philip's not here. He won't be home for another three weeks."

"Oh. Where is he?" Disappointed, Louise wondered if she should go.

"Still at school, the lucky sod. Mummy and Daddy wouldn't hear of *my* going, of course. Educating females is to their decadent minds a complete waste of time. So I'm left to my own devices until a suitable husband presents himself to take me off their hands." She made a little face, then smiled again. "A lot of rubbish. Tell me everything! How long have you been over? Where are you staying? What are your plans? And why on earth have you come to live in this dreary country? I *adored* Canada, especially the central heating. I'm always perishing here in the winter."

"I arrived the day before yesterday," Louise explained. "For the moment I'm staying in a hotel."

"Which?"

"This awful place on Cromwell Road."

"Oh, that endless row of hotels," Rachel said. "They look so frightful."

Encouraged by Rachel's sympathy, Louise admitted, "My place is pretty frightful. A tiny little room at the back with the bath along the hall and up three steps, and the toilet back the other way and two steps down. I've got to start looking for a place. The only problem is I don't know where to look or even what part of the city I want to look in. I was hoping Philip might be able to help."

"*I* can help!" Rachel offered. "I'd *adore* to,"

"That'd be wonderful, if you really would like to," Louise said. "I have no idea where anything is. I got lost three times just finding my way here."

"It's not so difficult to learn one's way around," Rachel said confidently. "We'll work from here, make this your starting point. In no time at all you'll be riding the underground, learning the buses." Narrowing her eyes slightly, she studied Louise for a moment or two before declaring, "I think you'd like South Kensington. Of course it depends on your resources. But that's none of my business, is it? I'm always in trouble for saying things one simply doesn't say. I'm afraid I'm frightfully non-U. Not on, not done, chaps; that sort of rubbish. Mummy and Daddy were hoping to marry me off before I turned twenty-one because they had the idea I'd make a complete shambles of my coming out." She laughed, then said, "I let them off the hook by conveniently falling ill. I've got no time at all for that foolishness. But they feel that time's running out and they haven't managed to persuade any of their eligible candidates to come to dinner more than once. They extend invitations, you see, then trot me out like a little pony. Except that I refuse to dress up or to play by the rules. They become just a bit more desperate with each birthday. I was twenty-one this past February, you see. Now they're actively praying someone'll come along to relieve them of being responsible for me."

"Isn't Philip's birthday in February, too?"

"That's right. Didn't the naughty boy tell you? We're twins."

"No kidding! That's terrific."

"I expect you're the only one who thinks so," Rachel said. "You're very dear. That's the impression I had of you when we met. Philip certainly thought so. Now, back to the matter at hand. How are you fixed, if you don't mind my bluntness."

"I do have some money," Louise said, enjoying the girl's charming eccentricity. "In fact I have to open a bank account so I can deposit this draft I've been carrying around, but I wanted to wait until I found an apartment so I could have a bank nearby."

"Perfectly sensible," Rachel said approvingly. "You'll want to get started straightaway, I should think. It's a waste, spending money on an hotel room. And you'll want to establish credit with a bank. That's very important. We'll have our tea and then, if you like, I'll show you South Kensington. If that doesn't suit, we can go on to Chelsea. Hampstead's nice but it's too far, really. At least, I think so. Mayfair and Belgravia are over the top, out of the question. Not fun people in any case. Have you any plans at all? And you haven't told me yet why you've come."

"My sister died a year ago," Louise said, feeling an ache in her throat saying the words. "I couldn't stand the city anymore. I wanted to get far away." It was Faye who'd told her to go, who'd suggested England. In a dream, Faye had sat cross-legged on her bed in pink baby doll pajamas and said, "England makes sense, Lou. You're a commonwealth citizen so you don't need a visa or work papers. Plus you speak the language. It's a good idea. You could start all over again." She'd never, as long as she lived, admit to anyone that her dead sister visited her in dreams, held long conversations with her, and offered advice. People would think she was crazy, even though it was the truth. She dreamed several times a week of Faye. It eased the ongoing pain, made the days bearable.

"Oh, how awfully sad," Rachel sympathized. "I am sorry. You must miss her terribly."

"I do," Louise said, the inner stabbing only slightly dulled after a year. "Anyway, I'm starting fresh. And first I have to find a place, then a job. After that, I've no idea. Just live, I guess."

"What sort of work do you do?" Rachel asked, wisely choosing to get past an area that was visibly painful to her visitor.

"Secretarial, Dictaphone typing, receptionist, that kind of thing."

"Well, I should think a secretarial agency would be the right place to go. I wouldn't mess about with newspaper adverts. An intermediary's always so much more effective, I think, regardless of the enterprise. Oh, this will be fun!" Rachel bubbled. Then, faltering, she said, "Am I being frightfully presumptuous?"

"Not at all," Louise replied. "You're just what the doctor ordered. As I said, I was hoping Philip might help, but this is better, if you've got the time and you honestly don't mind."

"Time," said Rachel, "is the one thing I've got heaps of. Oh good!" she declared as a middle-aged woman in uniform wheeled in a trolley. "Here's tea. And clever Molly's made all my favorite sandwiches: cress, and cucumber, and smoked salmon too. Thank you, Molly! You're a treasure."

The servant flushed with satisfaction, smiled, and went on her way.

"The really clever thing to do, if one has the resources, is to buy a flat. Real estate," Rachel said, "can only increase in value. Aside from being a tremendously good investment, it's collateral, in the event one needs it. Rather than pay rent, one's paying toward ownership of one's own property. A very sensible investment, and if one is clever, something that needs a bit of doing's ideal. You know: buy it, fix it up, then sell it at a profit, and move on to something better."

"How do you know these things?" Louise asked, noticing that the other passengers on the bus gave Rachel one puzzled glance and looked away. The English, it seemed, were too polite to stare. For the most part, so were Canadians. From the little she'd seen so far, the English and the Canadians were a lot alike.

"Daddy *is* a banker, you know. Or perhaps you didn't know."

"I didn't, as a matter of fact."

"Well, he is. International banking, but banking is banking. I begged him for a position but he wouldn't hear of it. That same rubbish about wasting education on women because we'll simply get ourselves pregnant and they'll have to go about educating someone else to replace us. In any event, I find it fascinating. And I'm also eminently practical. I've done very well with my investments. If you ever want to invest, let me know. I read the financial pages every day, and I subscribe to the *Wall Street Journal*. If Mummy and Daddy weren't such dolts they'd have let me go to the school of economics. But, no. They insisted it'd be too much for me. It's such a bore. They prefer to have me idle and permanently eligible for Mr. Right, rather than allow me to put my brain to good use."

"Are you a beatnik?" Louise finally asked, overcome by curiosity.

Rachel laughed happily. "I wish I were, but no. I admire them tremendously, though. Don't you? Mummy and Daddy would disown me altogether. As it is they barely tolerate my bare feet and plimsoles."

"What about the hat?"

Surprisingly, Rachel turned suddenly serious. "Hats are my armor," she said soberly. "They keep me safe."

"From what?"

"Here we go!" Rachel said. "This is our stop." She rang to signal the driver, then led Louise off at the front of the bus. "I have a feeling in my bones you'll like South Kensington. It's not so twee as Chelsea, not quite as U as Knightsbridge."

"What do the hats keep you safe from?" Louise asked again, intrigued by Rachel's mood shifts.

"Nanny crocheted me this dear little beret when I was about eight, and when I wore it I felt simply super. I've been raiding Mummy's wardrobe ever since. And of course I have some I've bought myself. But I prefer Mummy's. They're so . . . so Queen Motherish!" She laughed and took Louise's arm. "We'll go along here to Old Brompton Road, then cut through to Fulham Road so you can see if you care for the area. If you do, we'll find the nearest tobacconist and check the board out front. Local people tend to put their notices up on the nearest board. It's quite sensible, really, if you think about it. Obviously, if one's looking for something in the area, the practical place to begin looking is on one of the boards. You wouldn't consider *buying* a flat, would you?"

"That'd depend on how much they cost. I do have some money, but not a whole lot."

"We'll find you something to rent for now, then start looking for a place to buy once you're established. You're ever so lucky, Louise. I'd give anything to have a flat of my own."

"Then why don't you?"

"Mummy and Daddy would never allow it. I have no marketable skills, for one thing. Although I do have an income. Inherited, you know. But they insist I'd be unable to cope on my own, and I expect they're right."

"Why?"

"Oh, well," Rachel sighed. "I have these tiresome spells now and again, and have to go away."

"Spells?"

"Hmmn. Things become rather too much. I get frightfully muddled, then Mummy and Daddy ship me off to this tiresome place in the country until I'm well again. A lot of nonsense. Oh, now here's a board. Let's have a look, shall we?"

✦

"It's so green over here," Louise was saying in the coffee shop where they'd stopped to take a rest. "I've never seen a green anything like it. Even in the rain, it seems to glow."

"It's the damp, of course," Rachel said. "Wettest place anywhere, except for Ireland. We've got positively bloody weather, really."

"I don't mind, although it's pretty cold for June."

"Summer comes usually on a weekend in August," Rachel said drolly, "and if one isn't paying close attention, one could miss it altogether."

"It's not *that* bad, is it?"

"Wait, you'll see. It's perfectly foul. You've heard, haven't you, of our famous pea soup fogs? They're very real, my dear, I assure you. I usually spend most of each winter down with bronchitis. Mummy's had chilblains I don't know *how* many times. Daddy's bound to get gout, and

Phippy's forever got sniffles. I can't honestly think why we live here, why *anyone* lives here. All the really sensible people are in the Greek islands or the south of France. I'd adore to live in the south of France or in Italy. But of course it's out of the question. We're *rooted* in London. Dozens of generations of Townsends and Posts, the intertwining of the family branches and all that, you know, my dear," she said in mock lofty tones.

"Well, so far I like it. If you don't work and you're not at school, what do you do with yourself all day?"

"I try to rebel," Rachel said with a self-deprecating smile. "I'm not terribly good at it, but I do try. I read," she said, "and I meet up with friends and we go to clubs to hear jazz, listen to bad poetry, and drink foul coffee. Primarily, though, I'm bored witless. Which is why it's positively *providential* you've come along. Unless of course I'm being intrusive. You must promise to tell me the instant you feel I'm becoming the least bit of a bore."

"I can't imagine you ever being boring," Louise said truthfully. "So what do you think? Which place did you like best?"

"They're all impossible, really. But if we must pick, I think the bed-sitter on Onslow Gardens is the best of the furnished lot. If it was me, though, I'd take that flat in the Fulham Road over the antiques shop. I know it's unfurnished and in frightful condition but it has simply fabulous potential. It needs masses of work but for the price of the furnished bed-sitter you'd have two rooms plus what passes for a kitchen—I mean to say there is a grotty cooker and a sink—as well as your own bathroom. Of course you would have to buy some furniture, which might be beyond your means."

Louise drank some of her coffee, thinking. Rachel did have a point. The place over the antiques shop was more than twice the size of the room on Onslow Gardens, and a private bathroom was a definite plus. "How much was that unfurnished place?" she asked.

Rachel pulled a scrap of paper from her pocket. "Onslow Gardens was four pounds fifteen. The flat over the shop is four pounds seventeen and six."

"Brother! I've got to figure that out in money," Louise laughed, doing some mental arithmetic.

Rachel rhymed off the equivalent dollar rates, then put a hand on Louise's arm, saying, "Take the flat, Louise. I'll help you fix it up. In fact, I'm sure Mummy and Daddy would contribute a thing or two from the attic or the country house. They've got masses of bits and pieces squir-reled away, more than enough to furnish several houses, let alone one small flat. And when Philip's home from school we'll get him to round up some of his friends and put them to work building shelves and painting, fixing the place up. Although I'm far handier than Phippy. I do quite nice carpentry work. I made a birdhouse at our country place, and a jolly decent set of shelves too. I asked to take a carpentry course but naturally Mummy and Daddy said I wasn't up to it. They're tiresome, honestly. Won't let me do a thing."

"I don't know," Louise hesitated, thinking of the run-down condition of the place, the two grimy windows overlooking the street, the foul bathroom with its stained fittings, the scarred floorboards and tattered wallpaper. "It's such a mess. And there's no fridge, no cupboards, no closets."

"Yes, but did you see the exquisite molding on the ceilings? And there is a working fireplace in the front room. Oh, take it, Louise! I promise you you won't be sorry. I'll help you fix it up and it'll be charming. We'll strip off all that nasty wallpaper, paint everything white, clean the floors and windows. I know there are some curtains in one of the trunks in the attic that would do for the windows. You'll see! It has wonderful poten-tial. And think of the public service you'll be doing by giving me some-thing to do and a place to do it. Plus, I know where to get most of the things you'll need, aside from the endless trunkfuls of odds and sods up in the attic."

"You say it's a good neighborhood?"

"Oh, you can see that for yourself," Rachel said emphatically. *"And,"* she added momentously, "the number fourteen bus will bring you almost to our door. Or you could walk over in fifteen minutes. You'll also be well situated for work, say, in the City or anywhere in the Piccadilly area. Please take it. If you hesitate someone's bound to come along and snatch it up. It's a tremendous find. Nothing else we've seen was anywhere near as interesting."

"Okay," Louise laughed. "You've convinced me. Let's finish our coffee and go back to see the landlord again."

"I think you'll be jolly lucky too, to have such a super landlord. He was ever so friendly and nice. I even liked one or two things in his shop."

"The only problem is," Louise said, "I'm going to have to stay on in the hotel until we get the flat cleaned up and I can buy a bed. I probably should've listened to my grandmother. She told me to put everything in storage, that I'd want it one day. But I couldn't . . . Everything reminded me of Faye.''

''Poor you. I expect you did the sensible thing. And of course you won't stay on in that dreary hotel. You'll come to stay with us until the flat's in good nick. I thought you understood.''

''Rachel, maybe your mother and father won't like that.''

''My dear, they'd be delighted. Besides, they'll probably never even know!'' Rachel laughed. ''They're in Paris for another week before they go on to South Africa. They won't be home for a *month!* Philip will be back before they are. Honestly, it's quite all right. Phippy and I have friends stay all the time. In fact, I think we should go directly to your hotel after you've put your deposit on the flat. Do you have enough cash?''

''I think so.''

''Good. We'll do that now, then collect your things and be home in time for dinner.''

''Are you sure?'' Louise asked.

''Absolutely,'' Rachel said. ''I told Molly before we left that you'd be staying. She's already preparing one of the guest rooms.''

''You're very generous, Rachel. Are you sure you won't get into trouble?''

''I'm *always* in trouble, my dear. What difference will a spot more make? You will come to stay, won't you? Tomorrow we'll go round to some of the secretarial agencies and get you signed on. Then we'll find you a bank. You'll need a referrer, so I'll bring along my identification. It's quite sticky opening a bank account, for some reason. You'd think they'd be enchanted to have one's money. But no. One must have a responsible referring party, if you will. And I certainly qualify for that, if for nothing else. When all that's done, we'll take another good long look at your new flat and make a list of what needs doing. I expect laying in a supply of cleaning materials will top the list. It's far and away the *dirtiest* place I've ever seen. But wait and see, Louise! It's going to be super, absolutely super. Honestly, it will. Oh, I'm *so* pleased you've come to stay. We're going to be the best of friends. I just know it.''

''I think so, too,'' Louise said, thinking Faye had been right in telling her to make the move. She'd only been in the country two days and she'd already found a friend and confidant. She'd telephone Gramma before she checked out of the hotel, to let her and Uncle Bob know where to reach her.

CHAPTER

THIRTY-NINE

WEARING RUBBER GLOVES, LOUISE SCRUBBED AT THE grimy bathtub with scouring cleanser and a sponge, wondering why she'd let herself be talked into renting this place. From the looks of it, the tub hadn't been cleaned in years, nor had the toilet, the basin, or the lino-leum-covered floor. Some previous tenant had covered the window with a frost-patterned adhesive paper and there was no way to remove it from the glass. She'd have to hang curtains to hide the ugly window. Mr. Greeley, her new landlord, insisted the water heater was functional, but neither she nor Rachel had so far been able to figure out how to turn it on. As soon as she finished cleaning the tub she intended to go down to ask him for specific directions. She also thought she'd ask if he'd provide a refrigerator, or share the cost of one with her. She only wished she'd thought to ask before paying any money. But things were done very differently here. She hadn't had to sign a lease or put down a month's rent for a deposit. All she'd had to do was pay the first week's rent in advance and wait while Mr. Greeley set up a rent book for her. If he refused to contribute to the cost of a fridge, she'd do without, and have milk delivered daily. In the early mornings she'd seen the milkmen delivering half-pint and pint bottles. It was something she hadn't seen in Toronto since her childhood, and the clank and rattle of the bottles had become for her the sound of a London morning.

Mopping her forehead on her sleeve, she rinsed the tub, relieved to see much of the dirt draining away. She'd just have to live with the orange rust stain that appeared to have become ingrained in the porcelain. But at least she was making some progress. Now that her bed had been delivered she'd be spending her first night in the flat. She was looking forward to it, eager to be on her own.

Staying with Rachel had been an exotic interlude. She wasn't accustomed to being waited on, to having food prepared for her, to having her bed made and her laundry done. For Rachel, of course, being cossetted by a live-in staff of three was perfectly natural, but Louise felt slightly smothered by the constant, albeit often invisible attentions of the cook, housekeeper, and maid. She'd come to London to be alone, to make a new life for herself, and until she actually moved her bags into this flat and began acquiring the items that would personalize it she wasn't making any progress. It felt as if she were leaning on Rachel now, the way she'd leaned on Daniel throughout the previous year.

She'd spoken to him almost every day, and had seen him two or three nights a week, allowing him to envelope her in his love. Not that she hadn't cared for him. She had, almost painfully. But as long as she'd gone on using him as a kind of human shield to stand between her and the pain of Faye's death she was being dishonest. She'd known from the outset that she and Daniel had no future together. She'd needed him, and so she'd taken with both hands the comfort and consolation he'd offered, drawing strength from him until she felt strong enough to go forward alone. And then she'd told him her plans.

She'd expected him to try to dissuade her but he hadn't. He'd said, "It's a good idea, Lulu. You need to make a break," and he'd helped her. He'd gone with her to the steamship office to book the ticket; he'd shopped with her for luggage; he'd even accompanied her to the passport office. At times she'd wondered if he wasn't actually relieved that she was going, but she'd understood finally that he loved her so much he was prepared to do what he thought was right: He let her go. "You're so young," he'd said on their last evening together. "You're doing the right thing. I've had nine more years than you to work on myself, to find out what I want and don't want. You have to have that chance now. I love you and I'll always be here for you. If there's ever anything you need, let me know. I'll come running." And then he'd kissed her goodbye.

Now she was more than three thousand miles away, working herself into a sweat to turn a pair of filthy rooms into a home. She was overcome by a sudden intense longing to see her Gramma and Uncle Bob, to be back in Daniel's sheltering embrace. But she'd made her decision and she'd stick with it. She certainly wasn't going to become discouraged by something as elemental as dirt. Not when she had the means to clean it away. She was eighteen years old and independent at last. And tonight she'd begin staking a real claim on this pair of rooms that was going to be her new home.

Rachel appeared in the doorway, beaming. "Come see what a lovely job I've done on your cooker!"

Throwing down her sponge, Louise peeled off the rubber gloves and followed her new friend to the kitchen to admire her handiwork.

Using water she'd heated in a large pot she'd brought along, Rachel had cleaned the stove inside and out. The oven racks sat drying on some newspaper on the floor. In a rush of gratitude and affection Louise hugged her. "It's like new, Rachel," she said, overwhelmed by a sense of déjà vu for all the times she and Faye had worked together, cleaning the rooms on Manning Avenue. "Thank you," she got out, touched by Rachel's efforts on her behalf. She suspected it was one of the few, if not the only time in her life Rachel had performed this type of household labor, and she wondered what she'd done to inspire the girl. Perhaps if Rachel knew some of the things Louise had done over the past year she might not be quite so inspired. She thought again of Daniel, and stopped herself. She wouldn't think about him now. He was a grown man. She hadn't forced him to do anything he hadn't wanted to do. And he'd told her to go, told her it was a good idea. Everyone had said so, even Gramma, who'd insisted she have Faye's share of the St. George Street house money. "You're going to need it, honey," Gramma had said. "You can't go off to another country without a little nest egg, in case things don't work out right away."

"I'll take you out to dinner," Louise said. "It's the least I can do to thank you for all your help."

"Don't be a ninny," Rachel said, pleased. "Phippy's due back, remember? The three of us will dine at home. And do stop thanking me. I've *told* you: This is a treat for me. I'd be dying of boredom otherwise. You've lent an entirely new dimension to my previously tiresome life. Besides, it's such fun showing a complete stranger the city. I'm seeing it quite differently now as a result. And there's tons more you've yet to see."

"But the sheets and blankets, the towels, the dishes and pots and pans. You've saved me an absolute fortune."

"All I've really done is cleared some of the rubbish out of the attic.

Mummy and Daddy ought to be undyingly grateful. Next on the agenda I must search out those old curtains for the front windows. And we'll have a good look to see what other bits and pieces you might use. The place is looking better already, don't you think?''

Louise had to agree, although the light that poured in the newly cleaned windows merely pointed up the water-stained wallpaper and scarred wood floor. There was so much still to be done. Her list ran to two pages with only a few items so far crossed off. She'd applied for a telephone; she'd opened an account and deposited the draft Gramma had given her; she'd bought a bed; and she'd signed on with a secretarial agency in Brooke Street. She'd already done three days' work for a firm of chartered accountants near Oxford Circus and was scheduled for an additional two weeks there. With Rachel's assistance she was learning her way around the city and had met several of Rachel's friends.

"What next?" Rachel asked, looking around. "I suppose I'll have a go at this sink." She frowned, eyeing the free-standing basin. "We'll have to rig up some sort of counter space for you, as well as some shelves. I'll get this sink done while you finish up in the bathroom. Then let's assemble your bed, shall we?"

"You're not getting tired, are you?"

"I'm perfectly fine," Rachel said, with the fingers of her right hand adjusting the angle of the broad-brimmed, flower-bedecked hat she was wearing with her usual black pullover and slacks. "Please don't fuss over me," she snapped angrily. "I get quite enough of that at home, thank you very much."

"Sorry. I didn't mean to fuss."

"Now you're patronizing me," Rachel said, scowling. "I really don't care for it at all."

Startled by Rachel's abrupt change of mood, Louise smiled and said, "I don't even know what patronizing means."

"I suppose you think that's amusing."

"What's the matter, Rachel?"

"You know perfectly well what the matter is," Rachel insisted. "I'm not a child to be jollied along and I resent being treated like one. It's demeaning."

"That's not at all how I think of you."

"Then don't *treat* me that way. It's horrid. I'm not a child," she repeated.

"I know you're not. Whatever I said, please forget it. I didn't mean to upset you." She found herself becoming as upset as Rachel. "Honestly," she added, trying another smile.

"I do so hate being fussed over."

"You have my most solemn promise I'll never fuss over you again." Louise tried another, coaxing smile.

Relenting, Rachel's features lightened. She again adjusted the angle of her hat, saying, "Make sure you don't."

"Cross my heart," Louise promised, relieved. "I'll just go give the toilet a once-over." She made a face. "Maybe a twice-over," she laughed. "Then I want to run down and ask Mr. Greeley how to turn on the damned water heater." Thinking it best to leave Rachel alone for the moment, she went back to the bathroom. Retrieving her rubber gloves, she reviewed the brief episode, finding as she pulled on the gloves that her hands were shaking. For a minute or two, Rachel had seemed like a complete stranger. And Louise had floundered, frightened by how easily she'd inadvertently upset her friend's equilibrium.

✦

"Oh, dear," Mr. Greeley said. "I'll come up and show you. I should've thought to point out the switch. How are you getting along, Miss Parker?"

Louise smiled and said, "Very well, thank you. I've already started doing temporary work. And my bed's arrived."

"Enjoying our city, are you?"

"I like it very much." It was true. She did. She liked the parks and the historical buildings; she liked the double-decker buses and the Lyon's Corner Houses where she went for lunch. "The food's not very good, though."

"No," he said. "We British have never been famous for our cuisine. You'll have to dine with my wife and me one Sunday, have a proper roast beef dinner with Yorkshire pudding."

"That would be very nice."

"Yes, I must mention it to Isabel this evening."

In his early sixties or so, with a carefully trimmed moustache and goatee, Mr. Greeley was, in his own way, as charmingly eccentric as Rachel. He wore figured suspenders and well-cut if outdated suits, and was unfailingly kind, if not somewhat beleaguered by the logistics of being a landlord. He'd already explained to Louise that the previous tenants—a pair of young men—had been in place when he'd bought the building some four years earlier, so that all he'd done until now was collect the rent and sign the rent book. He'd never had to fuss with things like water heaters.

"There's no fridge, you know," Louise said as he put a sign in the front door. BACK IN FIVE MINUTES, it read. "I don't suppose you'd consider putting one in."

"Oh dear," he said, smoothing his goatee. "I don't know about that, Miss Parker."

"I was thinking that we could get a secondhand one or something, maybe split the cost."

"That's very decent of you. Let me make some inquiries, my dear. We'll see what's available."

Upstairs in the flat he went to the cupboard in the hallway that housed the water heater, felt inside along the wall, found the switch, showed it to Louise, and turned it on. "There you go," he said, shifting to survey his property. "Place is a bit of a shambles, isn't it," he grimaced apologetically. "But you've cleaned it up a fair bit. It's already looking better. Do let me know if there's anything you need, and I will make inquiries about a refrigerator. Oh, by the bye. If you need to use the telephone, please feel free to come down. And I'll be happy to receive any deliveries for you, Miss Parker."

"Thanks a lot, Mr. Greeley."

"Not at all. Good day to you, Miss Townsend-Post," he nodded to Rachel. "Must get back now," he said, rubbing his thumbs and fingers together as if to rid them of dust as he hurried down the stairs.

"The only cupboard in the place," Louise said to Rachel, "and it's wasted on the water heater."

"No, no, Louise. You're lucky. You've got a built-in airing cupboard."

"A what?"

"You see this shelf?" Rachel put one hand on the row of slatted boards over the heater. "You put your laundry and towels here and the heater keeps them lovely and warm. See! There are even several hooks up top there if you want to hang things to dry. It's a great bonus."

"No kidding! I hadn't even thought about laundry."

"There's a coin laundry up the road," Rachel said. "I spotted it the other day. And some not bad-looking restaurants in the neighborhood too. There's even a milk machine a few doors down, in case you run out. You're wonderfully well situated here.''

Louise was beginning to believe she might be right. But she still wasn't convinced. There were no streetcars or trolley buses; napkins were called serviettes; the subway was the underground; trucks were lorries; elevators were lifts; raincoats were macs. There was a great deal to learn.

Initially Philip didn't recognize her. But since she wouldn't have recognized him either, Louise wasn't bothered. He'd grown into a very tall, sandy-haired man of six-two or -three, with large perfect teeth like his sister's. He was soft-spoken, stooped slightly, and wore wire-rimmed glasses. He did remember their dancing together at the Royal York, and once past the awkwardness of being reintroduced by Rachel, he expressed an enthusiastic interest in helping with the flat.

"What needs doing?" he asked both girls.

"Everything," they chorused, then laughed.

"Phippy, couldn't you round up a few of your friends to lend a hand? With four or five of us, it'd take no time at all to strip the walls and floors, get everything painted. There's a bit of carpentry needs doing, as well. There's no countertop in the kitchen, not a single solitary shelf anywhere. The front windows have been painted shut. The kitchen window has several broken panes of glass. On and on, I'm afraid.''

"I expect I could dragoon a few of the lads into some unpaid labor,'' he said, "provided you lay on some food and plenty of beer.''

"I'd be more than happy to do that,'' Louise said, finding him as immediately likable as his sister. It seemed their only similarity. They bore no particular resemblance to one another. And where Rachel was quirky in her manner of dressing, Philip seemed very conservative in gray slacks and a white shirt with a school tie and a navy blazer. "The thing is, we'll have to do it evenings and weekends. I'm doing temp work for a couple of weeks for a chartered accountant.''

"I don't see that'll be a problem. I'll ring up Tony and Ben. I'm sure they'll be willing. And Rachel, what about Molly's son, Nick? He's a jack-of-all-trades.''

"Crikey! I hadn't even *thought* about Nick. What a clever monkey you are, Phippy.''

"You might not be so willing once you see the place,'' Louise said. "I still don't know why I let Rachel talk me into it. I'll probably freeze there tonight.''

"We'll lend you an electric heater," Rachel said. "I'll fetch one for you right now. And while I'm about it, I'll have a word with Molly about hiring Nick to do some of your carpentry." She jumped up and hurried off, calling for Molly.

"Well," Philip said, "Rachel seems to have taken you over. I hope she's not being a nuisance."

Mildly irked at this, Louise said, "She's been a godsend. And terrific company, not to mention working like a slave to get the place clean enough for me to stay in."

"Please don't misunderstand," he said. "I wasn't criticizing my sister. I adore Rachel. It's just that she has . . . certain problems."

"I know. She's told me all about her problems. I think you're very lucky to have her for a sister. I really do. She's good-hearted and lots of fun."

"Listen, Louise," he said, leaning forward on the sofa opposite, elbows on his knees. "I think you should know. Rachel's in one of her 'up' phases just now. When she's up, she's always good-hearted and lots of fun. When she's down, she's another person altogether, lost and confused and frightened of her own shadow. It's why we're all so protective of her. She's not a very stable girl. I'm delighted the two of you've hit it off so well. I only worry that she's taking too much on, and that she's given you a false impression."

"I'll keep an eye on her," Louise promised, "see to it she doesn't overdo. And my impression is that she's sweet and lovable. I don't think that impression's going to change because she hits a 'down' patch. I really *like* her, Philip. But I will look out for her. Okay?"

"That's very decent of you." He smiled and said, "It's lovely to see you again. Do you still dance, Louise?"

"I haven't lately, but I still like to."

"Perhaps one evening you'll let me take you to one of the clubs. There are some quite good bands about town."

"I'd love it."

"Good! For now I suppose I'd best get on to the chaps, see who'll pitch in."

Early Saturday morning while Louise was cleaning the bathroom floor for the third time in as many days there was a knock at the door. She opened it to find Rachel and Philip along with two of Philip's friends, all of them dressed in casual clothes, ready for work.

"Louise Parker," said Philip, "I'd like you to meet my friends Tony and Ben."

They all shook hands, then Louise invited them to look the place over. "It's in pretty sad shape," she said. "I honestly don't even know where to begin."

"I should think stripping off this tatty wallpaper's the first order of the day," said Tony. "Perhaps we could work in teams. Two of us will have a go at the wallpaper while two of us fetch in some paint and brushes, sandpaper, and whatever other tools we'll need."

"Has your landlord a ladder?" Ben asked.

"I'm sure he probably does," Louise replied.

"What about me?" Rachel said.

"Ah, Rachel," said Tony. "You'll be the swing worker, with whichever team needs you. Fair enough?"

"I suppose. So who's on which team and where do we begin?"

"I suggest," Tony said, "that Ben and I begin on the wallpaper while Louise and Phil go for the supplies. After all, Phil's the one with the vehicle."

"And what about me?" Rachel asked again.

"You'll come with us," Louise said. "We'd better make a list."

"It's quite a decent flat," Philip said judiciously. "I think you've done well to find it, Louise."

"Rachel found it," Louise said. "She's the clever one. I'm just obedient."

Everyone laughed at this, then Tony and Ben shifted Louise's bed into the center of the front room before surveying the walls.

"We'll need scrapers," Ben said.

"See if you can't rent one of those machines for stripping the wallpaper. It's a steamer sort of thing," said Tony.

A knock at the door interrupted them. Louise went to answer it, saying over her shoulder, "Somebody start making that list."

The young man at the door grinned, asking, "You Louise?"

"That's right."

"I'm Nick. Me mum said you've got some carpentry needs doin'."

He looked to be in his late teens or early twenties, with fair hair, brown eyes, and a jaunty manner, as if he was prepared to find fun in every situation.

"Oh, hi!" She extended her hand, and, looking startled, he shook hands with her. "Come on in," she said. "Everybody's here. We're just getting organized."

Breaking into a smile, Nick said, " 'Ello Rachel. How're you then, luv?"

"Hullo, Nick," Rachel smiled. "I'm fine, thank you."

"Keepin' busy, are you?" he asked her with evident fondness.

"Very, since Louise arrived."

"Nick," Philip said, crossing the room to shake his hand. "You've got your work cut out for you here, as you can see. These are my friends Tony and Ben. We've volunteered to help out."

"What're you lot plannin' on doin'?" Nick asked, his brows drawing together as if suspicious of their abilities.

"We thought we'd begin by getting the wallpaper down," Philip explained.

"You go tryin' to strip that paper," Nick said, "and the plaster's likely as not to come with it. What you want is to sand the walls, paper 'n' all, get the surface smooth for paintin'."

Everyone paid close attention.

"In these old buildin's you can't just go tearin' things down, see," he added. "You never know what you'll find."

"Perhaps you should supervise," Louise said, at once aware, as were the others, of this young man's natural authority. "We'll put you in charge and you can tell the rest of us what to do."

"Let's have a look round," Nick said. "Tell me what wants doin', then we'll see to organizin' you lot."

"Sounds fair enough," Philip said.

"Sounds jolly sensible to me," Rachel said, with another smile for Nick.

"Right, then. Take five while me'n Louise have a look-see," Nick said.

He agreed to install a counter in the kitchen with shelves above to hold food and crockery, to build a closet in the hallway next to the cupboard containing the water heater, to mount a shelf in the bathroom and additional shelves in the living room, and to replace the broken window glass and free up the front windows. "You'll either want to paint these floors," he told Louise, "or have me hire a sander and redo them. Cheaper to repaint. Less of a mess, too."

"What's cheapest and easiest?" Louise asked him.

"Buy a bloody carpet, darlin'," he laughed.

"I'm sure we can find you something in the attic," Rachel said. "I don't know why *I* didn't think of that."

"Rachel, you can't simply go helping yourself to things without consulting Mother and Father," Philip said.

"Don't be a ninny! I'll give Louise the old carpet from my bedroom. It's actually in very good condition, Louise," Rachel explained. "There's simply no reason why we can't give it to her, Phippy. It's merely sitting there collecting dust. Don't be such a prig."

"Be it on your head," he said. "Well, Nick. Tell us where you'd like us to begin."

"Right, then. We'll need a ladder . . ."

"Wait," Louise said. "You haven't said how much it'll cost."

With a laugh, Nick said, "Gettin' ahead of meself. Here's 'ow we'll do it. You'll pay for the materials as we go, and I'll charge you for my time. Fair enough?"

"Very. And I'll provide meals for everyone."

"I'll be the tea lady," Rachel announced.

"Now, as I was sayin', Tony and Ben will fetch a ladder. You say your landlord has one, Louise?"

"I think so."

"Right. So you two do that while Louise and Philip and me 'ead off to the lumberyard."

"But what about *me?*" Rachel asked.

"Put on the tea, darlin'," Nick told her with a smile.

With a feeling of satisfaction and a sense that things were finally going to begin, Louise went for her purse and her checkbook.

CHAPTER

FORTY

IF THE WEATHER WAS GOOD, LOUISE TOOK THE NUMBER 74 bus to Oxford Street and then caught another bus to Oxford Circus. If the weather was bad, which it was most days, she took the number 14 or 49 to the South Kensington station and got on a District Line train to Victoria Station, where she switched over to the Victoria Line to Oxford Circus. Either way took about the same amount of time, but she preferred the bus. She saw new things each trip, a piece of architecture or some shop caught her eye, even through the constant-seeming rain.

She actually didn't mind the rain; it suited her underlying state of mind, felt appropriate to the sorrow that lived, even thrived, just below the surface. For the benefit of her new friends and coworkers she resurrected the sunny attitude that once had come naturally. No one seemed to notice that her smiles were not, for the most part, spontaneous, or that it required a conscious effort for her to participate in conversations or to laugh. It struck her as profoundly possible that everyone might be consciously structuring their reactions to everyone else, that by the time most people reached the age of say, sixteen or eighteen, they no longer possessed the ability to respond spontaneously to any situation. She thought about this a lot during her trips back and forth to work. The concept fascinated her, and she watched people, trying to see if there were some visible demarcation between the real and what she considered the performance. She couldn't see it.

The English seemed unfailingly polite. Twice she encountered people who stiffened at the sound of her voice and asked straight out if she was American. When she explained that she was Canadian there was a complete change of attitude, an expression of relief overtaking the features of her questioners. It was something she'd encountered at home—not being mistaken for American, but the negativity. For some reason both the Canadians and the English had a low-grade animosity toward Americans.

She didn't understand why, and thought it probably had something to do with politics—never her strong suit—and couldn't imagine why people would judge individuals, would hold them responsible for their government's actions. She'd never actually met many Americans but thought they were probably a lot like everyone else. Still, she wished she'd thought to say she was American just to see what would have happened. She felt slightly embarrassed and a little guilty at the relief she'd experienced in being able to respond that she wasn't an American but one of eighteen million or so Canadians.

Her boss at the accounting office was a small, soft-spoken man in his mid forties with premature wrinkles that only heightened his boyish features. Every time she encountered him she thought she could tell exactly what he must have looked like as a boy. He was a very gentle man who treated her with great courtesy and praised her work each time she presented him with yet another batch of letters or profit-and-loss statements or balance sheets. He seemed both grateful for and somewhat astonished by her speed and efficiency, and after her sixth day invited her into his office to offer her a permanent position.

"We'd be delighted to have you stay on, Miss Parker. Your work is really very good and we do need someone on a full-time basis."

"I've enjoyed working here, Mr. Reeves," she said, choosing her words with care, "but I've only been in the country two weeks and I'm not really ready yet to take a permanent job."

"I quite understand," said the small man. "Should you change your mind, though, feel free to let me know."

The people in the office were all very friendly, particularly Annie, the tea lady who came around twice a day with a trolley and brought everyone tea or coffee and a sweet biscuit or two. Annie was in her late fifties, round and jovial, always smiling. The typists went to her with their problems and there was inevitably someone standing in the doorway of the minute kitchen talking to her while she brewed up an immense pot of tea or prepared individual cups of instant Nescafé.

Louise went out to lunch each day with one or more of the girls, to some place nearby that would accept their luncheon vouchers. The food for the most part was awful, but the desserts were invariably good: puddings of one variety or another drenched in hot custard. Louise stuck with sandwiches, preferring them to the eggs and chips or beans or spaghetti on toast the other girls ate. The coffee everywhere was dreadful, so she drank tea during the day and brewed herself a decent pot of coffee in the evening when she got back to the flat.

Each evening when she returned home she found some new item Rachel had brought over or had asked Nick to bring over in a borrowed van. So far Rachel had sent along a comfortable if somewhat shabby upholstered armchair and an attractive polished-oak side table, a set of wrought iron fireplace tools and a small black fire screen, a scratched brass log holder, a standing lamp with a pale yellow fringed shade, several mismatched teacups and saucers, and a square nightstand that Nick had immediately given a coat of glossy white paint. When Louise protested that she couldn't go on accepting the almost-daily gifts, Rachel shushed her, saying, "I'm having a lovely time searching things out. Don't spoil my fun by being a poor sport." Louise stopped protesting. Rachel really did seem to be having a wonderful time.

Nick worked in the flat at random hours while Louise was at the office, and was usually still around when she arrived home from work. She'd grown accustomed to finding him there and looked forward to having a cup of tea or coffee with him before he went on his way. She enjoyed his company and loved the way the place was shaping up.

When she arrived home that Thursday evening, she saw that Rachel had provided a six-foot runner for the hallway, and the promised carpet lay like a log in the middle of the hall. Smiling, she stepped into the doorway to admire her new home, thinking it was quite remarkable what a coat of white paint could do. She looked around the high-ceilinged rooms, able at last to see the potential Rachel had pointed out at first viewing. The front room seemed large and airy with the overhead light reflecting off the smooth freshly painted walls. Once the carpet was in place the room would look positively elegant. The shelves Nick had built on either side of the fireplace had been painted a glossy white, as had the bathroom and the kitchen. The hallway had been painted the same matte white as the front room and the entire apartment looked bigger as a result.

"You've done a wonderful job," she told Nick, watching as he finished mounting the countertop to the wall.

"I like to do good work." He was crouched beneath the counter, giving the mounting screws a final turn. "It says who you are, doesn't it?" He came out from under the counter and leaned his full weight on it to test it. "This'll hold a hundredweight easy," he told her, reaching for his cigarette in the ashtray on the windowsill. "Solid as a rock. Give 'er a wipe with a damp cloth and you're ready for business. That's the last of it, my girl. Everything's done."

"Would you like some coffee?" she asked, accustomed after nearly a week to his requests for a "cuppa" at frequent intervals.

"Wouldn't say no, ta." Moving out of her way, he said, "Place looks right nice, Louise. That lot did a decent job, once we got them organized. Dead empty, though, in't it?"

"I plan to buy things as I go along," she said, filling the percolator with cold water.

"It was me I'd get some lino for this kitchen," he said from the doorway as she got two blue-and-white-striped mugs from the shelf. "Finish it off right nice, that would."

She looked down at the floor, saying, "You're right. But I don't really want to spend any more money right now."

"Wouldn't cost you all that much. I know a bloke in Clapham who'll give you a good price." Pulling out his tape he began measuring the floor. "Eleven by fourteen. Say five square yards. Maybe fifteen, twenty quid, depending on the width, seams 'n' all."

"Could you do it?" she asked, thinking that was almost two weeks' pay.

"Sure. Dead easy. Just sand down the uneven bits of this floor, lay out the lino, trim it, cement 'er into place, and Bob's your uncle. Wouldn't take more than two, three hours, only cost you another couple of quid for labor. You might as well get it down now, girl, before you've got furniture in the way. If you like, I could borrow me mate's van, run you to Clapham Saturday morning and we could have it finished by late in the day."

Putting coffee into the basket, she smiled. "You're too persuasive."

"Aw, go on, girl. Have done with it all in one go. It'll niggle you otherwise."

"Niggle?" She looked again at the floor. "You're right. It will. All right. We'll go Saturday. What time?"

"I'll fetch you at nine. All right?"

"All right. The coffee'll be ready in a few minutes."

"Right. I'll put that carpet down for you in the meanwhile if you like."

"I'll give you a hand," she said.

They moved the few pieces of furniture out of the way, then shifted the carpet from the hallway into the center of the room. Nick cut the rope, saying, "Nice bit of Wilton, this. She's dead generous, is Rachel."

"It looks brand new, doesn't it?"

"I daresay it probably is. Knowing Rachel's mum I'd wager this lot wasn't down more than a year or two at most. She's forever 'avin' the place done over."

The carpet fit almost as if it had been cut to measure.

"It's wonderful," Louise said, once they had the furniture back in place.

"A bit of all right," Nick agreed, admiring the pale yellow deep pile carpeting. "I'll 'ave a quick washup, if you don't mind me usin' your bathroom."

"I don't mind at all."

While the coffee finished percolating she got out the cream and sugar, then took a deep breath and turned to survey the apartment. It was so wonderfully bright now with its newly cleaned fireplace and white-painted mantel, its high ceilings and glossy wood trim. And she had Nick Calley to thank for most of it.

He was one of the easiest, most affable people she'd ever met, always singing along to the radio as he worked, always ready with a smile. He obviously had a soft spot for Rachel, and she wondered why he didn't ask her out since it seemed quite clear that Rachel liked him too.

When he returned from the bathroom she handed him his coffee, asking, "Why don't you ask Rachel out, Nick?"

He looked shocked at the suggestion. "Oh no," he said. "That wouldn't be right."

"Why not?"

"Well," he faltered, "we're not the same, are we? I mean, she's Belgravia, isn't she? And me, I'm Battersea Park. The two don't go together, do they?"

"Why not? Come sit down," she said, leading the way to the front room and sitting on the floor with her back against the bed.

He came to sit beside her, positioning the ashtray to one side, holding his mug with both hands. "It's the way things are, in't it?" he said, thrown at having to explain the class system when he'd all his life assumed everyone knew how it worked. *"Her* mum and dad 'ave pots of money. They're upper class. *My* mum's their 'ousekeeper."

"I know all that," she said. "So what?"

He laughed and shook his head. "Things must be a 'ole lot different in Canada," he said. "Over 'ere, if your mum and dad 'ave pots of money you don't go dating the 'ousekeeper's son. That's just the way it is."

"But you obviously like each other."

"Sure," he said. "Me 'n' Rachel 'n' Phil, we've known each other all our lives, 'aven't we? I mean, me mum's worked for them twenty years come this August. But that don't make us the same, see."

"It doesn't make you different, either," Louise insisted.

"Ah, but it does. See, that's England for you, Louise. If you're like Rachel or Phil, you can do any bloody thing what takes your fancy. But if you're like me or me mum, you do what *they* let you do. No point lookin' to go 'igher."

"But of course there is," she argued. "You can do anything you want. It's up to you, not anyone else."

"Not over 'ere, my darlin'. Not over 'ere."

"But wouldn't you like to ask her out?"

With a smile he said, "It'll never 'appen. Not in my lifetime or yours."

"But wouldn't you?" she persisted.

"Crikey!" he said. "Like a bulldog, you are. Yeah," he admitted. "I've always 'ad a real soft spot for Rachel. Nutty as a fruitcake, she is, but good as the day is long. She'd give you 'er last sixpence, give you the shirt right off 'er back. The way I see it, she'd be fine if they'd leave 'er alone, let 'er 'ave a go at a thing or two. But they treat 'er like she's made of glass, always 'ave done. By now she's convinced there's nothin' she *can* do, if you get my meanin'."

"They don't seem to let her do much of anything," she agreed. "Why is that?"

"She gets depressed, see. Started when she was about eleven or twelve, I recall. One day she was 'appy as a lark. The next day all she did was cry. Mum said it was 'eartbreakin'. Everything set her off. If you said 'ello, she'd go to smile and start cryin' instead. But if you was always tellin' me, Don't do this, Nick, or Don't do that, Nick, or You'll make yourself sick, Nick, well after a while I'd start believin' it, too. The way I see it though, if they'd've left 'er alone, she'd be fine. Course they'll never leave her alone now, not since she tried to kill 'erself two years ago come Christmas. So that's the end of it, in't it?" He stared into space for a few moments, then asked, "What about you, Louise? What's brought you all this way from 'ome?"

"It's a long story," she hedged. "Why did she try to kill herself?"

"Dunno," he shrugged. "She took a couple of fistfuls of pills. Lucky thing Mum found 'er in time. She wasn't 'ardly breathin' by then. The ambulance come 'n' they rushed her off to 'ospital, pumped out her stomach. Said she was lucky she didn't suffer no brain damage." He shrugged again, then said, "You in a big 'urry, you can't tell your long story? Me, I've got plenty of time."

"I had an older sister," she said. "Faye died a year ago."

"That's a shame. What'd she die of?"

"A botched abortion."

"What a bloody waste!" he said feelingly. "I don't understand that, you know."

"What?"

"Why a bird can't just go'n' 'ave an abortion if she needs it. Why they've got to make everything so fuckin' difficult. Pardon me French. I *hate* stories like that. Must be the third or fourth time I've met someone lost a girlfriend or a sister 'cause some geezer with a sodding knitting needle did a bit of 'ome surgery. 'Ow come you girls don't get up on your 'ind legs and make a great bleeding fuss about it? Why is that, any'ow?"

"I don't know," she admitted. "I've never thought about it."

"It was blokes 'avin' babies they'd make a fuss, right enough. You can bank on that, girl."

"I still have trouble believing she's dead. It's been a very hard year."

"So you ran away, is that it?"

"I suppose. I just couldn't stand it anymore. Everywhere I went I kept seeing her; everything reminded me of her. I love Toronto; it's my home, but I couldn't stay."

"But don't you miss it?" he asked, lighting a fresh cigarette.

Her throat starting to close, she said somewhat thickly, "Don't get me started. I really can't talk about it."

"Fair enough," he said easily. "Let's talk about your nice new flat. If you decide you want to get a bit of furniture, a table and chairs, say, for your kitchen, let me know. I've got friends," he added meaningfully.

"What? You can get a deal on furniture too?"

"Get you a deal, darlin', on most any bloody thing you can think of," he laughed. "Place looks a treat now, Louise. Get a few pictures for the walls, a radio, some books for those shelves and it'll be real 'omey. You'll need a stock of wood or coal come the winter." He nodded at the fireplace.

"And you've got a friend, right?"

"That's right. You'll want to 'ave a word with the geezer downstairs, see if 'e's got a place where you can store your coal or firewood. Me, I'd go with wood, less messy."

"You'd better make sure I've got your number before you go," she said. "From the sound of it, I'll be needing you for all kinds of things."

He finished the last of his coffee and stood up, saying, "I don't reckon you'd fancy goin' out to a meal one night, would you?"

"Sure I would," she said at once.

"You would?" He looked surprised.

"Why not? We're friends. And I'm not English," she smiled. "I don't have your problem with class distinctions. Maybe I'll even talk you out of some of your fixed ideas."

"Never 'appen," he returned her smile. "But you're welcome to try."

She looked down at the carpet, saying, "I really should buy Rachel a little present. She's been so good to me."

"Be one of the only times anyone ever *give* her anything," he said approvingly. "Most of them what 'angs about, they just take what's on offer, don't they?"

"What d'you think she'd like, Nick?"

Breaking into a big grin, he said, "You'll never go wrong with an 'at, darlin'."

"That's perfect! That's exactly what I'll get her."

"Tell you what, Louise. Saturday, before we go for the lino I'll take you to the market in Portobello Road. You're bound to find somethin' there."

"What is it exactly?"

"It's a street market, darlin', with all kinds of things. Bring your checkbook. I wager you'll find an item or two for the flat. And if you like, Sunday morning I could take you to Petticoat Lane."

"Another market?"

"Yeah, but I reckon you'll like it. You can't come to London and not go to Petticoat Lane at least once."

"It sounds like fun."

"Tell you what," he said, getting into a festive mood. "I'll borrow the van for Sunday too. We'll get the flat kitted out all in one weekend."

"I don't want to spend too much money," she began.

"Don't worry about a thing. *I'll* be with you. We'll do some 'eavy bargaining, you find anything you fancy. Won't cost you more than a few bob and you'll pick up a picture or two, some bits and pieces, books and what-'ave-you for them shelves. Be a lark. You'll see."

"Okay," she agreed. "It *is* pretty empty in here."

"Not for long, my girl," he promised. "And you'll find 'ats galore for old Rachel. She'll be tickled pink."

"Why don't we ask her to come along?"

"Suit yourself," he said offhandedly.

"Would you rather I didn't?"

With a smile he pulled on his jacket saying, "Seems to me you're tryin' to do a bit of matchmakin', darlin'. Give it a rest for now," he said kindly. "It's England, remember?"

"We'll see about that," she said.

"Can't make a fish fly, my girl. Keep that in mind. Ta ra for now."

" 'Bye, Nick," she said, and stood at the top of the stairs watching him go.

As he was opening the street door Mr. Greeley was about to come in. They greeted each other, then Mr. Greeley started up the stairs saying, "Hello, Miss Parker. I wanted to let you know I've found you a refrigerator. Secondhand but in good condition. Chap said they'll deliver it tomorrow afternoon."

"That's terrific, Mr. Greeley, but I'll be at work."

"Not to worry. I'll let them in. Oh, I say! The place looks smashing! You *have* done a splendid job."

"Thank you. I really love it. And the fridge'll make it perfect. If you'll let me know how much I owe you, I'll write you a check."

"Oh, I wouldn't dream of allowing you to pay. Not when you've gone to so much trouble fixing up the flat. Not at all. May I look?" he asked.

"Sure," she said. "Nick just finished putting up the counter here in the kitchen." She showed him. "And we've got the carpet down too."

"It's all very nice," he said, pleased. "Do come down and have a look round the shop, Miss Parker. If there's anything you fancy, I'll give you a good price."

"Thank you, Mr. Greeley. I'll do that."

Going to the door, he said, "And I haven't forgotten about dinner. Isabel asks if Sunday week would be convenient for you?"

"That'd be great."

"Good. I'll give you directions closer to the time. Good night now, Miss Parker."

"Good night, Mr. Greeley, and thanks an awful lot."

When he'd gone she got the mugs from the living room, put Nick's in the sink and poured herself a fresh cup of coffee. Then she went to stand by the front window looking out at the rain-dark street, thinking it was real. She'd left home and was living now in London. And she was going to have to buy a diary to keep track of her appointments. Everyone she'd met so far seemed to have a small Lett's pocket diary. She wished she already had a telephone. She wanted to call Rachel and ask her to come along on Sunday morning. She wanted to prove to Nick that he was wrong. Later, she decided, after she'd fixed herself something to eat, she'd walk up the road to the pay phone and call. She couldn't imagine that Rachel would refuse.

✝

"I'd love to, honestly Louise," Rachel said, "but I couldn't possibly. Mummy and Daddy are having guests for lunch on Saturday. I've promised I'd be here. Perhaps another time."

"Sure," Louise said. "Anyway, thank you for the carpet and the runner. You'll have to come over and see. The carpet looks wonderful."

"I am glad. And by the way, Molly's just done hemming the curtains. They'll be ready by tomorrow afternoon. I thought I'd drop them by."

"Why don't you wait and come over in the evening? I'll cook dinner."

"What a lot of bother," Rachel said. "I haven't much of an appetite these days. Wouldn't you rather come with me to see the new film at the Paris Pullman?"

"Okay," Louise agreed. "What is it?"

"It's Italian, called L'Avventura. Phippy saw it in Oxford and says it's super."

"Fine."

"I'll bring the curtains and keep you company while you eat. Then we'll go see the film. All right?"

"I'll make enough for you too, in case you change your mind."

"I won't change my mind. I'm dieting at the moment."

"Dieting? What for?"

"I'm getting a bit pudgy. I've gone over seven stone and I hate it."

"If you're pudgy, Rachel, I'm obese."

"I am pudgy, and you are not obese. Must fly. See you tomorrow."

Walking back to the flat, Louise stopped on impulse at a cafe called Le Jazz Hot on the far side of Fulham Road. She could hear live music playing downstairs, but opted to have a cappuccino in the restaurant section upstairs where music was playing on a jukebox. She was feeling quite well until the record changed and an incredibly lonely piece of music began to play.

"What's that called?" she asked the waitress when she brought the frothy coffee.

The waitress listened for a moment, then said, "That's Acker Bilk, 'Stranger on the Shore.' Nice, in't it?"

Louise nodded, finding the sound of the clarinet somehow heartbreaking. She sipped the cappuccino. When the music ended, she got up and dropped a shilling into the box, selecting "Georgia on My Mind," by Ray Charles, "Let It Be Me," by the Everly Brothers, and "Stranger on the Shore." Then she sat back down and made her coffee last until the final notes of Acker Bilk had died away. She walked home thinking about Faye, missing her, the melody of "Stranger on the Shore" now forever linked in her mind to her own first two weeks as a stranger in another country.

*C*HAPTER

FORTY-ONE

THE HAT WAS A CLOCHE OF BLACK VELOUR WITH A LARGE black silk rose fastened to one side, and it came in a vintage 1930s hatbox in reasonably good condition. When Louise presented it to her the following Wednesday evening, Rachel initially wouldn't accept the box.

Looking confused, even suspicious, she asked, "What is it?"

"It's a present," Louise said. "For you," she added, since Rachel seemed not to understand.

"You bought me a present?" Rachel's expression now turned to one of near astonishment as she at last accepted the box. "Why?"

"Because I wanted to, because you've been so generous and helpful. I wanted to give you something in return." Louise was beginning to feel awkward. In spite of what Nick had told her, she hadn't expected to have such difficulty in giving Rachel this gift.

"But what is it?" Rachel asked, gazing down at the box now in her hands.

"Open it and find out," Louise suggested.

"Now?" Rachel looked around the flat as if for a previously unnoticed audience who might at any moment begin hooting and jeering.

"Right now."

Nervously, as if she'd never before received a present, Rachel set the box down on Louise's bed and removed the lid. Lifting out the hat, she held it with both hands, her mouth slightly open. "You bought this for me, Louise?" she said, her large brown eyes suddenly moist. "It's simply super," she added in a husky whisper, turning the hat this way and that. "Really super."

"Try it on," Louise prompted.

"You haven't a mirror," Rachel observed somewhat distractedly.

"Use the one in the bathroom."

"We must find you a mirror," Rachel said, again looking around, this time seeming to despair at finding the flat so lacking in amenities. "There's quite a nice cheval glass in the attic . . ."

"Go try it on," Louise laughed. "We'll worry about getting me a mirror some other time."

Rachel carried the hat to the bathroom, where she stood for a few moments admiring it. Then, facing the mirror, she took off her yellow straw boater with flowers and netting, set it to one side, and put on the cloche. "It's wonderful!" she crowed, "simply wonderful."

In the front room Louise smiled, pleased, as Rachel came rushing in to model her new hat. Clad all in black as usual, her eyes ringed in heavy black pencil, Rachel turned in a full circle, exclaiming, "It's the best hat ever, Louise. I adore it. Wherever did you find it, you clever girl?"

"Portobello Road," Louise explained. "Nick took me last weekend before we went to get the linoleum. You really like it?"

"I *love* it!" Rachel sang, throwing her arms around Louise to give her a fierce hug.

Hugging her back, Louise was startled by how small Rachel was beneath her bulky and concealing black clothes. She felt like a child in Louise's arms, her bones tiny and very close to the surface.

"*Thank you,*" Rachel said emphatically, stepping away to turn in another full circle. "I haven't brought anything for you," she said guiltily. "I meant to have another go at the trunks, but I forgot."

"Rachel, you've practically furnished this apartment," Louise said. "You don't have to bring something every time you come. It's good just to see you." She wondered for a moment if Rachel considered her regular offerings the price of admission, if she was in the habit of believing she had to buy friendship. Louise hoped not. It was too sad even to consider.

"Oh, and you got a table and chairs," Rachel noticed, one hand on the hat as if to reassure herself it was really there. "Did you get those at the market too?"

"Uh-huh, and those books, the secondhand radio on the bedside table, and some little pictures I haven't had time yet to hang. You should've seen Nick haggling with the stall owners! I only paid four pounds for the table and chairs. Nick insisted on painting them right away. And he decided I needed a row of hooks in the front hall so he put them up before he left on Sunday."

"You saw him Sunday too?"

"That's right. We went to Portobello Road on Saturday and Petticoat Lane on Sunday."

"He fancies you," Rachel said with a canny light in her eyes, a shrewd smile.

"We're just friends. He 'fancies' you, if he fancies anyone, Rachel."

"Don't be silly," Rachel said rather abruptly. "Nick's simply someone we've always known. Because of Molly."

"So what? He still likes you."

"And I like him," Rachel said. "But that doesn't mean he fancies me."

"Oh well," Louise shrugged, deciding to change the subject. "Are you eating today? I've got some pork chops I could cook."

"Not for me, thank you. But you go ahead. I'll keep you company."

"You're not really dieting, are you?"

"Absolutely. I weighed seven stone two last week. I can't be over seven stone. Two extra pounds on me is the equivalent to ten on anyone else."

"Rachel, seven stone two's only a hundred pounds."

"I never weigh more than seven," Rachel insisted. "But I will have some of your super coffee, if you're making some."

"I'll put the pot on," Louise said, while Rachel placed her old hat in the box, then put the box in the hallway by the door.

Coming to stand in the archway while Louise began fixing the coffee, Rachel said, "How old are you actually?"

"Eighteen. I thought you knew that."

"I may have done. I'm frightfully forgetful." Rachel crossed her arms and leaned against the wall, asking, "Are you a virgin? Or am I being unforgivably rude?"

"It's pretty rude, all right. Are *you?*" Louise countered with a smile.

"I'm afraid so," Rachel sighed. "I expect I'll live out my life as an old maid virgin, despite all the eligible bachelors Mummy and Daddy keep inviting round to meals."

Louise laughed, spooning grounds into the basket.

"It's no laughing matter," Rachel chided.

"Sure it is. You're only twenty-one, for Pete's sake. And you're very pretty. You've even got naturally curly hair, which I personally would kill for. I honestly don't think you're going to go into your dotage never having made love."

"I'll be twenty-two in February. That's less than six months away, you know."

"Stop rushing yourself."

"You're not, are you?" Rachel asked.

"I was involved with someone," Louise admitted.

"Oh, what was he like? Why did you break up? I'm *so* jealous!"

"I broke it up to come here. But I always knew we had no future together."

"Why not?"

"It's complicated," Louise said.

"Do you miss him?"

"Uh-huh. We write to each other, though. I've had four letters from him since I got here."

"That's wonderfully romantic."

"Not really," Louise laughed. "Come sit down," she beckoned, sliding into one of the chairs. "Daniel writes very encouraging letters, with practical suggestions, little philosophical/inspirational quotes to keep my spirits up. He tells me things like not to forget to visit the Tate and the Tower of London and Madame Tussaud's, and he mentions movies he's seen that he thinks I'd like.''

Sitting down opposite, Rachel crossed her arms on the table saying, ''I'm still jealous. The boys I meet are so . . . proper, so boring. They're all candidates Mummy and Daddy think would make good husbands. I wouldn't mind being married. I'd love to have children. But I haven't met a single one who doesn't spend all his time talking about himself, or about what smashing people Mummy and Daddy and Phippy are. The only boy who's even tried to kiss me had dreadful breath. I couldn't bear it.''

Louise started to laugh and Rachel slapped her on the arm. ''It isn't funny, Louise. It's all such a bore. You've no idea.''

''You could change your life, get a place of your own, take some courses, go to work somewhere, or start up some kind of business.''

''I couldn't,'' Rachel said grimly. ''I'd be hopeless.''

''You would not,'' Louise argued.

''I don't even know how to make coffee,'' Rachel said, ''let alone look after myself.''

''I know all kinds of people who can't make a decent cup of coffee, especially in this country. You don't need to know how to make it. You can buy ready-made coffee in restaurants, and you seem to look after yourself well enough.''

''That's because I've got Molly and Cathleen and Iris to do my cooking and cleaning, to pick up after me. No, Mummy and Daddy know best. I'd be hopeless,'' she repeated.

''Well I don't think so,'' Louise said. Then seeing that Rachel was on the verge of becoming upset, she said, ''I found a jazz club down the road. Want to try it out?''

''Oh, definitely!'' Rachel said, at once perking up.

''Good. I can have a sandwich while we listen to some music. We'll have to make it an early evening, though. I want to write some letters, and I've got work in the morning. They want me to stay on another two weeks to train the new secretary.''

''And then what'll you do?''

''Then the agency'll send me somewhere else.''

''You're very brave. I'd hate having to meet entirely new groups of people every few weeks.''

"I'm not brave at all, Rachel. It's just work. You tell the receptionist who you are and they give you a desk and get you started. At the end of each week I turn in my time sheet to the agency and they pay me. It couldn't be easier."

"The agency makes money off your services," Rachel said, thinking this through. "I expect they pay you one rate and charge the clients another, then keep the difference."

"That's right."

"Then," Rachel declared, "I should think you'd want to work for the agency and share in the profits. You'd be bound to make more money."

"I don't know how you can say you wouldn't be able to manage," Louise said, awed as ever by Rachel's financial acumen. "You certainly understand how businesses operate."

"I do," Rachel agreed with a show of pride. "It's unfortunate one can't make a career of it."

"But you could, you know. Banks always need people. You'd be a natural."

"Best we forget it," Rachel said quietly. "It's really out of the question."

"Well," Louise said, glancing over to see the coffee had finished percolating, "if you ever change your mind, I'll be happy to help you get started on your own, just the way you've helped me."

"You're very kind," Rachel said seriously. "I'm so glad we're friends. And thank you for my splendid new hat. My treat at the club."

"We'll go dutch," Louise said. "I can't let you pay for everything, Rachel. It makes me feel crummy."

"It shouldn't, but all right. We'll go dutch." Putting both hands to her head, she jumped up saying, "I must have another look," and ran to the bathroom to admire again her new hat.

⌖

The Greeleys lived in Chelsea, just a short walk from the flat. Following Mr. Greeley's directions, Louise went down Beaufort Street to Elm Park Road. For a pleasant change the day was sunny, if a bit on the cool side for July, and she enjoyed the ten-minute walk.

She'd only encountered Mrs. Greeley once in the shop, when she'd gone down to pay her rent. She'd offered a long, carefully manicured hand and Louise had admired her height and her graciousness. "Aren't you very young to be on your own, so far from home?" she'd asked.

"I'm eighteen," Louise had told her, having been asked this same question by a number of people including her supervisor at the temporary agency.

"I wouldn't have guessed you at more than sixteen," Mrs. Greeley had said.

"I know." Louise had smiled. "I get asked a lot."

"Well, I won't keep you. Obviously you've got something to take up with William. Lovely to meet you, Louise," the woman had said, and gone on her way.

The house was a two-story red brick with boxes of flowering geraniums in the front windows and a polished brass knocker. Mr. Greeley came to the door and with a smile invited her inside, saying, "Ah, Miss Parker. So glad you could come. Splendid day, isn't it?"

"It's great," Louise agreed, being led by Mr. Greeley into the lounge, which was furnished with a mix of antiques and traditional furniture, white net curtains over the windows, and a pale rose carpet.

Seated in a wing chair to one side of the fireplace was a man in his late twenties who at once got to his feet and smiled.

"I'd like you to meet my son, Stewart, Miss Parker."

Stewart bore a strong resemblance to his mother: tall, with exemplary posture, clear hazel eyes, and short side-parted brown hair. He shook hands, giving Louise a smile that in no uncertain terms indicated his immediate interest. Finding him quite attractive, Louise returned the smile. She'd learned a lot about male-female attraction since those days with Daniel at the lunch counter, and it intrigued her to be able to recognize now the first sparks of interest.

"Will you have a glass of sherry, Miss Parker?" Mr. Greeley asked.

"That'd be very nice, thank you."

Mr. Greeley went to a drinks trolley to get her sherry, as Stewart, still smiling, said, "I understand you're from Canada."

"That's right," she answered, "Toronto."

"Do sit down," he said. "I apologize for keeping you standing."

Louise sat in the companion wing chair and looked around the room.

"Quite a switch," Stewart said with a smile. "So many of the English are anxious to go to Canada or America."

"I've never liked to do what everyone else does," Louise said, which brought a laugh from Stewart and a smile from Mr. Greeley as he handed her a delicate little glass filled with dark amber liquid.

"I'll just give Isabel a hand," Mr. Greeley excused himself and left, presumably to go to the kitchen.

"So what do you do, Miss Parker?"

"Louise. I'm doing temporary secretarial work for the moment, until I find a permanent job. What do you do?"

"I work for the BBC."

"Oh? Doing what?"

"Assistant producer on a variety program."

"That sounds interesting," she said.

"Interesting," he said, smiling again, "is what one says when all other adjectives fail."

Louise laughed.

Encouraged, he went on. "One reads a book that's been highly recommended and it's tiresome and not particularly good. When asked, you say, 'It's terribly interesting.' The same applies to films, music, any area you care to name. My job, however, is decidedly *not* interesting. Frustrating, exasperating, tedious—yes to all of the above. Interesting, no."

"Then why do it if it's so awful?"

"Because," he said, "people keep finding my novels 'interesting.' "

"You're a writer?"

"I'd like to be. In the meantime, there's rent to be paid and so forth. I'll keep bashing away at it until I succeed, however. Have you made many friends since arriving?"

"A few," she answered. "I'm not seeing anyone in particular."

Plainly pleased by her forthrightness, he said, "Perhaps you'd care to have dinner one evening."

"That'd be very nice."

"We'll do that," he said with another smile. He took a pack of Peter Stuyvesants from his inside pocket and offered her a cigarette. When she declined, he lit one himself, then said, "Father says you've done quite a job on the flat. I had a look at it after the last tenants moved out, and I'd say you had your work cut out for you."

"It looks terrific now," she told him. "You'll have to come over and see for yourself."

There was a knock at the door then, and Stewart set his cigarette in the ashtray saying, "I expect that'll be Grace."

For a moment Louise felt a stab of disappointment thinking Grace must be his wife. But then he added, "My sister," and she was relieved.

Stewart Greeley reminded her slightly of Daniel, and she guessed they were close in age.

Grace also resembled her mother—tall, brown-haired and hazel-eyed —but was nowhere near as friendly as her brother. After being introduced to Louise she said somewhat archly, "Father's very taken with you, Louise. Now I can see why." She winked, which irritated Louise, then headed for the drinks trolley saying, "I'm desperate for a gin and tonic. The bloody Mini decided to act up in the middle of the Old Brompton Road. I had visions of people attacking me with spanners," she laughed. "I've simply got to get rid of it and buy something decent." Drink in hand, she went to sit on the sofa saying, "How are you, Stew, darling? Still struggling with the novel of the decade?"

"Don't be bitchy, dearest," Stewart said coolly. "I have no pretensions about my work. I simply want to write something publishable."

"Stewart," Grace told Louise, "has been writing novels since he was eleven. His first one was thirteen pages long and entitled *Curse of the Vampire.*" She laughed. "Easy to see the influence there. The last two, to be fair, haven't been half bad. I honestly don't understand why you haven't found a publisher yet, Stewart."

"Only you would remember something as mortifying as *Curse of the Vampire.* I hope you'll spare my biographers that tidbit."

"Assuming you warrant a biography. So Louise, how are you finding London?"

"I like it a lot," Louise said, bothered by the biting banter between older sister and younger brother. "I'm still finding my way around, but so far I'm doing pretty well."

"Louise is doing temporary work until she finds a suitable job," Stewart explained. "Grace is with an American oil company with offices in St. James's. Lucky girl gets to see the changing of the guard every day."

"Can you take dictation?" Grace asked.

"I do Dictaphone typing," Louise said.

"We're always looking for secretaries. I'll keep you in mind."

"What do you do, Grace?" Louise asked politely.

"Administrative. I'm assistant to the president of the London office. It's a super job. I get to travel a great deal. Of course it's always on an hour's notice. But I like it enormously. I've been with the company nine years now. Have you a telephone?"

"Not yet. You can leave a message for me with your father, though."

"I may do that. How good's your typing?"

Disliking being put on the spot, Louise was about to reply when Isabel Greeley exclaimed, "Good heavens! Surely you're not interviewing the poor girl. Shame on you, Grace."

Grace got up to embrace her mother, saying, "Sorry. Bad habit. But we're always desperate for good people. And Mr. Sherman would be tickled to have more North American staff."

"That'll do for now," Isabel said, turning to greet Louise, who'd got to her feet still holding her untouched glass of sherry. "How are you, my dear? I take it you had no difficulty finding us."

"None at all. Mr. Greeley's directions were perfect."

"Good. Well, come along, you three. The roast is ready."

Louise developed an instant passion for Yorkshire pudding and ate three helpings, to Mrs. Greeley's delight.

"It's obvious," said Grace, with raised eyebrows, "you're not watching your weight. Lucky you."

"I have a great metabolism," Louise lied pleasantly. "I burn off calories very quickly. Do you have to diet a lot?"

With a slight frown Grace looked down at her plate, saying, "Not as a rule. Of course, it's your age."

"It must be," Louise agreed with a smile, thinking Grace was the biggest bitch she'd ever met.

"You'll have to be careful as you get older," Grace said. "Your sort has a tendency to get a bit thick through the hips."

"It's funny you should say that," Louise said, maintaining her pleasant tone. "All the women in my family are actually very slim. So I guess our sort has changed its tendency."

Stewart snorted softly into his serviette, his eyes smiling approval at Louise. "So much for categorizing, Grace," he addressed his sister.

After what felt to Louise like an interminable length of time, they moved to the small garden at the rear of the house for coffee. Stewart and Grace continued their bickering, Grace accusing him of being a dilettante, Stewart countering by claiming she was an effete snob. Grateful to have Grace's attention turned elsewhere, Louise sipped at her demitasse of quite bitter coffee, longing to get out of there. Mr. Greeley kept spotting weeds and getting up to pull them from the flawlessly maintained flower beds. At Mrs. Greeley's urging, he created a small bouquet for Louise to take home. When finally Louise felt she could make a graceful exit, Stewart offered to give her a ride, saying, "I go right past the shop." So instead of walking, as she'd planned, Louise climbed into an ancient Morris with Stewart, who drove in sudden alarming bursts of speed and equally sudden applications of the brake.

"I'll be in touch," he said as a somewhat shaky Louise climbed out onto the pavement. "It was a delight to meet you. You certainly handled Grace nicely. Perhaps next week," he said, then shot off into the traffic.

Louise let herself in the street door, grateful the afternoon was over, although she was looking forward to seeing Stewart again. She wished she had a telephone. It would've made life a good deal easier.

She found a water glass for the flowers and placed them on the side table beside the armchair. Then she got the airmail paper and some envelopes and went to sit at the kitchen table to write her weekly letters to her grandmother and to Daniel. As usual, she had a lot to tell them.

CHAPTER

FORTY-TWO

THE FOLLOWING TUESDAY LOUISE ARRIVED HOME FROM work to find Stewart camped on the stairs, waiting for her. Getting quickly to his feet as she came through the street door, he said, "Took a chance I'd catch you. Are you free this evening, by any chance?"

She said, "Sure."

"Splendid. I thought we'd have dinner. There's a little French place up the road we could try."

"That'd be great. Why don't you come in while I get tidied up?"

"Actually I'd love to see what you've done with the flat," he said, following her up the stairs.

"Have a look around," she said. "I won't be long." Pleased by this turn of events, she went to the bathroom to have a quick wash and to brush her hair.

"You've done a smashing job," Stewart complimented her when she returned. "Although you don't have much in the way of furniture."

"No. I'm picking things up as I go along. A friend has given me most of what I have."

He sat on the side of the bed and gave a bounce, as if considering purchasing it.

"The bed's new," she said, somewhat amused.

"So's the carpeting, from the look of it," he said, rising. "Well done. I wouldn't have believed anyone could make quite such a charming silk purse from this particular sow's ear."

"It wasn't that bad," she said, looping her bag over her shoulder. "I'm ready if you are."

"Yes," he said, returning his cigarettes to his jacket pocket. "It's just a short walk up the road. Seems no point to driving."

"That's fine."

"So," he said as they headed up Fulham Road, "how goes the temporary work?"

"It's okay. I finish my current job at the end of next week. Then I'll go somewhere else. How's your novel coming along?"

"Ah well, I don't have all that much time to work on it, what with my job at the Beeb. But it's progressing. Perhaps you'd like to read it sometime."

"Sure. I'd love to. What's it about?"

He frowned and said, "I hate that question. It's impossible to answer. You'll read it and see for yourself. Actually, I've got a spare copy in the car. Remind me and I'll give it to you before I go."

"Okay." She wondered if he always traveled around with an extra copy of his manuscript. It seemed a pretty odd thing to do.

The restaurant was a few doors past Le Jazz Hot. A small narrow place with a row of tables along the wall to the right as one entered, most of which were unoccupied. Seeing this, Stewart seemed to reconsider. "Doesn't appear they're doing a booming business," he said in an undertone as the maître d' approached.

"It's early," she said.

"It's gone six. You'd think they'd have more customers than this."

"A table for two, monsieur?" the maître d' asked.

Looking decidedly unhappy, Stewart said, "Yes, two," and he allowed Louise to precede him to a table midway along the room.

After presenting them with hand-written menus and wishing them a bon appétit, the maître d' left.

"How bloody pretentious," Stewart muttered. "The entire thing's in French."

"It's okay," Louise said. "I speak French."

"You don't say!" Stewart looked somewhat put out at this, as if they'd suddenly embarked upon a game of one-upmanship.

"I'm from Canada, remember. French is compulsory. I did four years of it in high school."

"You're full of surprises, aren't you?" he said with a smile, getting out his cigarettes. "Well, I think I can muddle through this. Where's the bloody waiter? I'd like a drink."

Louise looked around over her shoulder. Two waiters were standing at the rear of the room.

"I think if you signal," she said, "he'll come over."

"That shouldn't be necessary," he said peevishly. "I loathe poor service."

Beginning to feel uncomfortable, Louise turned again, smiled, and lifted a hand. At once one of the waiters started forward.

"Have you a wine list?" Stewart asked.

"But of course, monsieur." The waiter hurried to the rear of the restaurant and returned in less than a minute with a cellophane-covered piece of paper on which were typed the wines on offer.

"Do you prefer red or white, Louise?" Stewart asked.

"Either one," she said, wondering why he was so irritated.

"We'll have a bottle of the burgundy," Stewart told the waiter, then turned to Louise saying, "So what did you think of Grace?"

"Well," Louise said, "I didn't find her especially friendly."

"She's a cow," Stewart declared. "I don't know how anyone puts up with her. Always taking potshots, always so bloody snide. I must say you put her in her place very nicely."

"I didn't enjoy it," Louise confessed.

"It appeared as if you did. I thought you handled her admirably. All that rubbish about dieting, and 'your sort.' She really is a frightful bitch."

Louise didn't disagree but felt uncomfortable enough with the subject not to want to prolong it.

After a moment, Stewart said, "So, what will you have?"

"I think I'll have the entrecote steak, please."

"Right," he said, squinting at the menu. "I'll try the *rognons.*"

Louise nodded, wondering why the English had such a fondness for kidneys. She hated the taste of them. Having tried steak and kidney pie once, she'd ended up carefully examining each piece of meat in order not to eat another morsel of kidney by mistake.

The waiter brought the wine and uncorked it. Stewart asked to smell the cork. Louise smiled but saw he was deadly serious. The waiter stood at attention pending Stewart's verdict. With a curt nod, Stewart indicated the man should pour a splash of the wine into his glass. Stewart took a sip, swished it around like mouthwash, then swallowed. "It'll do," he said, and the relieved waiter filled their glasses before retreating to the rear of the restaurant.

"It's got a bit of an aftertaste," Stewart commented, "but it's not altogether bad."

Louise drank some of the wine and said, "It tastes fine to me."

"A bit overripe," he said, at last lighting one of his cigarettes. Then, looking over at her, he smiled and said, "I must say, you don't look eighteen."

"I know." She was tired of her age as a subject of conversation.

"You don't miss Canada?"

"I do sometimes. But I like it here. I like the people. I find the English very funny. I mean, they've got a good sense of humor."

"I can't say, in general, that I agree with you. But then, doubtless, I've been overexposed. God knows, what passes for humor at the Beeb leaves me cold for the most part. Canadians must be a dour lot if you find the British good-humored."

"They are, sort of. My Uncle Bob says Canadians are more English than the English."

"And what does your Uncle Bob do?"

"He's a lawyer."

"Ah, that explains it."

Explains what? she wondered, but didn't pursue it. Stewart seemed neither as relaxed nor as jovial as he had at their first meeting, appearing on edge and prepared to be bothered by the slightest thing. It made Louise uncomfortable, and she smiled at the waiter when he returned to take their orders. She felt like apologizing for Stewart, who was behaving very rudely without cause. Her initial interest in him was rapidly waning.

And it vanished altogether when the waiter brought a bottle of ketchup to the table and Stewart asked indignantly, "What's that for?"

"For madame's *frites,*" the waiter replied.

"I don't recall madame asking for ketchup. Do you want ketchup, Louise?"

More concerned now with the waiter's feelings than with Stewart's, Louise, who would have preferred vinegar, said, "Yes, I do, thanks."

Disgruntled, Stewart said, "No restaurant worth its stars would dream of putting that stuff on the table."

"It's nothing," she said. "Why are you so bothered?"

"I expect you're accustomed to this sort of thing in Canada."

"As a matter of fact, I am. We've got these restaurants called Fran's where they bring an entire relish tray to your table when you order a hamburger. It's got everything from relish to sliced onions."

"That's as may be," Stewart said, "but you're not having a hamburger, are you?"

"No, but I am having chips."

With a smile, he said, "I'm surprised you don't call them French fries."

"They're chips," she said. "Americans call them French fries."

"Oh!" He stubbed out his cigarette, asking, "How do you enjoy having dear daddy for a landlord?"

Oh, brother! she thought. What next? "He's been very sweet," she said.

"He's no idea what he's doing," Stewart said. "The shop's nothing more than a whim. Not that he doesn't know antiques, but he's over his head when it comes to retail."

"I thought the shop was doing quite well."

"Pure luck, I think." He busied himself lighting another cigarette and Louise looked over at the door as a foursome came in and the maître d' rushed to greet them.

"It's starting to fill up," Louise observed.

Stewart looked around, then turned back, saying, "I hope the food's better than the service."

"I'm sure it'll be fine."

"So," he said, "you're not seeing anyone. That surprises me."

"I would've thought you'd be married," she said.

"Good God, no! I'm not ready yet for that particular game of chance."

"Game of chance?"

"Don't tell me you haven't noticed?" he said. "It could be a television game show, it's so farcical. Look at my parents, for example. Daddy using his savings to play about with that shop, and Mummy making out as if she isn't worried sick he'll lose every penny on the venture."

"They seem quite happy to me," she said, wondering why he had such a sour view of everything.

"Part of the game," he said. "Mummy acts out the role of good sport while Daddy gambles his retirement money on what, by rights, should be nothing more than a hobby."

"But the shop does very well. I'm always seeing customers in there."

"Luck, as I've said. Personally, I think he was a bloody fool to take it on. But he had his heart set on it. No one could talk him out of it."

"Do you like movies?" she asked, trying to change the subject.

"Rarely have time to go," he said. "I prefer opera. Do you care for opera, Louise?"

"I've never been to one."

Looking shocked he said, "You're joking."

"No. In my family, we're all moviegoers."

"Your education is sadly lacking," he said with a taut little smile. "I'll have to take you one evening to Covent Garden."

"We'll see," she said noncommittally, thinking there were at least a dozen other things she'd rather do. Not that she had anything against opera, she just didn't care for the idea of going with Stewart. They hadn't been together an hour and already she was wishing she'd thought to tell him she was busy. "Tell me about your book," she invited, thinking to get him onto a topic he liked.

"I can't discuss it with anyone until it's finished. I find talking about my work dilutes my efforts. I don't mind having it read. That's quite different. But talking about it, that's quite destructive, I've found. Mind you, I'll never again show Grace a single word I've written. She will keep dredging up that hateful story about my efforts at thirteen."

"I thought it was eleven."

"Eleven, thirteen, whatever."

The food came, and Louise attacked her steak hungrily. It wasn't especially good, thinly cut and rather on the chewy side. But the taste wasn't bad. Stewart took a bite of his *rognons* and appeared not displeased. Reaching for his wine, he said grudgingly, "At least they've managed to do the kidneys decently."

"Oh, good," Louise said, anxious now to get the dinner over with as quickly as possible.

"Care for a taste?" Stewart offered.

"No, thank you."

"Steak all right?"

"Very nice, thank you."

"Pity about the wine," he said.

"I think it's fine," she said cheerfully, wondering how people as nice as Mr. and Mrs. Greeley could have had two such awful children. Grace was a bitch, and Stewart was a born complainer. She couldn't think now why she'd found him attractive. He was good-looking but that was all. He certainly no longer reminded her of Daniel, and in fact she felt awful for having considered them in the same thought.

Somehow they got to the end of the meal and, after finishing cups of quite decent coffee, Stewart signaled the waiter for the check. When it came, he picked it up off the saucer, and Louise watched him suddenly go red as he looked at the total.

"Oh dear," he said, flushed with embarrassment as he got out his wallet.

"What's the matter?"

"This is frightfully embarrassing," he said in an undertone. "I've come away without enough money."

"Oh, that's okay. I'll lend you some. How much do you need?"

"That's very sporting of you," he said in a grateful whisper, eyeing the waiter and maître d' at the rear of the room. "Five would do it."

"Sure." She got a five pound note from her bag, promising herself she'd never see Stewart Greeley again. She didn't mind paying for her share of the meal, but she did mind the fuss he'd made over every moment of it.

"I'll repay you," he said, making a somewhat anguished face as she passed the money across the table to him. He glanced around as if hoping no one had noticed, and she thought he was the most horribly pretentious person she'd ever met.

"Don't worry about it," she said, wanting to be out of there.

"A damned good sport," he said again. "Shall we go?"

He insisted on seeing her right to her door, and stood on the top step, crowding her, while she unlocked the upstairs door. When she turned to say good night he was suddenly all over her, pressing a wet kiss on her mouth while at the same time clamping one hand over her buttocks and the other over the back of her neck.

Pulling back, she pushed at his chest, gasping, "Stop that! What're you *doing?*"

"Oh, come along," he said, eyes glittering. "You're not a child."

He made another grab for her and she swatted his hands away, saying, "Stop that, I told you!"

Refusing to be deterred, he again put a hand over the back of her neck as she took a step backward into the hallway. "I said no! What the hell's the matter with you?"

"Now, now," he said, as if cajoling a child, continuing to close in on her.

Jesus! He wasn't going to quit. Suddenly furious, she punched him on the arm, saying, "Can't you take no for an answer, you jerk? I said no and I mean no."

He went suddenly rigid and glared at her. "You little prick tease."

"Get the hell out," she said, "or I'll throw you down the goddamned stairs."

"Prick teasing little bitch!" Still glaring at her, he took one step away, then another.

Getting hold of the door, she used it to start pushing him backward. "Go home!" she said, furious. "Go on! Get out of here!"

"I suppose you'll go rushing to tell my father," he said, poised on the top step.

"You asshole!" she cried. And with that, she gave a mighty heave on the door and succeeded in getting it closed and locked.

She could hear him standing outside breathing heavily, but at last he turned and stomped away down the stairs. A moment later the street door slammed. "Jesus!" she exclaimed, angry and a little frightened. "What a jerk!" So much, she thought, for her first date in England.

CHAPTER

FORTY-THREE

O N HER LAST DAY AT THE ACCOUNTING FIRM THE GIRLS IN the office took Louise out to lunch, and before she left that afternoon they gave her a small box containing a pair of gold stud earrings. Moved, Louise took note of their names and numbers, promising to stay in touch with everyone, particularly Annie, the tea lady, who actually got tearful when it came time for Louise to go.

Louise was so touched by the send-off she had to wonder if she wasn't making a mistake in turning down Mr. Reeves's offer of a full-time position. But as she rode the bus home through the rain she told herself she was doing the right thing. She had no specific idea what she wanted to do; she only knew it was something more interesting than typing letters to Her Majesty's inspectors of taxes, and explanatory or mollifying notes to sundry clients.

She arrived home to find that Mr. Greeley had let Rachel in to wait for her.

"I hope you don't mind. I rather browbeat the poor man, but I was so anxious to see you. *When* are you getting a telephone?" Rachel asked as Louise came through the door.

"I wish I knew. I never dreamed it'd take so long," Louise answered, somewhat irked that Mr. Greeley would let someone in without her permission. He'd meant well, though, and she wasn't about to make a fuss over it. She just hoped he didn't make it a habit.

"I do hope it's soon," Rachel said fervently. "It's horribly frustrating trying to reach you."

"You could've called me at the office."

"Oh. I hadn't thought of that. Well, never mind. We'll have to hurry. I've booked us an appointment for seven."

"An appointment for what?"

"With Mrs. O'Brien."

"Who's Mrs. O'Brien?"

"She's this remarkable woman Mummy told me about. She's quite famous, really. Evidently she's read for a number of royals. Mummy says she's extraordinary, and we're very lucky to be able to get an appointment at all. One usually has to wait weeks, even months. But she had a cancellation, so she agreed to take us."

"Take us for what, Rachel?"

Rachel checked her watch and shook her head, saying, "We haven't time to do a thing if we're to get to Chiswick on time. I thought I'd go first. I'm *so* excited."

"Rachel, *why* are we going to Chiswick? What exactly are we having done?"

"Oh, sorry. I'm so excited I'm forgetting you don't know who she is. Mrs. O'Brien's a *clairvoyant*. We're having readings done."

"I don't believe in that kind of thing," Louise said with a doubtful smile.

"It doesn't matter if you believe or not. It'll be fascinating, Louise. I mean, what if she actually is able to see the future? Wouldn't you like to know what's ahead?"

"I don't know." A superstitious shiver traveled down Louise's spine. She'd heard and read all kinds of spooky stories in her lifetime, had taken them all with a grain of salt as nothing more than the products of people's overripe imaginations. "Maybe not. Even if it were possible for someone to foretell the future, it'd probably be better not to know."

"I disagree. Anyway, we're to be there for seven so we really should leave now. We'll have the devil's own time finding a taxi. I expect we'll have to take the bus."

"I don't know about this," Louise said again, wondering if Rachel was naturally enthusiastic or if she were more than a little crazy.

"Don't be such a priss," Rachel chided her. "What harm can it do?"

"None, I guess. But I want you to know I really don't believe in this kind of thing."

"Neither do I, really. But one never knows." Rachel gave her a mischievous grin, saying, "The possibilities are so delicious, though. Don't you agree?"

✝

Mrs. O'Brien lived in a tidy flat in a block on the High Street. She was a tiny, smartly dressed woman well into her seventies who spoke in a strong deep voice and moved with decisive energy. After greeting both girls at the door, she gave them cups of tea, stared into their faces one at a time, then said to Rachel, "I'll see you first. You'll wait in here," she told Louise, showing her into a cozy bedroom. She paused in the doorway for a moment staring intently, then smiled and said, "You're the strong one. You'll manage the wait," and closed the door.

Louise drank her tea and tried to ignore the hungry rumbling of her stomach as Mrs. O'Brien's voice murmured steadily on the opposite side of the door. What on earth was she doing here? she wondered, getting up to look at the framed family photographs on the dresser—a much younger Mrs. O'Brien with four children and a husband, individual portraits of the children at varying ages, shots of what had to be grandchildren. Why had she let Rachel bulldoze her into this? What would she have done if Louise had had another date? She couldn't imagine Rachel coming here on her own. But perhaps she would have.

Bored, she looked at the book on the bedside table. A novel by Taylor Caldwell, borrowed from the local library. Returning it to the table, she went to the window and looked out at the early evening traffic. Monday she'd be starting work for a small company near Shepherd's Bush. Charmion, her contact at the agency, had assured her it'd be more inter-esting than the accounting firm. Something to do with publicity, but Louise hadn't been paying very close attention. It was another three or four weeks' work at the same hourly rate of pay, which was fine. Eventu-ally she was bound to find something she liked and wanted to stick with.

Once more she wished they'd install her telephone. It'd been more than a month since she'd applied and put down the two hundred pound deposit. She'd never before realized how impossible it was to stay in touch with friends without benefit of a telephone. Nick left messages for her with Mr. Greeley. So did Rachel. Philip was back at school and wouldn't be home again until December. She hadn't heard a word from Stewart, but doubted he'd attempt to communicate with her via his father.

Suddenly she missed everything she'd always known: Toronto, decent hamburgers, kosher food from Switzer's delicatessen, her friends, her grandmother and Uncle Bob and, most of all, Faye. Here she was on a rainy evening in Chiswick, waiting to have her fortune told by a wiry little Irish woman with a deep booming voice and a piercing, rather unsettling gaze. It was absurd. No one could tell the future. No one knew a thing about anyone else. It struck her as sad that Rachel was so willing to believe in the impossible yet lacked the confidence to believe in herself. Perhaps she was looking for a miracle, or hoping to be told some kind of fairy tale. It would be so easy to trick Rachel; she'd likely volunteer all kinds of things that would make it very simple for that clever little woman to repeat them back to her in an altered, more palatable form.

Gazing out the window, Louise promised herself she wouldn't give anything away, not even the slightest hint. It would probably be the shortest "reading" in history. The voices continued to murmur on the other side of the door—Rachel's light tones, Mrs. O'Brien's heavier, more positive ones. Minutes were ticking away and she was stuck in an elderly woman's small bedroom wondering how she'd managed to get herself into this situation. She was too easygoing for her own good. But she hated to disappoint people. Rather than disappoint anyone, she often wound up furious with herself.

"Come along now!" the deep voice boomed at her back.

Startled, Louise turned, retrieved her empty cup from the dresser top and squeezed past Rachel, who smiled happily and went to sit in the slipper chair beside the bed.

"I'll just put this in the sink," Louise said, and took her cup into the kitchen.

"Put the kettle on while you're there, darling," Mrs. O'Brien said.

Pleased by the endearment, Louise did as she'd been asked, then returned to the lounge to sit at the side of the dining table as the tiny woman indicated.

"You're a good girl," the woman said, gazing at her again in that unnerving fashion. "You carry light with you; you've got a glow. Give me your hand."

Louise obeyed, asking, "Are you Irish?"

"Dublin born, darling," answered the woman in her rich voice as she studied Louise's hand, turning it front to back, then folding the fingers over. "And you're from Canada, says your wee friend."

"That's right." Louise hoped Rachel hadn't told the woman everything about her.

Dropping her voice to a confidential whisper, Mrs. O'Brien, still holding Louise's hand, said, "You're a good friend to that one. She'll be needing you. You won't let her down." Her pale green eyes fixed again on Louise's. "Lovely you are. Not just the look of you, but the heart of you. When I saw you at my door I knew you were the balance. Keep a watch over your friend, won't you? Ah, the kettle. You'll have another cup of tea. And you're hungry. I'll fetch you a bit of something." With that, she jumped up and scurried into the kitchen with amazing vitality.

Louise smiled to herself, then looked over at the bedroom door, wondering what Rachel was doing. In two or three minutes the old woman returned carrying a tray. "Clear a space, will you, darling?" Louise did and Mrs. O'Brien set the tray down saying, "I've fixed you cheese and crackers. Eat. I know you're hungry."

While Louise helped herself, the woman lit an aromatic Sweet Afton cigarette, watching Louise's every move. Louise could feel approval in her gaze and turned to smile, finding the apple-doll face wonderfully familiar now and strikingly attractive. "Would you like me to pour the tea?"

"That'd be grand," the woman said, exhaling a substantial cloud of smoke. "And when you've done, pick up those cards and shuffle them until you're ready to stop."

The tea poured, Louise picked up what looked to be an ordinary deck of playing cards and held them for a few seconds, her eyes connected to the old woman's. "Oh, yes," said Mrs. O'Brien. "Didn't I know it."

Feeling special, Louise smiled again, asking, "How long do I shuffle?"

"Stop when you feel it's time."

Perhaps she was being influenced by the woman's mesmerizing gaze, but as the cards passed through her fingers it felt as if brief electric shocks were being transmitted by them. She shuffled for quite some time, eyes on the cards, then abruptly stopped.

"Put them down!" Mrs. O'Brien ordered. "Cut them into two piles."

Louise did.

The old woman impatiently stabbed out her cigarette, her eyes now on the cards. Then she picked up the pile closest and began turning the cards over one at a time, laying them face up on the table. "Ah, it's a hard year you've had," she said, laying down several more cards before suddenly going very still, her eyes once again fusing to Louise's. "You've suffered a great loss, a great loss." Her eyelids lowering slightly, she paused for a moment, then said, "Someone very close, a woman, older, but not by much. A beautiful woman, fair, with smoky eyes and a tender heart. It put you on your knees."

Shattered, suddenly a believer, Louise whispered, "My sister."

Mrs. O'Brien nodded sadly. "It's not settled, dear girl. There's more to the tale. There's a document of some sort. Look to it for the answer. There's a great mystery here. Now." She set down two cards side by side; then, angrily, she said, "Jaysus! That one's the very devil. A terrible creature, terrible."

"My mother," Louise whispered.

Mrs. O'Brien shook her head mournfully, then went on. "Powerful women in your life, Louise. This one," she placed a forefinger on the queen of hearts, "is as good as the other's bad; as kind as the other's mean."

"My grandmother," Louise said, fairly flabbergasted.

The old woman nodded. "You've spent a fair time caught between the two. But the good will always win out for you, don't you know." When Louise failed to respond, she barked, "Do you *know* that?"

"Yes," Louise whispered, alarmed. This wasn't at all what she'd expected. She'd imagined some gypsy woman in vividly printed clothes, her neck festooned with chains, her hands laden with rings. But this was a quite ordinary-looking old woman with amethyst pierced earrings and a thin wedding band, a tweed skirt and a forest green pullover. No one's idea of a gypsy.

"There's not a thing I can tell you that you don't already know, dear girl. Not the past, not the present, and not the future. You know your own life, and you know your road. Don't you?"

"Yes," Louise replied, realizing it was true. She'd never considered it before, but she'd always had a powerful sense of her place in the scheme of things and of her own abilities. And she knew that her future was something to be shaped by her own efforts.

"This mother of yours," Mrs. O'Brien scowled. "She's given to using her fists when she can't get her way; she'll strike out as soon as look at you. And she'll use anyone to get her own way." The woman shivered and laid down another card. "Uses men, she does. Ah now," she said, tapping the uppermost card with one clear-polished fingernail. "Here's a dear fellow. But you've broken with this one. Don't give it a thought. It was the right thing to do. No harm's been done." She touched the queen of hearts, then smiled suddenly, sweetly. "Ah, but your grandmother has such a heart. She'll live a good, long time; long enough to see you with all your dreams come true. You, now, Louise," she said, quickly laying down three cards in succession, "you mustn't give in to your tendency to doubt what you know to be true. And go carefully with your tale-telling.'' She glanced over with a knowing smile. ''A fanciful nature, you have, dear girl. Mind how you go. There are men here. One, two, three, and a fourth. You've hardened your heart. Take care not to freeze it altogether, or you'll miss out on your dreams. This one,'' she indicated the jack of diamonds, ''can't live his life until you provide him with the key. A dark lad with fine features. You've done him a terrible wrong, Louise. But you'll right it eventually. Do you know one like this?''

''I think so,'' Louise answered, thinking of Raffie. But he was the one who'd wronged Faye; she hadn't wronged him. It didn't make sense and she wanted to know more, but the old woman was racing ahead.

''Don't be a hater, darling,'' the woman said with sudden kindness. ''You don't want to find yourself a duplicate of *that* one with the heart of knives. She's a horror, no heart at all, at all. Give me your hand again.''

Louise held out her hand and Mrs. O'Brien cupped it in both her own, tilting it toward the light. With a slight shake of her head, she said, ''You'll have great success, beyond your imaginings. Tremendous success. But it'll all be ashes in the mouth until you correct past wrongs. In the end, your heart will carry you through. Be sure to listen, dear girl. There's a point here''—she tapped Louise's palm with the tip of one finger—''when you'll have all your answers. Be sure to be listening, Louise. You've got greatness in you, greatness of mind and spirit. Don't let this past year turn you off course, cause you to doubt. You've got a good long life. Your heart and mind are perfectly balanced, perfectly, but you're to work to keep them that way. You could be a terrible breaker of hearts if you choose. People are drawn to you. Mind you don't lose patience, especially with a small dark girl with great haunted eyes. There'll come a time when you'll hold her life in your hands. Trust your instincts then, Louise. It's within your power to save a life others don't hold in particular esteem.'' She glanced up and Louise nodded her understanding. Folding her hands warmly around Louise's the old woman said, ''The one you've broken with, the one who worries you so, he'll marry another, darling. Have no fear for him.''

Without warning, tears flooded Louise's eyes. Mrs. O'Brien freed one hand to reach into her pocket and handed Louise a tissue. ''Remember to listen to your heart, dear girl. And promise you'll come to see me again soon. You and I are meant to be fast friends.''

''I will,'' Louise promised.

"That's my good girl," Mrs. O'Brien said as she looped an arm around Louise's neck and gave her a resounding kiss on the cheek. "My good girl," she repeated. "Now, fetch your poor friend before she dies of curiosity, and we'll have another cup of tea before I send the two of you on your way."

✝

While Rachel was in the bathroom, Mrs. O'Brien slipped Louise a piece of paper with her telephone number on it. "Your wee friend wouldn't understand," she whispered.

"I know."

"Be sure to ring me and come round," the old woman said. "I'll be counting on you, darling."

"I will," Louise told her.

"You're a ray of sunshine to these eyes."

"I feel a lot better now," she replied, realizing it was true.

"Mind what I told you about that one." Mrs. O'Brien indicated the bathroom. "You can make the difference to her life, Louise. You'll be glad you did the right thing. She's a troubled wee soul."

"I know. Her parents won't let her do a thing."

"She'll repay you a thousandfold. You'll never have a moment's regret."

"How do you know these things?" Louise asked, feeling an odd tugging at her heart at the thought of having to leave the warm haven she'd found so unexpectedly in this tidy flat.

"I know just as you know. I've simply had the years to take heed. Now, you won't forget about your old Evie, will you?"

"You know I won't. I could never forget my old Evie," Louise smiled, feeling, to her own surprise, as if she'd known the woman all her life.

Mrs. O'Brien pinched her cheek and gave her a crinkled smile. "You deserve to be loved, darling, even though you don't think so now."

Louise said, "Thank you," feeling humbled. She'd come here expecting trickery and had made a friend instead.

✝

"What did she tell you?" Rachel asked eagerly once they were on the bus.

Reluctant to admit just how much Evie had known of her life, Louise said, "She told me I'd be a great success."

"How extraordinary!" Rachel exclaimed. "She said I'd have a rough patch but then I'd be a great success, too. And it all had to do with you, Louise! Isn't that something?''

''She said that?''

''She did. She said I was a very lucky 'gorl,' '' she laughed, ''because you were going to mean more to me than I ever dreamed. I told her you were already my closest friend but she got quite stroppy at that. Did she bark at you? She did at me. Gave me quite a turn. 'It's more than friendship,' '' Rachel quoted. '' 'Trust in Louise,' she said. 'She'll always see you right.' It was a bit frightening, actually. What do you suppose she meant by that?''

''I don't know,'' Louise lied, sensing exactly what Evie had meant. ''But I don't think you need to be frightened. I wouldn't harm a fly.''

''Oh, I know that,'' Rachel said happily, linking her arm with Louise's. ''I told her I'd trust you with my life. And she said, 'Never say lightly what's meant in truth.' But I do, you know, Louise. Trust you, that is. You've been better to me than anyone ever has. Except Phippy, of course. But that's not the same. Are you glad now you came with me?''

''I really am. I thought it was going to be nonsense, but it wasn't. I loved her, Rachel. Thank you for taking me. I'm very grateful.''

''She's like a rather eccentric granny, isn't she?''

''Rather. Not like my Gramma, though. Someday you'll have to meet her. She's wonderful. And my Uncle Bob too.''

''You must miss them awfully.''

''I do. But it's time for me to be away from them now.''

''How do you know that?'' Rachel asked. ''I'm always impressed when someone has a sense of personal timing. I don't seem to have one at all. I'm forever saying and doing things at entirely the wrong times.''

''I just know it. And someday it'll be time for me to be with them again. And you do not say and do things at the wrong times. Has it ever occurred to you that maybe the other person's wrong, not you?''

''Does that mean you'll leave and go home?'' Rachel asked fearfully, ignoring Louise's question.

''Someday, Rachel. But don't worry about it. I only just got here, remember?''

''I'd hate you to leave, you know,'' Rachel said earnestly. ''You really are the dearest friend I've ever had. You've never once criticized me, or told me I'm silly or a coward or any of the things my other friends have said.''

"That's because you're not silly or a coward, and because you're a dear friend, too. Now could we please go get something to eat before I pass out?"

"Oh, that's right. You haven't eaten. Where shall we go?"

"Let's go over to Le Jazz Hot," Louise suggested. "I like the selections on their jukebox."

Rachel groaned. "You're going to play 'Stranger on the Shore' another half dozen times."

"I won't play it more than twice. Okay?"

"It's such a sad song, Louise."

"I know, but sometimes you need to hear sad songs so that you don't feel so sad anymore."

"That doesn't make sense."

"It does, you know. But don't ask me to explain it."

"I certainly won't," Rachel said, and sat back to adjust her hat. "I hate anything sad. I've spent too much time being sad. I'm certainly not going to pay money to buy more."

Louise laughed and said, "Remind me to show you what the girls at the office gave me as a going-away present."

"They gave you a present? But you were only there a month or so. How kind! You see! Everyone likes you."

"Not everyone," Louise said. "Just some peculiar people. Like you, for example."

"I am peculiar, aren't I?" Rachel said proudly.

"Definitely. It's why we get along so well. You're peculiar and I'm . . . I'm a good audience. It's true," she said. "And I enjoy you. We'll always be friends."

"Yes, always," Rachel chorused. "Here's our stop now!" She rang the bell and hurried to the front of the bus. "Hurry up, Louise," she said, and jumped off before the bus had come to a full stop. Louise had to hurry to catch up with her.

*C*HAPTER

FORTY-FOUR

ANTOINETTE "TONI" KING AND TERENCE REID OWNED AND operated a small public relations company housed in an office block in Shepherd's Bush. They arranged publicity primarily for actors and authors but took on clients in everything from theater to fashion, including a few society matrons wanting to ensure that their names made the right columns.

Having recently lost their longtime secretary, Toni and Terence had been making do with a series of temps until they could find a full-time replacement. The position required someone with unique attributes— flexibility, imagination, good basic office skills, and, most importantly, a sense of humor. Louise was offered the job on a permanent basis on the morning of her second day. She didn't hesitate and accepted at once.

King-Reid offered no employee benefits and didn't give out luncheon vouchers, but the work was fascinating, and the two partners were as flexible and imaginative as their new secretary. They also offered Louise somewhat more than the going rate of pay at thirteen pounds a week.

Toni and Terence were both extremely attractive, both in their late twenties, and both on good terms with a huge number of people in the media. Toni had long dark hair and fair skin and wore fashionable, good-looking clothes and dramatic makeup consisting of gray eyeshadow, black mascara, and bright red lipstick. She was frequently taken to be the celebrity rather than the publicist.

Terence was fair-haired and blue-eyed and also dressed well but with conservative elegance in custom-tailored three-piece suits, Turnbull & Asser shirts, and Sulka ties. He had a crooked front tooth that saved him from being too good-looking, and that reminded Louise of Faye. Every time Terry smiled, Louise felt oddly comforted.

They each had individual client lists and only occasionally worked together. Louise had to keep their contact books constantly updated; she typed up tour schedules for visiting authors, booked hotel rooms when necessary, and confirmed appointments. She served as liaison between clients and their companies, calling in advance of the promotions Toni or Terence had set up to verify arrival and departure times, and hire cars and drivers; depending on the budget, she ordered flowers and/or baskets of fruit to be sent to the hotel rooms of visiting celebrities; she arranged press conferences or baby-sitters or anything else that might be needed. She loved the job.

Because it was a small office, if she wanted Photostats made or stencils run off she relied—as did most of the other offices in the block—on the service office run by two girls on the ground floor. The place was usually chaotic, with people queued up waiting to use one machine or another or to have Jill or Susan do some typing. Often, frustrated at having to wait, secretaries went ahead and ran their own Photostats or stencils, then left a note on the desk saying how many copies they'd made. Jill and Susan were pleasant but almost pathologically inefficient. If she wasn't too busy, Louise would help out by doing some typing, or cutting and running a stencil for one of the other offices. Jill and Susan felt she was interfering with their business. But since they were invariably running behind, and Louise worked for free, they were in no position to complain.

Shepherd's Bush was quite close to Chiswick, so at least once a week Louise stopped in after work to visit Evie, who felt strongly that Louise had made a wise move in taking the job with King-Reid. "Something good will come of it, darling," she told Louise. "But it won't come from an expected direction. And it won't come quickly."

Louise was learning to accept the woman's pronouncements and kept a small notebook in which she wrote down the various things Evie said to her. The matter of Faye's death and the document Evie had mentioned still puzzled her. Aside from the death certificate the only document she had was the copy of the coroner's report, which was written in such arcane scientific language that it defied her comprehension.

With Evie's help, and with the job and her new friends, she no longer felt quite so crippled or enraged by Faye's death. She thought of her often, dreamed of her regularly, but the pain became less biting with the passage of time. And when in September she at last got her telephone and was able to call and talk to her grandmother whenever she liked, she felt better still. Nick phoned nightly to chat or to ask if he could drop by, and they fell into the habit of visiting the markets on the weekends, looking for items for the flat. Philip phoned every other week or so from Oxford, and of course Rachel called every evening. By Christmas she felt she was finally settled, that London was now her home.

On Christmas morning, Nick came by with the scooter and drove her to Chiswick so she could give Evie the box of Bronley soap she knew her friend liked. Upon opening the door, Evie asked, "Who've you left waiting downstairs?"

Surprised, Louise said, "My friend Nick."

"I'll put on the kettle. Fetch him up."

Having learned it was pointless to question Evie, Louise turned around and went back down to tell Nick that she wanted to meet him.

" 'Ow come?" he asked, locking the scooter. "She don't know me."

"I've talked about you. She wants to meet you."

"I dunno," he said, nevertheless following Louise inside. "We don't 'ave much time if you're to be at Rachel's by midday."

"We've got plenty of time," she laughed. "Are you nervous?"

"Dead right. I don't like meeting new people."

"Don't be nervous. Evie's like a crotchety grandmother. She'll probably bark at you, but that's just the way she is."

Evie took a long piercing look at Nick, then smiled and said, "Come along and have your cup of tea, dear. I've been wanting to meet you."

"Meet me? Why?" Nick asked, bewildered. "You didn't even know I was comin'."

Evie smiled and said, "You won't change a thing by being angry about it, you know. Best bide your time, my lad. The old ways are coming to an end. Louise, darling, pour the tea, will you? Did I tell you my Delia's fetching me in an hour's time? I'm to spend today and Boxing Day in Surrey with her and the grandkiddies."

"No, you didn't tell me," Louise said, pouring three cups of tea.

Nick looked at Evie, digesting what she'd told him, then said, "You're 'avin' me on, right?"

"Don't be tiresome! I haven't the time for jokes," she barked. "Give me your hand!"

He did so without hesitation and she studied it for a time, then said, "Clever with your hands, aren't you? That'll stand you in good stead when the time comes. You're a good boy with a kind heart. And you've been good to my darling girl. But you must learn to stop fussing over the rules. Realize they're made to be broken, and you'll have your heart's desire.''

Nodding as if hypnotized, Nick said, "I'll wager you scare the bleeding daylights out of most people."

"Only the foolish ones," she said. "And you're far from foolish." Releasing his hand she said, "There's no need to worry about your mother. She understands her position; she's not unhappy."

He sat back looking at his hand as Evie said, "This is for you, dear girl,'' giving Louise a package.

It was a box of fine airmail stationery.

"This is wonderful, Evie." Louise got up to give the old woman a hug. "Thank you."

"You're welcome. Now drink up, the two of you, and let me get on with my packing."

Before they left, Nick gave the old woman a kiss on her papery cheek, asking teasingly, "You a witch, then?"

"Of course," Evie laughed. "Come see me again. And mind how you go on that machine of yours."

" 'Ow'd you know what kind of machine I've got?" he challenged playfully.

"Just you take care," Evie said. "And look after my girl."

⋏

Because Molly had to work Christmas day preparing and serving the Townsend-Post dinner, it meant she wasn't able to celebrate the holiday with Nick, who came along every year to help so that his mother could get away a bit early.

"Useless bunch," he told Louise as he locked the Vespa in the street. "But me mum won't hear a word against them. I reckon you won't, neither."

"They've been very good to me, Nick. And from what I understand, they've been very good to your mother too."

"That don't mean she's their slave," he said bitterly. "Mum and Cathleen and Iris, they're *servants*. And the only one in the family what don't treat 'em that way is Rachel. It's not right."

"But it's what your mother and the others have chosen, Nick. No one forced them to go into service. And from what you've told me, no one else would hire your mother."

"Because she 'ad a kid in tow," he said. "I've been 'earing about it all me life. But that don't make it right. You 'aven't been 'ere long enough to see how it works, 'ow they keep us down, keep us in our places. I've 'ad to live me 'ole life that way and I'm fed up with it. It isn't right Mum 'as to work on Christmas, as well as every other bloody day of the year. Two days off a month she gets. It's bloody feudal, but she won't say a word to 'em about it.''

"I'm sorry," Louise said, not knowing how to deal with his complaints, or even if they were justified.

"Never mind," he relented. "It's got nothin' to do with you, 'as it? 'Ere," he said, pulling a small package from his pocket. "This's for you, from me."

Louise gave him a kiss on the cheek, then reached into the carrier bag she'd become accustomed to toting with her everywhere. "This is for you, from me," she mimicked him. "Aren't you coming in?"

"Servants' entrance," he said. "We're not good enough to come in the front door. Thought you knew that."

She felt suddenly a terrible combination of guilt on her own behalf and indignation on his. For the first time she had some real sense of why he was so permanently angry. "I'm sorry," she said again, glancing over at the wreath-bedecked front door. "This is awful."

"Forget it." He gave her a smile. "It's none of your doing, is it? I'll ring you tomorrow. Thanks for this." He held the package aloft as he descended the steps to the lower level of the house. "Ta ra, Louise."

Rachel was in black as usual but wore a Santa's hat pinned to her mass of dark curls and two brilliant green Christmas ornaments in her pierced ears. She seemed very excited, her features flushed, as she exchanged gifts with Louise. "You're to open yours this instant," she told Louise excitedly. "We finished with ours ages ago. Now it's your turn."

Rachel's parents sat benignly watching while Philip methodically cracked walnuts and dropped the shells onto a small silver plate. "Rachel's been panting for you to get here," Philip told Louise. "She's been like a four-year-old all morning."

"I have not," Rachel disagreed, her eyes somehow too bright. "It's Christmas, after all. It's supposed to be a festive time. I adore Christmas, don't you, Louise? Oh, do hurry up. You're taking far too long. Just rip the paper. There's no need to be so careful with it."

It all felt strange to Louise. Mr. Townsend-Post sat reading the *Times*, and smiled over every so often, while his wife paged through the latest issue of *Queen,* also rather absently smiling now and then. They were, in fact, like two indulgent parents witnessing the antics of a four-year-old. There wasn't anything particularly festive about the occasion, despite the exquisitely decorated tree positioned to one side of the grand piano in the bay of the front windows, and the discreet row of greeting cards on the mantel.

"Why don't you open your present?" Louise told Rachel.

"I will, after you've opened yours. Hurry, Louise!"

When Louise saw the small velvet-covered jewelry box she knew Rachel had spent too much money. She'd been hoping Rachel would give her some small thing, perhaps for the apartment. Instead she'd bought her a gold bar pin with a circle of seed pearls surrounding a small diamond. It was beautiful, but Louise was embarrassed by the extravagance.

"Don't you like it?" Rachel asked, attempting to read Louise's expression.

"I do, Rachel. It's beautiful. But you shouldn't have spent so much money. My gift to you is just a token, really."

"Don't be silly!" Rachel said blithely. "I know I'll love it."

"Well," Louise said, dry-mouthed, wishing she were out in the kitchen with Nick and his mother, "you'd better open it, then."

"I love it," Rachel declared of the copy of *To Kill a Mockingbird* Louise had bought her. "I've been wanting to read this. Thank you." She leaned over to give Louise a kiss on the cheek, then sat back, saying, "Look! Louise has given me a book."

"That's very nice, dear," Mrs. Townsend-Post said, smiling over. "Isn't that nice, Herbert?"

"What? Oh, yes. Very good of you, Louise."

"I'll start reading it tonight," Rachel said. "Do you really like your pin?"

"It's beautiful," Louise said. "But I wish you weren't quite so generous."

"It's Rachel's style," Philip said, coming to sit on the arm of the sofa next to Louise. "Care for a walnut?"

"No, thank you," Louise said, thinking her mouth was already so dry she'd probably choke if she tried to eat a nut.

"Something to drink now?" he asked, popping a walnut into his mouth.

"We've got champagne," Rachel said. "Have some champagne, Louise!"

"No, thanks. I'll wait and have something with dinner."

"I was wondering," Philip said, "if you're all booked up for New Year's Eve. If you're not, perhaps you'd care to join Rachel and me and a few friends. We're going to the Savoy."

"That's sweet of you," Louise said, "but I've already made plans." She hadn't, but knew she wouldn't feel comfortable on such an outing. She thought she'd ask Nick if he was free. Maybe they'd get together and go out for dinner or something.

"Oh, where are you going?" Rachel asked. "I was so hoping you'd come with us. It's going to be such fun."

"I'd love to, but I've promised Toni and Terence I'd go to a party they're having," she lied. "The party's at Toni's place and she's invited a lot of her clients and contacts." That much was true. And she had been invited, but she'd declined, feeling she'd be out of her depth.

"You could do both," Rachel said. "Spend a few hours with them, then come along to us at the Savoy to see in the New Year."

"I'll try, but I don't think it'll work out."

"Promise you'll try."

"Rachel, dear," her mother said, "do stop pushing at Louise. She's told you she's made other arrangements."

"That's okay," Louise told Mrs. Townsend-Post. "She's not pushing."

"No, I'm not," Rachel said childishly. "Phippy, tell them I'm not."

"She's all right, Mother," Philip said patiently. "If you change your mind, Louise, do please join us. There'll be dancing, and I thought you'd enjoy that."

"Thank you," she said. "I'll let you know if I change my mind."

Throughout the afternoon she continued to feel that mingled sense of guilt and indignation. Molly was as diffident but pleasant as ever as she and Iris carried platters from the kitchen and offered them around. Louise had glimpses of Nick in the kitchen, sleeves rolled up, arms plunged into a sinkful of soapy water, or waiting by the door to relieve his mother of a trayful of dishes.

The afternoon seemed interminable to Louise, who felt as if she was there under false pretenses. The only person who seemed at all real to her was Rachel, who appeared to be dieting with renewed dedication, taking only a tiny portion of turkey breast, declining the stuffing and roast potatoes, the brussel sprouts with chestnuts, the cranberries, the gravy, and everything else. She drank several glasses of champagne very quickly, which heightened her flush and made her even more animated, so that the other members of her family seemed all the more lifeless and stiff by comparison. Single-handedly she kept the conversation going, attempting to draw her father into a discussion of the current exchange rates but succeeding only in having him pat the back of her hand and say, "Now is not the time for that, Rachel dear."

She tried to get Philip to talk about his courses of study but he merely shrugged and said it was, "a lot of jolly hard work that wouldn't interest you."

Only Louise was willing to converse with her about her job and some of the more illustrious clients King-Reid represented. When Molly and Iris came in to begin clearing, Rachel said, "It was all superb, Molly. Three cheers for the cook!" No one joined in. Louise felt compelled to say, "It was delicious, Molly," which in turn prompted Philip to say, "Yes, delicious, Moll." This irritated Louise, who thought Philip sounded insincere and ungrateful.

Coffee was served in the lounge. Molly brought in the tray and set it down, then said in an undertone to Mrs. Townsend-Post, "We'll be goin' now, then."

"Ah, it's time, is it?" Mr. Townsend-Post said. "Good, good."

"I'll fetch the others," Molly said, on her way to the kitchen.

Rachel jumped up and rushed from the room, saying, "Don't start until I get back!" and Louise sat wondering what was going on as she watched Mr. Townsend-Post position himself near the fireplace.

Molly, Cathleen, and Iris, all in their street clothes, entered from the dining room. Before the door swung closed Louise caught a glimpse of Nick as he returned the candelabra to the now cleared table. His face was drawn tight and he looked angry and impatient. The three women stood to attention just inside the room, eyes on their shoes. Rachel came flying back with an assortment of gift-wrapped packages and proceeded to hand one to each of them, wishing them a merry Christmas and giving them each a kiss on the cheek, which, Louise noticed, caused her parents to frown.

Somewhat giddy with excitement, Rachel perched on the arm of the sofa next to Louise as Mr. Townsend-Post approached the women and gave them each an envelope and a quick handshake. "Happy holidays, girls," he said.

"Thank you, sir," the women chorused.

"Now, where's your Nick, Molly? You know we always like to include him."

"I'll just fetch 'im, sir," Molly said.

Before the door swung closed Louise was able to see Molly tugging at Nick's arm, whispering to him. Nick was shaking his head furiously. But a minute or so later a red-faced Nick appeared at his mother's side as the household staff remained awkwardly in position.

"Here you go, then, Nick," Mr. Townsend-Post said, giving him an envelope. "We know what a help you are to your mother."

Nick murmured a strangled, "Thank you," and looked everywhere but at Rachel and Louise.

"Off you go, then," Mr. Townsend-Post said, hands in his pockets, appearing pleased with the way he'd carried off his household duties.

"Thank you, sir," the women repeated, while Nick merely nodded. Then the group turned and retreated to the kitchen.

Louise was so embarrassed that she could barely wait to escape, and at four-thirty, she announced, "I'd better be going. My grandmother's going to be calling me in an hour, and I wouldn't want to miss her."

"Of course, dear," said Mrs. Townsend-Post.

"Good of you to come," said her husband.

"Don't forget New Year's Eve at the Savoy if you can possibly make it," said Philip.

At the door, Rachel murmured, "Horrid, wasn't it? I'll make it up to you, Louise."

"No, no," Louise said. "It was very nice." Swamped by sympathy for her friend, Louise embraced her, aware again of Rachel's thinness. "We'll get together in the next couple of days. Come over and see. I've bought a few more things for the flat. I found a terrific little desk and another armchair. So now we'll both have somewhere to sit when you come over."

"You've been to the market again with Nicky, have you?" Rachel asked, sounding as if she wished she could've gone, too.

"Next time we go, you'll come with us," Louise promised.

"Oh, that'd be super!" Rachel said. "What fun!"

Louise thanked her a final time for the lavish gift, then was outside in the cold rain, taking deep grateful breaths of the wet air. She wasn't expecting a call from her grandmother, but decided it would be a good idea to phone home. She suddenly had a strong need to hear loving, familiar voices.

As it happened, Nick planned to spend New Year's Eve with his mother. It was a long-term tradition. Every year he took her out to a good meal, then they went to their local and saw the old year out with friends and neighbors.

"Come with us, Louise," he said when they spoke on the phone the following day.

"That's very sweet of you, but I think I'll just go to Toni and Terry's party. You have a wonderful time with your mother."

"I'll see you before then," he reminded her. "It's not for another week yet."

"Sure. I'd better go now," she said. "I want to go to the Laundromat."

"Dead excitin', that is," he laughed. " 'Ave a good time yesterday?"

"It was very nice," she said, her guilt returning at the recollection of how he'd spent the afternoon. "Am I really stupid, Nick? I honestly don't understand any of this."

"Naw, you're not stupid. Not you. It's different 'ere, and you're not used to it, that's all. Any'ow, you're good for Rachel, and that's important. Christ knows that lot're no bloody use to 'er."

Louise couldn't disagree. Still, she felt even guiltier as she admitted, "They treated her like a baby. It was awful."

"One of these days, she'll get up on 'er 'ind legs and tell 'em all to get stuffed. Leastwise, I bloody 'ope so."

"So do I," she said. Then, not really knowing why, she added, "I'm sorry, about everything."

"Nothin' for you to be sorry about, is there? It's none of your doin'."

"Maybe, but I'm still sorry. I feel badly that your mother had to work on Christmas day, and that Rachel seems to be fighting a losing battle. I wish I could *do* something."

"You wait. Maybe you will."

"I don't know how, but I hope you're right."

"I've got a lot of faith in that girl, and in you," he said. "And never mind what that lot thinks."

"I've got faith in her, too," Louise said. "Thanks for calling, Nick, and thanks for the bath cubes and the soap."

"Thank you for the wallet. It's dead posh, it is."

They wound up, as always, by saying they'd speak to one another the next day.

In the end, she spent New Year's Eve of 1960 alone. She lit candles and sat in front of the wood fire with a cup of coffee and thought about the parties she and Faye had gone to at Kath's house, about the party room and the bands that played, and about how everyone had wanted to dance with Faye. She cried for a time, then got herself some fresh coffee, sat again in front of the fire, and promised herself the new year would be better than the one just ended. While she was getting ready for bed, she wondered how Terry and Toni's party had gone, and hoped Rachel was having a good time at the Savoy. She really wasn't at all sorry to have spent the evening alone. She'd have been rotten company.

CHAPTER
FORTY-FIVE

TONI CAME DOWN WITH THE FLU THE LAST WEEK IN JUNE. Terry was booked for a solid day's promotion with one of the leads of a new West End play about to open.

"We've got no choice," he told Louise. "You're going to have to escort Lydia Brinkley to her interviews today and tomorrow."

"Me? What do I have to do?" Louise asked, both excited and daunted. She'd been with Toni and Terence for over a year and had never even met any of their clients, let alone played escort to one.

"You've got the schedule. The car and driver are all set. All you have to do is take her round to the various places, make the introductions, and get her from one interview to the next on time."

It sounded simple enough. Louise said, "Okay. But what about the office?"

"We'll have to let the service take the calls and get caught up on everything else where and when we can. Miss Brinkley's last interview is at four, over tea at the hotel. It should take an hour or so. After that, you're through for the day."

"Then I'll come back here and get caught up on some work."

"Good girl." Terence gave her a smile. "I expect to be finished by five or so. I'll come pitch in." He looked at his watch, then at Louise as he reached into his pocket. "You'll need cash to pay for lunch and anything that crops up. Please make sure you get receipts for everything." He handed her twenty pounds, hesitated, then gave her another ten, saying, "If this situation arises again, we may have to think about getting you a credit card. Right, Louise. Be your usual charming self and nothing should go wrong. You've got half an hour to get to Brown's Hotel. The driver will meet you both there. Better take a taxi. And don't forget to get a receipt!"

She grabbed her coat and bag, a couple of copies of the schedule, and flew out of the office.

As she got out of the taxi on Albemarle Street, she saw several cars and drivers waiting. She approached each driver in turn until she found the one she'd booked for the day. "I'm Louise Parker," she told the man, giving him a copy of the schedule. "I'll be escorting Miss Brinkley today and tomorrow."

"Right you are, dear. I'm Malcolm. I appreciate having this," he said of the schedule. "Helps to know in advance where we're going. I don't know why more people don't think of letting the driver know the day's plans."

"We're due at the BBC in forty-five minutes," Louise said. "I'll go make sure Miss Brinkley's ready."

The concierge said, "I believe she's in the dining room. If you'll follow me." He led the way to a table in the small dining room where a well-dressed, middle-aged woman sat alone reading the *New York Times* and drinking coffee. To Louise's eyes she couldn't have been anything but American; everything about her, from her jewelry to her style of dress, declared it.

"Young lady to see you, Miss Brinkley," said the concierge, and left to return to his post.

"Good morning." Louise extended her hand. "I'm Louise Parker.

Mrs. King has come down with the flu so I'll be escorting you around town while you're here.''

Removing her reading glasses, ignoring Louise's extended hand, Lydia Brinkley looked at Louise with an expression of disbelief and said, ''How the hell old're you, anyway?''

''Nineteen.''

''Unbelievable. Sit down. You want some coffee?''

''No, thank you. We really don't have all that much time.'' Louise didn't know what to make of the woman, and hoped Miss Brinkley wasn't going to give her a rough time because of her age.

''You ever done this before?'' Miss Brinkley asked, coffee cup poised in midair as she again scanned Louise's face. She was a handsome woman with graying hair cut precisely to her shoulders, a direct gaze, a long narrow nose, and a generous mouth. She was wearing a simple black dress and a long rope of lustrous pearls. Once upon a time, Louise thought, she'd been beautiful. ''I've been with the agency for fifteen months,'' Louise replied. ''Primarily I work in the office. I do a lot of the booking,'' she added. ''As a matter of fact, I booked three of the interviews you're doing today and tomorrow.''

''You know you look about fifteen?''

Louise risked a smile. ''I get that a lot.''

Lydia Brinkley smiled back at her, shedding years in the process. ''Where're you from?''

''Toronto. And you're from New York.''

''How d'you know that?''

''I typed up your bio for the press kit,'' Louise answered. ''I'm one of those people who actually read what I type.''

Lydia laughed, took a swallow of her coffee, then reached for a black linen coat thrown over the back of one of the vacant chairs at the adjacent table. ''You'll do fine,'' she said. ''We'd better hit the road.'' As they were walking out to the car, she looked at Louise and said, ''So, Toronto, huh? Nice city. I've been there a few times on tour. What're you doing over here?''

''I've lived here for a year and a half.''

''You like the lousy weather and the rotten food?'' Lydia asked with a wry smile.

''The weather's terrible, but I like the people. This is Malcolm, our driver.''

Malcolm said, "Good morning, madame," and held the rear door open.

Once ensconced in the back seat of the car, Lydia asked, "You sure you've never done this before?"

Convinced she was messing up, Louise said, "I'm afraid so."

"Don't worry about it," the woman told her. "You're doing just fine. It's the first time I've been on tour when anyone bothered to find out the driver's name. I usually have to ask them myself. I don't shake hands, by the way," she said, and held out her hands for Louise to see. The fingers were twisted at an angle. "Rheumatoid arthritis," Lydia told her. "Too many eager beavers like to give you a crushing handshake to prove how damned earnest they are." With a pat on the knee, she told Louise, "It's nothing personal. You and I're going to get along like a house afire. So, what's first on the agenda?"

"BBC radio," Louise told her. "You did get your copy of the schedule, didn't you?" Louise had sent it by courier the previous day, along with a package of press clippings and a floral arrangement.

"I got it," Lydia confirmed. "You arrange for the flowers too?"

"They're from your publishers, I imagine," Louise lied. The publishers usually told King-Reid what they wanted and Toni or Terence took care of everything. "Were they nice?"

"Gorgeous. The Brits have style. Welcome to England. The only time my American publishers ever sent me flowers was when my first book hit the *Times* bestseller list." She laughed. "I guess they figured there was no need to welcome me to the States. Anyhow, that was a hundred years ago. Now I get a card at Christmas and my reprint house sends me something made of glass—a vase or a paperweight, whatever they're sending their top half dozen authors that year. I sound jaded as hell, don't I?"

"I don't think so," Louise said politely.

"I do and I am," Lydia declared. "Things are only exciting the first time they happen. After that, it becomes routine. You'll see. They'll all ask me the same questions. And I'll do my damnedest to make it seem like I've never heard them before. At least over here they usually take the time to read the book. I've pretty much stopped touring at home because about the best they can do is scan the press kit five minutes before airtime. Does *not* make for a great interview."

"I liked your book very much," Louise said. It was the truth. Lydia

Brinkley wrote biographies, and her latest was about D. W. Griffith. "I've always loved the movies. I thought it was fascinating."

"Canadians, you know, are the biggest moviegoing population per capita in the world."

"I didn't know that," Louise said.

"Neither did I, until I took on the Griffith bio. An amazing man. I mustn't get started or I'll be dull as dishwater for the interviews."

Understanding, Louise sat back and reviewed the schedule until they arrived at their destination.

At the BBC Louise went to the reception desk to say, "Lydia Brinkley is here for Roger Black," then sat with her client in the waiting room. Lydia lit up a cigarette and sat gazing into space, her crossed leg swinging rhythmically back and forth. Louise wondered if she was nervous.

"Do you have friends over here?" Louise asked her.

"Don't know a soul except for my publishers. This is my third promotion trip to London, and I've yet to meet anyone who wasn't connected in some way with my books. Two days, in and out, booked solid with almost no time to see anything."

"That's a shame. It's a terrific city," Louise commiserated. "If you like, I could try to get you a theater ticket for this evening. Is there anything you'd like to see?"

Lydia smiled. "I don't think that's part of your job, is it?"

"No, but I'd be happy to try for you."

"You're a damned nice kid, you know that?"

"Thank you. Would you like me to see if I can get you a ticket?"

"Tell you what. If you're free tonight, try for two and come with me."

"I'd love to," Louise said. "I'll see what I can do while you're having your interview."

She managed to get two seats in the stalls for *Stop The World—I Want To Get Off,* with Anthony Newley. And while she and Lydia had lunch back at Brown's, Malcolm went off with ten pounds of Louise's expense money to collect the tickets. Fortunately, Lydia signed for the lunch, which would, along with the hotel bill, be paid for by her publishers.

After lunch Lydia went to her room to freshen up, while Louise checked with the office answering service and left a message for Terence explaining that she was taking Lydia to the theater and wouldn't be able to get back to the office that afternoon, but would stop by early in the morning. Then she went downstairs to the ladies' room, thinking she could see now why Toni and Terry so enjoyed their work. It wasn't something she thought she'd like to do on a daily basis, but it was a delightful change.

Between interviews that afternoon she cashed a check at a branch of her bank to pay for dinner, then asked Malcolm to suggest a good place.

"Depends," Malcolm said, "on how posh you want to get."

"I'm really not dressed for posh. Someplace nice but not too-too," she told him.

"Well, let me see. There's Le Gavroche. It's French, as you might imagine. Might have trouble booking, though, but you could give it a try." They settled on Boulestin in the City. Malcolm agreed to stay on for the evening, so everything was settled, much to Louise's relief and satisfaction. She was pleased with herself for doing a good job.

It worked out perfectly. Lydia was plainly tired after a day of interviews, and Boulestin on Henrietta Street had a very relaxed atmosphere. She perked up over the menu and ordered crab with artichoke, while Louise had the duck.

"This is a nice change," Lydia said in the car on the way to the theater. "Usually I'm stuck in my hotel room eating food from room service and trying to find something decent on television."

"It sounds awful," Louise commiserated.

"It *is* awful, which is why I've cut my touring down to a minimum. I'm getting too old to be whiling my evenings away in sterile hotel rooms, reading anything I can lay my hands on. And what about you?" she asked. "What do you do with yourself?"

"Oh, I get together with my friends, this and that."

"No boyfriend?"

"Not at the moment."

"That surprises me," Lydia said. "A girl with your looks. I would've thought they'd be crawling all over you."

Louise laughed. "I've had a few dates, but nothing serious. I'm not all that interested, really."

"You don't want to get married and have children?"

"I've never wanted to get married."

"You might change your mind," Lydia said, but seemed unwilling to enlarge on the subject.

"I don't think so," Louise said carefully. "I like being independent, taking care of myself. I don't think," she continued, "that you can depend on men. They let you down one way or another. Except as friends. As long as you remain on a friendly basis with them they respect you. Once you become intimate, everything changes and you're dependent in some way or another, whether you want to be or not."

"That's a pretty harsh viewpoint to have at your age. I think you'll change your mind," Lydia said as the car pulled up in front of the theater. "Most women do."

"Maybe," Louise allowed. "But I'm not most women."

"Evidently not," Lydia smiled. "I definitely like your style. Most girls your age don't know their asses from their elbows."

Louise laughed. "I've been able to tell them apart since I was about six."

Lydia laughed with her. "You're a treat," she said. "This is turning out to be a most enjoyable evening, thanks to you."

"I'm enjoying it, too," Louise said, "especially the conversation."

⤙

"What did you do to Lydia Brinkley?" Toni asked two days later, coming to sit on the edge of Louise's desk.

"I didn't do anything to her," Louise said, alarmed. "Why?"

"She usually eats publicists for breakfast," Toni said, "but she was mad about you."

"She was?" Relieved, Louise caught her breath. "Thank God. You scared me half to death."

"A bit over the top going for theater tickets and dinner, but the publisher isn't complaining. Whatever possessed you to take her to the theater?"

"She was lonely," Louise said. "That didn't seem right to me."

"Well," Toni said, smiling her approval, "we may have to let you do this more often. You were a huge hit. Miss Brinkley raved about you."

"I liked her," Louise said, preparing to turn back to her typewriter.

"Obviously she liked you too," Toni said. "This just arrived for you." She put a package on Louise's desk and returned to her office saying, "Nice one, Louise. Well done!"

The package contained an exquisite Hermès scarf and a note.

I ran out this morning to get you a little something to say thank you for my best ever trip to London. Fondly, Lydia.

Rachel was mightily impressed by Louise's contact with a celebrity.

"Your life is so interesting, and mine's so horrid and dull," she complained. "Mummy and Daddy have run out of eligible men. Now they simply cast these reproachful glances at me whenever they're home, which isn't too often, thank heavens. I hardly see them, or Phippy, now that he's got his own place and is working in the City."

"You know what I think?" Louise said, trying not to be impatient at hearing the same complaint again and again. "I think it's time you signed up for a few courses somewhere. Your folks won't need to know, and it'll give you something to do. At least you won't be spending your life sitting around the house, bored out of your mind."

"Perhaps you're right. But I don't think I could do that."

"You could even learn something useful, like typing or bookkeeping. That way you'd have the skills to get a job and get out on your own."

"I might investigate the possibilities," she said cautiously. "Why didn't *I* think of that?"

"I don't know, Rachel. Maybe because everyone's always telling you you can't do anything. I don't happen to agree. I think you could do anything you set your mind to, including having a place of your own and living like the rest of us."

"Perhaps you're right!" Rachel said. "I'll think about it, perhaps ring a few places. In fact, I'll start tomorrow and let you know how I've made out."

"Just take it easy," Louise advised, suddenly afraid Rachel would try to take too much on. "You don't have to do it all in one day."

"Now you're sounding like Mummy and Daddy," Rachel told her.

"God! I wouldn't want to do that," Louise laughed. "All I'm saying is take it easy. Okay?"

"Yes, okay. Talk to you tomorrow."

That Friday evening Rachel came bursting into the flat, flushed with excitement. She'd signed on with a private business college to study computers and excitedly told Louise all about it.

"It's the coming thing, Louise. It's very exciting. One day, you know, computers will run simply everything. And I'll be a part of it."

"I think that's wonderful," Louise congratulated her.

"I'm very happy," Rachel said. "I must go now. I wanted you to be the first to know."

"But you just got here. Stay and I'll make some coffee."

"I can't. I want to look over some of the printed matter before I go to bed. There's masses of reading to do. Is this how you feel?" she asked. "Productive and purposeful?"

"I don't know about that. There are things I can do, and I take pride in doing them well. But you'll be way ahead of me if you're going to know everything about computers. Just thinking about them gives me a headache."

"I think you're teasing me, Louise. But this *is* serious business. I'm even considering buying stock in one or two of the better, more established companies. IBM, for example."

"Don't go crazy with it, Rachel."

"I've never been less crazy," Rachel said seriously. "If you were smart you'd invest a bit of money, too."

"I don't have enough that I can afford to play the stock market. You play it for me, okay?"

"You're being tiresome. I'm going to go now. I'll talk to you again when you're prepared to take me more seriously."

"Are you mad?" Louise asked. "I was only teasing, Rachel. Don't be angry."

"I don't know," Rachel sniffed. "Sometimes you can be quite cruel, really."

"Look, I love you and I'd never be cruel. You're tired, and so am I. Let's sit down and have a coffee and relax."

"It *has* been a full day, and I *am* tired," Rachel relented. "But I really don't want any coffee. I'm anxious to get home to my reading." She regarded Louise with large reproving eyes. "I hate it when people mock me."

"I've never mocked you," Louise defended herself. "I never would. I'm really glad you've found something that interests you. It's about time, wouldn't you say?"

"There've been tons of things that interest me, but Mummy and Daddy never approved. You know that."

"Yes, I do."

"Be happy for me, Louise," Rachel said imploringly. "I've got so little."

It occurred to Louise that despite Rachel's wealth, it was the truth.

Rachel had few if any outside interests, almost no close friends besides Louise, and endless time on her hands. "I *am* happy for you," Louise said.

"Sometimes it's hard to tell." Rachel sighed, then turned to go. "I was hoping . . ."

"What?" Louise asked.

"I don't know. I'll talk to you tomorrow."

"Are you mad at me?"

Rachel turned back in the doorway. "I'm mad at myself, Louise. I keep playing the fool."

"You're not a fool!" Louise stated, crossing to embrace her somberly clad friend. "You're tired. Go home and have a good night's sleep and we'll get together over the weekend."

"You won't tell Phippy, will you? About the course, I mean."

"Not if you don't want me to. It's your business, Rachel. You are an adult after all."

"I'm an old maid virgin." Rachel gave her a thin smile. "And now I really am going home. Will you call me?"

"Absolutely."

"Did I spoil your plans for the evening?"

"I didn't have any."

"Oh! Well, that's all right then," Rachel said.

"Take it easy now. Okay?"

After she'd gone, worn out by the exchange, Louise made herself a cup of coffee and went to sit in the front room, bothered by the way her friend had turned on her. It was a bit scary the way that happened. Since they'd first become friends, Rachel had reacted that way on one or two occasions. And it had upset Louise each time. She had the feeling she was suddenly sliding around in leather shoes on sheer ice, flailing about in an attempt to keep from falling on her face. So far she'd been able to bring Rachel around, to reassure her. But it scared her to think that one day Rachel would turn away from her, and that nothing Louise could say or do would work to put things right between them.

*C*HAPTER

F O R T Y - S I X

As 1961 DREW TO A CLOSE LOUISE BEGAN TO FEEL A KIND of ongoing agitation, a form not quite of restlessness but of a low-grade dissatisfaction. She wanted something but didn't know what. This wanting was like a physical urgency that kept her moving quickly all the time and made everything she saw appear not quite right. She wanted things to change, but didn't know which things, or in what manner. Nothing really pleased or displeased her; nothing *felt* the way it should.

When she sat down and tried to draw up a mental balance sheet of the pros and cons in her life, the pros far outweighed the cons. So why did she feel faintly edgy all the time? Why did she feel as if she wanted to fly but was held forcibly to the earth by the density of her own body? It was the end of another year. Soon she'd be twenty, but what had she accomplished? She had a small flat, a job she liked well enough, and friends. She should've been content with that, but she wasn't. Every time she thought of Faye she still felt the loss and pain of her absence. And when she thought of Daniel she felt guilty for having used him, and sometimes she felt a sexual ache, missing him. She missed her grandmother too, and Uncle Bob, and Kath, and the friends she'd left behind. But none of that really had to do with the continuing uneasiness she couldn't identify. There was some nameless thing that she wanted and the need for it seemed to grow a bit more every day.

At times she envied everyone she knew, convinced that no one else had this same little engine of discontent chugging away inside them. Why couldn't she enjoy what she had? She longed to settle, to have her life proceed in a calm, orderly fashion. Yet even when things seemed most stable, the urgency was singing in her veins, working in her lungs.

When she tried to describe it to Evie, Evie said, ''You're not one ever to settle, dear girl. Why are you working so hard to be ordinary?''

''Is that what you think it is?'' Louise asked her, anxious for some rational explanation she could apply like a soothing poultice to her malaise.

"I believe that's a part of it," Evie replied in her raspy voice. "You want something, you say, but you don't know what it is you're after wanting. I say it's your ambition urging you to get on."

"But I'm not ambitious," Louise said.

Evie laughed. "Get to know yourself, darling girl. You're fired up with ambition to do something. You simply haven't been presented with an opportunity that suits your needs. But it'll come. All your anxiety's about needing to get on, needing to make your mark."

"On what, though?"

"Ah, that I can't say. You'll know it when you see it. For now, Louise, all you can do is keep your eyes open. Don't let yourself be blinded by the urgency churning about inside you. Your time will come. Try to be patient."

"That's just it, though. I feel so . . . wild sometimes, as if I want to knock down walls with my bare hands or push over a bus. What the hell *is* that?"

"Youth," Evie laughed. "And you'll get over it. *That* I know for a certainty."

At Christmas she lied and told Rachel she'd been invited to spend the day with one of the King-Reid clients and that she'd had to accept for political reasons. Rachel was disappointed but understanding, and elicited Louise's promise that she'd stop by the house on Boxing Day. Louise agreed only because she couldn't believe that afternoon tea would be as dreadful as the Christmas ritual she'd witnessed the previous year.

She stayed home and spent the day reading and thinking about how her life had changed. The past year had gone well; she'd had a raise from Toni and Terence and was escorting clients on a fairly regular basis. She'd seen less of Rachel, who'd completed her first course and had immediately signed on for another. But since Rachel seemed pleased with herself, Louise could only be happy that she'd finally found some direction in her life. At moments she envied Rachel that newfound sense of direction. She seemed to have lost her own momentum, but she wasn't quite sure how or why.

She fixed herself a Christmas dinner of roasted chicken and potatoes and sat at the kitchen table with a glass of the wine she'd bought to celebrate the day. She telephoned her grandmother and Uncle Bob and afterward sat by the fire with a second glass of wine, deciding to bring her friends together for her second New Year's Eve in London.

She telephoned Nick to wish him and his mother a happy Christmas, then outlined her plan. It took a good deal of persuasion, but he at last agreed, saying, "You'll never bring it off, luv. But you're welcome to try."

The next afternoon, when she got a few minutes alone with her, Louise set about convincing Rachel to join her and Nick and his mother at the Golden Bough pub in Battersea.

"You know you really don't want to go to the Savoy again," Louise said. "You told me you hated it last year."

"I did, but Battersea?"

"It'll be great. At least you'll be with people you know and like, and you won't have to worry about getting all dressed up."

"How will we get home?"

Louise had to laugh. "Nick'll borrow a van. He'll drive us both home. Or you could spend the night with me."

"Oh, I couldn't do that. You've only got the one bed."

"Haven't you ever slept over at a friend's house, Rachel?"

"Of course I have. Phippy and I have spent weekends at lots of places."

"Big country houses where you had your own suite, I'll bet."

"You make it sound wrong somehow," Rachel said.

"Well, I don't mean to. I'm just saying you're welcome to spend the night with me. You could have the bed and I'd take the floor."

"I wouldn't dream of depriving you of your bed." Rachel looked dismayed. "I don't know why you're so determined to do this."

"Because," Louise repeated, "it'll be fun." What she wanted to do was to try to break down some of the barriers between Rachel and Nick, to illustrate to both of them that they had the right to see one another socially if they wished. And it seemed very clear to Louise that if the social barriers were removed, the two of them *would* want to see each other.

"I'm sure I'll regret it," Rachel said hesitantly, "but all right."

"Great! And I know you won't regret it. You'll probably have the best time of your life. Nick's a terrific guy."

"I've known him all my life," Rachel reminded her.

"That's not the same thing. Anyway, come at seven and we'll go together."

"What'll I tell everyone?" Rachel fussed. "They'll want to know where I'm going."

Patiently, Louise said, "Tell them you're going with me and a group of my friends. It's the truth, after all."

Still doubtful, Rachel at last agreed to all Louise's plans.

Next, Louise called Nick to confirm, and to her chagrin his doubt resurfaced. "I don't know as it's such a good idea," he said. "She won't like 'avin' bangers and mash and a pint or two. It's not what she's used to."

"That's the whole point. And don't you start giving me a hard time. Not when I've finally managed to convince her. We're coming with you and your mother, and that's that. It'll be fine. Will you be able to give us a lift home?"

"That's no problem," he said. "I just 'ope you know what you're doin'."

"All I'm *doing*," she said, "is trying to spend New Year's Eve with my friends. Now stop making such a big deal of it and tell me how to find the pub. We'll meet you and your mother there at eight. Do we need reservations or anything?"

At this he laughed. "Naw, you don't need no reservations. I'll 'ave a word with Flo, get her to save us a larger table." He paused, then asked, "Why're you doin' this, Louise?"

"God! You and Rachel are the two most difficult people I've ever known. I thought it'd be fun. Why are you making it sound as if I'm committing some kind of crime?"

"I've told you before: Belgravia and Battersea Park don't mix."

"And you've told me dozens of times how unfair you think that is. So we're doing something to change it. Besides," she sighed, tired of having to explain herself, "I'll be more comfortable with you and your mother than with Rachel and Philip's friends. The last time I went to a party with that crowd I felt like something from another planet. They meant well, I suppose, but my idea of a good time's not answering questions all night about the colonies."

"See," he said, "that's where you're wrong in your thinkin'. You're likely as not to get the same thing from our crowd. Only it won't be so polite."

"I think you're both wrong, and I'm sick of discussing it. We'll meet you at the pub at eight. Okay?"

"All right, darlin'. But I 'ave me doubts."

"Stuff your doubts," she laughed. "Just tell me what people will be wearing."

"Nothing too fancy."

"That's what I thought. Fine. See you Saturday."

Initially Molly and Nick were both a bit awkward with Rachel. Nick asked what they'd like to drink, and Molly murmured she'd have a pint of bitter.

"I don't know what to have," Rachel dithered. "Would I like bitter?" she asked Molly.

"Don't think you'd care for it, dear," Molly replied. "Why not 'ave a shandy?"

"Yes," Rachel said gratefully. "That's what I'll have."

"And what about you, Louise?" Nick asked.

Feeling bold, Louise said, "Scotch."

"Scotch?" Nick looked flabbergasted. "You sure?"

"I've had it before," Louise told him. She had, once, and hadn't especially liked it. But she wanted to reward herself for bringing these people together, and scotch had always seemed to her to be the epitome of grown-up drinks.

"You know best, darlin'. Scotch it is," Nick said, and put out his cigarette before going to the bar.

"You look very nice, Molly," Rachel said.

"Yes, you do," Louise agreed. It was the first time she'd seen Nick's mother dressed up. In a plain pink wool sheath with satin piping, with her fair hair in a French twist and some makeup on, Nick's mother looked very attractive.

Molly colored and looked down at the scarred tabletop. "It's nothin'," she said. "Just me once-a-year dress." Raising her eyes, she smiled at Rachel and said, "I see you've got your special 'at, Rachel."

Rachel put a hand to her head, beaming, then turned to Louise to explain. "This is the beret I told you about, the one Nanny made me. I wear it now only on special occasions."

"Lovely, she was, Miss Hastings," Molly said wistfully. "Nicest one of the lot, she was."

"I still miss her," Rachel said softly. "She was getting on, though. She'd have been close to ninety by now."

"I reckon," Molly said quietly.

"Will there be dancing?" Louise asked, looking around.

"Bound to be," Molly said, also looking around. "Starts out every year as a sing-along and winds up with couples dancin' like mad fools. Like to dance, do you, Louise?" Molly asked with a smile.

"Love it. It's how I met Rachel, you know. They were staying at the Royal York in Toronto, and Philip asked me to dance."

"You don't say!"

"Before we left, Philip gave me his father's card, and when I got over here I came to the house to look him up, and there was Rachel."

"You remember the day Louise came, Molly, and we had tea? We hit it off straightaway." Rachel gave Louise a fond smile.

"I remember," Molly said. "I was wonderin' how you two come to meet up."

"Now you know," Rachel said. "Louise is a wonderful dancer."

"So's my Nick," Molly said, as Nick returned to the table carrying drinks in both hands.

"So's your Nick what?" he asked, setting down his mother's bitter, his own light ale, Rachel's shandy, and Louise's scotch.

"A wonderful dancer," Molly told him.

"Wonderful," he confirmed. "Cheers, everyone!"

"I quite like to dance, too," Rachel put in quietly.

The scotch went straight to Louise's head, and, mercifully, it eased her constant-seeming agitation. Nick bought another round of drinks. They ate. Then they sang along to the piano and drums. "Maybe It's Because I'm a Londoner," and "Knees Up, Mother Brown," and "My Old Man." Louise didn't know the words to most of the songs but happily hummed along to the melodies. People jumped up and began to dance, and she danced several times with Nick. Before they returned to the table the last time, she told him he should dance with Rachel.

"Go on, Nick," she urged when he looked uncertain. "You know you're crazy about her. At least have a dance or two with the girl."

"You're a right mixer, you are," he said. "It's on your 'ead if there's a bill to pay."

"It's just dancing, for Pete's sake," she laughed, the scotch turning her loose-limbed and merry. "Go on and ask her."

"Fancy 'avin' a go, Rachel?'' he asked when they got back to the table.

Rachel didn't hesitate. She jumped right up, saying, "Yes, please," and Louise smiled, thinking she sounded like a little girl at a birthday party. Louise sat down and took another sip of her scotch, then smiled over at Molly, saying, "I knew this'd be fun."

Molly's eyes were on Nick and Rachel, her expression indecipherable. Louise turned to look, saw nothing exceptional, and turned back again, asking, "What's the matter, Molly?"

Molly lit one of Nick's cigarettes and took a long draw before meeting Louise's eyes. "The rate she's going, her mum 'n' dad are bound to find out what she's up to."

"What d'you mean?"

"She's studyin' night 'n' day, all them manuals 'n' textbooks, wearin' herself out. There'll be 'ell to pay," she said ominously.

"Why should they mind that she's finally doing something productive with her time?"

"It's not 'er time they're concerned with, see. It's 'er 'ealth. She's had a good long run now. It's been close on three years since the last time she was took ill. I know Rachel as well as I know my Nick, and I can tell when she's overdoin'. She don't 'ardly eat, and she's up early of a morning, off to that school, then 'ome late and studyin' those books to all 'ours. I'm worried about 'er."

"She'll be all right," Louise said.

"From your mouth to God's ear. So," Molly closed the subject, "you like our local, do you?"

Louise nodded, turning to look again at Nick and Rachel. Was there more to Rachel's illnesses than she'd been willing to believe? Rachel certainly looked well. If anything, she looked happier than Louise had ever seen her. And so did Nick.

"They make a nice couple," Louise said over her shoulder to Molly.

"I reckon I know what you're tryin' to do," Molly said with a sad smile, "and I think you're right good-'earted, Louise. But there's some lines as can't be crossed. And puttin' my Nick with Miss Rachel's one of those lines. 'E'll get 'is 'eart broken."

"Rachel's not a heartbreaker. I think she's really fond of him."

"She's 'er parents' child," Molly said meaningfully.

"That's where you're wrong," Louise disagreed. "Rachel's her own person. Or at least she will be."

"They'll never allow it, miss. Mark my words."

"But you wouldn't mind, would you?" Louise persisted.

"It's not up to me, is it?" Molly said simply. "T'were up to me it'd be a whole nother story. But it's not, see? It's the way things are done, the way they've always been done."

"Maybe all that's going to change," Louise insisted. "Would you like another drink, Molly? I think it's time I bought a round."

"I wouldn't say no," Molly smiled. "Mind 'ow you go with that scotch, though. That's a wicked brew."

"Oh, I'm fine," Louise said blithely, and pushed through the crowd toward the bar.

Louise got very drunk. At midnight, in spite of the fact that she felt in control of herself and of the situation, she burst into tears and wound up with her head cradled on Molly's shoulder as the crowd blew into noise-makers, and cheered, and kissed one another, and sang "Auld Lang Syne."

The last thing she remembered of the pub was falling asleep with her head on Molly's shoulder. She wakened briefly as the other three walked her out to the van, but was unaware of Nick dropping his mother home before driving her and Rachel over the bridge to South Kensington.

Snatches of Nick and Rachel's conversation came to her as if from a great distance as the two of them maneuvered her up the stairs and into her flat.

Rachel saying, "I'd best stop the night to make sure she's all right."

Nick saying, "You're sure? I don't mind runnin' you 'ome."

"I'm quite sure, Nick, thank you. I'll put the two chairs together. It'll be quite cozy."

"I fancy a cuppa. What about you?"

"I do, too, actually."

"I'll put on the kettle, then."

Their voices drifted away. A blanket settled over her. Louise turned her face into the pillow and slept.

Rachel said, "We'd best not put the light on. It'll disturb Louise."

"The 'all light'll do me fine. You fetch the cups, there's a good girl, while I brew up."

"You think she'll be all right?" Rachel asked, concerned, glancing through the archway to the front room where Louise lay soundly sleeping.

Nick laughed softly. "She'll 'ave an 'orrible 'eadache come the morning, but she'll be all right. 'Ow're you doin', Rachel?"

"Me? I'm perfectly fine. I had a super time. Mol . . . your mother looked lovely. You don't think she minded our coming along, do you?"

"Naw, don't be silly. Mum wouldn't mind. I never knew you was such a swell dancer, old girl." He lit a cigarette and leaned against the counter, smiling at her.

Rachel thought about how they'd kissed at midnight, about the spark of pleasure she'd experienced at having his mouth brush hers. It was the first kiss she'd enjoyed; she'd been disappointed at having it end. She was left with an impression of the softness of his lips grazing hers, and touched a fingertip to her mouth, but it felt rough by comparison.

"What you thinkin'?" he asked quietly, realizing it was the first time they'd ever been alone together.

Rachel flushed and said, "Oh, nothing."

"Know what I was thinkin'?" he asked.

"What?"

"I was thinkin' I wouldn't mind 'avin' another go at kissin' you 'appy New Year."

Rachel again looked over to the front room where Louise slept on, unmoving. "Do you like me?" she asked. "Do you think I'm pretty?"

"You 'avin' me on, darlin'?"

"Sorry?"

"Naw, you wouldn't," he answered his own question. "Course I like you, Rachel. Always 'ave done. An' you're better'n' pretty, darlin'."

"You think so?" she said, pleased. "I'm not as pretty as Louise, though."

The kettle boiled and he quickly removed it from the burner, turned off the gas, and poured the water into the teapot, saying, "You don't want to go comparin' yourself to other people. You're you, aren't you? And there's only one of you. D'you think I'm 'andsome?"

"Of course I do."

"Think I'm as 'andsome as those geezers your mum and dad're forever paradin' through the 'ouse?"

She smiled.

He said, "See what I mean?"

She nodded and opened the refrigerator for the milk.

"I've always fancied you," he said. "But there's no future in it, is there?"

"I don't know what to say to that," she said, flustered.

"D'you fancy me, Rachel?"

"Oh, dear," she said, embarrassed now as she handed him the milk. "I don't know what to say to that either."

"That's what I mean," he said confusingly. "So we'll have our cuppa, then I'll be on me way."

They drank their tea without speaking, each temporarily silenced by their thoughts. Nick drank his quickly, took a final puff of his cigarette, and prepared to go. "Tell Louise I'll ring her tomorrow, see 'ow she's doin'," he said as they moved toward the door.

In the hallway he took hold of Rachel's hand, and she waited expectantly to see what he'd do. He stood holding her hand with both his own, unable to look directly into her eyes. At last he said, "I didn't mean to 'urt your feelings."

"That's all right. My feelings aren't hurt."

"The thing is, they'd never let it 'appen, would they?"

She wanted suddenly to shout that it was her life and she could do whatever she damned well pleased. But of course she couldn't do that. She couldn't do anything, she thought wretchedly. "I suppose not," she said, wondering why, when it was just the two of them, the place felt so crowded.

" 'Appy New Year, Rachel," he said, and gave her another brushing kiss before letting himself out.

"Happy New Year," she whispered, and put the door on the latch. She wished Louise weren't sleeping. She longed to talk to her. Instead, she tidied the kitchen, then crept into the living room and curled up on the two chairs in front of the fireplace. She was suddenly very, very tired.

CHAPTER
FORTY-SEVEN

IT WAS A HARD WINTER, WITH FREQUENT THICK FOGS. One day in mid January it was so bad that Louise had difficulty finding her way home. People were colliding on the sidewalks and vehicular traffic had slowed to a crawl. It took her twice as long as usual to walk from the South Kensington tube station to the flat on Fulham Road. And in the fog she actually walked right past her own door.

When at last she made it inside, she unwrapped the yellow wool scarf she'd been wearing around her head to discover brown stains where the wool had come into contact with her nose and mouth. She stared at the scarf in disbelief, finally able to understand why Evie suffered so from bronchitis.

She telephoned Evie to say she wouldn't come over that evening. "The fog's unbelievable. I walked right past my own front door."

"Never mind," Evie said. "Come tomorrow. Will you do that?"

"I'll come straight from the office, but I'll phone you before I leave in case there's anything you need."

"You're a good girl," Evie said, then was overtaken by a coughing fit and gasped a goodbye before hanging up.

For a time Louise looked out the window, fascinated by the fog, unable to see a thing. When she turned from the window, the clarity of the air inside the flat seemed astonishing. She was very glad to be safely indoors, but felt her old familiar restlessness.

She peeled a potato and a couple of carrots and put them on to boil, then put a lamb chop under the grill and sat down at the kitchen table with her box of airmail stationery.

She reread the letter she'd just received from Kath, feeling very disconnected from her onetime best friend and all the things that had once been so familiar. Kath was in her third year of university but was thinking of switching over to the Ontario College of Art to study commercial design.

She was feeling, albeit belatedly, her mother's influence. "It's probably," she wrote, "got something to do with having grown up with the smell of linseed oil and turpentine, and of seeing jugs full of brushes like strange floral arrangements. Anyway, Mom thinks I should finish up and get my B.A. and then switch over to OCA if I'm still interested. She's probably right, but I hate the idea of putting in another year, taking courses that are just a grind.

"So tell me what you're up to. Are you seeing anybody? *Tell* me something! How goes the job, and how're your friends Rachel and Nick? Are you happy? I get the impression you like it over there but it's kind of hard to tell. . . ."

Uncapping her pen, Louise began: "Dear Kath," then sat and stared at the blank page. The water was boiling over; she got up and turned down the gas under the pot, checked the progress of her chop, then went back to the table. "Dear Kath." She tapped her teeth with the end of the pen, trying to think what to say. The double ring of the telephone startled her, and she jumped up and ran to the front room to answer.

"Oh good, you're there," Rachel said breathlessly. "Isn't it *foul?* I had such an awful time getting home. Didn't you?"

"Pretty bad. Did you just now get in?"

"Just this minute," Rachel said. "Isn't that simply incredible? It took me close on two hours to get from Bloomsbury. I've never seen anything quite like it. Mummy and Daddy are supposed to be arriving tonight from Frankfurt. I'm sure they'll be held up. What a bother!"

Louise thought she sounded genuinely unnerved. "Is something the matter, Rachel?"

"Oh, I don't know. The house is so empty. Molly's home with a cold. I hate being alone here."

"But Cathleen and Iris are there, aren't they?"

"Yes, but it's not the same. Ignore me. I'm being silly. I got frightened by the fog, that's all."

"Do you want me to come over?" Louise asked, looking through the archway at her dinner cooking on the stove.

"I couldn't ask you to come out in this," Rachel said, but with a hopeful note in her voice.

"If you're really bothered about being by yourself, I'll come."

"No," Rachel said, as if bolstered merely by the fact that Louise had offered. "I'm being a ninny. Don't you dare come out! I've a ton of reading to do. I'll have a cup of tea and calm down. I'll be fine."

"Are you sure? I could probably walk over and make it in about half an hour."

"I'll have a cup of tea," Rachel said, then asked, "Do you ever have the feeling that everyone but you is doing something with their lives and you're merely some kind of invisible bystander?"

"Is that how you feel, Rachel?"

"Just now I do, yes. I felt so . . . cut off by the fog. I feel cut off all the time, really, but the fog . . . I don't know how to explain it. I felt invisible, as if all the other people on the street could see each other but no one could see me. I know that's not the case. I mean, I know no one could see a thing. But people went past laughing and talking, making light of it, and I know they didn't see me. I had the feeling that if I'd spoken they wouldn't have heard me either."

"I felt a bit like that, coming home," Louise fudged, chilled by Rachel's word picture of horrible aloneness. "I'll bet everyone did."

"I expect you're right," Rachel said tiredly. "Shall we get together tomorrow evening?"

"I'm going to see Evie tomorrow. But we could do something Saturday night."

"I'm so jealous. She thinks you're special. Does she tell you bits and pieces out of the ordinary when you visit?"

"Not at all. It's like visiting anyone. We just talk. And you could come along, you know. I could call right now and ask her."

"No, don't do that," Rachel said, to Louise's relief. The truth was, she wasn't at all sure Evie would have welcomed Rachel. She probably would have, but Louise was reluctant to impose an unexpected third party on the woman when she wasn't all that well. "I'll see you Saturday. Actually there's a film I've been wanting to see, *Jules et Jim*. It's had fabulous reviews, and I love Jeanne Moreau, don't you?"

"Sure, that'd be great. Let's talk Saturday morning and we'll figure out where and when."

"Right you are," Rachel said with sudden briskness. "I'll be fine now. Bye-bye."

While she ate, Louise debated whether she should walk over to Wilton Crescent to make sure Rachel was all right. But Iris and Cathleen were there. It wasn't as if Rachel were actually all alone in that big house. She'd be fine, she told herself, going back to the kitchen to turn the chop and test the doneness of the vegetables.

Once she'd washed the dishes, she sat down and dashed off a letter to Kath.

"I'm fine. I adore my job. We're a bit quiet right now, but it's always quiet from about the beginning of December until the end of February. Nothing much is going on. Rachel's studying hard, and Nick's working on a housing estate in southeast London, so I only see him the odd Saturday morning when we go to one of the markets looking for bargains.

"My flat's great. It finally looks like someone actually lives here. I've got pictures on the walls and books on the shelves and I've acquired quite an assortment of knickknacks, mostly antique brass desk accessories—inkwells and stamp boxes, that kind of thing. They're cheap but interesting and look nice in little arrangements.

"I hear from Gramma and Uncle Bob every couple of weeks. They just got back from two weeks in Bermuda, but your mom probably already told you that. Gramma loved it. It was so British, she said, it gave her some idea of what it must be like for me over here.

"Daniel's still writing to me, still suggesting things I should see, even after I've been here all this time. He brings me up to date on the books he thinks I should read, and the movies he thinks I should see. Rachel's as crazy about movies as he is, and most of the time she drags me with her.

"I'm used to it here after two years but I still miss a lot of things, especially hot dogs and pizza. And there isn't a fish and chip shop anywhere around here. Isn't that something? I thought they'd be all over the place, but they're not. And they don't use halibut the way they do at home. Here it's plaice, or cod, or other fish I'm not used to. But all in all I like it here because it *is* so different.

"I have absolutely *no* love life. A few dates with friends of Philip's but nobody who excites me . . ."

Louise arrived at Evie's place to discover her friend had another guest.

"Darling," she rasped, "meet Tim Kelly. He's the son of one of my greatest friends."

Tim Kelly got to his feet to shake Louise's hand, saying, in a soft, lilting voice, "Lovely to meet you," as his eyes fastened to hers. He looked as if he'd been struck between the eyes by a rock.

"Good to meet you," Louise said, her hand warmly clasped by his.

"Tim's a doctor," Evie elaborated, hanging up Louise's coat. "Has a practice in Harley Street."

"Oh! What kind of doctor?" Louise asked, following Evie's direction to have a seat.

"Obstetrics and gynecology," he answered with a self-deprecating smile, waiting until both Evie and Louise were seated before resuming his own.

Louise was instantly fascinated. Everything about him bespoke wealth. A man of about forty, he had prematurely silvered hair, fine, almost delicate features, and deep-set, sad blue eyes. His aura of sadness was almost as powerful as the impression he gave of wealth. And it attracted her. His hands were slim and impeccably clean, with short, carefully trimmed fingernails. His sports jacket was cashmere, his shirt was crisp and very white, his tie was of figured silk. Even his shoes looked as if they'd be soft to the touch.

"Tim's mother and I were at school together," Evie said. "Will you have a spot of tea, darling?"

"I'd love some, Evie," Louise answered. "But I'll get it."

"She's such a good girl," Evie said to Tim as Louise got up to put on the kettle. "A lovely girl."

"Indeed she is," Kelly said in a hushed, melodious voice.

Overhearing, Louise smiled to herself as she set the kettle on the burner and reached for the teapot. Dr. Kelly was one of the most attractive men she'd ever seen, and the most appealing one she'd met since coming to England. She felt a clutching in her chest as she thought about the way he'd looked at her. The quiet music of his voice had affected her like a shout for attention.

"Delia's having me to stay in Surrey for a spell," Evie told her when she returned from the kitchen. "The damned bronchitis is hanging on and hanging on. Delia feels the fresh air'll do me a world of good. I don't know as it will, but it'll be a treat to have a visit with the grandkiddies."

"And what do you do, Louise?" Kelly asked. "Evie gives me to understand you're from Canada."

"That's right. Toronto. I work for a public relations firm."

"And do you enjoy that?" he asked, gazing at her with undisguised admiration.

"I do," she confirmed, warmed by the heat of his gaze as she heard the secondary conversation beneath the words. His eyes said he was taken with her; they asked if that distressed her at all. She met his gaze straight on, without hesitation. A visual positive response to the subliminal questions. "Especially when I get to escort a visiting celebrity around to interviews. I've met some fascinating people."

"I should think they'd find *you* fascinating," he smiled, as she poured the tea.

"For the most part I make them nervous," Louise laughed, absorbing his praise, drinking it in. It made her feel alive, gave her a sense of potency. "The first thing everyone asks is how old I am, as if I'm some helpless teenager who's going to mess things up." She was letting him know she was neither as young as she appeared nor inexperienced, and marveled at how well she'd managed to learn this coded language.

"I shouldn't have thought that," he said. "You're the least helpless looking woman I've seen in a good long while."

"Thank you. I agree."

"She's a very capable girl," Evie said, watching the interchange with considerable interest. "There's not a thing Louise couldn't do."

"Well," Louise smiled, "maybe not brain surgery."

"Ah, go on with you!" Evie laughed, which set the tiny old woman to coughing so hard, tears came to her eyes.

Louise went for a glass of water, came back and stood by her, anxiously asking, "Are you all right, Evie?"

"I want to put her on medication," Kelly said, "but she refuses."

"Don't want any damned drugs!" Evie wheezed, red-eyed.

"She's very stubborn," Kelly said to Louise.

"Jaysus!" Evie bellowed. "Don't be talking about me as if I'm not here!"

"Sorry," Kelly said softly, with a smile.

"Always were too smart for your own good, Timothy John Kelly," Evie said accusingly, accepting the glass of water from Louise.

"I think it might be a good idea if we had dinner another time," Louise said diplomatically, concerned for the old woman's well-being.

Reluctantly, Evie said, "It might be best. But sit down now and drink your tea."

Because Evie was so clearly under the weather, Louise cut her visit short. "I'd better be running along, Evie, and let you get some rest," she announced once her tea was finished.

At this, Kelly got to his feet, saying, "A good idea. I'll be going, too. Might I drop you somewhere, Louise?"

"I live in South Kensington," she told him, unsurprised by the offer, "if that's not out of your way."

"Not at all," he said, helping her into her coat. "I'll use your telephone if I may, Evie. Must check in with my service."

"Phone's in the bedroom," she told him.

While he was gone, Evie took hold of Louise's hand and whispered, "Mind how you go, Louise. He's a needy fellow and has a wife I wouldn't give you tuppence for."

"But I wasn't . . ."

"Stop with that!" Evie said impatiently. "I know what I know. Just don't harbor any false hopes. And don't allow that poor man to harbor any."

"All right, Evie," Louise said, cowed. "He seems very nice," she whispered, unable to suppress her interest.

"He fell in love with you on sight," Evie murmured with satisfaction. "Now mark my words and mind how you go."

"Nothing's going to happen," Louise said.

In answer, Evie gave one brief bark of laughter. "Hah!" she scoffed and shook her finger under Louise's nose. "Give Evie a kiss and get out of here. The both of you," she said, including Kelly who'd returned from making his call.

He had a Bentley. It was the first time Louise had ridden in one, and she complimented him on it, saying, "It's the most beautiful car I've ever seen."

"It's merely an automobile," he said dismissively. "I'm more interested in you, Louise Parker. Tell me about yourself."

"There's nothing to tell."

"Ah, but there's everything to tell. For example, I'll make no secret of the fact that I have a wife. We haven't been getting on for years, but we'll go to our graves as man and wife in the eyes of the Church. Have you someone, Louise?"

"I did, but I don't now."

"Do you know you have the most beautiful eyes I've ever seen?"

"Oh, they're all right," she said, never good at dealing with compliments. What other people saw rarely seemed to have any bearing on how it felt to live inside the housing that pleased or displeased others. It didn't change her basic belief that certain people saw past the surface and were attracted not to the externals, but to emotions they recognized.

He was quiet as he pulled the car over to the curb in front of the antiques shop as she'd directed. Then he turned and said, "They're beautiful eyes. You're a beautiful young woman." Looking out the window, he asked, "You live here?"

"Upstairs," she answered, rattled, wondering what would happen. She had the sense that something would. There was an inevitability to their having met, and to their continuing to meet.

"Well then, off you go," he said, and everything inside her that had lifted so expectantly crashed into the empty hollows of her body. Could she have been so far off the mark? Had she been vain to assume he found her as attractive as she did him? He was staring at her and she tried to think of what to say, when he smiled and said, "If I may, I'll call upon you sometime."

"If you like," she said, her confidence having been shaken by the way he'd appeared to dismiss her.

Turning to look at her again with his grieving eyes, he said, "I'd like to very much."

"My number's in the directory," she told him, offering her hand. "I enjoyed meeting you."

He accepted her hand and simply held it, gazing into her eyes for a very long moment. Then he said, "Beautiful eyes," and released her, getting out to come around and open the passenger door for her.

Standing on the pavement watching him drive away, she took in big gulps of air, feeling that she'd just come very close to drowning.

The following Tuesday she let herself into the flat to discover Dr. Kelly sitting, still in his overcoat, waiting for her by the electric fire.

"Don't be angry with the chap downstairs or with me," he said softly, getting to his feet. "I'm afraid I rather coerced him, told him I was your uncle." He smiled tentatively.

For a few seconds she was furious with Mr. Greeley. But then her pleasure at seeing Tim again was so intense that she forgot all about him. She set down her purse and carrier bag and walked directly into his arms. He held her, stroking her hair, for a long time.

"You're all I've thought of for days," he told her. "You've given me something to hope for. Is that too much of a burden for you?"

"I've been thinking about you too," she admitted, taken by everything about him, from his fluid, lilting voice to his gentle touch.

"I won't lie to you, not ever," he said earnestly. "There's only a limited sort of future."

"That's all right," she said, thinking it was perfect, absolutely perfect. "I'm not interested in anything with a future."

He held her face between his hands and again looked deep into her eyes, saying, "There'll come a time when you will be. Don't discount the possibility. But for now I'm most grateful. Beautiful eyes, but old, old. I know those eyes."

"I can't risk getting pregnant," she said, spontaneously responding to what they both knew was about to happen.

"Of course not," he said, with such sadness that she had to kiss him to try to make it better somehow for both of them.

He undressed her, commenting all the while on the sheer perfection of her. "Lovely, so lovely," he murmured repeatedly. "God, but you're lovely."

He kept his eyes on her as he removed his clothes, then he lifted her into his arms. She wound her arms and legs around him and buried her face in his neck, breathing in the fragrance of his flesh. For a time all her undirected energy had a focus and an outlet. She gladly enveloped him in her nakedness, reveling in the cadence of his words, the rhythm of his body, startled to learn she had an appetite that had been building without her realizing it.

CHAPTER

FORTY-EIGHT

SHE SAW TIM AT LEAST ONCE A WEEK. AFTER THAT FIRST visit she gave him a key so he could let himself in and wait for her. Often he telephoned her at the office to say, "I find I'll be able to get away later. Would that be convenient for you, Louise?" Most of the time it was. She had an insatiable craving for the sight of him, for the calming music of his voice. When she was with him time seemed to slow down; she was able to breathe more deeply; her senses were sharpened and she became more aware of sight and sound and scent. For however long she was in his company, she felt cherished and serene.

She'd arrive home and Tim would be sitting, still in his overcoat, in the chair by the fireplace, waiting. He never took the liberty of removing his coat in her absence or of switching on one of the bars of the electric fire.

There were occasions when she returned home from an evening out with Rachel or with Nick to discover that Tim had been in the flat. He'd have left a bouquet of yellow tea roses, or of cornflowers; or a copy of the *Evening Standard* sat folded on the table. He'd been reading while he waited. Once he left a box of Thornton's toffees because he knew she liked them. On another occasion she discovered a jeweler's box containing a fine gold chain necklace. But there were times too when he left behind no physical evidence of his having sat and waited. She simply knew he'd been there. The air in the flat was disarranged somehow, as if his presence had altered the atmosphere.

He was a secret she kept from everyone. Had anyone asked, she'd probably have admitted the truth: that she'd embarked upon an affair with a married man. But since she gave nothing away, no one questioned her. Sometimes she thought it would be a relief to admit to Rachel she was seeing someone on the sly. Telling would have lessened the weight of the secret. Yet all in all she didn't mind keeping this important piece of information to herself.

Sometimes they made love the minute she came through the door, shedding their clothes in fevered haste in order to be skin to skin, touching, as quickly as possible. Just as often they didn't make love at all, but sat with cups of tea or coffee and talked in front of the fire. Or she'd climb onto his lap and allow herself to be petted, like some oversized domestic animal deriving comfort merely from his attentiveness. His hands eased her inner turmoil, brought her thoughts into order. And his voice, like a coating of oil, smoothed the roughened surface of her mind. With Uncle Tim, as she occasionally, teasingly referred to him, she felt most at peace—with him and with herself. He was a man who liked her precisely as she was; he had no desire to change anything about her or about the manner in which she lived. And he instinctively refrained from inflicting himself, in however minimal a fashion, on her environment. Not only would he not take the liberty of removing his coat while he awaited her, he wouldn't even take so much as a drink of water. It was her home and he never intruded. She loved every moment of the time she spent with him.

Her twenty-first birthday was approaching and Rachel insisted Louise celebrate the occasion with her.

"Nick too, if he's free," she told Louise on the telephone the week before her birthday in April. "The three of us will go to a super restaurant, my treat, and we'll have champagne."

"We could get together here," Louise said, progressively more concerned about Rachel's health and state of mind. She'd finished her second course and was restless again. She wanted, on the one hand, to take yet another course, but on the other hand felt so tired all the time that she doubted she'd have the energy to pursue anything seriously. "I could make a casserole or something," Louise said, "and we could have a quiet time."

"You're not cooking on your twenty-first birthday!" Rachel said, as if scandalized by the thought. "We're going out, and you're to be waited on hand and foot by a bevy of fawning lackeys."

"You don't have to do that," Louise said.

"Of course I don't," Rachel laughed. "But I want to. And you're to allow me to treat you. And Nick too."

"I'll ask him," Louise promised, and rang off to call Nick.

"I'm working late every night for the next fortnight," Nick said, disappointed. "There's a push on to finish the estate. It wasn't for all the lovely lolly, I'd tell 'em to stick it. But I don't fancy gettin' into a bother with the union."

"That's all right. I understand."

"Sunday morning, though, I'll buy you a bang-up breakfast at the caff in the market," he laughed. "Much as you can eat, my treat."

"I've got a better idea," she said. "I'll make a picnic, and let's go to Hampton Court. I've been dying to see it."

"Right you are. 'Ampton Court it is."

Rachel said, "It's a shame he can't come. But never mind. I've booked us into the Louis XVI at the Ritz for seven-thirty. We'll be frightfully grand. I may even wear something special for the occasion."

"The Ritz?" Louise said. "Are you sure about this?"

"Positive. We'll meet in the foyer at seven-twenty. All right?"

"Okay."

"You'll recognize me," Rachel laughed, "by my hat."

✝

In the late afternoon on Louise's birthday Rachel entered Mr. Greeley's antiques shop to say, "I'd be so grateful if you'd let me into Louise's flat. I've a surprise for her birthday and the delivery man's waiting outside."

Mr. Greeley hesitated. "Miss Parker's specifically asked me not to allow anyone into the flat."

"I know. And I won't be staying. It'll only take a few minutes. It's a surprise," she repeated. "For her birthday. Please?"

"Well," he said. "I don't suppose any harm can come of it. Just a moment while I fetch the spare key."

The delivery man was waiting outside on the pavement with the new television set Rachel had purchased. Excited, she unlocked the street door and held it open. The set was hefted into the arms of the burly delivery man and he proceeded up the stairs.

"It's to go in the front room," Rachel told him as she opened the door to the flat.

Both of them stopped to stare at the overcoated man who got to his feet, an opened newspaper in his hands.

Startled and confused, Rachel said, "I had no idea . . . I'm Rachel Townsend-Post, Louise's friend."

The delivery man stood holding the heavy set while Tim Kelly tried to think what to say.

"You'd best put that down," Kelly said to the grateful young man.

"Stand's in the van," said the fellow. "I'll go fetch 'er up and be on me way." He loped down the stairs.

Kelly introduced himself to Rachel, extending his hand. "Tim Kelly," he said. "I was, ah, waiting for Louise."

"It's her birthday," said a flustered Rachel. "The television set's a surprise, you see."

"Yes, of course," said Kelly, trying to think of some valid explanation for his presence in the flat. "How very generous of you."

The delivery man returned with the stand, asking Rachel, "Where you want it set up?"

"I believe there's a point in the corner there, next to the desk," she told him, trying to imagine why this older man was sitting in his topcoat waiting for Louise. "I take it you're a friend of Louise's too," she said to Kelly, for some reason terribly bothered at finding him there.

"That's right," he said, and made a show of looking at his wristwatch. "I thought I'd stop by." It was on the tip of his tongue to say he was her uncle Tim, but thought how ludicrous that would sound, so he just looked at his watch again and said, "I'd best be on my way. Sorry if I startled you, Miss Townsend-Post."

The delivery man had the set on the stand, and announced, "It's all hooked up and ready to go, miss."

"Oh, thank you," Rachel said.

"Good day, miss, sir," the young man said, and hurried off.

"I must dash," Rachel said. "I've a taxi waiting."

"Oh, quite," said Kelly, holding the now-folded newspaper with both hands. "Good to have met you."

"And you," Rachel said, then hesitated for a moment, wanting to say something else, to ask what he was doing there. Instead, she left, closing the door at the top of the stairs quietly after her.

Exhaling mightily, Kelly sank back into the chair and swore under his breath. He thought he should leave. But since the damage had already been done, he decided to stay and explain the situation to Louise.

Louise sensed at once that something had happened. She could read it in Tim's face. She looked at him, then at the television set, and asked, "Did you do this?"

"I'm afraid I didn't," he said. "Evidently your landlord let in the young lady in order to deliver the set."

"Rachel?"

"That's right."

Louise crossed the room to look at the television set, picking up the license Rachel had thought to get and pay for. Holding it, she turned to Tim. "You were here?"

"It was extremely awkward. I am sorry, Louise."

"I've asked him so many times not to let people in," she said angrily.

"I think your friend's rather a persuasive young woman. And she did have a delivery man with her."

"She shouldn't have done it. I can't accept a present like this. God! What did the two of you say to each other?"

"We hemmed and hawed a bit. I am terribly sorry," he repeated. "I know it's your birthday and I stopped by to give you this." He reached into his pocket and withdrew an envelope. "I thought perhaps you might buy yourself something you fancy."

Staring at the envelope as he held it out, she asked, "What is it? Are you giving me money?" Her heart was suddenly racing.

"I've done the wrong thing, haven't I?" he said, the hand with the envelope dropping. "All the way round today, I've done the wrong thing."

"I'm not my goddamned mother, you know!" she railed. "You don't give *me* money. What the hell d'you think I *am?*"

Returning the envelope to his inside pocket, he said, "It wasn't my intention to offend you. That's the last thing I'd want to do."

"You want to give me money and you don't think I'd be offended? Are you joking? *She* bamboozles that idiot Greeley into letting her in with a damned TV set, and *you* . . . you want to treat me like a hooker. What the hell's the matter with you people?"

Wounded, Kelly said, "I think we all of us acted with the best of intentions. And I think each of us is sorry that our plans have, to put it mildly, gone somewhat awry. I have the highest regard for you, Louise. It's hurtful to think you'd interpret my gesture as an attempt to classify you as a woman who sells her favors. I apologize most humbly for the gaffe. I'll be going now."

"You don't give people *money*," she insisted, wanting him to know just how deeply offended she was.

"Evidently not. Again, my apologies." With that, having gone somewhat pale, he started for the door.

Oh, shit! she thought, feeling beleaguered. "Tim!"

He halted and waited to hear what she'd say.

She took several steps toward him, then stopped and said, "There are things you don't know, things I don't discuss, not with anyone. It's . . . unfortunate that you . . . I mean, I understand what you were trying to do." Looking over her shoulder at the television set, she said, "I know what Rachel was trying to do too." Her eyes returned to him. "Sometimes I feel as if I'm always running, trying to keep ahead of this angry crowd that's chasing me. If they catch me, I don't know what they'll do, but I know I'll be hurt. I feel that way most of the time. Even when I'm sitting at the office and the place is quiet, and I'm getting caught up on confirmation letters or schedules, whatever, I've got this feeling that I'm running. I can almost hear the wind whistling in my ears, and my side aches because I'm going as fast as I can. The only time I don't feel that way is when I'm with you.''

He nodded soberly.

"I didn't mean to yell at you or to upset you. It's just that you can't give me money. It *means* something. You understand?''

"I do,'' he said softly.

"And,'' she went on, "Rachel has to stop giving me things. She has to stop feeling as if she has to buy my affection. I should've told her about you. I don't know why I didn't. Did she seem upset?''

"That I can't say. The whole thing only lasted two or three minutes.''

Feeling remorseful now, she moved close to him and leaned against his chest. "I'm sorry, Tim.''

"I'm sorry,'' he said. "I forget sometimes how very young you are.''

"Not anymore,'' she said with a grim little smile. "As of today, I'm a legal adult.''

"If it were another time and another world, I'd marry you, Louise. I've loved you all my life. Can you understand that? You were rather like a film negative in my mind. And that evening at Evie's the negative suddenly became a positive print. The last thing on this earth I'd ever knowingly do is cause you pain. Today's been an unfortunate series of events. It's no one's fault. Not yours or mine, nor the chap downstairs, nor your generous young friend. Don't judge us too harshly because we try, in our ham-handed fashion, to demonstrate in tangible form our great affection for you.''

"My mother sleeps with men for money.''

"So I gather,'' he said with sympathy.

"I'm not like her,'' she said insistently.

"I don't imagine you are.''

"But for a minute there I felt like her. And I *hated* it.''

"That's not how I, or anyone else, I should imagine, thinks of you. You must believe that.''

"I believe it. But that doesn't change how I felt. I'd rather die than be anything like her.''

"That is something which, unfortunately, you must come to terms with on your own,'' he said wisely. "Life is filled with great ironies, you know, dearest Louise. I spend my days dealing with the miracle of birth, and no man ever wanted children more than I. But my wife never conceived. I hold newborns in my arms most days of the week, but I'll never hold one of my own. You have a disreputable mother and you harbor the fear that you'll become like her. I know otherwise, but I haven't the power to convince you. Only you have that power. Your young friend has a need to prove her friendship with generous gestures, perhaps because she doesn't perceive herself to be lovable when the truth is that she is. On and on. We all of us have our fears. We all of us must learn to live with them."

"You're not mad at me?" she asked.

He smiled finally and stroked her hair. "I love you far too much to be angry with you. I must be going. Enjoy your evening." He gave her a light kiss, then said, "Happy twenty-first, Louise," and smiled again.

"I'm sorry everything was such a mess," she told him. "Will you call me?"

"Of course," he said, and went off down the stairs.

Rachel was bursting with questions, and started in the moment she saw Louise. "Who *was* that this afternoon in your flat?"

"A friend," Louise answered, "someone I've been seeing."

"Why haven't you told me about him?"

"I don't know, Rachel. I haven't told anyone about him, except Evie. And she knows because she introduced us. Look, about the television set. You really shouldn't have done that. I can't accept such an expensive gift."

"Of course you can. Don't be silly!"

"Rachel, I can't."

"You have to. I'm certainly not returning it to the shop, and we've already got a set at home."

"All right, but I'm going to pay you for it."

"That's horrid! You most certainly will not."

"I'm not going to fight about it," Louise said firmly. "I'm going to pay you for it, and that's that."

"It's a twenty-first *birthday gift!*" Rachel exclaimed, as if that justified the expense. "One simply does not offer to pay for a gift."

"We'll discuss it later," Louise said. "I really don't want to get into a fight over it."

"Why didn't you tell me about that man? I honestly don't understand that. Didn't you want me to know?"

"I didn't tell you because the opportunity never came up. That's all. It's nothing personal."

"I thought we were best friends," Rachel pouted. "Best friends tell one another everything."

"I'm sorry I didn't tell you. All right? You look very nice," Louise said, trying to change the subject. Instead of her usual black trousers and black top, Rachel was wearing a black miniskirted Mary Quant dress, which went very well with her bright red beret. Her eyes were, as usual, heavily ringed in black, and she was wearing pale pink frosted lipstick. "It's a great outfit."

"You like it? I think my thighs are rather on the heavy side for such a short skirt, but I couldn't resist this when I saw it in the shop."

"Your thighs are like sticks," Louise said, always amazed by Rachel's distorted view of herself. "You look adorable."

"You honestly think so?" Rachel asked, pleased.

"Honestly."

"We'd best go along or we'll miss our reservation."

Somehow, while they were having their entrees, the conversation turned to Nick. And as she'd done any number of times before, Louise asked, "Why won't you consider going out with him? It's so obvious the two of you like each other."

"He's Molly's son, Louise."

"So what?"

"His mother's a domestic. Mummy and Daddy would go wild."

"Oh, for Pete's sake. You're twenty-four years old. What d'you care if they go wild?"

"They're my parents, Louise. I've got to care. And besides, I don't think Molly would be too keen, either. I still don't think she was particularly comfortable New Year's Eve."

"Unfortunately, I don't remember," Louise grinned. "I got a little blasted, remember?"

"I'm hardly likely to forget. It was quite something. Although Nick and Molly didn't seem bothered. Who *is* that man, Louise? Are you having an affair with him?"

"We see each other once in a while," Louise said. "It's an affair of sorts. It certainly wouldn't prevent me from dating someone else or anything like that."

"You're very difficult," Rachel said, looking hurt. "And secretive too. I never imagined you were quite so complicated."

"I'm not at all complicated. I'm sorry for not telling you, but it really wouldn't have made any difference to our friendship. I think you're overreacting, probably because you're bored again since your course finished. Maybe you should think about getting a job, putting your newfound skills to work."

"Why are you pushing me?" Rachel asked, her hurt look changing to one of distress. "First you want me to take up with Nick, which as you well know is simply out of the question. Then you want me to defy Mummy and Daddy and do something you know perfectly well they've forbidden. And you insist on repaying me for a gift when it gave me such pleasure to buy it for you. Are you trying to upset me?"

"Not at all. I'm just trying to help. You're very clever, Rachel. You need to keep your brain working."

Setting down her knife and fork, Rachel opened her bag, put two ten pound notes on the table, then got to her feet, her eyes suddenly brimming with tears. "I think you're being hateful. I was in quite a happy mood until you started all this."

"But I haven't started anything," Louise protested, thrown once again by the startling shift in Rachel's mood. "I didn't mean to upset you. Please sit down and forget everything I said."

"I can't do that, can I? Not when you've said such hurtful things. Why did you have to do that?" She pushed her chair aside abruptly and started from the dining room.

"Where are you going?" Louise asked, hurrying after her. "You haven't finished your dinner."

"I'm going home. You've been perfectly horrid."

"Rachel, I'm sorry. Don't go. It's a misunderstanding. The whole day's been full of them."

Rachel wouldn't listen, wouldn't be deterred. She marched out of the dining room with Louise at her heels, and straight out of the hotel.

"Taxi, please," she said to the doorman, who turned and waved one forward from the queue.

"Please don't leave," Louise said.

The taxi pulled up. The doorman opened the passenger door. Rachel pressed a coin into his hand and climbed into the back.

"I'll phone you tomorrow," Louise said.

"As you wish," Rachel said almost inaudibly, as the door closed and the taxi drove off.

"Damn!" Louise said under her breath.

"Taxi, miss?" asked the doorman.

"No, thanks," Louise said. She'd walk. She needed the time to think, to try to sort out what had happened.

The only thing she could think to do was to call Philip. Luckily he was in.

"Ah, Louise, hello," he said. "How are you? Haven't seen you in an age."

She described what had taken place at the restaurant, and he listened without interrupting. When she'd finished, he said, "Sounds as if she's going into one of her down periods. I was just this week thinking she's had a good long run, and that's in large part due to you, you know. No, don't feel badly, Louise. One never knows what'll trigger her. Usually it hasn't a thing to do with anyone else really. It's to do with Rachel. Don't be surprised if she's out of touch now for a time. I expect Mother and Father will ship her off to The Mansions if she's really bad."

"What's that?" she asked, more and more alarmed.

"A rest home in the country. She usually does quite well there. Dr. Hastings, Rachel's psychiatrist, runs the place. Good chap."

Louise felt terrible. "We were having an ordinary conversation and all of a sudden everything went wrong."

"As I've said, that tends to be her pattern, poor thing."

"I'll try to talk to her tomorrow, but in case she's still mad at me, will you keep me posted, let me know how she is?"

"Of course I will. And I promise you she's not mad at you. It's just that when she has one of her down spells she's angry with everyone. I'm glad you rang, actually. I'll give Molly a shout, warn her."

"Okay," Louise said dispiritedly. "Thanks a lot, Phil."

"Not at all," he said.

She hung up and sat staring at the television set, thinking it had been one of the worst days of her life.

*C*HAPTER

FORTY-NINE

AT ELEVEN THIRTY THAT SAME NIGHT THE TELEPHONE rang. Hoping it might be Rachel, Louise grabbed the receiver. It was her grandmother, calling to wish her a happy birthday. They talked for a minute or two, then her grandmother said, "Your stepbrother Mike is getting married in June, honey. We'd all love you to be here for the wedding. We thought we'd send you a ticket as your birthday present. It's been so long since we've seen you. This seems like a good occasion."

Initially Louise's reactions were mixed. But thinking it through, she realized a break from her new life might be a good idea. It would give her a chance to view everything from an actual distance, and suddenly she very much wanted that opportunity. "That's wonderful, Gramma. I'd love to come. It'll be great to see everyone."

"Kath will be home for the wedding. And you're invited to stay with them, if you'd like. Or with us, of course."

"I'll stay with you and Uncle Bob," Louise said at once. "I wouldn't dream of anything else. Is Nancy going to have a big party for them?"

Her grandmother laughed. "Naturally. You know Nancy. Any excuse for a party. I'm so pleased you'll come. We didn't want to send the ticket until we were sure you could get away."

"I'll talk to Toni and Terence next week, let them know so they can get in a temp."

"You're getting an accent, you know, Louise. You sound very English."

It was Louise's turn to laugh. "Not according to everyone I meet over here," she said. "They pick me out as a foreigner the minute I open my mouth."

"I know it's late there, so I won't keep you. I just wanted to wish you a happy birthday."

"Thanks, Gramma. I'm really glad you called. I love you. And give my love to Uncle Bob too."

Not five minutes later the phone rang again. Again thinking it might be Rachel, she picked up at once.

"Your line was engaged when I rang a few minutes ago," Tim said, "so I thought you'd likely still be up."

"I was talking to my grandmother in Toronto."

"Ah, that's lovely. And how was your evening?"

"It was a disaster. Rachel stormed out of the Ritz, furious with me. And I'm not even sure what I did."

"That is a pity."

"I wish you were here," she said, too agitated to go to sleep.

"Would you like me to come?"

"Could you do that?"

"I get late-night calls all the time," he said matter-of-factly. "I'll be round in twenty minutes."

This was a departure. He rarely called her in the evenings, and he'd never come to the flat late at night. She'd assumed he spent his evenings with his wife. But of course he'd be summoned for deliveries at all times of the day and night. She pulled on her robe and went to the kitchen to fill the kettle for tea.

He knocked at the upstairs door just as she was carrying the tray of tea things to the front room. Leaving the tray on the desk, she went to let him in, feeling for the first time the negative power of their illicit affair. He'd undoubtedly had to lie to his wife in order to get away.

"I feel guilty," she told him, hanging up his coat. "I shouldn't have asked you to come out so late."

"Not at all," he said, draping an arm across her shoulders. "I'm up late most nights. And I confess I was a bit concerned after the comedy of errors here this afternoon."

"I made tea," she said, taking him by the hand to lead him inside.

"That's very thoughtful. I could do with a cup. It's a cold night for April."

Once settled in the two chairs in front of the fireplace with their tea, she said, "My stepbrother's getting married in June. My grandmother's sending me a ticket so I can fly home for the wedding."

"How long has it been since you were home?"

"I haven't been back since I got here almost three years ago. This'll be the first time."

"I'll miss you," he said, running one finger around the rim of his cup.

"I'll miss you too," she said, suddenly wishing he could go with her. "It's a pity you don't have some international conference to attend or something."

"A pity," he agreed. "Perhaps sometime you and I will steal a few days and have a weekend in Paris."

"I'd love that," she said. "Maybe we will. Have you ever heard of a psychiatrist named Hastings?"

"I may have done."

"He apparently runs this place in the country called The Mansions."

"Ah, yes," Kelly said. "A rather fancy drying-out tank for monied inebriates. They do a bit of psychotherapy on the side, treating mild personality disorders."

"Is it a good place?"

"Has a decent reputation," he said. "Why?"

"Apparently that's where her parents send Rachel whenever she has what her brother refers to as a down period. I have a hunch that's where she'll wind up this time. I *wish* I knew what set her off. We were having a good time, then all of a sudden she turned. I've seen her do it a few times before, but this time she wouldn't snap out of it. She went off in tears, and I feel awful. Maybe I shouldn't have made such a stink about her giving me that damned TV set."

"Perhaps not," he allowed. "But there are times, and people such as yourself, who find it difficult to accept the grand gestures some of us make now and then." He gave her one of his self-deprecating smiles.

"I can't help it," she defended herself. "I'm used to making my own way. It makes me feel—conniving, sort of, to accept gifts. As if I'd somehow wormed them out of people by playing needy or something."

"That's not the impression you give, Louise."

"No? Well I'm glad to hear that. I'm not needy. I do have a little money of my own." In fact she had almost thirty-five hundred of the four thousand pounds her grandmother had given her when she left.

He smiled and drank some of his tea.

"What do you do in the evenings at home?" she asked, evidencing curiosity for the first time about his family life.

"Read, listen to music."

"What about your wife?"

"My wife goes about her business. She's very involved with charity work. And she has a wide circle of friends. We tend to go our separate ways. We share the house but not the master suite," he explained. "I took over one of the guest bedrooms some years back. Until I met you, Louise, I'd resigned myself to our rather alienated existence. Now I find I'm somewhat restless, impatient with the status quo."

"But nothing will change," she said, dreading to hear him say otherwise.

"Not in the immediate present. But it's not etched in stone that any of us must continue along a given course." He looked at his watch, then asked if he could use the telephone to call his service.

"Of course," she answered. "Help yourself. I'll get more hot water for the pot." She carried the teapot to the kitchen, thinking she'd be going home soon. It scared and excited her. On the one hand she longed to see her grandmother, her friends, old familiar places. On the other hand, she dreaded the memories those people and places might revive. All at once Faye's death was very fresh in her mind, and she felt herself curving protectively inward over the pain.

"I must go," Tim said, coming into the kitchen with his cup. "I've got a patient four centimeters dilated and getting ready to pop."

She smiled at this, and put her arms around his neck, saying, "Thanks for coming over. You've cheered me up."

"Happy to be of service." He gave her a kiss, then smoothed her hair, for a moment studying her eyes. "You mean the world to me, Louise. Is that impossibly selfish?"

"No. You mean a lot to me too. I like coming home and finding you here. It's a wonderful surprise every time."

"I like waiting for you, looking at your rooms, at the things you've chosen for yourself—the pictures, the inkwells. I'll ring you over the weekend if I'm able."

She kissed him, then walked with him to the hall to retrieve his coat from the row of hooks. "I'm sorry about the way I behaved this afternoon."

"It's forgotten," he said quietly.

"Drive carefully," she said, holding the door open.

"Sleep well," he replied, and went quickly down the stairs.

❧

When she awakened Sunday morning it was to the sound of rain drumming down on the roof and a high wind rattling the windows. Not the day for a trip to Hampton Court. She telephoned Nick to say, "Come here for breakfast. It's a rotten day."

He agreed to be there in an hour, and she tidied the flat before taking a quick bath. Dressed, she got the bacon started under the grill, and set the table. By the time he arrived, everything was ready and they tucked into the food she'd prepared. While they ate, she told him what had happened on Friday evening at the Ritz.

When she wound down, Nick said, "Phil's right when he says not to take it personal, Louise. It's got nothin' to do with you. When Rachel gets in a state anything'll set her off. It's like she's lookin' for someone to say somethin' she can 'ang it on, a reason like for why she's 'et up. So it doesn't matter what you say. I've 'ad 'er turn on me a time or two. It's a right shocker, but then in a way you get used to it."

"But I feel terrible. I admit I was kind of pushing her, but I really believe she'd be fine if she got out on her own and started being responsible for herself. Anyway, she started to cry and said I was being hateful. And from her viewpoint, I was, sort of. But I can't accept that things have to be the way they are for her. She *could* make changes if she really wanted to. I tried calling three times yesterday but she wouldn't come to the phone. Your mother told me she was staying in her room."

"That's what she does," he said. "She'll 'ole up in there for days. Then they'll bring in that Dr. 'Astings and 'e'll say it's time he took 'er off to that nut'ouse for a while. They'll give her shock treatments, fatten 'er up some, then ship her 'ome in a month or two. 'Orrible," he grimaced. "She comes 'ome all pale, her eyes like saucers, with her 'ands shakin'. She'll be like that for a few weeks, then gradual-like she'll come round to bein' her old self again."

"That's awful!" Louise was horrified. "Shock treatments?"

"She's 'ad 'em ten, maybe fifteen times, I reckon."

"Poor Rachel. I'll try to call her again after we finish eating."

"Won't do no good. Me mum says they called in 'Astings last night. They're shipping Rachel off tomorrow afternoon."

"Why didn't you *tell* me?"

"What difference would it make, Louise? You think there's anythin' you could do to stop it?"

"Yes, maybe."

"Yeah? Like what?"

"I don't know. Something. I could talk to them."

"Right, darlin'. And what'd you say?"

"I don't know," Louise admitted, feeling defeated. "Maybe if I talked to Philip."

" 'E's bloody useless," he said with contempt. " 'E'd as soon 'ave 'er locked away. That way she's not such a bloody embarrassment, is she? Give over, Louise. They're shippin' 'er off, and that's all there is for it."

"I shouldn't have pushed at her," she said, all at once repelled by the food. "Why didn't I just say thank you for the TV set and let it go?"

"Wouldn't 'ave made a blind bit of difference, my girl. It's got nothin' to *do* with you. Don't you get that yet? It's to do with *them,* 'asn't it? So it'll do no good your gettin' all worked up. Best forget it."

"How can I just forget it? She's my *friend.* I *care* about her."

"I know that. But *there's nothin' you can do.* Not one bleedin' thing. Whyn't we take a walk?" he suggested. "It's stopped raining."

"I could use some air," she admitted gratefully. "Just leave the dishes. I'll clean up later." She got up and went for her raincoat and purse.

Later that afternoon she called the house. Molly answered and Louise asked, "How's Rachel?"

"She's up in 'er room with the door locked."

"Molly, I've got to see her. Are her parents around?"

"They've gone out, luv. But I don't know as it's such a good idea."

"If I come over right now will you let me in?"

"Well," Molly said, thinking it through, "I reckon it couldn't do no 'arm."

"Thanks. I'll be there in fifteen minutes."

Rather than waste time waiting for a bus, Louise ran most of the way. Molly let her in, saying, "If she'll talk to you, see if you can't get 'er to eat a bit of something."

"All right, I'll try," Louise said, and went up the wide curving staircase and along the hall to knock on Rachel's door.

"I'm incommunicado," Rachel called in response to the knock.

"Rachel, let me in," Louise called back, knocking harder.

"I'm not seeing anyone!"

"I'm not leaving, so you'd better let me in!"

There was a silence. As it lengthened, Louise began knocking again.

"Stop making such an ungodly racket!" Rachel said, this time from closer to the door.

"Let me in!"

"You're being a bloody nuisance," Rachel said, turning the lock.

Louise waited for the door to open. When it didn't, she tried the knob. Rachel was sitting on a chaise longue with her knees drawn up to her chest and her arms wrapped around them. As usual, she was all in black, but her feet were bare, her toes curled under.

"Molly would like you to eat something," Louise said, sitting on the end of the chaise. "So would I."

Rachel shook her head and let her chin rest on her knees. "I despise this house," she said. "One can't get the least bit of privacy."

"Tell me what's wrong," Louise invited.

"Obviously, I'm depressed," Rachel said. "I'd prefer to be left alone."

"I like your hat," Louise said of the beige felt bowl-shaped creation atop Rachel's head.

"You're patronizing me," Rachel warned.

"Sorry." Louise looked around the spacious room, noting that the draperies were drawn. The only light came from a lamp on the bedside table. The top of the white French provincial desk was piled high with textbooks. "Talk to me," Louise said, putting a hand on Rachel's arm. Rachel closed her eyes. "Look," Louise said. "I'm sorry if I've been pushing Nick at you. I've been thinking about that and I guess I've been out of line. I didn't mean to upset either one of you. So if that's why you're mad, I apologize and I'll never do it again."

"You can't force people to be the way you want them to be," Rachel said dully.

"No, I know that."

"But everyone tries. I wish you'd go away, Louise. I'd prefer to be alone now. I'm tired and it's very difficult to think with people constantly battering at my door."

"But I'm worried about you," Louise said.

"You needn't be."

"I can't help it."

"I can't stop being depressed because you're worried about me," Rachel said with stubborn logic. "I don't care for the world just now. I expect I'll recover. I would simply *like* to be left *alone*."

Just then Molly tapped at the door and came in. "I've brought you some potatoes," she said, setting a covered bowl down on the table next to the chaise.

"Not cooked, I hope!" Rachel said sharply.

"No, luv. Raw, the way you like them."

"Thank you, Molly," Rachel said almost inaudibly. "I may have some later."

"Will you have some tea?" Molly asked.

"No, thank you. And Louise will be leaving shortly."

"Right you are," Molly said, and left.

"Raw potatoes?" Louise said.

"They're crunchy," Rachel said, as if that explained the matter to her satisfaction. "It makes my teeth feel good." Again, absently, she said, "I may have some later."

"Is this one of your down spells, Rachel?"

"Only a very mild one," Rachel said, then sighed. "Please won't you go now? I can't think with you here and I really must think."

Reluctantly Louise got to her feet. "Okay, I'll go. But it makes me feel terrible seeing you this way." She wondered if Rachel knew she was being sent to The Mansions, but was afraid to ask, afraid to upset her further.

"Don't give it another thought. A few days and I'll come round. I'd like to sleep now," she said, turning and settling in on the chaise. "Thank you for stopping by. I'll ring you soon." She pulled the hat forward over her face and closed her eyes.

"I'll call you tomorrow," Louise said, defeated, and walked across the thick carpet to the door.

⁜

"Don't you care, Nick?" Louise asked him the next evening on the phone, unable to understand his reaction to the situation.

"Yeah, I bloody care," he replied hotly. "Course I bloody care. I bloody love 'er, don't I? For all the good that'll do either one of us."

Touched at hearing this declaration, she was quiet for a moment, then said, "There ought to be something we could do for her."

"You ask," he said. "They might let you visit."

"And what about you?"

"Right!" he said sarcastically. "I can see it now. Ah, Nick," he said in put-on upper-crust tones, "lovely chap. Want to see our Rachel, do you.

Of course, of course. Delighted. We'd be enchanted to welcome you into the family. Jolly good show. Carry on, that's a good fellow.'' He laughed disdainfully. ''Dream on, darlin'! They wouldn't let me through the bloody door.''

''Of course they would,'' she insisted. ''I'll find out where this place is and we'll go visit her.''

''That might not be such a fine idea,'' he said. ''You might not care much for what you find.''

''I've seen sick people before, you know.''

''Not sick like this, you 'aven't. But it's up to you.''

''It's very good of you to be concerned, dear, but Rachel couldn't possibly entertain visitors just now,'' said Mrs. Townsend-Post.

''But aren't you planning to visit her?'' Louise asked. ''Isn't she allowed visitors?'' *Entertain?* What an odd way to put it!

''We feel it's always best for her to acclimate to The Mansions for a week or two. Of course she's allowed visitors. But we know from past experience there's nothing to be gained from attempting to see her prematurely.''

''I see,'' Louise said, thinking that Nick had been right. ''But would it be all right if I went to see her?''

''Well,'' Mrs. Townsend-Post drew out the word, ''I suppose there'd be no harm to it.''

''If it's okay with you, I thought I'd go next Sunday.''

''I really don't know . . .''

''Why not give me the phone number? I'll call up and ask if they think it'd be okay.''

''Yes, all right. Hold on a moment and I'll look up the number.''

Louise waited, halfway convinced Rachel's mother would come back on the line saying she'd changed her mind. She was gone for several minutes, and Terence signaled to her that she had a call waiting. ''I'll just be another minute,'' Louise told him, covering the mouthpiece with her hand. ''This is important.''

At last, Mrs. Townsend-Post came back, saying, ''Had a bit of a sticky time finding the number. Isn't that silly? Here it is, Louise,'' she said, and recited the number of The Mansions.

Louise thanked her, then switched to the waiting call, which was from the production assistant of a radio show on gardening, who wanted to confirm a booking for one of the agency's society matrons. Louise made a note of the confirmation, then waited for Terence to finish his call—Toni was out with a client—so she could tell him about needing to take time off in June.

"We can't function without you for an entire fortnight!" he complained with a smile. "We'll fall to pieces. How could you even *think* of leaving us?"

"You'll be fine," she told him. "We'll get in a temp, and you won't even notice I'm gone. I don't like to mention it, but I've been here almost three years and I haven't had one single vacation day. You people owe me about six weeks."

"Please don't say you want to take the six weeks now," he begged jokingly. "By all means take the fortnight, but no more. Please."

"All I want is two weeks."

"Perfect! Now be a pet and send this telex off to New York, will you?"

"Sure." She took the page on which he'd written out a message and went along the hall to the service office.

As usual, the place was chaotic. Jill was typing something for someone while Susan was sending a telex. One of the secretaries from the second floor was using the Xerox machine, and two other girls were queued up waiting for her to finish. When she did, she took up the pages, called out, "Six copies, Jill. Charge it to our account," and went on her way.

Louise stood by Susan's desk waiting for her to finish sending the telex, and watched people getting angry at the typical inefficiency of the place. It wouldn't have taken much to get things organized and running smoothly, but neither Susan nor Jill seemed to have any organizational skills whatsoever. They could type and run the machines, but they couldn't keep track of copies being made, or of telexes being sent, or of stencils being run off. If there had been another service office in the block it probably would have been doing a booming business, Louise thought. Every time she had to come in here she wanted to reorganize the place, establish some order.

By the time Susan had finally sent off Terence's telex, Louise had wasted close to half an hour. When she got back to her desk Terence was fielding two calls simultaneously. He smiled gratefully when she picked up the third line. What the office needed was another secretary, and what the entire block needed was someone efficient to operate the service office.

It was close to four before she found some free time to call The

Mansions. When she asked about visiting hours, the woman on the switchboard asked, "What patient were you calling about?"

"Rachel Townsend-Post."

"One moment, please. I'll put you through to Dr. Hastings."

"But—" Her protest was lost. Ringing started at the other end.

"Dr. Hasting's office."

"Look," Louise said. "I don't know why she put me through to you. I only wanted to know about visiting hours. A friend of mine's there, and I'd like to come see her."

"I see. And which patient would that be?"

"Rachel Townsend-Post."

"Yes. One moment, please. I'll put you through to Dr. Hastings."

"Oh, *brother!*" Louise muttered. Why did she have to talk to the doctor when all she wanted was to know the visiting hours?

"Hastings here."

"Dr. Hastings, this is Louise Parker. I'm a friend of Rachel . . ."

"Yes, Miss Parker. I understand you'd like to visit Rachel."

"That's right, I would. I was just calling to find out the visiting hours."

"I'm afraid visitors are out of the question at the moment, Miss Parker. Miss Townsend-Post's simply not up to it. Perhaps if you'd be good enough to ring in, say, a fortnight's time, our position might be more encouraging."

"You're saying she can't have visitors?"

"That is correct, unfortunately. Only family members may see Rachel for the next little while."

"I see."

"But I'll certainly tell her you rang."

"Well, thanks a lot," she said, and hung up to call Philip at his office. After they'd exchanged how-are-you's, she got right to the point. "Would you take me to see Rachel on Sunday?"

"I'm not sure I follow."

"I want to see her. Her doctor says only family members can see her. Surely if I go with you they'll let me in."

"I don't know," he hesitated. "We usually wait for Dr. Hastings to advise us as to when it would be wise to visit."

"You know," she said, "I don't get this. She's your sister. Don't you *want* to see her?"

"Of course, but Dr. Hastings knows best, really."

"So you won't take me. Is that it?"

"I'd have to consult with Mother and Father before I could agree to that, Louise."

"All right," she sighed. "Consult with them and let me know, please. Okay? I'd really like to go see her."

"I'll try, Louise. I know you're very fond of Rachel."

"I'm more than fond of your sister, Phil."

He rang off promising to get back to her in the next day or two. She sat and stared at her crowded desktop, sickened by the idea that Rachel was going to be lost to her. She vowed she wouldn't allow it.

When Philip called the next day, she was certain he was going to give her some kind of bum's rush, but in a light, almost conspiratorial mood, he said, "I've thought it over and I've come up with an idea. Our cousin Elsa is on the approved visitors list at The Mansions."

"Uh-huh."

"Well, the thing of it is, Elsa emigrated to Australia this past year."

"Uh-huh."

"So," he said, "you could visit Rachel as Elsa."

"But they'll know I'm not her."

"That's just it, you see. They won't. It's been better than four years since Elsa last visited Rachel at The Mansions. They won't remember after four years. It's perfect, don't you see."

"Phil, that's great! You're a genius."

"Oh, I say," he laughed. "Don't go overboard. At the weekends, one can go any time between nine and five. I'm booked up this weekend or I'd go with you. You did say you wanted to go on Sunday?"

"Yes, I did. Thank you, Phil. It really means a lot to me."

"It's odd, you know. But I have the idea it'll mean rather a lot to Rachel. You've been very good for her. Oh! And this'll be our little secret, won't it? I suspect Mother and Father would have fits if they found out."

"They won't hear it from me. Thank you," she repeated. "I'll give you dinner one night next week, if you like."

"There's no need for that. Just ring me, let me know how she is. Would you do that?"

"I'll phone you Sunday night when I get back."

After thanking him a third time, they ended the call. Terence was looking quizzically at her.

"A friend of mine's in the hospital," she said.

"Bad luck," he said. "Sorry."

"She's going to be all right," she said strongly. "She's going to be fine."

CHAPTER

FIFTY

THE TRAIN RIDE THROUGH THE COUNTRYSIDE REMINDED Louise of her ride three years earlier from Liverpool when she'd boarded the London-bound train and sat fairly mesmerized by the astonishing green of the countryside. On this overcast Sunday afternoon the countryside was no less green, no less astonishing. She hadn't been outside the city once since she'd arrived, and the wildflowers growing by the sides of the tracks drew her eyes, as did the weeds flourishing everywhere.

As the train clattered along on its way to Tunbridge Wells she was gripped by a powerful nostalgia—for her childhood and her sister, for the dusty summer streets they'd known so well, for the games they'd played and the secrets they'd shared. It all seemed very long ago, decades, centuries.

She thought of Daniel and felt a terrible longing for their lunches at the Kresge's counter. She'd been so perplexed by her emotions then, and so optimistically unaware of the darker of life's possibilities. Chuckie died, and then Blanche, and she'd mourned for her inability to mourn. Then her sister died and the inner strings that controlled the movements of her limbs and the traffic patterns of her thoughts had become hopelessly tangled. Daniel had helped her undo the worst of the tangles so that she was once again able to function. He'd guided her through what had felt like twelve months of midnight darkness, encouraging her to see the possibility of daylight, encouraging her to carry the bundle of her knotted strings to another country in order to begin again as someone without a sister.

While she waited for the bus in Tunbridge Wells she wondered what

Nick had meant when he'd said she might have seen sick people but she'd never seen anyone sick like Rachel. Maybe it was vain of her to believe that her affection for Rachel could make a difference. Love couldn't save people. It made them feel good; it made them behave out of character sometimes; but it wasn't a miracle cure. And it wasn't something she was sure she believed in. Tim often said he loved her, and she listened to him say the words, examined the way his features altered when he said them, and saw that uttering the words unraveled the strings inside him and made him somehow stronger. But she didn't feel that same possibility of intense satisfaction in repeating the words back to him. What she felt for him was dense and complicated, but was it love? Perhaps. But as with Daniel, she'd again chosen to involve herself in a futureless situation. She could only travel through the days as they arrived, putting her best efforts into each one while trying to cope with the perpetual feeling of being pursued by unknown assailants.

She'd gone to Wilton Crescent looking for Philip, and Rachel had from the outset inserted herself into a niche in Louise's feelings—not the dusty cavern where her love for Faye still resided, but a small place that had been empty for too long. And then, with powerful nesting instincts, Rachel had scooped out a larger place for herself and filled it with mementos, little souvenirs, images of their friendship. But until now, until this moment riding a rural bus along narrow roads, Louise hadn't acknowledged just how large Rachel's place inside her had become. Living daily with her absence was almost as painful as living with the finality of Faye's death. She wanted her friend, her slightly mad, wonderfully eccentric friend well and home again.

Stepping off the bus she had a sense of momentousness. Taking a deep breath of the fresh country air she approached the long driveway of The Mansions with a renewed sense of purpose. She was going to get Rachel the hell out of this place. Never mind that it didn't look in the least sinister, with its acres of lawn and well-tended flower beds. It was an institution, and Rachel didn't belong here—no matter what her parents wanted to believe. Rachel belonged out in the world, with someone like Nick to love her, with a home of her own, and work to do.

A receptionist sat in the marble-floored entryway and Louise announced herself as Elsa Bradbury. ''I'm here to see Rachel Townsend-Post.''

The receptionist checked a ledger, then said, "Have a seat, please. Someone will be along in a moment to escort you."

Escort me? Louise thought, wandering away from the desk to stand gazing out the open front door.

In a matter of minutes a nurse came along and with a smile said, "If you'll come this way, Miss Bradbury." She led Louise up the curving staircase to the second floor, then down a long hallway. Approaching an open door at the extreme far end of the hall, the nurse rapped her knuckles on the adjoining wall and leaned into the room saying, "You've a visitor, Rachel. Your cousin Elsa's come to see you."

Stepping into the doorway, Louise absorbed the sight of her friend like a blow to the stomach. In a robe and slippers, Rachel sat in a chair with her back to the window. Her hair ratty, her face pale, she looked up with dull eyes. She gave no sign of recognizing Louise.

"See if you can't get her to go out of doors," the nurse said in an undertone. "The fresh air would do her a world of good. She hasn't been outside this room once in the week she's been here."

"I'll try," Louise said thickly, realizing she'd never seen Rachel without either a hat or a full face of heavy makeup. Without them Rachel looked about twelve years old.

The nurse left and while Rachel watched her, Louise put down her purse and carrier bag and went over to drop down on her haunches, taking hold of Rachel's hand.

"How are you?" she asked, noting the deep purple pouches under her eyes. "Are you still mad at me?"

Rachel turned her head to look out the window, her hand limp under Louise's. "Who told you about cousin Elsa?" she asked listlessly, as if the answer wasn't really of any interest to her.

"Philip," Louise explained. "It was the only way I could get in to see you. Family only, no friends."

"Mummy and Daddy never come until after the first fortnight." Rachel blinked as the clouds passed and the sun emerged. "No one ever comes."

"You haven't answered my question. Are you still mad at me?"

Turning from the window, Rachel said, "Was I mad at you?"

"Furious," Louise smiled. "Spitting. Livid."

Rachel stared into Louise's eyes as if she might see through them into the interior of Louise's head. "The treatments destroy my memory," she said after a time. "I sit here and try to remember things, but I can't. It's the most frightful feeling."

"I'll bet it is. Would you like to come outside? It's really nice out for a change."

Rachel put a hand to her head, then lowered it to her lap. She moistened her lips, looked again out the window, then back at Louise. At last, she said, "The garden's very nice. Some of the residents work on the beds."

"Then let's go out," Louise said, giving Rachel's hand a squeeze.

"Oh, I couldn't," Rachel said anxiously, starting to chew on her lower lip.

"Where's your hat?" Louise asked.

"I don't know," Rachel said, and began to cry. "I can't remember."

"I'll tell you what," Louise said, pulling the scarf from around her neck. "Wear this. It's almost as good as a hat."

"I remember that scarf!" Rachel said with a sniff. "The American author gave it to you."

"That's right," Louise said, tying the scarf over Rachel's hair. "What d'you think?"

Again Rachel touched her head, her fingertips stroking the folds of silk. "It smells of you," she said, holding one corner under her nose. "It smells of fresh flowers."

"Blue Grass. My grandmother always wears it. It makes me feel close to her."

"That's lovely." Another tear rolled down Rachel's cheek. "My grandmother smelled of horses and leather. And my other grandmother smelled of dogs."

Louise laughed, drawing Rachel's eyes again to hers. "Was that amusing?" she asked.

"Very," Louise confirmed. "Let's go outside. Okay?"

"All right," Rachel agreed, and got up from the chair. "Do I look all right?"

"You look beautiful," Louise lied, keeping hold of her friend's hand.

"I must remember to call you Elsa," Rachel said, clinging to Louise, her hand no larger than a child's. "So many things to remember. Will I need a coat?"

"Let's take it just in case. Where is it?"

"I can't *remember*," Rachel cried, her face contorting. "I don't remember where my bloody coat is."

"It's probably in the closet," Louise said, letting go of Rachel's hand to have a look. "See," she said, removing it from a hanger. "Here it is. D'you want to wear it or shall I carry it for you?"

"I don't know. What d'you think?"

"Tell you what. Let's drape it over your shoulders for now. Okay?"

"Yes, okay." Rachel reached again for Louise's hand, and they went slowly out of the room and along the hall. Rachel moved like an old woman, her steps jerky and uncoordinated. "My joints ache," she said in a whisper, her free hand going to her head as if to reassure herself that it was properly covered.

"Poor Rachel."

In a whisper she said, "They strap you to the table, then they dab bits of jelly on your temples and put a padded stick in your mouth. And then they turn a switch. After that you don't remember anything. Each time I'm surprised that I wake up."

Louise gave her hand a squeeze as they descended the stairs. The front door seemed miles away, so slow was their progress. The front hall was empty but for the receptionist, who was on the telephone. Step by step they approached the door. Louise was gripped by the arbitrary fear that at any moment someone would come running out to denounce her as a fraud and send her packing. It didn't happen. They passed out through the door and Rachel sniffed at the air like a puppy.

"There's a bench along the path," Rachel said. "We could sit down."

"Okay," Louise agreed, and allowed Rachel to lead her along the gravel path between the flower beds where a number of other patients worked with forks and trowels, turning soil and weeding. No one took any notice of them.

Once seated on the bench Louise said, "I brought you some fruit. Would you like an orange?"

Rachel tilted her face to the sun, gazing straight into it. "I'll die here," she said softly, as if addressing the sun. "Next time or the time after they'll throw that switch and I won't come back. My joints will dissolve, my brain will empty like a washbasin, and I won't come back." She sighed heavily and lowered her head. "It might be nice not to come back."

"You don't mean that," Louise said, peeling an orange. "And I'd hate it. I don't know what I'd do without you. I'm used to talking to you every day.''

Without any change in her expression tears again trickled from Rachel's eyes. ''When I saw him I felt so desperately envious of you, Louise,'' she said. ''I thought how lucky you are, how lovely you are, and I envied you. It was fierce, like a wound. He looked so *nice,* and he was so wonderfully soft-spoken. I felt unutterably defective and foolish, like a clown. I *know* how absurd a picture I make. I know! But I wanted what you have. I wanted someone handsome and soft-spoken to sit and read the *Times* while he waited for me. All those stupid, stupid boys Mummy and Daddy paraded past me. I felt like something at the zoo, something flawed, on display, and for sale at a reduced price. Louise,'' she said, ''are you truly my friend?''

''Yes, I am,'' Louise said firmly.

''I always wanted a sister, you know. Someone to whisper with after the lights were out, someone to tell all my secrets to. It seemed so providential to me that first day you came. I opened the door and remembered you at once. I remembered how well you danced and I remembered your sister and your grandmother and her husband. I spent the entire evening watching you. It was I who suggested Phippy ask you to dance. You seemed so full of fun. I envied you then. And I envied you when I came with the delivery man and found that lovely-looking man in your flat. How do I get that for myself, Louise? How do I tell Mummy and Daddy they're destroying any chance I might have of a life? Just to be free, Louise. To be out of here, away from that room with the table and those straps.'' Pushing up her sleeve she held out her left arm to show the bruises on the inside of her elbow. ''From the needles,'' she said, one tear clinging to the tip of her nose. ''I wouldn't eat, so they fed me intravenously. And they give me drugs. My head aches from them. I don't want to be mad, Louise. I don't *feel* mad. They wouldn't listen when I tried to explain I was simply upset. I wasn't having one of my spells. They wouldn't *listen.* I just so terribly wanted what you have. Is that so very wrong?''

Louise had to swallow before she could speak. ''It's not wrong, Rachel. It's not even very much to ask. I'm sorry I didn't tell you about Tim. I should have. It was wrong to keep him a secret. But the thing is, he's married.''

''So what?'' Rachel said blankly.

"He has a wife," Louise repeated.

"So what?" Rachel said again. "He loves you. He sits and waits for you. Do you know what I'd give for someone who'd sit and wait for me?"

"Nick's sitting waiting for you."

"He thinks I'm pretty, you know. He told me that New Year's Eve. It's funny, I can't remember what happened last week but I remember New Year's Eve. He kissed me. Twice."

"He loves you, Rachel."

"They'd never allow it."

Louise handed her a section of orange and Rachel stared at it uncomprehendingly. "Eat it," Louise said gently. "It's not fattening."

"Yes, all right." Rachel bit the section in two. A bit of juice ran down her chin.

Louise got out a tissue and blotted her friend's chin. "Tell me what you want, Rachel," she said softly. "Tell me what you want most in the world, and then let's get it for you. You can do it, you know. All you have to do is decide that it's your right."

A nurse and bathrobed patient went past on the walk. Neither of them even glanced at Rachel and Louise. Across the way an elderly woman knelt before a bed of graded perennials and carefully trimmed dead leaves with a pair of nail scissors.

"I want to run away from home," Rachel said with a gulping laugh. "I want to tie a bandanna to the end of a walking stick, like someone in a Mark Twain story, and run far away. Why is it so hard to put one's hands firmly on something and keep hold of it?"

"It isn't hard. You just need practice."

"Is that what it is?" Rachel asked, accepting another piece of orange.

"I've been looking out for myself all my life, Rachel. Faye and I looked after each other. We had to. We didn't have anyone else, except Gramma. My mother's a cow, Rachel. When we were little she used to beat the hell out of me and Faye. And you know what? I'm probably way out of line to say this, but I think it's time I did. I think your mother and father are just as bad in their own way. Maybe they don't beat the shit out of you, but they've kept you all tied up in your insecurities, made you afraid to take two steps on your own. That's as sure a way of crippling someone as walloping them. I know you could do anything you wanted. All you've got to do is believe that."

"I'm afraid," Rachel murmured, holding the piece of orange in her lap. "I've been afraid all my life. I want to *stop*, Louise. How do I do that?"

"I'll help you. Decide what you want, and I'll help you. I swear to God, I'll do everything I can."

"I want so many things," Rachel said sadly. "I want my own flat, decorated the way I want it, not the way Mummy wants it. I want my own bedroom in my own flat, and I want to make love to someone in my own bed in my own bedroom. And I want to be able to remember it."

"First of all we've got to get you out of here."

At that, Rachel's face froze. "Oh," she said, alarmed. "I can't leave here."

"Why not?"

Rachel's mouth worked and she searched Louise's eyes anxiously.

"Why not?" Louise repeated gently. "What's stopping you? Have your parents committed you? Have they signed legal documents to keep you here?"

"I don't know," Rachel whispered. "Oh my God! I'm so frightened! What if they have? I can't bear it. If I have to stay here, I'll die. I'll die, Louise. They're killing me."

Louise put an arm around her shoulders to calm her, saying, "We'll get you out of here. I'll talk to Philip tonight."

"He won't help! No one will help me."

"I think he will, Rachel. It was his idea for me to come today as Cousin Elsa. Your brother loves you. He wants you to be happy. So do I and so does Nick. I'll do my damnedest to get you out of here, if it's what you want. But you've got to be willing to try to stand on your own once we do."

"But you'll be there to help me?"

"I'll always help you, Rachel. You're my friend. I love you. I hate seeing you here."

"Then talk to Phippy," Rachel said with sudden urgency, clutching Louise's hand. *"Get me out of here!"*

Louise all at once recalled their first meeting with Evie when she'd said Louise would be of great importance to Rachel. It was a little alarming to think of the trust Rachel was placing in her, but she knew she had to do whatever she could, because she believed her when Rachel said she'd die in this place. "I'll do everything I can," she promised. "One way or another, Philip and I will get you out. It might take a week or two, but you have my word."

An hour later she was walking back toward the bus stop, in her mind an image of Rachel being escorted back to her room by the nurse, going up the stairs one at a time but looking back over her shoulder with an expression halfway between hope and fear, one hand assuring herself that Louise's scarf was still tied firmly over her hair.

If it was the last thing she ever did, Louise swore to herself, she was going to get Rachel out of that place and standing squarely on her own two feet.

CHAPTER
FIFTY-ONE

"COULD YOU COME OVER HERE?" LOUISE ASKED. "WE really need to talk."

With an awkward, embarrassed laugh, Philip said, "Is that absolutely necessary? I'd rather hoped once you'd visited Rachel that would be the end of it."

"It's only the beginning," she said, working to keep her tone pleasant. "If you care at all about your sister, we've got to discuss the situation."

"Why are you becoming so involved, Louise?" He spoke the word "involved" as if it signified something untoward.

"Look, I've got a casserole I made up yesterday. I'll put it in the oven and it'll be ready by the time you get here. Humor me, please, and come over. There's no harm in talking."

"I suppose not," he said, still holding back.

"You don't have plans for the evening, do you?"

"Well, there is some work I was hoping to get caught up on."

"So you'll get caught up on it later," she said. "I'll put the casserole in the oven and expect you in about forty-five minutes. Okay?"

"Yes, all right, but . . ."

"Good." She cut him off. "See you then," she said, and hung up.

"Brother!" she said aloud to herself as she put down the receiver. She was going to have a hard time convincing him, harder than she'd anticipated.

After turning on the oven she went into the bathroom to have a quick wash, and looked at herself in the mirror. She looked angry, determined. That wouldn't do. She forced a smile at her reflection as she brushed her hair, then fixed it in a long single braid. She'd never encountered a family like Rachel's, people who required such convincing before they'd do the obvious, or right thing. It was work, genuine work. And she knew that Philip was going to resist her suggestions. It seemed, as Nick had said, that they preferred having Rachel tucked up out of the way in the countryside, being fed intravenously and having her brain electroshocked, to having her at home with them.

How to convince him? she wondered, going to the wardrobe to change into jeans and a white sweatshirt. What could she say or do to persuade him to act on Rachel's behalf, to help get her out of The Mansions?

As she pulled on a pair of white socks the answer suddenly came to her, and she knew it would work all right. But did she really have the nerve to do it? Philip was good-looking, but not especially appealing. On the plus side, he currently had a girlfriend, and Louise had heard, via Molly, that he planned to become engaged. That was a plus, because if she did go ahead with it, the last thing she wanted was to find herself caught up in an ongoing romance with Rachel's brother. Once or possibly twice would probably suffice. It wouldn't be the worst experience of her life, and if it helped Rachel it would be worth it.

God! Was she behaving like her mother? No, no. Never in her life had Maggie ever done anything for anyone else. Every last thing she'd ever done had been for her own benefit. This wasn't the same thing at all. And it might not even come to that. But if it did, she thought, tying her running shoes, if it came down to it, she'd do it.

"This is very good," Philip said politely of the casserole.

"I'm glad you like it." She smiled across the table at him, feeling the strain of having waited for the right time and mood to raise the subject of Rachel. "It's very simple. I can give you the recipe if you want it."

"Good grief," he laughed, showing his excellent teeth. "I'm hopeless in the kitchen. It's all I can do to brew up a pot of tea and fix some toast in the morning before I dash off to the City."

"Some more wine?" she asked, lifting the bottle. Always the perfect gentleman, Philip had brought along the Bordeaux.

"Lovely, thank you."

She refilled their glasses, then asked if he'd like any more of the steak-and-mushroom casserole.

"I've had my fill, thank you," he said, pushing back a bit from the table. "You've done a super job with the flat, Louise," he said, turning to look through the archway into the front room. "Hard to believe it's the same grotty digs the lot of us painted."

"I know." She smiled and took a sip of the wine. "You and your friends did a damned good job."

"It was all old Nick whipping us along," he smiled over at her. "You look jolly well, Louise. Your hair's grown very long, hasn't it?"

"Listen, Philip. We really have to talk about Rachel."

At this his expression tightened and he reached into his pocket for a cigarette, asking, "Do you mind?"

"Not a bit. I'll get you an ashtray."

She carried the dishes to the sink, got an ashtray from the shelf, and returned to the table. "We've got to get Rachel out of The Mansions. She's miserable there; she thinks she's going to die."

He made a face. "Rachel tends to be somewhat overdramatic."

"This wasn't acting, Philip. She can't remember things. She shakes; she can hardly walk. Is that what you want for her?"

"Dr. Hastings has helped her in the past."

"Well, he's not helping her now. She claims she wasn't even having one of her down spells; she was just feeling sad and dissatisfied. And I believe her. They're treating her when there's nothing really wrong with her."

"I wouldn't go that far," he said, neatly tapping the ash from the end of his cigarette. "Rachel does rather have a history, you know."

"Tell me something. Have your parents committed her to that place? I mean, have they signed documents or something? Or can she simply sign herself out and walk away if that's what she wants?"

"Why would she want to do that?" he asked with an air of genuine bewilderment.

"Because she hates it there. Have they committed her?"

He nodded slowly. "They sign her over to Dr. Hastings' care. At least that's what they've always done."

"Then sign her out," she said. "You're in a position to do that."

"I couldn't possibly contravene Mother and Father's wishes, Louise. That wouldn't go down at all well."

"Let me ask you a question," she said. "Do you want to see your sister spend the rest of her life in some fancy booby hatch, or would you like to see her living on her own like the rest of us?"

"Well, naturally I'd like to see her living on her own. But Rachel simply isn't capable—"

"She *is* capable," she said with quiet conviction. "All she needs is to believe in herself and to have the people she cares about believe in her. I don't happen to think that's too much to ask. Do you?"

"I suppose not, not when you put it in those terms."

"So sign her out. Drive up there with me and do it."

"It's not that simple," he said, looking uncomfortable. "Have you given any thought to what Rachel will do once she's left there?"

"What do you mean?"

"She's not going to be able to sail back into Wilton Crescent as if nothing's happened. Mother and Father won't allow it."

"Look," she said. "Correct me if I'm wrong, but Rachel has her own money, doesn't she?"

"That's right, she has an annual income."

"And is it enough to live on?"

"Oh, very comfortably," he said with a smile.

"And it's not tied in any way to your parents?"

"No, no. It's Rachel's outright."

"Okay. So she'll get a place of her own."

"Louise, forgive me. But you're simply not thinking reasonably. Given that I went along with what you're suggesting, Rachel's not going to be in any condition to set up housekeeping in a flat on her own. It usually takes her months to get back to herself."

"But that's usually because she's been locked up for months, right?"

"You have a point," he conceded.

"If we get her out of there, say, next weekend, she'll only have been in that place for a couple of weeks. She ought to be able to snap back in no time."

"Perhaps," he allowed. "But she won't be in any condition to go out with estate agents looking at properties. She won't be in any condition to do much more than sleep, I assure you."

"Fine. So I'll bring her back here. She'll stay with me and sleep for two weeks, or however long it takes to get the drugs out of her system."

"Here?" His eyebrows lifted.

"Sure. Why not here? I'll have you know my sister and I shared a one-room apartment that was about half this size, and we managed perfectly. Maybe it's not what you or Rachel are used to, but people do live quite nicely in small spaces, you know. Not everyone's accustomed to having an entire house to live in."

"Why are you doing this, Louise? Why can't you leave well enough alone?"

"Because it's not well enough," she said heatedly. "It's not good enough for Rachel. She deserves a chance to make it on her own, like the rest of us."

"That doesn't quite answer my question."

"I'm doing it because I want her alive and well, not shut up with a bunch of old people trimming hedges with fingernail scissors. That's why."

"Fingernail scissors?"

"Never mind that!" she said impatiently. "Will you please help me get her out of there?"

"I'll have to think about it," he said, putting out his cigarette.

"There's no *time* for you to sit around thinking about it. Don't you understand? She thinks she's going to *die* there! Doesn't that matter to you?"

"She's my sister," he said indignantly. "Of course it matters to me. There's no need to attack me."

"I'm sorry," she backed down, telling herself this wasn't the way to win him over. But hell! The mood was hardly right for a seduction, either. "It's just that I love Rachel and I want her out of that place."

"I'll have to think about it," he repeated.

"What will it take to persuade you?" she asked. "Is there anything I can say or do that'll make you decide right now?"

He leaned back in his chair and studied her appraisingly for several moments. Finally he said, "This is all very sticky. I really don't care for the idea of falling out with my parents by countermanding their wishes."

"What'll they do to you, Philip?" she challenged. "Will they banish you, tell you never to darken their doorstep again? What? You're a grown man. You've got your own flat, a good job, you're about to become engaged and start your own family. What will they *do* to you?"

"They *are* my parents, Louise."

"And Rachel's your *sister,* your *twin* sister, for Pete's sake!"

"I'm well aware of that. I must say I'm not especially enjoying this."

"I'm sorry. Neither am I. If I could think of some way to bluff those people and sign Rachel out of there myself, I'd do it. But I can't. I know it has to be a member of the immediate family. And that's you. Please do it. Please let her have the same chances you've had. Please?"

"I'll say one thing for you," he smiled. "I'd certainly want you on my side in a pitched battle. I admire your loyalty. My problem is, I don't know, in all honesty, that Rachel warrants it."

Nick was right, she thought, shocked. Philip really was embarrassed by his sister. Appealing to his sense of morality wasn't going to move him. She wasn't quite sure how to make the next move. Stalling, she said, "Would you like some coffee?"

"I would, thank you," he said, lighting another cigarette.

She got up to fill the percolator, trying to decide how best to make her approach. Should she go sit on his lap and put her arms around his neck? Or should she simply start undressing? How the hell did women do these things? In movies it always seemed so inevitable. The mood was right, the lighting was right, the victim was willing. Unable to help herself, she started to laugh.

Smiling reflexively, Philip said, "What is it?"

Getting the flame adjusted under the coffeepot, she turned to look at him saying, "I can't figure out how to seduce you."

His face turned very red, and his smile got wobbly. "Seduce me? I say! Whatever for?"

"Because I'll sleep with you if it'll convince you to help me help Rachel."

"Good God!" he said slowly. "You really are serious."

"Did you think I was just fooling around?"

"I'm not sure now what I thought, but I certainly never dreamed you'd be willing to go quite so far."

"Well, I am. I would."

"You are a remarkable girl," he said softly. "Truly remarkable."

She returned to her seat at the table, his eyes now following her every move. "No, I'm not," she disagreed. "I'm just a little desperate. I lost one sister, Philip. I don't want to lose the closest thing I'm ever going to have to another. Maybe you can't see what I see in Rachel, but you have to believe me when I tell you that she's worth it. I'd keep her here until she was well enough to look at apartments. And I'd find work for her to do. And, mark my words, in no time at all she'll be doing better than you ever dreamed. We all need people to believe in us, you know. Every one of us needs that. Without it, we might as well die. I believe in Rachel and I don't want her to die—not actually, not emotionally, which would be the same thing or maybe worse. So if I have to make love to you to get you to see that, then I'll do it."

"You don't have to do that," he said soberly. "I wouldn't want any woman under those circumstances, regardless of what you might think of me. But I'm . . . impressed, I suppose. I had no idea you felt so strongly about Rachel."

"Believe me, I do."

"All right, then, Louise. I'll help you."

"Honest to God?"

"Honest to God."

She got up and flung her arms around his neck and gave him a kiss. *"Thank you!* I swear you'll never regret it."

"Oh, I imagine I will, but I'll live with it," he said, unwinding her arms from around his neck. "Please go sit down now. You're making me frightfully nervous."

She laughed, kissed him on top of the head, and sat down beaming at him. "Okay," she said. "Let's work out the details."

⤞

The following Saturday morning she and Philip drove down to Kent. They were both nervous. "There's going to be hell to pay for this," Philip said several times in the course of the trip.

"It'll be worth it," Louise said. "You'll see."

"Easy enough for you to say. It's not your parents we're discussing."

"No, but it *is* your sister."

As they neared Tunbridge Wells, they again went over their plan. Louise was to go up to the room and get Rachel while Philip dealt with the head nurse on duty. Since Dr. Hastings was rarely at The Mansions on weekends, it was unlikely the nursing staff would make much of a fuss. But even if they did, legally they had no right to detain Rachel with a family member present insisting on signing her out. In the event that the staff protested her release and tried to contact Dr. Hastings, Philip would keep everyone distracted while Louise led Rachel out to the car. They agreed it was vital to do everything quickly.

Philip parked at the top of the driveway, saying, "I really do wish you could drive."

"Why?"

"I don't know," he confessed nervously. "I feel as if we're about to rob a bank."

"So do I." She gave him a shaky smile, dried her damp palms on her skirt and got out of the car. "I'll go first," she reminded him. "Give me five minutes before you come in."

Louise went up the front steps and sailed inside with a confident air. Without bothering to stop, she smiled at the nurse at the reception desk, said, "I'm here to see my cousin," and headed for the stairs. The nurse automatically returned her smile and went back to the novel she was reading. Her heart hammering, expecting the nurse to shout at her to stop, Louise flew up the stairs and along the corridor to Rachel's room.

As she had been on Louise's previous visit, Rachel was sitting slumped in the chair by the window. If anything she looked more despondent, less *present* than she had the week before. The only thing Louise took as even remotely encouraging was that her scarf was still tied around Rachel's hair.

"Rachel," she said, crossing the room and dropping down in front of her. "You're going to get dressed now. Philip and I are taking you home."

Rachel looked at her blankly. "Is Phippy here?" she asked in a tiny, exhausted voice.

"He's downstairs, signing you out." Louise went to the closet and pulled Rachel's clothes off their hangers. "Come on, kiddo," she said. "You've got to get dressed."

"Mummy and Daddy won't let me come home," Rachel said, plucking at the lap of her robe.

"You're not going home. You're coming to stay with me."

"But you've only got one bed," Rachel said tearfully.

"Come on, Rachel," Louise said urgently, closing the door before taking Rachel by the arms and trying to lift her out of the chair. "Get up. You've got to help. You've got to walk out of here on your own two feet. I can't carry you, and we haven't got much time."

Rachel stood unsteadily and put both hands to her head. "I'm very tired," she said, her arms falling heavily to her sides.

"You'll be able to sleep in the car," Louise told her, unbelting the robe and pulling it off her. For a moment she was so shocked by Rachel's thinness that she stared openmouthed at her friend's emaciated body. Rachel was cadaverous, her ribs visibly moving as she breathed, her hipbones jutting painfully against flesh that looked too tautly drawn to resist being penetrated by those prominent bones.

Going to the chest of drawers, Louise found some underwear and began maneuvering Rachel into it, saying, "Try to help, Rachel. Lift your leg. Come on. I know it's hard but in a couple of minutes you're going to be out of here. Hold up your arms for a moment," she told her, pulling a slip on over her head. God! she thought. This was taking forever. Any second someone was going to come in and demand to know what was going on. Maybe the rules had changed and they wouldn't allow Philip to sign his sister out. Anything could go wrong. "Just stand there for a minute," she said, holding Rachel steady with one hand while she reached for the black pullover she'd found in the closet, then pulled it over Rachel's head.

"Maybe we'll do this tomorrow," Rachel said, trying to sit back down in the armchair.

"No. We're doing it now," Louise said, on the verge of tears. She'd never had a more difficult time trying to do anything. "We've got to get your skirt on now," she said, trying to keep her tone pleasant and positive. Holding the waistband open at knee level, she said, "Step into this, Rachel. Come on. You can do it. Lift your foot. Come on."

With one hand on Louise's shoulder, and with aching slowness, Rachel lifted first one foot and then the other.

"Good girl!" Louise cried, quickly fastening the button at the waist. "Now your shoes."

Rachel managed to get her feet into the shoes. Louise fumbled to tie the laces, then, breathless, stood upright.

"Okay. We're going," she said. "All right?"

Rachel simply stood staring like a zombie.

Louise grabbed several vials of medication from the night table, jammed them into her pocket, then took Rachel by the arm and said, "We're going to walk now. Okay?"

"It's hard for me to walk," Rachel said. "I want to lie down."

"You can't lie down now," Louise told her, with an arm around her waist directing her over to the door. "Just remember, I'm Cousin Elsa."

"Elsa," Rachel repeated.

"If anybody says anything or tries to stop us, ignore them. We're walking right out of here."

"I'm scared." Rachel turned to look at her with darkly shadowed eyes.

"Don't be scared. I'm right here. It's going to be okay."

At an unbearably slow pace, with Rachel moving like someone of ninety, they inched along the corridor toward the stairs. From below, Louise thought she could hear Philip speaking to someone. Please let us get out of here! she prayed.

Suddenly there was the sound of footsteps pounding up the stairs and Louise's heart lurched with fear. What if they'd sent people to stop them by force? What if they dragged Rachel away and threw her and Philip out, or called the police? God! She was so frightened her stomach was threatening to overturn.

Philip appeared at the top of the stairs and came running toward them. "They're calling Dr. Hastings," he said. "They know perfectly well they've got no legal right to stop us, but they're going to try. Bloody hell!" he exclaimed at the sight of his sister. "Give her to me!" Louise stepped aside, and Philip hefted Rachel into his arms. They hurried toward the stairs.

"Don't stop, no matter what anyone says," Philip said, descending the stairs with his sister in his arms. "Go directly to the car. Hell!"

The reception area was deserted.

"Lucky break!" Philip said. "She's gone to get the head nursing sister. Hurry!"

Louise ran to get the rear passenger door open, and stood, agitated and trembling, while Philip deposited Rachel on the back seat. Louise slammed the door, then jumped into the front seat as Philip leaped behind the wheel and turned the key in the ignition. Nothing happened.

"What's the matter?" Louise cried, seeing through the open front door two nurses running into the reception area.

"Sod it!" he swore, throwing the car into neutral, then pulling out the choke before trying the ignition again.

This time the engine caught. He released the hand brake, popped the clutch, threw the car into first, and they shot ahead, the tires spitting up gravel. Louise craned around to see the two nurses reach the top of the driveway. Then the car rounded the bend and they were speeding toward the gates.

"We're home free!" Philip crowed as they slithered through the gates and onto the road.

"We did it!" Louise cried, turning to look at Rachel, who sat slumped on the rear seat staring straight ahead. "You can lie down now and go to sleep if you want, Rachel."

Like an obedient child, Rachel folded over sideways on the seat, pulled her knees up, tucked her hands under her cheek, and closed her eyes.

"I've never *seen* her in such frightful condition," Philip said quietly as Louise straightened and turned around. "You were right. Another fortnight and she might very well have died there."

"I wasn't kidding," Louise said, her heart still rapping at a wildly accelerated pace. "She can't weigh more than eighty pounds. You can see every bone in her body."

"Horrid!" Philip made a face. "I hope you realize we're both in for the row of the century with mother and father."

"I'll take all the responsibility," Louise told him. "You can blame the whole thing on me."

"I wouldn't dream of it," he said staunchly. "You're quite sure you're up to looking after her on your own?"

"I'll manage."

"I don't expect she'll do more than sleep for the next little while. That's usually the pattern."

"That's fine," Louise said. "She'll sleep and I'll try to get some food into her. I don't give a damn about anything except that she's out of that place." She turned again to see that Rachel was sleeping soundly. Louise leaned across to kiss Philip's cheek. "Thank you."

"No," he said. "Thank you, Louise."

*C*HAPTER

F I F T Y - T W O

"**H**OW DARE YOU TAKE IT UPON YOURSELF TO REMOVE
Rachel from The Mansions?" Mrs. Townsend-Post demanded.

"I didn't do it alone," Louise said quietly. "Philip agreed with me."

"You had no right," the woman insisted. "Rachel is *our* child, not
yours."

"Rachel's a grown woman who has a right to a life," Louise said. "I
don't understand why you don't want her to have a chance at leading a
normal one."

"She's not capable of looking after herself."

"Sure she is," Louise said, keeping her tone reasonable and friendly.
"She's not stupid. If anything, she's one of the most intelligent people
I've ever met."

"Intelligence hasn't anything to do with it. She's emotionally unreli-
able."

"That's not true, Mrs. Townsend-Post. She's got a chemical imbal-
ance, that's all. And I've got her medication here. I'm going to make sure
she keeps taking it."

"I can't imagine what you think you have to gain by this. But rest
assured, Rachel's trust income is accessible only to Rachel."

"That's not a very nice thing to say," Louise said, wounded. "I have
no interest whatever in Rachel's money. I'm her *friend*. I care about her.
She was *dying* in that place. Doesn't that matter to you?"

"What goes on in our family is no concern of yours, Miss Parker."

"What happens to Rachel is," Louise argued. "And it matters to
Philip too."

"Kindly leave Philip out of this. It's all too evident he was acting under
your influence."

At this, Louise had to laugh. "That's right," she said. "He was. I held
a gun on him and made him admit that he cares about his sister."

"We could have you charged with kidnapping!" Mrs. Townsend-Post blustered.

"Don't be silly. Rachel's a grown woman. I'm not holding her for ransom. I'm taking care of her. If you don't believe me, come and see for yourself. She's fine. Or at least she will be, once she gets over being drugged senseless."

"You'll hear from our solicitors," the woman threatened.

"Look, Mrs. Townsend-Post," Louise said patiently. "Threatening me isn't going to do anyone any good. Philip legally signed Rachel out. She's staying with me until she gets back on her feet. Your lawyer will probably tell you there's nothing you can do about it." Softening her tone, she said, "Maybe you don't realize what they were doing to Rachel there. If you saw her, you'd understand. She's nothing but bones. She can't stay awake for more than an hour at a time. I love Rachel," she said, starting to choke up. "I'm not interested in her money, or in making trouble. I just want her to *live*."

"One simply doesn't *do* things like this!" Mrs. Townsend-Post said, with somewhat less energy.

"One does if one cares. And I care. I know you're angry, and maybe I would be, too, if I were Rachel's mother. But please believe me when I tell you that I'll take the best care in the world of her. You're welcome to come and see her any time you like. I'm not trying to keep you apart. It's just that Rachel doesn't want to come home. She doesn't want to see you right now. She's terrified you'll force her to go back to that place. And to be honest, I think it'd be the worst thing for her. Give her a chance to get back on her feet, give her a chance to *breathe*. That's not a lot to ask, is it?"

"I resent your implying that we're not fit parents."

"That's not what I'm saying at all. Give her a chance to fend for herself, Mrs. Townsend-Post, to prove she can take care of herself."

There was a silence on the other end of the line.

"Tell Rachel to ring me," her mother said finally.

"Sure. I'll be glad to do that. I'll tell her to call you when she wakes up."

"I don't believe you're giving her our messages."

"Of course I am. But she doesn't want to talk to you now. I can't force her. Sooner or later, she'll call you. And in the meantime, I promise you, I give her every one of your messages. Why wouldn't I?"

"You have ulterior motives," the woman accused. "It's patently obvious to my husband and to me."

"If you choose to believe that, I can't stop you. But if you think about it, you'll realize the only motive I could possibly have is Rachel's well-being. I really do love her."

"You keep saying that," Mrs. Townsend-Post said, sounding exasperated and suspicious. "I'm beginning to wonder if it isn't the slightest bit unnatural."

"God! Now you're accusing me of being a lesbian? Is that what you're trying to do?"

"I'm not saying anything of the sort."

"I'm not a lesbian. I'm not after Rachel's money or her body. All I want is for her to be alive and happy. You're her *mother,* for heaven's sake. Isn't that what you want for her?"

"Naturally it is. How dare you?"

"We've been over all this before," Louise said. "I'll give Rachel your message when she wakes up. Okay? I don't know what else to say to you."

There was a long silence during which Louise listened to the woman breathing heavily. At last, Mrs. Townsend-Post asked quietly, "Is she eating?"

"Like a horse," Louise said.

"Well, thank heavens for that, at least."

"She's okay, honestly," Louise said.

Mrs. Townsend-Post sighed, said, "Well, I don't know," and hung up without bothering to say goodbye.

Louise collapsed in the armchair, sweating, and looked across to where Rachel lay peacefully sleeping. It was the fourth such conversation she'd had with Rachel's mother in the course of two days. Louise wished she had some way to turn off the telephone. She was exhausted from doing conversational battle with Mrs. Townsend-Post, both of them saying the same things over and over again. The only good thing was that Rachel slept right through it.

All Rachel wanted to do was sleep. She napped off and on throughout the day while Louise was at the office, then climbed into her half of the bed by six-thirty or seven and was still sleeping when Louise left for work at eight-fifteen in the morning. For eight solid days this continued. On the ninth day Rachel was awake when Louise came out of the bathroom.

"Are you leaving now?" Rachel asked.

"Not for another half hour. Want some juice?"

"Yes, please." Barefoot, Rachel followed her into the kitchen and sat down at the table. "I feel ever so much better this morning," she said. "For the first time I actually feel *awake.*"

"That's great." Louise set a glass of orange juice down in front of her. "Hungry?"

"No, thank you."

"Not even a piece of toast?"

"Well, perhaps toast."

"Good girl." Louise got out the loaf and placed it on the bread board. "You know, at some point you're going to have to talk to your mother. It's driving her crazy, talking to me. I'm amazed she hasn't hung up on me yet. To tell you the truth, I think she's actually getting used to the situation."

"She's jolly well going to have to, isn't she?"

"I guess so. But you'll have to talk to her, convince her you're really okay."

"I'll ring her this evening."

"Good. So, would you like to come to the office with me?"

"When, today?"

"Sure. I'll put you to work."

"Really?" Rachel asked wide-eyed.

"Absolutely. That is, if you feel well enough."

"I feel super today. What sort of work?"

"Well, let's see. You can spell, therefore you can file. The filing's stacked up all over the office. Plus we need someone to answer the phones. With your expensive voice, the clients'll be impressed as hell."

"Oh, I'd love it. May I really?"

"Yup. You'll have your toast, then get dressed and come with me." Elated, Louise went to give her a hug. "This is great, kiddo. You sure you feel up to it?"

"Honestly, I do. You're not going to fuss over me now, are you?"

"God, no!" Louise said at once. "Never catch *me* fussing."

"Well, just so long as you don't. I'd hate to have people think I was— incapacitated."

"I'd hate that, too," Louise said. "You're going to have to give Philip a call too, you know. He's been taking a lot of flak from your mother and father."

"I'll spend the entire evening on the telephone," Rachel laughed. "Oh, I *do* feel so well."

"Okay. Eat up while I get washed."

"All right," Rachel agreed docilely, reaching for the marmalade. "I'm actually hungry. I hope I don't get fat."

"Never happen," Louise said, and went off to the bathroom.

Louise said, "I need the help. I don't know what file clerks and telephonists make, but that's what you should pay her. Give her a two-week trial. If she doesn't work out, that'll be the end of it. If she does work out, which I know she will, we've got some intelligent extra help here."

Terence and Toni exchanged a look. Toni said, "Does she always dress like a Portuguese widow?" at which Terry smothered a laugh.

"Yes, she does," Louise said defiantly. "What difference does it make? Who's going to see her?"

"That was unkind," Toni apologized. "I agree we do need the help. What do you think, Terry?"

"We can't pay more than ten guineas."

"That'll be fine," Louise said. "I'll go tell her."

"She'd be lovely-looking if she went at the eye makeup with a lighter hand," Toni said.

"Then offer to make her over," Louise said. "She might let you."

"What's the story precisely?" Terry asked.

"She's been ill," Louise fudged. "And she needs the work."

"Yes, but has she ever done office work before?"

"No, but I'll supervise her. She'll be fine. She's got a certificate in computer studies. Rachel's no dummy."

"Computers," Terry said, impressed. "You don't say. I don't suppose she knows any bookkeeping?"

"I don't know. I'll ask her."

"Lord knows we need someone to bring the books current. We're months behind," he said. "Well, all right. Two weeks trial it is."

With renewed energy, Rachel signed up for an evening bookkeeping course, and took to it at once. "It's all so wonderfully logical," she told

Louise, sitting with her textbook at the kitchen table. "Profits on one side, losses on the other, factor in the income and expenses, and everything balances. It's really quite perfect."

"I typed dozens of balance sheets when I worked for the accounting firm," Louise said, standing by the stove with a cup of coffee. "Not to mention letters to Her Majesty's Inspectors of Taxes at Thames Ditton and sundry other places. To me, it was just tedious typing. I'm glad you find it so fascinating."

"Oh, I do," Rachel said enthusiastically. "I've almost got the office books up to date. I *love* the job! It's such fun."

"Rachel, we've got to start looking for a flat for you," Louise said, feeling that the time was right. It had been more than six weeks since she'd persuaded Philip to sign his sister out of The Mansions; more than six weeks since she'd been able to do anything more than talk to Tim when he stopped by—always announced in advance now—to have a cup of tea and inquire solicitously after Rachel's health; more than six weeks since the daily telephone calls from Mrs. Townsend-Post had started; and more than four weeks since Rachel had taken to spending anywhere from half an hour to an hour nightly on the telephone with her mother, assuring the woman she was perfectly all right and endlessly explaining why she couldn't and wouldn't be returning home. It was time to take the next step.

"I know," Rachel said, turning her textbook facedown. "When should we start?"

"I was thinking of this weekend. I thought maybe you could call an estate agent in whatever neighborhood interests you and we could look at some places on Saturday and Sunday."

"Have I been a nuisance?" Rachel asked worriedly.

"Not even a bit," Louise said. "But I'm not used to living with someone anymore. I've been on my own too long. And anyway it's time you had a place of your own. You need to prove to yourself you can handle it."

"You will come with me, won't you?"

"Are you kidding? Of course. Any idea where you'd like to look?"

"Chelsea, I think. That way we'll still be close."

"Terrific. So, will you make some calls tomorrow and set up some appointments?"

"Yes, I will," Rachel said decisively. "In fact, rather than rent, I think I'll look for something to buy. I'll feel more secure that way."

"Something that needs fixing up," Louise laughed. "Remember?"

"It's always a good idea. Buy low, sell high. And I could hire Nick to fix it up."

"Great. What'll you do about furniture?"

"Oh, buy it," Rachel said at once. "It's going to be the greatest adventure of my life."

"Your own flat, decorated the way you want it," Louise reminded her.

"Precisely! Oh, Louise," she said with a rush of emotion, "how will I ever be able to thank you?"

"Somebody said living well is the best revenge. We'll modify that and say living well is the best reward. Okay?"

Rachel got up to give her a hug. "I'll never know how you managed to convince Phippy to help."

"You want to know the truth?" Louise said. "I came right out and offered to sleep with him. He was so shocked he nearly dropped his teeth. But it got the point across, and he finally agreed."

"You wouldn't have, would you?"

"I don't know," Louise said. "Maybe. He's not the worst guy I've ever seen."

"Louise!" Rachel was positively titillated.

"Never mind," Louise laughed. "I was hopeless at seduction. But as it turned out, my coming right out with it did the trick. Thank God. I didn't really want to have to do it."

"I'm simply stunned." Rachel sank back into her chair.

"You think you're stunned," Louise laughed. "You should've seen your brother. It was hilarious."

Rachel covered her mouth with one hand and started to laugh. "I can imagine," she giggled. "Poor Phippy. I'll wager you scared him half to death."

"At least," Louise agreed. "But here you are, alive and well and learning how to keep books. Pretty good deal, eh?"

"A very good deal. I love you, Louise."

"I know you do, kiddo. And I love you too. Now I'm going to take a bath and get ready for bed. Don't sit here half the night. You don't have to learn everything all in one go. I don't want you overdoing it."

Rachel was already reaching for her textbook. "I know," she said. "I just want to have one last look at the debit and credit entry systems. My God, Louise! I'm simply staggered to think you offered to seduce poor old Phippy. The mind boggles!"

"Don't be too boggled," Louise laughed. "I didn't actually *do* anything. And I learned an interesting lesson. I'm not quite sure exactly what it is, but I did find out that men are basically cowards. At least, some of them. I *wish* you could've seen his face."

"You'll never know how much I wish it, too," Rachel said. "Positively amazing," she was saying to herself as Louise went off to the bathroom.

CHAPTER

FIFTY-THREE

THROUGHOUT THE FLIGHT BACK TO CANADA LOUISE WAS edgy, unable to relax. She couldn't help worrying about how Rachel would cope alone. She'd told Louise repeatedly she'd be fine. She had a great deal to do, what with working days at the agency, completing her bookkeeping course two evenings a week, and in her spare time overseeing the work Nick was doing on the small house she'd bought a month previously on Radnor Walk. On weekends she was shopping for furniture, selecting carpeting and curtain material. She'd never been busier or, she repeatedly told Louise, happier. She'd proved herself to be efficient and reliable and, once past their initial skepticism, Toni and Terence had grown very fond of her. Not only did she try very hard to do a good job, but she took such overt satisfaction in balancing the books, in keeping the filing right up to date, and in answering the telephones, that they found it impossible not to like her.

But still Louise was worried. She feared that Rachel might have taken on too much at once, that she'd become fatigued and as a result fall into depression. She fretted that the almost daily telephone calls Rachel received from her mother might convince her she really wasn't able to cope, that her current effectiveness was merely a temporary aberration, some bizarre manifestation of her underlying madness. But Rachel seemed to handle the calls philosophically. "You needn't fuss over me, Louise," Rachel told her. "I won't allow my mother and father to rule over me ever again. They can bribe and wheedle and threaten, but I'm never going home. It's a dangerous place for me. I know that now. And however much I might be tempted to go back and let them pamper me, all I have to do is think about the electroshock therapy and the temptation dies. They really didn't care what happened to me in that place so long as I was suitably sedated when I returned home. I'll never forgive them for all the years of that they subjected me to."

"I'll keep me eye on 'er," Nick had promised when they'd talked on the telephone the previous night. Then with a grin in his voice added, "It'll be my pleasure."

"You behave yourself," Louise had warned half-seriously. "She's still not a hundred percent."

"Who'd know that better'n me, Louise?" he'd countered, bristling. "I'm not about to throw 'er down on some bed just to satisfy meself. I 'appen to 'ave some morals, you know."

"I know," she'd said. "Don't get mad. It's just that I don't want her to take on more than she can handle."

"You've got to let 'er 'andle 'er own life now," he counseled. "You done the right thing gettin' her out of that nut'ouse. Now let 'er get on. You can't start in as 'er new mother."

The comment struck home. "You're right," she said. "That's what I've been doing, isn't it?"

"You got what you wanted for 'er, Louise. Now let 'er get on," he repeated. "I'll see she comes to no 'arm."

When she stopped worrying about Rachel, and about how the agency would fare in her absence, her thoughts turned with some trepidation to the two weeks ahead of her. Thinking about being back in Toronto heightened her sense of being pursued. She ordered some wine from the stewardess and drank the small bottle slowly, hoping to calm herself. But, irrationally, she began wishing instead that she could open a window and get some fresh air. She felt positively panic-stricken.

Tim had wanted to see her off, but he'd been unable to get away, so he'd insisted on sending a car and driver to take her to the airport. And he'd told her he'd be there to meet her when she arrived back. Thinking about him now, she wondered if to some extent her anxiety wasn't perhaps due to the fact that it had been almost two months since they'd made love. His visits to the flat had become purely social occasions, when he'd sit with her and Rachel and they'd discuss Rachel's progress, or speak of generalities. Even when Rachel tactfully removed herself from the flat to give them some privacy, neither of them could even think about making love. It simply seemed the wrong thing to do. So they talked some more. And Louise might allow herself the pleasure of sitting in his lap for fifteen minutes, holding him and being stroked, before she drew away and returned to the seat opposite.

A baby several rows back cried off and on throughout the flight. Its squalling irritated her unreasonably, and she wished the mother would feed her child or change it or do whatever was required to silence it. She needed the relative silence of the aircraft in order to marshal her thoughts. The harsh intermittent wailing kept distracting her, making her even more jittery. She didn't feel at all herself and thought for a few awful moments that she was like some watered-down version of her mother— itchy to have her own way and foul-tempered because she couldn't. That scared her. She told herself she was incapable of Maggie's brand of brutal- ity, of her unparalleled self-absorption. But the idea that she might, in any way, be like her mother hovered like a transparency being projected over her, creating a double image. She ordered more wine, and when it came, gulped down half a glass, anxious to put her emotions into some kind of order before seeing her grandmother.

But, God! She was having real trouble clearing her mind. Her thoughts roiled, rushing against each other like the old bumper cars at the Ex. Minor collisions that did no real damage, but jarred the senses, slowed and disoriented the reflexes.

Fortunately the plane was no more than half full and she sat alone in her row, with her novel untouched on the empty seat beside her. The stewardess had said if she'd like to stretch out all she had to do was raise the armrests. But Louise had no desire to stretch out. Instead she slid out of her seat and walked up and down the aisle several times, attempting to work off some of her churning energy. She wished more than anything else that she could attribute her anxiety to something specific. But every- thing that came to mind was additional fodder for her nervousness. What would Gramma think if she knew Louise was having an affair with a married man twice her age? What would she think about her interfering in

Rachel's life? Certainly Rachel's parents now viewed her as treacherous. And Philip had borne the brunt of their outrage, having had to answer for signing Rachel out of The Mansions. Stoically, he'd stood his ground, declaring his belief that it was time they stopped treating Rachel like a retarded child. But the situation was messy, and it was all Louise's doing. She'd created enemies. She was no longer a harmless child. More than anything else she wished she could have talked with Evie before leaving, but Evie was still in Surrey with her daughter Delia.

By the time the plane landed she was a bit drunk. Clearing immigration and customs, she felt everything had slid into a state of unreality. Sounds echoed in her ears, and she waited for her baggage feeling grimy and tired. She wished there were some kind of pill she could take that would wipe out everything negative and return her to the girl she'd been four or five years earlier.

She saw her grandmother and Uncle Bob before they saw her. And the breath caught in her throat at the sight of them. Her grandmother looked wonderful, her hair having turned more silver than blonde, her features softening with age. God! She was almost sixty. Time was moving too quickly, changing too many things. Bob was as distinguished as ever in a custom-tailored charcoal gray suit, a crisp white shirt, and a pale gray silk tie. She watched, waiting for them to spot her as she carried her suitcase out of the arrivals area.

Her grandmother caught sight of her and broke into a smile, lifting her hand to wave. They moved toward her. Louise put down her suitcase and went into her grandmother's arms, finding in her embrace everything familiar she'd forgotten: the fragrance of Blue Grass, the gentleness that transmitted itself through a caressing hand, the throaty softness of her grandmother's happy laughter. She had to fight not to cry as she embraced Uncle Bob, then stepped back to examine their faces as Bob reached for her suitcase, saying, "The car's right outside."

"I can't believe I'm here," Louise said, taking hold of her grandmother's hand as they went through the terminal. "The flight lasted forever. And there was a baby that cried nonstop."

Bob laughed and said, "That baby's on every flight. And it's always three rows back of where you're sitting. It cried all the way to Bermuda too, didn't it, Ellie?"

Delighted, Louise opened her mouth to laugh and, as had happened on several New Year's Eves, she cried instead, gulping down tears. There might not be a pill you could take to wipe out time and circumstance, but there were certain people who could effect a similar result. She felt twelve again as she climbed with her grandmother and Uncle Bob into the front seat of his latest sleek black Cadillac. Home was more than a place, she thought. It was where the people you loved lived. Without the people there was no home. Which was why, perhaps, she'd never missed the house on Manning Avenue, but why she thought often, longingly, of the small apartment she'd shared with Faye. It was why she could still see it so clearly, could recall where every last thing had stood, and how the afternoon sun had streamed through the window.

※

She'd forgotten that apartments could be so big. Everything in London was so scaled down. The apartment on Avenue Road was luxurious by British standards, with its three bedrooms and three bathrooms, its generous L-shaped living room. Entering the guest room with its pair of twin beds, Louise experienced a moment of backward time travel and actually expected to see her sister come out of the bathroom or walk in from the hallway. It was a painful inrushing of renewed hope that lasted only a moment. She opened her suitcase to get the gifts she'd brought for her grandmother and Uncle Bob then returned to the living room.

All the furniture was new. They'd redecorated. The carpeting was a thick creamy color, the sofa and matching occasional chair were in beige, nubby fabric. The coffee table was teak, as were a pair of end tables. The effect was light and airy; it suited the people who lived there.

"We thought we'd take you out to eat if you're not too tired," Bob said, bestowing one of his wonderful smiles on her, as if he couldn't get over the fact that she was actually there.

"I'd love to," she said, and went to give him a hug. "I'm so happy to see you. You don't look one bit different."

"You do," he told her, holding her by the shoulders to study her features. "You look grown-up and sophisticated."

"That's because I *am* grown-up and sophisticated," she laughed, thinking she sounded phony—her voice too high, too thin.

Coming back from the bedroom Ellen was jolted again by how strongly Louise's presence revived her memories of Faye. Their resemblance was more pronounced now that Louise was older. Of course there were differences. Louise was outgoing, self-confident, effortlessly poised. Faye had been softer, less formidable. And that was it, Ellen thought. Despite her comparative youth, Louise had become a woman of considerable power. She still looked younger than her age but she was leaner and her eyes were more knowing.

"We thought we'd walk down to Yorkville," Ellen said. "You won't recognize it. The whole area's completely changed."

"That sounds like fun," Louise said, thinking how odd it was to be standing there in three-inch heels and a dress when these were items she'd last worn in this place only on special occasions. The year following Faye's death, she'd gone to work every day with Bob and her grandmother wearing skirts and sweaters and flats. These clothes were the emblems of her independence: the nylons, the garter belt, the pair of short white cotton gloves. Even her ears, which she'd had pierced after the girls at her first temporary job had given her the gold studs, were different. "I had my ears pierced," she said, apropos of nothing, then laughed at her own foolishness and went to give her grandmother another hug. "The apartment looks fabulous. When did you get it done over?"

"Last year," Ellen answered. "And seeing how you've got pierced ears, I should give you my mother's earrings."

"That'd be wonderful," Louise said, thinking of the pearls draped around the neck of her sister before they'd closed the coffin. They'd been buried with Faye. "I keep wanting to cry," she said, and hugged her grandmother again.

"So do I," Ellen admitted with a laugh. "But let's not. Let's enjoy every moment of this."

"Open your presents!" Louise said, suddenly remembering. They sat down together on the sofa and she watched them remove the wrappings from the packages, fascinated by everything about them and feeling swollen with love at being with them again. It was as if she'd been away far longer than three years, so aware was she of the changes in them and in herself. Aside from the silvering of her hair and the softening of her features, her grandmother carried herself slightly differently now, as if her limbs were no longer quite so supple. And Bob's hair had gone completely gray. There were laugh lines around his eyes, and lines framing his mouth. They were fifty-four and fifty-nine; age had staked a visible claim on them. This realization gripped Louise like a hand squeezing her lungs; it was physically painful to think they weren't always going to be there.

Her grandmother was delighted with the three tins of tea from Fortnum and Mason. And Bob went at once to put on the paisley silk tie she'd brought him from Liberty's. While he was gone, Ellen said, "Daniel called wanting to know when you were arriving. He'd like you to call him when you get a chance."

"Okay. I'll call him tomorrow."

"And Kath called, of course. She's dying to see you. Everyone is, but we thought we'd have a quiet evening, just the three of us. You must be tired."

"I was before but I'm feeling more awake now."

Almost hesitantly, Ellie said, "Your mother phoned, too. She does now and then, you know. And I mentioned you were coming."

"I'll bet she didn't say she was dying to see me."

"She didn't say anything one way or the other," Ellen said. "She's impossible. I don't even know why she calls me. It's just every few months, all of a sudden, out of the blue. She moved again last year. She's in an apartment on Brunswick now, a little north of Bloor."

"Still working at the store?" Louise asked.

"Believe it or not she's at Creed's, in the lingerie department."

"*Creed's?* That's a major step up, isn't it? What about her other profession? She still working at that?"

Ellen made a face and toyed with her pack of cigarettes. "I wouldn't know," she said. "I'm the last person on earth she'd tell."

"That was rotten of me. I shouldn't have said that."

"No, it's all right. Don't give it a thought. I try not to think about Marg. It's a waste of energy."

"What about Raffie?" Louise asked, her heart beating suddenly out of synch. "Have you heard what he's doing?"

"I haven't heard a thing. Nothing." Ellen shook her head. "I stopped by the store a few times to say hello to Frankie. To tell the truth, I think my going there upset him, so I haven't been by in more than a year."

"Why should your going there upset him?"

"Probably," Bob answered, returning, "because of everything that happened. Quite naturally he associates your grandmother with Faye, and that reminds him of her and of how she died. He'd obviously prefer not to think about it. Are you two ladies ready to go? We've got an eight o'clock reservation."

Walking along Yorkville heightened Louise's edginess, deepened her sense of being pursued. The cars—larger than their British counterparts

—were long and unearthly; she'd grown unaccustomed to right-hand driving traffic. She felt like a tourist as she took in the sights and sounds, astounded at the changes the streets had undergone. Yorkville was alive in an entirely new way, with long-haired teenagers in headbands and beads, with American tourists, with boutiques and an amazing number of new restaurants; with specialty shops and panhandling hippies and street musicians. She felt a complete stranger to the place and kept covertly looking at her grandmother and Bob to see how they were reacting to the boisterous energy all around them. They seemed pleased and amused.

"How long's it been like this?" Louise asked finally, as they passed a folk club called the Riverboat.

"A while now," Bob said. "The hippies started moving in about a year ago, maybe more. Then the whole neighborhood began changing. I like it," he said decisively. "Ellie and I usually take a walk through the Village after dinner. We come along Yorkville, cut down Bellair to Cumberland, go back on Cumberland to Avenue Road. Sometimes we'll stop in one of the coffeehouses, or have dessert at the Gaslight."

"It's a nice change," Ellie agreed. "There are so many good new restaurants."

"We've gone to the Riverboat a few times, but the Gaslight's more our speed," Bob put in.

"He hates folk music," Ellen laughed. "They have a piano player at the Gaslight."

Their destination was Mr. Tony's at the northwest corner of Yorkville and Bellair. "We thought you'd enjoy this," Bob said as they climbed the stairs to the canopied front door.

Louise was more tired than she realized, because afterward all she could remember of the place was the flocked wallpaper and the cozy atmosphere. She remembered eating some kind of chicken and drinking several cups of coffee in an effort to wake herself up. But by the time they arrived back at the apartment she was yawning nonstop, and Ellen said, "You ought to go to bed, sweetheart. You're falling asleep on your feet."

"I think I'd better," Louise gave in, kissing them both before reeling off to the guest room where she plunged into sleep moments after undressing and slipping under the bedclothes.

Faye came into the room and sat cross-legged on the other bed and brushed her hair while she told Louise, "Gramma wouldn't understand about Tim, so it's not a good idea to tell her. I'm not sure I understand it myself, you know, Lou. He's not going to let things stay the way they are forever. What're you going to do when he leaves his wife and wants you to live with him?''

"He's not going to do that.''

"Even Catholics get divorced. Mr. Nolan did, remember?''

"But that was different.''

"Not all that different,'' Faye said consideringly.

"Well, I don't want to get married,'' Louise insisted.

"Nobody said anything about getting married. But if you think he's going to be satisfied sitting around waiting for you to get home for years on end, you're dreaming. One of these days it's all going to change.''

"So I'll deal with it when that happens.''

"Maybe you should tell him you love him.''

"I will not! Are you crazy? Then I'd never get rid of him.''

"You're such a liar!'' Faye accused, the hairbrush coming to rest in her lap. "You know you're scared to death he'll get fed up and get rid of *you.*''

"I am not!''

"You are too!''

"Go to sleep, Faye. I'm not going to discuss this with you.''

Faye started to laugh, and Louise asked, "What's so funny, eh?''

And Faye said, "I'm the one who always says that, not you.''

"Yeah, that's right,'' Louise said, and also started to laugh. "Things have turned around.''

"That's for sure,'' Faye said. "But I still think you should tell him you love him. You know you do.''

"Leave me alone, Faye.''

"Okay, I'll leave you alone,'' Faye said, and climbed into bed, pulling the blankets over her head.

It was so strange, Louise's dreaming self thought. She'd turned into Faye, and it was Louise under the blankets in the other bed. It was very strange indeed, but she was too worn out to think about it.

CHAPTER

FIFTY-FOUR

IT WASN'T ONLY YORKVILLE THAT HAD CHANGED. THE EN-
tire city seemed to be moving at a frantic pace into its adulthood. Live
entertainment was flourishing. Every restaurant and coffeehouse seemed
to have someone sitting behind a microphone, either at a piano or with a
guitar, singing and making music. Old buildings had been torn down and
there was new construction everywhere. The erection of the new city hall
was well underway—two curved buildings like eyelids opened around a
low separate rotunda. Viewed from above it was said to look exactly like
an open eye. The traffic was heavier, the traffic jams downtown growing
progressively worse.

And the people she'd known had also changed. At twenty-two Kath
was an imposing woman of six feet who strongly resembled her mother.
She was attending the Ontario College of Art, studying graphic design,
and engaged to a commercial photographer six years her senior. Daniel
was thirty now, and deeply involved with a divorcée with two small
children. They were planning to marry in late summer, before school
started.

He told Louise his plans over cups of cappuccino in a coffeehouse on
Avenue Road. And she felt such a stranger to the place and to this man
that she had to keep stealing covert looks at Daniel to remind herself of all
she'd once found so familiar: his dark good looks and liquid eyes, the
mobility of his mouth, his sudden frequent smiles. She felt a great fondness for him but the desire was gone. They'd evolved into friends, and she
listened to him tell about his soon-to-be wife, glad he'd found someone
with whom he'd have a future. She smiled, thinking Evie had been right.
She was surprised and gratified every time something Evie had predicted
came to pass. She only wished her own life were moving forward in a
more positive fashion. Everyone seemed to have a destination but her. She
was merely holding her ground, and acknowledging this made her agi-

tated, set the imagined crowds to chasing her again. She was supposed to be getting on, going somewhere. But where? She had a job she enjoyed but, like her affair with Tim, it had no significant future. Or was that the truth? Separated from him by three-thousand-odd miles she was no longer quite so sure of what was and wasn't true.

"What about you?" Daniel asked finally. "Will you ever come back here?"

"I don't think so," she answered. That much, at least, she knew. She had no desire to return to Toronto. She felt vaguely undermined by the high rises on all sides; she'd grown accustomed to the low-rise aspects of London. Toronto felt like a series of canyons to her now. Everything she'd once taken for granted about the city had become remote. Perhaps it was the lingering effects of jet lag, but she didn't feel entirely in contact with the ground. She was a visitor, not someone who belonged here. "I'm used to London now," she went on. "I've got my flat and my friends, the job. Whatever future I have, it's there. I'm out of touch with things here. I feel like a tourist," she smiled. "I still know my way around but the landmarks all seem to have changed."

"Are you seeing anyone?" he asked rather cautiously.

Perhaps because they'd been so close she felt safe in confiding in him. "There is someone. But it's a complicated situation."

"He's married," Daniel guessed.

"That's right."

"Is that such a good idea?"

She laughed and said, "I didn't choose it from a catalog, Daniel. It's just something that happened." Sobering, she said, "He's very kind, very respectful. He's a doctor, with a practice in Harley Street."

"So you don't hope he'll get divorced and marry you?"

"God, no!" she said at once. "That's the last thing I'd want."

"I see," he said, studying her eyes. "He's already safely married, and you prefer it that way."

"He's also twenty years older," she said. "You might as well know all of it."

He noted the defiance in her posture, in the thrust of her chin, and said, "You're not going to get an argument from me, Lulu. I'm in no position to be telling you what to do. If it's what you want and it makes you happy, then fine."

"No one over here knows about him," she said.

"I'm not going to tell anyone."

"No, I know that."

"That's why you told me," he said. "Isn't it?"

"Maybe. I do trust you, you know."

"I know," he said quietly. "I hope it works out for you."

"It's up to me how things work out."

"That's right, it is," he agreed. "I told you I'm not going to give you an argument. But I get the impression you're less than a hundred percent happy with things."

"Well," she admitted, "I'm still not over Faye. I dream about her quite often. We have conversations, talk about everything that's going on. Then I wake up and feel . . . cheated, because she wasn't really there."

"It's rough," he commiserated.

"I want to know why she died, Daniel. Oh, I know *how,* but I want to know why. There's no sense to it. I'm never going to be satisfied until I get some kind of an answer. Until this very moment I hadn't realized that. But it's the truth. I need to know why."

"Maybe you should talk to Raffie," he suggested.

"I've been thinking about it," she admitted. "Now that I'm here it seems like a good idea, but I'm nervous about seeing him. I've been thinking I might try to get in touch with him."

"I would," he said. "You might settle the issue once and for all."

"I'd like that. I really would. Ever since I stepped off the plane it's been hounding me. Sometimes," she confessed, "I'll get out the death certificate and the autopsy report and read them over and over, as if this time something'll leap out at me and it'll all suddenly make sense. But it's just still a bunch of medical mumbo jumbo."

He reached across the table and gave her hand a squeeze, saying, "Get in touch with Raffie, then. It might help."

Holding his hand, finding him familiar again, she said, "I'm happy for you, Daniel. I'm glad you've found someone."

"Don't you really want someone for yourself, Lulu?"

"I don't feel as if I do," she answered thoughtfully. "I feel as if there are all kinds of things I want to do, even *have* to do, but being with someone isn't one of them. I don't want to be all tied up in an involvement, planning my life around someone else."

"But what about children? Wouldn't you like to have a family?"

The strength of her reply startled both of them. "I don't want kids," she said. "I don't want to have to spend my life worrying about them, looking after them. I'd make a terrible mother. I'm too selfish."

"You're not at all selfish," he said with a smile. "But you sure are rough on yourself. I happen to think you'd make a damned good mother. Your instincts are all in the right place."

"I can't even imagine it," she said. "That's how wrong you are." The very thought of finding herself pregnant frightened her, made her palms grow damp, and dried out her mouth.

"Maybe you'll surprise yourself."

"I doubt it," she said confidently. "Growing up with a mother like mine would put anyone off having children."

"That doesn't make sense. Just because she was a bad mother it doesn't mean you would be, too."

"Let's drop it, okay? The whole subject makes my stomach turn."

"It's dropped," he said, holding his hands upright in a peace gesture. "Have I told you how wonderful you look?"

"Yes," she laughed, "but you can tell me again. It does my little heart good to think I finally look older than twelve."

"Sixteen, tops," he laughed with her.

"That's still better than twelve," she joked, her mind returning to the matter of Raffie. She was going to have to try to find him.

Throughout the wedding ceremony and the reception afterward at Nancy's house, Louise was preoccupied with the idea of seeing Raffie. She ran up imagined confrontations like little lace doilies, embellishing them with bits of scalloped trim, then unraveled them and ran up others. They got in the way of what was going on, held her back from enjoying one of Nancy's typically splendid parties. Celebrating another wedding in the party room reminded her of her grandmother's wedding day, and of her mother in that lurid red dress. That had been eight and a half years ago and she could still remember the jolt she'd felt coming out of the bedroom to see Ma in the living room in that dress. She was glad she wasn't going to have to see her mother now. Clots and clumps of words formed in her throat, almost choking her, at the very thought of having to see the woman. Although she was perversely tempted to take a walk down to Bloor and drop into Creed's to see for herself that her mother was actually working in that very exclusive, very expensive store. It seemed inconceivable, and she wondered what the management would do if they found out they had a prostitute in their employ. An aging one, at that. Maggie was forty-one. Louise wondered what she looked like now, but had no inclination to find out.

She danced with Bob junior and with Mike, with Uncle Bob and Jerry Nolan, and with several of Bob's and Mike's friends, losing herself in the music and the rhythm: "I Want to Hold Your Hand," "On Broadway," "Just One Look," "Jamaica Farewell." Old standards: "I Only Have Eyes for You," "Since I Fell for You," "I'll Be Around," and "Here's That Rainy Day," which was all at once unbearable. She excused herself, claiming to need air, and slipped out through the open door to stand on the patio looking up at the darkening sky: a deep blue, spangled canopy. Suddenly, without warning, she missed Tim. It was silly, she told herself. She didn't even know if he could dance, or if he liked music. There were so many things she didn't know about him; she'd refrained from asking direct personal questions because the less she knew the less bound she was to him. But exchanging personal information wasn't the binding ingredient. It was the silent exchange, the physical currency that tied you, regardless of your intentions. And here she was, tied; standing in Nancy Vickers Nolan's garden on the night of her stepbrother's marriage, all at once lonely for that lonely man three thousand miles away.

"Are you all right, honey?" her grandmother asked, her eyes also on the sky. "What a night!" she exclaimed softly, appreciatively.

"I'm fine, Gramma." She put her arm around her grandmother's waist and let her head tilt onto her shoulder. "I'm involved with someone. I wasn't going to tell you."

"Why not?"

"Because it's not what I think you'd want for me."

"What I want for you doesn't matter much," Ellen said. "It never does matter, because people have a tendency to go their own way."

"He's almost forty-two. He's a doctor, and he's married."

Ellen took a deep breath and let it out slowly. "As I said, people go their own way. Are you happy, Lulu?"

"I'm not happy or unhappy. I'm not anything. I didn't think I'd miss him but I do, and that kind of throws me. I don't even want to be thinking about him, for Pete's sake."

"Maybe you care more than you know."

"I don't have time to care, Gramma. I've got all kinds of things I want to do. I don't have a future with Tim."

"Does he have children?" Ellen asked hesitantly.

Louise shook her head.

"Well, that's something on the plus side."

"You think I'm awful, don't you?"

"I think you're very young," Ellen said, "and very angry."

"Me, angry? I'm not angry." Louise was thrown by the observation.

"Honey, you're burning with it, you're so angry. You have been since Faye died."

"I don't *feel* angry," Louise said wonderingly. "How can I be angry and not even know it?"

"It happens. I was angry for years without knowing it after your grandfather died. It took Bob to make me see it. Not that he said anything. It was just that having him in my life suddenly made me see how much I'd been missing and how angry I'd been about that. I'd have been as shocked as you are right now if someone had come up to me and said, 'You're angry, Ellen.' I'd have denied it. But that wouldn't have made it any less true. I was angry and so are you. It's not a bad thing, honey. It's not a criticism, just an observation."

"I am angry about Faye," Louise admitted, fascinated by her grandmother's statement. Was it anger that caused her to feel pursued and edgy all the time? Or was that something else? How remarkable, she thought, to be in a particular state and yet be completely unconscious of it. "But until you said it just now I didn't know what I was. Maybe that's it. I feel impatient all the time, Gramma, and I'm not satisfied with anything. Like my flat," she said, warming to the conversation. "It's twice the size of the one Faye and I had, but lately all I've thought about is having someplace bigger with a separate bedroom. I think all the time about having a bedroom. It's ridiculous. I don't *need* more space. I'd only have to fill it with things. And my job," she hurried on. "I love Toni and Terence. They've let me take on more and more responsibility and I ferry clients around all the time now. They've given me raises, so I'm making good money. And they're grooming me to deal with clients full time. But I'm still not satisfied. I want something else, something more, something that's mine." She laughed. "I couldn't begin to tell you what it might be. There's this nameless something I want and there are times when I want it so badly I feel as if I could take bites out of the walls or kick down doors with my bare feet.

"Then there's Tim. He's such a nice man, Gramma. You'd like him. I know you would. And he'd do anything for me. The problem is I don't *want* him to do anything for me. I want everything to stay as it is, and I know that's impossible. Nothing ever stays the same. Things have to change. I know that. So on the one hand I want to keep everything the same and on the other hand I want everything to change. I sound like a lunatic." She laughed again and gave her grandmother's waist a squeeze.

"You sound young," Ellen said. "At the risk of being repetitious, when you're young everything feels urgent and important. The older we get the less urgent things seem to be. It'll pass eventually."

"What if it doesn't? Every so often I feel as if I'm spinning like a top and one of these times I'll spin so fast I'll disappear altogether and go shooting off into the atmosphere in a puff of molecules."

It was Ellen's turn to laugh. She gave Louise a hug. "I don't think there's any chance of that. At least I hope not. Are you glad to be back, Lulu?"

"In some ways. In other ways it's rough. Every time I walk out of the apartment I look down the hall and think of Faye, expecting the door will open and I'll see her come walking out."

"I know. Bob and I have thought of moving quite a few times for that very reason. Seeing you at the airport gave me a turn," Ellen admitted. "You looked so much like Faye that for a moment I thought this time it really was her."

"Sometimes I *feel* like her. My dreams get all confused. She's me and I'm her. I came out because that song made me think of her and I got sad."

"Which song?"

" 'Here's That Rainy Day.' Whenever I hear it, it reminds me of Faye. All those plans she and Raffie had, so many dreams, where they were going to live, how their life was going to be, the children they'd have. She had every last detail of their life together worked out. She knew how Raffie would look going off to his office in the morning, and what she'd do during the day while he was gone. She was saving up for the right kind of towels and these dishes she'd seen at Ashley's. Leftover dreams, you know? Where do they go, Gramma? What happens to those dreams? Sometimes I imagine her floating around up there"—she pointed to the sky—"on a cloud of her dreams. And I've been thinking a lot about Raffie and how unfair I was to him."

"You were very hard on him," Ellen agreed softly. "He was devastated. The whole thing came as a tremendous shock to him. He adored Faye, Lulu. You know he did.''

"I know. And that's why I don't understand what happened. I need to know why she died. I feel as if once I know why, then I can get on with my own life.''

"Then maybe you should try to have a talk with Raffie,'' Ellen said.

"That's what I think too. It's just that the idea makes me nervous. I keep thinking he'll slam the door in my face, tell me to go to hell.''

"He wouldn't do that.''

"Maybe not. But if I were Raffie I wouldn't be in a big hurry to talk to me, not after the way I treated him.''

"You'll have to take the chance and find out,'' Ellen told her.

"Yeah,'' Louise sighed, "I will. We'd better go back in,'' she said, turning to look over her shoulder into the party room, feeling the music like a cushion at her back. "Uncle Bob'll be wondering where you are.''

"One of the nice things about a good marriage, Lulu, is that you don't have to watch each other every single moment. He knows I'll turn up at his side in a minute, because he knows there's nowhere else I prefer to be.''

"You're so lucky, Gramma.''

"Yes,'' her grandmother smiled, "I am. And I'll tell you something, sweetheart. I think one of these days you'll be lucky, too. It's a hunch I've always had about you. So don't let yourself get down. Things'll work out one way or another. I've always had the greatest faith in you, and that's not going to change. Concentrate on what you want; don't worry about what you think other people might expect of you. It's such a waste, trying to anticipate what other people might expect. The truth is, they're too busy worrying about themselves most of the time even to think about anyone else. We each have to live our own lives. All I've ever wanted for you is to see you happy, Lulu. And it's up to you to decide what makes you happy.''

⅄

The closer she got to the store the more nervous she became. But when she walked through the door it was Aldo she saw, not Mr. DiStasio.

"Hey, Louise!'' Aldo gave her a big smile. "Long time no see, eh? How the hell are you, anyhow? You slumming?''

He was older and beefier and somehow cruder than she'd remembered.

She smiled and said, "Hi, Aldo. I'm in town visiting and I thought I'd stop by. Is your father around?"

"Nah. Pop's out on deliveries."

"Oh, that's too bad. I was hoping to say hello. What about Raffie? Is he around?" She looked over at the staircase.

"Raffie? Hell, no. He hasn't been around for years. I thought you knew that. After Pop gave him the heave-ho he went to stay with our grand-mother, eh? Pop wouldn't give him the time of day. Last I heard Raffie headed off to the States. I heard the old lady paid some hot shot immigration specialists to get him a green card, and off he went."

"Oh!" Raffie was gone. "Where abouts in the States?" she asked.

"Don't know. Maybe New York. Some cousin or something lives in New York and the old lady shipped Raffie off to them." He shrugged, then said, "So I hear you're a limey now."

"No. I'm a Canadian who lives in London," she corrected him, irritated by his manner and by his remarks.

"You got an accent, you know that?"

"So people have been saying, but I don't hear it." It was a struggle to be polite to him.

"Yeah. You sound like a real limey," he said with a smile. "So how long're you in town for?"

"I leave the day after tomorrow."

"Oh. So I guess you don't have time to get together, eh?"

"No, I'm afraid not," she answered, thinking she'd rather run barefoot through a swamp full of crocodiles. "I guess I'd better be going," she said, giving him a smile she didn't feel. "Say hello to your father for me."

"Sure. He'll be real disappointed he wasn't here to see you. Take it easy there, Louise."

"Right," she said, making for the door.

"Hey!" he called. "You want a nice peach, an apple maybe?" He extended his hand toward the front window display.

"No, thanks, Aldo. See you," she said, and left the store. She was so disappointed she felt like weeping. Now she might never learn the truth of why her sister died.

Too tired suddenly to walk, she flagged down a cab.

Her grandmother and Uncle Bob were still at the office when she got home. The apartment seemed strangely empty, slabs of sunlight filled with dancing dust motes falling through the windows. She made herself a cup of tea and stood looking out at the view, pinpointing Casa Loma up on its hill. Then, on impulse, she put down the cup and went to the telephone to put in a call to Tim.

His nurse said, "He's with a patient right now."

"Oh. Tell him Louise Parker called. Okay?"

"I'll give him that message, Miss Parker."

"Thank you," Louise said, and hung up to pace the length of the living room. She was suddenly anxious to get back to London, to Tim and Nick and Rachel, to her flat, to her life. If she'd ever had any doubts about her life in London this trip had erased them all. She knew for certain now that she'd never again live in this city. She was so anxious to leave she wished she could be on her way there and then. Maybe Tim would see something significant in the autopsy report. Why hadn't it occurred to her before to show it to him?

God! She was so agitated she couldn't stop pacing. Then suddenly she remembered the way Ma used to pace up and down in the kitchen on Manning Avenue and she made herself sit down. She couldn't see Raffie, but maybe she could find out what she needed to know without him. One way or another she was going to learn why Faye died.

CHAPTER
FIFTY-FIVE

SO GLAD WAS SHE TO BE RETURNING TO LONDON THAT for once she was able to relax, and as a result slept through most of the flight. As the plane descended into London to a typically rainy morning she felt a bursting elation at the thought that she'd soon be seeing the people who mattered most to the new life she'd structured. Tim would be waiting for her at the arrivals area and she couldn't wait to be with him. While her three years away from Canada had felt like decades, her fortnight away from London had felt like months. And what she saw most clearly was that she'd been taking Tim for granted, going along on the assumption that he'd always be there, regardless of how much effort she put into the affair. She didn't think necessarily that she wanted to put more into it now, but she did very much want to be with him. She'd even brought him back a gift, a duty-free bottle of the single malt scotch he preferred.

Pushing a trolley with her luggage out the NOTHING TO DECLARE exit she looked about for Tim but saw instead a uniformed driver holding aloft a card with her name printed on it. She approached him and identified herself. The driver said, "I'm to tell you Dr. Kelly had an emergency and sends his apologies. He'll ring you later this morning."

Let down, she sat in the back of the Jaguar and looked out the window as the car traveled through the heavy traffic heading into the city. It was the first time one of Tim's emergencies had bothered her. Birth, she'd learned, was an unpredictable business and, except in the case of scheduled cesarean sections, came at often inopportune times. Still groggy and somewhat stiff from sleeping with her head tucked at an unnatural angle into the tiny airline pillow, she tried to tell herself it didn't matter. But it did. She'd built herself up to see him, and now he might not be free for several days. It was a mistake to become too involved, to care on more than a casual level. Once you did, you were asking to be disappointed. She glanced at her wristwatch. Eight-twenty. Rachel would be on her way to the office by the time Louise got to the flat. She sighed and told herself she'd take advantage of the chance to take a nap and try to get her physical clock caught up. Toni and Terence weren't expecting her at work until the following day. And Nick was busy remodeling the kitchen and bathrooms of Rachel's new house. As far as she knew Evie wasn't due to return from Surrey for at least another week. So whether she liked it or not she wasn't going to be seeing anyone in a hurry.

The driver carried the bags up to the flat. Louise gave him a pound tip and he went on his way. Leaving her luggage in the hall, she stepped into the front room to see that Rachel had left a jug of freesias on the mantel and a note.

Welcome back to another dreary day. I'll ring you this afternoon to be sure you've arrived home safely. Plan to dine out this evening with Nick and me. Lots of love, Rachel.

Smiling, Louise breathed in the flowers' perfume then went to change into jeans and a T-shirt. She unpacked, leaving the presents she'd bought on the kitchen table. Duty-free cigarettes for Nick and his mother, a bottle of Joy for Rachel, the scotch for Tim, and a silk scarf for Evie. Everything put away, she made a pot of coffee, and while it was percolating she got the bathwater running.

She was just toweling dry when Tim startled her, appearing in the doorway.

"I did knock," he explained, "but I expect you didn't hear. Shall I wait for you in the front room?"

"No," she said, seeing the way his eyes seemed to absorb the sight of her. She let the towel drop and held out her arms with a smile. "I was so disappointed that you weren't at the airport."

Gathering her into his arms, he said, "No more so than I."

"I missed you," she admitted, kissing him on the mouth. "I'm not supposed to miss you."

"Oh? And why not?"

"Because I think your life has enough complications and because my life has no room for them. I'm getting your suit all wet."

"That doesn't matter," he said, aligning his body to hers, his hands skimming down her sides. "It'll dry." He kissed the side of her neck, her throat, her shoulder.

She started tugging at his clothes, whispering, "How much time do we have?"

"Not very much."

"Then hurry!"

She locked the bathroom door while he threw off his clothes. Then he lowered the lid on the toilet seat and sat down. She climbed across his lap, held his face between her hands, and kissed him again. "Not very dignified," she murmured as he opened his mouth over her breast, "but I don't care. Do you care?"

He sat back and looked at her with his sorrowing eyes, his hands stroking her thighs. "It's of no concern to me," he said. "I'd be with you anywhere."

Reaching between them, she directed him, lifting forward to make the connection, then held still for a moment, savoring the feel of him inside her. Then she wound her arms around him, fastened her mouth to his, and gave herself up to a tremendous need to move.

They finished very quickly. She lay collapsed against his chest, her mouth open on his neck, her heart racing, her legs trembling. "I missed you," she said again, placing quick kisses across his shoulder and up the side of his neck.

"And I you," he said softly, smoothing her hair. "I'd give the world to be able to come home to you every day."

"Don't say things like that, Tim."

"But it's the truth."

"Maybe, but it's not going to happen, so what's the point of talking about it?"

"One never knows, darling girl, what might happen. I hate to say it, but I must dress and leave. I've an appointment due in the office in twenty minutes. As it is, I'll be late." Reluctantly, he lifted her off his lap and moved to the sink.

She turned on the water, reached for the soap, and handed it to him, then sat on the side of the tub and watched him wash and dry himself.

"I've spoiled your bath," he said, starting to dress.

"Never mind. I like having the smell of you on me."

He gazed at her for a moment, eyes wide, then ducked down to kiss her before he quickly finished dressing. "When does Rachel move into her new house?" he asked, tucking in his shirttails.

"Two more weeks, if Nick's working to plan."

"I'll look forward to that. It's been rather a long haul." His hand on the door, he said, "Forgive me for this, won't you?"

"There's nothing to forgive." Pulling on her robe, she walked him to the door. "I told you, Tim. I missed you."

He smiled, and it reached his eyes. "That makes me very happy."

"Oh, wait!" she said, and ran to the kitchen. "I brought you back a present." She gave him the scotch and he accepted the boxed liquor looking as if she'd given him something beyond value.

"That's very kind of you, Louise," he said in his hushed voice. "Very kind indeed."

"I know you like it," she said, awkward in the face of his gratitude.

"You're a lovely creature. I do adore you." He touched one hand to her cheek before hurrying away, promising to ring her later.

She stood at the top of the stairs watching him go, for the first time wishing they could have more time together. Finally she closed the door and went to pour herself another cup of coffee. Energized by their hasty lovemaking, she decided she'd take her dirty clothes up the road to the Laundromat.

The office was in perfect order. Rachel was at work on the books. Terence was out with a client for the next two days. And Toni was busy setting up interviews for an author tour and for the proprietor of a new nightclub. There were several schedules that needed duplicating so Louise went down the hall to the service office to find Jill and Susan in the midst of packing boxes.

"What's happening?" Louise asked them.

Susan, ever the more forthcoming of the two, said, "We're shutting down. We've run so far into the red our accountant's advised us to close the door."

"But what about all the equipment and everything?"

"Most everything's leased," Susan said, shoving handfuls of bills into an envelope. "The companies'll come and take back their machines."

"Wait a minute!" Louise said, trying to keep control of her sudden excitement. "You're telling me you're just closing the door and walking away?"

"That's about the size of it," said Jill from across the room.

"I'll buy the business from you," Louise said. "I mean, it *is* a properly registered company and everything, isn't it?"

Both Jill and Susan stared at her.

"Isn't it?" Louise repeated.

"Well, yes," Susan said, looking over at her partner. "We hadn't thought of selling it." She looked back at Louise. "We didn't think anyone would be interested in buying it."

"Well, I'm interested. Get together with your accountant and figure out an asking price. I'll get my accountant in to go over the books and we'll see if we can come up with a fair price. Okay?"

Fairly dumbfounded, Susan again looked over at Jill, who shrugged and said, "Can't see why not."

"In the meantime," Louise said, "keep the place running. We don't want to lose any business while we negotiate." She was so keyed-up her hands were buzzing and she could scarcely catch her breath. "I'll make some calls and get organized."

Hurrying back to the office she was so agitated—alarmed by the impulsiveness of what she'd done and exhilarated at the prospect of having a business of her own—that she whispered to Rachel, "I'm going to buy the service office down the hall."

"What?"

"That's right," Louise said. "I just made them an offer."

"But for how much? And why?"

"We'll have to work out the price. I'm going to need your help for that. And why? Because I can make that place work. God! I'm so excited. I've got to call Mr. Reeves. Remember the accounting firm I worked for when I first arrived? I need an accountant. I'll do that, then we'll talk some more. Okay?"

"Louise," Rachel said, noting Louise's high color and feeling her palpable excitement, "are you quite sure you know what you're doing?"

"I have no idea what I'm doing. But I know it's the right thing."

She spoke to Mr. Reeves, who remembered her and said, "I'm sure our Mr. Dickens would be able to assist you, Miss Parker. Hold on a moment please and I'll see if he's free to speak to you."

After she explained the situation to a young-sounding Mr. Dickens, he said, "It sounds as if their books'll be in a shambles, if they're as disorganized as you claim."

"I'm sure they are, which is why I want an accountant in on this from the outset. I don't want to pay more for the business than I should."

"Look, Miss Parker. Get the name of their accountant and his number, and I'll get together with him to go over the books. Then we'll make an offer based on the figures."

"Thank you. I'll do that right away."

"You're quite sure," he asked, "you want to take this on? Sounds a bit of a losing proposition to me."

"It won't be," she said confidently. "Not with me running it." She thanked him, said goodbye, then got up to go again to the service office to get the information about Jill and Susan's accountant.

On her return, Toni said, "What's going on? There seems to be a good deal of scurrying back and forth."

Unable to contain herself, Louise said, "You might as well know up front. I've made an offer on the service office. If it works out, I'll be taking over the business."

Toni's attractive face fell. "You're leaving us?"

"I'm sorry, but yes. If it works out."

Toni sat down heavily, saying, "This is unexpected, to say the least. Would you consider staying on? Terence and I have discussed the possibility of making you a partner, taking you into the company. We'd hate to lose you, Louise."

"I really want to do this, if it's possible, Toni. It's a chance for me to have a business of my own."

"But that office needs at least two people to function. And God knows it certainly doesn't function with those two. How are you going to manage it alone?"

"I won't. I'll hire . . ."

"I'll be working with her," Rachel said from her desk. "Isn't that right, Louise? We're going to be partners."

With a sudden lumping in her throat, Louise looked across at Rachel, then back at Toni. "That's right," she said huskily. "Rachel and I are going to be partners."

"You both will at least stay until we can find replacements?" Toni asked, looking shattered and a little angry.

"Of course. It'll take at least two weeks before we sort out Jill and Susan's books. And then another two weeks, I imagine, to get through the legalities."

"Four," Rachel put in.

"Right," Louise said. "So we'll be giving you six weeks' notice as of Friday."

"That's right," Rachel said, smiling widely.

"Bloody hell!" Toni got up and went to sit behind her desk. "I suppose we'd better get on to a personnel agency straightaway so Terence and I can start interviewing."

"I'll take care of it," Louise said, for the first time wondering how much it might possibly cost to buy the business. She didn't have all that much capital. But perhaps she'd be able to get a loan. For a long moment she sat paralyzed with anxiety, wondering if she was taking on more than she could handle.

After an energetic round of negotiating handled with dazzling efficiency and knowledge by Rachel and Mr. Dickens, the sale price was agreed upon. Then Louise became really frightened. Her half was several thousand pounds more than she had.

"I'll lend you the money," Rachel said.

"No! That's out of the question. You're already going to be a full partner. If I borrow the money from you for my share, you'll wind up

owning seventy-five percent of the business. I want us to be *equal* partners, Rachel. I'm going to have to come up with the money, that's all. I'll
go talk to my bank manager.''

The bank manager listened politely, then said, "Unfortunately, Miss
Parker, your capital cannot be used as collateral against a loan, since it's
going toward the cost of the acquisition. And failing additional collateral, I
very much doubt you're going to find any bank willing to advance you the
sum you're seeking.''

"But why? If I'm putting in three thousand, why can't the bank match
my commitment?''

With an indulgent smile, he said, "I'm afraid that is not how banks
operate, particularly not when dealing with someone so young as yourself
with so little in the way of business experience. No responsible institution
would view you as a viable risk, I'm sorry to say.''

Louise got the same response from each of the five other banks she
approached.

"I'm too young and inexperienced," she complained to Tim. "I've
talked to Nick, convinced him to come to work with us as a courier. And
he's got five hundred to put in, to make him a minor partner. So that's
good. But it still means I've got to come up with another twenty-five
hundred pounds.''

"Let me help you," Tim said quietly.

"Absolutely not! I didn't tell you this because I was trying to hit you
up for the money.''

"I know you didn't," he said evenly. "And please don't speak to me
in that tone of voice. I don't care for it.''

Thrown, she said, "I'm sorry.''

"Let me help you, Louise," he said again.

"I can't do that. It wouldn't be right." Taking money from him would
make her a whore.

Angry, he got up and took several steps across the room, then turned
to confront her. "You're taking on something that you claim has potential," he said. "You're striving for independence, but without assistance
you simply can't do it. If you fail to come up with the additional funding
your project will die. This service office will shut down and that'll be the
end of it. You have two choices: Either you let the matter go, or you
accept my help. Actually, there's a third choice. You accept my help or I
remove myself from the picture. I refuse to continue this relationship as it

stands. I'm not so besotted with you that I've forgotten myself, Louise. Perhaps it hasn't ever occurred to you, but there's something inescapably ignominious about my role in your life. I come here of a late afternoon and wait, on the off chance of seeing you. I've been doing this for months on end. I feel like a beggar at the gate, hoping for kitchen scraps. I have another life, dear girl. And in that life I'm a highly respected medical practitioner, with offices in Harley Street and a home in Mayfair.

"You give yourself in small pieces," he said with a sad shake of his head. "And I've been content to accept those small pieces because my affections are in play. But I'm too old to act out the role of the middle-aged fool lovesick over the beautiful young maiden. It palls, Louise. It sickens. It plays hell with the image I hold of myself. Bad enough to have a wife who despises me. I won't continue on with someone whose only connection to me is sexual. I can't. I'm beginning to lose respect for myself."

"I never wanted you to feel that way," she said, stunned.

"You haven't wanted to know my feelings," he said flatly. "I care for you. I want to help you. If you reciprocate my feelings on some level, accept my offer. If you don't, then we'll call it a day."

"That's blackmail."

He smiled and resumed his seat. "Not at all, darling girl. It's the crude use of power to determine my standing. I need to know I'm not making a fool of myself here. If I am, I'll put a stop to it. I can't bear to play anyone's fool, not even yours."

"I don't want to stop seeing you," she admitted, feeling all at once too young to cope with what he was asking and with what she'd voluntarily taken on. Maybe she was in over her head and was too stupid to know it.

"We'll make it a loan with interest. You'll repay it in proper monthly installments as you would to any bank," he said. "Have you another choice? Or would you prefer me to leave? It's entirely up to you."

"A crude use of power," she repeated.

"To determine my standing," he said again. "Louise, only saints go on faith alone."

"And you're no saint," she laughed.

"That I'm not."

With no warning, she found herself in tears. She slipped onto his lap and accepted his handkerchief, wondering why she couldn't tell this man that she cared for him. Why was it such an awful admission to make? It wouldn't kill her. "I don't want you to go," she said. "I'm sorry I've made you feel foolish."

"I've made myself feel foolish, don't you know," he said, holding her. "It's a talent middle-aged men seem to have. See it as the gesture it's intended to be, Louise. I want you to allow me some small involvement in your life. Because I love you. And because I suspect you have some small feeling for me."

"I have more than a small feeling for you," she admitted, clinging to him. "It's hard for me, Tim. I get scared."

"That I can understand. We all get scared when our feelings are on the line."

"Is that really how you see yourself? As a middle-aged man with a mistress half his age who doesn't give a damn?"

"No one wants to act out a cliché. It comes under the heading of one's worst nightmare."

"I know I can make a success of that business," she said fervently. "I know I can. Rachel's a financial wizard; she'll keep track of every penny. And I'm fast and efficient. Adding the courier service'll bring in additional income. Plus Nick will do the remodeling and look after things like the Xeroxing when he's not on a delivery. It'll work. I *know* it will."

"Then accept my offer of a loan and be done with it. I have confidence in you. I believe you can make a go of it. I admire your spirit."

"All right," she relented. "But I want it down on paper. And I'll pay you back monthly, with interest."

"Agreed. Now, if you'll forgive me, I must check in with my service." He eased her off his lap and went to use the telephone.

She dried her face and refolded his handkerchief, feeling wrung out.

"No emergencies," he said, returning with a smile. "Fancy a bite to eat?"

"I do care about you," she said. "I do. A lot."

"Yes," he said. "I knew that."

"If you knew it, why did you put me through all this?"

"Because I needed to *hear* it," he said. "Surely you can understand that." Smiling, he said, "I swear Evie's a witch."

"What? Why?"

"She brought us together, didn't she? I've known the woman all my life, and I've never known her to do anything without a reason."

"You mean she knew we'd become involved?"

He laughed, something he did very rarely, a light musical peal. "I'd have to say she did. Come give me a hug and tell me you're not upset with me."

She hugged him, then gave him a kiss. "Next time you need to know where you stand," she said. "Just ask me. Okay?"

"And will you admit to your feelings?"

"I don't know," she said. "But ask me."

"Hungry?"

"Starving."

"Then I'll buy you dinner."

"What would you have done if I'd said no?" she asked, going for her purse.

"Why, I'd have gone away," he said, surprised. "It wasn't a game, Louise. It's never been a game."

"You'd have stopped seeing me, just like that?"

"I'd have been unhappy for a good long time, but yes."

She was selfish, she thought, recalling her conversation with Daniel. "I'd have been unhappy, too," she said, thinking that no matter what happened she wanted to keep him. And that was selfish. Wasn't it?

CHAPTER
FIFTY-SIX

WORKING EVENINGS AND WEEKENDS, THEY REORGANIZED the layout of the office. Nick built a counter just inside the door that ran the width of the place, with a hatch to allow access to the work area. Then he built shelves to accommodate the reams of paper for the Xerox machine, the Gestetner stencil machine, the telex, as well as general office supplies and typing paper.

They instituted a system whereby customers took a number and were assisted in order. A stack of request forms sat on the counter, to be filled out by those requiring service: company name, type of service, number of copies, and so forth, with a space provided for a signature and the amount of the charge. Every individual was expected to fill out a form. At month's end, his or her company would receive a statement of the accumulated charges. Louise and Rachel set up a schedule of fees covering everything from sending a telex to the price per page for typing. Rachel started a new set of books, with accounts receivable set up for the various offices in the block that used their services, and accounts payable to cover everything from their own hourly rates of pay to Nick's charges for courier service, which were based on mileage averaged with the cost of petrol.

From the outset, Wordworks ran smoothly. Their clients were pleased with the billing system and with the overall efficiency of the revamped service office. Louise worked late most evenings and often all weekend in order to ensure that jobs were delivered on time. The courier service flourished, and Nick was on the go from first thing in the morning often straight through until close of business at six. Rachel tallied the requisition forms nightly so that the accounts were always up to date. Within three months they were breaking even.

"Three more months and we'll be into the black," Rachel announced in December. "It's unheard of," she said, looking both pleased and somewhat amazed. "I calculated we'd run in the red for at least twelve months, but at our current rate of income we'll actually be showing a profit by March first."

"I knew we could do it," Louise told her. "I knew this place could succeed with a little reorganization."

"We'll need additional help if we're to continue building," Rachel said shrewdly. "We'd do well to consider taking on a typist. With someone to do the typing, you'd be free to solicit new business from the other offices in the block."

"But they have their own equipment."

"Perhaps so. But there are always rush jobs, last-minute work needing to be done. With a typist on staff, we'd be able to offer more in the way of service. At some point, we'll want to expand, you know. The whole point of business is to keep increasing the profit line. In order to do that we hire more staff, expand our premises, perhaps branch out into other locations."

"Until I repay Tim we can't think about taking on additional expenses," Louise said. "And even if I double what I'm paying him monthly, it'll still be a year before I'm able to do that."

"That loan's a legitimate business deduction, Louise," Rachel explained patiently. "It offsets our profit, allows us to reduce our tax bite. Don't worry about the loan. All companies have accounts payable. They're necessary."

"But I don't like owing him money."

"Learn to live with it," Rachel advised blithely. "It's a business venture, not a personal commitment. I know he sees it that way."

"How do you know that?"

"Because he's not the sort of man who'd see it in any other way."

With a smile, Louise had to ask, "When did you become such an expert on men?"

"I'm anything but, as you very well know. But I do know Tim, and I know how he feels about you. Good heavens, Louise! All those afternoons when he came to visit, and there I was like the proverbial fifth wheel, don't you think I got to know him?"

"I suppose you did."

"Of course. And I'll tell you what else I got to know. He'd get rid of his wife in a minute if you gave him the slightest encouragement."

"I'm not going to be responsible for breaking up anybody's marriage," Louise said with some alarm.

"Oh, don't be a nit! That marriage was gone for a Burton before you ever came along. The man practically worships you. It makes me quite sick with envy. I can't for the life of me think why you're so cavalier about him."

"I'm not cavalier about him."

"Well, you certainly don't fawn all over him."

"That's not my style," Louise said.

"I'd fawn all over him, if it were me," Rachel grinned. "He's positively delicious." She closed the ledgers, announcing, "I'm going home. I've had enough of this place for one day."

"I've got to finish this report," Louise said, looking at the several pages still remaining to be typed.

"Finish it in the morning," Rachel said. "Come home with me and we'll eat at a reasonable hour like civilized people."

"I can't," Louise said. "I've promised it for first thing in the morning."

"You see," Rachel said, as if her point had been proved. "We need a typist."

"I thought you said March."

"I did. But it might be wise to go a little into the red for a few months to ease the workload."

"No. We'll wait," Louise said. "I don't want to start going backwards, not when we've made such a good start."

"Up to you," Rachel said. "But you'll wear yourself out."

"I'll survive. It's not going to be for the rest of my life."

"You never leave here before nine or ten at night," Rachel said. "When d'you have time for poor Tim?"

"He stops by late now and then."

"It's dreary. I think you should make time for him."

"There'll be time later on, Rachel. Right now, this business comes first."

"Well, I'm going," Rachel said, locking the books in her desk drawer. "Nick said he might stop by." She looked at the time. "Hell! It's already past seven. I hope I haven't missed him."

"He'll wait for you," Louise said. "He always does."

Rachel blushed and fussed with her coat buttons. "I'm soon going to be a twenty-five-year-old virgin. I don't know whether to have a party or slash my wrists."

"You're joking, I hope."

"Only partly. I wish I had some of your savoir faire."

"I have no savoir faire whatsoever. I'm just not shy."

"Is that what it is?" Rachel asked interestedly. "I'm horribly shy." She touched a hand to her hat, a lime green turban, saying, "I've died of embarrassment every time I've had to have a physical examination."

"Why?" Louise asked. "You've got a very good figure."

Rachel's blush deepened. "You're so *not* British. Don't you know that English women don't *have* bodies? Supposedly, we do the dirty deed for queen and country, and grit our teeth while it's happening. Then, when it's done, we say, 'There! Feel better now, do you, dear?' "

"God, what a picture!" Louise laughed. "Go home and give Nick something to eat. I'm sure he'll be waiting. I'll see you in the morning."

"Don't stay too late," Rachel said from the door.

"Just until I finish this thing," Louise said, fingers already flying over the keyboard.

By mid March they'd hired a typist, but Louise continued to spend evenings and weekends at the office. Rachel had had a flyer printed advertising Wordworks' services and had it distributed to nearby office blocks. It brought in additional work, so Louise put in the extra hours.

She only took time off on her birthday in April because Rachel insisted. "We're going to celebrate," she declared. "You're not to work this evening. We're going out to dinner."

"But I promised I'd see Tim."

"I rang him at his office and he's going to join us. We four are going to Wiltons in Jermyn Street. I've booked a table for seven. So you're to leave here promptly at five to go home and put on one of your pretty frocks. Tim and Nick will meet us at the restaurant."

"But there's all this work—"

"Doreen's agreed to work overtime," Rachel cut her off with a self-satisfied smile. "No excuses," she said, waggling her finger. "You're to celebrate whether you like it or not."

"How did you talk Tim into this?" she asked.

"He leapt at the invitation," Rachel said, "as I expected he would. Why do you look so surprised?"

"It's just so . . . public. It's not the same as our going to some small local restaurant," Louise said.

"Oh, I think he's long since come to terms with that," Rachel said with a worldly air.

"What d'you mean, come to terms with it?"

"Just that, Louise. It astonishes me you don't realize it."

"Realize what, for Pete's sake?"

"You're such a ninny!" Rachel said fondly. "He's prepared to change everything for you. Don't you know that?"

"God, Rachel! Don't say things like that!"

"Why should that scare you?"

"It does, okay? I don't want him to change anything for me."

"I don't think you've got much say in the matter at this point," Rachel said. "He seems to've made a commitment. And I haven't noticed you dating anyone else, my dear."

"That's because I don't have *time*."

"Rubbish! It's because you're head over heels for darling Tim. Just as I'm head over heels for Nick, in my own dismal fashion."

"I don't have time now to discuss this with you." Louise turned back to her typewriter.

"As you like. Just be sure to be at the restaurant at seven."

"I'll be there."

"Good." Rachel went back to her accounts receivable.

Nick and Tim had brought gifts, to which Rachel added hers, saying, "If you make any sort of a fuss about this I'll make you pay for the dinner. And to be sure it's a whopping bill I'll order *three* bottles of Dom Perignon."

"I won't make a fuss," Louise promised, wishing she felt more festive. All the late nights and weekends of work seemed to be catching up with her, and she kept swallowing back yawns. "I'll take everything you three have bought and say thank you. All right?"

"That'll be a pleasant change," Tim said.

"Indeed!" Rachel sniffed. "She's most ungracious as a rule."

" 'Ere!" Nick said. "Let's 'ave a toast then." He raised his glass and the others followed suit. "Cheers, Louise," he said. " 'Appy twenty-second, old girl."

They all drank some of the champagne, and Nick said, "Go on, then. Open your presents."

"What, now?"

"When if not now?" Nick asked. "We're all sittin' 'ere waitin' to 'ave you tell us 'ow much you like 'em."

"I feel like an eight-year-old," Louise laughed. "Which one should I open first?"

"Tim's," Rachel said, shooting a smile across the table at him. "I'm dying of curiosity."

"Ah, my dear," he said, returning the smile. "It's not worth dying over. Merely a wee token of my affection."

Louise undid the wrappings, and opened an elongated velvet box to see a strand of pearls with a simple gold clasp. At once she thought of her grandmother's pearls and of Faye, and tears came to her eyes. "They're beautiful," she got out, and leaned to one side to kiss Tim's cheek. "Thank you."

"They're super," Rachel exclaimed. "Do put them on! They go perfectly with your dress."

"Here," Tim said, and fastened them on for her. "You're pleased, are you?" he asked.

Looking down at the necklace, she couldn't speak for a moment. "They're wonderful," she said thickly, wondering what she'd ever done to inspire such caring in this man. "Thank you," she said again.

"Get on with it," Nick prompted. "I'm 'ungry. The geezer won't bring the food til you're finished with that lot."

"He's right," Rachel concurred. "Get on with it."

"Which one next?" Louise asked.

"Open mine last," Rachel said.

Nick's gift was a book of poetry by Anne Sexton, *All My Pretty Ones*. Louise asked, "How did you know I like her poetry?"

" 'Ere," he said. "Who was it built your bookshelves, then?"

Louise laughed. "I had no idea you were such a snoop. Thank you. This is great."

"Now mine," Rachel said, pushing the package toward her. "And I swear, you'll pay if you make a fuss. Read the card first."

The card read: "You've made all the difference to my life. I'll always love you for that. With every good wish and all my love, Rachel."

The box contained a pair of dainty diamond stud earrings.

"My God, Rachel!" Louise said. "You shouldn't have done this."

"I warned you," Rachel said threateningly.

"I won't offer to pay you for them," Louise said with a shaky laugh. "I don't think I could afford to."

"That's right, you couldn't. Now let's get on with the eating and drinking. Nick and I are simply ravenous." Rachel and Nick smiled fondly at each other, then Rachel lifted a hand to summon the waiter.

Wearing only the pearls and her new diamond earrings, Louise pressed her face into Tim's belly, then dipped her tongue into his navel. Slipping lower, she stroked him with her hand, then bent to put her mouth on him. A soft hissing sound escaped from his lips and his hands stroked her head. She kept on until every muscle in his body was taut, then she sat up and looked at him, her lips glistening. He looked almost frighteningly vulnerable as she held him steady with one hand and lowered herself over him.

"God!" she whispered, feeling him pulsing inside her like a nether heart. "God!" He was reaching for her, drawing her down on his chest, and she was gliding forward, gripped by a sudden desire to say I love you. What was this? she wondered, awed by his great kindness and by his unapologetic love for her. She cradled his head on her arm and gazed into his cool blue eyes, the words pushing into her mouth. "I love you," she said, then was seized by fear, as if she'd admitted to a fatal weakness. She held herself poised, his body solidly joined with hers, waiting to see how he'd respond.

It was wonderful and awful. All at once the sorrow left his eyes and they were suddenly full, brimming. He closed them tightly for one long moment, then, rather than risk ruining the moment with words, spoke to her through his body. He shifted, reversing their positions, and held her from beneath while he made slow, concentrated love to her. Her eyes remained fixed on his until the very last, when they rolled slowly closed and her arms held him locked tightly to her.

Some time later, after he'd checked in with his service and ascertained there were no urgent messages, he sat beside her on the bed and took hold of her hand, saying, "Tell me to do it, and I'll divorce my wife."

The fear rushed back over her and she said, "I can't tell you to do that. I don't want to be responsible."

"But you are responsible," he said. "As am I. We're each responsible for our actions, for our emotions. It's a fact of life, Louise. Whether we want to or not, we cause other people to feel certain ways. I love you. I'd like to be free to be with you. Or am I too old to nurture such dreams?"

"You're not too old for anything," she said. "But I'm not ready to tell you to do something as important as divorcing your wife."

"And if I did it? What then? Would you consider coming to live with me?"

"I don't know," she said. "I just don't know. It scares me when you say something like that."

"Ah, don't be scared," he said with an understanding smile. "I won't push you. We'll discuss it again another time."

"Tim, would you do something for me?"

"Anything."

She simply had to sit up with a smile and kiss him. "Don't be so agreeable," she said. "I might ask you to do something you wouldn't want to do."

"That couldn't happen."

"Would you read something and tell me what it means?"

"Certainly."

She slipped off the bed and went to the desk to get the autopsy report. "I want you to take this with you and look at it when you have time, then explain it to me."

"What is it, Louise?"

"It's the autopsy report on my sister."

He shivered as if suddenly chilled, but accepted the envelope and placed it on the chair with his clothes, then returned to the bed, saying, "But it's my impression you're aware of how she died."

"I know *how*. I'm hoping there might be something in that thing that'll tell me why."

"I doubt that. Unfortunately, quite a number of girls die as a result of botched abortions. But I'll read it and let you know my findings. You miss her still," he said.

"I'll miss her for the rest of my life. But I can't help feeling I'll be able to get on with my life if I understand what happened to Faye."

"And what if that document is of no help to you? Mightn't it be best to let it lie?" he asked gently.

"I can't," she said helplessly. "I wish to God I could but I can't. It seems to get worse all the time. I need to know."

"Perhaps you never will. What then, Louise?"

"Then it'll haunt me," she said. "You have to understand how close we were, Tim, the kind of childhood we had with my mother. You have to know what it was like for us, trying to make sense of a woman no one could ever make sense of. All we had was each other and our grand-mother. And Gramma couldn't be there all the time to look out for us. We were on our own. We looked out for each other. I thought she'd always be there. Then one night I came home and my sister was bleeding to death on the sofa. A little while later she was dead, and the one person who was always going to be there for me was gone forever. I still can't *believe* it. Sometimes I see some woman on the street and from the back she looks like Faye, and my heart gives this big leap. I go to call out to her and then I remember. It's not Faye. It could never be Faye. But that doesn't stop me from being tricked over and over. So if I can't have her back, at the very least I need to have some idea why she had to die."

"All right, Louise," he said very softly. "I'll do my best to find you an answer."

"I did mean what I said," she told him, breaking into tears for the second time that evening. "I do love you, Tim. God! Look at me! I'm shaking all over from saying that."

"It'll be all right," he said, holding her. "I won't push you. We'll just go along for now."

She grabbed the sheet and mopped her face, then embraced him, holding on to him with the feeling that her life had slipped slightly out of her control.

CHAPTER
FIFTY-SEVEN

"COME OUT TO LUNCH WITH ME," RACHEL SAID THE next day.

"What, now?"

"Yes, now. Doreen will look after things, won't you, Doreen?"

Doreen, the typist, was a pretty nineteen-year-old brunette with slanted green eyes who'd proved herself to be not only efficient but unfailingly pleasant. "Go on to lunch," she said. "It's quiet now."

"What's going on?" Louise asked as they settled into a booth at the small restaurant they frequented nearby. "You look very perky today."

Flushing becomingly, Rachel leaned forward across the table and whispered, "I am no longer a twenty-five-year-old virgin!"

Breaking into a big smile, Louise exclaimed, "Hah! You naughty girl. Tell me all about it."

Unable to stop smiling, Rachel said, "Let's order first."

The waitress came over to take their orders, and the minute she'd gone, Rachel again leaned close to Louise saying, "It was the champagne, I swear. If I hadn't had that third glass I know I'd never have done it."

"You don't look sorry."

"Oh, I'm *not!*" Rachel assured her. "After all these months of seeing Nick every day at the office and his stopping by most evenings, I've thought such a lot about what it would be like. But I was scared to death. And I knew he'd never do more than kiss me good night unless I gave some sign I was willing. Last night, thanks to the champagne, I was willing.'' She laughed into her hand, then said, ''It wasn't quite what I expected and I haven't got the hang of it yet, but it was smashing, really smashing. I think it was riding home on the back of his scooter that did it. You know? We seemed to be going so frightfully fast, and I had to hang on especially hard when we went round corners. I was sitting on the back of the Vespa with my arms round Nick's waist and I felt so wonderfully *free*. And suddenly I thought I'd never had a better evening or been happier and I didn't want it to end.

"So,'' she said, drawing in a long breath, "when we arrived at my house I asked him straight out if he'd like to stop the night.''

"You didn't!''

"I did! Boldest thing I've ever done, Louise. You should've seen his face. He said, 'Whot?' '' she mimicked him. " ' 'Ave you gone round the twist, luv?' '' and I said no, I didn't think so, and if he didn't make up his mind in a hurry I'd lose my nerve. So was he coming in or wasn't he?'' With a giggle, she said, "I thought he'd break his neck he was in such a hurry to lock up the scooter. Anyway, it was fine once we got inside. Thank heavens he knew what to do, though. I was hopeless.'' She put her head down on the tabletop and laughed wildly for a few moments. Then she raised her head. "He thinks I'm beautiful, Louise.''

"You are beautiful, dummy.''

"You only think that because you're my friend. But he's a *man*.''

"I had noticed that.''

"Don't be mean, Louise. You've had masses of experience. You know about these things and I don't. I told you: I was hopeless. There's no established protocol, for heaven's sake. I mean, I've read about it in books and no one ever writes about the *logistics*: Who undresses first, do you stop to remove the bedspread? I felt like such a ninny, but he was so sweet. This morning I opened my eyes and he was right there, sleeping like an angel. It seemed positively miraculous. After a while I got up ever so quietly and made tea before I woke him. He sat up and took his cup of tea and said, 'Ta, luv,' and I thought it was the most perfectly wonderful moment of my entire life. There was this fair-haired angel sitting in my bed drinking tea and smiling at me, saying, 'This is a real treat. I've imagined this.' Can you bear it? He'd thought about me, Louise. Oh, I'm so happy. I've asked him to move in with me.''

"Isn't that a little fast?''

"I don't care if it is."

"What did he say?"

Glowing, she said, "He asked me was I sure, did I really know what I was doing? Had I thought about the fact that my parents would probably have massive coronaries? And I said I didn't care what they did. But was he worried about what Molly might say? And he said, 'Naw. Me mum knows I've been 'ead over 'eels for you for years.' "

"So he's moving in?" Louise asked.

Rachel nodded. "This weekend. Isn't that simply fabulous?"

"It's terrific, kiddo."

"You really think so?"

"I think it's about time the two of you got together," Louise told her. "Thank God for champagne and scooters, eh?"

Rachel giggled, then adjusted the little yellow hat she wore that resembled a yarmulke with beads and netting. "I feel so *wicked,*" she said, "so wonderfully, wonderfully wicked."

"I hope you're being careful."

"About what?"

"You know," Louise said. "Using precautions."

"Oh, definitely. Nickie had some in his wallet. Do you suppose all men carry them around?"

"Only the intelligent ones."

"Does Tim?" Rachel asked.

"Tim doesn't need to. I take birth control pills. He prescribed them for me quite a while ago."

"Oh! Was it your idea?"

"Of course it was," Louise answered. "It would hardly be fitting for me to make the man a father at this stage of his life."

"How odd. I imagined he had children. He's the sort who'd be a super father, so very low-key and sympathetic. What a great pity."

"His wife can't have children."

"Wouldn't you like to have children, Louise?"

"No, I wouldn't," Louise said flatly as the waitress came with their food.

"Well, I would," Rachel said. "I'd like to have at least three."

"Right now we've got a business to run," Louise reminded her.

"I know that," Rachel said. "I wasn't planning to start having them tomorrow. I mean to say, Nickie and I haven't even discussed children yet. First I want to learn how to do it all properly. It takes some practice, I think. I always imagined it simply *happened*. Two people put their bits together and flamingos soared into a tropical sunset.''

Louise laughed and said, ''Never mind. You'll figure it out. Congratulations.''

''Thank you. It did hurt rather,'' Rachel confided. ''Made rather a mess of the sheets too. But I don't mind. In a way that made it that much more significant. Did it hurt your first time?''

Louise shook her head. ''But my sister Faye said the same as you.''

''Did you talk about absolutely everything?'' Rachel asked enviously.

''She was very shy. I used to drive her crazy asking questions.'' Louise smiled, remembering their late-night conversations in bed. ''She used to say she wasn't going to discuss it. But I always managed to pry it out of her. She was fourteen her first time.''

''That's very young.''

''I was seventeen.''

''That's still very young.''

''I didn't think so at the time. I still don't. I loved Daniel,'' she said, realizing as she said the words that she *had* loved him, and in a particular way she always would. But she'd never told him so. ''He was there at a time when I needed him. He got me through that year after Faye died. I don't know what I'd have done without him.''

''That's good,'' Rachel said, eating with appetite for a change. ''I love Nickie. And last night he told me over and over how much he loves me. I had *no idea,*'' she said wonderingly. ''None. Isn't that extraordinary?''

''I tried to tell you, but you'd never listen to me, either one of you.''

''Well, you were right,'' Rachel said. ''And nothing else matters. I don't care what anyone thinks. Nickie and I are going to be very happy together.''

''I'm glad, Rachel,'' Louise said sincerely. ''You deserve to be happy.''

''Yes,'' Rachel said. ''I quite agree.''

''So far as I'm able to ascertain from this document,'' Tim said cautiously, ''there's every indication that your sister sustained vaginal tearing as a result most likely of a forcible assault.''

''What does that mean?'' Louise asked, wincing at the idea of vaginal tearing.

"It means, I'm sorry to say, that there is every likelihood she was raped."

"*Raped?*" She was horrified.

"According to the coroner's statement there was recent vaginal scarring of a nature consistent with rape."

Her chest felt hollowed with shock; she could scarcely believe what she was hearing. "Raffie would never have raped Faye," she said in a low, stunned voice.

"I'm afraid it appears that someone did, Louise. The scar tissue was relatively recent at the time of her death. I take it you knew nothing of this."

"Poor Faye," she said, a sudden tremor in her hands. "God! I had no idea. She never said a word, not a thing. Tim, you're sure about this?"

"As sure as one can be given the evidence of this document." He set it down gingerly on the desk, then turned back to her. "I am sorry to be the bearer of such unpleasant news."

"Who could have done it? When?" she wondered. "God, Tim! Maybe you were right. Maybe I should've left it alone. I *hate* knowing this. It makes everything so much worse."

"I'm terribly sorry," he said again, an arm around her shoulders. "I had thought quite possibly you'd known of it."

"No." She shook her head, dazed, questions rushing through her mind. How? Where? Why? Most importantly, who? Had someone dragged Faye off the street into an alley? It was too horrible to consider. Oh, *Faye,* she thought, why didn't you *tell* me? But, instinctively, she knew why: because Faye had been too ashamed to tell. "My poor sister," she said, her tongue feeling numb. "She was so shy, Tim, such a sweet, gentle person. It makes me *crazy* to think of something like that happening to her."

"I'm sure it's frightful," he sympathized. "It's why I've put off for so many weeks giving you my interpretation of the report. I wish there were something I could do to ease the pain."

Louise wasn't listening. She was adding facts, totaling them like columns of numbers: Faye had been raped. She'd become pregnant as a result. And she'd had an abortion to rid herself of the rapist's baby. The abortionist had injured her, and she'd died. One nightmare after another. The last weeks of Faye's life had been an ongoing horror.

"I have to think about this," she said. "It changes things."

"What things specifically?"

"I don't know, Tim," she snapped, fraught. "Things in general."

"It might be best if I run along now," he said tactfully. "You're very upset."

"Upset doesn't begin to cover it," she said, trying not to take her anger out on him. "It might be a good idea if you went. I need some time to try to sort through everything."

"Of course," he said, giving her a kiss on the forehead. "We'll talk tomorrow. Good night, my dear."

"Good night," she said distractedly, not getting up to see him to the door. It was almost eleven and she felt suddenly exhausted, the weight of her new knowledge bearing heavily upon her. Nothing was as she'd imagined it to be. She'd done Raffie a horrendous injustice, had wrongly accused him of being responsible for Faye's death. And she had been wrong without question, because the one thing she knew for an utter certainty was that Raffie was incapable of intentionally harming anyone, but especially Faye. As Gramma had said, Raffie adored Faye. He was basically sensitive, fundamentally good. He'd never so much as even swatted Faye's arm in a playful moment, had always treated her with total deference. Which meant that someone else had forced himself on her sister.

In tears, she curled up on the bed and pulled the blankets over her. She wanted to sleep, to dream; she wanted Faye to come to her as she so often did, to talk. She willed Faye to penetrate her dreams and reveal the secret she'd taken with her into her death. But she dreamed instead that she was talking to Rachel and while they talked, Louise's teeth began to loosen and started, one at a time, slipping from her gums. In minutes she had a handful of teeth. Rachel didn't seem to notice and Louise didn't want to open her mouth to speak.

She went to sleep thinking of Faye and awakened thinking of her. It became a pattern. Her nights were filled with images of her sister being dragged into a dark alley, and she struggled for Faye, battling off her attacker. She failed every time and found herself barred from the alley by a steel gate, from beyond which she could hear her sister's screams. The images haunted her waking hours, and the only relief came in work and in those few stolen hours each week she was able to spend with Tim. In order to keep her mind off the matter, she took on more and more work, spending increasingly longer hours at the office.

✝

In November of 1964 she received a call one afternoon from Grace Greeley.

"You do remember me, I hope. It was quite some time ago that we met."

"Sure, I remember you. How are you, Grace?"

"Very well, thank you. I've been hearing about Wordworks. I hear business is thriving. Which is why I'm ringing. You'll recall that I work for an American oil company?"

"Uh-huh."

"Well, we've just moved into a new suite of offices in a block in Bayswater, and the thing of it is, the tenants are rather in desperate need of something along the lines of Wordworks. Since the block's fairly new, there's still space available and I was wondering if you'd given any consideration to expanding."

"My partners and I have discussed that possibility," Louise said, not allowing her sudden excitement to color her voice. "In fact, we've been talking quite a lot about it."

"I think you might be interested in coming along here to have a look. There's a definite need. If you like, I'll be happy to show you round, introduce you to some of the other tenants."

"We'd be very interested," Louise said, rolling her eyes at Rachel, who'd put down her pen and was following Louise's end of the conversation. "When did you have in mind?"

"How would tomorrow afternoon suit?" Grace asked. "I'm free between one-thirty and three. Perhaps you could stop by here and I'll ask the rental agent to be on standby."

"One-thirty tomorrow. Great," Louise said, making a note of the address. "Thanks a lot, Grace. We'll see you then."

"What, what?" Rachel asked the instant Louise put down the receiver.

"That was Mr. Greeley's daughter, Grace. She thinks we might want to open a branch in her office block."

"We most certainly do," Rachel said at once. "I expect your landlord must have commented to her on how well Wordworks is doing."

"He must have. What worries me is whether we're really in a position to lay out the money for a second office. And who's going to run it?"

"It's quite simple, Louise. If the location's good and it seems as if there'll be enough business to support a second Wordworks, we'll shift

Doreen over there, hire a new typist for this office, and you and I will take turns overseeing the running of the second location. Perhaps Nick has a friend who'd be interested in operating the courier service. I'll ask him when he gets back.''

"You think Doreen's capable of running an entire office on her own?''

"My dear, I think Doreen could run parliament. And if this *does* work out, we'll have to give her a substantial increase in salary.''

"Let's not go wild,'' Louise said. "How substantial?''

"We're currently paying her thirteen. I'd say we give her a rise to seventeen.''

"That sounds fair. But we'll need another typist here and a second typist there. Our overhead's going to double.''

"You're forgetting the income potential. Plus, I've a good mind to approach our various leasing companies and ask for a price break on the equipment. Certainly we'll get a better price on our supplies if we're doubling our orders. I'll sit down this evening and work up some numbers. We may initially have to pump in a bit more capital, but it should only be for the short term—depending, of course, on the sort of rent we'll have to pay. This *is* exciting. We're about to *expand!*''

"You really think we can do it without going up to our ears in debt?''

"Quite sure,'' Rachel said confidently. "We've been running in the black for eight months. You're a good collateral risk now, so we ought to be able to get direct financing from our bank. And you've only a few more months before you're clear of your debt to Tim. Which means you'll easily be able to carry your half of the company liability. It's brilliant.''

"No, you're brilliant,'' Louise told her. "Your father was crazy not to let you work in his bank.''

"He certainly was,'' Rachel agreed. "They're singing quite another tune these days. Although they still fuss at me, wanting to know am I taking my medication? Am I getting enough rest? Am I sure I'm not overdoing? As if I'd forget my medication,'' she scoffed. "Oh, I'd *adore* a stay of two or three months at The Mansions. Honestly. They're dotty, the pair of them. I don't know why I never realized it before.''

"So you're pretty sure we can do this?'' Louise said.

"Oh, I'm very sure, Louise. We're about to branch out. Isn't it thrilling?''

"It's thrilling all right. And scary as hell. I hate being in debt.''

"Stop fussing. All companies have debt, as I told you. It's the way of the financial world. I can't wait to tell Nick! Aren't you going to ring Tim with the good news?"

"It hasn't happened yet," Louise said with caution. "I'll tell him once we know for sure it's going to work out."

"I don't understand you," Rachel said. "I'm always desperate to tell Nick *everything*. But you save things up. Don't you want to tell Tim?"

"I'm not quite in the same position with him that you're in with Nick. You seem to be forgetting he has a wife."

"He wouldn't have if you'd give him the slightest encouragement to get shot of her."

"I'm not going to do that, and now's not the time to discuss it." Louise looked down at the schedules she was typing for Toni. "I've got work to do."

"Sometimes," Rachel said, "I have the feeling you're attempting to bury yourself in what goes on here. You're not taking enough time to yourself."

"I have as much as I need, Rachel."

"Will you come to dinner tomorrow evening?"

Louise thought for a moment, then said, "I can't. We've got that annual report coming in for typing."

"Let Doreen do it and come for dinner."

"No. We'll have to be out of the office for a couple of hours in the afternoon. I can't take off the evening too. We can't afford to lose that much time. Let's make it another evening."

"All right. Saturday."

"Latish Saturday. I'll come right from the office."

"Seven Saturday," Rachel said, "and don't you dare cancel at the last minute. Nick and I will cook up something super. Feel free to invite Tim."

"He can't ever get away on weekends."

"Ask him! He might surprise you."

"Fine. I'll ask him," Louise agreed. "Now let me get back to work. Okay?"

"Testy, testy. Okay. Go back to work." Rachel gave her a meaningful smile.

"What?" Louise asked.

"Nothing. Go back to work."

"What are you up to?"

"Nothing. Go *back* to *work*. I've got to go to the loo." Rachel got up and lifted the hatch, then let it down lightly, humming to herself as she went off along the hall to the ladies' room.

Louise watched her for a moment, then returned to her typing, wondering what Rachel was up to.

CHAPTER
FIFTY-EIGHT

TIM SAID, "I'D LIKE VERY MUCH TO JOIN YOU FOR DINNER Saturday."

"You would?" Louise was surprised. She'd fully expected him to refuse.

"I would," he confirmed. "Actually, I was wondering if I might stop round for a few minutes. There's something I'd like to discuss with you."

Louise looked at the clock. It was almost nine-thirty and she'd just arrived home. "I haven't eaten yet," she said. "Have you?"

"I have, but I'll take you out for a meal."

"I'm not up to it. Come keep me company while I scramble up some eggs or something."

"I'll be there inside of twenty minutes."

"Okay, Tim." She hung up to go look in the refrigerator. There were some chops but she couldn't be bothered. Nothing appealed to her. She looked at the tins on the shelf, then gave up and got out the bread. She started a pot of coffee going, then sliced two pieces of bread from the loaf. Her back ached from almost twelve hours of nonstop typing. And her head ached from the figures Rachel had thrown at her after they'd viewed the Bayswater office block. They were going to go ahead with the expansion, and she and Rachel planned to visit their bank in the morning. Nick did indeed have a friend with a scooter who, he was certain, would be very interested in coming to work for them. "As a matter of fact," Nick had said that afternoon, "there are so many deliveries now that I've been thinkin' we need a second bike for this office. I'm wasting a lot of valuable time comin' back'n' forth. With a second bike, we'll cover each other, like. Less wasted motion.''

"Nick's right," Rachel had said. "I'll factor that into my costs. It's a jolly good idea. With a second bike at this office and another at Bayswater, Nick can work back and forth between the two offices and supervise the courier services.''

"This thing's growing like an amoeba," Louise had said nervously. "Do we really know what we're doing?''

"My darling Louise," Rachel had said imperiously, "empires are not founded by timid souls. Of *course* we know what we're doing. Don't you trust me?''

When Tim arrived and Louise told him of their plans, he echoed Rachel, saying, "I'd trust her judgment, Louise. Rachel's got an exceptional head for business. Is that all you're having?" he asked of her toast and coffee.

"I'm not very hungry. And anyway, I couldn't be bothered cooking an entire meal for myself at this time of night. Would you like some scotch with that coffee?''

"I think not, thank you," he said, holding his mug with both hands. He seemed atypically nervous.

"What's the matter?" she asked, spreading lemon curd on her toast.

"I'm afraid you're about to become embroiled in rather a mess," he said, looking a little pale around the mouth.

"What's happened?" she asked, putting down the toast.

"Moira's decided to sue for divorce and she's named you corespondent. I don't know how she learned about you. I've tried to be very discreet. But I think she guessed some time ago I had formed, shall we say, another interest. I suspect someone saw the four of us together at Wiltons. I'm sorrier than I can say about this, Louise. The last thing on earth I want is to have you dragged through the courts.''

"Is that all?" she said, very relieved. "I thought you were going to tell me something really awful.''

"But this is awful," he said, taken aback by her reaction. He watched her push the hair behind her ears before retrieving her piece of toast and taking a good-sized bite. "Your name will be blackened.''

"Tim, I don't have a 'name.' That's just silly. Your wife can say whatever she likes about me. I don't give a damn. But how do you feel? You're going to be single. Are you glad?"

"Naturally I am," he answered. "I feel badly at not having taken the initiative myself. I was intending to. Time rather got away from me. So you're not undone at the prospect of being labeled the other woman?"

"I could give a care," she said honestly. "It means we'll have more time together, won't we?"

"That we will," he said, venturing a smile. "I take it you're pleased by this turn of events."

"I guess I am." She returned his smile, then leaned across the table to give him a lemony kiss. "I'm used to you," she said. "And to tell the truth, when Rachel was talking about Nick the other day, I actually felt a little jealous because she gets to see him every day. I'm lucky if I see you more than once a week."

"You do love me," he said very softly, pleased.

She looked somewhat embarrassed and said, "I told you that."

"Yes," he said. "I recall the occasion."

"So, okay," she said. "You know I do."

"I'm moving to an hotel," he said. "Moira's to keep the house. I'll have to find time to look at some flats."

"You're going to have your own place."

"It does appear so. And I was wondering if I could possibly persuade you to share a flat with me."

The toast was suddenly hard to swallow. She drank some coffee, her heart rate accelerating fearfully. "I don't know about that, Tim. I'd certainly be glad to help you fix up your new place. But I don't think I want to move."

"I quite understand," he said, visibly disappointed.

"Don't be mad at me," she said, reaching for his hand. "There's so much going on right now I can hardly think straight. Moving's a big step, especially moving in with you. I just don't know. And you haven't lived alone for years. You might find you really like it, that you don't want someone in your way all the time. We'll keep on seeing each other, won't we?"

"I would hope so."

"Well, then, so okay. You'll have your new place and I'll be here. And we'll be able to see each other whenever we want. Can we leave it that way for now?"

"Of course," he said. "I think if you don't mind, I will have a bit of that scotch."

"Sure," she said, and got up to fetch the bottle and a glass. "I'll even have some with you, to celebrate."

"I must say you're taking it exceedingly well."

"Are you kidding?" she laughed. "It makes me sound very grown-up and dangerous: the other woman. I love it. Moira can go to hell. What's she like, anyway?" she asked, taking a swallow of the Glenlivet. Now that Tim was to be free of the woman, Louise felt safe in asking about her.

"Moira?" He took an appreciative sip of the single malt scotch, letting it slide down the back of his throat. "How do I describe her?" he said, looking up at the ceiling. "She has milk white skin and jet black hair, large blue eyes, perfect features. She's very beautiful. It's been, I would say, her undoing. All her life, from earliest childhood, people have been telling Moira how beautiful she is. That knowledge has shaped her into a woman whose entire focus is her own image. She dresses with exquisite good taste. Every last item that goes on her body is chosen with all due deliberation, including her cosmetics. I've known her to spend hours selecting a new shade of lipstick. I'm making her sound shallow," he said. "And she's none of that. She's generous, and devotes a good deal of her time to worthy causes, volunteering many hours a week. But she's embittered and I'm afraid it shows in the set of her mouth. Tiny lines," he said, touching a forefinger to his upper lip. "She plans to have cosmetic surgery to remove them. Moira's very literally terrified of becoming old. Evie loathes her," he said with a laugh. "I only took Moira to see Evie once. Evie rang me at the office the next day to say I was never to bring her again. 'She's a cow,' he bellowed in imitation of the irascible old woman. 'She's a vain cow and I won't have you bringing her round, Timothy John. You'll live to regret the day you took up with that one,' she told me. And she was right."

"I haven't seen Evie in weeks," Louise said. "Maybe we should go see her."

"I'd like that," he said. "I always enjoy Evie. She reduces me to a twelve-year-old in knickers." He chuckled and drank some more of the scotch. "I love you so very dearly, Louise. Will you grow tired of me soon and look for someone younger?"

She got up and came around the table to sit in his lap. "Don't be stupid," she said. "Nobody younger would know all the terrific things you do. You're a very smart fella. That drink went right to my head."

"You've got no head for alcohol," he said. "It always affects you straightaway."

"It turns me amorous," she said, stroking his smooth cheek. "You're very good-looking, you know. How do you know I don't worry you'll find somebody nicer than I am, or richer, or prettier?"

"Do you worry about that?"

"I've thought about it," she allowed.

"You take a lot of studying," he said, slipping his hand up under her skirt to caress the sleek warmth of her inner thigh.

"That's what you like about me," she said, letting one foot slip to the floor as she loosened his tie. "Do you have to call the service?"

"I rang before I left." His hand reached the top of her thigh. She shifted, working on his shirt buttons. "I needn't ring again for at least half an hour."

"Good," she murmured, pulling her sweater off over her head, then getting his shirt open to spread her hands over his chest. "Good." She undid his belt, then stood up to slip off her skirt and underwear. "Hurry up!" she said with a laugh, removing his jacket, then his shirt. "We have to celebrate your emancipation."

He dipped his finger in the Glenlivet then painted circles around her nipples. She shivered as he licked away his artwork.

"No one else," he said, bending her backward over the table, "could possibly excite me the way you do." He poured several drops of the scotch into her navel, then bent his head to dip his tongue into the tiny well.

Her legs dangling, she closed her eyes and gripped the sides of the table.

"We've got great news!" Rachel announced after dinner.

"You're getting married," Louise guessed.

"Yes, we are!" Rachel said happily, an arm around Nick's waist, his arm across her shoulders. A black velvet beret sat atop her curls.

"We're getting married," Nick said, "and we're 'avin' a baby."

"My God!" Louise said, reacting with immediate fear to the announcement. "When?"

"In seven months. June sometime," said Rachel.

"Ah, lovely," Tim said and got up to give her a kiss on each cheek. "That's splendid news." He shook hands with Nick, saying, "Congratulations. Well done, Nick."

"Will you take me on as a patient?" Rachel asked.

"I'd be honored," Tim said. "Ring Monday and we'll schedule you for an appointment. Isn't this splendid!" He looked at Louise to see she appeared somewhat less than pleased.

"The timing could be better," Louise said. "We're just expanding to a second location, in case you'd forgotten."

"By the time the baby's born it'll be well underway," Rachel told her. "Aren't you happy for me, Louise?"

Louise forced a smile. "Of course I am. I am." Why did she feel so frightened? "You'll have to swear to me you'll take very good care of yourself," she told Rachel. "You're going to have to start eating like a normal human being."

"Exactly what I've told 'er," Nick concurred. "No more nibblin' bits of carrot, but proper meals, includin' breakfast. We wanted you two to stand up for us," he said looking first at Louise and then at Tim.

"It would be an honor," Tim said at once.

"I'd love to," said Louise, finding everything suddenly unreal.

"It'll be a quick ceremony at the registry office and a party here afterward," Rachel told them. "Phippy said he and Deborah will come. And mother and father are 'taking the matter under advisement.' On the one hand, Mother's thrilled witless about the baby, but on the other hand she's fairly aghast that Nick's the father. They're trying not to show how appalled they are at having Molly as an in-law housekeeper. It's really very funny."

"What about your mother, Nick?" Louise asked him.

"Aw, me mum's over the moon," he grinned. "Dead tickled, she is. She's already started knittin'. You knit, Louise?"

"Sorry, no." For some reason, Louise felt like weeping. She couldn't determine if she was very happy or terribly sad.

"Right," said Rachel. "Now that the announcements are out of the way, we'll bring on dessert and coffee. We've got a scrumptious chocolate cake from Fortnum's and imported raspberries. Come help me in the kitchen, Nick."

The two of them went off and Tim turned to Louise saying, "You seem decidedly put off."

"I don't know how I feel," she whispered. "I wasn't expecting this. About the baby, I mean. It's kind of frightening."

"It shouldn't be. Rachel's young and healthy. We'll fatten her up a wee bit, start her on a course of multivitamins, and she'll be fine."

"Everything's changing," Louise tried to explain. "Every time I think things are finally beginning to be settled, they change again. I had a letter from my grandmother today telling me another friend of mine's pregnant. Kath? You've heard me talk about her."

"I have," he confirmed. "And are you fearful for her as well?"

"A little."

"You needn't be," he said gently. "No harm will come to them."

She took hold of his hand and looked deep into his eyes, searching for something but unable to identify it. "Will you spend the night with me?" she asked. "You could leave my number with the service. I mean, it won't matter, will it, now that I'm officially the other woman?"

"I'd be delighted," he said, giving her hand a squeeze. "I've always wanted an opportunity to sleep at your side."

"You're hopelessly romantic," she said. "You know that?"

"Would you prefer I weren't?"

"I like you the way you are."

"And I you," he said. "Are you thinking of your sister?"

Tears came to her eyes and she let her head tilt onto his shoulder.

"It's a happy time, Louise," he said, lifting the hair back from her face. "Don't allow old pain to blind you. Rachel's going to be perfectly fine."

What did she feel? she asked herself. Was it possible that the slight interior stabbing might be envy? She'd told so many people so many times that she didn't want a child that she'd left herself no room for the possibility of changing her mind. And what was this? She had no intention of changing her mind. She didn't want children. *What* did she feel?

┴

In bed much later that night Louise said, "I can't help worrying about Rachel and what she's doing. Here we've made the commitment to expand the business and she goes and gets herself pregnant. We've got months of hard work ahead. This is no time for her to be having a baby."

"It's a perfect time for her to be having a baby," he disagreed softly. "Don't lose sight of the human factor, Louise. Rachel's almost twenty-six. She's had a truly difficult time of it for most of those twenty-six years. She and Nick have found something very good together. It has nothing to do with your business arrangements. This is *personal.* It's her life, her happiness. I should've thought you'd be happy for your friend.''

''What if something goes wrong? If anything happened to her, I don't know what I'd do.''

''Nothing's going to happen to her. You have my most solemn promise I'll take the very best care of Rachel.''

''You promise?'' she asked, curling up against his side.

''I promise.''

''I love Rachel,'' she said quietly.

''I know you do, Louise.''

''I don't want anything to happen to her.''

''All that'll happen is she'll be delivered of a perfectly healthy infant sometime in June. One way or another she'll become a mother. It's wonderful.''

''What d'you mean 'one way or another'?''

''I suspect, given her size, she'll be one of my scheduled cesareans. But that shouldn't offer any difficulties.''

''You can tell that just from looking at her?''

''I'm guessing,'' he said. ''But she has a very narrow pelvic structure. I'm merely saying it wouldn't surprise me, upon examination, to discover that a cesarean's in order. Now you, on the other hand, have a perfectly splendid pelvic structure.'' He placed his hand in the cradle between her hipbones. ''You'd have no difficulty whatever in delivering, should you ever choose to have a child. A lovely long birth canal, good bone structure.''

''No kidding,'' she said, imagining herself laboring to push out something the size of a basketball. ''Well, that's good to know, I suppose.''

''No charge for the consultation,'' he quipped.

''I have to be up early. I've got a full day's work tomorrow.''

''But tomorrow's Sunday. Surely you're not going to spend the entire day working. I'd rather hoped we'd spend some time together.''

''I can't, Tim. If I don't stay on top of it the work'll start backing up and before we know it the place'll be chaotic the way it used to be when Jill and Susan ran it.''

''We must avoid chaos at all costs,'' he said with such irony that she didn't know how to respond.

''Are you joking?'' she asked him.

"I am teasing," he told her. "I admire your diligence. And sundry other of your attributes."

"Let's go to sleep."

"Thank you for this," he said. "It's been a very long time since I shared anyone's bed."

"Every time you say something like that it makes me want to cry."

"Ah, don't do that. I was simply stating a rather dismal fact, not making a plea for sympathy."

"I know. That's why I feel like crying."

"Shut your eyes and go to sleep," he said, holding his hand lightly over her eyes. "Don't waste your tears on me."

"You swear she'll be all right?"

"I will do everything in my power to guarantee that." He eased her over against him and held her. "Now go to sleep."

She dreamed again of the rape and made herself wake up. Careful not to disturb Tim, she slipped out of bed and went to the bathroom. Then she came back and sat for some time on the floor beside the bed watching him sleep in the dim glow from the streetlight outside. She thought of Rachel describing the first night she'd spent with Nick, of how ecstatic she'd been at waking to find him in her bed. Louise gazed at Tim and felt guilty and a little sad; the two emotions merged to tug at her insides. I love you, she thought, studying his handsome, sleeping features. Why did it feel so dangerous?

Her feet cold, she climbed back into bed after a while, fitting herself to Tim's warmth. "I love you," she whispered, then settled in to sleep again secure in the lee of his body.

CHAPTER
FIFTY-NINE

FROM THE MOMENT THEY SIGNED THE LEASE FOR THE NEW premises it seemed they were constantly on the run. On weekends Nick worked in the Bayswater office, building a hatched counter and shelves.

Rachel was setting up the books and arranging contracts to lease the machines. Louise traveled the underground back and forth between the two offices, interviewing typists, being on site to sign for the delivery of the equipment as it arrived, and in between times handling, with Doreen, the work as it came into the Shepherd's Bush office.

The second Wordworks held an open house wine-and-cheese party on the fifteenth of December for the tenants of the Bayswater block, several of whom, including the administrator of the American oil company where Grace worked, sent plants and congratulatory cards. On the morning of the sixteenth, with Doreen and a junior typist in place, the office opened its doors for business and a short queue immediately formed.

Louise was on the telephone to Doreen at least three times a day, and when there was a backlog of work, she either got Robbie, one of the new couriers, to run her to Bayswater or hurried over on the underground to lend a hand. She felt she was in constant motion, even when she was seated in a restaurant with Tim or attempting to relax for an evening at the movies.

Instead of going home from the office she went more and more often directly to a movie. She'd sit in the dark in the stalls and let her mind go blank as she gazed at the screen. It was comforting. She came to look forward to each day's end so she could hurry to some theater to see *Becket,* or *Dr. Strangelove;* she saw *The Pumpkin Eater, The Americanization of Emily, The Servant, A Hard Day's Night.* Anything, just so she didn't have to go home and see the condition of the flat. Dust was accumulating everywhere and she resented the time it took to carry the bed linens and her dirty clothes to the Laundromat. It was time she could be spending seeing a movie, time spent letting her mind float among ideas that were in no way related to her reality.

When she lay down at night her brain began reviewing a lengthy list of worrisome items: her portion of the Wordworks' debt, her inadequate salary, the absence of any savings; Rachel's pregnancy; a near-miss accident Nick had had with the scooter. Her anxiety was heightened by dreams in which she was summoned to the hospital late at night only to find Rachel strapped to a table in a corridor; her eyes sunken and darkly shadowed, her body writhing and twisting as a baby emerged. The urgency Louise had been feeling for several years was growing worse. Her sleep was restless, nightmare-filled, and she began awakening at least twice a night, headachy and sweating, to go stand barefoot on the bathroom floor, letting the cold tiles bring down her body temperature.

When she complained to Rachel one afternoon in March about her lack of time and about the state of the flat, Rachel said, "Why didn't you tell me? What you need is a char, you ninny. I think mine has a free day. I'll speak to her. You'll see. It'll make a world of difference."

So Louise became the once-a-week employer of Hazel, who whirled in at eight every Thursday morning and spent the day cleaning. She even took the sheets up the road to the Laundromat, thereby relieving Louise of that chore and allowing her even more time to indulge in secret trips to the movies. Upon request, Hazel would leave Louise a meal that only required heating in the oven. It helped. But Louise still felt hounded by unseen crowds and by a perpetual lack of money.

Tim rented a furnished flat on Lowndes Street in Knightsbridge; the divorce was going through uncontested. Rachel's pregnancy scarcely showed—just a slight swelling of her abdomen. She radiated well-being and hummed over her account books, periodically showing Louise and Bridget, their new typist, the latest outfit Molly had knitted up for the baby. Nick was building a cradle with rockers, spending hours of his free time lovingly carving designs into the sanded oak before applying several coats of glossy white enamel paint to his creation. One of the bedrooms was in the process of being converted to a nursery and whenever Louise visited the house in Radnor Walk Rachel took her upstairs to show her how it was coming along. The walls were done in pale yellow, the furniture was all white, including a rocking chair with a cane seat Nick had found in Mr. Greeley's back room.

Louise was afraid to buy anything in advance of the baby's birth. Admittedly it was superstitious, but she had the idea it would be bad luck to purchase any of the lovely little garments she was suddenly noticing in shop windows. She covertly watched Rachel for even the slightest sign that she might be unwell, but Rachel was blossoming into an entirely new version of herself. She gave up the heavy black eyeliner and pale frosted lipstick and most days went without makeup at all. Her hair growing long, she wore what appeared to be an endless series of brightly colored crocheted berets pulled down low, to keep the lengthening curls out of her way, and she developed a fondness for flowing Indian cotton print dresses and what looked like riding boots. She read every book she could find on childbearing and periodically grabbed Louise's hand and pressed it to her belly, ecstatically saying, "Feel! It's kicking."

Louise felt the movements inside the small hard mound of her friend's belly with a mix of wonderment and alarm. "Doesn't it hurt?" she asked, concerned.

"It's lovely," Rachel said. "It's the most wonderful feeling I've ever had. Tim says it's going to be a small baby, but it's coming along brilliantly. Who'd have imagined I'd become accustomed to regular internal examinations?" she laughed. "I climb up on that table as if it's nothing. And he's so kind. Why don't you *marry* him, Louise? I swear if I didn't have Nickie I'd fling myself at Tim. He's such a super doctor. You should see all the women in the waiting room. Most of us are pregnant and we talk while we're waiting, and every one of us thinks he's the most heavenly man alive. And here you are, keeping the poor man on tenterhooks. I swear I don't understand you."

"He's not suffering," Louise said. "He's enjoying his new flat. If anything, he's positively chipper these days."

"You want to take care," Rachel warned. "He might get tired of waiting for you to make up your mind."

"If that happens, it happens," Louise said. "I've already got enough on my plate. Sometimes I wish I'd never made Jill and Susan that offer. I feel like I'm on a treadmill."

"Oh, dear. What you need is some time off."

"When would you suggest I take it?" Louise snapped.

"Don't bite my head off, Louise. You could take a few days off any time at all. We'd manage."

"We'd fall behind."

"We wouldn't," Rachel said calmly. "We could always get in a temp for a day or two or three. You look tired. It might not be a bad idea for you to take a break. You're working far too hard."

"When we're out of debt I'll take some time off. Right now, we're working for the bank."

"Of course we're not," Rachel argued. "We're building equity in a thriving limited company. Why, we could sell the company next week and realize a profit. Don't you understand what good will is *worth?* We're very successful, Louise. By my estimation we'll be ready to branch out to a third location within six months. And I think we ought to start considering possible locations fairly soon. As a matter of fact, I've come up with rather a brilliant idea.''

"God!'' Louise said. "I'm afraid to ask.''

"No, it's brilliant,'' Rachel said with certainty. "Nick thinks so, too. Once we've got a third location established, we set up the means whereby individuals who want to open a Wordworks service center could purchase a franchise from us. We'd get the franchisee set up and organized, then they'd buy the business from us in monthly increments. That way we could have offices all over London, even expand to other cities like Birmingham and Manchester. We've structured a very efficient operation. It works. And the bookkeeping's essentially very simple. Someone approaches us. We enter into a contract. We get them set up, and they purchase the office from us. It's sheer genius,'' she congratulated herself.

"You amaze me,'' Louise said, both impressed and wearied by Rachel's vision. "It's a fantastic idea. But I'll probably drop dead of exhaustion long before we ever get to opening a third location.''

"You ninny!'' Rachel chided. "The whole point of the franchising is to reduce the workload on us. We'll have the original two or three offices up and running with you and me overseeing managers in each place. We'll be *corporate,* Louise, supervising from on high, as it were. The managers will report to us, and you and I will concentrate on the broader picture. We'll get into leasing equipment on a larger scale, purchasing supplies for broader discounts. And the franchises will acquire everything through us. We'll have personnel to tend to the nuts and bolts of the daily operations. *And* we get a percentage of all the profits!''

"It sounds phenomenal, but for now let's concentrate on the two offices we do have. I'd like us to get to the point where I'm able to draw a halfway decent salary each week instead of having to plow money back in order to cover the bank loan and the operating costs. I hesitate now about buying even a new pair of shoes.''

"Why didn't you *say* something?'' Rachel said. "There's no need for you to be skimping. There's sufficient income for you to be drawing more money. I simply assumed you had enough.''

"Well, I don't,'' Louise said tiredly. "I never have had. Until I had the bright idea to buy this place I was withdrawing an extra couple of pounds every week from my savings account. But since I had to put up my savings to buy the business I've had nothing to fall back on. You keep telling me we're in the black, but I'm not seeing any of it. And now with the second office open I don't see how I'll ever see any of it."

"I'm sorry, Louise. Is that why you've been putting in such impossible hours?"

"Of course it is. I assumed you were making up the difference for your own expenses out of your trust income."

"I am, I do," Rachel said. "But it can be changed. I'm going to rework this at once so that the business starts paying you a better salary."

"But that's not fair. Then I'll be making more than you, and we'll no longer be equal partners."

"I'll increase both our salaries," Rachel said calmly, "give us each an additional, say, five pounds a week. Will that be enough?"

"It'll help a lot. Can we afford it?"

"We can. I'll simply add it to the accounts payable and make the accounts receivable tally accordingly. I expect Nick could probably use a rise too. This is entirely my fault, Louise. I'm sorry. I've been forgetting that you and Nick aren't in the same position as I."

"It's nobody's fault. But if we can take a little more out of the company without putting ourselves in any kind of jeopardy, then for Pete's sake, let's do it."

"You should have said something. I had no idea."

"Don't take it so personally, Rachel. Everything's been getting me down lately."

"That's because you're overworked and need some time off. If you don't take a few days I'll have a word with Tim, tell him to take you away somewhere."

"Is that a threat?" Louise laughed.

"Oh, dear. Isn't it?"

"He's been trying to get me to go somewhere for a weekend for months, kiddo. Telling Tim won't do you a bit of good."

"You ought to marry him," Rachel said seriously. "I would, if I were you."

"What makes you think he's asked me?"

"I'd stake my life on it. He has, hasn't he?"

With a sigh, Louise admitted, "He has. About sixty times."

"Then why won't you?"

"I can't. And besides, he's not divorced yet."

"He will be soon."

"I'll worry about it when he is."

"Why on God's earth do you think I brought the two of you together?" Evie bellowed. "Because," she answered her own question, "he needed a respite from that pretty fool he married. And because you needed the comfort and security he could offer you. Jaysus, but I never thought you'd go the route you have, Louise. You're miles off course, darling," she said more temperately. "What's happening to you?"

"I don't know," Louise answered. "Evie, would you do a reading for me?"

Evie regarded her through the smoke of her Sweet Afton for some moments. Then, crushing out her cigarette, she said, "Fetch me the cards from the drawer in the sideboard," and cleared the area in front of her on the dining table. "Shuffle them until it's time to stop," she told Louise, her eyes focusing on the near distance as Louise began shuffling the cards. "Concentrate!" she said sharply, placing one surprisingly large hand firmly on Louise's shoulder. "Settle," she said. "Settle. Come back into yourself, girl."

Louise paid attention to the cards. It was the first time since they'd met that she'd asked Evie to read for her. The worn cards slipped back and forth in her hands, their corners slightly frayed. When she stopped, Evie said, "Cut the pack."

Evie picked up the closest pile and held the cards with both hands for several moments, her eyes fusing to Louise's. "You've gone backwards," she said, her eyes traveling to the cards as she began laying them out on the table. "So much apprehension, too much. You've taken to holding too much to yourself. Everything here is in twos. Past and future. Pairs. There's a great ugly pair from the past. Do you know now who they might be?"

Louise shook her head, unable to think.

"The one," said Evie, her mouth curling in disgust, "is thick as mud. The other has hidden kindness. Look to him for an answer, darling girl." Evie laid down two cards. "There's a journey here of some great distance. It's off down the road a ways, but it's here." She tapped one card with her forefinger. "It's here," she said. "And one, two, three, four men." She laid the cards down more quickly now. "Four," she repeated. "And the last will be your salvation." She turned another card and slowly placed it face up on the far side of the others. "Mind how you go, Louise," she cautioned. "A child is waiting."

Feeling a sudden boundless despair, Louise began to cry. Reaching into her pocket for a tissue, she tried to laugh at her own foolishness but couldn't bring it off. "I never used to be afraid, Evie," she said, reaching to hold the old woman's hand. "Now I worry about everything. Everyone keeps telling me what a fool I am not to grab Tim, but I *can't*. It isn't the right time."

"No," Evie agreed, setting aside the cards, "it isn't. But take heed of the time, darling. It's passing ever more quickly. And Tim's more aware than you might think of his age. He's at a point when he's feeling its bite. You keep him young, don't you see. You give him all he missed those years with that vacuous bitch. Had I not felt the rightness of it, I'd never have brought the two of you together."

"I know that. But maybe I can't give him what he needs, Evie. I don't even know what *I* need. I want to be able to relax, but I can't, not even when I'm sleeping. I know Rachel's all right, but I can't stop worrying that something might go wrong. And Nick just narrowly missed being hit by that car. He could've been *killed*. As it was, he got badly scraped and bruised in the fall. I'm so afraid for everyone. Why is that?"

"There's only so much you can control, my darling girl. You've lost sight of that. And you've taken on enormous burdens, but not unwisely. The reward will be there for you. You're having a crisis of faith. You've discovered things are not what they seem, and it's pulling you down. But many things *are* indeed what they seem. Go off with Tim when he asks you again. Take the time to know the man," she counseled strongly. "You'll never regret it. Step outside your life for a bit, Louise. You've lost sight of your role."

"I'm so tired," Louise admitted. "I'm starting to feel old."

Evie emitted one of her barking laughs. "You're coming on to twenty-three. You're a *child*! In another fifty-five years you'll think back to this day and if you've a brain in your head you'll have the grace to be embarrassed." Caringly she patted the back of Louise's hand, saying, "You're needing to rest, darling. *Take the time.* You'll always regret it if you don't. And don't ever be misled by Timothy John's soft spokenness and quiet ways. He's got a fine temper."

"I know. I've seen it a time or two."

"And he's a man, don't you know. You don't ever want to be forgetting the role their pride plays. It's a powerful and ridiculous thing, that pride, but men have it and Tim's no exception. He's the sort who'll turn his back rather than be played for a fool.''

"I'd never do that."

"The waiting game can make a man feel the fool, girl. He's put years of precious time into you. It costs you nothing to give a wee bit back and in the process sweeten the atmosphere. I've loved Timothy John since he was a lad. He was a dolt to take up with that vain cow. He's paid with his heart. And you in your way are paying with yours. Watch how you go, Louise, and mind what I say.''

"I will, Evie." Louise sat forward across the table to kiss the old woman's cheek. "Thank you for reading the cards."

"It's your right to be happy, darling. Somewhere along the line you've forgotten that. Do what you know to be right and you'll never go too far wide of the mark.''

Upon arriving home, Louise sat down to call Tim. The phone rang three, four, five times and she was about to give up when he answered, sounding out of breath.

"You sound as if you've been running."

"Just came charging up the stairs to answer the phone. I hoped it might be you."

"Well it is. How are you?"

"I'm better for hearing your voice. And how are you?"

"I've just come from seeing Evie."

"Ah! And how is the old dear?"

"She's wonderful." She had a choice, she thought. She could steal a couple of hours and go to see a movie, hide out in the dark for a while. Or she could heed Evie's advice. "Tim, I was wondering . . . Could I come over?"

"Here? Now?"

"Bad idea?"

"No, no," he said. "A lovely idea, super. Would you like me to come fetch you in the car?"

"No. I'll throw my toothbrush in a bag and grab a taxi."

"You'll stop the night?" He sounded astonished.

"Maybe the whole weekend, if you've got nothing planned."

"Wonderful! I've stocked up on food, as luck would have it."

"You really don't mind? I thought I'd take the weekend off for a change."

"I'll come round to fetch you right now," he said eagerly. "Bring a change of clothes. We'll take a drive to the country on Sunday, get some fresh air. What a lovely surprise, Louise! I'll be there in twenty minutes." He rang off and she put down the receiver, moved by the realization of how very little it took to make him happy. Evie was right, as usual. Maybe she'd start taking a weekend a month to be with Tim. She'd still be able to see one or two movies during the week.

On impulse, she called Rachel. "I wanted to let you know I'll be at Tim's for the weekend, in case you're looking for me."

"Oh, you naughty girl!" Rachel laughed. "You're actually taking some time off. See there! Nick's just fallen over in a dead faint. Why don't you come by tomorrow night, the two of you? Nick and I are going to try making beef burgundy. We'll let you sample our efforts."

"I'll see what Tim says. I've got to go now. He's on his way over."

"I want you to remember that we're discussing a man who spends every day examining naked women." With a wild laugh, Rachel said, "That ought to give you something to think about."

"You're a fruitcake," Louise laughed.

"Yes, but a blissfully happy fruitcake. Let me know if you're coming tomorrow."

"I will."

Louise put some clothes in a straw carrier bag and was waiting downstairs when Tim pulled up.

"This is wonderful," he said, hurrying to open the passenger door for her. "I've told the service to ring me only in case of an emergency."

After throwing her bag on the back seat she straightened to look at him. His eyes were very alive, without a hint of sadness. She touched his cheek, then kissed him. "I'm glad to see you."

Exuberantly he hugged her, saying, "I'm always glad to see you. You may never know how much."

"I think I do." She kissed him again, and said, "Let's get out of here."

CHAPTER
S I X T Y

THE FOLLOWING MONDAY MORNING THE OFFICE WAS BUSY. Louise was getting caught up on the work left over from Friday; Bridget was at the Xerox machine; Rachel as usual was at work on the books. Robbie and Nick were both out on deliveries, and there was a short queue waiting for service. Louise had just finished sending a telex when a woman walked into the office and, ignoring the queue, approached the counter. Louise smiled automatically, first because the woman looked so totally out of place among the secretaries and typists, and secondly because for a few moments Louise thought she was Vivien Leigh. Which was absurd. What would Vivien Leigh be doing in their office? But still, the woman bore a remarkable resemblance to the actress. She was incredibly beautiful, with shoulder-length black hair and an exquisite heart-shaped face, eyes of a blue so deep they were almost purple. And when she spoke it was in a throaty voice that had everyone's immediate attention.

"I'm looking," she said, "for Louise Parker."

Louise said, "Hi. That's me. Can I help you with something?"

The woman smiled—no more than a tipping up of the corners of her mouth—and her head tilted slightly to one side. "I hadn't realized you were American."

"Canadian," Louise corrected her, absolutely fascinated. The woman's makeup was subtle and flawless. Her suit looked like Chanel. Small pearl earrings graced her earlobes. Her beauty was as intriguing as anything Louise had ever seen. She knew she was staring, but she simply couldn't help herself.

"Canadian," the woman repeated. "Oh, I see." She said it as if that made some sort of difference to whatever she was thinking.

"Can I help you?" Louise said again, aware that everyone in the place was following their exchange.

"I doubt it. I'm Moira Kelly," she said with chilly authority. "I merely stopped by to have a look at the slut who's been sleeping with my husband.''

Louise felt as if a pair of cymbals had clashed together inside her chest. Her smile felt stitched into place, as if tiny tucks were holding her lips to her cheeks. She couldn't speak.

"I have nothing to say to you," Moira Kelly said, already turning away. "I simply wanted to have a look at you. It was scarcely worth my time." And with that she left.

Louise stood rooted in place, sensing everyone's eyes on her. She felt as if she'd been stripped naked and wanted only to get away. Lifting the hatch, she fled down the hall to the ladies' room, where she closed herself into one of the stalls and sat down, stunned, on the lid of the toilet seat.

All she could think of was what a fool she'd been, and how stupid. Tim's wife had never been real to her, had never been an actual walking, talking person who might have the audacity to make her feelings known in public. "God!" Louise whispered, sitting with her arms wrapped around herself, utterly humiliated. Moira Kelly had called her a slut. The word was like an electric eel in Louise's brain, slithering through the coils in her skull and leaving a charged slime in its wake. "God!" She wanted to be a thousand miles away.

"Are you all right?" Rachel asked through the door.

"No," Louise said hoarsely.

"I didn't imagine you would be," Rachel said. "That was quite something. Straight out of a drawing room comedy."

"Comedy?" Louise got up and opened the stall door. "You thought that was funny? The most embarrassing thing that's ever happened to me, and you thought it was funny?"

"Oh, Louise," Rachel smiled, "it was pure farce. She's a pathetic middle-aged former beauty."

"I didn't see anything 'former' about her."

"Admittedly she's well put together. But it was just theater, Louise. Everyone's laughing like mad over it."

"Laughing at me, you mean."

"No, laughing at the scene. You mustn't take it so seriously."

"Are you kidding? She comes into the office and tells everyone I'm the slut who's been sleeping with her husband, and I'm not supposed to take it seriously?"

"Well, that was rather harsh," Rachel conceded. "But taken overall, it was strictly Noel Coward. Honestly."

"I feel like a complete imbecile," Louise said, going to the sink to splash cold water on her face. "And I can't believe this is you. A year ago you'd have been in there"—she pointed to the stall—"hiding with me."

"A year ago I was someone else," Rachel said mildly. "People change. You have. A year ago you'd have been laughing your head off. You really mustn't allow this to upset you. Try to see it from the outside."

"I can't," Louise said dully. "I was on the inside."

"Come back to the office and try to put it out of your mind. One day, you'll see, you'll look back on this and howl. I mean to say, did you *see* that outfit? Chanel with rickrack, and white gloves, patent leather court shoes, and that *hat!*" Rachel laughed. "You should've seen your face! You looked as if you were seeing an alien from another planet. Come back to the office," she said again, crossing the room to put an encouraging hand on Louise's arm. "I promise you no one'll say a word against you."

"I wish I could go home," Louise said childishly. "I feel like hiding."

"You can't do that, Louise. You've been involved with Tim for a long time now and you've known all along he had a wife. Today you had a singular opportunity to meet her. The poor woman must've rehearsed her lines for weeks. It was a shockingly bad performance, purely for effect. I got the impression she really didn't give a damn. She was merely doing it because somewhere, somehow it was expected of her. Think of it this way: It could've been a great deal worse."

"That's true," Louise agreed, still shocked every time she recalled Moira Kelly's throaty voice calling her a slut. "But still, it was awful."

"Come back in laughing, Louise," Rachel advised. "Don't let anyone know it bothered you. If you make a drama of it, it'll become one. If you treat it all as a joke so will everyone else."

"When did you suddenly become so worldly-wise?" Louise asked.

"When one wears the sort of gear I do every day, one becomes adept at turning insults into jokes. Do you think I've been unaware all these years of how people look at me? I may be crazy, but I'm not stupid. Now, give me a hug, put on your best face, and come along."

Still not entirely convinced of Rachel's logic, she went with her back to the office, and entered smiling. Bridget burst out laughing, saying, "Wasn't she just too ridiculous?"

"It was pretty funny all right," Louise agreed, amazed by the general reaction. No one was going to point a finger or hurl nasty accusations at her. Breathing deeply in relief, she went to deal with the next person in the queue. She decided, as she looked over the several pages of typing to be done, that she wouldn't mention the incident to Tim. But she would in future listen more closely when he spoke of his soon-to-be former wife. It stung every time she recalled Moira Kelly's self-satisfied expression when she'd seen her insult strike home. Louise had been publicly branded as someone not much better than her mother. It sickened her to think about it.

Rachel worked at home during the final weeks of her pregnancy. And Louise, fearful in spite of Tim's as well as Rachel's insistence that she was perfectly well, phoned at least twice a day to hear from Rachel herself that all was indeed well.

"You're becoming worse than my mother," Rachel laughed. "Aside from the fact that I look rather like an ocean liner coming in to dock, I'm in top form. I never dreamed you'd turn into such a fussbudget, Louise. What on earth's got into you lately?"

"I can't help it," Louise told her. "I have to be sure you're okay."

"The only thing that bothers me is not being able to make love," Rachel confided. "We've had to stop. It's become a physical impossibility."

Embarrassed by her own ignorance, Louise said, "I'd assumed you'd stopped months ago."

"Don't be a nit! There was no need to stop. We simply worked out new positions. I thought you had more imagination than that."

"It's not harmful to the baby?" Louise had an unpleasant vision of the infant awash in the fluids generated by lovemaking.

"Not a bit. It kicks up a storm, I'll admit. But parents have rights, too, you know."

"I didn't know."

"You should try it. Having a baby, I mean. Aside from the discomfort of carrying the weight and feeling as if your ribs are splitting, it's lovely being in the club. People give you their seats on buses and the underground, and they smile at you. Everyone's so much friendlier. I expect I'll do it again quite quickly."

"When will you ever have time for the business?"

"Baby's are portable, Louise. And there are such things as nannies. I'm well aware we have a business to run. Stop worrying so! I'm not going to abandon you.''

''I told you. I can't help it. Anyway, as long as you're all right, I'll get back to work.''

''As you know perfectly well, the delivery's scheduled for the morning of June twelfth. Until then I'll be right here, making sure the books stay current. Feel free to come see for yourself. Visitors are always welcome.''

''I'll stop by tomorrow on my way home from the office.''

''Good. Now go away and leave me be. I'm bringing the accounts receivable up to date.'' With a laugh, Rachel said goodbye.

Louise told herself Rachel was right; so was Tim. But every morning and afternoon she had to hear Rachel's voice, to make sure nothing had gone wrong. During those last days before the baby was due, Louise found herself thinking of how much Rachel had changed, and of the wedding in particular, and of how adeptly Rachel had handled everything: her parents holding themselves apart from the proceedings; Philip and his wife, Deborah, caught in the middle with Tim and Louise; and Nick making sure his mother didn't also hold herself apart. It had been a strained ceremony, mercifully brief. But once everyone got to the house on Radnor Walk and had been urged by Rachel to have something to drink, the barriers had come down, at least temporarily.

The house had been crowded with friends, both Rachel's and Nick's, and the plentiful champagne had been the leveler. The hi-fi had played nonstop while the catering staff circulated with trays of hot and cold hors d'ouevres, and in short order—aside from the differences in accent—it was hard to tell who belonged to the bride's or the groom's set. Rachel and Nick, both in white, had formed a human bridge to span the classes. Nick had danced with Rachel's mother. Mr. Townsend-Post had actually danced with Molly. Rachel danced with everyone, and Louise stood in awe at the completeness of Rachel's transformation from someone afraid of asserting herself to a woman of happy certainty.

Louise wished she had her own former certainty. Having taken on the business, she felt she'd lost some vital element of her basic confidence. She knew she could do the work; she was as competent as she'd ever been; but she couldn't envisage, as Rachel so readily could, a point in time when she'd be free of the burden of her obligations. Matters weren't helped by her obsessive concern with Rachel's well-being, her endless scraping to make her salary cover her expenses, or her periodic efforts to unscramble the puzzling clues in Evie's last reading. She scanned the letters from home in the absurd hope of finding some additional enlightenment. And that, she told herself repeatedly, was a waste of time. But then she received a letter from her grandmother, with an enclosed clipping from the Toronto *Star,* telling of how Aldo and Anthony and two other young men had been arrested for extortion. In a variation on the old protection racket, the four had been forcing local restaurants to purchase their produce from the DiStasio market in return for the right to do business without fear of having their customers harassed or their windows smashed. The four were currently awaiting trial.

"Frankie must be very upset," her grandmother wrote. "But since it's been so long since we were in touch, I didn't feel quite right about calling him up. He's been completely cleared of any charges. It seems that Aldo was the ringleader, and apparently the whole thing had been going on for quite some time. The police set up an undercover operation and arrested Aldo and Anthony on the spot. All four of them are being held in the Don Jail pending trial. Bob says they'll probably get very stiff sentences."

Louise wasn't surprised by the news. She'd always expected Aldo to wind up in trouble of one kind or another. But she read and reread her grandmother's letter and the clipping, wondering if Raffie knew, and if he did, what he thought of the whole thing.

Her resolution to spend more time with Tim failed after the visit from his wife. She began to feel guilty about her role in the breakup of the marriage, even though Tim assured her it had died long before he'd ever met her. She lied and said the business kept her too busy to see him more than once or twice a week. He seemed to accept that, but she noticed the old sadness creeping back into his eyes. She felt powerless to change anything.

She again took refuge at the movies: *The Collector, The Pawnbroker, A Thousand Clowns, Juliet of the Spirits, Dr. Zhivago, The Spy Who Came in from the Cold.* In the stolen hours she studied the behavior of strange celluloid heroes and heroines, finding a logic on film that too often escaped her in reality. She adored the little boy in *A Thousand Clowns* and hummed "Yes, Sir, That's My Baby" as she fed papers into the Xerox machine or typed annual reports. New players took center stage in her dreams and she viewed these nighttime events with an ongoing curiosity, wondering if

Rod Steiger or Richard Burton or Claire Bloom might make an un-scheduled appearance.

✦

Curled up in the armchair in her bathrobe, Louise sipped at some of Tim's Glenlivet, so tired she thought she might fall asleep right there. Tim sat in the chair opposite, a glass of scotch held in both hands, his legs extended straight in front of him, and watched her as she stared unblinking at the fire.

"Once the baby's safely born," he said, "you should take some time away."

"That's the time when I'll be most needed," she replied, her eyes still on the fire. She wanted to see *Darling* with Julie Christie, and hoped to be able to get away from the office at a reasonably early hour the next day. "With Rachel out for at least a month I'll be up to my ears in work."

"You're becoming driven," he said soberly, even somewhat angrily. She looked over at him. He was very good-looking, attractive enough to be a film star. His voice now and again reminded her of Richard Harris. "The baby and that business have become your sole focus. It's not healthy, Louise. Everyone needs time away."

"You don't seem to understand that everything I have is tied up in the business. I can't *afford* to take any time off."

"Then come away with me. We'll go somewhere for a fortnight. Italy, perhaps."

"And you'll pay for everything."

"I'd happily allow you to pay were that possible," he said equably, crossing his ankles. "Nick manages to deal with very similar circumstances with admirable aplomb. He pays for what he can and, with no loss of self-esteem that I'm aware of, allows Rachel to pay for the rest."

She thought about that for a moment, remembering how guilty she'd felt for pushing Nick and Rachel at each other, then said, "That's true. But I don't think I can be like Nick." Nick and Rachel had never once displayed any anger toward her, had never accused her of meddling in their lives. God! She'd taken incredible liberties.

"The West Indies perhaps," he said. "Or the Bahamas."

"Don't tempt me," she said with a smile, almost able to smell the heavy tropical air.

"I'm not trying to tempt you. It's an outright invitation. We both deserve a break. I'm tired of Moira's imbecilic demands, of her impossible

claims on my income, and of constantly being on call. And you're working yourself to the point of collapse. By the end of June the decree will be
final. Let's take a holiday. Wouldn't you like some sunshine, Louise? God
knows, I would.''

"I'll think about it. Okay?" She *really* wanted to see *Darling,* and hoped
nothing would come up to keep her late at the office.

"Think hard about it. And in the meantime I'll get some brochures.
One way or another I'm going to take some time.''

"Are you saying you'd go alone?" She studied his face, which was half
in shadow, trying to get some feeling for what he was really saying. But
she was distracted by the pleasing shape of his mouth and the squared
aspect of his chin. It was a pity she was too tired to make love. He always
attracted her. He was like a film that played only for her benefit.

"If I must. It's been a long tiresome year. I'm also sick of that flat and
of living with someone else's furniture. Once the decree is final I intend
to find something unfurnished. While you're thinking about whether or
not to come away with me, think about a change in our living arrangements too. Neither of us is entirely happy with the flats we do have. So
let's make a change. Come help me find a place we can both live in.''

"I would like to move," she said, looking around. The living room
was in need of painting. The storage space was inadequate, as was the
kitchen. "It's such a big step.''

"Not really, Louise. Either you want to be with me or you don't. It's
very simple. I'd like to be settled. To be candid, I'm finding the sheer
transience of the current setup somewhat disturbing. I want a home and
I'd like to have you in it. I'm tired of rented chintz with overstuffed
armchairs and dried floral arrangements.''

"I need to think about it." The mere idea of moving exhausted her.

"I must check in with the service," he said, glancing at his wristwatch.

"Sure. Help yourself." She sat staring at the glowing embers of the
fire, thinking about what he'd said. She did want to move, and she did
want a holiday. But who'd supervise the two offices if she wasn't there?
What if some problem arose that neither Doreen nor Bridget could handle? Rachel would be around, and so would Nick. Maybe it would be
possible.

"I'm going to have to go," Tim said, putting down the receiver. "I've
got a possible premature delivery." He seemed atypically agitated.

"You're getting fed up with me, aren't you?" she asked, rising to see him to the door. She was going to have to start paying closer attention to the things he said. It alarmed her to think he might give up on her and let her go.

"I'm getting fed up with things in general," he said, "but not with you, Louise. The problem is, dear girl, I want more—more time, more of you, more of a life. I love you and I want to do things for you, but for a variety of reasons you find it close to impossible to allow that. I understand. But I'm rather worn out from doing battle with you for the simplest things. It's not a lifetime commitment on your part if you agree to go abroad with me."

"I know that."

"Then stop fighting and say you'll come along. And say you'll make the time to look at flats with me. I want a life, Louise. And I want you in it. Sometimes, you know, words simply cannot convey all they're meant to. I have to battle my inclination to accept the status quo because I believe we could have more. I think you want more too. But it falls to me to orchestrate it. I don't mind accepting that role. It seems I must, because it'll do neither of us good if I give in to any degree of complacency where you're concerned."

"I know what you're saying. And I know you're right. But I'm so tired, Tim. I feel as if I'll never live long enough to catch up on all the sleep I've missed. I can't even think straight now. Please, let's talk tomorrow," she said, taking hold of his hands. "I'll think everything over and let you know what I decide. Okay?"

"Okay," he agreed, then kissed her goodbye, and quickly left.

Seize the day, Louise thought, preparing for bed. She remembered the phrase from grade ten Latin. *Carpe diem.* It was more than a little frightening to think of putting out both hands and taking hold. Why did she feel that way? Rachel was the one who'd been apprehensive about life's possibilities. Not her. Certainly there were times when she felt as if she'd slipped into Rachel's brain and was viewing everything and everyone through her friend's eyes, with her friend's former reticence. She could do so many things Rachel had always feared. She could throw off her clothes and wind herself around Tim's body like a contortionist. But Rachel had given her heart away, and she couldn't. Moira Kelly had called her a slut. And since then there were moments, sharp slivers of time, as she opened her body to Tim, when she felt whorish, wanton. Then she'd look at Tim's rapt features, at the raw emotion deepening his eyes, and think, No. She was simply demonstrating her caring in the best way she knew how. Words were treacherous. Love was potentially lethal. Silence was safe.

The telephone rang. She snatched up the receiver to hear Nick say, "Rachel's 'avin' the baby! She started spottin', so Tim's gonna do the cesarean right now. Get on over 'ere! I'm 'avin' a bloody stroke!"

"I'm on my way!" Louise threw down the phone, pulled on some clothes, grabbed her bag, and ran out into the street to flag down a taxi.

When she arrived at the hospital, Nick was nowhere to be seen. Inquiring at the nurse's station, she was told that Dr. Kelly would be out shortly to see her.

Too nervous to sit down, Louise paced up and down for almost forty minutes, imagining the worst. Something had gone wrong. Rachel and the baby were in trouble. One or both of them had died. Dread was like acid in her mouth. She paced the length of the waiting room, perspiring and whispering to herself, ignoring the several other occupants, who all watched her with curiosity.

At last Tim appeared, still in his surgical garb, and Louise ran to him, asking, "What's happened? Is she all right? Is the baby all right?"

Taking her by the hand, he said, "Come along with me now, Louise."

"Where are we going? How's Rachel? Where's Nick?"

"Calm yourself," he said kindly. "Nothing's gone wrong. We're simply a day or two ahead of schedule. Come along here now." He guided her down the corridor and through a pair of swinging doors. "Rachel's in the recovery room," he explained. "And Nick's in the waiting room there. Come in here," he said, showing her into a scrub room, "and put these on." He handed her a gown, then fastened a mask over her face and one over his own. "Give your hands a wash," he told her, proceeding to wash his own.

When they were both scrubbed and gowned, she followed him to the nursery.

"This," he said, lifting an infant from its cot, "is Nicola Louise Cal-ley." He placed the baby in Louise's arms, then stood by, eyes smiling above his mask.

The baby was enchanting, its tiny features symmetrical and serene. Louise held the infant in her arms and felt something breaking inside her, something large and solid that seemed to crack her ribs as it shattered. "Nicola," she whispered, awed by the weighted reality of the child.

"Rachel's all right?" She looked up at Tim. His eyes were full of wonder. He dealt with babies every day. Did he look like this every time? What an incredibly caring man he was, she thought, loving him more at that moment than she ever had.

"Rachel's fine," he said, returning the baby to its cot, then leading her out, untying his mask as they went back along the corridor. "She'll be coming round about now. You'll be able to see her shortly."

Following his instructions, she deposited the mask and gown in a bin and accepted his invitation to have some coffee in the doctors' lounge. Halfway there, she reached for his hand and pulled him to a stop.

"Tim," she said, feeling liquid replacing the solid mass that had dissolved in her chest. "I shouldn't be, I know, but I'm frightened of saying yes to you. I know nothing bad's going to happen, yet I have this feeling that if I say I'll go away with you, that I'll live with you . . ." She was so afraid, she couldn't complete the thought aloud.

"Come in here," he said, leading her into his darkened office. Sitting her down on the edge of his desk, he put his hands on her shoulders and said, "Look at me now, Louise. Listen carefully. Were your sister alive and here today, I have every expectation she'd tell you she had no regrets for having loved. What happened to her was unfortunate, tragic. But it didn't happen because she loved that young chap. It happened because someone—and you may never know who—violated her. Her death was an accident, not the result of anything she did or didn't do. I hold your life more dearly than my own. So far as it's within my power, I'll never allow anything untoward to happen to you. Do you believe me?"

She nodded, feeling the tide rising within her.

"Tell me," he said. "Do you love me, Louise?"

"You know I do," she got out, the words causing a pain in her throat.

"Then come away with me, live with me. Let me care for you."

She nodded again, the liquid spilling upward, outward. She tried to laugh; it emerged as a great sob that shook her, had her hiccuping just the way she had years before when Ma would finally stop hitting her.

She hugged him, thinking maybe now she could stop being so afraid; maybe now she could start making decisions again and get back to being the person she used to be. That other Louise seemed so far away, like someone she'd known in childhood and had lost touch with. She wanted her back again.

CHAPTER
SIXTY-ONE

AFTER THREE WEEKS AT HOME RACHEL CAME BACK TO
work, bringing the baby with her. Louise frequently had to stop whatever
she was doing to look at her.

"You've gone positively gaga," Rachel said, amused. "At this rate
you'll never get anything done."

"She's so beautiful," Louise said, gazing at Nicola in her carry cot.

"She looks like Nickie, don't you think?"

"I think she looks more like you."

"Pick her up," Rachel said indulgently. "I know you're dying to."

Louise lifted the baby into her arms and gazed at the satiny features,
touching with a fingertip the dark downy hair, the chubby cheeks that
made her want to laugh and cry. The baby was a bundle of sleeping
sweetness, talcum scented, wonderfully fresh. There was something in
the purity and innocence of the infant that drew at Louise as nothing else
ever had. It wasn't just that Nicola was Rachel and Nick's child—that in
itself seemed sufficiently miraculous—but the child herself. No one
would ever beat this baby or lock her out of the house; she'd have the
opportunity to grow up with two people who loved her. And that seemed
more significant than anything else. It was so fundamental, so profoundly
simple: Out of love you created life. So simple, yet until Nicola's birth
Louise had been unable to see it. She'd believed, without any real basis in
fact, that she'd be an appalling mother merely because her own mother
had been. The truth was, it didn't have to be that way.

Reluctantly returning the baby to its cot, she went back to her desk.
Her fears for Rachel had been replaced by unanticipated envy. Each time
Rachel retreated to a far corner of the office and turned her back to nurse
the infant, Louise gazed at her, noticing the loving bend of Rachel's head
and thinking perhaps it wouldn't be so awful to be a mother after all.

Rachel's transformation seemed to have been made complete by mother-hood. She was calmer, her movements slower; she radiated happiness.

When Louise commented to him on the effect Nicola seemed to be having on Rachel and Nick, Tim said, "Babies are the only immortality we can hope to attain. What's always struck me most ironic about Moira is that for all her yearning after a child she'd have been a frightful mother. She's much too vain ever to take second place to anyone, even a child."

"Maybe she just used the issue as an excuse," Louise said. "Maybe she only claimed to want a baby because she knew she couldn't have one."

"Maybe so," he said, intrigued by her reasoning. "Are you changing your mind, Louise?"

"About what?"

"About marriage and children."

"I don't know. I never thought I'd care as much for the baby as I do. I get this feeling when I look at her, when I hold her, as if . . . As if I want to run away with her and keep her for myself." She sighed, then said, "Anyway, what difference does it make? It's academic." What if she got pregnant? She experienced a *frisson* of excitement and fear. What would she do? The idea of an abortion frightened her far more now than the idea of having a child. Which surprised her. Nicola was changing everyone.

"So," he asked. "Have you given any thought to where you might like to go?"

"Not really. It'll be at least another month before I dare take any time away."

"But you will come look at flats with me this weekend?"

"I can't think about it now. There's too much work."

"So, you're changing your mind," he said coldly, let down.

"Not exactly. I just can't set a specific date. I promised Evie we'd stop by on Sunday afternoon."

"Did you now?" He smiled.

"Why're you smiling that way?"

"You made plans for us as a couple," he said. "It's an encouraging sign, one of the few I've seen recently."

"If I were you I'd have given up on me a long time ago. You know that? And I'll tell you something. Sometimes I wish I'd never made an offer to buy that damned business. It's such a tremendous responsibility."

"And what would you do if you didn't have the business?"

"I'd work for somebody else."

"You'd hate it at this point. Whether you admit it or not, I think you actually like the challenge."

"I do and I don't. Every so often I get the feeling the whole thing'll fall down and suffocate me."

"That's only because you're overtired. Two weeks in the sun and you'd view things quite differently."

"Don't you ever get tired of your work?" she asked him.

"Never," he said emphatically. "Every time I deliver another baby I'm thrilled."

"Doesn't it make it worse for you?"

"That I don't have one of my own? Not really," he said thoughtfully. "I've long since come to terms with the reality of my situation. I've given up that particular dream. I'm working on one or two others."

"I never had any dreams," she said. "All I ever wanted was to be grown-up and to get away from my mother, to be on my own." She remembered telling Daniel that she expected to be an interesting woman, and had to smile.

"What?"

"I once told someone I intended to grow up to be an interesting woman. I was about fourteen at the time."

"And you have," Tim said. "You're very interesting indeed."

"I'm ordinary. Rachel's *interesting*. So is Nick, and so are you. But I'm ordinary. I'm a plodder and there's nothing interesting about that."

"You're very much mistaken," he said, surprised by her view of herself. "You're far more than that."

"No, I'm just someone who's willing to work hard. But when it looks as if it's going to get a little too hard, I get scared."

"Can this really be how you view yourself?"

"Sure it is. How do you think I should view myself?"

"Ah, now." He folded his arms behind his head and gazed at the ceiling. "The view," he said at length, "is of someone passionate and determined, ambitious and caring. A bit tricky when it comes to accepting, but openhanded when it comes to giving. Nervy and bold. A thoroughbred."

She laughed and said, "Not according to your wife."

"Pardon?"

"Your wife," she said. "She came marching into the office a while back and said she wanted to have a look at the slut who was sleeping with her husband.''

"Good God!" He turned to stare at her. "Why have you never told me before?"

"Because it was stupid. Rachel was right. I was mortified when it happened, but now that I've had some time to think about it, I can see how silly the whole thing was."

He shook his head in disbelief. "You should have told me, Louise."

"Why? What would you have done?"

"Had a word with her. Something. I don't know."

"It doesn't matter. Honestly. In a way, it's kind of a good thing it happened. At least she made herself real to me. Up to that point she didn't really exist. She was this woman you talked about sometimes, not an actual person."

"You should have told me." He sat up and looked at his watch.

"Are you mad that I didn't?"

"I'm bothered by the cliché," he said, smoothing his hair with both hands. "You know how I loathe clichéd situations."

"Rachel said it was pure Noel Coward," she said, hoping to jolly him out his suddenly dour mood. "No one took it seriously."

"You did, Louise," he said, turning to look directly into her eyes. "You're making light of it now, but you took it to heart. I know you that well at least."

"I shouldn't have told you. I didn't intend to, ever."

He dropped his head into his hands. "I *loathe* scenes," he said vehemently. "Bloody Moira thrives on them."

"Tim, it's over now. You're divorced from the woman. Forget I said anything."

"I thought by not contesting the divorce I'd spare you any unpleasantness."

"I don't care," she said. "Why're you getting so upset?"

"I don't really know," he answered. "I must check in with the service."

He got up, pulled on his shorts, and went to the telephone. She sat on the bed with her arms wrapped around her knees, wishing she'd kept her mouth shut. She'd never imagined he'd get so upset.

"I'm going to run along," he said.

"Is there a call?"

"No, but I'm tired."

"Don't go. Leave this number with the service and stay here."

He sat down on the side of the bed holding his trousers and said, "I've got to get away."

Alarmed, she asked, "What's the matter?"

His shoulders slumping he said, "I wanted to protect you."

"Nobody protects anybody," she said, a hand on his shoulder. "I'm not a little kid, Tim. I knew from the start you were married, and I didn't care. I'm really sorry I told you. I had no idea you'd react this way. I don't even know what you're upset about."

"Neither do I," he admitted. "Which is a good reason why I should go home."

"Please don't," she said. "Or at least stay and talk to me until we settle this. You're making me feel stupid."

"You're not stupid," he said quietly. "Neither of us is. I'm feeling old this evening." He reached for his shirt and fitted his arms into the sleeves. "Another few months and I'll be forty-four. You're twenty-three. I've got no right to want you."

"You're making me sad," she said softly, getting up to fit herself into his arms. "Don't go home."

He threaded his fingers through her hair. "It's simply an attack of melancholia. A night's sleep and it'll pass."

"Call the service and leave this number. You're staying. I'm sorry I mentioned your ex-wife. This is all my fault. Call the service."

He smiled tiredly and said, "Yes, all right. I'm sorry to have become so lugubrious." He went again to the telephone. She slipped back into bed.

Something was happening, she thought, straightening the bedclothes as she tried to decide what it was. Then it came to her with a jolt, and she turned to watch Tim removing his clothes. She liked his body. He was broad in the shoulders and chest but very lean, his legs long and well-shaped. She liked his face, with its delicate features, his silver hair. She especially liked his hands, which were always scrubbed clean, long-fingered like a pianist's. She imagined her life without him and felt a sudden panic burst in her chest. The degree to which she loved him shocked her. Her entire being seemed suddenly filled with it. It seemed to swell inside her, making her skin feel all at once too tight.

"Come to sleep," she said, opening her arms to him, cradling his head on her shoulder.

"I do apologize for that little scene," he said. "It was childish."

"Don't apologize. You put up with all my garbage and never complain."

"I love you," he said simply, almost helplessly. "It's what one does."

"Exactly," she said, drawing him closer so that his warmth began to penetrate her flesh. She inserted her knee between his, relishing his weight, her hand gliding the length of his arm to find his hand. "Are you too tired?"

"Evidently not." He laughed softly, one hand closing over her breast. "Louise, you're going to have to make a decision, let me off the hook. I'm finding it increasingly difficult to continue on the way we are."

"I will think about the trip," she said, hoping to avoid an argument. "I know I keep changing my mind on you, and I'm sorry. But there's such a lot going on."

"I appreciate that. But ultimately you're going to have to decide on your priorities. I'd like to be one of them, but I'm not so egotistic that I'll ride along on assumptions. One week we're on, the next week we're off. I know all your reasons, and they're all valid. So are mine for wanting some small commitment from you. Let's agree you'll give me your decision by the end of next week."

"And if I can't?"

"Then we'll have to consider alternatives."

"All right," she said, frightened by what she could only view as an ultimatum. "I'll let you know."

All her caring was seeking an outlet, urging her to claim him once and for all. Her hands touched him with new sensitivity and she became aware that she was caressing him now in the way he always caressed her: gently, with awareness, with love. At once she regretted how blinded she'd been for so long by so many fears. From one moment to the next her perception had been completely altered and she understood how much she wanted to keep him, to comfort him, to care for him and make him happy. So why couldn't she capitulate finally?

When the telephone rang, she groaned and whispered, "Hell! It's your damned service."

"Sorry. Shall I answer it?"

"Might as well. It's for you."

He got up and went to the telephone, listened for a moment, then held out the receiver. "It's for you, Louise."

"Is it Rachel?" she asked, unable to think of who else would be calling after eleven at night.

He shook his head. She took the receiver and was astounded to hear, "It's Uncle Bob, Louise."

"Oh God," she said, instantly alarmed. "Is everything okay?"

"I'm afraid not," he said. "It's about your mother, Lulu."

"What about her?"

"I'm sorry to say she's dead."

"What?" It wasn't possible, she thought. Maggie would never die. She'd go on forever.

"There was an . . . accident. Your grandmother and I just learned of it a few hours ago. I think you'd better come home, honey."

"Okay, Uncle Bob. Is Gramma all right?"

"Well, she's upset. You can imagine."

"Yes, I can. I'll call the airlines right away, then call you back to let you know when I'll be getting in."

"The funeral will be the day after tomorrow," he told her. "We'll explain everything when you get here."

"Okay. I'll call you back."

She hung up and looked over at Tim.

"Bad news?" he asked, already in his shorts.

"My mother died," she said, dazed. "Some kind of accident. Jesus H. Christ! I've got to book a flight to Toronto."

"I'm terribly sorry," he said, bringing over her robe and helping her into it.

"I can't believe it." She sank down into one of the chairs. Maggie was dead? It wasn't possible. What kind of accident?

Tim poured some Glenlivet into a glass and handed it to her. "Drink this. I'll ring the airlines. I imagine you'll want to get on the next available flight."

"Tim, I don't have any money."

"Don't worry about that. I'll take care of it."

"I'll pay you back."

"We'll discuss it later." He rang directory inquiries and got the numbers of Trans Canada and several other airlines. Then with a notepad and a pen, he sat down and began making calls. Within five minutes he had

Louise booked on a 7 a.m. flight. "I'll take you to the airport," he said, belatedly pouring himself a drink. "Are you all right?"

"I can't believe it, but I'm all right. God! I thought she was going to live forever." She gave a hoarse laugh. "I thought she'd end up the world's oldest hooker. That's awful. Forget I said it. Oh, but it's the truth. She was the most hateful person I've ever known. Completely selfish. I wonder how she died. All Uncle Bob said was that it was an accident. Look at this!" She held out a trembling hand. "I'm shaking, for Pete's sake. I didn't even *like* her. I haven't seen her since my sister's funeral six years ago. Now she's dead."

Tim took hold of her hand. "I'm sorry," he said again.

"God! Don't be, Tim! I'm not. I'm a little thrown. I mean this was the last thing in the world I was expecting. But I'm not sorry. I know that sounds terrible. But you had to know Maggie. You had to know her." She gave another hoarse laugh and said, "She even had to make a show out of Faye's funeral, making an entrance at the last minute, dressed for effect. She didn't give a damn about Faye or about me. God! She's dead. And I've got to go home in the morning." Remembering, she said, "I'd better call Uncle Bob back."

She made the call, giving Bob the information Tim had written down, then said, "I'll see you tomorrow afternoon."

"Was that your friend Tim who answered the phone before?" Bob asked.

Louise looked over at Tim. "That's right," she replied.

"Tell him we're looking forward to meeting him sometime. See you tomorrow, honey."

"Uncle Bob would like to meet you sometime," she told Tim.

"That's very gracious."

"Will you let Rachel know? I don't want to call now and it'll be too early in the morning when we leave."

"I'll take care of it," he said calmly. "Have some of that," he indicated the glass on the table.

She took a sip. "I'm having a lot of trouble believing this," she said. "When I was little and she pounded me or locked me and Faye out of the house, I used to cry and say I wished she'd die. I know all little kids say things like that, but I *meant* it. I hated her, but I kept on trying to please her. We'd clean that goddamned house and she'd come home from the factory and say what a lousy job we'd done and make us do it all over again. She wore only the best clothes, and dressed me and Faye in cheap garbage from the sale annex. Nothing we ever did was good enough. And if anything happened, no matter how minimal, it was always either Faye's or my fault. She's dead,'' she said, trying to wrap her mind around the concept. "She died. I'll bet my grandmother feels terrible. I feel badly for Gramma,'' she said, searching Tim's eyes. "You think I'm horrible, don't you?''

"Not at all,'' he said in his hushed voice. "You seem very angry.''

"That's what Gramma said. She said I was angry. I didn't even know I was. At the time I thought it was about Faye. But it wasn't. I'm angry about every damned thing she put us through. She was a monster, Tim. I promised myself when I was a kid that I'd never get married and have children because I didn't want to grow up to be anything like her. It's so stupid. As if getting married and having kids would make me like her,'' she scoffed. "How could I be so dumb?''

"You've had a bad time of it.''

"Maybe I did once upon a time,'' she said. "But I've had a pretty easy time of it since I came over here. I admit the business has been getting me down, but you were right in what you said a while ago. I wouldn't want it any other way. Why am I seeing everything so clearly all of a sudden?''

"It's the shock.''

"I want to see her in a coffin. I want to make sure she's actually in it. Maybe once I do I'll be able to get over being angry and anxious and get on with my life. I feel as if I will.''

"Perhaps you will then.''

"You've been so good to me,'' she said, setting down the glass to climb into his lap. "I'll pay you back for the ticket.''

"And if you don't,'' he said. "Will the sky fall in?''

"Maybe.''

"I promise you, it won't,'' he said. "Perhaps you might just say thank you and be done with it.''

"Is that what you think I should do?''

"It is.''

"Okay, Tim. Thank you.''

"Good girl,'' he said with a smile. "Well done. Now I think it might be wise if we tried to get a little sleep.''

"I am tired,'' she admitted.

"Then to bed with you," he said, easing her off his lap. "You've got a long day tomorrow."

She drank down the remaining Glenlivet all in one go, shuddered, then took off her robe and got into bed.

"I wish you were coming with me," she said, curling up against him.

"I wish I could, but it's not possible."

"I know," she sighed.

"Just think about what we've discussed while you're away. That's all I ask. I do realize the timing's deplorable, but we've got to settle matters."

"I'll think about everything," she promised. "I will."

CHAPTER
SIXTY-TWO

Bob WAS WAITING FOR HER WHEN SHE CAME OUT OF THE arrivals area. He greeted her with a hug, then took her bag and led her out to the car. "Your grandmother's waiting at home," he said. "She wasn't quite up to the trip."

"Is she very upset?" Louise asked.

"She's more in a state of shock than anything else. This was so unexpected."

"It certainly was."

"I'm afraid it's not very pleasant," he said, stowing her bag in the trunk of the Cadillac.

"Somehow I didn't think it would be. Was she murdered?"

Bob paused in the middle of putting the key into the ignition and looked over at her. "I guess it's not unreasonable for you to think that," he said. "But no." He got the car started, put it into drive and pulled away from the curb. "She didn't show up for work for several days. One of her coworkers became concerned, and when she couldn't get any response either by phoning or when she went to knock at the door of Marg's apartment, she went and got the super, who called the police.

They unlocked the door and found her. She'd been dead for four or five days.''

"God! What happened?"

"Evidently she'd had too much to drink. She slipped and fell in the bathroom, hit her head on the sink, and knocked herself out. While she was unconscious she aspirated." He glanced over. "She choked on her own vomit."

"That's awful." Louise made a face, imagining the scene.

"Not a pretty picture," he agreed. "Your grandmother's taking it pretty hard. I think she hoped one day Marg might see the error of her ways, and there'd be a reconciliation."

"Ma would *never* have changed."

"I tend to agree with you. But it's hard to lose your only child, Lulu. Even if that child is a difficult, disagreeable woman."

"You never liked her, did you?"

"I found it impossible to like your mother. It's terrible to speak ill of the dead, but she wasn't likable."

"Poor Gramma."

"She's coping very well, all things considered." He smiled over at her. "And of course she's anxious to see you. You look wonderful, honey."

"So do you, Uncle Bob."

"The circumstances notwithstanding, everyone's anxious to see you. Kath wants you to call her right away. And Daniel called this morning. He read the obituary in the paper. We're planning a short service followed by cremation. Ellie's been taking care of some of the last-minute details. Oh, and you might be interested to know that Aldo DiStasio's been sentenced to eight years in the Kingston Pen."

"Eight years," she repeated.

"The others got six years each. Grievous bodily harm was added to the charges against Aldo. Nasty piece of work that young man, according to the newspaper reports."

"He was always pulling stunts," Louise said. "All the kids in the neighborhood were terrified of him and the twins."

"I was hoping you'd help your grandmother go through your mother's things. Her apartment has to be cleared out."

"Sure, I'll help."

"We had a quick look but couldn't find a will. It's one of the things we're hoping to find."

"Why?"

"To know how to dispose of her property."

"Can't we just give everything to the Salvation Army?"

"Not," he said, "if there's a properly executed will."

"I can't imagine Ma making out a will. She probably thought she'd live forever. God knows, I certainly thought she would."

"How do you feel?" he asked.

"You want to know the truth? I'm relieved. Two years ago I kept dreading I was going to run into her on the street. I knew that if I saw her I'd probably want to turn and walk in the opposite direction, or I'd start shrieking at her for every rotten thing she ever did. It actually gave me butterflies, thinking I might run into her. Now I never have to worry about that again. It's only lately, you know, that I've begun to realize how much I disliked her. She never did a decent thing for anyone in her entire life. I'm not going to be a hypocrite, Uncle Bob, and say I'm sorry. Because I'm not. I'm sorry for Gramma's sake because this is one more thing Ma's put her through, but I'm not sorry she's dead. I know she didn't actually have anything to do with Faye's dying, but that doesn't stop me from feeling as if she did. If she hadn't been the way she was, maybe Faye would still be alive today. I feel a lot of different things right now, but I'm not sorry."

"I can't blame you," he said quietly.

While her grandmother emptied the closets, Louise went through the desk. Ellen began filling cartons with Maggie's clothes, marveling at the size of the wardrobe her daughter had acquired.

When the telephone rang, Louise automatically answered, to hear a man's voice say, "Hiya, Baby. How're you doing?"

"Who did you want to speak to?" Louise asked, glancing over at her grandmother, who'd come to the doorway.

"Is that you, Margaret?"

There were any number of rude things Louise was tempted to say, but in deference to her grandmother she remained polite. "I'm sorry," she said, "but Margaret passed away."

"What? Are you kidding me?"

"No, I'm not."

"Well, I'll be," said the man. Then, as if realizing he was speaking to a stranger, his voice and attitude changed and he said, "Sorry to trouble you," and hung up.

"Some friend of Ma's," Louise told Ellen.

Ellen nodded and went back to the bedroom.

Louise stared at the telephone for a moment, then continued her search of the desk.

She couldn't believe the things her mother had kept—business cards, old telephone and hydro bills, sales receipts dating back to 1952. And bank books, four of them.

"Gramma," she said, taking the books into the bedroom, "look at this!" She showed her grandmother each one. "Toronto Dominion Bank, a balance of sixteen thousand, four hundred and fourteen dollars. The Bank of Montreal, balance eleven thousand, nine hundred and ninety two. The Bank of Nova Scotia, fourteen thousand, three hundred and twelve. The Royal Bank, nine thousand, six hundred and eleven. And there's a checkbook that shows a balance of over four thousand. She had a fortune saved."

"Good heavens," Ellen said, gaping at the multicolored books. "I had no idea she had that kind of money. She was always complaining about not having enough. The last time I spoke to her, a few months ago, she was saying she'd have to move because they were going to raise her rent."

"Obviously," Louise said without thinking, "business was good."

Her grandmother looked stricken and Louise apologized at once. "I'm sorry, Gramma. But we both know where she got the money. She must've saved every penny."

"Any sign of a will?"

"Not yet. I'll keep looking."

"I need a break," Ellen said, following her back to the living room to get a cigarette from her handbag. Sitting down on the sofa she observed, "Expensive furniture. Marg certainly didn't skimp when it came to herself."

"She never did," Louise said, finding a folder of what looked like important documents. "Maybe it'll be in here," she said, tipping the contents out onto the desk. "Let's see. Some kind of insurance policy for the apartment. Health insurance. Our birth certificates." She set these aside. "Her marriage license." She set this aside as well. "A storage receipt from a fur company for a Persian lamb coat. It's dated April this year, so that means there's a coat to dispose of. For Pete's sake, here it is!

She actually had a will." Scanning the pages quickly, she said, "It's from *1943!* D'you think it's still valid?"

"Bob will have a look at it," Ellen said, accepting the document. "I seem to remember when she did this. It was after John left her and Marg went to see a lawyer about getting a divorce. I remember her complaining that the lawyer insisted she have a will drawn up to protect you and Faye in case anything happened to her. She was furious at having to pay the extra money, but she obviously did it. I'll be damned. I'd completely forgotten about that."

Louise went to sit beside her grandmother, saying, "This must be horrible for you."

Ellen turned to take a long look at her, curving her hand over Louise's cheek. "Your mother did two wonderful things in her life," she said. "You and Faye. For that, I can forgive a lot of the less-than-wonderful things she did." Withdrawing her hand, she put out her cigarette. "Come give me a hand in the bedroom. I'd like to finish this as quickly as possible. I'm not enjoying it, and you must be tired. You've had a very long day."

"Why don't you go through the rest of the papers and I'll do the bedroom?"

Casting a grateful smile at her, Ellen agreed.

As it happened, Louise was glad she'd made the offer. It spared her grandmother the sight of a drawerful of condoms, as well as several dildos, an assortment of lubricants, and a number of what appeared to be belts of varying sizes, many of which were too small to fit around anyone's waist. Sickened, Louise gazed at the evidence of her mother's career. Maggie Parker, who'd hated men, had stockpiled a considerable amount of money by catering to their sexual whims. She had to wonder how Maggie had justified her activities to herself. Or had she merely hated men more for being willing to pay her? Judging from the telephone call she'd taken only minutes before, it was obvious she hadn't stopped seeing them. Forty-three years old and she'd still been selling herself. It struck Louise as grotesque, both that her mother would do it and that the men were interested in her shopworn wares.

In a hurry to hide the tools of Maggie's trade from her grandmother, Louise pulled out the entire drawer and dumped everything into a garbage bag, then started on another drawer. At the bottom, still in its original Morgan's box, she found the scarf she and Faye had gone to so much

trouble to buy. The sight of it revived her anger and her hurt, triggering
memories of that day she and Faye had pooled their savings, and of the
gracious saleswoman who'd helped them make their selection. The scarf
went into the garbage, along with a collection of expensive lacy undergar-
ments Louise couldn't bring herself to touch. Again, she simply tipped
out the entire contents of the drawer. Sweaters went into the cartons,
along with sundry nightgowns and blouses. All Maggie's cosmetics and
perfumes also went into the garbage. Louise had to talk herself out of
stopping every few minutes to wash her hands. The temptation was
almost overwhelming.

"If there's anything you want," Ellen said from the doorway, "take
it."

"There's nothing here I'd want," Louise said, repelled by the idea of
wearing anything that had belonged to her mother. As it was, she could
scarcely bear handling the dead woman's things.

"No," Ellen said softly. "I can understand that. Are you about done?"
she asked, looking a bit pale. "I'd like to get out of here."

"I'm finished," Louise told her, folding over the flaps of the last of the
boxes. "I'll find a bag to put the papers in and we can leave."

"I've already done it," Ellen said, hefting a shopping bag to show her.

"Then let me wash my hands and we'll go," Louise said. "We could
both use some fresh air."

She stepped into the bathroom, looked at the tile floor, imagined her
mother lying there, and stepped back out again, going instead to use the
kitchen sink while her grandmother waited by the front door, plainly
agitated and as eager as Louise to be gone from the place.

"I saved a box of photographs," Ellen said as they walked back down
Brunswick in the last of the late-July light. "I thought you'd want them. If
not, I'll keep them."

"We can look at them later," Louise said, slipping her arm through
her grandmother's. "It's pretty hard to believe, isn't it?"

"Bob wouldn't allow me to see her. He made the identification. He
looked green around the gills when he came out of the morgue. I've told
the funeral home to seal the coffin."

"Let's stop somewhere and have a drink," Louise suggested. "I think
we could both use one."

Her grandmother stared at her for a moment, then laughed and shook her head. "That threw me," she said. "I keep forgetting you're a grown woman."

"So do I," Louise admitted.

They went to the roof bar at the Park Plaza. Louise ordered Glenlivet and felt a pang, missing Tim. She wondered what he was doing at that moment. Her grandmother ordered a Tom Collins, then sat back with a sigh, the shopping bag at her feet. "Bob and I drop in downstairs to hear Peter Appleyard play now and then. But I haven't been up here in ages. It's very pleasant."

"Yes, it is."

"A handful of bankbooks and some old documents," she said. "That's all that's left of Marg." Her eyes filled and she opened her bag for her cigarettes, blinking the tears away. "What a waste," she said sadly.

What a way to die, Louise thought, having disposed of the empty bottle of Cointreau along with the contents of the refrigerator. She'd packed up the sundry boxes and tins of food to give to the super and his wife. Tomorrow everything Maggie had lived with would be carted off on a Salvation Army truck. And that'd be the end of Maggie Parker, except for a handful of old photographs and a surprisingly large cache of money.

As if reading her granddaughter's mind, Ellen said, "The money will go to you, Louise."

"You read the will?"

"I didn't have to. You're her next of kin. After all these years of working with Bob I know that much about the law. How do you feel about that?"

How do I feel about that? Louise asked herself, thinking she ought to be repelled by the very notion of accepting money her mother had earned on her back. But common sense and practicality won out. She'd be able to pay her own way, to breathe more deeply without having to fret constantly about building the company while at the same time sliding ever deeper into debt. And she'd be able to contribute to furnishing the new flat. Tim wouldn't have to pay for every last thing. "I'll take the money," she said. "God knows, I could use it. I'm up to my ears in debt. The money'll pay off the loans I took out to start the business and let me take a vacation. Tim's been after me for months to take some time off."

"Are you happy, Lulu?" Ellen asked, taking a sip of her drink.

"I think I'm going to be," Louise answered carefully. "Tim wants me to move in with him."

"Are you going to?"

Louise hesitated for a moment then said, "Yes, I am."

"Do you love him?" Ellen asked.

The question triggered a rush of emotion. Gripping her grandmother's hand she said, "It's an aching inside, Gramma. Is that how you feel about Uncle Bob?"

Ellen nodded, studying Louise's eyes. "A sweet ache," she said, able to see a new maturity in her granddaughter that hadn't been there two years before.

"The longer I know him the more I care about the way he feels. He drove me to the airport this morning and we sat in the car for a few minutes. Not talking. Just holding hands. And for the second time in just hours I had this terrible feeling of panic, not knowing what I'd do if I didn't have him. It reminded me of that day when you came to pick me up at school. Remember? That awful snowstorm, and you were so worried about Uncle Bob. You let me cook the dinner and every few minutes you kept going to look out the window. That was exactly the way I felt leaving Tim. He got out to get a skycap and I watched him with this terrible twisting sensation in my chest. He's so *kind,* Gramma. And he's been so sad for such a long time. Sometimes his eyes clear. I can see it happen. It's like something dark slides out from behind his eyes and the light suddenly shines through. And I feel so—elated, because I know I'm responsible. I made him laugh. Or I said something that got him thinking in a new direction. He does the same thing for me. I've been a wreck this past year, what with the business and worrying about Rachel. Worrying about every little stupid damned thing, really. He's never been impatient or bored or uninterested. I love the way he sounds on the telephone, for Pete's sake." She laughed. "He keeps me grounded, in a way. Like you do, Gramma, and Uncle Bob does, too."

"You love him," Ellen smiled.

"I have trouble with love," Louise said, "with the words anyway. I blame Ma for that. All that stuff she was always spouting when we were little. Never trust a man. There's not one of them worth the powder to blow him away. The one who loves you is the one who puts food on the table and keeps a roof over your head. I *believed* her, Gramma. Faye didn't, but I did. It all kind of seeped in through my pores. I mean, that year I was with Daniel I felt guilty because I was convinced I was using him. But that wasn't the truth. I loved Daniel. I'd been in love with him for years. But I couldn't admit that because it would've made me a sap in Ma's book. And I never wanted to be a sap, because then I'd be just like Ma. I was trying so hard not to be like her that I was turning into a basket case." She stopped, thinking again about the devices she'd found in her mother's drawers. "She was *pitiful*. I'm sorry if my saying that hurts you, Gramma. But she was. Why the hell was she the way she was?"

"I'll go to my grave asking myself that, Lulu. She was always hard to handle, right from the time she was old enough to talk. I spent years trying to see what part I might have played in her turning wrong, but I could never get to an answer."

"You're not to blame for her," Louise said with heat. "How could you even *think* that?"

"I'm her mother, Lulu. Someday maybe you'll understand the implications of that. It's hard to accept that sometimes people go wrong for reasons that have nothing to do with you. As the parent in question, you have to wonder why. No one was ever closer to Marg than I was. But I couldn't begin to explain her thinking or her actions. I never understood her. The only person who ever had any genuine affection for Marg was Blanche DiStasio. And I think that was because she knew Marg when she was first pregnant with Faye and still happy with John Parker. Maybe Marg showed a side of herself to Blanche that she never showed to anyone else. I really couldn't say. But I do know Blanche always thought well of her."

"Blanche loved everybody. She was wonderful."

"Too many deaths," Ellen said, looking into the depths of her glass.

Respectfully, Louise remained silent, thinking of Chuckie, that thin, neglected little boy. She could remember every last detail of that morning vividly: how she'd run across the street anxious to have a showdown with Shirley for stealing Ma's money; the very stillness of the street and the fullness of the trees; Shirley's mother's face. Chuckie was dead. Now all these years later Faye was gone; so was Ma, and she and her grandmother seemed suddenly cocooned in a bubble of silence in the dimly lit bar. The scotch left a ripe taste on the back of her tongue; she was aware of her own slow breathing.

She looked at her grandmother, recalling the sound of Bob's voice over the crackling long-distance line and her own sudden sick fear that he was calling to say something had happened to her grandmother. But it had been Ma. Gramma was here in a white summer dress, with her hair in a soft coil atop her head and her eyes focused on some remote vision, thinking no doubt about her dead daughter, drowned in her own vomit.

Louise leaned over to kiss her grandmother's cheek, murmuring, "I'm sorry, Gramma. I love you more than I'll ever love anyone else."

Ellen sighed deeply, took a swallow of her drink, then put the glass down, saying, "I'm sorry, too. I thought time would change her, change her view of things. But she'd only have gone on in the same way. I couldn't ever completely let her go. She was my child. No matter what she did, she was always my child. It's a terrible feeling, terrible." She looked at her watch and said, "We should go. Bob'll be wondering where we are."

"I think he'll understand, Gramma. Let's sit quietly and finish our drinks."

"Perhaps you're right," Ellen said. "We'll do that."

Louise gave her grandmother another kiss, then lifted the glass of Tim's favorite scotch to her lips.

CHAPTER
SIXTY-THREE

INITIALLY LOUISE THOUGHT NO ONE WOULD COME. SHE and her grandmother and Uncle Bob sat near the door of the small chapel of the funeral home in awkward silence. It was as if the coffin at the front of the room contained a live Maggie who was trying to get out, and the three of them were ignoring her unheard complaints. Louise's eyes were drawn repeatedly to the coffin, and she thought about the woman inside —trying to understand who she'd really been and how she'd come to be so hateful. Even dead, Maggie was making her presence felt.

Ellen got up to go outside for a cigarette and Bob and Louise automatically got up to go with her. After the flower-scented, air conditioned atmosphere inside, the heat of the July afternoon was actually a relief. They stood under the portico and Louise looked at the passing traffic, guiltily wishing she were back in London. Not that it wasn't good to be with her grandmother and Bob. It was. She knew that in the future she'd always be returning to see them. But she had a business to help operate, and she'd left matters dangling with Tim. He wasn't going to look at flats without her, because he didn't want to risk buying a place she mightn't like. It was important to him that she be happy with their new home. It gave her an odd feeling to think of having a home with Tim. It was such a permanent move, living together as a couple. She thought she wanted it, but couldn't help wondering if the matter of children mightn't become an issue. She was no longer quite so terrified by the prospect of finding herself pregnant. Yet she couldn't imagine herself in that condition.

She'd watched Rachel's body change, watched Rachel herself change; and she'd fallen in love with the infant Rachel's body had produced. She'd discovered that she actually liked children, and could even visualize herself and Tim living with one. The projected family portrait made her edgy, but she was able to view it with some measure of satisfaction—because it would make Tim happy. The idea was like a small hand-bell ringing in her ears. It unnerved her, made her ask herself if she really knew, after all, what she actually wanted.

She turned to look at her grandmother and Bob, holding hands by the door. They were talking in undertones, their fingers intertwined. In love. Married, close, pledged to one another. It seemed absolutely right for them. It was right for Nick and Rachel, too. Perhaps if she married Tim, they'd attain the ultimate closeness. The idea no longer alarmed her. If anything, she suddenly knew that the edginess she felt was a need to state the words, take the actions that would accomplish it. Her ongoing interior urgency had turned in Tim's direction, and she wanted to hurry the present proceedings along, to be rid of Maggie once and for all in order to get on with her own life. She looked again at the street and saw a very pregnant Kath approaching with her mother and Jerry Nolan. She ran down the steps and along the sidewalk to greet them.

Ellen and Bob went inside with them while Louise remained under the portico, waiting, thinking. The street was relatively empty of pedestrian traffic. Cars continued to go past, the sun glinting hotly off the metal. When she looked again at the street, Daniel was approaching and she smiled, lifting a hand to wave.

His embrace was still familiar, but different. They'd both grown accustomed to the feel of other bodies, the scent of other flesh, the sound of other voices.

"How is it?" he asked, knowing all too well her feelings about her mother.

"Weird. I want it over. We all do. How are you?"

"I came in case you needed a hand to hold."

"You've done a lot of that for me," she said, smiling at him. "How's your wife?"

"She's great. How is Tim?"

"Fine, so far as I know. I'm going to call him later, when all this is over." She looked past his shoulder to see a hulking figure from her childhood moving along the sidewalk. Bruno.

"Are you going to marry him?"

"I was just thinking about that," she said, looking back at Daniel. "I can't help thinking it's so hard to do, such a monumentally big step to take. But no one else seems to be having any trouble. Only me. I keep vacillating in great big swings back and forth."

"He sounds good for you, Louise."

"He is. I'm the one who's been holding back, not Tim." There was a peculiar buzzing in her hands, as if the urgency had reached the underside of her skin and was searching for an outlet. "This is strange," she said. "I'm having very mixed emotions." She looked through the door into the interior of the funeral home. "Not about Ma, but about everything else."

Bruno arrived at the bottom of the steps.

Seeing her eyes turn to Bruno, Daniel said, "I'll go along inside," and his hand slipped out of hers.

Looking uncomfortable in a brown suit, a shirt and tie, Bruno came up the stairs saying, "My ma read in the paper about your mother. She told me, eh? So I thought I'd come, pay my respects."

"It's good of you to come, Bruno. How are you?" She held out her hand and he enclosed it in his own enormous one.

"Oh me, I'm good. Got married, eh?" He smiled shyly. "We got a boy, two."

"That's great, Bruno."

"Yeah." He looked down at the toes of his shoes. "You heard about Anthony and those guys?"

"I heard."

"Anthony, I was always telling him Aldo was gonna get him in trouble. But he'd never listen. We weren't talking the past couple a years. Ma threw him outa the house. I quit hanging out with Aldo a long time ago, after what he done to Faye. I didn't like that. It wasn't right. I always felt bad about it.''

"To Faye?" She put her hand out to grip the wrought iron railing. She was suddenly so dizzy she thought she might fall. "What do you mean?"

He looked up at her with round brown eyes. "I thought you knew. I figured she told you all about it."

"She didn't tell me," she said, having trouble breathing. "What did Aldo do to her?"

"Jeez! I thought you knew," he said apologetically. "He hurt her, eh? Anthony, he was gonna hurt her, too, but I wouldn't let him. I made them let her alone, put her in a taxi, and sent her home. She was real scared. That Aldo." He shook his head, his mouth thinning. "He always liked to hurt girls. But it was mostly hookers, you know. He'd go with 'em, then he'd beat 'em up. I tried to talk to Mr. D. but he wouldn't listen. He threw Raff out of the house and Aldo didn't say one word. But I really thought you knew, Louise. I figured you and her being so close, she'd of told you."

"I didn't know," she said, her mouth so dry she couldn't swallow. "Thank you for telling me."

"Maybe I shoulda kept my big mouth shut."

"No, no. You did the right thing." Her body was fighting to contain a shrill scream that she could hear echoing inside her head.

A pair of women were coming up the walk and Louise recognized Flo and Bets from the factory.

Bruno said, "You mad at me, Louise?"

"I'm not mad at you, Bruno. Please go inside. We'll talk more about this later. Thank you for telling me. I've been . . . needing to know." How was she going to get through this? Tears were raining down inside her, sheeting down her insides. And that scream went on and on, rever-berating, bouncing off the bony dome of her skull. If she wasn't very careful, when she next opened her mouth that shriek might escape. She swallowed several times, suppressing it.

"Okay," Bruno said, and stepped in through the door.

"Remember us?" Flo asked uncertainly.

Louise hugged each of them saying, "Of course I remember you. Thank you so much for coming today. Please go inside. The service will be starting in a few minutes."

Alone again, Louise leaned against the iron railing, her heart knocking hard and very fast. *Aldo.* Why hadn't she guessed? Because the last thing in the world you'd ever want to believe about someone you'd known all your life was that he was a rapist. But he was. And Anthony would've been too, if his brother hadn't stopped him. God! Faye must've gone to the store to meet Raffie and Raffie for some reason had been late. Mr. DiStasio had probably been out making deliveries. And Aldo had taken advantage of the opportunity to attack Faye. He'd hurt her so badly he'd torn her flesh, leaving scars. *God!* She'd thought she wanted to know, but now she wished she didn't. It was like clutching handfuls of razor blades —countless small stinging injuries each drawing blood. There was a metallic taste in her mouth and she could hear her heartbeat in syncopation with the rhythmic screaming that went on and on like a fierce winter wind battering at her ears.

Ellen came to the door to say, "We're about to start, Lulu."

Louise looked at her grandmother and forced back tears. She hadn't told her what Tim had said about the autopsy report. She hadn't wanted her grandmother to know what Faye had been through. She couldn't spring it on her now. "You've been through such a lot, Gramma," she said, taking hold of her grandmother's hand, feeling a terrible rush of sympathy for her. "I wish this hadn't happened."

"We'll all get through it," Ellen said, searching Louise's eyes. "What's wrong, Lulu?"

"Nothing. It touched me that Flo and Bets would come. And Bruno."

"Here's Frankie," Ellen said, as the small man came rushing toward them.

Louise's surging sympathy spread to encompass the man and she put her arms around him saying, "Hi, Mr. DiStasio. How are you?"

"I'm okay, Louise." He extended his hand to Ellen. "How you, Ellen?"

"I'm well, Frankie. Thank you for coming. We'd better go in. The service is about to begin."

Grateful for the timing, Louise held her grandmother's hand as they returned into the chapel.

✦

Throughout the service Louise thought about Faye, and about Raffie. The wound of Faye's death gaped open, fresh as yesterday, like an incision running from her breastbone to her pelvis. She tried not to think about how Faye had suffered, concentrating instead on the monstrous wrong she'd done to Raffie. She reasoned that if she'd grieved these past six years trying to understand the how and why of Faye's death, then Raffie had to have despaired, too. He deserved to know the truth, and he deserved her abject apologies. In all her thoughts of Faye's manifold dreams, she'd neglected to consider Raffie. He'd dreamed along with Faye; together they'd nurtured ideas and plans for the life they'd live together. And in the end it was Raffie who'd found himself the lonely beneficiary of those leftover dreams. Why had she failed to see it?

She cried during the service. It was a convenient, albeit ironic, circumstance. Not a tear for you, Ma, she thought. But for Faye, and for Raffie. Poor Faye, her poor sister, raped by that odious scum Aldo DiStasio. Her fists clenching, she was overcome by a desire to kill him. A lucky thing he was already in prison, or she'd have gone out looking for him. She saw herself stabbing him repeatedly, saw herself grinding her high heels into his eyes. She wanted him castrated, dead. And she wanted, more than anything else, to find Raffie and tell him how sorry she was for the accusations she'd flung in his astonished face.

After the service she approached Frankie to ask, "How is Raffie?"

Frankie shrugged and said, "Don't know. I got no boys no more, Louise."

"Frankie, Raffie never did anything wrong. He wasn't responsible for Faye's dying. You should know that."

"He done wrong," Frankie insisted. "He made her pregnant."

"No, he didn't," she said, feeling her way. "You'll have to take my word for it, but Raffie didn't do *anything* wrong. I really want to see him, Mr. DiStasio. Do you know where he is?"

He shook his head, having difficulty accepting what Louise was saying. "You gotta ask his grammother. She tell you."

"How do I get in touch with her?"

"Your grammother, she knows."

"She does?" Louise looked over at Ellen in surprise.

"Sure. They friends, huh?"

"Thank you."

"You take carea yourself," Frankie said. "I gotta get back to the store."

"Thank you for coming."

"I liked your mama, cara. She was a good friend to my Blanche. You mama and my Blanche they alla time have fun, long time ago. Before

Raffie's born, before Faye's born. The twoa them out to here''—he made
a bulging stomach with his hands and smiled. "She had a hard time, your
mama," he said, sobering. "Bad guy, that John Parker. Used to beat her
up real bad. Lotsa times I gotta go down there, say, What you doing, huh?
When he go away I think, *'Basta!* It's good he goes.' But your mama, she's
not happy he goes. Me, I never understand women. Only my Blanche."

"She was lovely," Louise told him.

"Yeah," he agreed sadly, and turned to go. "Ciao, Louise," he said
over his shoulder.

"Ciao, Mr. DiStasio." She watched him head off up the sidewalk to
where his truck was parked, then turned hoping to speak more to Bruno,
but he'd apparently gone off while she was talking to Frankie.

The small group dispersed quickly and Louise joined her grandmother
and Bob to witness the cremation.

Louise watched the coffin travel along the conveyor belt, moving toward a
distant fire. This was the end of Maggie, she thought, imagining she could
feel the heat from the fire. John Parker used to beat his wife. She couldn't
conceive of anyone daring to strike Ma. But he had. What kind of man
beat a pregnant woman? What kind of person had her father been? In
twenty-three years she'd given almost no thought to John Parker. He was
nothing more than an epithet her mother spat at them when they were
children. He was a shadow figure, someone who'd never been real. There
had been times in her childhood when Louise had wondered if there'd
ever actually been a John Parker. But there had been, and he'd seduced
sixteen-year-old Maggie. What the hell did anyone know at sixteen? she
thought, watching the coffin make its steady progress toward the blaze. At
sixteen you were just a kid. Maggie Parker: married at seventeen, a
mother at eighteen, abandoned at twenty, a child-beater at twenty-two,
turned prostitute at roughly thirty-four, dead at forty-three. That was the
story of Ma.

It changed things knowing John Parker had beat his wife. It didn't make
her care any more for her mother, but it made Maggie slightly more
forgivable. Maybe sleeping with men for money became Ma's way of
getting back at all men. Because one thing was certain: Ma didn't give a
damn for any man, so the sex was meaningless, an act purely of pleasurable friction for which she'd charged the highest possible price. And she'd
have gone on charging, making them pay, until the end. Now she was

dead and no doubt the phone in the Brunswick apartment was still ringing. In a way, a very small grudging way, she had to admit Ma got her
own back for John Parker. It didn't excuse her countless cruel stunts, but
it explained a few things.

"Goodbye, Ma," Louise whispered as the doors closed behind the
coffin.

Her grandmother turned and wept inside Bob's arms. Louise stood at a
respectful distance, her head aching slightly as if from the burden of
everything she'd learned that day. Not a single goddamned thing was ever
the way you thought it was. Not a thing. Everyone had stories to tell, not
all of them nice. She'd contributed to Raffie's story, given it a direction it
needn't have taken, and she was obligated to make whatever amends she
could. Maybe it would ease the murderous rage she felt every time she
thought of Aldo.

When she looked, she saw that her fingernails had left deep, blood-
rimmed impressions on the palms of her hands.

"Gramma, I need to find Raffie," Louise said later that evening. "I need
to see him, talk to him."

"I have no idea where he is, Lulu."

"No, but his grandmother does."

"You want me to call Leonora and ask her?" Ellen looked uncertain.
"Why?"

"It's my fault Frankie threw him out. I went into the store and point-
blank told him Faye was dead and that he was responsible. I had no idea
what I was talking about, Gramma. But Frankie believed me, and look
what happened. I was completely wrong. Somehow I've got to try to
make that up to him. I can't go back to England without trying to set
things straight."

"Ellie," Bob said, "I think you should ask Leonora."

Ellen looked at him, then back at Louise. "What aren't you telling me,
Lulu? Something happened this afternoon. I could tell by looking at you.
Did Frankie tell you something? Or was it Bruno?"

"I don't think this is really the right time to go into it," Louise said,
reluctant to add to her grandmother's grief and barely able to cope with
her own.

"No. This is as good a time as any," Ellen said, reaching for her
cigarettes. "I saw you talking to Bruno. What did he say?"

Louise looked at Bob, who nodded slightly as if to say, Your grand-mother's stronger than you think. Say what you have to say.

"Aldo raped Faye," Louise said bluntly. "That's what Bruno told me." She was so enraged that she wanted to cry, to protest, to beat her fists on the walls. All these desires battered like children at a locked door.

Ellen managed to get her cigarette lit, then sank back against the sofa with a sigh. She was silent for several moments, then pushed herself up saying, "I'll call from the bedroom. Or would you prefer to ask her yourself?"

"I don't know her," Louise said. "You do."

Ellen nodded and went off down the hall.

Louise turned to Bob saying, "I didn't want to tell her. It felt like too much."

"It's all right, honey," he said. "Your grandmother and I guessed it had to have been something like that. Faye would never have tried to abort Raffie's baby. They'd have discussed it, and they'd have arranged to get married."

"You knew?" Louise was flabbergasted. What he said was the simple truth, yet she'd never thought of it herself.

"We only suspected," he said. "There was no other reasonable expla-nation. The only question was who."

"Why didn't you ever say anything to me?"

"You were in no condition to hear the two of us speculating on the subject. Were you?"

Louise had to admit, "No, I wasn't."

"This answers the question once and for all. And if it'll make you feel better to make your peace with Raffie, then you should do it, by all means."

"Why don't we ever talk about all the things that are so important?" she said, holding the fingers of her right hand to her throbbing temple. "Today was one jolt after another. My head's aching."

"I'll get you some aspirin."

"No, I'll go, Uncle Bob. Thanks."

She got up and went into the master bathroom and opened the medi-cine cabinet. It staggered her to think her grandmother and Bob had had an answer of sorts all along. Here she thought she'd been shielding her grandmother, but in fact her grandmother had been protecting her. She took two aspirin tablets with a handful of water, realizing she'd forgotten to call Tim and now it was too late. It was after 3 a.m. in London. He worked such long and irregular hours that it would've been unfair of her to wake him for the purely selfish purpose of hearing the sound of his voice. She dried her hands and returned to the living room. Her grandmother was still on the phone in the bedroom. Bob was in the kitchen fixing a pot of coffee.

"Want some help?" Louise asked.

"Everything's under control, honey."

"No, it isn't," she said huskily. "Nothing's under control. Every other minute I think I've got answers, that I can handle everything. Then, the next minute, I can't handle a thing."

He set the pot down on the burner and Louise went over to embrace him. "You're tired," he said, stroking her hair. "It's been a hell of a day."

"Yes, it has," she agreed. "Ma's gone and I can't believe it. And Aldo, that son of a bitch . . . God! What he *did!*"

"I was sure your mother would go on making trouble for a lot more years. She used to call up every so often and upset your grandmother, always pleading poverty. Ellie would give her money, and here she had close to sixty thousand dollars socked away. I can't tell you how mad that makes me. Not that I object to whatever Ellie chooses to do with her money. I've got no right to object. But it infuriates me to know how badly Marg took advantage of her own mother. How do you feel about the money, Lulu?"

"I feel fine about it," she answered, sure at least of that. "In a way, I feel as if I earned it."

"In a way, you did," he concurred.

"I'll repay Gramma what she gave Ma."

"You don't have to do that."

"Yes, I do," Louise said firmly. "It's one thing for me to take the money ma squirreled away. It's another thing for me to take Gramma's."

"Fair enough. Whatever you're comfortable with. The will's pretty cut and dried. It won't take long to clear. But you'll have to declare it as income over there, I think."

For the first time that day Louise felt well enough to laugh. "I'll be more than happy to declare it," she said. "I'll be happy just to *have* it. I've been broke for too long."

"You should've said something."

"No. It was my decision to take on the business. I made that particular bed."

"Well," he smiled, "now you'll be able to afford a few blankets."

Ellen came to the doorway with a piece of paper in her hand. "Raffie's in New York," she said, handing Louise the paper.

Louise turned to Bob saying, "Will you lend me the airfare to New York, Uncle Bob?"

"Sure," he said readily. "When do you want to go?"

"Tomorrow," she said. "With luck I can go down in the morning and come back in the evening. I really can't stay away from the office for too long. This way, if it works out, I can book a flight back to London for the day after tomorrow."

"Stay one extra day," her grandmother said. "Spend it with me."

"Okay, Gramma. One extra day."

CHAPTER

SIXTY-FOUR

SHE KNEW IT WAS ONLY FIVE IN THE MORNING IN LONDON but she had to call. She needed to hear the sound of Tim's voice. And there were things she wanted to say to him.

He answered on the second ring and she knew she'd awakened him.

"I'm sorry to be calling so early. It's Louise."

At once his tone brightened and he said, "Ah, Louise. How's my darling girl?"

"I don't know. I'm all right, I guess. How are you?"

"Lonely for you. When will you be back?"

"In three days. I promised my grandmother I'd stay an extra day and spend it with her."

"And so you should. You don't get to see her often enough."

"I don't get to see you often enough, either."

"That's a lovely thing to say."

"Tim? I've been thinking . . . about us, about the flat . . ."

"And?" he asked, a certain hesitancy in his voice. "Have you changed your mind again?"

Just say it! her inner voice dictated. "No," she answered. "I was thinking . . . if you still want to, maybe we should get married."

"Aaahh," he said slowly. "Were you now?"

"You haven't changed your mind, have you?"

"Never. This is great news," he said, sounding wide awake now. "I'm very happy. Had you some date in mind?"

"Not really. I just think we should."

"Then we shall," he said definitely. "We most certainly shall."

"I'm going to New York tomorrow to see Raffie."

"I see."

"Just for the day. I'll be back in the evening. I've got to set things right, or at least try."

"You must of course do what you feel is right."

"Will you be able to meet me at the airport when I get back?"

"Certainly," he said. "What flight will you be on?"

She consulted the paper where she'd written out the information and gave him the flight number and scheduled arrival time.

"I'll be there to collect you."

"I can't wait to see you," she said. "I love you, Tim."

"I know you do, and I love you. I'll see you the day after tomorrow."

"Go back to sleep. I'm sorry I woke you."

"Don't be sorry. It's the most delightful call I've had in an age. Look, give me your number again—I know it's here someplace, but give it to me again—and I'll ring you tomorrow evening."

She gave it to him, and he asked, "What time is it there?"

"Midnight."

"Off to bed with you now," he said. "Sleep well."

"I love you," she said again, feeling shaky with emotion and fatigue.

"I know you do, dear girl. I know you do."

✢

Her flight wasn't until eleven. Bob offered to wait and go into the office late so that he could drive her to the airport but she said, "No, I'll take a cab. You can't be spending all your time ferrying me back and forth to the airport. And I'll grab a cab home this evening. With any luck I'll make the five o'clock flight and be home by seven-thirty or so."

"Let me give you some cash," he said. "You're going to need it for all those cabs. And I've got some American money you might as well take with you."

Seeing Louise about to protest, Ellen said quietly, "Take it, Lulu. You'll need it."

"I feel awful going off and leaving you this way."

"I'll be going back to work the day after tomorrow," her grandmother told her. "I plan to spend a little time taking it easy, maybe putting that box of photographs into some kind of order. Don't give it another thought. And give my love to Raffie when you see him."

"Give him my best, too," Bob said, preparing to leave. "You can fill us in over dinner tonight. I'll make a reservation for nine. Just remember the streets go east and west, and the avenues run north and south. New York's a pretty easy city to find your way around."

"I'll be back in a moment," Ellen told Louise, and went to walk Bob to the elevator.

Louise went into the kitchen to pour herself more coffee, then stood looking at the dull American money Bob had given her. As kids, she and Faye had called it "funny money," because it lacked the color and pictures they were accustomed to.

She was going to the States, a trip to another country that, according to Bob, required nothing more than some proof of her residency. Since she didn't have a driver's license, she planned to take her passport. She was going to a place called Il Mondo on East Fifty-second Street. It sounded like a restaurant, and she wondered what Raffie was doing there.

"Have you ever been to New York?" she asked her grandmother when she returned from seeing Bob off.

"Bob and I went for a long weekend last summer. He had to see a client on the Friday, so we decided to make a trip of it. Dirtiest city I think I've ever seen." Ellen's nose wrinkled as if recalling a bad smell. "And I've never known such crowds, everyone in a big hurry. The salespeople were the rudest I've ever encountered. But the restaurants were good and we saw two terrific shows, *The Subject Was Roses* and *Hello, Dolly!* We stayed at the Canadian Club at the Waldorf, which was very nice. Sunday we walked around a bit, had lunch at the Plaza, then we flew home in the afternoon. I wouldn't break my neck rushing to get back there, but we had a good time."

"I'm nervous," Louise admitted. "What if he tells me to go to hell?"

"Raffie?" Ellen smiled and shook her head.

"He might, Gramma. If I was Raffie, I don't think I'd ever forgive me."

"But you're not, and he will. Leonora tells me he's married."

"Married?"

"Two years ago May," Ellen said. "They have a baby girl."

Louise couldn't help smiling. "Raffie a father. Where has all the time gone?" Faye had been dead for six years, but it felt much more recent.

"It'll be fine, Lulu. You'll see."

Because the passengers went through U.S. customs and immigration in Toronto before boarding the plane, Louise was able to leave the terminal at La Guardia directly after arriving. Following the overhead signs, she went outside to the taxi rank.

On the ride into the city she looked first out one window then the other, seeing nothing remarkable. A lot of middle-income houses and low-rise apartment buildings, factories. But once they left the highway and entered Manhattan she felt a sudden rush of excitement. Somehow the dirt and garbage everywhere didn't matter. There was something exhilarating about the skyscrapers, about the apartment buildings with the uniformed doormen, about the people on the hot summer sidewalks, and the shops, the tremendous crush of vehicular traffic; cars and trucks double- and triple-parked. The noise was formidable: horns honking, people shouting, music drifting above it all like an afterthought. In contrast, Toronto seemed almost sleepy, suburban, and positively pristine.

Il Mondo was an unprepossessing restaurant from the outside. Nervousness had her sweating in the close afternoon air, and her hand was unsteady as she opened the door.

Inside, the place was elegant, subdued. The maître d' approached and Louise said, "I'm looking for Raffie DiStasio."

"We're very busy right now," the man said.

"I can see that." Louise looked at the packed tables and smiled. "I won't take much of his time."

"Perhaps you could wait, signorina? In one hour he will be free to speak with you."

Louise again looked into the dining room, wondering if Raffie was possibly one of the waiters. "Could you tell him I'm here?"

Somewhat annoyed, he asked, "What is the name? I tell him."

"Louise Parker. I'll wait at the bar, if that's all right."

"Certainly," he said curtly, then turned and worked his way between the tables toward the rear of the place.

Her hands wet, Louise slid onto a vacant bar stool. At once the bartender slid a small napkin in front of her, asking, "What will you have?"

She didn't dare drink on an empty stomach, especially when she was so nervous. "A Coke, please."

The bartender smiled, whipped up a glass, scooped up some shaved ice, then flipped the top on a bottle of Coca Cola and poured it into the glass. He decorated the rim with a slice of lime, added a swizzle stick, and set it down on the napkin in front of her.

She took a sip and looked back in the direction the maître d' had gone. The door pushed open and a tall, well-built man in a chef's outfit came through. With a jolt, Louise realized it was Raffie. She slid off the bar stool and stood clutching her purse.

He stopped about three feet away and stared at her. Then he said, "You look so much like Faye," and held open his arms.

She stepped into his embrace, then moved back to look at him, asking with a rather giddy laugh, "You're the chef?"

He nodded and took hold of her hand. "Come back to the kitchen. I can't stop to talk to you now. Have you got time?"

"Sure. I only came here today to see you."

"Good. If you don't mind waiting in the office, the rush'll be over in about forty minutes and then we can sit down and talk." He led her between the tables and out to the kitchen, where several men in chef's outfits were moving at a frantic pace.

Off the kitchen was a small office containing a desk and two chairs. "Sit down here, Louise," he said, showing her inside. "Have you eaten? Are you hungry?"

"You sound just like your mother," she said, knowing everything was going to be all right. He was still Raffie. He hadn't changed.

He smiled and said, "I'll fix you something," then slipped away to the kitchen.

Some fifteen minutes later he ducked in with a plate of food in one hand and a napkin and cutlery in the other. "Try this," he said. "It's the house specialty. Let me know how you like it."

She hadn't realized she was hungry until she started on the veal in brandy cream sauce with shallots and a touch of tomato. The food was superb and she ate slowly, savoring the delicate flavors.

"Good, eh?" He grinned, popping into the doorway.

"Wonderful."

He removed the plate and set down fresh cutlery and a white bowl filled with raspberries. "Eat this," he said. "By the time you finish we'll be able to have some coffee and talk." He paused a moment, then said, "It's great to see you, Lou. Really great. Back in about ten minutes. Okay?"

"Okay."

He ducked out again, and she ate the raspberries one at a time, enjoying the novelty of eating an exquisite meal in that tiny office. Her nervousness was gone and she waited for Raffie to return, knowing she'd done the right thing in coming.

At last, Raffie reappeared with two cups of espresso and two small glasses of amaretto.

"*Salute!*" he said, touching his glass to hers.

"Cheers," she said, and took a sip of the liqueur.

"This is some surprise," he said. "I've been wondering what you were up to. I heard from my grandmother that you were living in London."

"That's right. I didn't even know my grandmother and yours were friends."

"They always knew each other," he said, "but they got pretty close after Faye died." His features firmed up at the mention of Faye's name, then he relaxed and smiled at her.

"Raffie," she said, putting a hand on his arm, "I came to see you because I owe you an apology. More than an apology. I was so wrong about everything. I know now none of it was your fault."

"It's okay, Lou. I know you didn't mean it. You were upset."

"You have to know what happened," she said, the urgency overtaking her again. "You can't just say it's okay, you know I didn't mean it. Because I *did* mean it. I thought you got Faye pregnant, that it was because of you she died. But now I know you had nothing to do with it."

He sat up straighter, asking, "What d'you mean?"

"The whole thing bothered me," she explained. "So I asked a close friend who's a doctor to look at the autopsy report. He read it and said that Faye had been raped."

At this, Raffie's head jerked back and his eyes widened. He looked both horrified and fearful.

"That was my reaction too," she went on. "Anyway, I'm home—at least I came back to Toronto a couple of days ago—because my mother died.''

''Oh, that's a shame.''

''I don't know about that. But the thing is, Bruno came to the funeral. And he told me what happened. He told me that Aldo raped Faye.''

Raffie's face became suffused with color, his features going hard. One arm wrapped itself around his belly and he closed his eyes, bending forward over his arm as if in sudden, terrible pain. He remained in that position for quite some time, then opened his brimming eyes.

Stricken, she whispered, ''Please don't cry. If you do, I will, too, and I might never stop.''

He nodded slowly, swallowed, then said thickly, ''Aldo? Bruno told you that?''

''I believe him.''

''Yeah,'' Raffie said, gradually straightening, his arm staying wrapped around himself. ''So do I. That rotten son of a bitch!'' He rocked forward again as if in an effort to ease his abdominal pain. ''That stinking son of a bitch. Jesus! I could kill him.''

''I feel the same way,'' she said quietly. ''But at least now we both know what happened. I had to come; I had to tell you how sorry I am for the awful things I said to you.''

''Aldo,'' he repeated disbelievingly. ''He put his filthy hands on her? *Jesus!* This is hard to take, Lou. If I'd known . . .''

''She was too ashamed to tell any of us, Raffie.''

''Faye,'' he said softly, his eyes again glazing over. ''I loved her so much. Another year and we were going to get married. We had everything planned. And that bastard destroyed it all. If only I'd *known*. She should've *told* me. I'd've *killed* him. I'd've murdered him with my bare hands. Six years I've been trying to make sense of it, trying to figure out how she could've got pregnant. Somehow, I should've known, Lou. Why didn't I know? We were so close. I could read her moods just by looking in her eyes, or by the way she said something. Why didn't she tell me? I'd have understood.''

''She couldn't tell you.''

''No,'' he agreed sorrowfully. ''There would've been bloodshed. It would all have come out into the open. It would've killed her.'' Hearing what he said he went silent and stared at Louise, his deep brown eyes filled with sadness. ''He ruined everything.''

"But you have another life now," she reminded him.

"Every damned thing I've done has been because of what happened to Faye. For three solid years all I thought about was your sister, Louise. My whole life fell apart. I worked because I knew I had to, but I didn't give a damn about anything. I came to New York to work for my cousin, who owns this place. I tended bar. It was perfect. I had this handy barrier between me and everybody else. I worked and thought about Faye. I went home and thought about Faye. I went to sleep and dreamed about her, got up in the morning and she was the only thing on my mind. I couldn't believe I was still living my life and she was gone."

"It's been the same for me," she said gently. "Somehow, you go on. You can't believe it, but you do. And now you have a wife and a baby."

"Yeah. Lindsay. We've had a lot of problems. Faye kept getting in the way. I had this feeling that I was cheating on her. You know? I couldn't get it into my head that she was gone forever. When I saw you out there time shot backwards and forwards all at once. You were Faye the way she'd have been now. You look a lot like her, you know."

"I don't see it, but Gramma thinks so, too."

"You do," he said. "But now that we're talking, there's no mistake: You're Louise, all right. I appreciate your coming to see me this way."

"I had to," she said simply. "I treated you abominably. I owed you an apology, a big one."

"That prick Aldo. Jesus! This really throws me. Does Pop know?"

Louise shook her head. "I doubt it. I tried to talk to him but it seemed as if I was confusing him. I think he'd like to see you, though, Raffie."

"He'd probably throw me out on my ear."

"I don't think so."

"I don't know. I'll have to think about it." He gazed at her for several seconds, then asked, "What about you, Lou?"

"I'm going to get married," she said, smiling at the thought of Tim. "To my friend, the doctor I mentioned before."

"No kidding! That's terrific."

"Have you got any pictures of your wife and baby?" she asked.

It took him a moment to respond, as if he had physically to drag himself forward out of the past. He shifted to reach into his back pocket for his wallet. "This is Lindsay," he said, pulling out a photograph and handing it to her. "And this is Faye," he said, handing her a second snapshot.

"Faye," she repeated, looking first at him then at the picture of the baby—a dark-haired chubby little girl chewing on her fist. "She's beautiful, Raffie. And so is your wife." The photograph of Lindsay showed a strong-jawed very pretty blonde who bore a strong resemblance to Faye. She was less rounded and thinner; her features taken individually were not the same, but viewed as a whole, the resemblance was unmistakable.

"Lindsay looks like Faye," he said, confirming her impression. "But she couldn't be more different. She's a Connecticut Wasp from a wealthy family. She was a regular customer, and Sal, my cousin, introduced us one evening. We got married eight months later. She's got a nice family, good people. One of these days we're planning to open a restaurant in Connecticut—our own place. Lin's very sharp. She's already got her eye on a location she thinks would be ideal."

"She knows about Faye?"

"Oh, sure. I poured my heart out to her on our second date. Lin's something else. We've had some ups and downs, but we're working things out. This'll help. I feel guilty, as if I should've been there to protect Faye. But at least now I know once and for all it wasn't because of anything I did. That does make a difference."

"I'm glad," Louise said. "I know it does for me. I feel as if I can finally start breathing properly. All these years it's hounded me, not knowing why she died."

"Maybe one of these days me and Lin and the baby will take a trip up to Toronto and see Pop."

"I think he'd be glad to see you, Raffie. I really do."

"Yeah," he said. "Maybe we'll do that, introduce him to his granddaughter."

"Do you forgive me?" she asked, again putting a hand on his arm.

"I forgave you a long time ago, Lou," he said earnestly. "It's kind of rough, this business about Aldo. If the little shit wasn't locked up, I'd be tempted to go up there and kick his teeth in. But at least, as you say, now I know why. Are you staying in town for a while?"

"I've got a five o'clock flight back," she told him. "I only came down to make peace with you. I didn't feel I could go back to England without trying."

"I'm very damned glad you came."

"So am I," she said. "You haven't changed."

"Yeah, I have," he said. "And so've you. We've all changed. But that's okay. And you know something funny?"

"What?"

"Things are okay. I love the restaurant. I love cooking. I think of my Mom all the time I'm at the stove. In a funny way, it's like an act of love. You know? All that time she was sick and I did the cooking, I never minded because I was helping her. Now, here I am a chef and a lot of what I know is what Mom taught me. I'd have made a lousy engineer." He smiled.

She smiled back at him. "My grandmother and Uncle Bob send you their love," she said.

"Send them mine. I always loved your grandmother. She was so nice to me and Faye. I think a lot about those Sunday dinners she used to make. After Mom got sick, it was the only place I could go where it felt like family. You know? And Bob was a terrific guy. Maybe if I come up to see Pop, I'll stop in and see them too."

"They'd like that, I know."

"You'll stay in touch now, eh?" he asked.

"Absolutely. Sometime, I'd like to meet your family."

"Maybe we'll take a trip to England."

"It's good to see you doing so well, Raffie. I guess I'd better be going. I thought I'd walk around for a while, have a quick look at the city before I head back to the airport."

He pulled over a piece of paper and wrote down his home address and phone number. She did the same. Then they traded papers.

"We'll stay in touch," she said, walking with him through the now fairly empty restaurant.

"You bet," he said, stepping out into the hot sunshine with her. "Take care of yourself, Lou." He gave her a hug. "Thanks for coming all the way down here to see me. I feel like I just shed about twenty pounds."

"So do I. Give Faye a kiss for me," she said, then hugged him again before setting off down the block.

As she walked, feeling wonderfully unencumbered, she thought about Tim and was filled with a longing to see him. The day after tomorrow they'd be together. He'd meet her at the airport and in the time to come she'd demonstrate actively how much she loved him. She couldn't help smiling as she glanced into shop windows and sidestepped pedestrians hurrying along the pavement. Faye's death was finally a thing of the past. She could think of her sister without feeling that grating anxiety. And she'd made her peace with Raffie. She'd soon be out of debt; she'd be moving into a new flat with someone she adored; everything was going to be all right. She'd go on missing Faye, probably for the rest of her life, but at least now she knew the truth.

On impulse, she stopped in a hat shop and, thinking of Rachel, knowing she'd approve, bought a wide-brimmed white straw hat festooned with flowers. She wore it out of the shop, feeling closer to everyone she loved. Checking the time—coming up to three-thirty—she flagged down a taxi to take her to the airport.

Throughout the hour-long flight back to Toronto she thought about her sister. She looked back, fondly recalling those times Faye had taken her to the Ex, patiently doling out dimes after Louise had spent all her money. She thought of the countless nights when they'd sat in bed with books propped on their knees, exchanging secrets; Faye growing red in the face at Louise's probing questions. They'd lived and slept side by side for so many years, sharing each other's thoughts, their lives complexly intertwined. She'd never expected it to end. She'd imagined they'd grow old, live out their lives in that same side by side fashion. But their childhood companion had destroyed the future they should have had.

She remembered with anger that afternoon at Sunnyside Beach when Aldo had tormented her and she'd stormed away over the sand, stepping on a piece of broken glass. Everything had gone wrong that day, but Faye had been there to hold her hand, to see her through. There'd been no one to hold Faye's hand at the end. She'd traveled alone, and she'd carried her terrible secret away with her.

It was all over now. All of it. Ma was gone, reduced to a pound or so of ground-down powder Gramma had taken to the roof of the apartment building and scattered into the night wind while Louise and Bob had stood, silent witnesses to the act. And the festering place where she'd resided inside Louise had been lanced, drained. Her poison was gone. All men weren't scum. Pregnancy didn't kill you. It was all right to care. She pressed a hand into her belly, wishing with sudden fervor that she could carry a child of Tim's, could give him living proof of her caring for him.

Strange to think how different things would have been if Faye hadn't died. She'd never have gone to London, never have gone to call on Philip only to find dear Rachel instead. She'd never have gone with Rachel to meet marvelous Evie, never have met Tim. How terrible it would have been never to have known him, never to have come to know his instinctive kindness and generosity, his loving sadness.

She thought of seeing Faye's body in the emergency room, the colorless beauty of her features, the sightless eyes, the sweep of lowered lashes over those gray-blue eyes; poor shy Faye stripped naked on a gurney, blue-white in the harsh glare of overhead lights. Louise mentally covered that small still form as she had in reality, drawing the thin cotton hospital blanket up under her sister's chin, shielding her from the eyes of strangers.

I wish you could know, she thought. I wish I could tell you about my life, about the people I know and love. You'd have been so surprised by how it's all turned out, Faye.

She looked out the airplane window at the cotton candy banks of clouds, wondering if perhaps Faye already knew these things. Did she see them from wherever she was? Was she real when she came to Louise in dreams? Would she stay eighteen forever there, in that place? *Gramma has a box of photographs that are all that remain of the life we lived on Manning Avenue. Pictures I remember of you and me that somebody took in the schoolyard, on the front porch one snowy winter afternoon, on the merry-go-round at Sunnyside, in our best dresses with Gramma and Uncle Bob one evening at the Royal York. And I know there are pictures of Ma, too. But none of John Parker. Ma cut him out of every single photograph. There are just odd shapes and irregular outlines of where he once fit into the pictures. Two little girls in snowsuits with mittens on strings, sitting on the front steps of that old lopsided porch, our hands shaping snowballs. A picture of Blanche with the four of us following after her like baby ducks.*

A voice announced they'd be landing shortly in Toronto and would everyone please extinguish all smoking materials and fasten their seatbelts. One more day. She'd spend it with her grandmother. Then Louise would board another plane and fly back to London, where Tim would be waiting. God! She wanted to see him so badly. She'd been wasting precious time. Tim was going to be forty-four. They might have a good thirty or so years together, if they were lucky. She was all at once greedy for time, thinking there'd never be enough of it. But one thing was for certain: She was through wasting it. The minutes counted now, just as Faye's eighteen years had counted for so much.

She lied to the customs officer, saying she had nothing to declare. Her wonderful new hat wasn't so much an acquisition as a necessity. It made her feel buoyant and free as she sailed through the baggage claim area and out to get a taxi. She couldn't wait to see her grandmother and Bob, to tell them about her visit with Raffie and about her new sense of herself. Time, she thought. It was so important to recognize the significance of every passing moment, to make each one as meaningful and worthwhile as she was able. No more wishing she'd never taken on the business, feeling slightly bitter and beleaguered as she sat through a Sunday afternoon typing documents. She and Rachel would keep working and expand, even perhaps build that empire Rachel could so readily envision. And she'd work at making a good marriage with Tim. She'd erase forever any hint of sadness from his eyes.

By the time she got out of the cab in front of the apartment building on Avenue Road her mouth felt crowded with the many things she wanted to say. She was eager to embrace her grandmother and Bob, to tell them again and again how much she loved them; she wanted to bask as long as possible in the warmth of their communal affection, to carry their love away and keep it with her just as she kept Faye close in her mind.

All the way up to the twelfth floor in the elevator she was anticipating her reunion with her grandmother. It felt as if she'd been away for months, not just the space of one day. She hurried down the hallway and opened the door to see her grandmother on the sofa with some man, and Bob in the armchair.

The three people in the room turned to look at her and she felt as if she were having some sort of seizure. Shock unlocked her jaw. Her mouth fell open and twin reactions overcame her so that she laughed in amazement then burst into tears, frozen in the doorway with her hand still on the knob.

She watched the three of them get to their feet—Bob, her grandmother, and Tim—and laughed again, gulping down the cry of astonishment that swept up from her chest. Taking flight, her hat toppling from her head, letting her shoulder bag fall to the floor, she soared through space to be enclosed in Tim's embrace, asking tremulously, "What are you *doing* here? I can't believe this!"

He smiled, his hand as always reaching to stroke her hair.

Bob, smiling too, went to close the door while her grandmother moved to retrieve Louise's hat and bag with an expression of immense satisfaction.

"I came to ask for your hand in marriage," Tim said in his hushed voice, but with an elated laugh. "It seemed the proper thing to do."

"But when . . . how did you get here so quickly?" Louise couldn't let go of him. If she opened her arms he might dissolve like smoke.

"I took the early morning flight," he explained. "After you rang I knew there was no possibility of my going back to sleep. I got up and went directly to the airport and rang your grandmother when I landed this afternoon," he smiled over at her. "She told me to come ahead. So I did." He pulled his handkerchief from his pocket and pressed it into her hand. "I take it you're not displeased."

"I'm in a state of shock," she laughed, blotting her face, then going on tiptoe to look into his eyes before giving him a kiss. "It's a lucky thing I don't have a bad heart."

"Ah, you've got a fine strong heart," he teased.

Louise broke away from Tim to spread her arms around both her grandmother and Bob, a giddy three-way hug. Then she had to go back to Tim, to thread her fingers through his and look down at their joined hands before looking again at his eyes. Clear, untroubled, filled with amusement and delight.

"What about your patients?" she asked him, her heart completely out of synch.

"Called in a locum," he said. "He'll manage until I return."

"I can't believe you did this," she said again.

"One of my better impulses."

"We have a dinner reservation," Bob said.

"Great," Louise said, then turned back to Tim. "Where are you staying?"

"Here," he answered. "Your grandmother insists."

"In the second guest room," Ellen said. "I didn't see the point of his spending good money on a hotel when we have plenty of room here. We'll just freshen up, honey," she said. "Then we'll go." She and Bob went off to the master suite.

Louise looked at Tim, who seemed unable to stop smiling. "Rather old-fashioned of me," he said, "but after your call I wanted to make myself known to your family."

"Ever since I left, I've been thinking about you, wanting to see you. And here you are!" She gazed at him, drinking in the sight of him. "This is so wonderful."

"Perhaps tomorrow you'll show me around your city."

"I'd love it, just love it."

"I take it your trip was a success."

She smiled and shook her head, saying, "I can't get over this. Yes, it was a great success. Tim, I love you so much." Her tears started up again. "I was thinking on the plane that if we're very lucky, we might have thirty or forty years together, and I want them. I couldn't wait to get back to you. I wanted it to start right away, and here you are." She kissed him on both cheeks, then again on the mouth. "Thank you for doing this. I'll never forget it, never."

Late that night, fairly certain her grandmother and Bob were asleep, she crept barefoot to the second guest room. Getting the door open noiselessly, she shut and locked it, then crept across the room intending to slip into bed with Tim without waking him, eager simply to be close to him.

But he was awake and sat up, whispering, "I've been waiting and hoping you'd come."

She got in beside him, trailing her fingers over his face in the darkness, shaping the line of his eyebrows, his nose, his mouth and chin.

"Do we dare?" he asked, glancing over at the door.

"Yes," she whispered, sitting up to strip off her nightgown.

Having brought no luggage, Tim was wearing only his shorts. She tugged them down over his hips, then stretched out on top of him, lining her body up with his. She rested her head on his chest and listened to the steady surging of his heart as his hands caressed the length and breadth of her back.

Tomorrow she'd show him her city, all the places she'd known growing up: the ballpark, the CNE grounds, the house on Manning Avenue, her high school, even the fish and chips shop.

"It's so silly," she whispered, her hand moulded to the strong curve of his shoulder. "I want to show you everything, the whole city. There'll never be enough time. But I want you to see everything I've ever seen, to know how it all looks, so that years from now, when I talk about the stores on Queen Street, you'll have a picture of them in your mind. When I talk about Harbord, you'll know what my school was like. I want to open my mind and take you in, the way I can take you inside my body.''

He gave a little shiver and held his hand to her lips. ''I'm where I most want to be,'' he whispered. ''So long as you are, too, nothing else matters.''

About the Author

Charlotte Vale Allen was born in Toronto, Canada and, after living for three years in England, emigrated to the United States in 1966.

In her early life she had a variety of careers including actress, model, waitress, salesperson, insurance broker, secretary, and nightclub/cabaret performer. It was as a singer that she first came to the U.S., working in clubs throughout the Midwest before moving to New York in 1968.

She began writing in 1971 while pregnant with her daughter, and published her first novel, LOVE LIFE, in 1976. Since then she has been a full-time writer. LEFTOVER DREAMS is her twenty-seventh novel.

Although she has made her home in Connecticut for more than twenty years, she maintains close ties with friends and family in Toronto.